BOUND BY HONOR

Book Two in The Clan Donald Saga

REGAN WALKER

BOUND BY HONOR

Paperback ISBN: 978-1-7354381-2-2

PRAISE FOR REGAN WALKER

"The writing is excellent, the research impeccable, and the love story is epic. You can't ask for more than that."

—*The Book Review*

"Regan Walker is a master of her craft. Her novels instantly draw you in, keep you reading and leave you with a smile on your face."

—*Good Friends, Good Books*

"Ms. Walker has the rare ability to make you forget you are reading a book. The characters become real, the modern world fades away, and all that is left is the intrigue, drama, and romance."

—*Straight from the Library*

"Walker's detailed historical research enhances the time and place of the story without losing sight of what is essential to a romance: chemistry between the leads and hope for the future."

—*Publisher's Weekly*

"...an enthralling story."

—*RT Book Reviews*

"Spellbinding and Expertly Crafted...Walker's characters are complex and well-rounded and, in her hands, real historical figures merge seamlessly with those from her imagination."

—*A Reader's Review*

ACKNOWLEDGEMENTS

I am indebted to photographer Robert Gibb for the magnificent photograph of Loch Voil at Balquidder in the Scottish Highlands that provided the background for the cover, the same photograph on the book's page on my website.

The wonderful talent of illustrator Bob Marshall is shown in the map he did for *Summer Warrior* updated to include new locations mentioned in this story. He also did the new map of Ulster as of 1300 A.D.

I must also thank Dr. Katharine Simms, author of *Gaelic Ulster in the Middle Ages*, for her invaluable assistance in helping me to understand the history, customs and players in Ulster at the time of my story. She graciously engaged in an extensive email correspondence with me that provided much useful information.

Ian Ross Macdonnell, author of *Clan Donald & Iona Abbey: 1200-1500,* helped me to understand that Iona Abbey, as we see it today, and the abbey church, the *"Cathedral of the Isles"*, are Clan Donald's legacy, which the Macdonalds built, protected and maintained as their ancient ecclesiastical capital. In addition to his scholarship on Iona's significant role in the lives of the Lords of the Isles, Ian also helped to verify Angus Og's considerable role at the Battle of Bannockburn which, sadly, is neglected by many historians. As with Dr. Simms, Ian graciously engaged in an extensive email correspondence with me that provided much useful information.

For Ian's kind assistance and abundance of information, I thank him.

As always, I cannot forget my beta readers. In Canada, Liette Bougie, one of my readers, has a fine eye for detail.

The Clan Donald badge is used with the gracious permission of Clan Donald's High Commissioner.

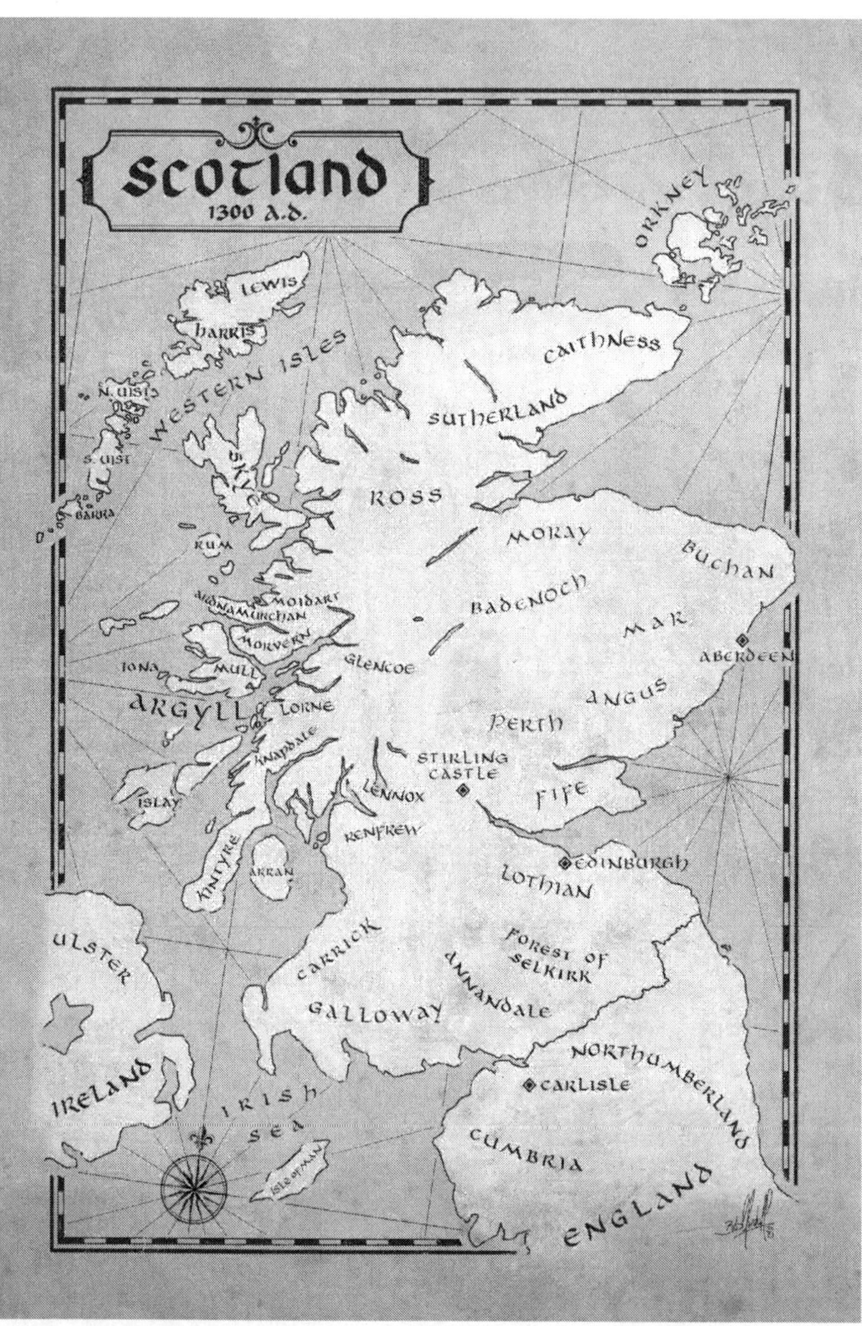

Scotland
1300 A.D.
ORKNEY
LEWIS
HARRIS
WESTERN ISLES
N. UIST
S. UIST
BARRA
SKYE
RUM
CAITHNESS
SUTHERLAND
ROSS
MORAY
BUCHAN
BADENOCH
MAR
ABERDEEN
MOIDART
ARDNAMURCHAN
MORVERN
GLENCOE
IONA
MULL
ARGYLL
LORNE
ANGUS
PERTH
KNAPDALE
STIRLING CASTLE
FIFE
ISLAY
LENNOX
RENFREW
EDINBURGH
KINTYRE
ARRAN
LOTHIAN
ULSTER
CARRICK
FOREST OF SELKIRK
ANNANDALE
GALLOWAY
NORTHUMBERLAND
IRELAND
CARLISLE
IRISH SEA
CUMBRIA
ISLE OF MAN
ENGLAND

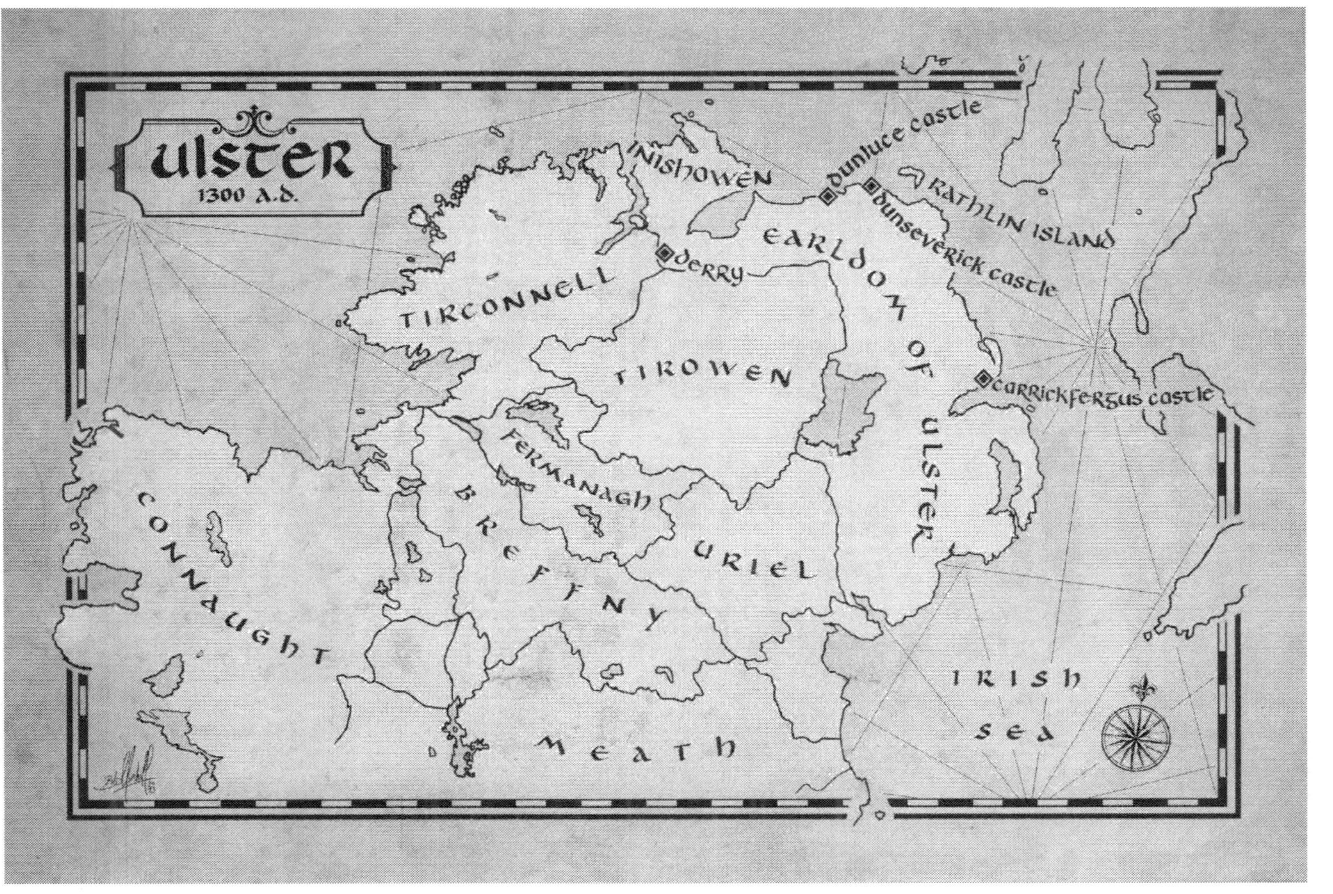

Ulster
1300 A.D.
Inishowen
Dunluce castle
Rathlin Island
dunseverick castle
derry
Earldom of Ulster
Carrickfergus castle
Tirconnell
Tirowen
Fermanagh
Breffny
Uriel
Connaught
Meath
Irish Sea

CHARACTERS OF NOTE

ANGUS OG MACDONALD ("Og" means "the younger"), Lord of Kintyre, eventually Lord of the Isles

ÁINE O'CAHAN, daughter of Lord Cumee O'Cahan ("Áine" is pronounced "awn-ya")

SIR ANGUS MOR MACDONALD ("Mor" means "the great" or "the elder"), Angus Og's father and Lord of the Isles

HELEN CAMPBELL MACDONALD, wife of Angus Mor, Lady of the Isles

ALEXANDER MACDONALD ("Alex"), Angus Og's elder brother, Lord of the Isles after Angus Mor

JULIANA MACDOUGALL MACDONALD, wife of Alexander Macdonald and Lady of the Isles

JOHN SPRANGACH MACDONALD ("John the Bold"), Angus Og's younger brother, eventually Lord of Ardnamurchan

LORD CUMEE O'CAHAN, Áine's father, Lord of Ciannacht, Chief of the Name of O'Cahan and senior subking to the King of Tirowen

NIALL O'NEILL, "The O'Neill", King of Tirowen, Áine's first husband

AGNES ("Nessa"), Áine's handmaiden

DERMOT O'CAHAN, Áine's brother, eventually Lord of Ciannacht, Chief of the Name of O'Cahan and senior subking to the King of Tirowen

TURLOUGH O'DONNELL, King of Tirconnell and Angus Og's nephew

RICHARD DE BURGH, Earl of Ulster and friend of Edward I

MARGARET DE BURGH, Countess of Ulster

ELIZABETH DE BURGH, daughter of Richard de Burgh, who became Queen Consort to King Robert I

DUNCAN MACALASDAIR MACDONALD, cousin to Angus Og, nephew to Angus Mor

SIR ROBERT BRUCE ("Rob"), son of Robert Bruce VI, Earl of Carrick, and grandson of Robert Bruce V ("Robert the Noble"), eventually Earl of Carrick and then King of Scots

BRIAN BALLOCH O'NEILL, son of Áine O'Cahan by Niall O'Neill, King of Tirowen

ALEXANDER MACDOUGALL, Lord of Argyll and Lorne (sometimes just Lord of Lorne or Lord of Argyll)

DUGALL MACEANRUIG, the "chief man" of Glen Coe

SORCHA MACEANRUIG, daughter of Dugall MacEanruig and mother of Iain MacDonald, natural son of Angus Og

DONALD MACKAY, seer on the Rhinns of Islay (pronounced "eye-la")

RUAIDHRI MAGUIRE OF FERMANAGH ("Rory"), one of Áine O'Cahan's suitors

MARK, BISHOP OF THE ISLES (succeeded by ALAN)

FIONNLAGH, Abbot of Iona

The chiefs of the lordship mentioned by name:

TORMOD MACLEOD, chief of the Macleods and his son, MALCOLM

NIALL MACNEIL, chief of the MacNeils of Barra and his son, NEILL

MAOLMUIRE, chief of the MacMillans of Lochaber

MALISE, chief of the Macleans of Duart on Mull and his son, MALCOLM

MALCOLM MACDUFFIE of Colonsay, chief of the Macduffies, and his son GILCHRIST, who became chief

LAIRD JOHN MACNICOL of Lewis

RUAIRI MACRUAIRI, chief of the MacRuairis

CHRISTINA MACRUAIRI, heiress of the MacRuairis

King Robert I's companions aka "the inner circle" (in addition to Angus Og):

SIR EDWARD BRUCE, his younger brother, who becomes Lord of Galloway and Earl of Carrick

JAMES DOUGLAS, aka "the Black Douglas", a squire but eventually knighted by King Robert

SIR GILBERT HAYE, eventually made High Constable of Scotland

SIR NEIL CAMPBELL, chief of the Campbells of Loch Awe
MALCOLM, EARL OF LENNOX
SIR ROBERT BOYD of Kilmarnock
SIR THOMAS RANDOLPH, King Robert's nephew, eventually Earl of Moray and Lord of the Isle of Man
WALTER STEWART, High Steward, son of James Steward and cousin to James Douglas
WILLIAM LAMBERTON, Bishop of St. Andrews

THE CLAN DONALD SAGA

Their roots were in ancient Ireland with its high kings, in the Isles where the Norse settled and in ancient Dalriada, the Kingdom of the Gaels. They were the great sea lords, plying the waters in their longships and galleys, ruling the western Highlands and the Hebrides for four hundred years.

From Somerled, the first Lord of the Isles, to the Macdonalds who fought alongside Scotland's kings and, later, at Culloden for freedom, to those who came to America to help win her independence, they were known for their courage, honor and constancy.

These are the tales of their chieftains, men of great deeds, and the women they loved. Their stories are worth remembering. In bringing them to the world of historical fiction, I write about my own clan, my own heritage, hoping to inspire my fellow Clan Donald members and my readers who love all things Scottish.

BOUND BY HONOR

The friendship that changed the destiny of a nation…

In the waning years of the thirteenth century, two young noblemen form a bond that forever changes their destiny and that of Scotland's. Their shared pledge of honor would endure for a lifetime to secure power in the Isles for Angus Og Macdonald and a crown for Robert Bruce. This is the story of their friendship, their times and the battle that secured their future.

Standing beside them would be two women from Ireland, Áine O'Cahan, the dark-haired beauty from Ulster, who captured the heart of the Lord of the Isles, and Elizabeth de Burgh, the fair Norman heiress who stood by her man, King Robert Bruce, though it would cost her dearly.

Enter the world of medieval Scotland and live the adventure!

It is no joy without Clan Donald,
It is no strength to be without them;
The best clan in the world;
To them belongs every goodly man.

The noblest clan ever born,
Who personified prowess and awesomeness;
A people to whom tyrants made submission;
They had great wisdom and piety.

A brave, kind, mighty clan,
The hottest clan in the face of battle,
The most gentle clan among women
And most valorous in war.

A clan who did not make war on the church;
They feared being dispraised.
Learning was commanded
And in the rear were
Service and honor and self-respect.

A clan without arrogance, without injustice,
Who seized naught save the spoils of war;
Whose nobles were men of spirit,
And whose common men were most steadfast.

~ Gaelic lament by Giolla Coluim mac an Ollaimh, a MacMhuirich bard
Book of the Dean of Lismore, 1493

CHAPTER 1

Ardtornish Castle, Morvern, Scotland, 19 September 1286

WITH HIS BACK to the stone tower on the rocky shore of Morvern, Angus shielded his eyes from the sun as he watched his father speaking to the captain of his great galley resting on the shore.

To where does Father sail?

No one had told Angus the purpose of his father's voyage or why his elder brother, Alexander, had arrived from Islay the day before. Yet their whispered conversations before the fire last night told Angus something of significance was in the making.

He had sailed with his father, Angus Mor Macdonald, Lord of the Isles, many times to visit the clans that were a part of the lordship but he did not think this was one of those voyages. As a younger son, he had sometimes been left behind. He had not minded before but he did now, for he sensed this time would be different. This would be important.

At fourteen, Angus was already good with a sword, long-handled sparth axe, bow and spear, taught by his father's constable, the head of the galloglass warriors. In letters, he had been tutored by his father's chaplain, Michael Dominici, so that he could read and write in Latin and French. He spoke French sufficiently well to converse with Normans, which was sometimes a necessity when in Ireland.

Surely, he was ready to enter his father's world. Alex, named for Alexander III, King of Scots, was twenty-six and their father's heir, but Angus, too, had an interest in matters of state.

As his father began the climb back to the castle, Angus walked down the slope to meet him. "Father, may I ask to where you and Alex sail this day?" Angus half-expected the answer to be Ireland for his father had oft traveled there in recent months.

"Aye, you may," his father said, stopping in his stride. "We are for Turnberry Castle."

Turnberry. He had heard his father speak of the Bruce castle in Carrick on Scotland's western shore but he had never been there. "Might I go with you?"

His father, tall, strong and fierce in his fourth decade, with shoulder-length red hair set aflame by the sun, returned Angus an assessing gaze. Running his hand over his short beard, the Lord of the Isles nodded. "Aye, you are of sufficient years. Though you'll not attend my meeting with the Lord of Annandale, mind."

"Might I at least know what will be discussed at the meeting?" Angus was on tenuous ground in asking but he thought his indulgent father might tell him and he was curious to know.

"Scotland's future, lad. I cannot say more. Now, best tell your mother you are sailing with us. Get your sword and satchel. Bring a change of clothing adequate to be presented to nobility. We will be away for a few days."

Angus' spirits soared. "Thank you, sir!"

His father resumed his tread toward the castle, then paused in mid-stride and turned. "As I recall, Robert the Noble, Lord of Annandale, has a grandson your age, another Robert, of course." He chuckled. "The eldest sons of the Bruces are all Roberts. Mayhap, you and he can keep each other company."

Like Angus' father, Robert Bruce, fifth of the name, the old Lord of Annandale, had more than one son and, apparently, more than one grandson. Angus twisted a strand of his copper-tinged light brown hair in his fingers, contemplating this younger Bruce.

He knew from his tutor that since 1266 and the Treaty of Perth, the overlordship of Argyll and the Isles, though never a strong one, had been transferred from Norway to Scotland. And, while his father considered himself a baron of Scotland, control of the Isles was effectively left to his lordship. To think his father was meeting with the Lord of Annandale, a close relative of the King of Scots, who had died only months before, to discuss the future of Scotland was significant indeed.

Just then, his younger brother, John, came running up to him. His hair, the same color as Angus', flying about his face. "Are you going with Father?"

"Aye," Angus said, pride in his voice. "To Carrick."

"You must tell me about it when you return."

"All right." They were friends as well as brothers. Angus looked out for John. Wrapping his arm around his brother's shoulders, they walked back to the castle. "I promise."

September often brought mild, sun-filled days and Angus was pleased the fair weather held as they sailed south from Morvern. The crew pulled hard at the oars, their chanting providing the rhythm for their rowing, carrying him, his father and Alexander over the deep blue water. With his father's guard and two men on each of the twenty-six oars, the galley carried nearly sixty souls.

They sailed past Lorne and Knapdale to Dunaverty Castle, a Macdonald fortress on the southern end of the Kintyre Peninsula. Angus' father had several castles, each located with an eye for defense. It was why their ancestor, Somerled, the first Lord of the Isles, had sited the castles on promontories where enemy ships could be seen from afar.

The sun had already begun its descent, spilling its golden light on the waters of the bay, when they neared the shore beneath Dunaverty Castle. Angus turned to gaze south across the Straits of Moyle. Beneath the sunlit clouds, the long dark shape of Ireland rose in the distance. Ulster, a frequent destination of his father, was a mere twenty miles away.

As the crew beached the galley, his father announced to his captain and crew, "We'll overnight here and sail to Turnberry early on the morrow."

Angus gazed up at the rectangular keep rising above the high curtain wall. When he was a young boy, his father had assured him that once the drawbridge was raised, the castle was nearly impregnable. Of all his family's castles, Angus considered this one the most magnificent.

Turnberry Castle, Carrick, Scotland, 20 September 1286

THE NEXT DAY'S voyage from Dunaverty was a short one, just across the Firth of Clyde to the Scottish mainland. Since his father's meeting was expected to occur upon their arrival, Angus had dressed in a fine linen tunic and blue woolen surcoat, the steel sword at his side a gift from his father.

As the galley approached the Ayrshire coast, Angus fixed his eyes on the castle coming into view. The great stone edifice rose from the surrounding cliffs and crags as if a part of them. On the shore rested several fine galleys, their pennons bearing the badge of the lords who owned them.

The castle itself stood on a rocky spit of land covered in a carpet of green. Its high wall was crowned with a battlement. Each corner of the keep was braced by a tall slender tower that flew a red and gold pennon.

"Are those the Bruce colors?" Angus asked his brother.

"They are, though the Bruces hold the castle and the earldom of Carrick through Marjorie, Countess of Carrick, the wife of Robert the Noble's son and heir. The Bruces have other castles. Lochmaben is the main seat of the lordship of Annandale."

"Well, this one is impressive," remarked Angus, staring up at the castle.

His father nodded. "Aye, needs must with the English close at their backs, sometimes an ally and sometimes an enemy." The same could be said of the MacDougalls, thought Angus, their kinsmen who were often more enemy than friend.

As they sailed closer, a huge arched opening in the rock beneath the castle loomed before them like a great yawning mouth open to the sea. The portcullis had been raised, leaving only the tips of its iron teeth showing. The crew took down the sail and, moving to the oars, rowed the ship through the great sea gate. Angus felt like he was being swallowed by a giant fish.

Once inside the belly of the fortress, the crew maneuvered the ship next to a stone quay where three servants waited.

One, dressed in a fine crimson surcoat embroidered in gold thread such as a seneschal would wear, bowed to Angus' father. "Welcome to Turnberry, my lord. We have been expecting you."

The saffron pennon flying a black galley with furled sails confirmed the ship belonged to The Macdonald, the Chief of the Name, but the seneschal's warm greeting suggested his father had been here before.

"'Tis a fine day," said Angus' father as he stepped from the ship to the ledge with Alex and Angus following.

The thin, dark-haired seneschal inclined his head. "We could not have asked for better weather for those arriving by ship. Your baggage will be delivered to your chambers, my lord. The other guests await you in the great hall." He gestured to the stone stairs. "The Earl of Carrick asks that your men beach the ship next to the others."

"Aye," said Angus' father, turning to give orders to the captain to see it done.

"Your crew will have lodgings just outside the castle within the palisade."

Angus' father thanked the seneschal before exchanging a nod of agreement with his captain. It was a great honor for an Isleman to captain the Lord of the Isles' galley. This captain was one of Angus' father's most worthy warriors, elevated for his skills and loyalty.

They took the stairs that wound upward to a door giving entrance to a great hall. Herbed rushes on the polished stone floor gave off a pleasant smell as Angus stepped into the room and gazed up at the timbered ceiling high above them. The walls beneath were paneled oak and displayed Bruce banners and tapestries depicting hunting scenes. A large fireplace dominated one wall already laid with wood ready to be lit.

At one end of the hall, a minstrels' gallery of carved oak was set above the chamber. Dark and silent now, Angus imagined it filled with musicians like songbirds in a tree high above the forest floor.

In the center of the hall, a dozen men in opulent attire stood around a long wooden table. Their surcoats were embellished with embroidery and, in some cases, jewels. They spoke in hushed voices as they drank from goblets of silver.

The men turned as the Macdonald men entered. An older man separated himself from the group and crossed to them, his smile wide. Angus assumed this was their host, Robert the Noble, Lord of Annandale. His dark hair and slight beard were thick with silver and his gray eyes shone with welcome.

He offered his hand to the Lord of the Isles. "Angus, my good friend! You are the last to join us."

"We are not late, I trust?" said Angus' father, a note of amusement in his voice.

"Nay, more like on time to your thinking." The Lord of Annandale chuckled. "We have only just begun to pour the wine."

"You know my lawful heir, my eldest, Alexander," said the Lord of the Isles.

"I do," replied Robert the Noble. His gaze shifted to Angus. "You bring another fine son?"

His father laid his arm across Angus' shoulder. "My middle son, Angus Og. I thought he might spend time with your grandson, Robert."

The Lord of Annandale raised his thick brows. "An excellent thought. I will summon him." Calling a servant, their host issued instructions before turning back to Angus' father. "I believe you and Alexander know all here save some of the elder sons who accompanied their fathers."

Angus had not yet been told to leave, so he followed behind his father and brother at a discreet distance as they walked toward the men who were gathered around the table. It occurred to him that whatever these noblemen were about, they expected it to affect the next generation or the lords would not have brought their sons.

The Lord of Annandale then introduced them. "For those of you who do not yet know him, meet Sir Angus Mor Macdonald, Lord of the Isles and a longtime friend. He brings with him his eldest son, Alexander, and his middle son, Angus Og."

"Angus Mor is also a friend of mine," said a younger man with dark red hair and trimmed beard, who was of an age with Angus' brother.

"Doubtless, you know every man here, de Burgh," said the elder Robert Bruce. He turned to Angus' father. "The Red Earl of Ulster was instrumental in calling us together so you know he must be in need of something."

A few of the men hid their laughter behind their hands.

Angus had heard his father speak of Richard de Burgh, Earl of Ulster, many times. A Norman, he was a friend of England's King Edward called Longshanks for his long legs.

The Lord of Annandale beckoned to two men with dark hair standing nearby. "Angus, you have met my son, the Earl of Carrick, before. And my other son, Richard, who is most often with King Edward."

"Aye", said Angus' father, holding out his hand to Annandale's sons, first one and then the other. Angus wondered if Richard Bruce kept the King of England informed of this meeting. Doubtless the English king would have insisted upon it.

As he studied Annandale's two sons, Angus thought neither had the presence of their powerful father, unlike his own brother. As a small lad, Alex had been a hostage of King Alexander for their father's good behavior after the Battle of Largs. More than a decade separated him and Angus. He respected Alex as the acknowledged heir who would one day take their father's place as Lord of the Isles.

When Angus was born, his sisters, Mary and Mora were grown and already married. So when his younger brother, John, came along, they became friends.

Robert the Noble then introduced another man who Angus judged to be in his seventh decade. His eyes were blue and his hair and beard full gray and wiry. "Patrick, Earl of Dunbar, has come from Lothian with three of his sons, Patrick, John and Alexander." The sons, somewhere in their fourth decade, dipped their heads to the Lord of the Isles.

"We were glad to hear you were coming," said the Earl of Dunbar, his deep voice resonating about the hall.

"I would never fail to heed Annandale's call," said Angus' father, directing a grin at their host. "The Macdonalds stand with the Bruces."

The face of the eldest Robert Bruce softened with a pleased expression as he continued, "I believe you also know Walter Stewart, Earl of Menteith and sheriff of Dumbarton, but you may not know his two sons, Alexander and John." The earl, who looked to be in his fifth decade, had a prominent nose and dark brows to go with his dark hair. The two sons were of similar appearance and, in age, somewhere between Angus and his brother.

"Aye, Walter and I are well known to each other," said Angus' father, offering his hand to the earl. "It is a pleasure to finally greet your sons."

"Walter's nephews, James Stewart, High Steward of Scotland, and most recently one of the Guardians, and his brother, John, have come, too," said their host.

Angus was aware that the Stewarts' father, Alexander, had just died, which was why, he assumed, the two sons were here in his stead. If a Guardian, James would be one of the new ones appointed to tend the affairs of Scotland since the country now lacked a king.

Both Stewarts, somewhere in their twenties, possessed the look of warriors. Thin-faced, they wore their brown hair long and their beards short.

"I am sorry for the loss of your father," said the Lord of the Isles to the two men.

"Thank you, Lord Angus," said James.

In all this, Angus was virtually ignored and his brother merely acknowledged with a dip of heads. It was their father to whom the nobles and their sons paid tribute. It came to Angus then that Angus Mor Macdonald truly was a magnate of Scotland, respected by all. There was something these men wanted from him, something only he could supply.

"Finally," said the Lord of Annandale, "another has come from Ireland, Thomas de Clare, Lord of Thomond." De Clare was fair of coloring and his eyes light but his face was browned as if he spent most of his time in the sun. About forty in age, he carried himself like a soldier though he was dressed as a peer.

The Lord of Thomond chuckled. "By the King of England's grant, I have lands in Ireland and my lady wife and I are often there, but to find peace, we have recently been sojourning in England with our children."

"Ah, yes," said the Red Earl, "and that brings us to my reason for our meeting."

"And to mine," said their host. "But first a toast to this day!" The Lord of Annandale ordered wine to be poured for the newcomers.

A liveried servant entered and whispered to their host, who beckoned Angus to him. "My grandson, Robert, awaits you outside the castle, Young Angus."

Angus bowed. "Thank you, my lord." And with a glance at his father, he followed the servant out of the hall.

Outside, the servant pointed to a patch of green where a lad of an age with Angus stood staring out to sea, his hands clasped behind him as if contemplating a weighty matter. His chin-length russet hair blew about in the wind. Angus wondered if he had been made to change his clothing for his surcoat was of dark green wool and his hosen a madder red, not the clothing of a boy who had been at play when called. At his side was a man's sword much like the one Angus wore.

Angus strode forward and the boy turned.

"I am Angus Og Macdonald."

"They told me who you were. I am Robert Bruce, the seventh of that name." His eyes were the same gray as his father's, but with a spark his sire's eyes did not possess. Angus and this Bruce were of the same height, tall for their age. They met each other's gaze unflinching.

Angus reached out his hand and they clasped forearms in fulsome manner. "Are you, too, barred from the meeting of the lords?"

"Aye," said the younger Robert. "But it saddens me not. I expect their conversation will be quite dull."

"Not I," said Angus. "I have never seen so many nobles from Scotland and Ireland gathered together in one place. Are you not curious as to why?"

"Not really." He shrugged. "My grandfather is always meeting with some noble or other, especially since King Alexander fell off his horse and died." His look said he had no respect for a man who could not keep his seat. Sliding his sword from its sheath, and facing the sea, he brandished it about. "Besides, I will soon leave to become a squire."

Though his father had been knighted, Angus did not seek the distinction. He had trained with his father's galloglass warriors whose fierce prowess in battle was valued by the kings of both Scotland and Ireland. Still, he liked this Bruce's bravado. Mayhap he had found a kindred spirit.

Angus kept his own sword sheathed. "I, for one, would like to know what business such men are about this day."

"You do?" came Robert's reply, an incredulous look on his face. Puffing out his chest, he sheathed his sword. "I can arrange it."

Angus leaned forward. "You can? How?"

Robert shifted his gaze to the castle ramparts behind him. "I was born in this castle. I know every inch of it. There is a hidden access to the minstrels' gallery where we can hear all that is said in the hall, no one the wiser."

Anticipation coursed through Angus. A surreptitious eavesdropping appealed to him. And it would not exactly be attending the meeting. With a sweep of his hand, he said, "By all means, lead on, new friend."

Robert smiled, obviously pleased he had thought of it. "Follow me."

They entered by a side door and crossed through the kitchens to the chagrin of the cook, who frowned and shook her head at them. But what could she say to the master's son?

A short way on, they ventured into a dark passage. Angus followed on Robert's heels until they reached a wooden staircase where he paused. "Up here," he whispered, "but be quiet."

At the top of the stairs, Robert dropped to his knees. "Keep down and mind your sword," he said in a low voice. "They cannot see us as the parapet is solid oak."

Angus had seen the gallery from below and knew this to be true. He dropped to his knees and followed. As they carefully found their way onto the narrow platform, Angus could hear voices rising into the air.

"We must first acknowledge," said the Lord of Annandale, "that Scotland's king, now dead, has left no male heir and only the possibility that Queen Yolande's pregnancy will lead to a male child. Otherwise, it falls to his wee granddaughter, the one they call the Maid of Norway, to uphold the crown."

"There is no precedent for female succession even should Margaret of Norway grow to adulthood and there is no other heir," said a deep voice Angus recognized as belonging to the Earl of Dunbar.

Angus grew excited at hearing these words. *Their business is the successor to Scotland's throne!*

Then, from below, he heard Robert Bruce, Earl of Carrick, say, "My father, Lord of Annandale, is of royal blood, a descendant of King David and second cousin of the late King Alexander. Moreover, he has the stature to command the loyalty of his fellow Scots."

"Aye, there is none more suited to wear the crown." The familiar voice was that of Angus' father.

"John Balliol will challenge your claim," said a voice Angus thought he recognized as that of Walter Stewart, Earl of Menteith.

"Balliol is aligned with the Comyns who are joined in purpose with the MacDougalls, the enemies of the Macdonalds," said Angus' father.

"Then we can count on the support of the Lord of the Isles?" said the Lord of Annandale.

"You have always had it," said Angus' father.

"Should King Alexander's descendants fail, Guardians of the Realm must be appointed to serve until a new king is chosen," said the deep-voiced Earl of Dunbar.

"And in the choosing," said the Lord of Annandale, "there will likely be war when I put forward my name. For that, we will require soldiers such as you, de Burgh, and you, Macdonald, command—the famed galloglass."

"And the ships to bring them to Scotland's western shore," said one who Angus thought might be Walter Stewart, Earl of Menteith.

"Just so," replied Robert the Noble. "Angus, you have more ships than anyone."

"Aye, I'll not dispute that," replied the Lord of the Isles.

"As long as we are speaking of soldiers and ships," said the Earl of Ulster, "we in Ireland have enemies who would have us dead. Our own forces, barring any help from England, are insufficient."

"I see that my ships and galloglass will be much in demand," said the Lord of the Isles, a note of humor in his voice. Angus pictured his sire with a wry smile on his face. He must have known, or at least suspected, why the Macdonalds were invited to this meeting.

"Your Islesmen are known to be fierce fighters," said de Burgh. "I would hardly want to go to war without them. But I would ask that henceforth, you not supply your galloglass to my enemies."

"Add my voice to that of de Burgh," said Thomas de Clare, Lord of Thomond. "I have been trying to hold on to the Irish lands King Edward gave me for seven long years without success, which is why I'm in London instead of Ireland."

"Agreed," said Angus' father. "No longer will the lordship supply mercenaries to any Irish lord who opposes the Earldom of Ulster."

A rustle of parchment rose to Angus' ears.

"With that in mind," said the Lord of Annandale, "I have taken the liberty of drawing up the text of a band to which we might agree. The allusion to the Scottish crown is left intentionally vague should this be discovered, but knowing the needs of de Burgh and de Clare, which are aligned with King Edward's, the document mentions both of them specifically."

"Read it aloud for all of us to hear," said Walter Stewart, Earl of Menteith.

"Very well," said the Lord of Annandale, and he began to read.

We inform all of you by our present writing that we have bound ourselves and have faithfully promised – and by swearing a bodily oath, touching the holy Gospels, and by pledging our faith, we have strengthened our promise to unfailingly adhere to the noble persons, the Lord Richard de Burgh, Earl of Ulster, and the Lord Thomas de Clare in all their affairs; and with them and with their accomplices we shall faithfully stand against all their enemies saving our faith unto the Lord King of England and saving our faith unto him who, by reason of nearness of blood unto Lord Alexander, King of Scots, lately deceased, shall possess and obtain the kingdom of Scotland, according to the ancient customs which have hitherto been approved and used in the kingdom of Scotland.

"A canny document," said Angus' father. "Masterful in saying as little as possible while complying with what I perceive is the intent of this gathering."

"Aye," agreed the Earl of Menteith.

Annandale's eldest son, Robert, Earl of Carrick, said, "And you, Father, have preserved your right to claim the throne by your blood relation to our dead king."

"In exchange for our pledge," said James Stewart, the High Steward of Scotland, "there will be things we who are not mentioned would ask."

"Of course," said Annandale's lord. "But let us defer those discussions until after dinner. Then, if all can be made acceptable, we can affix our signatures."

Murmurs of agreement rose from below the gallery where Angus kneeled, stunned at what he had heard. His new friend nudged him, gesturing toward the stairs leading down from the gallery.

They retraced their steps and, once outside, retreated to the same swath of grass overlooking the Firth of Clyde. The wind had picked up but the day was still full of sun.

Angus looked around and seeing they were alone, said, "Your grandsire wants to be the next King of Scots!"

The younger Robert Bruce furrowed his brows. "Aye, so it would appear."

Angus was puzzled at the bland expression on his friend's face. "You do not seem surprised."

Robert let out a sigh and stared at the toe of his leather shoe which he dug into the grass. "Nay, not surprised. If the throne comes vacant, the crown should be his by right. Yet I know my grandfather spoke the truth when he said it will mean war if he makes a claim to be king."

"And you are not yet a knight, is that it?"

"Aye, in part. I would want to fight for my family."

Angus raised himself to his full height and, remembering his father's words about the Macdonalds being aligned with the Bruces, he put his hand on the hilt of his sword and declared, "The Macdonalds stand with the Bruces. And I, Angus Og, will stand with you, bound to you by my honor."

His new friend smiled and nodded. "Very well. I will be glad of your friendship and your pledge, Angus. And you may call me Rob."

Pleased they were of one mind, Angus thought to remind Rob of their families' long-ago connection. "Did you know that Somerled, the first Lord of the Isles, my great-great-grandfather, was a friend of your ancestor, King David?"

"I have never thought about it but likely my grandfather knows of it. He speaks often to our sennachie who keeps the family history."

Angus would have this new friend aware of the Macdonalds' illustrious beginnings. "Somerled was Lord of Argyll and all the Isles as well as King of the Isle of Man. He never paid homage to the Scots king but I am told he pledged his honor to David and was true to that pledge, fighting with the king at the Battle of the Standard in England."

His new friend's face took on a look of chagrin as if he were recalling an unpleasant truth. "The first Robert Bruce fought on the side of England in that battle but the family's fortunes rose when the fourth lord married Isabel, a daughter of King David. And that is how my grandfather, the fifth Robert Bruce, claims his right to the throne."

Robert raised his head as a liveried servant strode toward them in efficient manner. "You are summoned to dinner, Master Robert, along with the young Macdonald."

The servant hurried back toward the castle and Rob said, "Well, at least tonight I shan't have to dine with my younger siblings. I think

I have you to thank for that."

"I, too, am glad of it," Angus said as they returned to the castle. "The food will be better and when they send us out so they can continue their discussions, we can have a game of chess."

"Aye," said Rob. "My grandfather says chess is good practice for planning battle strategy."

"True," replied Angus, and then with a smile he added, "but as my father reminds me, the most powerful piece on the board is a woman."

Rob chuckled. "He must have met my mother, the Countess of Carrick."

They shared a laugh as they entered the great hall to find the long table now turned and placed at one end. Two trestle tables had been added at right angles to the head table. All were covered with white cloths. Candles flickered on each table and a fire burned steadily in the stone fireplace, filling the air with the faint odor of wood smoke.

Rob's father, the Earl of Carrick, left the servants he'd been speaking with and strode toward them. "As you two will be the only younger sons in the hall tonight, I thought you might like to serve the wine before taking your seats at the lower end of one of the trestles."

Rob nodded his head. "As you wish, sir."

Angus nodded his assent. He had only been asked to serve once before but he knew it was often a task given to the younger sons of noblemen. Importantly for this evening, it also provided a way to hear the conversations of the lords as they dined.

The same nobles and their sons he had seen earlier began to trail in from the stairs leading from the upper chambers to take their seats. Added to their number was a woman clothed in a gown of mulberry-colored silk with a jeweled belt and a veil that partially covered her auburn hair.

"'Tis my lady mother," said Rob, "the Countess of Carrick. Have you met her?"

Angus gazed with approval at the slender and very pretty countess who he judged to be in her early thirties. "Nay, but I would like to."

Rob urged Angus forward. They arrived in front of the lady of the castle and Angus bowed before her.

"So, you are Angus Mor's middle son," she said, her eyes alight with interest as she perused his person. "Welcome to Turnberry." Behind those blue eyes, Angus sensed a woman of great strength.

"Thank you, my lady."

"I can see that you and Rob are enjoying each other's company. My son has served at our table before when we've had visiting noblemen so he can direct you." She gave her son a passing glance and glided back to her husband where she took her place at the head table.

"When we finish serving," said Rob, "and are playing our game of chess, I will tell you how my mother won my father's marriage proposal. It is a story oft told to my father's amusement."

In the gallery above the great hall where he and Rob had hidden earlier that day, minstrels began to play their harp, lute and lyre.

Angus eagerly joined his new friend in serving the wine to the seated nobles, catching snippets of their conversation that he now understood related to the meeting earlier that day.

"You could force the issue by seizing a few castles in the southwest," said the Earl of Menteith to the Lord of Annandale. His voice had been pitched low but, listening attentively, Angus had overheard.

"I have been considering such a move—" began Robert the Noble.

Angus did not hear the rest as the aged Earl of Dunbar, sitting to the right of the Earl of Carrick and his countess, beckoned him. When he finished pouring for Dunbar's earl, he cast a glance toward the trestle tables and noticed that the two nobles from Ireland, the Red Earl of Ulster and Thomas de Clare, had their heads together, whispering beneath the sound of the minstrels. Turning from de Clare, the Red Earl leaned over to Angus' father to speak in his ear.

Angus and Rob had just finished pouring the wine and assuring the flagons set before the guests were full when servants entered the hall bearing great platters of food. The smells of herbed meats filled the air making Angus very hungry. He had eaten nothing since breaking his fast at Dunaverty Castle that morn.

"Let us find our seats," said Rob, coming to him. "I am famished."

They claimed the last seats across from each other at the end of one trestle and began to fill their trenchers from the sumptuous feast set before them. Dinner was everything Angus had hoped it would be. Trout in white butter sauce, chicken with cumin and cream sauce and beef served in a wine currant sauce were among the offerings. These were accompanied by leeks with walnuts, herbed beets and parsley bread. By the time Angus finished, he was sated and rubbing his stomach.

"When my mother leaves the hall," said Rob, looking in her direction, "it will be time for us to retire to our chess game."

A short while later, they had left the hall for their game. As Angus bent over the chessboard, contemplating his next move, his new friend began to tell him of how his parents came to marry. A candle flickering at his side cast Rob's face in shadow as he spoke.

"My mother was first married to Michael de Kilconquhar, who died at Acre while on crusade. She was told of his death by one of his companions-in-arms who arrived at Carrick with the news. As it happened, the messenger was my father, who was, I am told by my mother, a handsome man in his second decade. My mother was only fifteen at the time but she knew what she wanted." He paused before adding, "She is still a formidable woman."

Angus thought of the auburn-haired woman he had met earlier and tried to imagine what a formidable woman looked like at fifteen. Neither of his older sisters could be so described.

"Anyway," Rob went on, "as the story goes, she was smitten with my father and decided to hold him prisoner at Turnberry until he agreed to marry her."

Angus forgot the bishop he was holding in his hand. "What?"

Rob smiled. "They were married the next year."

Angus shook his head. "That is some story."

"My mother told me the tale herself."

"'Tis amazing."

Their chess game continued and was followed by two more as they shared more family stories. When the games ended, Angus had won two of the three and he and Rob had become fast friends.

CHAPTER 2

Dunseverick Castle, northern coast of Ulster, Ireland, May 1289

ÁINE DREW HER fur-lined cloak around her against the sharp wind as she took the path along the edge of the promontory on the cliff high above the sea where Dunseverick Castle stood, the seat of the O'Cahans.

A gust of wind whipped her dark hair across her face. She drew it back to glimpse the blooming yellow gorse interspersed among the thick green grass. The sun on the wildflowers was a welcome sight after days of rain. Smiling to herself, she inhaled the sweet smell of the blossoms.

Hundreds of feet below, skirting the cliffs, the blue sea sparkled like a sapphire jewel.

She gazed north, across the Sea of Moyle, to Rathlin Island ten miles offshore where a colony of puffins lived.

Most often, Áine and her wolfhound, Finn, she had named after the King of the Fairies, walked the clifftop early in the morning so she could be alone with her birds before her father's men-at-arms took to the practice yard. Many of her feathered friends made their homes on the cliffs and in the surrounding waters, particularly in the spring, and she looked forward to their return each year.

Gray and white herring gulls and the smaller but stocky fulmars abounded on the cliffs. From their nests, the fulmar pairs cackled to one another. Together with black cormorants, they swooped in front of the sheer cliff face, putting on a great show. Puffins, too, had come to nest here. Their whimsical appearance could keep her entertained for hours. Soon the noisy kittiwakes would be arriving for the summer.

The gulls greeted her with raucous cries as she neared their nests. Finn regarded them with only mild interest as he walked at her side. She recognized the gull with the unusual black mark on his gray wing as he flew above her and dropped a small starfish at her feet.

An offering from a friend.

Finn sniffed at it and then looked up at her, his copper-colored eyes suggesting he perceived no trait worth noting. She stroked his wiry gray head and reached down to pick up the starfish, holding it in the palm of her hand. "'Tis a marvelous creature, Finn, one worthy of your respect." The starfish was cold and damp to the touch. She would return it to the cove at the foot of the cliffs where her favorite gull doubtless had found it.

She fancied all the birds knew her. Sometimes, she sang to them and, though the wind swept away her words, she often spoke to them. She had no other friends. Her only sibling, her younger brother, Dermot, was now fostering with the de Burghs at Dunluce Castle down the coast.

A sigh escaped her lips. In a month, she would be sixteen, an auspicious age when her father would be seeking a marriage for her. The idea caused her to feel both excitement and fear.

Knowing the day would come, she had oft wondered who her future husband might be. When the eyes of one of her father's soldiers had followed her, she wondered if one of them might be hers. But no, her father would never give her to a man without lands or title. He would want an alliance of importance for the O'Cahans. Mayhap a younger son of one of the nearby lords. She prayed whoever he was he would be someone she could love.

"My lady!" shouted her handmaiden running toward her. "Your lord father is asking for you."

"No need to be overexcited, Nessa. I am here." Then, holding out the starfish, she said, "If I am to go to the castle, it must be you who returns this little one to the waters of the cove."

Nessa tucked a stray curl of her brown hair beneath her kerchief, as if to avoid taking the starfish, and turned up her freckled nose. "Me?"

"Here," Áine said, reaching out her hand, "take it and do not delay or it will not live."

Her handmaiden curtseyed. "As you wish, Mistress." Reluctantly, Nessa took the starfish onto her palm and held it out before her as if it were a serving tray as she took the path down to the cove.

Amused, Áine beckoned to Finn and they hurried on, past the guards who greeted her with a nod, and entered the castle.

The light in the hall was dim after the full sun outside. Pausing to allow her eyes to adjust, she glimpsed her father standing in front of the fire, staring into the flames. His arms were crossed in front of him, the stance he always took when pondering something. His hair, dark brown like hers, curled to his shoulders over his red-brown surcoat of fine wool.

Laying her hand on Finn's head, she commanded him to "Wait". Walking forward, she said, "Father, you wished to see me?"

He turned and gave her a small smile. In his fourth decade, Cumee O'Cahan was a handsome man with strong features. He was also a man who commanded the respect of other men. The O'Neill, King of Tirowen, entrusted him with the defense of the northern, western and eastern approaches to the O'Neill territory.

"I did. We are to have guests this eve, the Earl of Ulster, his wife, Lady Margaret de Burgh, and The O'Neill. I want you to wear your finest gown and act my hostess."

"Of course, Father. I will see all is made ready for your guests." He had an odd look on his face, almost nostalgic and mayhap tinged with regret. Was he thinking of the past? The loss of his much-loved wife? Áine knew that sometimes when he looked at her, he was seeing her mother whom he oft told her she resembled in appearance.

Áine had only known her as a small child but remembered her scent of flowers. She died in childbed trying to birth a second son. Mayhap it was her memory that had clouded his thoughts. Certainly, it was not his request for Áine to act as hostess, which was most reasonable. Now that she was considered a woman and her mother no longer living, it would be proper for her to act the hostess for her father's guests and she often did. "Will they stay the night?"

"I do not know. We must be prepared should they decide to do so but, with fair weather and their lands so close, they might return home after the evening's entertainment."

Her father was not only Chief of the Name of O'Cahan but Lord of Ciannacht and senior subking to Niall O'Neill, King of Tirowen, whose large territory lay to the south. Their overlord, Richard de Burgh, Earl of Ulster, had several castles, Dunluce on the coast, where her brother was fostering, being the closest to Dunseverick.

By the time she returned to her chamber, Nessa was there, her kerchief having been discarded to let her brown curls fall free.

"Nessa, we are to have noble guests in the hall this eve. I must meet with the cook to see about the menu and to speak to the seneschal. While I am gone, please have a bath drawn for me. I think the crimson silk gown and my mother's pearls would be appropriate for tonight. I must honor my father with my appearance in serving as his hostess."

Nessa curtseyed. "You will, I am certain, my lady." And then with a smile, she added, "I will see to it!"

Her handmaiden was at her best in dressing Áine as a lady. "Did my little starfish arrive safely in the tidepool at the cove?"

"Aye, Mistress, he did."

A smile on her face, Áine headed for the door.

Later that day, her tasks finished and having bathed and dressed for the evening, Áine came down to the hall to assure all was ready. Finn was asleep beside the fire, no doubt sated by his dinner. He raised his head at her entrance and then laid it down on his front paws, keeping his alert eyes focused on her.

Torches set into brackets on the stone walls illuminated the shields, banners and tapestries. One of the tapestries, stitched in cream, blue and green, was Áine's own design and featured her birds, her favorite herring gull in the center.

Candles on the head table and sideboard and a fire in the stone fireplace added a warm glow to the large chamber and took the dampness from the air. She was pleased at all she saw, knowing the dinner she had planned would also impress their guests.

"All looks to be in order, Áine," said her father when he arrived.

"Thank you. I was hoping you would find it so."

The two of them were still conversing when a servant came to tell them a carriage had arrived. The O'Neill might come by horse but since the earl was traveling with his countess, Áine expected the carriage to be theirs.

The castle door opened and the guard escorted the two inside. Richard de Burgh, Earl of Ulster, was a slender man of thirty years with ruddy countenance, dark red hair and well-trimmed beard. He wore the fine clothing of a nobleman, a dark blue tunic with green surcoat and a jeweled belt. Though he was born in Ulster, the Red Earl, as he was called by many, had been raised in England and was now, with the blessing of England's king, the most powerful Norman in Ireland.

His countess, Lady Margaret, the daughter of the Earl of Kent, was of fair coloring and her figure shown to advantage by a gown of green damask. A gold chain and jewels worn around her neck identified her as an Englishwoman of high rank. Áine liked the countess for the smile on her pleasant face was always genuine.

Irish women, whose long flowing hair was the subject of bards' poems, did not often wear veils or head coverings, even the married ones, but since Margaret de Burgh was English, she covered her flaxen hair with fine linen.

"Welcome to Dunseverick," said Áine's father, reaching his hand to the earl. Inclining his head to the countess, he said, "Lady Margaret, you grace my hall."

Áine curtseyed. "My lord, my lady."

"'Tis good to see you, Áine," said the countess, giving Áine an appraising look. "You have grown into a fine young lady."

Áine thanked her but before she could say more, de Burgh inquired, "Has The O'Neill arrived yet?"

"Not yet," said Áine's father. "I expect he will be riding up to my door at any moment with his guard. Meantime, let us partake of some good French wine."

A servant brought a tray of jeweled silver goblets filled with red wine and offered them first to their guests. When the tray was offered to her, having many duties this eve, Áine took a goblet but did not intend to drink the wine until dinner.

"How is my son doing at Dunluce?" Áine's father asked the earl.

"I am told he is a sturdy lad and diligent in his training," said de Burgh. "As well, he has a gift for languages at which he excels."

Her father smiled at the earl's words.

Áine was happy to hear the report concerning her brother. Dermot had been anxious about doing well at Dunluce before he left.

Just then, the heavy castle door swung open. His dark blue eyes alight with fierce intent, The O'Neill strode in on a gust of wind that swirled around the hall, scattering flames in the fireplace.

Tall and elegantly attired in black velvet and silver, a jeweled dagger at his hip, Niall O'Neill's presence filled the room. His fair skin bore lines etched by time, but he still had the body of a warrior and the determined look of a man who was ever on a mission.

Áine had been told that at one time, at war with his brother for the kingdom, Niall had shaved the front of his head and allowed the remainder of his hair to hang long down his back, the sign of a warrior's oath. The nickname "Culanach", given him then, meant "of the long back hair". The description no longer applied as he now wore his ginger hair only to his shoulders and his beard short. Áine was too young to have known him then. Now, the silver in his hair and beard marked his fifth decade.

To Áine, all the O'Neills looked alike with their reddish hair, some lighter than others, and their penetrating eyes and bold features. They acted alike as well, often at war with each other over Tirowen, their large kingdom in the center of Ulster.

"At last, The O'Neill graces my humble hall with his presence!" announced her father, a note of amusement in his voice as they were good friends. "Welcome."

"'Tis my honor, Cumee," said the King of Tirowen, bowing more deeply than courtesy and his superior rank called for. "And greetings to you, my lord earl, and to your countess." He inclined his head to King Edward's man and bowed to Lady Margaret.

"My lord," Áine said, curtseying before him.

Keeping his eyes on her, The O'Neill handed his cloak to a waiting servant and reached for her hand, touching his lips to her knuckles. The gesture, which she considered oddly intimate, made her uncomfortable. She was unused to such greetings from her father's friends. When she looked up, his gaze lingered on her person.

Six years ago, when Niall's brother was slain, Niall's second cousin, Domnall O'Neill, had seized the Tirowen kingship. In reaction to Domnall's perfidy, and with the O'Cahans' full support, de Burgh had deposed Domnall and installed Niall as King of Tirowen in his place. Áine was but a girl of nine years then. Her father had told her the story.

She had seen Richard and Margaret de Burgh occasionally over the years and Niall O'Neill in passing at last summer's fair but she had not spent much time in their presence. Not since Niall had been inaugurated as King of Tirowen at Tullyhogue three years before. Áine had attended the ceremony as the O'Cahans had a necessary role in the installation of a new king. At the feast held afterwards, she had met many Irish nobles and their children.

The servant, who had previously served wine, brought a tray with a goblet for The O'Neill.

"'Tis French wine," said her father. "A good red from Bordeaux."

Niall lifted the goblet from the tray and held it to her father in salute. "I would expect nothing less from Cumee O'Cahan."

Her father had ordered his minstrels to appear and they began to entertain them from the far end of the hall.

As they drank their wine, the men's conversation turned to affairs in Ireland and Scotland. Áine listened, often glancing at Margaret de Burgh. The countess stared into her goblet, rarely looking up. Áine could not tell if it was disinterest on Lady Margaret's part or because she had heard it all before. Mayhap it was her preference to say little when in the company of men.

De Burgh was speaking as Áine turned her attention to the men. "It seems I may soon be welcoming my friend Sir Angus Mor Macdonald and his son Angus Og to Ulster."

"And why is that?" asked The O'Neill.

De Burgh took a sip of his wine before replying. "He has sent me a letter telling me of his plans to intervene in Tirconnell in support of his grandson, Turlough, whose mother is one of Angus Mor's daughters. Apparently, as a part of the marriage bargain, Donnell O'Donnell, the old King of Tirconnell, promised the kingship to her firstborn son. But Aodh, the son of O'Donnell's first wife, believes the crown should be his."

"The O'Donnells are an unruly lot. They have ever been at war with the O'Neills," put in Niall.

Earl Richard nodded. "Sadly, my family has been keenly aware of that for decades. You realize, of course, that Angus Mor tells me this not because it will please me. He knows it will not, but because he does not want me to interfere."

"Will you?" asked Niall.

"Not unless I must to keep the peace. Angus Mor knows how to handle himself. I trust him not to make a mess of it."

"If the Lord of the Isles brings his galloglass with him, he will surely prevail," said Áine's father. Áine had heard much about the Macdonalds who controlled the Hebrides and were known to have strong ties to Ulster. Some of the Macdonald galloglass served Irish lords as guards and mercenaries.

"I agree," said Earl Richard. "That is why I mention it. We may as well be prepared for them to descend on Ulster. Since your lands border theirs, Niall, I wanted you to be aware. Now that I think on it, I might invite Angus Mor to Dunluce. The Lord of the Isles is one Scot whose favor we should cultivate. He was one of the barons invited by King Alexander to attend the parliament he held in Scone five years ago."

"Where the king persuaded the Scottish magnates to accept his granddaughter, Margaret, as the heir to the throne?" asked Niall.

"The very same," replied de Burgh. "For Angus Mor's support, the king granted him the Ardnamurchan Peninsula in Lochaber. Why is not difficult to understand. Angus Mor commands more than a hundred and fifty galleys and thousands of Islesmen."

"The Lord of the Isles is known to me," said Niall, "as he must be to all. His army of warriors and galloglass can move as swiftly over water as migrating birds."

Earl Richard said, "So you understand why he is an ally I can ill afford to lose."

Áine's father and The O'Neill nodded to the earl, who said, "On another matter of some interest to us, I have received a message from King Edward."

The other men waited, their gazes fixed on the earl. Áine was certain Richard de Burgh received many missives from the English king. Why would he share this one?

"The king writes concerning the Isle of Man. Apparently, the Manx have petitioned Edward for his protection from the Comyns of Badenoch and the MacDougalls of Lorne. The king wants me to obtain an oath from the isle's leaders binding them to him as their sovereign lord."

"The Macdonalds will have mixed feelings about that," said Áine's father. "Both they and the Bruces consider the Comyns and the MacDougalls their enemies, and for good reason. Moreover, the Isle of Man once belonged to the Macdonalds."

"True," agreed de Burgh. "Ironically, Robert the Noble and the Comyns have come together for a purpose of keen interest to King Edward. At this very moment, the Lord of Annandale and the Earl of Buchan are traveling to Salisbury to flesh out the details of a treaty of marriage between the Maid of Norway and Edward's son, the young Prince Edward."

The O'Neill drew back with furrowed brow. "But that would eventually put Scotland under England's control."

"Aye, it would," said Áine's father. "And though King Edward would be pleased, many in Scotland would not."

"As long as you mention the Lord of Annandale," said The O'Neill, "I am curious. I heard he had attacked the Balliol castles of Dumfries, Wigtown and Buittle. How goes that?"

"Well enough to make the Balliols more vulnerable in their Lordship of Galloway," replied de Burgh.

Áine's father chuckled. "Balliol is in a bad position with his lands located inconveniently between the Bruces' lands of Annandale and Carrick."

Earl Richard looked down at his wine, his expression thoughtful. "Indeed."

"As far as the Bruces go," said Niall, "I am told the Guardians of Scotland are standing firm against their challenge of Balliol."

"That news has come to me, too," said Earl Richard. "The Bruces' little war may end with them handing back the castles they've taken. It is too early for them to lay claim to the crown since the Maid of Norway is still heir."

"What age is little Margaret now?" inquired Áine. Everyone who cared about affairs in Scotland knew of her, the daughter of Norway's king and granddaughter of the dead king Alexander. "Is she not just a child?

All eyes turned to her as if surprised she had spoken.

"She is but six, Lady Áine," said Earl Richard with a kindly look, "too young to rule. Which is why Scotland has Guardians at the moment. When they can manage to agree, they act as regents, governing the Kingdom of Scotland, until the young queen comes to her majority."

The O'Neill inclined his head toward Áine. "Young Margaret has held the throne since she was three when the queen of the deceased King Alexander failed to deliver a living child."

A servant approached Áine and said, "Dinner is ready, my lady."

She nodded to the servant and turned to her father. "If our guests are ready to dine, Father, the meal is ready to be served."

"Well then," said her father, turning to his guests, "shall we adjourn to the table?"

"Your men," she said to Earl Richard and The O'Neill as they began to follow her father, "will be escorted to the kitchens where they will be fed."

They thanked her and, together, crossed the hall to the dais where the head table had been graced with a white cloth and set with silver.

Áine's father took the center chair with the de Burghs on his right and The O'Neill on his left. Niall beckoned her to take the chair next to him on the end.

Though the food was sumptuous, she ate sparingly as her attention was focused on the dishes being served, their guests' exclamations of delight and the servants efficiently attending to everyone's needs.

For most of the meal, The O'Neill spoke to her father, sometimes in hushed tones, but when the minstrels paused in their music to allow their bard to come forward, The O'Neill leaned toward her and said, "You have become a great beauty, Áine, as I thought you would."

Embarrassed at his flattery, Áine dropped her gaze to the trencher she shared with him. He had placed many slices of roast game and venison on her side. Most she had left untasted. The heat of his presence was tangible, for he was not a small man. Intimidating, not only for his size, but because he was the King of Tirowen and his very title commanded respect.

"You are too kind, my lord."

He lifted his goblet to his lips and took a drink before answering. "Not so kind as discerning, I think. Surely you cannot help but notice the way men look at you."

"Most of the men I know are my father's soldiers or his friends. They are always respectful."

"You are young, Áine, but you are a woman full grown if I judge correctly. You should know that a man will take note of a beautiful woman no matter his station."

Áine was becoming uncomfortable with their conversation and was glad when the bard took his seat before the dais and began to recite a poem to the playing of a harp.

Once dinner and the entertainment ended and the men stood again before the large fireplace with their wine in hand, talking, Áine invited Margaret de Burgh to step outside the castle. "'Tis magnificent at this time of night but we will want our cloaks." The countess consented and with the permission of her father and Earl Richard, Áine led her outside.

The sun hung low over the horizon and its descent had painted the sky a vivid salmon color.

"I see what you mean," said the countess, looking to the horizon. "We have beautiful sunsets at Dunluce but this one is exceptional coming as it does on a rare clear eve."

"I like to walk the cliff path at this time of day," said Áine, "and in the early morning." As they talked, they began to walk the familiar path. Finn had followed them outside and now walked beside Áine.

The countess inclined her head toward her. "Can you see yourself leaving your father's home one day?"

With a sigh, Áine replied, "I suppose I must at some point but I would miss all this and my father."

"I anticipated the same when I married Richard yet now I have more splendid views than in England and a life where I can contribute more. You will, too."

Áine drank in the sky and the sea, overwhelmed by God's creation, and wondered how she could ever have a more beautiful place to live than this.

"Your father will choose well for you, of that I am certain, for 'tis clear he loves you much."

"Ah, but that is not always the reason for marriage, is it?" Áine was young but she knew the way of the world for women of noble birth. She turned to the countess whose face reflected the warm light of the setting sun.

Lady Margaret smiled. "You are correct, of course. It is rare a woman can choose. Even noble English widows are considered the king's wards and can be bargained off for lands and alliances."

Áine was suddenly chilled. "Should we go inside? The air grows cold."

"Probably a wise idea. The men will be wondering if we fell off the cliff."

They laughed as they walked back together yet a foreboding came over Áine and she reached out to pat Finn's head. She sensed her life would soon change did she want it to or not.

Their guests decided to depart that eve, the sky giving sufficient light for their travel.

Áine bid them Godspeed, waving from where she stood next to

her father on the road in front of the castle.

"You did well tonight," he said. "The earl and The O'Neill both spoke highly of you and your proficiency as a hostess."

She waited for she knew he would say more.

They walked into the castle and, without looking at her, he said, "The O'Neill has asked for your hand in marriage."

For a moment, Áine could say nothing as her mind reeled with the shock of his words. "But Father," she protested, "he is older than you by a decade! I am not yet sixteen and he is more than fifty. Surely you do not mean to give me to him?"

"'Tis true, Niall O'Neill has waited long to marry and sire legitimate children. But he is now firmly ensconced as the King of Tirowen and in great favor with the Earl of Ulster and King Edward. The value of the alliance to the O'Cahans is immeasurable."

Her father's voice was not stern. He was rarely stern with her. But in his kindness she sensed his resolve and heard the door slamming on her dreams. Her eyes filled with tears. She blinked them back, yet one lone tear betrayed her, streaking down her face. She brushed it away.

He must have seen it. "The O'Neill has vowed to treat you well," he assured her. "I believe him, for he has loved you for some time. He thought you enchanting as a young girl at his inauguration three years ago. I told him then I would not consider a marriage for you until you reached your womanhood."

Suddenly it came to her. This was the fate the countess had alluded to. She must have known what was coming. And this was the cause of the regret she had seen in her father's eyes. The whole evening had been arranged to bring about this result.

"This is God's choice for you, Áine. Consider that one day your son may be the King of Tirowen."

She made no reply. Whether it was God's choice, she could not say. Clearly, it was her father's.

"You will have the summer, Áine, but prepare yourself. In early autumn, you will become the wife of The O'Neill...and his queen."

She turned sixteen in June and thereafter time moved all too rapidly.

Determined to make the most of her remaining days of freedom, she left her wedding clothes to Nessa and others, who cared about such things, while she and Finn took long walks and lingered on the clifftop where she spent time among her birds.

At night by candlelight with Finn curled up at her feet, she read the poems of the bards, drinking in the history they recorded, some concerning her own family. One poem, in particular, struck her, the lament recording the death of her grandfather, Magnus O'Cahan, at the Battle of Down. The sadness in the bard's words spoke to her heart:

Five of the active Clan Cahan
Fell in the slaughter besides Magnus;
The fall of five burst the battle array.
Alas! Are they not losses!
Though to me each man is a grief
For O'Cahan the yellow-haired I most grieve.
He is the wound of the artery of my head.
This is the blood which I cannot bear.
Grievous to our children and women
Is the killing of Magnus O'Cahan.

Ireland had ever been the land of warring clans and men who, from jealousy or want of power, would kill to gain another man's title, another man's office. Was it their destiny to always be so? In marrying The O'Neill, would she be dragged deeper into such conflicts? For her, it was a futile inquiry.

In those long summer days and the months that passed, Áine matured. She supposed it was the sadness of this passage into adulthood and the coming unwanted marriage that aged her. She had accepted her fate but it did not bring a smile to her face.

The O'Neill paid her two visits that summer. The first, she was convinced, was merely to assure himself she had consented to his suit.

"I trust you are looking forward to our marriage?" he asked as they went riding one dreary day. He had taken pains with his appearance, dressing in fine garments and his graying ginger hair neatly trimmed.

She looked straight ahead wondering where her birds were. "My father has agreed and I know my duty, my lord."

"Call me by my given name, Áine. After all, we will soon be wed."

"Yes, my lord," she said absently.

Her reply called forth a chuckle from him.

The second visit was, to her mind, an effort to court her. He was eager; she was resigned. As they walked the clifftop path, he had taken her hand and she had not pulled it back, for soon he would take far more liberties with her person. She dreaded her wedding night, but then what girl bartered for lands or an alliance did not? Those who married kings were never given a choice. At least the King of Tirowen wanted her and, if what she saw in his dark blue gaze spoke truth, he desired her as well.

Before he left that day, he placed in her hand a golden ring brooch studded with gems. "Think of me when you wear it."

"I will, my lord."

On the day they were to leave for Tirowen and her marriage to its king, the dark clouds overhead that portended rain mirrored her mood. She lingered long on the clifftop, saying goodbye to her birds. They would never understand where she had gone and that was as it should be. Finn and Nessa would come with her but all else she cared for would stay behind.

When she could delay no longer, she faced the sea that mirrored the gray clouds and inhaled deeply of the fragrance of home, wanting to never forget. With a last look at her birds, she turned and slowly walked to where her father waited by the carriage.

CHAPTER 3

Tirconnell, Ulster, Ireland, early October 1290

TO ANGUS, IRELAND seemed a world apart from Argyll and the Isles. He stared wide-eyed at the rugged sea cliffs looming above the white-tipped waves as he and his brother and their cousin, Duncan MacAlasdair, sailed down the west coast of Tirconnell.

A wild coast, it challenged the best seaman. Braving high winds and the churning Atlantic the thirty galleys the Lord of the Isles had brought to Ulster were so pressed at times that Angus and his companions took to the oars to give some relief to the oarsmen.

Angus was glad his cousin had joined them as Duncan was good company and cheerful in the worst of times. His father, the brother of Angus Mor, though a Macdonald, had given his sons the surname MacAlasdair, beginning a new clan.

Cherub-like in appearance with his honey-colored hair, green eyes and ruddy cheeks, Duncan could, at times, be a bit of a rogue when it came to the lasses. But he was a strong hand Angus counted upon in times of trouble. When a powerful wave crashed over the gunwale, ripping an oar from a crewman's hand, Duncan dove for the oar and handed it back to the seaman, saying "I wonder when the hot wine will be served." That produced smiles and a few lusty remarks from the crew.

By late afternoon, wet and tired, they reached Donegal Bay and sighted their destination. Angus was never so happy as when he fixed his eyes upon that long stretch of sand.

Once the ships were beached, Angus Mor drew his captains to him. "See that no man steps over the boundary into Tirowen. The Earl of Ulster tells me the O'Neills are at war with each other just now." Angus could see his father had taken the warning seriously when he added, "I have no wish to enter that fray."

At the captains' nods, the Islesmen, galloglass and archers took up their weapons and followed their lord inland. Donning his helmet and shouldering his long-handled axe, Angus beckoned John and Duncan to follow. The three of them trudged over the sand dunes.

Some distance on, they entered a pine forest and were soon engulfed by a heavy mist.

"'Tis a cold that seeps into a man's bones," said John, walking at his side.

"Aye," said Duncan, "and we were not dry to begin with. It reminds me of the damp fog that rolls in over Skye." Then, with a grin, "When a man seeks a warming fire and a willing lass."

Other than the vague anxiety Angus always experienced before a coming battle, he did not fear the O'Donnells. Not when he would be fighting alongside so many galloglass and Islesmen. Years of fighting with them had given him confidence in his skills. Still, he regretted yet another battle involving his kin. It was bad enough they were constantly at war with the MacDougalls of Lorne, who were also descendants of Somerled. Now, they could add to their enemies the O'Donnells of Tirconnell.

This time, Angus had not asked to be taken along. His father had sought him out. "You'll be sailing with me, Angus. I expect I will have need of your sword arm and axe before this task is done."

When Angus had asked if his older brother, Alex, now thirty, would be going with them, his father shook his head. "He'll stay on Islay. Should I not return, he must take my place. 'Tis enough you will have the company of your cousin and the responsibility for your younger brother."

As they walked through the pine forest, Angus stole a glance at John, pleased to see no fear shadowed his face. With each passing year, Angus and John had grown more alike in appearance with their blue eyes and light brown hair that took on a reddish cast in the sun. It was nothing like their father's vivid red, of course, which made sense when Angus thought of it. Their mother was a Campbell and had the brown hair of that family. Their sisters and older brother favored their mother more than did Angus and John.

Gripped by a sudden need to protect his younger brother, Angus determined to keep him close. He had helped in John's training and the lad had done well, gaining the nickname "Sprangach", meaning "the bold", but he lacked experience in battle. Today would change that.

Once through the forest, they set out over the moors, heading toward the woods where they were told Turlough, the son of Angus' oldest sister, Mary, would be waiting. She had married The O'Donnell when he reigned as King of Tirconnell. Mary was young at the time and his second wife. A son had been born of each marriage and that was the source of the conflict once the old king died.

Angus had only met his nephew once before. They were of an age, neither yet twenty. They shared their Macdonald lineage, their faith and their Gaelic language. But there was one difference between them, and that had to do with history.

Angus could still hear the gruff voice of Michael Dominici when the chaplain had been his tutor. "Enough from General Caesar for today," he said, as he closed the book in the solar at Ardtornish. The priest was paid to teach Angus Mor's sons the gospel and Latin but he often strayed from the classics to the politics he believed a son of the Lord of the Isles should know. "So tell me, young Angus—who are the Gaels?"

Angus answered without hesitation. "The first people in Ireland, Western Scotland and the Isles."

"The first people, aye. Who else came to live in these lands? Did the Romans, like our General Caesar?"

Angus had thought carefully before answering. "Aye and nay. The Romans invaded Scotland but not the Isles. And they were beaten back from Scotland and never returned."

"Very good. Who else?"

"Well, my ancestor, Somerled, was partly Norse."

"Aye, you do well to remember. And he was also of royal Irish blood and the great Gaelic kingdom of Dalriada. Who else?"

Angus pondered for a moment. "The…Normans?"

"Correct, at least so far as Scotland east of the Isles is concerned. Unlike Ireland where the Normans invaded, King David *invited* them into Scotland. And they all became Scots. The Bruces are descended from them as well as King David. But in Ireland only some of the Irish joined with the Normans. Others remained independent—like the O'Donnells in Tirconnell."

"And so did the Isles for more than a hundred years," Angus had offered proudly.

The old voice faded as a large group of men slowly emerged out of the mist like ghosts. Angus knew by the men's unguarded and open approach, devoid of menace, that this group was not the enemy.

Some wore quilted tunics, or aketons, to which they'd added chainmail and shiny helmets, much like Angus and the Islesmen. Others wore no armor at all, their legs naked beneath their tunics, and they carried spears. Galloglass that had been a part of his sister Mary's dowry were present as well with their long-handled sparth axes.

Angus spotted archers among this group. Like the archers that had come with the Lord of the Isles, they were lightly armored and carried short poplar bows looped over the shoulder, their quivers full of arrows with goose feather fletching.

Most, save the archers and the galloglass, had only swords or spears and a long, fearsome dagger.

Angus' father removed his helmet and shook out his flaming red hair.

"Grandfather!" Turlough strode forward, a look of relief on his face. "I knew you would not fail me." The would-be King of Tirconnell had dark coloring like his mother, his hair worn long to his shoulders. But he dressed more like his Irish kin, his tunic embroidered in Celtic design.

Angus' father laid a hand on his grandson's shoulder. "I'd not see your inheritance denied you, lad." The relationship was one of long standing as Turlough's father had fostered with Angus Mor's father, Donald.

Turlough smiled at Angus and John. "Greetings, Uncles." Then he acknowledged Duncan with a nod, for he was also kin. Looking past them to the Islesmen that filled the woods, Turlough said, "You have many with you."

"More than a thousand," said Angus' father.

Turlough nodded. "It will be enough. Aodh cannot have more than seven hundred. As you can see," he gestured behind him, "many stand with me." Behind Turlough stood several hundred men. "I like to think 'tis because they favor me as their king but it could be due to their knowledge the Lord of the Isles has come to enforce the bargain made long ago."

"Is your mother well?" Angus' father inquired.

"Aye, though she is in hiding at the moment and much concerned. We had hoped Aodh would agree to our request that he step aside. He has long known the way it was to be. Alas, our pleas went ignored. I took to the forest after that, expecting to be slain. If today goes well, you must see Mother before you leave."

"I will. But first, we will dispatch this man who would disregard the old king's pledge."

Angus Mor beckoned his captains to him and Turlough gestured toward a clearing where a small table had been set upon the grass. As they walked to it, Angus saw a parchment had been placed on the table and held down with rocks.

"I have drawn the land and the water," said Turlough. "My spies tell me Aodh's forces are camped north of us along the River Eske." He used the tip of his dagger to trace the path of the river north. "I think we can take them here," he said, pointing to a spot on the east bank of the river. "We'll have the high ground."

"I cannot argue with your strategy," said Angus' father, studying the drawing.

"I suspect Aodh thought you would come," said Turlough. "He's had spies watching the coast for weeks."

Angus' father asked a few questions about the distances, how Aodh and his men were armed and what Aodh was like in a fight. Seemingly satisfied with what he heard, he turned to his captains who stood around the table. "This is what we will do..."

The instructions given, the captains returned to their warriors while Turlough relayed the instructions to his own men.

Angus' father ordered the galloglass forward with the archers in the lead, as the army of the Lord of the Isles made its way north over the heathered moors.

"Stay close, Angus," said his father. Angus had planned to guard his father's back and he was glad they were of one mind.

To John, Angus said, "Stay between me and Duncan for as long as we can manage it."

His brother and cousin nodded and the three of them joined the others.

A few hours later, one of Turlough's men, who had been sent ahead, returned with news confirming a large force gathered on the bank of the river a half-mile on.

Angus' father ordered the archers to position themselves in the woods on the west bank of the river. Then he waved the galloglass on ahead to await his order to attack. Angus knew his father used his fiercest warriors to strike fear in the hearts of the enemy before the rest of the army rushed in behind them.

Once the archers were in place, Angus' father emerged from the trees to raise and lower his sword, the only signal the archers were to receive.

A rush of arrows followed, arching through the air toward the O'Donnell force covering the banks of the river. Many fell with the first volley and more with the second.

Confusion reigned in the enemy ranks for long minutes.

Then the Lord of the Isles gave one sound on his horn and, with a great shout, his army, led by the galloglass, rushed forward, out of the woods and down the hill to where Aodh's men were scrambling to face them.

Excitement rose within him as Angus gripped his axe and ran

behind his father, determined to strike all who threatened the Lord of the Isles. John and Duncan ran with him.

Protecting John on his left as best he could, Angus slashed through the warriors coming at him as if he were harvesting wheat. Soon, he was covered in O'Donnell blood.

One hulking brute hurtled toward John, his sword raised to strike. Angus veered to meet him, swinging his axe with both hands to slice the man's throat. A look of shock froze in his dark eyes as blood spurted from his neck and he collapsed to the ground.

"To me!" Angus shouted to John. His brother joined him and they hurried forward to catch up with their father who had gone ahead. On the riverbank, Angus saw his father surrounded by three men, closing in on him with their swords poised to strike.

Angus broke into a run, cutting down one man as John engaged another. Duncan joined them to ward off others as John defeated the O'Donnell he was battling.

Tall and defiant in his stance, Angus Mor faced the third soldier who looked like a galloglass with his great size and fearsome countenance. One of Aodh's mercenaries.

A sword in one hand and a long dagger in another, the Lord of the Isles blocked the warrior's blade streaking toward him and rammed the dagger into his throat just above his mail. A jab to his middle with the hilt of his sword sent the man sprawling.

More warriors poured into the fray erupting all around them. When the fighting became close, Angus dropped his long-handled axe and unsheathed his sword. The sound of metal on metal rose in the air as blades clashed in the close fighting around him.

It was inevitable that many would die. The galloglass were the elite of Angus Mor's army, highly disciplined and ruthless. Though he was the son of the Lord of the Isles, Angus had learned their ways.

Ultimately, their greater numbers and greater skill forced Aodh's army to give way. When it was clear Turlough and the Lord of the Isles' army would prevail, Angus paused to wipe the blood from his face, grimacing at the coppery scent rising to his nostrils. His mail was streaked with the blood soaking the field of battle.

He had never become accustomed to that smell.

Bodies were strewn on the grass between the forest and the river. Some floated face down in the peat-darkened waters.

Angus was relieved to see his brother and cousin, having become separated from him in the last of the fight, were still alive and coming toward him. Looking them over and seeing the blood on their mail, he said, "Tell me you are unwounded."

"Aye," they both said at once.

Angus heaved a sigh of relief and seeing the smile on his brother's face said, "You did well."

"Aye, I survived."

Just ahead, his father pulled off his helmet and turned, raising his brows to Angus in inquiry.

Angus wrapped his arm around his brother's shoulder. "We are all well, and you?"

Angus Mor wiped his brow with the back of his hand. "A few scratches. Nothing more." He scanned the men still standing, as if searching. "Have you seen Turlough?"

"Aye, just there," Angus said, pointing to the edge of the woods. Turlough had been well guarded by galloglass, which, Angus assumed, had been his father's earlier instructions to them. Angus Mor would not risk losing the reason he had come.

It took some time to dispense with the bodies and assure that the few prisoners taken were appropriately confined. Their physicians would see to the wounded.

Angus found his long-handled axe and washed both his axe and his sword in the river.

Meantime, Turlough had been ensconced in the elaborate manor house of the chief of the O'Donnells, surrounded by the fortifications that now marked him the King of Tirconnell.

When the men took to the river to bathe and set up camp fires, Angus and his companions joined his father who was speaking to Turlough. "We'll sup with you and my daughter tonight and leave at first light."

Turlough nodded, his dark hair tangled but his blue eyes full of affection for the man who had come to his aid. "I thank you, Grandfather. The victory this day is as much yours as mine."

Glancing down at his blood-splattered mail and tunic, the Lord of the Isles smiled. "That being the case, after we have bathed and cleaned the blood from our clothing, we will help you celebrate. My men have ale but we will require food."

With a chuckle, Turlough said, "Do not worry, sir. We will kill the fatted cows and net the river upstream for fish. The village women were none too fond of Aodh, so I expect at least the ones who did not lose their menfolk today will be glad to help."

"Good. Tomorrow when I depart, I will leave with you some of my galloglass and a ship. Together with your army, that should be sufficient to secure your future. The rest of my ships and my men will return to the Isles, save for my own ship. I am for Dunluce with Angus."

Turlough raised a brow. "To visit the Red Earl?"

"Aye. I am overdue."

Angus' father had told him that Richard de Burgh's warning to avoid the O'Neill lands of Tirowen included an invitation to come to Dunluce Castle. As Angus had never been there, he was eager to see the great castle on the north shore of Ulster he had heard so much about and to see again the Norman earl he had met at Turnberry four years before. Though they might like to go along, it was best that John and Duncan return to Dunaverty to await him.

THE NEXT MORNING, his feet firmly planted in the stern of the ship, Angus' spirits rose with their return to the sea. The waters of the Atlantic were again stirred to a wild froth by the currents and a biting wind. Still, he was content to be back in his element.

A full day of sailing north along the jagged coast of Tirconnell and then east, past the Inishowen Peninsula, brought them into calmer waters and to Dunluce Castle.

Perched high above the sea, the castle looked out on the narrowest expanse of the Atlantic between Ireland and Scotland. Grass covered the tops of the cliffs, so deep a green it reminded Angus of green velvet. He knew such a color could only be produced by constant rain. They were fortunate not to have had any.

The wind blew all day, scattering the gray clouds across the sky in a random manner like an artist's erratic paintbrush. At the horizon, the sun turned the sea into liquid gold. It was his favorite time of day when he was happy to have his ship beached on a friendly shore with a warm fire and a good meal awaiting him.

As they passed in front of the seaworn cliffs, a large cave suddenly appeared before them leading into the belly of the headland. On either side lay a rock-strewn beach. Waves crashing onshore and larger rocks offshore, half-hidden, rendered the approach precarious.

Angus' father knew the sea and ships as well as any Isleman and yet Angus had observed that more often than not he placed his confidence in his hand-picked crew. His steersman, one of the finest in the fleet, took hold of the rudder just as Angus' father turned to Angus, fixing him with a steady gaze. "You bring her in."

Angus stared back at his father, knowing words of appeal would not suffice. It was so like his father to throw him into deep water and expect him to swim just as he'd taught him to swim in the Sound of Mull as a lad. Angus had beached ships before but this situation was more treacherous and called for more skill.

Seeing his hesitation, the Lord of the Isles said, "I have seen you observing me often enough. Did you think I had not noticed?"

His father was right. Angus could recite commands in his sleep. His gaze slid over the crew. Every face was turned toward him. Even the lookout on the bow watched over his shoulder, waiting expectantly.

Angus took a deep breath to steady his thumping heart, filled his lungs and bellowed, "Hands prepare to wear!"

The faces vanished as every man bent to his assigned line. Their obedience was gratifying. Angus' heart filled with pleasure at their trust. Now, he must earn it.

The call from the crew chief came on the wind. "Ready!"

Glad for the remaining light enabling him to see clearly the hazards, Angus watched the narrowing gap between the ship and the rocks, his every nerve on edge, until he judged that the distance was right. There was no time left. "Ease away larboard! Haul away starboard!" As the mainsail yard came around, he turned to the helmsman beside him. "Helm alee!"

The steersman gave him a nod and shifted the heavy tiller, keeping his eyes fixed on the sail, as he should, lest some errant shift of wind take control.

"All well!" Angus called. "Hands to douse! Ease halyard! Haul starboard!" The heavy yard swung around as it slid down the mast, the sail collapsing into a stack of thick wool, pulled by crewmen into folds as it fell. The sail and main yard settled onto the trestles, and Angus braced his feet wide apart as the deck lurched underfoot.

With the long steady crunch of the keel on the rocks, the ship rode up onto the beach and came to a satisfying stop.

His father's hand clapped his shoulder. It was the best reward Angus could have had. Smiles from the crew assured him he had done well.

Once the galley had been secured onshore, they scrambled over the rocks, too large to be called shingle, and began the long climb to the castle. As they drew closer to the edifice perched on the edge of the cliff, Angus glanced up to see two round towers and rectangular stone buildings. Each had been constructed of rocks of various shapes, which was hardly surprising given their abundance, but some of the structures had an unfinished look as if the earl were still in the process of building.

"I expect most of the earl's visitors prefer to arrive by land," Angus said to his father with a smirk.

His father nodded. "Aye," then shot him a speaking glance. "Only the best sailors would venture an approach from the sea, although that cave might be useful when resupplying stores in time of siege. I could have mentioned there is a wide sandy beach a few miles away but then you would have missed the test."

Angus shook his head. "I should have guessed."

They reached the summit where a narrow bridge led across a deep gulf to the castle proper. At the sight of two score armed men approaching, the guards gave them a wary look and stepped into their path with crossed spears.

"Angus Mor Macdonald to see the earl," announced Angus' father, "at his invitation."

The guards obviously knew the name for they relaxed, withdrew their spears and beckoned them to enter. "Your men will be seen to once you are inside, my lord."

Gesturing to Angus, his father said, "This one is my son."

The guard acknowledged this information with a curt nod.

Angus' father whispered a word to his captain before they followed the castle guard into a large grass-covered area surrounded by buildings. The crew was directed one way and Angus and his father another.

Inside the great hall, Angus and his father were asked to wait so that the earl could be informed they had arrived. Servants gave them curious looks as they bustled around setting the head table for dinner. Enticing smells from the kitchens made Angus' mouth water.

He and his father walked to the large stone fireplace where a fire burned steadily, the flames sending sparks up the chimney. The familiar scent of burning wood was pleasant.

Three gray wolfhounds strolled toward them, sniffing at their tunics and weapons.

Angus scratched one large hound's head, and then turned to stretch his hands toward the heat while scanning the immense hall. Several tapestries and a few paintings hung on the walls. Candles were set on side tables. Carpets, woven in patterns of blue and red, added color to the stone floor. Otherwise, the vast space reflected the cold dampness of the rock of which it was made.

Angus and his father turned at the sound of boots on the stones. Richard de Burgh crossed the hall and held out his hand. "I am heartened to see you have arrived unscathed."

Angus' father gripped the earl's hand. "Aye, a day's work done. You know my son, Angus Og, from our meeting at Turnberry some years ago."

Angus remembered the dark red hair and beard that gave de Burgh the nickname "the Red Earl". He had changed little in the years since Angus had first seen him at Turnberry Castle. Though the earl was now about thirty in age, he was still young for his position and the power he wielded.

"I remember him, yes." The earl smiled at Angus. "You have

grown from a lad to a man."

Angus dipped his head. "It would seem so, my lord." When the earl had first met him, Angus had a smooth jaw and had not grown to his full height, a few inches over six feet.

Turning to Angus' father, the earl asked, "And is Turlough now the King of Tirconnell?"

"He is, as was intended by his father, the former king."

De Burgh shrugged. "I will not ask what it took to accomplish that feat, my friend. Rather, I will invite you to dine with Margaret and me and to stay the night, for we have much to discuss."

"Your kind invitation is accepted and most gratefully. I would rather not navigate around those rocks below the castle in the dark."

The earl laughed. "Yes, well, most of our visitors arrive and depart when there is light. And then we are often at our castle at Carrickfergus, which is more welcoming to visitors arriving by ship."

A servant approached the earl. "Your guests' chambers are ready, my lord."

"Very well." Then to Angus' father, the earl said, "He will show you to them. But, as dinner is close, do not be long."

After a brief time in their chambers to refresh themselves and change their attire, Angus and his father returned to the great hall where they found the earl standing with his wife, Lady Margaret, elegantly dressed in a crimson silk gown that set off her fair coloring and white head cloth.

The earl presented his wife to Angus who had not met the countess previously.

He bowed before her. "My lady."

The countess' welcome to Angus was gracious, considering he was only a younger son. "Welcome to Dunluce, Angus Og."

"Most of our children are still quite young," said de Burgh, "so you will not see them this eve, but Dermot O'Cahan, son and heir of Cumee O'Cahan, Lord of Ciannacht, is fostering here. I've asked him to join us for dinner as he returns to his family's home at Dunseverick tomorrow."

Just then, a handsome lad of medium height and dark coloring crossed the hall to join them. If Angus judged correctly, Dermot was the same age as Angus' brother, John.

Dermot bowed before the Lord of the Isles. "My lord," he said before rising to acknowledge Angus.

"An O'Cahan, eh?" said Angus' father. "'Tis a great family, one with a long and proud history."

"Thank you, sir," said the young O'Cahan, who did not smile at the compliment but his dark brown eyes conveyed his pleasure.

"The lad has done well here," interjected de Burgh. "He is a scholar among us, yet he is also skilled with a sword. Doubtless, he will be a knight one day if he desires."

To be a knight and a learned man was not unheard of. Angus himself loved to read and, since Dermot would one day take on the mantle of his father, a knowledge of the masters might serve to render him a worthy leader of men.

"Do you want to be a knight?" asked Angus, looking into Dermot's unfathomable brown eyes.

"I will seek my father's guidance, my lord, for he is a wise man."

Angus' father exchanged a knowing look with the earl. "Well said. He who accepts a wise man's advice will never go wrong."

A servant approached and nodded to Lady Margaret, who turned to her guests. "Dinner awaits us."

A group of minstrels began to play on one side of the great hall and de Burgh offered his arm to his wife. With Angus' father on the earl's left, the three of them walked to the head table. Angus followed with Dermot, close enough to the three ahead of them to hear their conversation.

"Your message to me spoke of war among the O'Neills," said Angus' father. "We were careful to avoid Tirowen. Does the war still go on?"

"'Tis a nasty business that. Domnall O'Neill, who might be of interest to you as his mother is a MacDougall, has deposed his cousin, Niall, who I made king in Tirowen. Niall has retreated to Inishowen where he was once king. I am about to intervene to see that Domnall is not rewarded for his treachery."

"It has ever been so in Ireland, kin fighting kin," said Angus' father, a sad note in his voice. "I would never trust the son of a

MacDougall. While I would rather not be a part of it, if you should need my galloglass to succeed, I am happy to send them."

"They would be most welcome. Send them soon before the cold weather sets in and they can winter here. I will not deal with Domnall's perfidy until spring."

"You shall have them, at least two ships' full."

At the table placed at one end of the hall, de Burgh took the center chair with his lady wife on his right and Angus' father on his left. Angus was glad when the earl suggested he sit next to his father as he wanted to hear more of what the earl had to say.

Lady Margaret asked for Dermot to take the chair next to her. "It will be my last opportunity to talk at length with the lad."

The servants began setting platters of food before them. Wonderful smells of spiced meat, vegetables and hot bread filled the air.

Reaching for his wine, Angus heard the earl say, "I suspect things will very soon be in Scotland as they are in Ulster."

Angus' father paused in contemplating the food before him. "What news do you have that suggests such a thing?"

The earl turned to him with a look of surprise. "Ah, you must not be aware. The Maid of Norway has died in Orkney on her way to claim the throne of Scotland."

Angus paused in his eating to listen.

His father's face fell. "Nay, I did not. When?"

"Nearly a fortnight ago but the news only reached us two days ago."

Angus' father heaved a sigh as he stared into the hall. "I see only a difficult road ahead. There will be many contenders for the throne, not the least of which will be Robert the Noble and John Balliol, each of whom claims descent from King David."

"True," said de Burgh. "Each has a valid claim, yet by our band at Turnberry we are bound to the Bruces."

"Aye, and no regrets," said Angus' father.

Angus was heartened that his father affirmed his bargain sealed at Turnberry years ago. For his own part, Angus had not forgotten his pledge of honor to his friend, the youngest Robert Bruce.

"Though we are bound to support the Bruces," said the earl,

"Robert the Noble is in his seventh decade and less malleable than Balliol, who is much younger. If I know Edward, he will want someone he can control. And one cannot dismiss the fact Balliol will have the support of the MacDougalls and the powerful Comyns."

"Two of the Comyns now serve as Guardians of the Realm," said Angus' father, "but that hardly commends Balliol to me. What of the Bruce's son, the Earl of Carrick?"

"At the last news, he and the youngest Bruce were in England at Edward's court where young Robert is expected to be made a knight."

Angus lifted his goblet ever so slightly in toast to his friend, for to be a knight had been Rob's goal when last they'd met.

"And there is this," said de Burgh, "what Edward hoped to gain through the marriage of his young son to the Maid, he may now think to gain in another manner."

"What are you thinking?"

"Nothing specific, but we both know Edward is wily. He has already had me claim the Isle of Man for himself. His eye has been on Scotland for some time. He needs men to fight his wars in France and money to refill his coffers."

Angus cringed at the loss of the Isle of Man as it had once been a possession of the Macdonalds. Though losing Man to the English might be inevitable, to think the King of England had his eyes on Scotland was more worrisome.

"Do you believe Edward will use the potential for civil war to intervene?" asked Angus' father.

The earl contemplated the wine in his goblet. "Quite possibly. But he may not have to venture that far if the Guardians of Scotland come to him, as they might to avoid such a war."

Once dinner ended, they gathered before the fire and spoke of other matters. Angus had only a few moments to talk to Dermot O'Cahan but, in that time, he learned more about the friendship between the O'Cahans, the O'Neills and the Earl of Ulster.

"My sister is married to Niall O'Neill, the rightful King of Tirowen the earl spoke of," said Dermot, "which is why we are grateful he has promised to restore Niall to his kingship."

"We just came from Tirconnell where we helped to restore my nephew, Turlough, to his kingship. It seems the way of things in Ireland, does it not?"

"Alas, it does." Then with mirth in his brown eyes, Dermot said, "But our families are both allied with the Norman lords supported by King Edward, and there is some safety in that." Dermot had told Angus he was the only son of Lord Cumee O'Cahan and thus the heir. "I have yet to speak with my father but I assume he is eager for me to learn the skills I will need to one day assume his role."

"I hope he lives a long life," said Angus. "I, at least, have an older brother who will succeed our father when the time comes."

Dermot returned Angus a shy smile. "Being the only son carries a responsibility unshared with others."

Angus was quick to agree and they parted as friends. The next morning, he was informed by his father that they would be sailing together only to Dunaverty. His father intended to go on to gather galloglass for de Burgh's assault on Tirowen. Meantime, Angus was to sail from Dunaverty to Turnberry Castle in Carrick, where his brother, Alexander would be witnessing a charter.

"You have proven you can fight and captain a ship, now you must see to a statesman's business. This one is with men of the cloth. It is time you join your brother in such tasks. Watch him carefully for he is ever gracious to the clergy."

Angus supposed he had just been paid a compliment. The Lord of the Isles did not give them often.

CHAPTER 4

Derry, Inishowen Peninsula, Ulster, Ireland, October 1290

ÁINE DIDN'T MIND the move to Inishowen. The peninsula's rugged coast, jutting into the Atlantic Ocean, with its stony green hills and blue waters beyond, reminded her of home. For all its beauty, Inishowen was a smaller place than Tirowen, less than half its size.

Though he spoke little of it, Áine knew Niall resented deeply the change in his status. He was a proud man who had known defeat before; but the unceremonious ousting from his kingship by Domnall O'Neill had come as a surprise. Niall faulted himself for trusting too much in the power of the Norman Earl of Ulster to protect him.

Left no other choice and facing a larger army, when it was clear he could not win the day, he had fled to Inishowen with Áine, their servants and those of his men who survived.

In Derry, they lived comfortably if not lavishly. The town had been built on a small hill named after an oak grove that had once stood on an island in the River Foyle. It was a place of commerce for surrounding farms and ships coming from places far away to trade. Derry boasted a large stone cathedral, built by Columba's successor.

For Áine, it became a quiet retreat.

Their timber-framed house, whitewashed and topped with a thatched roof, was large enough to accommodate Niall and her as well as Nessa and the visitors who came often. Their cook, servants and Niall's loyal men-at-arms lived in cottages nearby.

Niall was well-liked by the people whose farms were small but whose hearts were large. They were simple folk, not unlike the O'Cahan families in the lands surrounding Dunseverick. She often experienced a longing for her father and the castle that had been her home, even her birds, yet she had found purpose in her new life.

The women of Inishowen had opened their arms to her. While she did not have a lifetime of wisdom to impart, she bore them smiles of encouragement and good wishes for the health of their families, and she did what she could for them.

She could be happy here but Niall never could, having been king of a greater realm.

The sound of laughter rang in Áine's ears. She turned to see Nessa laughing with Flora, who came from the village each day to cook for them. Nessa's brown curls and Flora's red hair mingled together as they bent over the table, kneading dough.

Áine's handmaiden had found delight in doing things she had never done before. She had been very frightened when they were forced to leave Tirowen earlier that year but she laughed often now that she was safe. Áine, too, had known fear then, though not so much for herself as for Niall. As the daughter of the powerful Lord Cumee O'Cahan, she knew Niall's cousin would not harm her. But as long as Niall lived and was de Burgh's—and thus King Edward's—preferred choice as King of Tirowen, he would remain a threat.

After they arrived in Derry, they had paid de Burgh a visit at his castle at Dunluce. The Red Earl had been furious at what had taken place. "Domnall will not long succeed in his treachery. Only be patient, Niall, and I will see you restored to the kingship."

Áine gazed out the window to her garden where she had planted vegetables. *Would she be here to harvest them?*

Notwithstanding de Burgh's promise, their future remained uncertain, making her worry, especially now. Resting her hand on her belly where the child grew, she stretched her gaze beyond her garden to the waters of the River Foyle that flowed into Lough Foyle before traveling north to find their home in the Atlantic.

"What do you think, Finn?" she inquired of her faithful hound, lazing at her feet. He was another reason the O'Donnells had been reluctant to approach her, for he had stood a snarling guard at her side. "Will I have a male child and will he be born here?"

Finn gazed up at her, his soulful copper-colored eyes inquiring but not understanding.

If the child were a boy, his life would be in constant danger as the heir of the man who had once been, and could be again, King of Tirowen.

While Áine might hope for a daughter, Niall desperately wanted a son.

"He will one day be able to claim the kingship," he had told her. She well understood the affairs of men and their need for sons to follow after them. It was ever so. And, while Niall had not been her choice and their first months had been awkward, he had been kind and patient. For that, God willing, she would give him sons. After all, she was only seventeen with many years of childbearing ahead of her.

The child would be born in early spring. *Where will I be then?*

The cathedral bells rang, reminding her it was time to leave. She must visit the priest who often prayed with her for she would need God's help in the coming days.

Dunaverty Castle, Kintyre Peninsula, October 1290

WITH HIS COUSIN by his side, Angus waved farewell to his younger brother who stood in the bow of their father's ship as the crew rowed hard from Dunaverty for deeper waters.

Angus and his cousin began the climb back to the castle and Angus extended his gaze south, across the water, to where he glimpsed the coast of Ulster.

With his father's instructions still fresh in his mind, he said to Duncan, "I will not be long in Carrick. After all, how long can it take to witness a charter?"

"That depends on who is to witness it and for what purpose."

"'Tis a matter of the Church," said Angus. "I am to join my brother, Alex, at Turnberry Castle where we are granting a charter to Paisley Abbey for the kirk of St. Queran on Kintyre. That reminds me, I must find the Kintyre clerk named Patrick. He is to go with me."

Duncan looked down, shaking his head, causing his golden curls to fall into his face. "Well, you may be there for some time. Clerics are rarely quick to do anything. They love much ceremony and many words. And if you are at the Earl of Carrick's castle at Turnberry, there will be a bevy of notables."

"I confess I am curious about this granting of charters. I am hoping Robert Bruce, the earl, will be in attendance but I have heard he and his eldest son are in London." With the thought they might have returned north, Angus looked forward with eager anticipation to what might now be a reunion with his friend Rob and not just a dull meeting of churchmen.

The next morning, a thick mist surrounded the beach on Kintyre as he and Patrick, the Kintyre clerk, left for Turnberry Castle, thirty miles to the east.

As they reached the Firth of Clyde, the mist cleared but, above them, clouds were gathering. He was glad when the crew finally rowed the ship through the seagate that led into the belly of the castle.

The same thin dark-haired seneschal who had greeted Angus and his father before was there to welcome him. "Welcome, Angus Og. Your brother, Alexander, arrived by ship not long ago. The clergy from Argyll will have come by land. I presume they are gathering in the great hall but I must remain here to await Sir Maurice, the vicar of Arran. You know the way?"

"Aye, I have not forgotten." Angus spoke a word to his captain and then turned to ascend the stone steps that wound up to the hall, Patrick following on his heels. "Tell me," he said over his shoulder to the Kintyre clerk, "do you know the vicar of Arran and the others who are likely to be among the clergy here?"

"I know the vicar. He is a good man, humble for all his raised status."

"Who else might be here for the charter?" Angus asked.

"I expect the Abbot of Crosraguel Abbey will be here." With a note of amusement in his voice, he added, "He is yet another Patrick. The abbey is tied to Paisley Abbey, of course, but since the Bruces established Crosraguel, they watch over it, and the friars there are loyal to the family."

"Who will accept the gift of the kirk of St. Queran?"

"Doubtless it will be Laurence, the Bishop of Argyll."

Angus knew the bishop to be a MacDougall but, since he was a Dominican priest, one of the Black Friars, Angus would not hold his clan against him. "The bishop must be very old now."

"Aye, he is, nearly three decades in office but not too old to affix his seal."

As they continued up the stairs, Angus recalled that four years ago, his father had affixed his galley seal to the document that bound the Macdonalds to the Bruces, the Earl of Ulster and other nobles in a common purpose. Now his brother would bring his seal to the grant of the Kintyre church.

At the top of the stairs, Angus stepped into the great hall, which was just as he remembered it: the familiar aroma of herbed rushes, the paneled oak walls and the Bruce banners and tapestries. Windows at one end cast a soft light around the room.

Angus handed his damp cloak to a waiting servant and looked longingly toward the fire blazing in the stone fireplace. Before he could step in that direction, however, his attention was drawn to the other end of the hall where a group of black-robed clergy and well-dressed nobles turned to see who was joining their number. He was glad he'd worn his best clothing, a woad blue tunic embroidered in silver and his sword belt, though worn with good use, was well made.

Recognizing his brother, Angus crossed the hall to him. For the occasion, Alex, too, had taken pains with his appearance. His dark brown hair fell in neat waves to his shoulders and his cinnamon tunic was of fine wool. A new leather belt held his sword.

Angus' weapons were not so new but in Tirconnell, they had proven their worth.

The smile on Alexander's face was genuine. "'Tis a surprise to see you here, younger brother."

"Father's idea." With an amused grin, he added in a low voice, "He thinks it time I learned some statecraft from you."

"Aye, you might learn something here," said Alex in the manner of an older brother counseling a younger one.

In a louder voice, Angus said, "I bring Patrick, one of our clerks on Kintyre."

Alex greeted Patrick before turning to the others. "At our father's request, my brother, Angus, joins us with Patrick, a clerk from Kintyre."

"Welcome, Patrick," said Robert Bruce, the Earl of Carrick. "We will surely have need of your skills. And greetings to you, Angus. I recall the last time you were among us. Of course, you know my son."

Appearing from behind a cleric to stand next to his father was Angus' friend, Rob. The gray eyes were the same but he looked older, his russet hair more auburn in color and shorter. His face displayed the beginnings of a dark brown beard.

Rob smiled and so did Angus. "Aye, we are friends," said Angus.

Rob offered his hand, the smile in his eyes telling Angus he was glad to see him. "I was hoping you might come."

The earl began to make the introductions. Patrick had been correct in the list of clergy who would attend, including the old Bishop of Argyll with his white tonsured hair and beard and deeply wrinkled face. Much deference was paid him by the others.

Angus greeted each one as his station required, including Sir Maurice, the vicar of Arran, who had just arrived. As soon as the greetings were dispensed with, he again found Rob.

"You must stay the night so we can bridge the years," said the youngest of the Robert Bruces.

"Over a game of chess mayhap?" asked Angus, realizing he had decided to accept the invitation, which would make him delayed in rejoining his cousin.

Rob smiled. "That, too."

The clerk then read the charter granting to Paisley Abbey the kirk of St. Queran. The formalities involved in the grant were as dull an affair as Angus had expected, though one day such duties as witnessing charters and bestowing them would be his and thus he followed carefully the details and listened to every word his brother spoke. Alex impressed him with his easy manner among the dour clerics and the respect they paid him.

The Macdonalds had long been in the business of establishing abbeys and endowing monasteries. Somerled, his ancestor, had contributed St. Oran's Chapel to Iona and conceived the idea of Saddell Abbey on Kintyre. His son, Ranald, carried through with his father's dream. Watching the somber-faced men of the church in their ecclesiastical black and white finery, Angus knew with a certainty he could never be one of them and was glad his father had not destined him for the church.

Had that been a part of his father's purpose in sending him here? In showing him what he was not, the Lord of the Isles had revealed more clearly what Angus was—an Isleman born to ship and sea and the people who were his responsibility, whose freedom he must ever secure. Too, his father might have wanted him to understand the responsibility they had to support the Church, as they did on the Isle of Iona, constructing and maintaining the great abbey there.

In the end, Alex affixed his seal "as son and heir of Angus, Lord of the Isles," for all to remember. "So that this grant does not sink into blind oblivion," he said, "Laurence, Bishop of Argyll, and Robert Bruce, Earl of Carrick, have agreed to witness the grant and affix their seals as well."

The business of the day concluded, the men raised goblets of wine in tribute to a task well done and, afterwards, lingered in small groups to speak of the affairs of the day.

Angus and Rob stood to one side, listening. "They speculate about who will next wear Scotland's crown," said Angus.

"Aye, and my grandfather's chances of wearing it."

"Which are good, one would suppose," said Angus.

Rob shrugged. "My grandfather thinks so but John Balliol and the Comyns will resist. To avoid war, there is talk that King Edward will be asked by the Guardians to decide among the many claimants."

Angus tried to imagine such a process and failed. "That will be a messy business."

Still watching the others, Rob nodded.

Angus wondered what his friend was thinking. If his grandfather, Robert the Noble, were to become King of Scots then Rob would himself be in line for the throne one day.

That afternoon as Angus was about to settle down to a game of chess with Rob at the far end of the hall, Alex came to bid him goodbye. "Do you sail to Islay?" Angus asked.

"Nay, I sail north to the coast of Lorne and Dunollie Castle."

Dunollie! Angus could not fathom a mission that would take his brother deep into enemy territory. Excusing himself to Rob, who was just setting up the chessboard, Angus drew his brother aside where they would not be overheard.

"I know you are my elder by more than a decade, but still, I must ask. What business do you have at Dunollie, a MacDougall holding?"

His brother's eyes glistened with excitement. "My business, younger brother, is a matter of the heart. Dunollie is where Juliana MacDougall lives and I plan to spend the winter wooing her."

"You cannot mean it!" Angus hissed, incredulous. "You wish to marry a daughter of our enemy when you could have your pick of any lass in Scotland…or Ireland for that matter?"

"I do not want any lass. I want Juliana," Alex insisted. "She is beautiful and educated. Besides, she will become a Macdonald. That is all you need to know."

Seeing the look of determination on his brother's face, Angus heaved a sigh. "I hope you know what you are about. Father will not be pleased and I see no good coming from such a misalliance. The MacDougalls stand with John Balliol and the Comyns."

"You have yet to love a woman, Angus. When you do, you will understand."

Angus watched his brother stride from the hall, tall and proud, the heir of the Lord of the Isles, obviously eager to be about his "wooing", as he called it. Shaking his head, Angus returned to where Rob had just finished setting up the board.

"What is it?" asked Rob.

Taking his seat, Angus let out a sigh. "I fear my brother is about to make a mistake of serious consequence. But let us not speak of that." He glanced up at his friend. "What of you? I thought you were in London where I hear you are to have that knighthood you have long sought."

Rob moved a red pawn forward. "Aye, so my father tells me. We were in London just before we came to Turnberry. It was there I learned King Edward plans to bestow his favor upon me, and I am to be knighted early."

Angus brought one of his own white pawns forward. "Doubtless you have earned it. Will you return there?"

"Aye, I must. We came north for this charter and to see my mother. The Crosraguel Abbey is of importance to my family. The Bruces endowed it and my father wanted to remind the bishop of that fact since Paisley Abbey has not always done right by the smaller monastery."

Angus was aware of the squabbles between clerics, mostly over money, but he wanted to hear about Rob's time in London as he had never been there. "What is it like to live in London at the court of the English king?"

Rob studied the chessboard, then made his next move, a canny one. "The accommodations are small but then I am a squire in training to become a knight so it hardly matters. I spend little time in my chamber. At the court, there is much pomp and extravagant clothing. Edward collects precious jewels and his garments, typically of red and white, are covered in them. The throne room is decorated overmuch and every occasion requires an elaborate ceremony."

"What is the king like?"

"He can be ruthless and terrifies everyone. But there are beautiful ladies to dance with, fine horses and abundant food that make it tolerable."

"Is there a girl you are fond of?" Angus moved another pawn, a risky move but it might gain him a lead.

"No. Most days I am so tired after training and jousting and keeping my knight's armor and his horse in good order that I can scarcely keep my head from falling into my trencher at dinner." Rob eyed one of Angus' pawns, finally taking it. "Still, we are required to learn courtly etiquette, music and dance, as well as skill with a sword." Looking at Angus over the chessboard, he said, "I expect you have gained some skill since we last met."

"A bit. I will admit to adding a few weapons to those I carry from my training with the galloglass."

"Galloglass? I hear they are fearless."

"Aye, they are. My family trades in their skills. They are much in demand in Ireland where the feuding is continual." Angus moved his bishop to an active square and thought about Rob's pawn. "But tell me more of London town. I understand it is a great city."

Rob sat back in his chair and let out a sigh. "The town is dirty and assaults one's senses with wretched smells, but it holds many allures. You can find anything you desire in the stalls of London's merchants."

"Would you ever want to live there?"

The chess game forgotten for the moment, Rob leaned forward and said in a low voice, "For now, my future and mayhap that of my family are tied to England's king, so I must spend time there, but London could never be my home. I would miss Scotland."

That night, Angus had difficulty finding sleep. His brother's words kept repeating in his mind. It was true. Angus had never loved a woman, not in the way his brother meant. He supposed he had begun to look more closely at the lasses he met, not unmindful of their lingering gazes and their flirting. But, like Rob, his path to manhood had not allowed him time for serious courting. Still, somewhere in his future, he hoped for a lass who could hold his heart, a woman he would want by his side, a woman he could love.

Tirowen, Ulster, Ireland, spring 1291

"'TIS A SON, MISTRESS!" Áine heard Nessa's words through a fog as she sank back against the pillows, relieved the long and painful birthing was finally over.

The babe's cry broke the air as the first rays of sunlight streamed in the window, illuminating the face of the swaddled bairn Nessa held out to her. "He has The O'Neill's hair and your bow-shaped lips," said her handmaiden, "and don't they look fine on such a handsome lad?"

"God bless him," said the midwife in the ancient tradition of the words that must follow such a compliment to preserve the babe's safety.

Áine would not have called her newborn son handsome with his wizened face and reddish down hair on the top of his head, yet he was most beloved. She took him in her arms and cuddled him close, helping him find her breast, where he latched on with voracious hunger, making her laugh. "I was the one doing all the work but it is the lad who is hungry."

"Just like the master," said Nessa as she and the midwife scurried about changing linens and helping Áine to look presentable. "The O'Neill is always eating."

"He is always practicing his skills with weapons," said Áine in her husband's defense. "Is Niall about?" At one point when the birthing went on longer than might have been hoped for, Niall had been dragged off by a few of his men for a drink but he would want to know she'd given birth to a son.

"Aye, and pacing like a lion downstairs."

"Well, best let him in."

The midwife opened the door and shouted down the stairs, "Lord Niall!" A moment later, Niall rushed in. "'Tis a lad," said the midwife. "You've a fine son, my lord."

"God be praised." Niall turned toward the bed. "And my wife?"

Áine smiled, seeing the concern on his face. "I am well, my lord."

Niall strode to the bed and dropped to her side, staring in wonder at his son. He touched the babe's tiny hand, marveling at the splayed fingers. "Thank you, Áine," he said, leaning in to kiss her forehead. "I could not have asked for more."

"What shall we name him?" she inquired.

"What about Brian? 'Tis a proper name for a king in Ireland."

"You do not wish to name him for one of our fathers?"

"No, I would rather my son be his own man."

Given what Niall had been through, she well understood. "Then Brian O'Neill he will be." She gazed at her young son who had opened his eyes and smiled. "Niall, he smiles at us!"

"And why not? He is the heir to Tirowen. The world lies before him."

A month earlier, Richard de Burgh and his army had managed to drive off Niall's cousin, Domnall, and restore Niall to the kingship but Áine still had an uneasy feeling about their return to Tirowen.

Dunaverty Castle, Kintyre Peninsula, summer 1291

ANGUS CRUMPLED THE parchment in his hand and pondered the voyage he must take north. "My father asks that I attend Alex's wedding in his place, though it will take me to Dunstaffnage Castle, the seat of Alexander MacDougall, Lord of Lorne and Argyll."

"I would not have you go alone," said Angus' cousin, Duncan, who had joined him at the battlements to gaze upon the sea. A clear blue sky above and the warm air around them spoke of high summer.

Angus leaned his forearms on the stone wall. "Surrounded by MacDougalls, your presence will be comforting."

"Take heart. The wedding will soon be over and then we can sail to Glen Coe where I have business for my father with Dugall MacEanruig, the chief man of Glen Coe."

"Aye," said Angus, "'tis the least I can do for the favor of your accompanying me to enemy territory. But I would go first to Ardtornish to see my father. He will want a report on the wedding."

"A visit to Ardtornish Castle would be most welcome. I have not seen my uncle in some time."

Angus wondered if his father had chosen not to attend Alexander's wedding because of the company he would be forced to keep, for he had made clear he disapproved of Alex's choice, or whether it was due to their father's ill health. Angus had received a message from his mother telling him the Lord of the Isles was not well, though she did not say what ailed him.

Early the next morning before Angus and Duncan set sail, Angus addressed his crew. "We go to my brother's wedding where, following the vows, there will be the usual celebration with much food and drink. Eat, but drink little. Keep your wits about you, for we know not what treachery the MacDougall fools may be planning. I do not trust them once they are full of ale and wine."

"Will we stay the night at Dunstaffnage?" asked his captain.

"Nay. Too much can go awry. I do not know my brother's plans for his bride but Morvern is close so we will sail to Ardtornish Castle and tarry there for the night."

Understanding appeared on the faces of the crew and each man nodded.

They arrived into the Firth of Lorne late in the afternoon and then sailed up the coast of Lorne to the entrance to Loch Etive where the stone castle of Dunstaffnage sat on a promontory. To the west, across the firth, lay the Isle of Lismore, the seat of the bishopric of Argyll and MacDougall territory.

As the ship's hull slid over the shingle beach, Angus looked up at the castle, a large stone fortress painted with yellow lime. It stood on a spit of land watching over the waters of the western seas. It had been built decades ago by Duncan MacDougall, Lord of Lorne, grandson of Somerled.

Many galleys were drawn up onshore, including those belonging to MacDougalls, flying a raven pennant. Three he recognized from the Galley of the Isles pennons as belonging to the Macdonalds.

Duncan paused to look at the three ships. "I expect your brother has brought Islesmen with him for more than just a celebration."

"Aye," said Angus, "I would hope so. 'Twould be the wise thing to do when wedding an enemy's lass. Just being here gives me an uneasy feeling, as though we are entering the wolf's den."

They climbed to the top of the promontory where in front of the castle a large crowd had gathered. Villagers as well as nobles and clan chiefs had come for the wedding. The excitement in the air was tangible. Highlanders loved summer weddings as much as fairs. It was a chance to enjoy good food and drink and to be with those they might not see the rest of the year.

Angus was pleased the Macdonalds had come in force. From their waves to him, they were glad to see him as well.

Spotting his brother near the trees at one end of the grassy area,

Angus strode to meet him. "Greetings, Brother."

Dressed in his finery, Alex's smile beamed his happiness. "I am glad you have come. You, too, Duncan. And Father?"

"He is unwell and asked me to stand in his stead. Mother remained behind to be with him."

Alex's brow furrowed. "I hope 'tis not serious."

"I cannot say but I sail to Ardtornish from here and will soon know." He did not want to admit to his brother that their father would not want to greet the Lord of Lorne except on a battlefield. Their older sisters were married and now lived with their husbands so they were not expected to attend. John, their younger brother, had remained at Ardtornish, per his father's message. "And you, Brother? To where do you take your bride when the celebration is over?"

"I had thought to spend our first night here. Alexander MacDougall has given us the guest tower. Then I would sail to Islay tomorrow, though mayhap we'll stay a night or two in Ardtornish on the way so that Father can meet Juliana."

Angus did not try to dissuade his brother from his plans but decided to wait and see what developed.

"You never told me," said Angus, "what was Juliana's dowry?"

Alex's smile was wide. "The Isle of Lismore."

Taken aback, Angus nonetheless nodded his approval. "A prize to be sure." Angus shifted his gaze to the isle whose name meant "Great Garden". A small isle strategically located between Morvern and Argyll at the mouth of Loch Linnhe. He could not imagine the MacDougalls giving the seat of the Bishop of Argyll to the Macdonalds. "Why would the MacDougalls allow the Macdonalds to be so close?"

"To gain the future Lord of the Isles as husband for his daughter, the Lord of Lorne had to offer something of great value or his daughter would be shamed. Mayhap he prefers that to coin."

Angus shot a sideways glance at Duncan. "Aye, mayhap."

Just then, a piper struck up, turning all eyes on him and the couple that walked in his wake. Alexander MacDougall, Lord of Lorne and Argyll, a man in his fourth decade, strode forward with a lass on his arm. By her green silk gown, the wreath of yellow and white flowers on her head of long brown hair and the smile on her face as she gazed toward her intended, it was clear this was the beautiful Juliana. Following in their steps was a bevy of girls older than Juliana, each with a basket of flowers they scattered along the path.

Though he walked with pride, his chest jutting out beneath his dark red tunic that was nearly the color of his hair and beard, Alexander of Lorne looked none too happy. His clenched jaw spoke volumes to his men whose dour looks matched his own.

Angus' brother left his side and crossed the swath of green to offer his arm to his bride, who happily took it. The two headed for the woods where, presumably, the chapel could be found. Alexander MacDougall and his family followed along with the guests, including Angus, Duncan and the other Macdonalds.

Dappled sunlight pierced the canopy of green to light the path through the woods. Every now and then, patches of sky could be seen where the trees gave way to a small clearing. As he walked along, Angus sought a word with Alex's captain, Conall, a stern man who Angus knew to be a seasoned warrior and a good seaman. "I trust you have taken precautions should the MacDougalls have a mind to deny Juliana her husband this night."

"Aye. We have. And more than enough men and weapons to see Alexander and his bride quickly away."

Angus was pleased to hear it. "Assuming the lass has packed a chest, might I recommend your men load it on Alex's ship and post a guard? Remember, Ardtornish is just a short sail down the Sound of Mull, should the need arise."

"Aye, good idea. But should Alexander decide to stay the night, we will guard the tower assigned to him and Juliana, alert and ready to fight."

"Your very presence may hold the wolves at bay. That and too much drink." He looked up to where the sun's rays were the brightest. "The sun will not set for many hours, providing ample time for the MacDougalls to drink their fill."

The captain returned Angus a wry smile. "I am counting on it."

As the crowd reached the large stone chapel in the forest, the piper stopped playing. Alex and Juliana paused in front of the wooden door. There, to Angus' surprise, stood the old Bishop of Argyll, ready to perform the marriage.

"Lismore is, after all, the bishop's residence and an hour's row across the firth," said Duncan.

Angus considered his cousin's words. It was reasonable for the bishop to be the one to perform the ceremony since he was a MacDougall and the MacDougalls had, before the dowry, possessed the isle. But what did the bishop think of the isle being part of a marriage bargain with the Macdonalds? That could not have gone down well.

The crowd of well-wishers closed in behind the happy couple, Juliana's father and family standing to one side. When the vows were said and the rings exchanged, the bishop led the now-married couple inside for another ceremony and Mass.

The guests waited eagerly for them to reappear and, when they did, erupted in loud cheers.

"Now for the hard part," said Angus to his cousin. "Staying sober during what is sure to be hours of drunken revelry."

"Aye, I remember your admonition," said Duncan with a grin. "We eat, but drink little."

Angus moved through the crowd to congratulate his brother and wish him and his bride a happy life and many sons. Juliana's face glowed with happiness.

As he turned to leave, Angus whispered into Alex's ear, "I have asked your captain to secure your bride's things aboard your ship should you need to leave in haste."

His brother gave him an incredulous look.

"It pays to be prepared, elder brother. You are not among friends except those you brought with you."

Alex and Juliana were swept away with the crowd that boisterously escorted them back to the castle. Angus and Duncan followed, mindful of the MacDougalls around them.

The day was sunny and warm so Angus was not surprised when they emerged from the woods to see tables covered in white cloths standing on the grass in front of the castle's curtain wall. Servants were setting out platters of food and jugs of ale and wine.

At the head table, set at a right angle to the others, the bride and groom were soon seated. Angus and Duncan took their places next to Alex, with Alex's captains next to them. On Juliana's other side sat her father, mother and siblings.

Angus rose and introduced himself to Alexander MacDougall, Lord of Lorne and his wife, Marion Comyn, the Lady of Lorne. Angus was dismayed to be reminded that not only had Alex married into the MacDougalls, but now he was also tied to the Comyns who controlled much of northeast Scotland.

The MacDougall daughters spoke their names as Angus greeted them. He inclined his head to Juliana's brothers, all of whom were older than him.

He resumed his seat and Duncan leaned in to say, "Juliana's sisters are comely, and their eyes followed you as you walked away."

"MacDougalls, every one, Duncan. I'd not make my brother's mistake. Besides, Juliana has three brothers, all in their prime fighting years, or did you not notice?"

"Aye, I noticed, but my eyes were on the lasses."

Angus shook his head, unsurprised, and turned his attention to the trencher he and Duncan shared. The food was plentiful, roast pork and duck, dressed in herbs and spices, and fish from the loch as well as summer vegetables. Honey cakes followed.

Angus sipped his ale sparingly while he scanned the tables where the wedding guests celebrated. Save for a few exceptions, the Macdonald men sat together, apart from the MacDougalls. He only hoped it would stay that way.

When the meal was finished, the dancing began, the first being a sword dance by Juliana's brothers to the piper's lively tune accompanied by the quick beat of the drum. Angus knew well the dance called *Duncanlie Callum*, first devised by Malcolm Canmore more than two hundred years ago after slaying one of his enemies.

The dancer crossed his own sword over his victim's on the ground, making the sign of the cross, and then high-stepped over, but never touching, the blades. Angus was half-expecting the MacDougalls to ask for Macdonald swords for the dance. The insult would not have been tolerated so it was well they did not. However, he had also heard the dance was often performed before a battle with auspicious omens if the dance was completed without touching the swords, which the MacDougall men only just managed to do.

Mayhap, thought Angus, I am being too suspicious. It was a day of joy and merriment after all. Still, remembering the stories of the MacDougalls' past treachery, he determined to remain guarded.

CHAPTER 5

HOURS LATER, following numerous toasts to the newly wedded couple and songs sung in their honor, the guests began dancing on the grass in front of the castle to the lively music of pipes and drums.

The spirited revelry continued until everyone was thirsty and resorted to the tables where jugs of ale and wine stood waiting.

Joining Duncan, Angus crossed his arms over his chest and leaned against a food table while watching the wedding guests reach for refreshment. "Now the serious drinking begins."

"Aye, and since the night will be warm, they will care not where they end up when sleep overtakes them."

"Under the tables most like," said Angus. He was pleased to see his brother's men as well as his own were showing restraint when it came to the ale and did not touch the wine. Water was available though few of the guests would indulge in what they considered too paltry a drink for a wedding.

On the other side of the farthest table, Angus heard shouting. He turned to watch. The argument was between a MacDougall and one of Alex's Islemen. "I had best see what this is about," he said as he strode toward the altercation. Duncan followed on his heels.

As they ventured closer, Angus heard the MacDougall say with slurred words, "Do ya th…think we are so stu…stupid as to let a Macdonald keep the isle where *our* bishop lives?"

This produced ribald laughter from his companions.

"He's not *your* bishop, you idiot," replied the still sober and now angry Isleman. "The Bishop of Argyll serves the whole diocese."

"He is *our* bis…bishop!" With these words, the MacDougall took a swing at the Isleman but, because of his drunken state, was not able to make contact and stumbled. His friends came to his rescue, propping him up. One MacDougall, a huge hulk of a fellow, stepped forward to enter the fray.

Angus would have none of it. Soon it would be a brawl. "Now, now," he said, moving between the two men but speaking to the MacDougalls and mindful of the gathering crowd. "I am certain the Lord of Lorne would never suggest that his family is anything less than honorable. A promise made and dower lands given cannot be taken back without disgrace to the MacDougalls."

"And who are you?" barked the MacDougall's beefy friend. One of his companions, recognizing Angus, tugged on the man's sleeve but to no avail.

"Angus Og Macdonald, brother to Lord Alexander Macdonald of Islay, Juliana's husband."

Hearing this, the MacDougalls hushed up their drunken friend and pulled him away.

Angus turned to the angry Isleman. "Let it pass. I will make sure Alex is aware. Tell your captain about this and remind him to post guards this night."

The man nodded and headed to where Conall stood watching from the other side of the grass beneath the trees.

Angus shook his head. "So that is their game. Think of it. In the Highlands, where a man's word is his bond, they do not intend to honor Juliana's dowry. The lass will be sad to hear her family would dishonor her so and Alex will be furious. Should the MacDougalls carry through with such a despicable act, my father will have something to say as well. Steps will have to be taken."

"Aye," said Duncan. "And that will not end well."

Once Angus had spoken to his brother who confirmed he intended to stay the night, Angus made sure guards would be posted to deal with any more drunken fools. Then he sailed to Morvern, anxious to be away.

The sun was hanging low in the sky as they entered the Sound of Mull that separated the Isle of Mull from Morvern. It was still hours before dark, yet Angus was tired from the long day and regretted the news he must give his father.

His mother met him and Duncan at the door to the castle on Ardtornish Point. Helen Macdonald, daughter of Sir Colin Campbell of Loch Awe, and younger than her husband by many years, was a handsome woman yet Angus could see her strength had been affected by whatever ailed his father. While her nut-brown hair lacked strands of gray, her face bore lines of worry, and the spark in her blue eyes had waned since he'd last seen her. "Mother," he greeted her with a kiss on the cheek, "how is Father?"

"He will be better now that you are here. Come, he sits by the fire, awaiting your news from Lorne."

Angus crossed the large hall to his father while his mother put her arm around Duncan and welcomed him to their home.

"Father," said Angus, taking the seat next to him. The two deerhounds lying next to his father rose and accepted a pat from Angus.

"Ah, you are home, Son. Well and good. And I see you bring my nephew. Greetings, Duncan."

"And to you, Uncle," said Duncan who came to stand behind Angus.

Meeting his father's weary expression, Angus asked, "Are you unwell?"

"Brought low, more like, for Scotland's affairs worsen."

Angus pondered what he knew. "Is it the Guardians' request to King Edward to mediate the claims of those who would be king that concerns you?"

His father gave Angus an impatient look. "Not the request, Son, but what England's king demanded for his agreement to do so."

"What was that?"

"He required each of the candidates for the crown to accept him as Scotland's overlord, which, damn their eyes, they did, even Bruce."

"That, I'd not heard. What can it mean?"

"It means that whoever is named king after what promises to be an unduly long process, will be bowing to Edward, who sees himself as no mere arbitrator but, rather, a judge."

Angus' heart sank. "Has it begun? …the 'process'?"

"Aye, Edward sits as head of the hundred auditors who will advise him on who has the strongest case. Hearings begin next month in Berwick."

"What do you think of Bruce's case, my lord?" asked Duncan. "Will Robert the Noble prevail?"

"He has submitted his claim, a good one, but not being senior in proximity of blood, he is not the favorite. 'Tis John Balliol, a weak man if ever there was. Worse, he is more Englishman than Scot."

Angus' brow furrowed beneath the weight of such a possibility. "That would be ruinous. Tied as they are to John Balliol, the Comyns and the MacDougalls would become unbearable were Balliol to gain the throne."

"Aye, they would. And I would never bend the knee to John Balliol." His father returned his gaze to the fire for a moment and then looked up. "By the bye, how went Alex's wedding?"

Angus suggested Duncan pull up a chair. "The tale is a bit long but I'll not spare you the details." Whereupon Angus relayed all that had happened at Dunstaffnage Castle and his concern about the Isle of Lismore. "I fear my brother may never see that dower property come to him."

His father put his hand to his red-bearded chin and let out a deep breath. "It would be in keeping with the MacDougalls' character to plan such a mean trick. I did not want Alexander to marry the girl for my distrust of her people, but he is thirty and too old to be forbidden. Ah, well. The deed is done. What did you think of her?"

"A pretty lass," said Angus, remembering the bride on her father's arm and after the vows were said when her happiness was clear to all.

"Biddable, I would suspect," added Duncan, "being as she is a daughter of the Lord of Lorne. She would have been raised to follow orders."

"Mayhap, through her," said Angus' father, "the MacDougalls hope to gain our title." His blue eyes flamed. "'Twill never happen!"

He was glad to see his father's spirits rising with his anger. Whatever ailed him, he had not given up the fight.

Just then, Angus' mother glided into the hall and laid her hand on her husband's shoulder. "Shall we let these two refresh themselves before dinner? They must be hungry and we are nearly ready to eat."

Angus' father patted his wife's hand. "Aye, 'tis later than I thought."

Not wishing to discourage his mother's enthusiasm for what would likely be a wonderful meal by speaking of all he had consumed at the wedding, Angus rose. "That sounds good to me, Mother." He shot a glance at Duncan. "I am certain my cousin will not object."

"I am always ready to eat," said the good-humored Duncan.

They had intended to remain at Ardtornish for only a few days to enjoy the company of Angus' parents and his brother, John, and to allow those of the crew from Ardtornish time with their families. But when Alex arrived the next afternoon, Angus and Duncan decided to extend their stay.

Alex and his new bride were so smitten with each other no one wanted to cast a pall on their happiness by asking Juliana about her family. The Lord of the Isles had already received the report of the wedding and did not appear interested in hearing more. Instead, Juliana fairly charmed all and was most respectful to Angus' mother.

"'Tis beautiful here," Juliana enthused at dinner, her cheeks rosy with health. "The hills are so green and the sound's waters so blue." Taking a breath, she gazed at Alex and added, "I saw a white-tailed eagle fly over the galley as we arrived at Ardtornish Point!"

"Aye," said Angus' father, obviously pleased she had noticed, "they have an eyrie in the tall pine tree nearby. Their fledglings are nearly ready to be on their own."

Angus wondered if his father thought the same of his sons. They were all men now and would soon be completely on their own.

Angus' mother expressed delight at having time with her new daughter-in-law. "With my two daughters grown and living away, I have been lonely for a daughter."

While Juliana spent time with the Lady of the Isles, the men hunted deer on the heather-clad hills and fished for salmon and sea trout in Ardtornish Bay.

Angus' father had recovered and was well enough to join them one golden summer day. The trees were rich in green leaves bathed in sunlight as they wended their way to the River Aline.

It seemed to Angus that time stood still that day.

They enjoyed each other's fellowship without many words as men sometimes do. They sympathized with John when he missed his shot at a red stag he'd been stalking for hours, and they laughed at Duncan's antics when he slipped on the bank and ended up drenched in the water.

Angus could not remember such a glorious time with his father and brothers and was glad Duncan was there to share it. As if they had agreed to an unspoken truce, they did not discuss political matters or the quest for the crown. Nor was mention made of the ongoing rivalry between the MacDougalls and the Macdonalds or what might become of Lismore.

The next day, Angus wished Alex and Juliana Godspeed and waved to them as their ship headed west down the sound. Angus was sorry they had stayed only a few days but he considered they were recently wed and wanted to be alone.

August had just arrived when Angus and Duncan departed for Glen Coe, sailing east down the sound to Loch Linnhe. Once in the loch, they headed north, past Lismore, to Loch Leven. At that point, the crew lowered the sail and took to the oars, pulling hard, to carry the ship to where the River Coe met the loch. A short way up the river, they beached the ship. It was midday, the sun high in the sky.

Signaling the crew to follow, Angus grabbed his satchel and he and Duncan strode farther inland. "Do you know this man Dugall MacEanruig with whom you are to meet?" Angus asked his cousin.

"I would know him to see the man as I met him once. But I know little about him, save he is the chief man of these parts."

Angus nodded. "Then, mayhap our arrival will be welcome."

"Aye, he is aware I come on a mission for my father, a matter of the church MacEanruig is most interested in."

"Let's hope they dine well. Bargaining can give a man an appetite."

Duncan laughed. "So it does. And a great thirst!"

At the end of the road, they found no castle, only a large whitewashed manor flanked by cottages and what looked like stables on the far side. A garden of vegetables and herbs was thriving on one side of the manor.

When the few men standing outside learned their identity, Angus and his cousin were greeted with smiles and escorted inside. Angus asked his captain to keep the crew outside until they knew more of what lay ahead.

Inside, Angus looked around, admiring the clean hall and rushes. Though no hearth fire burned, the scent of wood smoke permeated the air. "Wait here," their escort said.

Soon, they were greeted by a young woman in a green tunic, a bonnie lass with long curling copper-colored hair worn loose about her shoulders. Her eyes matched the green of her garment. The quality of her clothes suggested she was not a servant. Angus judged her age to be about seventeen.

She fingered her green and red plaid shawl, draped loosely over her arms. "You are welcome here, Angus Og Macdonald and Duncan MacAlasdair." She gave Angus a penetrating look. "The Lord of the Isles' galleys are well known to the people of Glen Coe since they frequently ply the waters of Loch Linnhe and those off the coasts of Morvern and Mull." Then to both of them, she asked, "Why have you come?"

Duncan said, "I come on business for my father, Alasdair Macdonald of Saddell. Dugall MacEanruig should be expecting me. Is he about?"

"Nay, he is hunting with some of the men. He will return in time to roast meat for dinner, of that you may be certain. You'll stay the night?"

They had little choice. With the long days of August, dinner could be late in coming if the men chose to hunt all day.

"Aye, said Duncan. "If that is an invitation, we accept."

She returned him a coy smile. "'Tis."

"And my crew?" Angus inquired.

"They can sleep in the stables or in the hall, as they choose. I will see you two have chambers in the manor. There will be room enough for all at dinner. I have asked the servants to bring you ale and see to your needs." With that, she turned on her heels and crossed the large room, leaving through a door. Angus thought it might lead to the kitchens though, at the moment, there was no smell of cooking.

He puzzled at her odd behavior. "Did she give us her name?" he asked Duncan.

"Nay, I do not recall it. A woman of few words." He smiled. "How rare."

Or evasive, thought Angus.

A manservant brought them mugs of heather ale. "I'll make sure your men are seen to and when I return, I will take you to your chambers."

"Pardon," interjected Angus, "but might I ask, who was the lass who was just speaking to us?"

"She be Sorcha MacEanruig, the chief man's daughter, his only child."

The servant walked away and Duncan said, "Well, that explains it."

"Explains what?"

"The only child would speak with authority even though that child is a lass."

"Aye," said Angus, "but I wonder what happened to her mother. I cannot think of a Highland family where the chief man has only one child."

"'Tis unusual. Most would have remarried to produce more."

Once Angus and Duncan had been shown to their simple but well-appointed chambers where they left their satchels, they went outside. There, Angus found his crew happily imbibing the heathered ale, which was excellent. For the better part of an hour, he and Duncan sat around talking with the men of Glen Coe.

"We've some fine garron ponies if you have a mind to ride through the glen," said one. "They are sure-footed through the hill passes where we keep our cattle at this time of year."

"A grand idea," agreed Angus, rising from the stone on which he was sitting. With Duncan and a few of their crew who wanted to go, and a Glen Coe man named Owen who knew the valley well, they rode along the River Coe through the wooded glen.

On either side of the road, soaring moor-clad hills and sheer rock faces rose high above them. The bracken was already turning a dark gold. From the slopes and ledges flowed magnificent waterfalls, long columns of white water thundering to the rocks below.

In one place, Angus paused to bat away swarming midges that had been vigorous in their attack. Hoping to avoid them, he stepped closer to the cool mist the waterfall spewed into the air. A red squirrel sitting on a nearby boulder eyed him as it nibbled on a nut.

"It fair takes my breath away," said Duncan, looking up at the waterfall that began its descent hundreds of feet above them.

"The coast of Tirconnell in Ulster is a place that moved me to this same awe," said Angus, "though Skye and Mull have some magnificent waterfalls."

They rode on until their guide took a sharp left turn, leading them over a small bridge across the river. "You are in luck," said Owen, "for we've not had much rain, else the path could be blocked by the swollen river. We'll leave the ponies here and walk on."

A short distance away, a herd of two score shaggy black cattle grazed lazily. "However do you get them up here?" asked Duncan.

"And why?" added Angus. The Macdonalds kept cattle but mostly on low-lying pastureland.

"We bring them up in the spring before the heavy rains. It takes a few of us to accomplish it. We keep them here in the summer where they are hidden from reivers. They do well on the poor pasture and, more importantly, they are out of sight of the MacDougalls."

"The MacDougalls are a problem?" Angus asked.

"Aye, from time to time," Owen answered with a shrug. "They consider all of northern Argyll theirs and we must remind them it is not."

"Do you have help at such times?" Angus inquired.

Owen shot him a glance but gave no name. "There are those who aid us when we have need."

The midges had become oppressive and Angus was glad when they returned to the ponies and began the journey back down the magnificent glen.

An hour later, they arrived at MacEanruig's manor where a heavy mist had begun to settle on the hills.

The hunters, too, had returned. Dugall MacEanruig, with the same copper-colored hair of his daughter and a bushy brown beard, held his hand out in welcome. "I know your father, Angus, and yours, Duncan. Both are good men. I am pleased you have come on business of importance to me, but let us enjoy each other's company tonight and leave the business until morning."

"A welcome plan," said Duncan.

Angus had no qualms about what MacEanruig proposed. His midge bites, gained in the glen, were starting to itch. Mayhap he could get a quick bath in the river before dinner and apply the salve his mother had given him.

"Did you enjoy your ride through the glen?" the chief asked.

"Aye," said Angus, "there is no place quite like it."

"We feel the same," said MacEanruig, as he welcomed them into his hall.

The large room was filled with men and women gathered for the evening meal. To Angus, the people of Glen Coe seemed a happy lot. They might lack the wealth of the Macdonalds but they had enough to feed their families and care for their houses, horses, ponies and cattle, which was more than many had. And, above all that, they lived in a magnificent glen with waterfalls to delight a man's eye.

"We've a good life here," MacEanruig remarked as they dined later that evening in the hall lit with candles and flames in the fireplace. The day had been warm but now the air was cool and the fire welcome.

Duncan sat on the chief's right and Angus on his left. Next to Angus was Sorcha MacEanruig, who chatted of her skill at embroidery and cooking. "Only when I want to, mind. We have cooks aplenty in Glen Coe."

A musician playing a stringed instrument with a bow, different from the lyre Angus was used to, sent a beautiful, though sad, melody through the hall. When it ended, Sorcha rose and said, "A livelier tune for our guests, aye, Father?"

The MacEanruig nodded whereupon the girl went to a side table and lifted a hand drum of animal skin stretched over a circle of wood affixed with small bells. She motioned to a piper who had just entered. As he began to play, Sorcha danced, beating on the small drum with her hand, which caused the bells to make a sharp tinkling sound. All eyes were upon her as she twirled around the hall, her long copper hair catching the light of the fire.

When the music stopped, other dancers flooded the center of the hall, eager to take part.

Sorcha came to stand in front of Angus, beads of sweat on her brow. Reaching her hand toward him, she said, "You must dance!"

Angus glanced at Duncan.

"Do not worry about him," she said. "He will have a partner." Just then, another girl reached her hand toward Duncan. He took it, laughing in merriment as the girl dragged him away.

"Best go with them or they will not be satisfied," said MacEanruig.

"Very well," said Angus and allowed Sorcha to lead him onto the floor where, as best he could, he copied her steps. The dance differed from the ones he was used to but that did not seem to matter overmuch. Soon, he was swept away with the music, the effects of the ale, and the girl's joy as she danced, her green eyes never leaving him.

Many dances with Sorcha and other lasses followed when, exhausted, Angus begged a rest from his current partner.

Sorcha returned to his side and he told her, "I could use another tankard of that fine heather ale. The lasses of Glen Coe have worn me out."

"I doubt that is true, Angus Macdonald. All of them wanted to partner with you and you were kind to accommodate them."

"'Twas my pleasure," he said, inclining his head.

She glanced up at him from beneath her lashes. Angus knew a flirt when he saw one. "'Tis just having a new man about, especially one they have heard of. You are a curiosity."

He smiled at that and left her to wend his way through those still dancing to the table where her father sat talking with Duncan. How long his cousin had been there Angus could not say but Duncan showed no signs of fatigue so he could not have been dancing for the hours Angus had.

He sat and talked with them as he drank another tankard of the ale but soon found his eyelids drooping. Setting down his empty tankard, he said, "'Tis time I seek my bed." With good humor, he said to MacEanruig, "Your hospitality is most gracious, and I am your willing, if exhausted, guest."

The chief laughed, a deep hearty sound. "Leave us if you must. I expect you will be fully restored in the morning, son of Angus Mor." The jolly chief smiled as he observed his guests enjoying themselves.

With that, Angus wished them goodnight and climbed the stairs to his bedchamber, leaving Duncan drinking with their host.

In his chamber, Angus shed his clothes, thankful a fire burned in the hearth, and slid between the sheets, remembering to place his dirk beneath his pillow. Moments later, he was fast asleep.

Sometime in the dark of night, he was awakened by the sound of footfalls. He was not alone. Slowly, he reached his hand beneath his pillow and grasped the handle of his knife. Opening his eyes, he glimpsed a cloud of white moving toward his bed. The fire had burned down and the moon's faint light cast the chamber in dark shadows.

Now fully awake, he sat up and lifted his dagger to face the intruder. "Who are you and why are you here?"

The white cloud, which he now realized was a linen gown, disappeared to be replaced by what looked like a naked woman, her face and most of her body hidden in shadow.

She spoke in a low whisper. "For such an important guest, the chief provides a woman to warm your bed."

In the meager light, he thought he glimpsed full breasts and a slim waist. Before he could speak, she lifted the bedcover and slid in next to him, her warmth adding heat to his suddenly aroused body.

"Do you do this willingly, lass?"

"Aye," she said, the whisper growing seductive.

A warm hand reached out to touch his chest, her fingers playing in the hair she found there. Still speaking in a whisper, she said, "You're a handsome man, Angus Og Macdonald, and you have the air of a prince about you."

"A prince?" He nearly laughed. "I am but a younger son."

"Aye," she said, sliding her hand beneath the bedcover and down his body, "but a younger son of the great Angus Mor."

Angus still had hold of his dirk and was about to set it aside when she whispered again. "You can put away the blade. You'll not be needing it this night."

Never before had a woman boldly come to his bed and, though he lacked experience, he knew enough of coupling to take the lead. "I'll not turn you away if this is the chief's provision and you insist upon offering yourself."

"'Tis my desire."

For a servant offered to honored guests, he did not think her movements were very practiced but she made up for it in enthusiasm.

He slept little that night.

When he awoke for the last time, muted light streamed into his chamber from what had to be a gray morning. His head ached as he lifted it off the pillow. A movement drew his gaze to the door where a girl hastily donned a dark cloak over her white chemise and slipped out. But not before he glimpsed the long copper curls belonging to MacEanruig's daughter.

Horrified, he hurriedly donned his clothes and splashed water on his face. Between the ale and the lack of sleep, his mind was slow to respond. But he could not help asking, *Why?*

He considered the possibilities. Were her actions designed to trap him into marriage? Would the chief man of Glen Coe demand retribution from the Lord of the Isles? Or, was Sorcha merely a rebellious daughter who wanted to defy her father?

In the hall, some of MacEanruig's men and Angus' crew were eating together. Angus greeted them and scanned the hall. Neither Sorcha nor her father was in view. Duncan stood at the open door staring out on a gray day with lightly falling rain.

Coming up behind him, Angus said, "Have you spoken with the chief about your father's business?"

His cousin turned. "Aye, the matter of a new kirk for the glen has been agreed to." Duncan gave him a long perusal. "You slept late and judging from the look of you, I'd say you did not sleep alone."

Angus rubbed the back of his neck, recalling the night before. "Nay." He did not want to mention Sorcha's name for fear of bringing reproach upon her. "Did you?" Mayhap one of Sorcha's friends had visited his cousin's bed.

"Aye, I went to my bed very late. Before I did, I saw MacEanruig's daughter ascending the stairs and, seeing the way she looked at you all evening, I had to wonder about her destination."

Inwardly, Angus chided himself. "Until this morning, I had no idea the woman who snuck into my chamber was the chief's daughter. I certainly gave her no invitation. In the dark, her voice was different, a low whisper. She made herself out to be a servant offered to me by the chief."

"A plausible explanation."

Angus saw the flaw. "Yet no such offer was made to you, the expected guest."

Duncan placed his hand on Angus' shoulder. "If there is a plot afoot, we will soon know it. Have you eaten?"

"Nay, and I am fair hungry."

Duncan tossed him a smirk as they walked to the table where they had dined the night before.

Angus sat and a servant placed cooked eggs and fried trout before him. Trout was a favorite delicacy and he was quick to partake.

On the table were a jug of ale and a crust of bread and butter. Duncan reached to pour himself ale and Angus noted there was no food before him.

"You have eaten already?"

"Aye, while I spoke with MacEanruig."

"Did the chief man of Glen Coe leave?" Angus could not imagine Dugall MacEanruig was aware of his daughter's actions or he would have demanded retribution.

"He and his men went riding out soon after our meeting. I have not seen his daughter all morning."

So, she had said nothing. Mayhap that was best. If Angus were to meet her in the light of day, he was not certain what he would say. He hoped she had no designs on him for he had none on her. Still, he chided himself for not seeing through the ruse.

Later, as they were returning to their ship, a young lad of serious demeanor came running to Angus. "Are you Angus Og Macdonald?"

"Aye," he said, wondering at the mission of the boy.

Thrusting a folded piece of parchment at him, the lad said, "This is for you."

Angus accepted the missive and the boy turned and ran back toward the manor. Opening the folded parchment, he read, *'Twas I who shared the night with you, son of Angus Mor. And I would do it again should you desire it. – Sorcha*

Angus looked up, his brow furrowed.

"What is it?" asked Duncan.

"It seems Sorcha wanted me to know 'twas she who shared my bed."

Dunseverick Castle, northern coast of Ulster, Ireland, late summer 1291

THUNDER RUMBLED in the distance as Áine stood at the castle window, staring at the rain that had begun to fall. At her neck, she pressed her fingers into the cold metal of the golden ring brooch Niall had given her. She had been so chilled when she returned from her walk she had yet to remove the woolen mantle. The brooch was all she had left of his many gifts, except for the most important one.

Had it only been a sennight since she returned from Tirowen? She had lost track of time.

She remembered that terrible night and shivered. The sounds of war erupting all around her, men shouting, dogs barking, swords clashing and women screaming.

Niall had quickly armed himself and rushed to the door. "Stay inside!"

She had used the precious minutes she had while the battle raged to don her cloak and rouse Nessa and the babe's nurse.

Caught unaware, Niall's men fought bravely but were losing to the enemy's greater numbers. Watching through the window by the light of the full moon as the battle waned, she saw Niall fighting one man as another attacked him from behind. She recognized the cowardly one who drove his sword through Niall's back—his cousin, Domnall O'Neill.

Áine had covered her mouth and swallowed her scream as one of Niall's captains rushed into the house. "Come…now!" he yelled. "We must get you away while there is still time! Through the back!"

She did not hesitate. Clutching Brian to her breast, with Finn close at her side, she ordered Nessa and Alma to come with her. The three of them followed the captain into the night.

The sight of Niall lying face down in the dirt was one she would never forget. In the moonlight, his blood had been colored black. His murder left her stunned. But for his men, she might not have left when she did. It was only due to their quick action that she and her son escaped the chaos.

Áine arrived at Dunseverick, shaken but relieved, as her father welcomed her into his arms. "Thank God you and the babe are safe."

She buried her head in his broad chest. "His men managed to recover his body and have brought it for burial."

Her father held her away, looking into her face with sympathy. "He will be buried with much ceremony and solemnity and his men are welcome to stay on O'Cahan lands."

"Thank you, Father. The O'Neills will be grateful."

The next day, Richard de Burgh, the Earl of Ulster, had sent a message of support, vowing to remove the man who took her husband's life. Revenge might satisfy the earl but it would do nothing to strip from her mind the image of Niall lying bloodied on the ground, forever imprinted on her soul. Nor would revenge return to her son his father.

In the span of three years, she had been a reluctant bride, wife, queen, mother and now widow. Could one live so many lives in so few years and not be much changed?

"Come, sit by the fire, Mistress," said Nessa, quietly approaching.

"I've hot spiced wine for you. 'Twill warm your bones."

"Thank you, Nessa. That would be most welcome."

Slowly, she crossed the hall to the chairs in front of the blazing fire in the large stone fireplace. Finn came to sit at her feet. It seemed she did everything more slowly in these last days as if she were reluctant to take a step toward the future. "Brian?"

"The babe is with Alma, sleeping protected by his angel."

"'Tis a blessing he is too young to have been aware," Áine said, taking a seat and opening her cloak as she accepted the wine. "Sit with me, Nessa. Your company is a comfort."

Nessa glanced around the hall. "Well, I suppose your father will not mind seeing 'twas you who asked."

Áine smiled to herself and gazed into the goblet of wine warming her cold hands. "No, he will not mind. He is happy to have us here, no matter the dire circumstances that brought it about." Inhaling the familiar smell of cinnamon, ginger and cloves, she sipped the honeyed drink that brought warmth to her inside.

"Aye, a pleased man is Lord Cumee. 'Tis true he lost a friend and his daughter a husband but your father has you, his son Dermot, and his grandson together under his roof."

Áine's brother was now a man grown and sharing the responsibilities with her father that would one day be his own. She found solace in her family and the familiar surroundings of home and thanked God for the refuge they provided. The priest in Derry had once assured her all would be for her according to God's will. At the time, she'd had no idea this would be the path she would take, but she did not doubt God was still with her.

The burial took place two days later at Dungiven Priory, the place where O'Cahans were laid to rest.

Her father's bard had written a lament for Niall and that night after dinner, he recited it as a harp played in the background. There were many verses. Some spoke of Niall's bravery from the days before she had met him. As the bard came to the end of the lament, his voice rose.

O king of heroes, heroic child!

You did smite our foe in battle wild,
You did right all wrongs, O just and mild!
And who lives now—since dead is Niall?

In place of feasts, alas! There's crying,
In place of song, sad woe and sighing,
Alas, I live with my heart a-dying,
And you beneath the sod!

You were skilled all straits to ravel,
Thousands brought from death and cavil,
They journey safe who with thee travel,
And you now safe with God!

Tears welled in Áine's eyes. 'Twas a sad yet fitting tribute to a man who had been loved by his people but whose reign was cut short by a kinsman's treachery. As for herself, the thought occurred, *better for me, so much evil have I found, that I should have been a poor man's wife.*

Niall's colored cloaks, his gold rings and all but the most loyal of his warriors were gone. In song, at least, the fallen King of Tirowen would be remembered. And he would live on in his son.

When the bard's verses ended and the harp fell silent, her father patted her hand and leaned close. "I know it seems like the end of all things, Daughter. But, in truth, your life is just beginning."

Áine wondered if that were so. She was young yet she had no desire for anything save to care for her son. It heartened her to think that young Brian O'Neill would have his grandfather and his uncle to guide him. Still, she had once hoped for so much more.

CHAPTER 6

Dunaverty Castle, Kintyre Peninsula, June 1292

FOR ANGUS, THE remaining months of 1291 passed swiftly. As autumn descended, bringing its cooler days and nights, the Macdonalds prepared for winter.

Typically, MacFinnon, the master of the Lord of the Isles' household, would call upon their tenants on the scattered Isles to ensure their needs were met before rents were collected on Martinmas. Since MacFinnon was occupied with other business for Angus' father and Alex was newly married, the task fell to Angus.

"'Tis time our people see more of you," said his father as he issued the instructions.

That his father trusted him to meet with the tenants pleased Angus. Such a voyage would also give him a deeper understanding of their lands and the people who worked them. Some might need help with roofs or crops or slaughtering of cattle to feed them through the winter and Angus was eager to offer help if it were needed.

"Might I take John with me?" Angus knew his younger brother would be eager to accompany him.

"Aye, take the lad."

By late October, Angus had completed the visits to their tenants and returned to Ardtornish to report his findings. He summarized the list by saying, "With the exception of the few cattle lost to sickness and one failed crop, the tenants are thriving and ready for the coming months."

His father nodded. "You have done well and I can see young John was happy to be taken along." John did, indeed, look happy. He had a talent for bringing joy to people with his pleasing demeanor and his questions that demonstrated his genuine interest in their lives.

The next day, with his father's shouted Godspeed echoing off the waters of the Sound of Mull, Angus waved goodbye to his brother and sailed for Kintyre. In late November, he was joined by Duncan, who rode south from his home at Saddell Castle to spend the winter with Angus at Dunaverty.

On the rare days of little rain, they practiced their sword skills with the castle garrison. Or, since Angus kept a falconer and several hawks at Dunaverty, they might go hawking, a pastime both had enjoyed from their youth.

In deep autumn, when the bracken turned the hills golden brown, the wind stripped the branches of the trees, leaving a carpet of gold, red and yellow on the forest floor.

Storms rolled in from the sea, turning the waters of Dunaverty Bay the color of slate, and cold rain beat on the castle's stone walls. Duncan and Angus, wrapped in their woolen cloaks, sought refuge before the fire where they read to each other from favorite books. When reading failed to hold Angus' interest, he persuaded Duncan to join him in a game of chess.

"That's two games you have had of me," said Angus' cousin.

"Then, mayhap you will find solace in some spiced wine, and we can discuss the reports I have just received from the hearings taking place in Berwick. It must have put to sleep those nobles assembled to listen to the auditors droning on about their research into the lineage of those seeking the crown."

A total of fourteen claimants had stepped forward. Most were dismissed at an early stage. One of these was John Comyn of

Badenoch, nicknamed "the Red" for his red coat of arms to distinguish him from his uncle, Alexander "the Black". The Comyn's dismissal caused Angus some little joy.

"The rejection of Comyn's claim comes as no surprise," said Duncan, "and, though you find it an occasion for joy, 'tis likely not much of a disappointment to him. Remember, he is married to a sister of John Balliol. If Balliol prevails, so do the Comyns."

"Aye," agreed Angus, his joy ebbing away, "a dismal thought. And the elimination of more contenders will soon leave Edward with a simple choice between Balliol and Bruce."

Duncan nudged a log in the fireplace with the toe of his boot. "That may be but the hearings will drag on as all will want to be heard."

"Edward is doubtless pleased with the delay, for it leaves him that much longer in control of Scotland."

"That is the true outcome he desires," said Duncan. "Now that he has Wales under his thumb, he has fixed his eyes on who becomes King of Scots, though with all the candidates swearing allegiance to him, that signifies little."

His cousin spoke the truth. 'Twas clear to Angus the English king looked upon Scotland as a vassal kingdom. And while this saddened him, if he had to choose between King Balliol, aligned with the enemies of the Macdonalds, and King Edward, the choice just might be Edward.

The Bruces, too, would make the same choice. After all, his friend, Rob, now Sir Robert, was in London serving the English king. Rob had once told Angus the future of the Bruces might be tied to King Edward. And so might be the fate of the Macdonalds—the only way to save their lands should Balliol become king.

In the early spring of 1292, as the first primroses were blooming in the woods and the gorse painted Kintyre's meadows a rich gold, Angus' father sent for him. The message arrived as he and Duncan were standing at the castle wall watching a mated pair of sea eagles in their ritual display, the male's loud calls echoing off the water. On the horizon, Angus could just make out the faint outline of Ulster.

A courier approached and handed him a sealed parchment. "From

Lord Macdonald."

Angus thanked the courier and sent him to the kitchens for a meal. Opening the message, he quickly read the summons. Glancing up at Duncan, he said, "It seems Father has yet another task for me and requests my presence at Ardtornish. Will you come?"

"Aye, of course. I will send a message to my father that I am on business for Angus Mor. He will not question it."

The next day, Angus and Duncan sailed north for Morvern. The rain that followed them was light and, thankfully, did not linger. Nor did it discourage the dolphins that swam alongside the ship, leaping in the air as they rode the bow wave. Angus always suspected the creatures were drawn to the crew's chanting when they took to the oars.

The afternoon Angus and Duncan arrived, the wind was blowing hard as they stepped ashore in the shadow of Ardtornish Castle. Angus' younger brother, John, who must have been watching them sail down the sound, waved from where he stood on the shore.

John brushed a strand of his light brown hair from his eyes. "It took you long enough."

"Father's message said nothing of haste," said Angus. "Besides, you would not expect us to sail here in a day. We stopped at Claig Castle." The massive sea fortress on *Fraoch Eilean*, the Heather Isle just off the coast of Jura, was built by Somerled to defend the Sound of Islay. Now, it served the Macdonalds as a convenient place from which to extract a toll from ships passing through the sound.

While Duncan described for John their brief stay at Claig, Angus made a studied assessment of his younger brother. In the year since they had hunted together in Morvern, John had grown taller. Mayhap he was anxious to be included in more of the family business. "Are you longing for another adventure, younger brother?"

"I am," said John. "Father wants you to sail again, something about the chiefs. I am hoping you might take me with you."

"I will if I can," said Angus, his attention drawn to the calves grazing on the green hillside. "We have added to our herd, I see."

"Aye. Father is pleased so many were born this spring."

The sun had just broken through the clouds as they climbed the great headland to the castle. The day's light persisted as Angus, his brother and cousin sat down to dinner with Angus Mor and his wife.

Angus' eyes grew wide as a young servant girl set before him a platter of roast trout wrapped in bacon, winking at him as she walked away. It was one of his favorite dishes, as his mother well knew.

"Cook has been waiting for you to arrive," said John, "and, by chance, I caught several trout this morning, one of which you are eating."

Angus speared a piece of trout with his dagger and drew it to his mouth. "You may miss a shot at a deer from time to time, but you are a skilled fisherman and, for this delicious trout, I thank you."

When they had eaten their fill, Angus said, "You spoil us, Mother."

Duncan, whose mouth was full, nodded.

"I suppose it is ever the case that I must wait for my sons to gather around me before I can expect such a grand feast," said Angus' father with a look of feigned offense.

"Not so, my lord," chided his wife in a friendly manner, "and you know it. Why, Cook would do this for you any day should you but request it."

"All the same, 'tis good to have you home, Angus, no matter the meal. I could have told you of the task in a message but I wanted to see you. And glad I am you came, too, Nephew," he said to Duncan. "The task I have for you is important in light of our troubled times."

Angus paused in his eating to capture his father's next words.

"I want you to call upon the chiefs and the others who will gather on Islay for the Council in early autumn. The sennight before Michaelmas will do, I think. Share with them what we know of what is taking place at Berwick where Edward decides who will wear the Scottish crown. Gather the mood of our chiefs. Answer their questions if you can. We will have a full discussion when we meet at Finlaggan."

The Council of the Isles, the governing body of the lordship, met on an island in Loch Finlaggan on Islay. There, the chiefs debated matters of great import and rendered decisions on disputed matters. Angus always looked forward to the gatherings, so he was not displeased with his father's request. "Aye, I will gladly undertake such a mission."

"I would go along if you allow it, Uncle," offered Duncan.

"'Tis good you do," said Angus' father. "I have been in contact with my younger brother, your father, but what you learn will add to his knowledge, as I expect it will add to mine." With a glance at Angus, he said, "Take John with you as well. 'Twill be an opportunity for him to better know the chiefs and for them to remember I have three sons."

Angus tossed his younger brother a grin. "It would be my pleasure."

"If you can find him at home, it might be advisable to visit Donald Mackay on the Rhinns of Islay. He is a seer I have consulted before. I have not been sleeping well and he may know the reason."

Angus could not recall his father having spoken of a seer but he knew the peninsula in the west of Islay called the Rhinns. "I will do as you request."

"Then, on your way back to Ardtornish, stop at Iona to call upon Fionnlagh, the abbot. He, too, will attend the Council's meeting at our invitation. Tell him I will send a galley for him. The Bishop of the Isles will attend as well. But I will see to his invitation myself."

"Very well," said Angus.

Angus' father set down his wine. "I believe our clan and the chiefs will stand united with the Bruces, but I will be glad to have that confirmed by the Council." Mirroring Angus' own thoughts, he said, "In truth, I would rather be allied with a strong King Edward than a weak John Balliol, particularly since Balliol will further empower the Comyns and MacDougalls."

Thus dispatched, the next morning, Angus, Duncan and John set sail under a blue sky streaked with thin white clouds. Heading west down the Sound of Mull, they reached the open sea and sailed north to the Isle of Skye where they had decided to begin their calls upon the chiefs.

Angus intended to speak only about the status of the proceedings before King Edward and urge the chiefs to attend the Council's meeting in September. If he happened to learn something of the chiefs' views that would be all to the good.

Skye was an isle of dramatic contrasts. From its rugged sea cliffs that rivaled those of Tirconnell in Ulster to the Mealt Falls in the northeast that sent water plunging nearly two hundred feet to the ocean below to the Black Cuillin mountains in the south that were often shrouded in mist, there was much to admire.

It was late afternoon when Angus' crew beached the galley on a shore in the far northwest of Skye next to a rocky summit at the head of Loch Dunvegan, the abode of Tormod Macleod, aging chief of the Macleods. Though the Macleods dominated the Isles of Harris and Lewis, Angus' father had advised him that the clan's most recent castle was located at Dunvegan on Skye.

Angus and his companions, as emissaries of the Lord of the Isles, were given a hearty welcome. "Greetings, son of Angus Mor," said Tormod, who, with his son, Malcolm, met them at the castle door.

A giant of a man, Tormod's silver-laced fair hair fell to his shoulders. His eyebrows and beard were a bushy white. His eldest son was also fair in coloring. More than the other clans, the Macleods still retained the look of their Norse ancestors.

Tormod eyed Angus with an appraising look. "You've become a man since I last saw you at Ardtornish. What is your age now?"

"Twenty," replied Angus.

"And I suppose this is your brother, John. The resemblance grows more sure with the years."

"Aye," said Angus, for the truth of it was apparent. "And this fair handsome beast, looking for all the world like a Macleod, is my cousin, Duncan MacAlasdair."

Duncan, being in good humor, smiled.

"I know your father, young Duncan," said Tormod, "the brother of the great Angus Mor."

Tormod offered his hand and each of them shook it in turn. "Come into the keep. I'll see your men are offered refreshment and provided lodging with my own."

"Thank you," said Angus with a nod toward his captain.

As they walked up the hill to the castle, Tormod remarked, "As chance would have it, John MacNicol is visiting me, so you can speak with him, as well."

"We had planned to call upon Laird MacNicol next," said Angus. "You have saved us a trip to Lewis." The MacNicols were an ancient clan with roots in the kingdom of Dalriada like Angus' own. He knew his father would want them to attend the Council.

Tormod preceded Angus and his companions into the great hall where they greeted Tormod's wife, Fiona, and his son's wife, Alyse.

Once the men and women were seated, Tormod said, "MacNicol and I have just been discussing the events playing out in Berwick."

John MacNicol, a shorter and younger man than Tormod but of fair countenance like the Macleod chief, agreed. "We are anxious to know what you have heard."

Tormod's brow furrowed above his intense blue eyes. "I assume my good friend, Angus Mor, has been watching the events taking place on the English border where King Edward holds court?"

"Aye," said Angus. "He has followed closely how the field of candidates narrows. 'Tis a slow process as Edward seems in no hurry to make a choice. We but wonder at the outcome."

"Do you think the Guardians are so foolish as to believe Edward will forget the oaths of fealty he demanded of them once a new King of Scots is chosen?" asked MacNicol.

"They may forget their oaths, believing them replaced by their oaths to the new king," said Angus. "But I am confident Edward will not.

With a chuckle, Duncan added, "The English king forgets nothing that is in his interest."

"Aye, 'tis as we suspect," said Tormod. "Much can go wrong and likely will. I look forward to meeting with the other chiefs at the Council. All will want to hear what Angus Mor has to say."

Their conversation was interrupted by the wives' questions about Angus' family and Duncan's. The political discussion was only taken up again over dinner. Angus and Duncan participated freely. John said little but Angus noted his eyes were alight with interest.

Sitting back in his chair, Laird MacNicol took up his silver goblet, turning it slowly in his hand as he stared at the logs burning low in the fireplace. "King Edward dallies."

"So it would seem," said Angus. "Still, given the claims he has already rejected, we may have a decision by year's end."

"The Council meeting in September will be timely," interjected Duncan.

"I will be there with my family," the laird assured them.

Tormod nodded. "I as well, accompanied by my son and our wives."

The next day, Angus bid his host goodbye and sailed west from Skye to the small isle of Barra, the seat of the MacNeils. Rain descended on them as they arrived, and they were glad to be welcomed into the tower house by Niall, the clan chief and his son, Neill.

The MacNeils, like the Macleods, were descendants of the Norse raiders who had plied the waters off the Western Isles in Somerled's time. They were fair in coloring like the Macleods.

Once they had shed their wet cloaks and been refreshed, the conversation quickly turned to the Scottish succession.

"This Council meeting will be one of importance for years to come," said the MacNeil chief. "We are poised on the edge of a cliff and must take care not to plunge to our ruin. I see difficulty no matter which way we turn."

Angus did not disagree for he knew the very kingdom was at stake. "So, we may expect to see you in the days before Michaelmas?"

"Aye, the MacNeils will be there."

They did not tarry on Barra but the next morning, they thanked their host and sailed east to Lochaber, north of Morvern.

"Have you met all the chiefs before?" asked John as they watched the coastline coming into view.

"At one time or another," said Angus.

"Me as well," put in Duncan, "though I have not seen some of them for quite a while."

In Lochaber, they sought out Maolmuire, chief of the MacMillans. The bold chief with black hair and beard had endured many battles and was not eager to see another. "I do not wish to see the lordship dragged into a civil war in Scotland but if Balliol becomes king, I see no way to avoid it. Still, I would hear from the other chiefs. Before the leaves begin to turn, my son and I will sail for Islay."

Their voyage next brought them to the Isle of Mull and Duart Castle on the other side of the isle. Perched on a high crag jutting into the Sound of Mull, the castle, shrouded in fog this day, was home to the Macleans. Sea otters that ringed the shores of the isle were much in evidence.

The crew pulled the galley onto the grass growing near the shore and Angus and his companions climbed to the castle. He tried not to notice the Isle of Lismore just off the coast, knowing it should be his brother's but likely was not. Instead, he focused his attention on Malise, the aging Maclean chief, who met them in front of the castle with his son, another Malcolm. Both were pleased to see Angus and his companions.

"I would recognize that galley pennant anywhere," said Malise, whose dark hair was beginning to turn gray. He beckoned them to follow him and his son into the great hall. "We are not so far apart in miles, your father and I, but alas, we do not see each other as often as I would like. You must stay the night, a few days if you can, and tell us the news of the Macdonalds."

Urged on by the looks his companions gave him, Angus decided a few days here would not be ill-spent. "We would be happy to accept your invitation. We are visiting all the chiefs at my father's request in advance of the Council meeting he has called for early autumn."

The east coast of Mull where Duart Castle was located was a good place to break their voyage. The isle was known to have a healthy herd of red deer and there was rich fishing offshore that would appeal to John.

Over dinner, they discussed Alex's marriage. Angus could see Malise chose carefully his words. "Lismore for a dowry. Now, that will be a treasure if the Macdonalds can wrestle it from the MacDougalls. I'd rather have Alexander Macdonald just offshore of my castle than that treacherous lot. But I cannot see the dowry coming to Alexander without a fight."

Angus agreed but had no desire to dwell on that subject, so he described for the Maclean chief where King Edward was in the process of choosing a new king.

Hearing the explanation, the old chief frowned, uttering a low growl. "Doubtless King Edward expects us all to swear allegiance to him, but it is not a move I favor. I must know what other choices we have."

"The Isles have always been rather independent no matter the king," said Duncan.

While Malise was of an age with Angus' father and had fought with him at the Battle of Largs in 1263, his son was near Angus in age and was quick to express his opinion. "We are now part of Scotland and Scots must have a king of their own," said Malcolm, "but we Macleans pray that man is not Balliol, for if Edward chooses him, the Isles will erupt in war."

"It is to be hoped we can avoid that," said Angus, "but if war comes, the clans must be united and ready."

"Have no doubt, young Macdonald," said the old chief. "We will be ready. United is another matter. I will not see my clan join a foolish venture."

"Nor would my father," said Angus. "He seeks what is best for all in the lordship."

"Aye," said Malise Maclean. "You remind me Angus Mor is the wisest among us." Slapping his palm on the table, he said, "Very well, Angus, tell your father, the Macleans shall attend the Council meeting where we can discuss our choices. Meantime, enjoy the hospitality we offer you and your men."

Angus, his companions and crew passed several agreeable days with the Macleans under mostly fair skies before taking up their journey.

This time they sailed south to the Isle of Colonsay that lay north of Islay. Colonsay was home to the red-haired Macduffies, who were held in high esteem by Angus' father. As the recordkeepers for the Macdonalds, they always attended the Council meetings, but Angus still thought it appropriate to let their chief know where things stood on the quest for the crown.

Malcolm Macduffie had long led his clan, the gray in his red hair a testament to his age. He greeted them warmly with his son, Gilchrist, who was a few years older than Angus. "It has been awhile, Angus," said the Macduffie chief.

"Aye. Duncan and I have been at Dunaverty; only John here has been with my father at Ardtornish."

Inside the keep, the Macduffie chief invited them to sit. "Tell us what brings you to our isle."

"Scotland's future and who will wear the crown."

"There are many Scots who would be king," said Gilchrist, his dark amber eyes hinting of his amusement. "But, to my way of thinking, King Edward manipulates the choosing of our king for his own purposes."

The Macduffie chief nodded.

"My father would invite you to a Council meeting just before Michaelmas."

"Aye," said the Macduffie chief, "we will gladly attend. And whatever the Council decides, we will stand with the Macdonalds." Angus was not surprised to hear this as the Macduffies had ever been loyal to his family.

"We are grateful for your support for the waters into which the lordship is sailing are dangerous."

At the chief's invitation, they stayed a few days on the isle. His son, Gilchrist, joined them on their excursions. One afternoon, they walked across the tidal strait to visit the small isle of Oronsay where there was a monastery established by St. Oran. Angus enjoyed Gilchrist's company, for he was full of information about the isles that were his home. Above that, the son of Colonsay's chief was good fun.

"The walk is worth it, no?" asked Gilchrist.

Angus gazed at the ancient priory rising from the grassy mound overlooking the blue sea. "Aye. My father spoke of it but I have not been here before."

"Columba stopped here on his way to Iona," said Gilchrist. "For that reason alone, it is worthy of your visit."

They returned to Colonsay and, like the quiet before a storm, the wide golden beaches, heather-covered hills and light breezes lulled Angus to linger. He walked the beach alone early each morning, inhaling deeply of the scent of salt, fish and kelp. At those times, he thought of the future and what role he might have in the lordship.

Certain that difficult years lay ahead, he vowed to support his father and elder brother. And, if there came a time when he could take up arms with his friend Robert Bruce, he would hasten to do so.

At night, he often laid on the sand, his hands behind his head, looking up at the sky where thousands of stars twinkled from the black canopy. The sound of the sea lapping at the shore was so familiar to him at times he forgot it altogether. But on Colonsay, he remembered.

Though he could have stayed longer, they had to move on. Bidding goodbye to the Macduffies, Angus and his companions sailed to Islay where Angus intended to visit Alex and his new bride. Beneath a blue sky, the winds picked up as they neared the coast, and he remembered the task his father had given him.

"First, I must pay a visit to Donald Mackay, the old seer my father asked me to visit. He lives on the Rhinns on the west side of the isle."

Angus was to regret finding Mackay at home. The brooding, dark-haired seer with the wizened face was kind enough, inviting them into his cottage set near the large hillfort. There, he lived with an old servant and a great rough-coated hound that Angus thought a handsome beast.

Once Mackay realized they were Macdonalds sent by the Lord of the Isles, he asked no questions. Instead, he invited them to sit and offered them ale, dispatching his servant to offer some to Angus' crew. "I am not surprised Angus Mor has sent you, young Angus, for a cloud hangs over the land and the winds of change are blowing. A wise leader, such as your father, would sense it."

"Do you have words for my father then?" Angus asked, not sure he wanted to hear them for the seer wore a dark expression.

"Aye. There are words I would speak." Mackay paused for a long moment before staring straight ahead, seeing what, Angus could not say.

The old man then began to speak in a quavering voice, drifting into a trance. "A king will rule with uneasy scepter. Scotland will be imperiled as chief attacks chief. Treachery will abound as ancient conflicts are renewed and a foreign ruler will slaughter many. Two chiefs will die before a new one rises with a new king. Only then will

Scotland know peace."

The seer's words left Angus stunned. What could it mean but chaos and death?

They did not stay long after that but thanked Mackay and, being assured they would see him at the Council meeting, quickly departed.

"Good Christ," said Duncan, as they climbed aboard the galley. "What a gloomy vision."

"Aye," said Angus. "Mackay paints a dark picture, one I will never forget and which I am loath to share with my father."

"I would not tell him," put in John. "The warning of the chiefs' deaths might make Father ill."

True though that might be, Angus knew he could not withhold the seer's vision even though it predicted woe. "I must. After all, Father sent me to the seer and surely knew he might speak of sad tidings."

Duncan shrugged. "Aye. Mayhap Angus Mor knows all too well what lies in store for the lordship."

"Say nothing of Mackay's vision to Alex," warned Angus. "My father must be the first to hear the seer's words."

With heavy hearts, they sailed to the south side of the isle where Dunyvaig Castle stood on a rocky outcropping facing the azure waters of Lagavulin Bay on one side and the Atlantic on the other.

It was at this castle that his brother preferred to live rather than at Finlaggan in the middle of the isle. Dunyvaig, meaning the "fort of the galleys", had long been the stronghold that guarded the bay where the Lords of the Isles anchored their galleys. From here, the Macdonalds controlled the eastern reaches of the Atlantic and the seas around Argyll and the Isle of Arran, beyond which lay Carrick and the mainland of Scotland.

In addition to Lagavulin Bay, Dunyvaig also had a sea gate that allowed a galley easy access to the castle. He ordered the crew to beach the ship in front of that opening and then to pull the galley onto the grassy slope.

Angus' mood lifted as he jumped down from the ship, walked up the stone steps and sighted his elder brother striding toward him. Alex's face glowed with happiness.

"I see you find marriage agreeable," Angus teased.

"Aye. Marriage to Juliana is much to my liking. She and I are well content. We are blessed, as well, for she will soon deliver our first child."

Duncan chuckled. "Wasting no time, Cousin?"

"Upstart! And why should we?" Alex replied in good humor. Casting a glance at their younger brother, he said, "You have young John with you. Good! We shall have a grand time."

"I do hope so," John teased. "I was counting on it."

The three brothers and their cousin climbed up the hill to the castle in good spirits. That night they dined as family, unencumbered by the need to represent the clan to others or act as emissaries, ever watchful of their speech. It was evident to Angus that his brother, whose hand held that of his wife when it was not needed to cut his food, was truly enamored with Juliana, who was now great with child.

"What has brought you to Islay?" asked Alex.

"Father asked the three of us to call upon the chiefs to take their view of things in Scotland before the Council meeting he has called for September in the days before Michaelmas. Because you were newly married, the task fell to me. Will you attend?"

"Aye. Father will expect me to be there. What have you heard in your travels?"

"All eyes are on Berwick and Edward. They are anxious, as are we, for they fear the decision will not be in favor of Robert the Noble. We have always known that Bruce's connection to King David was not as strong as Balliol's, though Robert the Noble would have it otherwise. There is also concern among the chiefs that whoever is named King of Scots must bow the knee to England's king since he required the pledge of each candidate as a condition of mediating the competing claims."

Alex nodded. "Edward's insistence on holding the reins of power does not bode well for an independent Scotland. And given Balliol's allies, if he is Edward's choice, it will go worse for the Macdonalds."

Angus watched Juliana's face for any angst about her kin's close relationship to John Balliol but she displayed a calm demeanor. In an attempt to bring a lighter mood to their visit, he asked, "Have you a name for the child yet?"

Alex turned to his wife, who smiled shyly and said, "Only for a lad. We have chosen Ranald."

"'Tis from Somerled's son, the ancestor of the Macdonalds," added Alex.

"Aye," said Angus, "I know the name. A good choice."

Duncan and John agreed, smiling broadly.

Hoping to make Juliana more comfortable, Angus said, "You are gracious to entertain so many of us Macdonald men at your table, Lady Juliana. But have some of our women offered you friendship since you came to live on Islay?"

"Oh, yes."

"And you will meet more who will come with their husbands to the meeting of the Council," said Alex.

"I hope to see your lady mother again, too," said Juliana." Placing her hand on her bulging belly, she said, "By then, her grandchild will be with us."

Angus did not wish to mention that the women who would come, like their husbands, would consider the MacDougalls to be enemies. He could only hope that Juliana, being a charming young woman, would win them over as she had his family.

They stayed on Islay for a few days, enjoying Alex and Juliana's company, and then returned to Ardtornish and the Sound of Mull. Along the way, they stopped at Iona where the dark-tonsured abbot told them he was looking forward to the Council meeting. "My father will send a galley for you," Angus told him.

The abbot thanked Angus and then blessed him and his companions before they sailed for Morvern.

At Ardtornish, Angus suggested his father walk with him. Outside the castle under a cloudless sky, Angus gave his father a report of his travels.

In response, Angus Mor said, "I am heartened to hear the chiefs are committed to the meeting."

"I had no sense of any support for Balliol," said Angus, "though the Maclean chief wants to hear more about his choices."

"Aye, he would. But I am still encouraged there is hope for the unity of the lordship. You have done well."

Angus then spoke briefly of Mackay's prediction, hoping his father would not be overly concerned with the seer's dire words.

His father's countenance darkened as he received the prophecy. "He sees more that I would hope to avoid. Conflict and war among the clans may be inevitable but I do not want it. King Edward's cruelty is well known so a slaughter would not be unusual for him. But where and how many? And this 'new king'. Who might he be?"

"The future is in God's hands," Angus gently reminded his father. "'Tis what your chaplain always tells me."

His father placed his hand on Angus' shoulder. The weight of it was comforting. "So it is, my son."

The next day, Angus and Duncan bid John goodbye, knowing they would see him at the Council meeting in September. As they sailed southeast for Kintyre, rain followed them but there was an occasional rainbow to marvel at.

By the time they arrived at Dunaverty Castle two days later, they were pleased to be home, most especially his crew whose families were standing on the shore to meet them.

Once the ship was beached, Angus and Duncan climbed the rocky headland to the castle, eager to find a warming fire. He had only stepped inside the great hall and handed his wet cloak and sword belt to a waiting servant when his seneschal approached, bearing a folded parchment. "Sir, this arrived after you left. Seeing no urgency, I thought to hold it for your return."

He thanked his seneschal and took the message to a chair in front of the fire where the heat from the flames helped take away the chill.

Duncan accepted two goblets of hot wine from a servant and brought them to where Angus sat, taking the chair next to him. Placing one goblet on the small table between them, Duncan said, "This will be waiting for you."

Angus mumbled his thanks and stared at his name written in script on the folded parchment, recognizing the handwriting he had seen only once before. Drawing a steadying breath, he broke the beeswax seal.

I think of you often, Angus Og Macdonald, and would that I could see you again. There is more than one reason for that but the one you may care most about is that I have borne you a son. He has your eyes and there is a look about him that speaks to me of you. I have named him Iain.

Sorcha
7th of May 1292

He looked up and encountered Duncan's puzzled expression. "Is it bad news?"

Angus sat back and shifted his gaze to the fire, remembering the Glen Coe lass. He wondered if the bairn had her fiery red hair. "That depends on whether fathering a child out of wedlock disturbs you."

"What?"

Angus returned his gaze to his cousin. "It seems my trip to Glen Coe was not without consequence." He glanced again at the date on the letter. "In the spring, Sorcha gave birth to a son. She claims he is mine."

Duncan stayed silent for a moment. "Do you think the child could be another's?"

Angus heaved a sigh. "I may never know. She says he has my eyes and the look of me. The timing is right. But it matters little, for I'll not doubt the lass."

"Will you marry her?

Angus picked up his goblet and sipped the wine, the honeyed spices sweet on his tongue. There had been no love between them, only pleasure and that for a single night. "Nay, nor will I formally acknowledge the lad, else he would be my heir."

"I see," said Duncan. "Well, the nobles of the lordship have been known to keep lemans and concubines."

He detected no judgment in his cousin's eyes but Angus' thinking lay along an entirely different path. "I will have only one wife, as my father and my brother. And no lemans or concubines."

"Will you go and see the child?"

"Eventually, but not now, else Sorcha's father might, at sword point, insist I wed her. He must realize I did not force her, but whether he knows the truth of it, who can say? It matters little as I will provide for the lad." Looking again at the message, he said, "I will let Sorcha know she need have no worry for his future."

Duncan returned Angus an incredulous look. "Very generous of you, considering."

"Or, a costly lesson well learned."

CHAPTER 7

Dunseverick Castle, northern coast of Ulster, Ireland, early September1292

ÁINE GAZED OUT the castle window and smiled. The rain that had come in the night with rumbling thunder and gusts of howling wind had departed, leaving the air pleasantly cool and the sky a cloudless blue.

She turned to address her young son, who was sitting on a woolen blanket next to a chair on which Áine had been sitting. Busy with his playthings, Brian was a happy child. "What do you think, Little Prince? Shall we visit the birds on the cliffs?"

The boy, who had been walking for only a few months, pulled himself up using the chair leg and grinned. The freckles on his face, just beginning to emerge, were framed by his bright red hair. The dark blue eyes that looked back at her were those of his father.

"Birdies?" she inquired, knowing this word, at least, would get a reaction.

"Bir-dee," he mouthed the familiar word.

Whenever the weather was fair, she took Brian with her on her walks to see the birds she loved to watch.

Her wolfhound, Finn, who was very protective of her son, was always with them. Finn rose from his place by the fire and came to stand before her, his copper-colored eyes gazing at her expectantly.

"Finn," said Brian, pointing to the hound. His name was one of the first words Brian had spoken.

"Well, if we are agreed, let us go and visit our friends. Come, Finn." Lifting Brian into her arms, with the hound on her heels, she swept out the door a servant opened for them, past the guards and into the bright sunlight. The brilliance of it rendered the wide swath of grass a rich green.

The wind carried the sound of the noisy kittiwakes and the raucous cries of the gulls to her ears. Autumn brought many birds to Dunseverick. Geese and ducks abounded as well as curlews and sandpipers on the shores below the castle.

As they took the path around the promontory, the sound of the waves breaking against the rocks hundreds of feet below joined the chatter of the birds for a splendid chorus.

She set Brian down but kept hold of his hand, putting herself between the cliff edge and him as he toddled along. With Finn following closely, she spoke to her son of his people, the O'Cahans and the O'Neills, as she often did.

"The O'Cahans are a people of great valor, Brian, a family you can be proud of. So, too, are the O'Neills. Your father, Little Prince, was a great warrior and a good king." How much Brian understood, she could not have said but she would keep speaking of it, for she had determined her son would be raised to know of his birthright.

As the time for his nap drew near, she observed Brian's steps flagging, his little legs slowing. Finding a seat on a nearby bench, she pulled him into her arms, rocking him as she sang an old hymn long known to her family. "Be thou my vision, oh Lord of my heart..." Soon, her little lad fell asleep. Observing his sweet face, Áine breathed a deep sigh of contentment. She had no complaints about the path her life had taken. Not now anyway. She thanked God for her family and her son and the place high above the sea she called home.

She had begun to doze when Nessa's voice stirred her to awareness. "Oh, there you are, my lady," said her handmaiden. "I've come to tell you that your father's guests have arrived."

"The ones from Fermanagh?"

"There are two of them is all I know, lords by the look of them."

"Is Father with them?" Áine did not want to be left alone with men of high rank who her father had invited to the castle in the hope one would appeal to her as a husband. Since her mourning had ended, her father had turned his attention to another match.

"He speaks with them now, my lady. It was your father who requested your presence."

Áine rose and handed her sleeping son to Nessa. "He will sleep for a while yet."

"I will see his nurse watches over him."

Áine tossed Finn an inquiring glance. "Stay with Brian if you like." With that, Finn turned and trotted after Nessa. She did not begrudge Finn his newly divided loyalty.

Smoothing the wrinkles from her indigo tunic, she entered the castle but could do nothing about her wind-tossed hair that hung long down her back.

"Ah, my daughter comes," said Áine's father. He stood by the fireplace with two men, one older and one younger, dressed in fine tunics embellished with gold and silver threads. "Áine, meet our guests, Donn Maguire, King of Fermanagh, and his grandson, Ruaidhri, who, I am told, prefers 'Rory'. They are well known to the Earl of Ulster." Which was her father's way of saying he approved of them. The two men appeared refreshed. Mayhap they had stopped for the night to take shelter from the storm.

Áine curtseyed before them.

Her father had lured a great prize to his castle for her to consider. Fermanagh was a kingdom whose importance was on the rise and, except for challenges from the O'Connells of Tirconnell, was at peace and allied with the O'Neills.

She smiled and extended her hand to the king whose graying brown hair was clipped to just below his chin. His beard, salted with silver, was well-trimmed. She might have guessed he was a king by his presence that spoke of regal confidence.

The king bowed over her hand.

Mindful of what she must look like, she said, "Please forgive my appearance, my lord. I was walking the promontory and the wind—"

He straightened. "Only a woman as comely as you are, Lady Áine, could bring the sun with her when she enters a hall. If the wind had anything to do with it, my grandson and I pay homage to the wind." He smiled in the way an older man would to a young woman he found attractive.

Áine was certain her cheeks were now scarlet, which only added to the reddening of her skin from the sun and the wind. "You are too kind, my lord."

"Your father," the king went on, "has been telling my grandson of your love for the birds that live on these high cliffs and dive into the sea beneath."

Áine shifted her gaze to the one called Rory, whose dark red hair suggested his name. She guessed he was somewhere in his twenties. Like his grandfather, he wore an elegant embroidered tunic, his fingers bejeweled. He had a pleasant face and a nice smile but his presence stirred nothing in her. Was she being too dismissive of a man her father thought a worthy suitor? In truth, her heart was reluctant to consider any man.

Rory's brown eyes fixed her with an assessing gaze. "I have been eager to meet you, my lady."

"And so you have," she said with a slight smile. Despite her lack of interest in a suitor, she would not fail them as hostess. "Fermanagh is far and you must be weary. Allow us to refresh you with some wine."

"And some food for our guests!" added her father enthusiastically.

Calling a servant to her, Áine gave instructions for the meal, which was already in progress, and to remind the servant to prepare their chambers. Meantime, her father poured wine for their visitors, a look of satisfaction on his face. He had told her the choice of a husband this time would be hers, but what if she wanted no husband at all?

Loch Finlaggan, Isle of Islay, September 1292

THE ATMOSPHERE was that of a harvest fair. Pennons and banners of every color waved in the breeze in the sloping valley that rimmed Loch Finlaggan. The day was sun-filled and gaiety prevailed among the teeming throng gathered for the meeting of the Council of the Isles.

Angus strolled with his cousin, Duncan, amid the nobles and dignitaries and their families mingling on the largest isle in the loch, enjoying his clan and his people, all the while knowing the merriment could not last.

Although the chiefs Angus had visited were keenly aware of the serious nature of the matters to be discussed when the Council finally got down to business, they would not deny their families the celebration and fellowship that always accompanied the meetings. A time of levity was expected and served to strengthen the bonds between them.

The unusually mild weather allowed for all manner of games and contests, as men vied for fame and the attention of the lasses. Angus was tempted to enter the archery contest as he was a fair shot with a bow. However, there was much to see so he continued on.

Bards, musicians and jugglers, practicing their skills, drew many to observe their offerings. Here also were representatives of the Church, so essential to their lives. Every chief had his chaplain who sailed with him. But for such a gathering as this, the Bishop of the Isles and the Abbot of Iona being in attendance added solemnity to the proceedings.

The Lord of the Isles and his chiefs, whose prayers were laid before God, were those who fought and won battles for the others. The host of men and women who supported them, who kept the cattle, sheep and pigs and tended the crops that grew on nearly every isle, depended on the chiefs for their security.

At this gathering were also the shipwrights and smiths who, from Somerled's days, built the galleys that allowed the Lords of the Isles to conquer the seas.

Angus and Duncan paused next to the two-story great hall with its slate roof rising above the others on Eilean Mor, its highest point flying the Galley of the Isles banner of the Macdonalds. From here, they could see the loch's shores already crowded with people.

"I am grateful we have lodging in the family quarters," said Duncan, looking out on the boisterous crowd. "So many have come that extended families and retainers will doubtless be forced to camp along the shores of the loch."

One hundred feet across, Eilean Mor was the largest of the two islands in the freshwater loch named for St. Findlugan; Eilean na Comhairle was the smaller. Each was accessible to the mainland and to the other by a bridge and causeway.

The larger isle was home not only to the great manor and hall but to the kitchens, servants' quarters, chapel and chambers for the Lord of the Isles' family and other nobles. Unlike the castles in the lordship, most of these buildings set on stone foundations had timber walls and thatched roofs. Loch Finlaggan needed no curtain wall, for it was a well-protected haven.

The smaller isle, Eilean na Comhairle, named for the Council meeting place, was occupied by three buildings. The largest was the rectangular stone keep where the Council met. There was also a storehouse and a residence where Angus' father housed the Bishop of the Isles and the Abbot of Iona to provide them a quiet place of retreat.

On the shores of the loch itself stood the guardhouses where a contingent of Macdonald galloglass would reside while the Council was in session, along with the guards that accompanied the chiefs. Since many chiefs enjoyed hunting with hounds, there were also horses and stables to house them and kennels for the hounds. His own father had brought two hounds.

The sights, sounds and smells of the festive atmosphere were familiar to Angus, for he had attended most of the Council meetings with his family since his youth. A short distance away, Angus spotted the table where the sword makers to the Macdonalds displayed their wares. "I am eager to see the new swords the McEacherns have brought with them but it might have to wait until after the Council meets tomorrow."

"I could use a new blade if they have one that suits," said Duncan. "God knows it will be well used in the coming years."

A group of giggling girls passed by Angus and his cousin, sending them furtive glances. Their brightly colored tunics embroidered with threads of silver and gold and matching ribands streaming from their long tresses spoke of their status as daughters of high-ranking clansmen.

"Have you noticed that we are the subject of much conversation among the lasses?" asked Duncan, looking over his shoulder to smile at the girls.

"No more than usual. 'Tis always the same at the Council gatherings. The members bring their families, including their daughters."

"You are failing to see the significance, Cousin. With Alex wed to a MacDougall, surely you realize that you have become the man every lass wants. And so it will be for John in a few years."

"And you, Duncan, if that be the case."

"To a lesser extent, aye," said Duncan. "There are doubtless many chiefs here who thought to increase their standing by marrying one of their daughters to the eldest son of Angus Mor. Disappointed, they will now cast their hopes for their dowered daughters to the rest of us." In a voice Angus recognized as sarcastic, Duncan added, "What father would not want his daughter to marry a Macdonald lord, a commander of hundreds of galleys, a prince of the clan respected by kings? After all, ours is a clan that endows monasteries, trades widely and lives lavishly, aye?"

Angus laughed. "Not so lavishly as some might suppose. Besides, with all that comes responsibility—for the people and the land and all those galleys you speak of. This year, the burden of it has grown heavy. And I am not a Macdonald lord, nor the heir, merely a Macdonald son."

"At Finlaggan, that places you high in the chiefs' eyes. By the bye, where is your younger brother?"

"With his friends and likely flirting with some lass." Angus scanned those gathered beneath the afternoon sun. He did not see his brother among the girls dressed in their finery. "I have known most of these since they were wee lasses."

"Aye, but look closely, Cousin. They are no longer *wee* lasses, are they?"

To Angus, they all looked like versions of Sorcha and he had vowed never again to dally in that direction. "They are young. Aside from that, I have yet to meet a woman I would want for my wife."

"There is time, Cousin. You are only twenty, as am I. With things so uncertain in Scotland, mayhap 'tis not the best time for either of us to wed."

"Aye. Given what the seer told us, this gathering has the feel of a last feast before Lent."

Duncan laughed. "You are still thinking of Mackay's message?"

"That and what will come from King Edward's court at Berwick."

"Well, we can do nothing about either at the moment. By the by, how did my uncle react when you told him of the seer's vision?"

"He appeared unsurprised but downcast all the same. He interpreted the unsteady scepter as a Balliol kingship. As for war between the clans, he hates the idea, as do we all. If the foreign king is Edward, his cruelty is well known as shown in his treatment of the Welsh. My father said nothing about the death of two chiefs and wondered at the mention of a new king." Angus paused and looked around for his father. Not seeing him, he continued, "I know he has not slept well since I brought him the seer's words but then he rarely does when the future looks ominous. The lordship's fate is closely tied to that of Scotland."

That evening, the chiefs and their families dined in the great hall on Eilean Mor. Lit by a hearth fire and a multitude of candles, the hall's tapestries, some made long ago, depicting birds and wild creatures on Islay, drew Angus' gaze to the walls. There was history in this place, a history his family had shared for generations. With God's grace it would continue for more.

Musicians played in one corner, their lyre and harp a soft sound against the many conversations.

Angus found his seat at the head table between his mother and John. On his father's other side were Alex and Juliana. A sumptuous feast of salmon roasted in wine and spices, thick slices of roast beef and pork pies with leeks and coriander was set before them.

The barnacle geese that had begun to arrive on the isle in great numbers also found a place among the dishes served. Rubbed with spices and roasted slowly, they were delicious. Vegetables, fresh from Islay's gardens, as well as breads and cheeses adorned every table. In addition to ale, there was mead and wine to satisfy each noble's preference.

Seeing Duncan sitting nearby at one of the long tables, he remembered Duncan's description of the lordship and smiled. Admittedly, they did dine lavishly when the Council met.

Angus glanced across his mother and father to Juliana, who glowed with happiness. Leaning toward his mother, dressed in a cinnamon-colored tunic with jewels at her neck, he said, "How was Alex's bride received by the women?"

"Well, I think. All remarked on her bairn's sweet face and smiled when they heard his name. Juliana was gracious. When asked what she would do if her MacDougall kin came to blows with her new Macdonald family, she answered well."

"I suppose 'twas inevitable they would ask. What did she say?"

His mother smiled, telling Angus she approved of Juliana's answer. "Fortunately, she did not mention the contention over Lismore, which has still to be resolved. Rather, she said that when she consented to become Alexander's wife, she placed her heart and her loyalties with him and his family. Then, in a most certain manner, she announced that both she and her children will be Macdonalds."

"No one could fault her for that," said Angus.

His mother smiled. "None did."

Angus remembered that Alex had spoken the same words when he responded to Angus' challenge of the decision to court Juliana. "'Tis good she and Alex are of one mind. Still, she will need our support, for her clan will give her none."

"I have assured her she has it," said Helen Macdonald. Angus reminded himself his mother was a strong woman who had challenged her husband when she thought it right to do so though he was the Lord of the Isles.

That night, peat fires burned long on the shores of Loch Finlaggan against a sky of muted colors left behind by the setting sun. The sound of the roosting geese could be heard along with the conversations of clansmen renewing old acquaintances. Angus listened from Eilean Mor, content the lordship was in good hands.

The next morning after breaking his fast, Angus trailed behind his father and Alex as they joined the chiefs to cross the causeway on foot to Eilean na Comhairle.

The day was fair and the wind slight, giving Angus hope this would be another fine day. As he walked along, his thoughts drifted to the future. Things would change for the Macdonalds and the Bruces if John Balliol became King of Scots. And not for the better. He was eager to hear what his father had to tell the chiefs.

Inside the Council chamber, Angus Mor took his place at the front of the room between Mark, the old Bishop of the Isles, who had been installed by King Alexander, and Fionnlagh, the gaunt, black-robed Abbot of Iona.

The Lord of the Isles then asked the bishop to lead them in prayer, which he did, asking God to guide their deliberations and give them wisdom in making decisions. The bishop ended his prayer with a line from the Psalms. "Lead us in the paths of righteousness for your name's sake."

The chiefs and men of rank took their seats around a square stone table. Angus found a bench next to the wall where he sat with Duncan and the other younger sons, who were invited to observe but not to speak. On the other side of the room, Donald Mackay, the old seer, sat half in shadow with his arms crossed over his chest.

Angus' father, still standing, reminded those gathered that they were at a significant point in the history of the kingdom. From the look of grim determination on each face, it was clear the chiefs had come prepared to do hard business.

"We are a part of Scotland," said Angus Mor, "yet never dominated by it. Even when we were arguably subject to Norway's kings, we were independent sea lords, reigning over the Isles and the western shores with no ties save those we ourselves sought.

"Since we set aside our crowns to become barons of Scotland, we are warmly welcomed at the court of the King of Scots. But all that may soon change. I asked my son, Angus, to visit each of you before this meeting so that we have common knowledge as to where things stand. England's king will soon decide who rules the Scots. If it's to be Robert the Noble, the eldest Bruce, then I believe we will have strong and worthy leadership. But should John Balliol be chosen, I fear the Comyns and MacDougalls will seek to expand their power at our expense.

"We cannot hope what is coming will pass over us like a fast-moving storm. Rather, I perceive it may linger to our detriment. We must decide today what our position will be before events take their course. I would ask that your deliberations be open, respectful and honest. Whatever the decision of the Council, all must abide by it. 'Tis our way."

The Lord of the Isles resumed his seat and many heads nodded in agreement.

Tormod Macleod slowly got to his feet. Angus was not surprised that he should speak first, for it was fitting the elder chiefs would do so.

"I have seen much in my days and my ancestors even more. I do not wish to live through another war between clans but I fear one may be coming. In this, we who are a part of the lordship must stand as one. As for me and the Macleods, we stand with the Bruces. That will not alter should the English king select John Balliol or, indeed, another."

The next member of the Council to speak was Maolmuire, chief of the MacMillans. The proud chief got to his feet, his black hair and beard defining his sharp features. "As most here know, the MacMillans have their roots on Iona in the Columban Church. Our allegiance to God and to our people has never wavered. We must pray God gives us a worthy king. I have brought my brother, Duncan, with me this day so that he can mark my oath to serve God and the lordship."

As he returned to his seat, Malise Maclean rose, his dark hair and beard, streaked with gray, conveying his status as one of the elders. "The Macleans, too, stand with the Bruces if that be a choice. And we have ever stood with the Macdonalds. Whichever candidate King Edward selects will be forced to bow the knee to him and that is troublesome, particularly if that man be a weakling like Balliol. We must anticipate this and be prepared to fight."

Others spoke, echoing the words of the elder chiefs so that the discussion continued for most of the morning. A few wanted to see how Balliol, if chosen, might do, but even they, after some discussion, were convinced that with Balliol so tightly aligned with the Comyns and MacDougalls, there was little chance the Macdonald lordship would be well considered.

As the meeting drew to a close, the younger chiefs rose and called for the Isles to be ready with galleys, weapons and galloglass should war come.

No one disagreed.

When it was clear how the Council would decide, Angus Mor rose, wisdom and strength in his face, the gray strands in his red hair speaking of his years of leading the lordship. A hushed silence fell over the assembled group as he began to speak. "My heart is gladdened to see we have come to agreement and are of one mind. 'Tis the result I had hoped for. I speak for the Macdonalds when I say we are with the Bruces, bound by a bond made years ago, which my sons are pledged to honor. We will not falter and we will not fail. And we will not serve a Balliol king. I agree with Malise Maclean. We must be prepared to fight if it comes to that."

Pride rose in Angus' chest as he heard shouts of acclimation and the pounding of boots stomping in agreement.

The chiefs stood as the Bishop of the Isles was asked to pray for their future. The prayer that followed was a somber reflection of the dark cloud hanging over the future and the need for God's guidance.

Following the prayer, Angus' father invited those present to drink a toast to their decision. Angus joined the others, lifting his goblet, and thinking of his own pledge to the youngest of the Robert Bruces. He would have to find a way to tell his friend that the Lord of the Isles and the clans of the lordship would stand by his family.

Ardtornish Castle, Morvern, December 1292

"I'LL NOT GO and that's an end of it!" shouted Angus' father as he ripped in twain the summons from King Balliol's new Sheriff of Lorne, Alexander MacDougall. Tossing it into the fire, he said, "Balliol may be king by Edward's decree but he mocks me if he thinks I will pay him homage. At the summons of his lackey Alexander MacDougall, no less!"

Angus watched his father in silence, recalling the Mackay seer's vision of a wobbly scepter, which had surely come to pass. November had brought unwelcome news, much of it bad for both the Macdonalds and the Bruces. Early in the month, Marjorie Bruce, the Countess of Carrick, died. Angus remembered the captivating mother of his friend, whom he had met at Turnberry Castle six years before, and wondered at the cause, for she had died young.

As if her death were an omen of worse tidings to come, in Berwick, Robert the Noble's claim was rejected. He was quick to react. "We inform all of you that we have granted, and totally surrendered, to our well-beloved son Robert Bruce, Earl of Carrick, and his heirs, the whole right and claim that we had, or could have had, to sue for the realm of Scotland."

In turn, his son, Robert Bruce VI, Earl of Carrick, resigned the earldom to his oldest son. Thus, two generations of Bruces passed the torch to another, making Angus' friend, Rob, an earl at eighteen and a contender for the crown.

The final blow, by then expected, occurred on the seventeenth of November when, in the great hall of Berwick Castle, King Edward pronounced in favor of John Balliol. Angus remembered his father's face going pale at the news.

The Scottish nobles, particularly those close to Balliol, hurried to crown him. On St. Andrews' Day, the last day of November, John Balliol was enthroned on the Stone of Destiny at Scone Abbey in the manner of all Scottish kings. Of no surprise to Angus or his father, King Edward was not present to witness the ceremony, which doubtless held little interest for him. However, Edward was quick to demand the new King of Scots kneel before him at Newcastle, which John Balliol did all too readily.

"A King of Scots who kneels to another king is no king at all," Angus' father had said at the time.

Angus recognized the weariness in his father's face, the frustration that, of late, had grown worse with all that had happened in so short a time. With Balliol now king, the Comyns took control of the government and the spoils of high office went to them and their allies, among them the MacDougalls.

In furtherance of his new power, Balliol named three sheriffdoms: William, Earl of Ross, whose mother was a Comyn, was made Sheriff of Skye. Alexander MacDougall, Juliana's father, was made Sheriff of Lorne with jurisdiction over much of Argyll so that he controlled the southwest coastline. And, in the southwest, James Stewart, High Steward of Scotland, one of the signatories to the Turnberry Band, was made Sheriff of Kintyre. The expansive territory of the Macdonalds meant that they were under the authority of both Stewart, a friend, and MacDougall, an enemy.

Before December's end, Balliol had ordered Alexander MacDougall to summon Angus Mor to pay homage to the new King of Scots. It was this summons that Angus' father had just tossed into the fire.

"What about the parliament in February?" asked Angus.

"Neither I nor the Bruces will attend."

Apparently King Edward held little respect for his newly chosen King of Scots. As the year was drawing to a close, the English king announced, as Lord Paramount of Scotland, he would hear appeals from judgments made in Scotland. By this, he made clear he viewed himself as Scotland's overlord.

And so it was that Angus' brother, Alex, appealed to King Edward the MacDougalls' refusal to convey Juliana's dower lands at Lismore. Edward, surely happy to be overruling his puppet, agreed that Alexander Macdonald should have the dower lands on Lismore. Balliol unwisely ignored Edward's judgment.

CHAPTER 8

Dunaverty Castle, Kintyre Peninsula, late February 1293

IN EARLY FEBRUARY, John Balliol held his first parliament at Scone. Like the Bruces, the Macdonalds avoided the meeting they would otherwise attend.

Angus' father was busy building a stone kirk at Kilchoman on the west coast of Islay, and Angus was consumed with affairs at Dunaverty. As a result, when Alex's news reached Angus on a cold and dreary morning, it came as a shock.

Angus,

There is no way to soften the blow. Father was suddenly taken ill and died. By God's grace, Mother was here on Islay with him until the last and was comforted that he had the good death.

His chaplain, Michael Dominici, performed the last rite sacraments and his physician, Macbeathadh, and the priests prepared his body for burial.

Tomorrow, I sail with Mother, the chaplain and some of the household to Ardtornish to get John and thence to Iona for the burial.

Bring Uncle Alasdair and such of his family as may be able to come to Iona. I have sent messengers to the chiefs and others who will want to attend. I expect the burial to take place within a fortnight.

Alex

For a moment Angus stared at the parchment, unable to move. His hand went to his chest where a heavy weight had settled. *It cannot be!*

Tears welled in his eyes. There had been no warning, no impending battle, no treachery. His father was still a virile man. Yet, in Angus' mind, he saw his father as he was the last time they were together, his red hair salted with gray as he spoke to the Council, the lines of worry in his face that had come with the seer's predictions and his pale countenance when word reached him that John Balliol had been chosen king.

"When did my brother give this to you?" he asked the messenger who stood waiting.

"Last evening, my lord. He told me to sail at first light, that it would take time for the chiefs to arrive, and to let you know he will await you at Iona."

"Aye, there is time."

The messenger turned to go, then paused and turned back. "All Islay mourns his passing, my lord."

"Thank you."

Pushing away his grief, Angus found his captain and issued orders to make ready to sail the next day to Saddell, halfway up the Kintyre coast. To his seneschal, he said, "Have several casks of wine and rounds of cheese loaded on my ship for the Iona monks will be housing many they did not expect." Others, too, would bring food and there were cattle on the isle but Angus wanted to contribute. To do something.

There was much weeping at Saddell Castle when Angus conveyed the news of his father's passing. His frail uncle, Alasdair Mor Macdonald, remained stoic, though his red-rimmed hazel eyes betrayed his deep sadness as he comforted his wife. "Only Donald and Duncan are with us," he told Angus, acknowledging the two standing before him. "Hector is in Ireland. Duncan may go with us to Iona but I need Donald to remain here to guard the castle and manage my affairs."

Angus turned to his cousins and greeted them in somber manner. Then, drawing Duncan aside, he said, "I did not anticipate this, not so soon."

"'Tis a sad truth," said Duncan, his face lined with grief, "the great ones will not always be with us."

"'Aye," agreed Angus, still feeling the shock of his father's death. "I cannot believe he is gone. Already, I miss him."

"This means your brother, Alexander, is now—or soon will be—The Macdonald, Lord of the Isles."

Angus nodded. "As it should be. Alex will be a worthy chief of the Macdonalds and a wise leader of the lordship. He is well respected by all and his loyalties are those of our father and the chiefs who met in Council last autumn. He has proven himself in combat, most valiantly and skillfully. And he stood strong against the MacDougalls, who assert their new power over lordship lands."

The next day, they left Saddell for Iona, the air cold but the sea calm beneath a cloud-filled sky. The crew took to the oars with vigorous strokes, there being insufficient wind to raise the sail until they rounded the tip of Kintyre.

As they proceeded north toward Islay, the wind picked up and the men shipped the oars and set the sail. Duncan and his parents drew their woolen cloaks tightly around them against the chill. Angus had donned trews beneath his tunic and wrapped himself in a fur cloak as the winter day was very cold. Though he was going to bury his father, he still carried his sword and dagger.

The voyage was a somber one, the mood of all matching the weather. The crew wore long faces as many of them or their fathers knew Angus Mor. Their chant this day was a dirge.

Angus was glad they'd not encountered a storm, for it would have made things worse for his passengers. Still, there had been rain and rough water so that all were soaked despite their cloaks. He was glad they were stopping for the night at Claig Castle at the head of the Sound of Islay. With the shortened days, it was gloaming when they finally beached the ship.

The castle sat on the flat summit of *Am Fraoch Eilean*, the Heather Isle. Once inside the great hall, Angus shed his cloak and warmed himself by the great fire as he conveyed the news of his father's death to those who kept the castle for the Macdonalds.

Again, there were many tears for their lord was well loved. Some expressed fear for the future of the lordship. Angus assured them there was no cause for concern, that Alex was prepared to assume the role of chief. Though the other chiefs had to confirm this, Angus had no doubt Alex would be their choice.

On the morrow, the rain gave way to a brilliant rainbow as they sailed north through the Sound of Islay, past Colonsay to the tiny but significant Isle of Iona off the east coast of Mull. The cold wind blew hard as they neared their destination. The ocean spray made Angus shiver beneath his cloak.

The crew pulled the galley onto the beach at Martyr's Bay, named for a Viking attack centuries ago. Angus gazed at the wide stretch of sand, already lined with many galleys set close together in a long row like sleek greyhounds eager for the hunt. Angus recognized the pennons of the chiefs he had visited the year before. The burial of the Lord of the Isles would draw many to this hallowed place.

He had known from his boyhood that Iona was sacred to the Macdonalds. Dedicated to God, it was the place where they buried their lords since Somerled's time. Michael Dominici, his tutor, had taught him that the isle's spiritual history began even earlier. The Irish prince, Columba, exiled from Tirconnell in the sixth century, came to Iona to found a monastery, following the steps of Oran, the Apostle of Colonsay.

From Iona, Columba had sent missionaries to the Picts and the Gaels of Dalriada. These monks brought the good news of the gospel of Christ to the land that would one day be Scotland.

Angus' tutor had told him it was Somerled's son, Ranald, the *Rex Insularum*, King of the Isles, who founded the great Benedictine abbey on Iona, providing land, building materials and funds for construction. Later Lords of the Isles and their master masons completed the project. It was the abbey where Angus and his family and the chiefs and their families would stay while awaiting the burial. Had it been summer, many would have set up tents but, with the bitter cold, the monks would shelter some in the abbey. The women who came alone could be housed in the Augustinian nunnery on the isle. Bethoc, Somerled's daughter and Ranald's sister, had been the first prioress.

Angus, his aunt and uncle and cousin left the shore and, bent into the wind, proceeded over the stone path that was part of *Sràid nam Marbh,* the Street of the Dead. It was the path leading from the bay across the windswept grass to the abbey. Their servants and Angus' crew followed, carrying the baggage, wine and cheese.

Passing the nunnery, they came to a small building made of red granite with a steeply pitched roof covered in stone tiles. Angus knew it to be St. Oran's Chapel, the burial chamber of the Lords of the Isles built by Somerled nearly a hundred and fifty years ago.

The chapel stood within the ancient graveyard of *Reilig Odhrain,* where isle chieftains were buried along with Norse, Scottish and Irish kings.

Illuminated by the low northern light was a magnificent carved stone cross, taller than the height of two men. Angus recalled the words of his father's chaplain one Sunday after his message encouraging them to live for Christ. "On St. Oran's cross is carved the image of Daniel in the lion's den, which reminds us that God will save those faithful to Him."

Angus had not been born when his grandfather, Donald, died, but he had once been to Iona with his father, who had explained that St. Oran's Chapel and the graveyard comprised the most sacred place on Iona.

Casting a glance at the stone chapel, he said to Duncan, "My father's body lies in state there. I will go to him after I have seen your parents to the abbey and paid my respects to the abbot and my mother."

"If you will allow it, I will go with you," said Duncan, the cold wind blowing his honey-colored hair across his face. An earnest look shone from his green eyes.

Angus returned his cousin a grateful nod. It was a comfort to know that he and Duncan were walking through this time of grief together.

Until the funeral service in the abbey church, his father's body would remain inside the chapel where, for eight days, the monks would continually chant psalms and prayers. Because of the gusting wind, Angus could not hear the monks' voices but he was certain they were singing as they stood vigil.

Angus' party proceeded on until the magnificent red granite abbey loomed before them. In front of the great edifice stood St. Martin's cross, as tall as the one dedicated to St. Oran. There were other crosses there as well that were dedicated to St. John and St. Matthew. All were carved with Celtic designs and scenes from the Scriptures.

To his right, Angus glimpsed the blue-gray waters of the Sound of Iona and, beyond them, to the Isle of Mull. The winter sun had dropped low in the sky but the remnants of its red and gold light were reflected in the water. It was the end of a day and the end of a life. As he walked on, heaviness hovered about him like an unwanted cloak.

The gaunt, black-robed Abbot Fionnlagh welcomed them at the abbey door, greeting first Angus' uncle and aunt. Behind the abbot, Angus heard voices echoing off the abbey's stone walls. "Others have arrived," said the abbot, looking over his shoulder, "including the Bishop of the Isles. Lord Alexander, Lady Juliana and Lady Helen are with them now." Then, gesturing to a table to one side, he said, "You may set your things here and they will be placed in the chambers we have readied for you."

Angus' uncle thanked the abbot and took his wife's elbow to escort her inside while their servant placed the baggage as instructed.

"We brought wine and some food," offered Angus, gesturing to the casks and large rounds of cheese his crew had hefted to their shoulders.

"Most thoughtful," said the abbot. "Your men can set them here as well and we will take them to the kitchens where the evening meal is being prepared. There will be many to feed this next sennight. With God's grace, we will see it done."

Angus entered the abbey, relieved to be out of the wind. He went to his mother, whose tear-stained cheeks and red-rimmed eyes spoke loudly of her loss, and embraced her. "Father is with God and the angels now."

Her sad eyes looked into his. "I know, my son, but life is hard without him."

He acknowledged the truth of her words. "Aye, his loss is a great one." Others came to console her and, blinking back tears, Angus spotted his brothers and moved toward them, knowing his mother was cared for in her grief.

He spoke briefly with his brothers, seeing in their eyes what he had glimpsed in his mother's. "I knew this day would come but I did not think it would come so soon."

"None of us did," said Alex. "But he would expect us to go on for the sake of the lordship."

"Aye, he would." Telling his brothers he would see them later, he found Duncan and, together, they went to the chiefs and thanked them for coming. When this was done, he, John and Duncan went to the chapel to pay their respects to Angus Mor, a man larger than life in many ways, the first of the name Macdonald.

The black-robed monks did not cease their chanting as Angus and his companions entered but acknowledged them with their eyes. Candles burned on the altar and flickered along the rails of the wooden frame suspended over the body, the heat of the flames lifting the air above the body.

Covering the earthly remains of Angus Mor was an ivory silk pall with a long-shafted Celtic ringed cross appliquéd in golden fabric. Beneath the pall, his father's body would be wrapped in a white winding cloth.

His father had been so vibrant in life, Angus could not picture him in death. He could only conjure images of him as he lived: the kindhearted high chief of the clan, speaking wise advice, smiling at his sons, laughing with the chiefs, angry at injustice, and proud to the last. There had been times when his father had left his other duties to spend time with his young sons. It was not often but it had been enough.

Angus did not remain long in the chapel. He and his companions crossed themselves and turned to leave, inclining their heads to the monks whose chanting continued unbroken.

The dinner that night became a tribute to Sir Angus Mor Macdonald, his mighty deeds remembered along with his courage and his character. Tormod Macleod told stories of their battles together for both had fought at the Battle of Largs in 1263. Angus' uncle, Alasdair Macdonald, recounted his older brother's exploits in Ireland where the Irish praised Angus Mor's graceful galleys, dubbing him "the scion of Tara", a reference to his royal Irish roots. Malise, the aging Maclean chief, whose predecessors were buried on Iona, told of the times he and Angus Mor had hunted the red deer together on the Isle of Jura. Angus had not heard some of the stories before and it warmed his heart to know of them. Like small unexpected treasures, he would keep them to savor later.

Angus sat between his two brothers, encouraged that they would face the future together. "Whatever you need," he told Alex, "however I can help, I am your man."

"Thank you, Angus. Your loyalty means much. Already I feel the weight of the burden Father carried but rarely spoke of."

"I wish I could have been with him when he died," said Angus. "But at least you and Mother were there. Some chiefs die in battle with no one to comfort them save the angels who bear their souls to Heaven."

A wistful expression crossed Alex's face. "At the end," he said, "he spoke of you and John. He said he was leaving the lordship in good hands."

Angus looked long at his elder brother, his dark hair and eyes so like their mother's and his noble face showing the marks of his grief. "I believe he did."

The next days passed as the burial preparations were accomplished by the monks. More chiefs arrived. Many remained unsmiling, their faces like stone, as they respectfully greeted the family.

On the morning of the eighth day, Angus awoke to see the isle covered in snow, the sun reflecting off the frozen ground. It seemed fitting somehow that the ground should be hidden beneath a mantle of white like the pall draped over his father's body.

Quiet surrounded them. Even the wind, which had been unrelenting, dwindled to a mere breeze and the sky above was a clear blue. Fortuitous signs to Angus as the burial was to be today.

Leaving their footprints in the new snow, Angus, Alex, John and Duncan carried Angus Mor's body on a bier from the chapel to the abbey church and placed it on a table in the sanctuary while the monks' choir chanted.

The Requiem Mass for Angus Mor was presided over by the abbot and the bishop before the grand marble altar with the tall arched window behind them. The walls of the church were painted with scenes from the Scriptures. The arches on the side of the main sanctuary were decorated with brightly colored tiles, some with colored glass. It was a fitting place to celebrate the life of so great a leader who was now with God in Heaven.

After the Mass, the bier was carried back to the chapel in preparation for the burial.

Garbed in his finest tunic he had saved for this day and his fur-lined woolen cloak, Angus set off toward the chapel with his brother, John. Their boots crushed the snow beneath their feet.

The lofty church tower pulsated with the ringing of the large bells his father had commissioned as they crossed the rock path that formed part of the Street of the Dead. The stones were now covered with a layer of snow but Angus remembered his father telling him the large smooth rocks, pressed into the ground, had been there for centuries.

Squinting against the sun, Angus glimpsed the bishop ahead of them in his mitre and vestments of white and crimson walking beside the black-robed abbot. They were followed by Alex and Juliana with Angus Mor's widow between them. Helen Macdonald was tearful but her countenance resolute. It was clear she had summoned all her courage to face this day.

Behind Angus, John and the rest of the family and the chiefs and their wives walked, wrapped in warm cloaks against the chill of the morning.

The mourners, who had come to honor Angus Mor in death, pressed into the small chapel. When there was no more room inside, those left outside gathered at the arched stone doorway to watch the solemn proceedings.

Two long narrow windows, one on either side of the altar, facing north and south, allowed winter's light into the chapel. Candles set on the altar, now covered in a white cloth, added a warm glow to the cold chamber. More candles had been placed on the wooden frame suspended above the body, symbolizing the upward ascent of the offered prayers for Angus Mor's soul.

The monks, who had been chanting, fell silent. The only sound remaining was the women weeping.

Abbot Fionnlagh took his position beside Mark, the Bishop of the Isles, who held the crucifix before the body as he spoke of Angus Mor Macdonald and led them in prayer.

Angus experienced a great emptiness inside. Life was short, fragile and uncertain. None knew how long they had on this earth. Death was the only certainty. But, with the bishop's words that spoke of the afterlife, Angus consoled himself that there was hope for all who believed in the risen Christ. Heaven awaited beyond this life and he would see his father again one day.

Hearing the prayers in his mind, Angus stared at the long grave slabs of his ancestors, Ranald and Donald, that covered the shallow tombs set into the paved floor. Each was carved with a long-shafted Celtic ringed cross and an aristocrat's sword. Ranald's also had a pilgrim's staff and Donald's an intertwining Celtic plant scroll.

Somerled's older, more substantial monument sat heavily on top of his tomb, the large block of sandstone from Mull was shaped to resemble the chapel with its high-pitched, coped roof. Carved into the stone were the words Angus had read on his first visit to the chapel:

ór don anmain
somhairle giolla bride
rig innsi gall

A PRAYER FOR THE SOUL OF
SOMERLED [mac] GILLIBRIDE
KING OF THE ISLES

The prayers trailed off and the bishop called Alexander forward. As the heir, it was his solemn duty to remove the bones of his grandfather, Donald, from the tomb that had been opened the day before by the monks. Donald's grave slab had been moved to a new place in the chapel near his final resting grave.

The voice of Angus Mor's bard, one of the MacMhuirichs, sounded out clear and strong as he began to recite in chanting rhythm the Lords of the Isles' long ancestry accompanied by the harpist Alex had brought from Ardtornish to Iona.

The chant continued as generation by generation, from Angus Mor, back to the ancient Conn of a Hundred Battles, the great Macdonald's lineage was remembered.

When the bard finished, without aid from others, Alexander lifted Angus Mor's body, draped in the white winding sheet, cradling it for a moment before lowering the body into the same grave previously occupied by Donald's bones.

Angus' father had once explained that at a lord's burial three kings are present: the father, the son and the grandfather, a trinity reinforcing the everlasting lordship.

When he had first arrived on Iona for the burial, Angus had spoken to Alex about their father's grave slab. "I would have it ready for the burial."

Alex agreed. Given the importance of the lord being buried, Iona's leading artisan had set his other work aside to accommodate their request. In addition to a sword and a cross, per their instructions, carved into the sandstone was a sleek galley with high prow and stem and doused sails, a fitting tribute to a great sea king.

As the new grave slab was rolled into place on old oar shafts dedicated to the purpose, the monks' chants rose, filling the chapel with the ethereal music. Their singing spoke to Angus of the celestial realm, now the abode of his father's soul.

When the ceremony was concluded, the monks' chanting died down and the abbot said a last prayer for the soul of Angus Mor.

Angus left the chapel with a heavy heart. He knew his father would live again but he was gone from this world. In his mind, Angus heard the words of Donald Mackay, the seer: *Two chiefs will die before a new one rises with a new king.* Was his father one of those chiefs? And, if so, who was the other?

That night, they dined in the abbey with the monks on a meal of roast venison and pork, consuming the last of the wine and cheese Angus had brought.

The talk drifted from the actions of John Balliol, the new King of Scots, who was recognized by all as no great leader, to Edward of England, a strong king but with cruel proclivities as evidenced by his brutal conquest of Wales, to Alex's impending position as Lord of the Isles. For the latter, there was much enthusiasm.

The next morning, Angus sailed for Kintyre with John and Duncan and his parents only to depart for Islay a fortnight later. A Council meeting had been hastily called for the second week in March to be held at the seat of the Macdonalds at Loch Finlaggan. It was the place of ceremony to install a new Lord of the Isles. Others, not present at the burial of Angus Mor, were in attendance. Among these were the chief poet, musicians and bards as well as the chancellor, judges and bailiffs. Beyond them, thanes and squires from around the Isles had gathered to see the new chief installed. The Marischal, Chief Gilbride MacKinnon, who was also the Macdonald standard bearer, had come with his ceremonial axe inlaid with silver.

Once all had arrived, they assembled next to the chapel on Eilean na Comhairle, the Council Isle. With the Bishop of the Isles again presiding in his official vestments, mitre and ring, Alex was made Lord of the Isles in a ritual as old as the lordship itself.

Clothed in a white tunic to show his innocence and integrity of heart, and to assure his clansmen that he would be a light to his people and maintain the true faith, Alex set his foot into the depression cut into a square stone where others before him had set their foot.

Facing the chiefs, he said, "I will walk in the footsteps and uprightness of my father and his forbearers." Then he received the white rod of kingship in his hand, indicating he had the power to rule, not with tyranny and partiality, but with discretion, sincerity and purity.

After this, the bishop placed Angus Mor's sword in Alex's hand, signifying that his duty was to protect and defend the clan from its enemies in peace or war. With war ever on the horizon, Angus expected all viewed this a particularly significant moment. Alex would now be the one making decisions for the clans.

With the ceremony concluded, those in attendance poured out their prayers for the new lord's success.

"'Tis done," Angus said to Duncan and John. "We have a new Lord of the Isles."

"Aye, and now to Mass," said John.

"And the blessing of Bishop Mark and the mandatory seven priests," added Duncan with his usual good humor.

Angus did not mind the lengthy process as it made firm his brother's position and confirmed the support of all the chiefs.

After the Mass, as they were dismissed, Alex invited all to a great feast, which was to last for a sennight. During that time, Alex made Angus the Lord of Kintyre and gave gifts to the monks, poets, bards and musicians.

Despite the celebrations and his new status, in which he delighted, with affairs in Scotland so uncertain, a wave of melancholy swept over Angus as he and Duncan left John and Alex on Islay to their shout of Godspeed and sailed back to Kintyre.

CHAPTER 9

Dunaverty Castle, Kintyre Peninsula, June 1294

IT HAD BEEN over a year since the burial of Angus' father. During that time, Angus had become Alex's right arm, undertaking tasks that called for dealing with the clan chiefs and keeping an eye on the waters where the MacDougalls and their allies might be tempted to raid.

With grave concern, Angus and Duncan had followed closely the events unfolding in Scotland. In an effort to curb the growing power of Alexander MacDougall of Lorne and the MacRuaris of Garmoran in the northwest, both kindred enemies of the Macdonalds, King Edward had turned to Angus' brother, Alex, naming him one of the English king's bailiffs. And so the Macdonalds and the Lordship of the Isles were aligned with the King of England against the Balliol-Comyn-MacDougall faction that reigned in Scotland.

In May of the prior year, Edward had summoned King John to London, demanding to know why he was ignoring Edward's judgments, including Alex's own appeal concerning Lismore. Balliol, who had once sworn fealty to Edward, tried to reverse course, saying he could not agree without consulting the Scots nobility. But, confronted with the fierce English king, whose disdain for so weak a ruler must have been intense, Balliol swiftly conceded and affirmed his vassal status as "your man of the realm of Scotland". News of this spread throughout the Highlands and the Isles where it was met with dismay.

Imagining the scene of Balliol kneeling before an outraged King Edward caused Angus to recall what his friend, Rob, had said about the King of England. *He can be ruthless and terrifies everyone.*

Balliol's weak behavior could hardly serve to pacify a king like Edward, who promptly sentenced King John to lose three of his castles. He went further, demanding that Balliol provide personal military service to him in France where Edward was engaged in a war with King Philip the Fair over Gascony.

Faced with Edward's demands, like a lamb before a snarling wolf, Balliol said nothing. This caused Scotland's nobles to be increasingly disillusioned with their new king.

In Ireland, trouble was brewing in Ulster, so that Alex now summoned Angus to Islay with a call for action.

Angus,

Matters have worsened in Ulster with the resumption of the old feud between the de Burghs and the Geraldines. Richard de Burgh calls for our help in defending his lands being decimated by the lawless John fitz Thomas Fitzgerald.

With my duties for King Edward, I cannot go but you must. John is with me on Islay and he would go, too. Come with your Islesmen and galloglass as soon as you can.

There is more to tell you.

Alex

Since he had become Lord of Kintyre, Angus had gained a small fleet of galleys and many galloglass were now at his beck and call. These days, his cousin was often at Dunaverty and had accompanied him on most of his voyages. Angus expected Duncan would want to be a part of this one as well.

Angus did not know the number of warriors fitz Thomas could call upon but if the Earl of Ulster needed help, it must be many, mayhap a thousand or more. Angus could call upon hundreds of Islesmen, thousands if the Isles were threatened, but with Balliol and the Comyns seeking vengeance on the Macdonalds, he could not take more men with him than his brother could do without. He would leave some of his fleet at Dunaverty for defense of Kintyre.

It took but a day to gather Duncan from Saddell. Returning to the Dunaverty, they joined Angus' other ships and sailed for the southern coast of Islay. In the sheltered Lagavulin Bay with its wide rocky shore next to Dunyvaig Castle, they beached the galleys.

Angus, Duncan and Angus' guard strode to the castle whose oak door was left open on this fine summer day. Inside the great hall, Angus found Alex hunched over a wooden table poring over a large parchment.

"Planning my voyage to Ulster?" asked Angus in an amused tone.

Alex raised his head. "Good day to you both. Nay, not planning but judging the strength of our forces scattered throughout the Isles. You know that Alexander MacDougall left his Argyll stronghold to plunder our Isles. What you may not know is that he has gone so far as to breach sanctuaries and burn ships under the protection of Holy Church."

"God save us. It is worse than I thought. Are you certain you want me to go to Ulster?"

"You must. I promised aid to Earl Richard."

Then looking beyond Angus, and seeing only his guard, Alex asked, "Did you bring a large number of men?"

"Aye. Fifteen galleys. And more than crew I brought archers and two physicians, Arthur MacNulty and Peter Bethune. I left five galleys at Dunaverty to guard the eastern approaches should you have need of them."

"I might. Soon I must leave for Skye where MacDougall harasses and kills. Do you have more galloglass with you than your guard?"

"The entire crew of my lead ship is now galloglass and the other crews have many among them."

Alexander nodded. "That is good." Glancing around the hall, he said, "John's around here somewhere and is anxious to see you. You've only a thirty-mile sail to Dunseverick but I would not delay."

"Dunseverick?" The name was familiar, something his tutor had mentioned. Thinking hard, he remembered. Dunseverick had once been the capital of Dalriada, the Gaelic kingdom that had extended from Ulster to Skye. It was that kingdom Somerled had reconquered over a hundred years ago.

"Aye. 'Tis the castle of Cumee O'Cahan, an Irish lord and friend of the Earl of Ulster. It sits on a headland six miles north of de Burgh's castle at Dunluce where your friend, the Earl of Carrick, will be staying."

"The youngest Robert Bruce is coming to help the Red Earl?"

"His father, who is in Norway visiting his daughter, has sent him and it seems King Edward gave his permission for the young Bruce to be in Ireland for some months."

It was the Turnberry alliance playing out before him but Angus made no mention of it since his brother did not know he and Rob had listened in as the nobles committed themselves to the agreement that bound them to the aid of each other years ago. The band called for support not only for the Bruces and any claim they had to Scotland's throne, but also for the Earl of Ulster and Thomas de Clare who, even then, had adversaries in Connaught.

"Is the fitz Thomas you spoke of in your letter from Connaught?"

"Aye. A lawless troublemaker but a powerful one with estates in Leinster as well as Connaught and ambitions for more. He attacks the earl's men throughout Ireland. I'm told that fighting has broken out in Tirconnell as well. Our nephew, Turlough, will doubtless be happy to see you."

"If they are friends, I assume the O'Cahans at Dunseverick will support de Burgh."

"They have many Irish warriors at their command and have already sent men to Dunluce. So, aye, both Lord Cumee and his son, Dermot, will stand with Earl Richard. I suggested Dunseverick for you since there is a long sandy beach just north of the castle where you can secure your ships. That way, you will not be arguing with de Burgh about where to lodge your men. I am certain his army occupies all the space he has. From Dunseverick you can borrow horses to ride south to Dunluce where Earl Richard will explain the current situation."

"I met Dermot O'Cahan once with Father when we were at Dunluce on our way back from installing Turlough as King of Tirconnell. He struck me as a most reasonable young man."

"Well, then, you will be at home there. You had best be sailing if you want to dine with Lord Cumee tonight."

"And you, Brother? How is it with you? Are you and Juliana content?"

"We are. Our second child, John, born while you were at Kintyre, has a head of hair so black we call him John Dubh, 'Black John'." Then with a smile, he added, "Juliana is expecting another child."

"Well done, Cousin Alex!" said Duncan with his characteristic grin.

"Aye," agreed Angus. "A man could not ask for more than two sons and mayhap another soon to follow." It was obvious Alex was well pleased with his growing brood. Then, glancing at the parchment before his brother, he asked, "Do you have enough men for the tasks Edward has given you? Enough ships to defend the Isles?"

"I do. As long as the English king continues to send funds, we will have ships and men to rein in the MacDougalls and MacRuaris."

"Then I bid you good day," Angus said to his brother. To Duncan, he said, "We had best collect John and be off."

John was waiting for them just outside the castle door dressed for battle, in a padded coat, tunic and mail. Like Angus, he wore a sword at his side and a dagger secured at his waist. In one hand, John carried his helmet and in the other a long-handled axe. Though years younger than Angus, he had already achieved his height of six feet, a wee bit shorter than Angus.

"I am glad you are coming with us," said Angus with an approving smile, "and that you are prepared. It is well you trained with Father's galloglass as I expect this fitz Thomas will have many in his army."

Retracing his steps to the bay and his ships, Angus sailed due south to Ulster. Remembering the treacherous waters below Dunluce

Castle, he was relieved his destination was a long stretch of sand to the north.

It was afternoon and the sun still hours from setting when Angus spotted the castle looming before him set high above the blue sea on a promontory green with summer's grass. As he stared at the stone edifice, he wondered what he might find there.

Dunseverick Castle, northern coast of Ulster, Ireland, June 1294

IN THE AFTERNOON, Áine went to the nursery to see her young son. Brian was sleeping peacefully, watched over by his nurse. Assured he was in good hands, Áine turned to the tasks before her.

Ever since the feud between John fitz Thomas and the Earl of Ulster had flared, her father's chiefs had been coming to the castle on a near daily basis so that she rarely knew how many would be joining them for dinner. Rory Maguire of Fermanagh was also a frequent visitor and brought with him his personal guard.

As a result, she instructed the cook to prepare more food than she would have had it been just her family and members of the household. The harp player, bard and minstrels had been warned so often of arriving guests they now expected to perform every evening so she need not pay them a visit. But she still had to speak to her father's seneschal about supplies and fresh rushes for the great hall.

When she had finished these tasks, she stepped into the afternoon sun, intending a brief walk around the promontory. Days without rain were rare and she wanted to take advantage of this one to visit her birds.

Finn followed at her heels though more slowly these days as he was old for a wolfhound and most often stayed by the fire. Sometimes she glimpsed a sadness in his eyes when he looked at her as if he knew his remaining days on earth would be few. Her heart broke to think of losing him but, she reminded herself, it was the way of all living things. She only hoped his passing would be peaceful.

Outside the stone walls, the sun was warm on her face. It was summer, that glorious time when the birds returned to nest on the cliffs. "Finn, we must see how our fulmars are doing. As well, the puffins arrived more than a fortnight ago."

At the end of the promontory, she let her gaze drift from the cliffs to the sea. To the east lay Rathlin Island, less than ten miles offshore, where a colony of puffins nested. Shifting her gaze from Rathlin to the north, she was amazed to see a fleet of galleys in full sail emerging out of the mist and moving swiftly toward Dunseverick.

From the lead ship, which was larger than the others, a gold pennon flapped in the wind, making it impossible for her to discern its design. As she watched, the ships veered east across her line of sight. *They must be making for the beach at White Fields Bay.*

She counted fifteen galleys, each with thirty oars except for the lead ship, which had thirty-four. Hastening to the castle, Finn at her heels, she sought out her father and found him speaking to one of his chiefs. When they were finished and the chief bid her a good day, she turned to her father. "I have just seen a fleet of galleys nearing the coast."

"Ah. That may be Angus Og Macdonald and his Islesmen. They are expected but I did not know their timing."

"The largest of the ships carries thirty-four oars and a golden yellow banner though I could not see clearly its device."

"If it is Angus Og Macdonald's fleet, the largest ship is his and the golden pennon bears the black Galley of the Isles, the symbol of the lordship."

Áine had never met the men of the Lordship of the Isles but Dermot had and spoke of their prowess in battle. "Are these the Macdonalds that Dermot spoke of, the ones you and he met at Dunluce?"

"We met The Macdonald, the chief, Angus Mor, and his middle son. Earl Richard has advised me Angus Mor has since died and is widely mourned. The eldest son, Alexander, has taken his place as Lord of the Isles. According to Earl Richard, Angus Og, the middle son whom we met, is bringing his warriors to join the earl's fight against fitz Thomas. He will have many galloglass with him. I told de Burgh we could see to their needs while they are here."

"Oh." She took a step back. "But Father, he brings a small army—

fifteen galleys and, judging by the oars, five hundred men! I planned to feed many mouths but not an army. They will be hungry and need a place to sleep."

"They are too many to house in the castle. They may camp on the beach or Angus Og may prefer to keep them close, mayhap in the heather nearby the castle. But he and his guard will have chambers in the castle. Will you arrange it?"

"Of course. How long will they be with us?" Áine was still thinking of feeding the Macdonald army. Men carried meager rations when on campaign but their expectations would be higher when camped so close to the castle.

"For only a short while, I should think. Until de Burgh sends them after fitz Thomas. We can feed them for that time. We've cattle and sheep. And, if need be, they can fish and hunt."

She had best instruct the cook to begin making more bread. The chiefs' wives would help as well. Telling her father she would return shortly, she went to the kitchens to see the bread would be made. Then she went to her chamber to change into clothes more appropriate for greeting guests.

In her chamber, she found her handmaiden. "Nessa, we are to have guests tonight. Even now they come." Then recalling the number of men, she added, "More like a small army."

"An army in the castle? Who are they?"

"The Macdonald Islesmen, who come to help Earl Richard. But only a few will be housed in the castle."

Nessa grew thoughtful. "The Islesmen are great men of the sea."

"They are and from what I hear, formidable warriors as well. 'Tis their galloglass who serve the Irish lords."

"Let me help you dress," said Nessa. "I set out the blue silk, should that please you."

Áine nodded and, with Nessa's help, donned the silk gown of deepest azure set slightly off her shoulders but still modest enough for her father. She dressed with care for her appearance, thinking of the Lord of the Isles' brother, who was allied with the Norman Earl of Ulster. She must do all she could to present herself well for her father's sake. Her only jewels were those in the sapphire pendant he had given her.

"Here, let me brush your hair," said Nessa. "You have been out in the wind and look more like one of the village girls than the chatelaine of the castle."

Áine laughed. "Very well, brush my hair."

Picking up the brush, Nessa ran it through Áine's long thick tresses, very dark brown in color except where the sun had touched them. Once this ritual was finished, Áine left her hair to curl around her shoulders and hang long down her back.

"Will you see that Brian's nurse stays with him this evening?"

"I will do more than that. I will take Finn to the lad and tell both of them a story. Brian likes the stories you tell him. Surely I can conjure one from my memory."

"Thank you, Nessa." Her handmaiden had grown close to Áine's young son since they'd left Tirowen.

"Here," said her handmaiden, holding out a small dish, "I crushed some wild strawberries for your lips."

"That was thoughtful," she said, taking the dish and dabbing her lips with the sweet juice. "I suppose I often look pale and this small bit of paint will give the priest nothing to frown upon." Áine blotted her lips with a small cloth. Since her eyes were dark and her lashes long, she never applied anything to them. She turned to her handmaiden. "Do I look the proper hostess?"

Nessa stood back with her arms crossed over her chest and gave Áine an assessing look. "I will just say this, Mistress. Whatever fish you are hoping to catch, he is already in the net."

Áine chuckled at her handmaiden's clever way with words. "I think to catch no one, Nessa, only to make Father proud. I have dressed in the same manner for all of his chiefs and even for Rory of Fermanagh, who would be my suitor."

"Yes, Mistress, you have. It is just that you grow more beautiful with each passing year yet you do not see it."

"Your flattery will certainly add color to my cheeks."

"Mayhap my words will cause you to think yourself a woman greatly desired. You can have your choice of suitors, you know."

Áine shook her head. There was no convincing Nessa but she had to say it. "I am content with my life as it is."

"'Tis possible God has other plans."

Áine left her chamber, reflecting on her handmaiden's words. At Dunseverick, she was needed, appreciated and loved. Her father and his chiefs could protect her from the petty wars that swirled around them and her brother would always offer her a home where she could raise her son. She turned her wedding ring on her finger, the ring she still wore. In truth, she was afraid to leave so warm a nest. Once before, she had done so with dire consequences.

By the time she entered the great hall, their guests had arrived. She paused in the shadows to consider the scene before her. Three men, bristling with weapons, stood with her father and the captain of his guard. Behind them were six giant galloglass, heavier in stature though no taller than the three in front of them. She frowned, thinking of what it would take in beef, sheep and butter to keep such men fit for their battles.

The galloglass, with hair falling in waves to their shoulders, wore the uniform of their occupation: saffron tunics, padded coats, knee-length mail and gauntlets. They had weapons aplenty, belted swords, daggers and each gripped a long-handled axe. Irish galloglass might leave legs and feet bare but these wore hose and leather shoes.

The three speaking with her father were like the galloglass in the weapons they carried, save for the axe which they must have left behind with their padded coats and mail. They were elegantly garbed in brightly colored woolen tunics. The tall one in the middle, whose tunic was a rich crimson, wore a gilded leather belt from which hung a fine-looking sword.

As she stepped from the shadows, they turned and the conversation ceased.

"Ah, my daughter," said her father. "Come, Áine, allow me to introduce you to our Macdonald guests."

The men's gazes followed her as she slowly stepped forward. She walked with her head held high, a daughter proud of her father.

Of the three with her father, two were similar in appearance though one was younger. The elder of the two had an air of confidence about him. His fierce countenance reminded her of a golden eagle. Both had blue eyes that glistened like the sea. Brothers, she assumed, and handsome. Their hair was a red-brown streaked with gold from the sun. Their skin bore the look of seamen who spent much time in the sun, their jaws etched in well-trimmed beards. The third had hair the color of ripe wheat. His eyes might be green or hazel. All three were smiling broadly at her, their white teeth on display.

"Áine," said her father, "this is Angus Og Macdonald, Lord of Kintyre," gesturing to the one with the gilded belt, "and his brother, John, sons of Angus Mor. Their cousin, Duncan MacAlasdair, comes with them."

She inclined her head and held out her hand to the Lord of Kintyre. "You are most welcome in our home, good sirs. We will do all we can to accommodate you and your men."

Angus Og held her gaze for a long moment before addressing her. "My lady," he said, bowing over her hand. He placed a gentle kiss on her fingers, his warm lips sending a sudden ripple of sensation coursing through her. She could not recall having experienced such before.

His stormy blue eyes fixed her with a piercing look as he rose. He seemed to hesitate and then said, "When my brother, Alexander, bid me come to Dunseverick, he failed to mention that hidden behind its walls was a rare jewel of unmatched worth." Slowly releasing her hand, he turned to her father. "You honor us, Lord Cumee, in allowing us to meet your lovely daughter, for I have not encountered a more beautiful woman in all of Scotland and the Isles."

Used to flattering words from men, Áine was tempted to dismiss these as well. He was not much older than she but his outward appearance was that of a rough warrior, one skilled in warfare who had come to do battle. Yet he had the calm assurance of a man content within himself and the regal posture of one used to giving orders and having them obeyed. His voice and manners were cultured and his compliment seemingly without guile. She decided to accept his overly lavish praise as a kindness. "You honor me with your unmerited praise, my lord."

CHAPTER 10

ANGUS WAS CERTAIN the ground beneath him had moved, so strong was the current that drew him to Áine O'Cahan. The first time he gazed upon her loveliness his breath caught in his chest. Words came with difficulty.

He had been searching for a woman with whom he could share his life never thinking he would find her. Could O'Cahan's daughter be the one? All this while, she had been here in Ulster, less than a day's sail from his castle at Dunaverty.

It was not just her beauty that drew him, though he had spoken truth when he said he had never seen a more beautiful woman. She moved with the fluid grace of a noblewoman and her words were kindhearted and humble. Yet there was something about her he could not explain that pulled him to her like a strong undertow.

Her eyes were dark pools that glimmered on the surface and her skin was like cream, her berry-colored lips enticing. Framing all was her long hair hanging in waves like a curtain of midnight embracing her white throat and shoulders.

"My seneschal will show you to your chambers, Lord Angus,"

said O'Cahan. "I expect you will join us for dinner?"

"Aye and we thank you." Angus glanced at O'Cahan's daughter, for he could hardly look away. "But I must first see to my men who are still with my ships. Might they set up camp in front of the castle?"

"They can and we will do our best to feed them. But you can also billet them in the homes of my chiefs if you prefer. They would be welcomed, coming as they are to serve Earl Richard."

"I would be pleased to meet your chiefs but, as for my men, I prefer to hold them together and close until I know the earl's plans and where he would send us. I told them to fish as I set off for the castle. By now, they should have dinner in hand."

Lord Cumee laughed. "I admire a warrior who looks ahead and cares for his men. Go and return to us when you've seen to them. We can at least supply them with bread and honey and ale to quench their thirst."

"I will see it done," said Lady Áine.

"May I borrow horses for me, my companions and my guard so that we may be quickly gone and quickly return?"

"Of course," said Lord Cumee. "We have a fine stable. And should you need carts and horses to pull them, those, too, can be at your disposal. My steward will meet you outside to assist you."

Angus bowed to his host and smiled at the daughter. The smile she returned him was winsome. Already, Áine O'Cahan was fixed in his heart.

Outside the castle, while awaiting the steward, Duncan tossed Angus a smirk. "The most beautiful woman you have ever laid eyes on? Where did *that* come from? You, who barely notice women?"

Before Angus could reply, John said, "Well, she *is* lovely is O'Cahan's daughter."

Duncan shook his head. "Angus, mayhap you failed to notice that when she held out her left hand to you, on her right hand she wore a wedding ring."

Married! He frowned. "I confess I did not see it." Angus chided himself for assuming such a woman would be unwed.

"If she is her father's chatelaine, mayhap her husband is away fighting for the earl," offered John.

Angus knew his brother was trying to help explain the absence of a husband but it did not lift Angus' spirits. To come so close to a woman who might be the one he had been searching for only to find she was the wife of another soured his mood.

He was still pondering this as the steward arrived to escort them to the stables.

It took the rest of the day for Angus to bring his men from the ships and see them ensconced in the valleys around Dunseverick. By the time he was ready to return to the castle, the heather-clad land was dotted with tents and campfires where his men roasted the fish they had caught along with meat they had brought from Kintyre.

As Angus, his companions and guard were leaving for the castle, a group of servants arrived bearing loaves of bread, honey and ale. "From Lady Áine with her blessing," said the one in charge.

"My men will be most grateful, and I will be certain to thank her for her kindness." From the number of servants and the amount of provisions, it seemed the O'Cahans knew how many ships were in his fleet and the number of Islesmen he had brought to Ulster.

At the entrance to the castle, Angus, John and Duncan were welcomed by the guard and, together with Angus' guard, shown into the great hall where their satchels were taken from them.

"They will be in your chambers," said the servant.

Once inside, Angus realized that Lord Cumee must have called for his chiefs to join him as there was a crowd of two score men standing about. They were richly attired in splendid tunics and jeweled belts. With them were well-dressed ladies Angus assumed were their wives.

Áine O'Cahan approached him. "Lord Macdonald, you and your two companions are welcome at the head table this eve. But before you take your seats, I would have you greet my brother, Dermot. I believe you have met him before. My father is with him and can make the rest of the introductions. As you can see, there are many chiefs here tonight so, before you begin so laborious a task as meeting all of them, I would offer you refreshment for your thirst."

"Thank you, my lady, and please use our given names."

She smiled as if amused. At her summons, a servant approached with a tray holding goblets of wine.

Angus released his galloglass into the hall with brief instructions and accepted the wine. "Thank you for your kindness to my men. Your gifts were much appreciated."

"You are most welcome. We are fortunate to have had a good honey season though some of the honey and bread came from our chiefs' kitchens. Did your men have enough food?"

"Aye, they are well fed."

She acknowledged this with a smile and turned toward the fireplace, crossing the hall and passing through the midst of the gathered chiefs. Looking beyond her, Angus could see her father standing some distance away with her brother Dermot in front of the great hearth where a fire burned steadily.

Pausing, she gestured to a large wolfhound lying beside the hearth. The hound raised his head and fixed his copper-colored eyes on Angus and his companions.

"Finn is my wolfhound. He is old now but still takes seriously his duty to protect me and my son."

Son? Not only married but with a son. Taken aback, Angus said, "I did not know you had a son, my lady."

"There is no reason you should."

Áine O'Cahan was a young woman so she must have been very young when she was wed. Before Angus could inquire as to the child's age or her husband's whereabouts, she turned and proceeded the short distance to where her father and brother stood. Light from the many candles set about the hall reflected in her long dark hair that fell to her waist, shimmering like waves at sea on a moonlit night. In her blue gown, she might have been an elfin princess, one of ethereal beauty. But she wore another man's ring, so Angus turned his attention to her father.

As they reached Lord Cumee, Lady Áine bid Angus and his companions a good eve, saying she would see them at dinner.

"You have returned to us," said Lord Cumee, greeting Angus. "I trust all is well?"

"It is, thank you."

"You know my son, Dermot."

"I do." Angus held out his hand.

Dermot took it, smiling warmly. "We dined with Earl Richard at Dunluce four years ago. I am sorry for the loss of your father, Lord Angus."

"He is greatly missed." Angus then introduced Dermot to his brother and cousin. "I believe you and John are of an age." It was true and both Dermot and John seemed delighted to realize it. They were of dissimilar heights, Dermot being slight and of medium height while John was nearly as tall as Angus.

"My chiefs are eager to meet you, Lord Angus," said The O'Cahan. "Your family is well known to them. Some fought alongside your father in past times. I expect the young ones will want to fight alongside you."

There were many chiefs to meet. Angus had just accomplished this when it was time to be seated for dinner. He was pleased with the arrangement that placed him between The O'Cahan and his daughter, though he considered it sweet torture to be so close to her.

Duncan sat on her other side. Dermot took the seat on his father's right, as was proper for the heir in the absence of the lord's wife, with John on Dermot's right and O'Cahan's constable next to John.

The dinner was a sumptuous feast of roast beef and herbed lamb with many side dishes of spiced vegetables. Bread and honey were placed on every table and, though some drank ale, at The O'Cahan's table they drank wine.

Lord Cumee quickly engaged Angus in conversation so that Duncan entertained Lady Áine. For that advantage, Duncan would tease him later.

"Earl Richard will be glad you have come," said Lord Cumee. "He is in need of men despite those we have sent him."

"My brother tells me de Burgh's people are being attacked all over Ireland," replied Angus.

"Fitz Thomas' ambition knows few bounds. The fighting ranges from Kildare in the south to Tirowen and Tirconnell in the north."

"Tirconnell? My nephew, Turlough, is their king."

Lord Cumee gave Angus a serious look. "You should be aware his reign is threatened."

Worried for his nephew, Angus was eager to reach Dunluce. "May I borrow your horses again to ride to Dunluce at first light to consult with the earl?"

"Of course. You may have the ones you rode earlier today or select others. We have horses aplenty to serve you. The distance is not great, less than seven miles, but Earl Richard may invite you to stay the night all the same. Do not worry about your men. We will see to their needs and, when you return, they can be ready to sail or march, as you see fit."

ÁINE KEPT ONE EAR on the conversation Lord Angus was having with her father while listening to Duncan MacAlasdair's description of Dunaverty Castle and his home at Saddell on Kintyre. She found Duncan to be congenial and quick-witted. His remarks were often humorous, but it was Angus Mor's middle son who intrigued her. His being a Scot and obviously a warrior caused her to wonder. Scotland now had a king but Angus Og, Lord of Kintyre, was allied with Edward's man in Ulster. *Why?*

As soon as he turned to her, she asked him.

His reply came without effort. "King John Balliol is joined with the enemies of the Macdonalds who, even now, would wreak havoc on our Isles. Moreover, we are bound to the Earl of Ulster and the Bruces by an agreement forged long ago and, more recently, we are bound to the Bruces by assent of our chiefs. My brother, the Lord of the Isles, has been appointed one of King Edward's bailiffs."

"I see." And she did. She liked that he did not dismiss her inquiry concerning a matter of war as coming from a mere woman but treated her as someone to be taken seriously, someone with whom he would share his business.

"I would know more about you, Lady Áine."

"There is not much to tell. Dunseverick has been my home except for the few years I spent in Tirowen and Inishowen. My mother died when I was young, so I have been my father's chatelaine for many years."

"That is to your credit but surely while your husband is away you engage in pastimes that do not involve the business of the castle."

"I am a widow, Lord Angus."

A wave of relief swept over him. *A widow.* "Yet you wear a wedding ring?"

She looked down to the golden band. "It tells others my wedding vows were said in a church." She shot him a glance. "Not all are. And it serves to let others know I am content."

"You are not looking to remarry?"

"No."

A long silence stretched between them.

"To answer your question about my pastimes, Lord Angus, the tapestries you see are my designs and those of my mother. The ones with birds are my creations. I'm very fond of the birds that come to Dunseverick's cliffs."

"I did notice the tapestries decorating the walls. They are magnificent. I would like to see the birds that inspired them."

"I would be happy to show them to you. A walk around the promontory at sunset can be very pleasant on a day like this one."

"I would look forward to that."

Áine was happy to think Angus Og would want to see her birds. She was not so naïve as to think it was only the birds he was interested in. She could see the interest in his eyes. But he accepted her expression of contentment so mayhap they could be friends. With the long days of June there would be light enough after the evening's entertainment to show him her nesting birds.

"The bard has planned a special poem for you and your companions," she said. "It is a poem written in memory of your father."

Soon thereafter, the bard took his place before them with the harpist. When the conversations ceased, he began to recite,

> *There is not in Ireland nor in Scotland an Aonghus like thee, thou graceful form.*
> *Thou hast come round Ireland; rare is the strand whence thou hast not taken cattle.*
> *Graceful long ships are sailed by thee, thou art like an otter, O scion of Tara.*
> *The house of Somerled, the Race of Godfrey, whence thou art sprung,*

who did not store up cattle,
O fresh-planted orchard, O apple branch, noble is each blood from which thou comest.
There is not in Ireland nor in Scotland an Aonghus like thee, thou graceful form:
the Aonghus of the dew-dappled sod of the Brugh send thee gifts, O Aonghus.

ANGUS LIFTED HIS GOBLET in toast as the bard finished his poem and the harp fell silent. "Well done, good sir." Echoes of the same sounded in the hall. That the bard would commend his father's cattle raiding reflected their respect, for raiding was a celebrated practice in both Ireland and the Isles. And to remember the Irish roots of their noble family was the highest of praise coming from an Irish bard.

Lord Cumee leaned in to Angus. "'Tis not often all of my chiefs are gathered into my hall. Many came in response to my invitation because they wanted to meet you. For a man in the middle of his second decade, you have drawn their approval, and I commend you."

"I am humbled by your praise, Lord Cumee. I do not claim to deserve it."

"Are there many chiefs in the lordship?" asked Lord Cumee.

"Aye. We have holdings and castles from Kintyre to Skye and farther north in the Outer Hebrides. At my father's bidding, I frequently engaged with his chiefs. 'Tis only more so with his passing now that I serve my elder brother. Angus Mor trained his sons well in all things to do with ships and the sea, our obligations to the church and men of the cloth, the nature of kings and nobility, the building and provisioning of castles and, not least, the way to fight."

"That is all to the good." Scanning the tables where the others were eating, Lord Cumee said, "Your guard seems to be enjoying themselves. Are there more galloglass with you than these you brought here tonight?"

"Aye. They are among my Islesmen camped below the castle. I left some at Dunaverty with my other ships. And my brother, Alexander, keeps some on Islay. The rest are distributed throughout the Isles when they are not working for Irish lords." This last he said with a smile. Angus had the impression he was listing his credentials to satisfy Lord Cumee's curiosity. But then another thought occurred. Could it be that the daughter may be content to remain unwed but her father was not? "Your daughter has kindly offered to show me her birds. If you are agreeable, I would like to do that while there is light."

"She did, did she? A rare offer is that. Well, then I will not delay you. The chiefs will be enjoying the conversation of your brother and cousin while you are observing the birds." Then, with a chuckle, he added, "But do not be long else my chiefs will have successfully bargained away the services of your galloglass guard."

Angus' smile spoke of his confidence. "Doubtless they will try but these are loyal to me. Some of them trained me in the use of the long-handled axe years ago." Rising from his chair, he offered his hand to Lady Áine. "Shall we visit those birds you spoke of?"

ÁINE TOOK THE Scot's hand and they departed the castle together, her wolfhound trailing behind. Unlike the hound's reaction to some visitors, Finn had no concerns about his mistress being alone with Angus Og.

Outside, she gazed toward the horizon where the sun had already slipped beneath the sea. In its going, it had left a fiery tail of gold stretched across the western sky, turning the clouds above an unusual lavender and leaving the sea a magical indigo.

"What a splendid sight," she remarked, inhaling the breeze.

She felt his eyes on her as he said, "Indeed, it is."

They strolled to the edge of the clifftop and, though she was comfortable in the silence between them, Áine was very aware of his presence. She paused to peer down to the water lapping at the rocky shore. The sound of the gentle waves breaking far below was soothing. The cliffs were mostly quiet of bird calls and shrieks that filled the air during the day.

"The seabirds have settled for the night," she said. "Now they make only soft sounds. During the day, they can raise quite a clamor."

"Now, there is a sight," he said in his deep voice as he pointed to the rocky beach at the foot of the cliffs. "A great white egret at the water's edge."

She followed his gesture. In the blue mist that hugged the coast, the egret waded in the waters near shore. "'Tis very unusual to see them here."

"I have observed them on occasion in the far north of our Isles but, even there, they are rare. I shall take it as an omen of good fortune."

In the glow of the sun's dying light, she glimpsed a smile on his face.

He pointed to the east. "Do you see that long stretch of land hiding behind Rathlin Island?"

"I do. When it is not clouded with mist, or we are not in the middle of a storm, I see it every day."

"'Tis my home, Kintyre, but a short sail for a galley."

"I was aware that the land beyond Rathlin was Kintyre but, of course, I had not realized it was the home of Angus Og Macdonald." She had said this in a tone that conveyed amusement, but Áine knew then she would never again gaze east toward Kintyre without thinking of him. "Since your home is so close, mayhap we will see you more often at Dunseverick." She could not recall inviting a man to visit her home before but she would be pleased to see him again.

"Should I survive de Burgh's war with fitz Thomas, I will."

"You must survive," she blurted out. Realizing her reply had been too quick and might have revealed more than she intended, she said, "After all, we have yet to share a game of chess."

His mouth quirked up at one end. "Aye, I would like that. Besides, how could I stay away now that I have discovered the rare gem that resides at Dunseverick?"

ANGUS HAD TO FIGHT the urge to take her in his arms and kiss her. The night was magical and she was so lovely. When the wind blew her hair across her face, he reached out and brushed it from her eyes. "Despite that you are content with your life, my lady, I assume you have many suitors."

"Some." She said this shyly with downcast eyes as if she were reluctant to disclose such a fact. He was certain there were many. A woman of great beauty with a kind heart and the manners of a noblewoman who had already proved she could bear a son would be in great demand. She had told him he must survive the coming battles and that had given him hope that it mattered to her that he did.

"I would not venture onto a field of battle if the day has already been won by another."

"There is no field of battle concerning me, Lord Angus, and nothing has been won." Her gaze flitted away.

"I do not mean to embarrass you."

She returned her beautiful eyes to him. "You did not but you move like lightning where others would proceed slowly especially since I give no encouragement."

"They are fools and, while I am not slow, I can be patient."

They resumed their walk and she pointed out the nesting fulmars and other birds that found sanctuary in the clefts of the rocks.

"We have many seabirds in the Isles," he said.

She gazed north. The sun's golden streak was gone, leaving twilight's muted shades. "I have never traveled to your Isles but I have heard much of them."

"One day, you must see them." He hoped to be the one to show them to her. Searching for another subject as they neared the castle, he said, "Tell me about your son."

"Brian is three, a delightful child, happy and eager for adventure. He has the red hair of his father, an O'Neill trait." Then facing Angus, she said, "My husband was Niall O'Neill, King of Tirowen, slain three years ago."

Angus could see the pain reflected in the depths of her eyes and knew she had experienced something horrible. "Were you there?"

She nodded and shut her eyes tightly. "He was cut down before me. Even now, I can see it in my mind." Opening her eyes, she said, "My son and I barely escaped with our lives."

He took her hand and held it to his chest. "If I have anything to say about it, Lady Áine, you will never experience anything like that again."

CHAPTER 11

ANGUS AWAKENED as a breeze from the sea wafted into his chamber, carrying with it the morning's meager light. Remnants of his dream flickered through his mind, images of a dark-haired beauty smiling up at him. The blood in his veins coursed with new vigor. His world had changed. Áine O'Cahan had changed it forever.

Rising, he splashed water on his face and peered through the arrow slit facing the sea. The castle was sheathed in mist beneath a cloud-filled sky. Impatient to be about the day's business, he dressed in his tunic, padded coat and mail then went down to the great hall where he accepted the bread, cheese and ale servants hastily set before him.

Soon he was joined by his brother and cousin, lifting their heads in greeting as they silently slipped onto the bench across from him.

Observing their bleary eyes, he asked, "Have you no words for me this morning?"

Duncan slowly let out a breath as if pained. "You have no idea the sacrifice we made for the sake of diplomacy last eve. When you went for a walk with Lady Áine, we sat around drinking with the O'Cahan chiefs and your galloglass."

"Aye," agreed John, his hands cradling his head. "Overmuch, I fear."

Angus was tempted to smile at the "great sacrifice" but, instead, said the one thing he thought might encourage them. "Well, at least we do not face battle this day." He had come in from his walk with the beautiful Lady Áine the night before to speak briefly with her father and the O'Cahan chiefs before going to his chamber. Thus, he had avoided the rounds of drinking that must have ensued.

Hearing footsteps, he looked up to see his galloglass guard filing into the hall. Angus acknowledged them with a nod as they joined him at the table, appearing only slightly more alert than his brother and cousin.

The door leading to the kitchen swung open. Áine O'Cahan glided into the hall in a yellow tunic that shone like bright gorse, cheerful on this cloudy day. She must have been awake for some time as her lovely eyes were bright and her smile engaging. In her arms she carried a platter of cold meats.

Smiling at Angus, she set the platter on the table. "Good morning."

A lord's daughter typically would not be serving guests, which made Angus appreciate the gesture more than he could say. "And to you, my lady. I trust you did not rise with the dawn just for us?"

"I am here for you and your men who ride to Dunluce. After all, warriors cannot perform on bread alone and the earl may not offer you food until evening."

His guard, still waking up, nodded their approval. One of them covered a yawn as he reached for a slice of cold meat.

Duncan, too, stabbed a piece of beef with his eating knife. "We thank you and your father for your hospitality, my lady."

Angus agreed. "Aye, you have been gracious. But, to help, I will ask my men who remain behind to fish and hunt to feed themselves and add to your larders."

"We will gratefully accept their gifts," said Lady Áine. "With many men away, there are fewer to hunt and fewer to tend the fields and the cattle, sheep and pigs. But I will send some cheese, salted pork and ale to your men to add to what they have."

She did not linger in the hall but ascended the stairs. Angus watched her go and wondered if she went to her young son. Were he not committed to meeting with the Red Earl, he would have stayed and met the boy. Instead, he ate hurriedly so that not long after, he and his company were mounted and ready to ride.

From where he sat atop his horse, Angus gazed up at the sky. The mist was dissipating but the gathering clouds were dark, the chance of rain great. He hoped it would hold off until they reached their destination.

He turned his horse to go and, suddenly, Lady Áine was there, looking up at him, an earnest expression on her face. "I wish you Godspeed, Lord Angus."

"Thank you, my lady." Captured by the mystery within her dark eyes, he had a vision of her wishing him Godspeed from the shore at Dunaverty. If God granted the desire of his heart, it would be so. Reluctant to go, yet knowing he must, he smiled at her before urging his horse forward.

He and his companions descended the path to where his captains stood waiting. Their words in response to his inquiry assured him they had food enough for the morning meal.

"The lady of the castle will send you more but you will need to hunt and fish to feed all the men. It will give them something to do besides wrestling and swordplay. If you can, help to fill the castle's larders. I go to speak with the Red Earl at Dunluce. Expect me to return on the morrow with news. Should he send us to Tirconnell or Connaught, we will take the ships."

Given the options, he expected the earl would need him and his men where he could bring his ships. To march an army south a far distance in what would surely be a damp Irish summer would not be his preference.

Angus set a fast pace as he took the path along the cliff that followed the coast west. His brother and cousin rode alongside him with his guard following. On his right, a hundred feet below, the gray sea was calm. On his left, as far he could see lay green fields, some ripe for the scythe. June was the time when hay was harvested. He thought of the farmers, knowing they always suffered in times of war. He hoped the battles to come would not make their lives more difficult.

Dunluce Castle, north coast of Ulster

THE APPROACH TO Dunluce from the tops of the hills gave Angus a view of the castle and surrounding area he had not had years before when he and his father had climbed the headland from the rocky shore. Now, open pasture stretched before him, providing fodder for a herd of grazing black cattle.

With Dunluce's stone walls in sight, Angus rode hard for the outer bailey perched high on the sea cliff. After identifying himself, his companions and his guard to the guard at the gate, they were admitted to the wide field of grass crowded with hundreds of warriors and knights sparring with each other. "Why are so many men still here?" he asked from atop his horse.

"The earl and his family are in residence, my lord," said the guard. "When he leaves, these men will go with him."

Angus was glad to know Earl Richard was still at Dunluce, but he would have thought the earl's family would be safely ensconced behind the thick stone walls of Carrickfergus Castle on the east coast. Mayhap they had been caught unaware when the fighting began in the south.

"Is Sir Robert Bruce, Earl of Carrick, still here?"

"He is, my lord. You will find him in the great hall with the Earl of Ulster's advisors."

They rode to the far end of the bailey and dismounted, handing the horses' reins to the waiting grooms. Angus asked his guard to occupy themselves while he, Duncan and John continued on to the castle.

A narrow bridge led across a deep gulf to the rock on which the castle stood a hundred feet above the pounding surf. The slate-colored sea surrounding the promontory opened before them. Above, the sky was an expanse of gray and the air redolent of rain.

Inside, the castle was as he remembered it with carpets of red and blue and tapestries hanging on the walls. A new mural in bright colors of red, yellow, blue and green featuring elegantly attired men and women standing around fruit trees was in the process of being added to a white-plastered wall.

The great hall bustled with servants and men, their voices echoing off the stone walls. One of the earl's wolfhounds came up to Angus with a sniff and a tail wag.

A long wooden table, set in front of the fireplace, dominated the room. Men in jewel-colored tunics sat and a few stood around it deep in discussion. Before them was a map or diagram that had drawn their attention.

Angus stepped forward and Richard de Burgh rose from his chair. "Angus, Lord of Kintyre, you are a welcome sight! Have you come with your army of Islesmen?"

Angus strode to meet him, recognizing as he did that his friend, Robert Bruce, was one of the men at the table. "Indeed, Earl Richard. I come to Dunluce with my cousin, my brother and my galloglass guard. But to your inquiry, five hundred Islesmen are at Dunseverick awaiting my orders."

"Excellent! We were just discussing how we might disperse our forces to deal with my rebellious vassal, fitz Thomas, and his treacherous allies. They would have Connaught and all of Ireland for themselves if they could. Our plan is to have fitz Thomas contained in the south and his allies defeated in the north."

Briefly, Angus introduced his brother and Duncan then described his ships and the number of men, galloglass and archers he had brought to Ulster.

"Wonderful," said the earl. "Now, meet the others."

Angus' friend, Rob, known to these men as Sir Robert Bruce, Earl of Carrick, rose from his seat and held out his hand. "It is good to see you, my friend. At the moment, we argue about what chess pieces go where on the landscape of Ireland. But tonight, I claim a game of chess with the Lord of Kintyre."

"You shall have it," said Angus, shaking his hand.

The others who had come at Earl Richard's call included both Norman and Irish lords, all apparently willing enemies of John fitz

Thomas.

Earl Richard addressed the men at the table. "Meet Angus Og Macdonald, Lord of Kintyre, brother to Alexander, Lord of the Isles. Lord Angus has with him his younger brother, John, and his cousin, Duncan MacAlasdair. Besides these, he has brought us five hundred Islesmen, many galloglass among them."

Smiles and murmurs of approval accompanied this announcement.

Then turning to Angus, the earl said, "Join us and partake of some ale as I introduce those gathered here. We are sharing our thoughts as to where each of us will go to meet the threat we face."

Angus and his companions found places at the table and, thirsty from the long ride, gratefully accepted the offered ale.

The earl gestured to two men, who, like Earl Richard, were in their third decade. "My brother, Theobald, and my cousin, William Liath, have proposed that they join me and my army in Connaught."

Angus had never traveled to the ancient kingdom of Connaught southwest of Tirconnell but he was aware it had been under the control of the de Burghs for decades. That John fitz Thomas intended to wrest it from the Red Earl, a friend of King Edward, seemed an outrageous move, one not likely to succeed.

Earl Richard's brother, Theobald, had the look of the earl and the same blue eyes, but his chin-length hair was brown.

"Do we know how many men fitz Thomas has?" asked Angus.

De Burgh's cousin, William Liath, whose light eyes were assessing as he took in Angus and his companions, said, "The spies we have sent forward say he has a thousand marching with him for he has stirred the whole countryside against the Anglo-Normans."

"And on our side?" asked Angus.

"Not quite that number," said Earl Richard, "not counting your men. But our forces are better trained and better equipped. Both sides will have cavalry and, though most of the knights are ours, Sir Piers de Birmingham, Lord of Athenry, fights with fitz Thomas."

Robert Bruce frowned, his auburn brows drawing together. "King Edward will have something to say about that."

"Indeed," said Earl Richard before shifting his attention to another man. In his middle years, the man the earl introduced as Aed O'Connor, by his dress was an Irish lord. His features were sharp, framed by long dark hair. His green tunic bore silver Celtic designs. "The O'Connor is King of Connaught by my choice," said Earl Richard. "Once imprisoned by fitz Thomas, Aed has asked to lay siege to fitz Thomas' castle at Sligo."

"I do it most heartily," said the Irish lord with a wry smile. "'Twould be gratifying to tear it down and deal fitz Thomas a blow at his seat of power. Connaught is not only my home but the place of my youth and I'd as soon see him gone from it."

Heads nodded at the choice of Aed O'Connor to attack Sligo Castle.

"Last, and of great importance to me," said Earl Richard, "I present Sir Thomas de Mandeville, Seneschal of Ulster, and Sir Hugh Bisset, Lord of the Glens of Antrim. Both have served me faithfully for many years."

Sir Thomas, a man of fair countenance, looked very English to Angus with his high cheekbones, aquiline nose and pale skin, reddened from the sun.

Angus acknowledge Sir Hugh with a dip of his head. They were already acquainted, as Sir Hugh Bisset had married one of Angus' older sisters when Angus was quite young. The older knight had graying brown hair and narrow eyes beneath bushy brows. The Bisset's family was originally Norman and, once, were nobles in Scotland. Banished for their suspected involvement in the murder of some noble, they went to Ulster where they used their wealth to acquire lands in Antrim in the northeast of Ulster. It was the place where Angus' ancestor, Somerled, had been born.

"Only a few years ago," de Burgh went on, "these two helped me to install Brian O'Neill as King of Tirowen. The previous king was Niall Culanach O'Neill, Brian's uncle. Niall, some of you will recall, was foully murdered by his cousin Domnall O'Neill."

"Whose mother was a MacDougall," put in Angus, remembering he had learned that the first time he'd visited the Red Earl.

"Ah, yes. I would expect you, a Macdonald, to recall that," said Earl Richard.

"'Twas a grave sin to murder his kin," muttered Sir Thomas, running his hand through his hair that was the color of flax.

"But not beneath Domnall O'Neill," added Sir Hugh. "The sooner he is dealt with the better."

"I am familiar with that history," said Angus, recognizing the name Niall O'Neill. Once King of Tirowen, he had been the husband of the lovely Áine O'Cahan and the father of her son. He could regret the man's death at the hands of kin, especially a MacDougall, but not that it left Lady Áine free to wed.

"If these go with me and the main army to Connaught," said Earl Richard, "that leaves the north to defend. For now, Brian O'Neill is safe in Tirowen but Turlough O'Donnell's kingdom of Tirconnell is hanging by a thread."

Angus leaned forward to hear the earl's thoughts.

"What do you think, Lord Angus, if I send you and your five hundred men to Tirconnell to aid your nephew who must fend off his half-brother, Aodh O'Donnell? As I remember, you accompanied your father to rescue Turlough once before."

"Aye," said Angus. "My father and I helped secure the promised kingship for Turlough. I would do so again."

"Good. Turlough needs reinforcements," replied the earl. "If Tirconnell does not hold, then Tirowen to the east will be threatened, for the enemies of Brian O'Neill are also the allies of fitz Thomas. I cannot risk the north falling to them."

Earl Richard was about to move on when Angus said, "If he is willing, my lord, I would have the Earl of Carrick accompany me."

Earl Richard glanced at Rob, who nodded his assent. "King Edward told me to lend you my sword," he said to de Burgh, "he did not say where that was to be."

"That being the case, since you agree, you shall join Lord Angus and his Islesmen in Tirconnell." Facing Angus, the earl said, "With the number of warriors you have, you will not need O'Cahan's men he sent to me earlier. I can use them to bolster our defenses in the east of Connaught."

"Agreed," said Angus, "with the exception of the young O'Cahan chiefs still at Dunseverick. I am told they would sail with me."

Earl Richard nodded. "Fine. Any who do are yours to command."

"If Earl Robert wishes to ride to Dunseverick with me," offered Angus, "we can sail to Tirconnell from there tomorrow."

"A ship to Tirconnell would be welcome," said Rob.

Earl Richard nodded. "The sooner the better." And to Angus, he said, "There are a few good places to beach your ships near Turlough's base at Kilmacrenan in the northeast. I do not know how many men the O'Donnell allies of fitz Thomas have in Tirconnell," said de Burgh. Turlough will know, of course. If need be, support can be found with Brian O'Neill to the east in Tirowen."

"Let us hope it does not come to that," said Angus.

"We can all agree with that," said Earl Richard. Looking around the table, he added, "We have our assignments. What about the arrangements for supply wagons, weapons, grooms to tend the horses?"

"They are well in hand," said his brother, Theobald, "as well as siege equipment for The O'Connor."

Richard de Burgh nodded. "My castle at Shrule in Connaught can serve as a place to send me messages. It stands strong against our enemies."

That night at dinner, the men were joined by Lady Margaret, the Red Earl's fair countess, whom Angus had met the first time he visited Dunluce. In what the earl allowed as being an exception to his usual rules for his children, the de Burghs' three eldest children were allowed to join them.

All were daughters: Aveline at fourteen had her father's red hair; Eleanor at twelve was fair like her mother but tending to plumpness, a favorable trait for a wife. And then there was Elizabeth with her long golden hair and her large green eyes that reminded Angus of Ireland's hills. A very pretty child, obviously aware of her charm even at ten years of age. She fluttered her eye lashes outrageously at Angus' younger brother, John, who found it most amusing. "I think the lass likes me."

"That one will leave a trail of broken hearts," Angus told his brother.

"A small fish," put in Rob. "You had best throw her back into the sea until she is grown."

That produced a laugh from all who heard it, save Lady Margaret, who cautioned, "I warn you, Elizabeth is made of stern stuff. She will make a strong wife one day for a great lord."

The men, suddenly quiet, gave the young girl another look. Angus wondered what Lady Áine looked like at that age. Even then, her beauty and kind heart must have been evident.

After dinner, Angus and Rob settled down to their chess game. Angus' mind drifted to the fighting to come. "If we ride to Dunseverick at first light, we can sail from there to Tirconnell tomorrow. The earl tells me if we beach the ships on the banks of the River Foyle in Derry, we will be close to Tirconnell yet still on the Red Earl's lands."

"Earl Richard knows well those lands," said Rob. "However, he mentioned to me that there is a long beach west of Derry on Tirconnell soil. It would mean less walking for us."

Angus considered only for a moment before replying. "I expect my nephew, Turlough, will be at Kilmacrenan in the north of Tirconnell, so the long beach you speak of west of Derry would do well."

ÁINE WAS IN the inner bailey to meet the Macdonalds when they arrived early the next morning. Another man she did not recognize had joined them. A knight by all appearances. His mail was finely woven and polished, and he was accompanied by a fair-haired squire.

Almost as tall as Lord Angus, the knight was introduced to her as Sir Robert, Earl of Carrick. He spoke to her in Gaelic, which was not surprising as Carrick was known to be Gaelic in large part, but she suspected he spoke several other languages, as did she. He wore the gilded belt of an earl and his manners were more like de Burgh's, telling her the knight might be a Scot but he was also Norman.

"My lady," the auburn-haired earl said, bowing over her hand.

Sensing haste from the expression on Lord Angus' face, she asked him, "Do you sail soon, my lord?"

"Aye, to Tirconnell."

She looked up at Lord Angus. "Then 'tis well I have ordered the servants to load a cart of provisions for you. They will accompany you to White Fields Beach and bring back the cart and the horses." Áine had been working since Angus Og's departure for Dunluce to make sure all would be ready. Though his men had brought game, rabbits and fish to the castle, they would need other provisions she could supply. "I have also included oiled cloths for the rain you will surely encounter and an oiled cloak for you, Lord Angus." Gazing up at the sky of gray clouds, she added, "It is not raining now but the day is still young."

"Ah, yes, Ulster's rain," said Lord Angus, meeting her gaze. "Worse than Scotland's, I believe. Your foresight and kindness are welcome, my lady. I will wear the cloak and think of you."

Áine wanted to say more but contented herself with helping him as she could. "The young chiefs, who want to go with you, are waiting with your men. My brother wanted desperately to go as well but Father forbade him. Dermot is the only heir, so my father holds him close."

"Understood," said Lord Angus. "As I recall from my first meeting with him, your brother is also a scholar."

She smiled, for she was proud of her younger brother. "A good one."

Brian ran up to her just then and, from behind her skirts, peeked out at the men, his dark blue eyes wide as he took in the four tall men armed for battle.

"Is this handsome lad your son?" Lord Angus inquired.

Brian giggled.

"He is, my lord. Brian, come forward and make your bow to the Lord of Kintyre and his friends."

Still holding her skirts with one hand, Brian stepped forward shyly and bowed, his three-year-old body only recently having learned how.

Lord Angus offered his hand, bending in order to do so.

Brian let go of her skirts and put his small hand in that of Angus Og Macdonald. The Lord of Kintyre's display of gentleness with her young son pleased her. Many visitors to Dunseverick paid the boy no attention at all despite he was a prince of Tirowen.

"Master O'Neill," said Lord Angus, "I bid you good day. Alas, we must soon depart. We go to aid a friend who is also kin. You understand, I trust?"

Brian nodded solemnly.

To her, Lord Angus said, "I would introduce the Earl of Carrick to your father if he is available."

Áine turned to a servant and asked that her father be told the Lord of Kintyre was here.

A short while later, Lord Cumee appeared and introductions were made.

"I wish you success on your venture, Lord Angus," said her father. "Do not fail to return to me the half-dozen young chiefs who go with you. Their fathers will be anxious."

"My galloglass and I will protect them with our lives. And the Earl of Carrick is quick with his sword."

Áine asked a servant standing nearby for the small parcel wrapped in linen cloth he had been holding for her. She handed it to Lord Angus. At his raised brows, she said, "Meat pies for you and your close companions. They will keep for a few days."

"Again, you think of our needs. Thank you, my lady."

Áine was glad she had included a fourth meat pie, an extra for Angus Og that he could now give to Sir Robert.

She waved to the men as they mounted and headed down the path to the glen below where his army stood ready to march. He sat his horse in proud fashion, more like an Irish horseman of noble family than a Scot used to being on the sea. Her voice was a mere whisper as she prayed, "Lord, go before him, make his path straight that he might return safely to Dunseverick."

Brian took her hand, his bright red hair blowing in the breeze. "Will he come back?" he asked in his small voice.

"God goes with him, Little Prince, so there is hope Lord Angus will return." She thought of him pressing her hand to his chest where his heart beat strong as they stood alone on the promontory. And she remembered his promise to spare her the hurt she had once experienced.

Touching her hand to her forehead, she crossed herself.

Brian, his trusting face looking up at her, did the same.

Kilmacrenan in the northwest of Tirconnell, Ulster, end of June 1294

UNCERTAIN OF THE land in the hazy onset of evening, Angus might have missed the small village that surrounded the manor house if his men had not spread out in search of Turlough and what army he had with him.

They had followed the Leannan River, traveling west for the last stretch of the long trudge from where they had beached the ships. Only twice did they rest and then not for long. They had seen nothing save green fields, some ready to harvest. Villagers, likely afraid of so great an army of foreign warriors, had made themselves scarce.

He was glad for the small meat pies, which he shared with Rob, Duncan and John, and wondered how she knew there would be four to eat them. The cloak she had given him was a great prize, quickly becoming the subject of much teasing from his brother and cousin.

"She must favor you," said John.

"Or, she just had a spare cloak lying about," said Duncan with a smirk.

Angus thought it might have been a customary gift for a lord from outside Ireland but, secretly, he hoped the gift represented more.

With the coming of twilight, the midges began to swarm, making him thankful for the light rain that began to fall.

"My lord!" One of his men came running to him. "We have found Lord Turlough. He awaits you just ahead."

"That is welcome news," said Rob, striding alongside him. "I feel like I have walked half the width of Scotland." Then with sarcastic good humor, he added, "Oh, where, pray tell, is my horse?"

Angus chuckled. "Indeed. Remind me, what is it a squire does when there is no horse to tend?"

"The list is a long one, my friend. He must tend my mail, my sword and my clothes," said Rob in all seriousness. "And for himself, he must learn to fight and to joust. When we are at court, he must be acquainted with music and dance."

Angus had learned all that under the watchful eye of the Lord of the Isles.

"Even so," said Rob, "I am hopeful I shall not long be without a horse."

"Nay, you will not. I expect Turlough will have horses, at least for some of us. This is Ireland, after all. Still, I prefer to travel by ship when I can."

Turlough came out to meet them, the dirt on his face smeared by the rain but, otherwise, he was whole and happy they had come. "Uncle! What a grand sight you are." Gazing beyond Angus, Turlough added, "So many men! We are down to a few hundred so your army is much needed."

Though they were of an age and Turlough was half-Macdonald, he had the look of an Irishman. He wore his saffron tunic long and pulled up around his waist to fall in folds over his belt where he carried a large sword sheathed in leather. From his shoulders hung a cloak festooned with braided Celtic trim. Both his hair and beard were brown as Angus remembered but they were now darkened by the rain.

Grasping his nephew's hand, Angus said, "Earl Richard sent us and I was glad as it would have been my choice." Gesturing to his companions, he added, "You know Duncan and John from our journey to Tirconnell a few years ago. But you may not know Sir Robert Bruce, Earl of Carrick, a good friend."

"Duncan, John," said Turlough, acknowledging them. Then, offering his hand to Angus' friend, he said, "I know not this Robert Bruce but I know of the Bruces of Carrick and the Lords of Annandale. My grandfather spoke of your family often. Welcome to Tirconnell."

The two men shook hands as the rain started to fall in earnest. Turlough suggested they go inside. "I can offer you food and your men can eat with mine. As you will see, we have a village here but with so many in your retinue, I assume you have tents?"

"Aye," said Angus, following his nephew. "Do you think we would come to this place of continuous rain without tents?"

Turlough laughed. "Wise uncle."

Angus issued orders to his captains and his guard before following Turlough into the whitewashed house that stood in the middle of the small village.

"My housekeeper and her husband," Turlough said, introducing the man and woman who were setting dishes on the table that dominated the room. Stairs at one end led to a second story.

"Sit!" said Turlough. "You must be hungry after your travel. Did you come from Earl Richard's castle at Dunluce?"

"Aye," said Angus, "and talk of war."

"The earl worries about fitz Thomas and Connaught," said Turlough, "but we worry more about my half-brother, Aodh O'Donnell."

"He has not given up?" asked Angus. "After we sent him running, I would have thought he'd learned his lesson."

"Nay, he persists. Worse, he has gained men to his cause and has promised them much. My scouts have discovered where they hide and we will soon be upon them."

"They have galloglass, do they?" asked Angus.

Turlough nodded. "More than before."

Angus noted that in the years since he'd seen his nephew, Turlough had grown in stature as a leader and likely in his skills as a warrior.

Shifting his attention to Rob, Angus said, "Doubtless you have bested many a knight in tourneys and melees, my friend. This will be different. A galloglass' reach with the sparth axe is longer than yours with a sword. You will have speed and the skill of a knight but, as you raise your steel to strike, the sparth axe has already hit with devastating force. And when our axe blade is lodged in some man's flesh or is set aside, we still have our sword."

"So this is to be a test, is it?" asked Rob undaunted.

"Aye, 'twill serve," said Angus. "Stay by my side and you will win the day."

Rob laughed, his gray eyes sparkling. "Must I?" He patted the hilt of his sword. "Do you have so little confidence in this sword of mine?"

"Nay, 'tis just that I have more in my long axe and those of my galloglass guard who will fight with me. If you want to learn to fight against galloglass, you must remain by my side. I do not intend to lose you, my friend."

Rob let out an impatient but good-humored sigh. "Oh, very well.

I suppose I could find some time to practice with your galloglass as we head toward the O'Donnells."

"'Twould be wise." Then, as an afterthought, Angus said, "You could always try to best *me*. I promise it will be more exciting than chess."

Turlough and the others laughed.

Rob lifted his gaze to the ceiling.

Angus was certain it would be their last moment of levity for some time.

Tirconnell, Ulster, September, 1294

IN MID-JULY, A GREAT storm swept across the country. Angus had never endured so much rain. It pounded crops until they lay dying on the ground, soaked beyond saving. For days, he and his men were rarely dry. The downpour persisted through August and into September. Many days, he thanked God for Áine O'Cahan's foresight in giving him the oiled cloak and cloths to cover their provisions.

In the rain's wake, famine stalked the land. So desperate were people for food they risked encounters with Turlough's army and Angus' galloglass to beg for sustenance. Angus and his men shared what they could. It did not help that King Edward, indifferent to the plight of the peasantry, continued to ship what grain there was to England to feed his armies preparing to invade Gascony.

Angus' men managed to hunt while game could be found. The rivers gave forth fish and that added to their meals. Some days, they existed on rabbit stew and wild plants.

Despite the rain, a few encounters with the O'Donnell army had taken place, though none were conclusive. As soon as the fighting waned, their enemy was off into the woods. While there had been injuries among Angus' men, there had been no deaths. Still, the physicians he'd brought with him were kept busy.

After days in the woods tracking O'Donnell's army, they had set up camp, taking shelter in their tents, glad for a respite from the constant rain. There, a messenger from the Red Earl reached Angus and Rob with reports of the fighting in the south.

"The earl has left the siege of Sligo Castle to Aed O'Connor and his men," said the dripping messenger. "It goes well and The O'Connor is optimistic the fitz Thomas castle will not long stand. As a result, the Earl of Ulster has taken half the army and ridden southeast to Kildare with Sir Hugh and Sir Thomas."

"What has happened in Kildare?" asked Angus.

"One of the earl's scouts reported that fitz Thomas has unleashed his Irish allies on the town. The followers of one William Donyn have broken into the castle and robbed it and the surrounding town of money, cloth, grain and livestock."

Rob shook his head. "Food and supplies Kildare could ill afford to lose with the famine."

"The earl worries they will burn the castle," said the messenger.

Angus did not hear more of the report as the shrill sound of a sentry's horn sounded, interrupting the messenger. Sharing a quick glance with Rob and Duncan, Angus jumped up, responding to what could only be a call to battle. Arming himself with sword and dagger, he reminded Rob to stay close.

John came running into their tent. "O'Donnell's men are attacking! We are summoned to arms!"

Angus threw his oiled cloak around his mail and, grabbing his axe, raced from the tent with Duncan and Rob on his heels. There was no time for horses that might slip and slide on the muddy ground. No time to organize beyond a few shouted commands to his galloglass and his captains who came to him.

In the dim afternoon light, Angus peered through the rain to see the O'Donnell forces pouring across the open ground like a squall from the sea, clashing with the combined forces of Turlough and the Macdonalds. Angus shouted to his archers, "Into the trees and high ground!"

There was no time to think, only to fight. His galloglass warriors were already wielding their axes, cutting down the men streaming toward them. He joined them, slicing through the necks he could reach with his axe.

The next two hours were a blur as Angus fought hard to defeat the Irish warriors while protecting John when he could and assuring that Rob was not felled by an axe. Duncan, he prayed, would hold his own.

Swinging his axe in a wide curve, he wounded one man's arm, inflicting a terrible gash. His axe found the necks of others. Soon it was dripping blood.

Rob fought at Angus' side, wielding his blade with a knight's skill to find openings in their enemies' armor. The sounds of metal clashing and men's grunts as they took a blade filled the air in the clearing.

Angus' galloglass fought with them, cutting down any of O'Donnell's men who escaped the blades of Angus, his companions and Islesmen. He had tasked some of his galloglass with protecting the young O'Cahan chiefs should he not be able to do so. He trusted them to cling to their charges.

His archers had made it to the trees and were launching arrows through the air that were inflicting a toll on the enemy.

When a galloglass he did not recognize came charging toward him with his sparth axe poised to strike, Angus crouched and swung his axe low, slicing across the man's legs. With a groan, the galloglass dropped to the mud.

At his side, Rob blocked the swords of the men rushing toward him. But against a sparth axe, he did not have the advantage. When a galloglass targeted his friend, Angus came from behind the enemy and, holding the handle of his axe at either end, he swung the wooden haft over the head of the galloglass and, with a sharp pull back, broke his neck.

Rob smiled his thanks and turned to confront another O'Donnell swordsman.

From what Angus could see, John was prevailing against his opponents. He had learned much since his first fight with their father.

The field of battle was soon full of clashing blades and men's shouts. The fighting grew close. Bodies were pressed in so tightly it was difficult to tell who was friend and who was foe. Exchanging his axe for his sword, Angus shouted to his companions, "Backs together!"

The four of them stood back-to-back, a mighty bulwark against the fierce enemy whose swords and axes were bent on their destruction. Keeping to the tight formation, they defeated all who came close. But not without injuries. Angus took a blade to one arm, slicing through his cloak though his mail prevented a crippling wound. Duncan sustained a blow from the flat side of a sword.

When the fighting subsided and the air gave rise only to the groans of the wounded, Angus scanned the battlefield. The rain that was now subsiding had washed much of the blood from the mail of those still standing. Turning to his companions, he asked, "Are you all well?"

"Aye," came from his cousin and brother.

"Only scratches," said Rob. "However, I think I should have taken you up on the chance to practice against your sparth axe. I see what you mean about their reach."

Angus was glad his friend could find humor in all of this. Gazing across the battlefield, he saw bodies strewn upon the ground. Looking for who stood and who did not, he glimpsed Turlough not far away. Blood ran from a cut on his face but he was standing and otherwise sound. His galloglass were with him, bloody but whole.

Finding his own galloglass he'd left to guard the young chiefs, he asked, "Do they yet live?"

"Aye, my lord. A few have wounds but none threaten their lives."

Relieved, Angus thanked God and his faithful men. He did not want to carry the body of any young chief back to Dunseverick and Lord Cumee. Let them learn a battle lesson that came at no great cost.

The day ebbed and, as darkness fell, both sides limped away to tend the wounded and count their losses. Angus cleaned his sword on the tunic of one of the fallen enemy and retrieved his axe.

"I have posted more guards around our camp," said Turlough, "though I expect Aodh will lick his wounds for what remains of this night."

CHAPTER 12

Tirconnell, Ulster, late December 1294

THEY HAD JUST won a battle against the O'Donnells, though regrettably the man himself, Donnell O'Donnell, had escaped, when news from the south reached Angus. Fitz Thomas' castle at Sligo had been destroyed by Aed O'Connor, at Earl Richard's urging. Angus was elated, thinking they would soon accomplish their goals and he could return to Dunseverick to celebrate Christmas with Áine O'Cahan.

His elation was short-lived.

Turlough had gathered Angus, Rob and the other leaders into the manor house at the end of the day to escape the sodden ground. They met by candlelight in a room warmed by a blazing fire. While they were discussing strategy, a messenger arrived from the south. Angus recalled seeing him before in Earl Richard's retinue. Tired, hungry and wet from days on the road, his cloak dripping rain, he did not ask for food or drink before blurting out what he'd come so far to say. "Fitz Thomas has raided the town of Kildare, burning the castle and slaughtering the people."

Gasps echoed around the room.

"There is more," he said, brushing his dripping hair off his face. "On the eleventh of this month, fitz Thomas captured Richard de Burgh and his cousin, William Liath."

Turlough stared open-mouthed, apparently unable to speak.

"Grave news, indeed," said Angus, gazing around at the long faces illuminated by the fire. The sound of the flames devouring blocks of dried peat filled the silence in the crowded room. "What has the villain done with them?"

The messenger shed his sodden cloak and accepted a cup of ale. "He has taken them to Lea Castle southwest of Dublin where 'tis said he holds them prisoner."

"King Edward will never allow such an atrocity to stand," said Rob, clenching his fist on the table until his knuckles were white.

The messenger nodded and cleared his throat. "Earl Richard's brother agrees, my lord. 'Twas Theobald who sent me. Word has been dispatched to King Edward of the earl's capture. All Ireland holds its breath to see what will happen."

"What is the state of de Burgh's army?" asked Angus, fearful all would be lost if the army had been destroyed.

The messenger frowned. "Well enough to be pursuing fitz Thomas with a vengeance as he presses into Connaught chasing after Aed O'Connor. Theobald now leads our army and is fast on the rebel's heels."

Rob crossed his arms over his chest and leaned back in his chair. "Fitz Thomas has stirred a hornet's nest. If he thinks to take Connaught while he holds the earl in prison, he makes a grave mistake."

"Can we free the earl and his cousin?" inquired Angus, wanting very much to be about such business. He was not familiar with Lea Castle but if the bulk of fitz Thomas' army was in Connaught, mayhap the castle was not fully manned and they could rescue the two men.

"Lea is a towered keep," said Turlough, "protected by walls, portcullis and drawbridge. The stone edifice rises four stories and is flanked on each corner by a circular tower. It cannot be easily attacked. Aside from that, we lack the equipment but Aed O'Connor will have it."

"That is one reason I have come," said the messenger, his gaze fixed on Angus. "Aed O'Connor stands with Theobald and both ask that you remain in the north. Our spies tell us that Domnall O'Neill, empowered by fitz Thomas' success and the capture of the earl, is preparing to attack King Brian in Tirowen."

"God's blood, the world has gone mad," said Angus. "A half-MacDougall attacks The O'Neill in Ireland while the rest of that treacherous clan attacks the Lordship of the Isles in Scotland."

The messenger nodded his agreement. "The fighting spreads as the Irish who resent the Normans are rising. There are rumors that those in the mountains, at peace for many years, have wasted Leinster and are attacking Newcastle."

Angus regretted they could do little to help Earl Richard much less Newcastle. "We must trust fitz Thomas is not so stupid as to harm King Edward's man in Ireland. Given the threat in Tirowen, our duty is clear. We must leave the south in Theobald's capable hands if we are to aid Brian O'Neill."

"I must stay in Tirconnell," said Turlough, "for the battles here will continue. But you should go. Tirowen must not fall."

Heads, cast in shadow by the firelight, nodded in agreement.

"Where might we find Brian O'Neill?" asked Angus. Tirowen was as large a kingdom as Tirconnell. Brian could be anywhere.

"When last we had word," said the messenger, "he was at Creeve, just west of the River Bann near Coleraine."

Angus pondered the location. Though he did not know it well, he thought it part of the territory the O'Cahans guarded for The O'Neill. Shifting his gaze to Ryan O'Docherty, one of the young chiefs who had been invited to the meeting, he asked, "Do you guard that land for Brian O'Neill?"

"That and more," said O'Docherty, raising his chin.

"Then it is there we must go. How close can I get to Creeve with my ships?" They could have walked east to Tirowen as it bordered Tirconnell, but Angus did not want to leave his ships vulnerable to the O'Donnells.

The young O'Docherty chief said, "The River Bann is wide and flows into the sea in the Red Earl's territory ten miles west of Dunluce. You can sail its waters south all the way to Creeve."

Angus shot a look at Turlough. "Under the circumstances, I would ask to take the O'Cahan chiefs with me and as many of their men as you can spare since we are the reason they are not in Tirowen to defend their king."

"You have given me a hundred men, Uncle. If you take the chiefs, I can make do with the rest."

"I will not leave you undermanned," said Angus. "For every O'Cahan man-at-arms I take from the hundred I gave you, I will leave you one of my Islesmen." Then with a smile, he added, "Treat them well. I will leave a ship for them, hidden near where we beached the ships at Rathmullan, until they are ready to sail. Tell them to sail for Dunseverick. If I am no longer there, I will leave word with Lord Cumee."

Turlough offered his hand and Angus grasped it. "Agreed."

At dawn the next morning, Angus, his companions and his men, save those he left with Turlough, retraced their steps east and sailed from Rathmullan in Tirconnell around the Inishowen Peninsula to the mouth of the River Bann.

Dunseverick Castle, northern coast of Ulster, late December 1294

ÁINE WAS STANDING in the great hall with her father and brother when Conor O'Docherty, one of the O'Cahan chiefs, came striding into the hall, his steel gray hair tousled and his face a mask of worry. His tunic and hosen were splashed with mud, doubtless from racing his horse across the boggy countryside. "Lord Cumee, have you heard of the battle that rages west of the Bann at Creeve?"

Her father narrowed his dark eyes. "What battle?"

"All I know was told to me by a villager fleeing the carnage. Domnall O'Neill attacked Brian, king of Tirowen. In the fighting that ensued, King Brian was slain along with many others. I must know what has happened to my son! He went with Angus Og Macdonald. Might they now be in Tirowen?"

Áine covered her mouth with her hand to hold back her gasp. It seemed every time a messenger or one of her father's spies returned it was with news of war, battle and death. She often thought of Angus Og Macdonald and the young O'Cahan chiefs who rode with him, knowing they had gone into danger. Daily, she offered up prayers for their safety. "Were they not in Tirconnell?"

Her father shook his head. "I cannot say where Lord Angus is now." His face twisted into a frown. "This is the result of that rebel John fitz Thomas Fitzgerald capturing Earl Richard! In the absence of the cat, the mice are demanding their day." Lowering his dark brows, he added, "I will soon know what Domnall has wrought."

Áine had seen that look in her father's eyes before. His fury rising, he would hold accountable all those who disturbed King Edward's peace.

Turning to his seneschal, her father asked him to summon the constable, his personal guard and his physician. When they appeared, he ordered his constable, "Assemble the men, every warrior who is not needed to guard the castle. We ride for Creeve within the hour." Then to his physician, "I do not know what we will find. We can hope some are only wounded but it might be wise to take a priest with us."

As the men hurried from the hall to fulfill his requests, she spoke her thought aloud. "Father, you will not arrive until twilight. Let me pack some food for you to take."

"Be quick, Áine. We dare not dally."

She stepped away to make her requests known to the servants. When she turned back to her father, he was speaking with her brother.

"No, Dermot, you cannot go. You must stay to command the castle should the fighting spread north to Dunseverick. Dunluce is still free, I think, so we should be safe but I will not leave our home or your sister and my grandson unprotected."

By his lowered eyes, Áine could see Dermot was disappointed not to be going but he would accept their father's will. Raising his chin, he said, "I will guard them with my life."

"Good." Her father strode to the stairs calling for his armor-bearer to bring his mail and weapons.

Áine turned to her brother. "He did not say that for my sake, Dermot, but knowing how you value your honor, he knew you would not fail to rise to the challenge. He knows well, as do I, that you are needed for more important things than my protection or even my son's. In our father's stead, you are now lord of the castle. You *are* The O'Cahan should he not return. The men will follow your orders without question."

He tossed her a grateful smile. "I shall comfort myself with that knowledge though I would rather join the fight."

She went to the kitchens to see that the food was ready. A short while later, her father descended the stairs in full armor, his sword and dagger at his side, his dark, silver-streaked hair combed back from his face and his helmet in hand.

Áine followed him outside and handed him and his guard the parcels that the servants had given her, enough food to sustain them for a few days. More of the small packages were handed out by the servants to the men who would ride with her father.

Though the Bann would supply water to drink and fish, if they had time to catch any, with the famine still raging across the land, they could not be assured food would be available. The unrelenting rain that had begun the year before continued so that crops were ruined and all of the country was suffering. Áine and the chiefs' wives did what they could but often it was not enough.

With a heavy heart, she walked back to the castle, sadness and worry weighing her down like a heavy cloak. In the midst of war and concern for those she loved, there would be no celebration of the Lord's birth, only prayers for her father and his men. And, to add to her sorrow, Finn was dying.

Creeve on the River Bann, Tirowen, Ulster, January 1295

THE SKY POURED rain and the air off the sea had been chilling as Angus' galleys left the coast and entered the waters of the wide River Bann. Miles later, nearing Creeve, the rain tapered off, leaving drops falling from the trees.

Angus' crews pulled the galleys onto the soggy grass at the edge of the river. As they trudged up the banks, trying not to slide in the mud, they heard the moans of the wounded.

Strewn across a grassy field were scores of bodies. Groans emanated from the few who yet lived.

Rob came to stand by his side, shaking his head as he stared at the grisly scene of blood-soaked bodies covering the wet grass. "Some think it a favored position to arrive late to battle. I say not, especially when 'tis an ally you come to rescue."

"Aye," said Angus. "By the look of this, Domnall struck unexpectedly. Some fought without mail, as if unprepared." Angus made it a habit never to take off his mail when anticipating war.

"Had we but arrived earlier…" Rob's voice trailed off.

Angus ordered his men to search for the living and call the physicians to them. Spotting a helmet several feet away bearing a silver crown, Angus walked toward the fallen king. The body had been pierced through many times, more like an execution than the death of one killed in battle.

He crouched next to the body. "This must be Brian O'Neill." In death, the king looked younger than his thirty years, his face unlined, his brown eyes fixed open in a glazed stare. Angus crossed himself and closed the king's eyes. "May God rest his soul." Standing, he said to Rob, "Slain by the same Domnall O'Neill who killed his uncle Niall Culanach."

Angus had expected a pitched battle in which he and his men would fight for Tirowen's rightful king. He had not expected to find the battle over and the king lying dead in his blood surrounded by the bodies of his men. A terrible end to the hope of a young life.

"He should have a king's burial," said Rob.

Angus nodded. "'Tis the least we can do."

Duncan and John came striding across the grass. "Those left alive," began Duncan, "say that Domnall talked of going to Coleraine to celebrate his victory."

Angus gazed off in the direction of the town across the wide river. "How many men does he have?"

"A few hundred," said John.

Angus sighed. "What of the villagers?" Creeve was not a large settlement but Angus could see cottages in the distance nestled among the trees. Yet he'd seen no peasants since they had arrived.

"Fled," said Duncan. "Most likely hiding their women, waiting until Domnall and his bloodthirsty lot depart."

"At least Domnall has not torched the town," offered Rob.

Angus inclined his head to his friend. "It would be most foolish to do so if he plans to reign in Tirowen. My thought is to let Domnall and his men drink their fill in the taverns of Coleraine while we tend the wounded and bury the dead. Then, as night descends and they are swaying on their feet, we will surround the town and see what we can. What say you?"

Rob scanned the battlefield and let out a sigh. "We came to fight. It hardly seems right to turn and go when the villains who did this are still close by. Yes, let us do as you suggest."

"Very well," Angus said to his companions, "Duncan, ask some of the galloglass to stand guard while we see to the wounded and the dead."

Duncan dipped his head and turned to go. Angus thanked God his cousin was a stalwart soul, one he could count on.

The physicians were busy attending the injured. Those who had survived the battle now sported white bandages and were being led to the nearest cottages to recover.

It took a few hours for the burials to be accomplished. Angus joined in the gruesome task, knowing it was his Christian duty to honor the dead. The threatening rain had yet to resume.

When the dead had been laid to rest and Brian O'Neill's body had been wrapped in a linen cloth for later burial, Angus encouraged his men to eat but he forbade cooking fires so as not to announce their presence to the enemy.

He was standing with Rob and Duncan, chewing on a stale crust of bread when he heard hoofbeats. Casting the crust aside, with his hand on the hilt of his sword, he looked up to see a large contingent of armed men riding in from the north, their helmets and mail visible in the waning light.

John came running up, his face smudged with dirt. "'Tis Lord

Cumee!"

Angus strode to meet Cumee O'Cahan, sitting astride a handsome black courser. He had never seen the Irish lord arrayed in mail and weapons, prepared for battle. 'Twas a formidable sight.

"We came as soon as we heard," said Angus. "But, as you can see, we were too late to save Brian O'Neill."

Lord Cumee and his men dismounted. "A sad end to the young king. The people will feel Brian's loss. And what of Domnall O'Neill?"

"The wounded tell us he and his men hied off to Coleraine to celebrate their victory."

Lord Cumee looked toward the town as his men gathered around him.

"Is there a place near that is fitting for King Brian's burial?" asked Angus.

"The Abbey of the Bann in Coleraine would serve and 'tis close," said Lord Cumee. "None can object as the abbey was founded by us. I will have my men see to it." Then searching the group of men who had come to stand behind Angus, Lord Cumee said, "What of the O'Cahan chiefs who came with you?"

"They are all here, my lord," Angus assured him. "Some of your O'Cahan men were wounded in battle in Tirconnell but none of the young chiefs have wounds of grave concern."

"That is a relief. Their fathers begin to inquire of their wellbeing."

Angus turned and beckoned Ryan O'Docherty to him. The young chief stepped forward. Splashed with mud and blood from his labors at Creeve, he bowed before Lord Cumee. "My lord."

Lord Cumee smiled at the young chief and reached out to squeeze his shoulder. "Your father is the reason I am here." To Angus, he said, "Do you have a thought as to what we should do concerning Domnall?"

Angus nodded. "Earl Robert and I have discussed what's to be done." Then they explained what they had planned, and Angus said, "What is your preference, Lord Cumee?"

"If I know Domnall, he is well into his ale by now and the townspeople who have not fled are serving his needs, willingly or otherwise." Then, with a smile that verged on a smirk, he added, "Let us pay the villain a visit."

A short while later, with their five hundred men waiting outside, Angus followed Lord Cumee and Rob into the Coleraine tavern where they were told they could find Domnall O'Neill.

Loud conversations and sounds of merriment filled the darkened room that smelled of sweat, blood and spilled ale. Angus' two companions made a fearsome pair, one a respected Irish lord who wore an invisible cloak of authority, the other a battle-tested knight of noble birth. Angus was proud to be in their company.

With a nod of his head, Lord Cumee gestured to a man holding court amidst a group of men, still streaked with the dried blood of the slain. A woman sat on his lap, her long dark hair hanging in tangles about her shoulders. Whether she was willing, Angus could not say but as O'Neill grabbed at her tunic an expression of fear crossed her face.

Lord Cumee stepped forward in a bold manner and the boisterous conversations died. From the look on Domnall's face, it was clear he had expected no opposition, no pursuing army.

Angus was content to let Lord Cumee speak as he had responsibility for guarding these lands and, hitherto, the O'Cahans had been at peace with the O'Neills.

Domnall abruptly stood, throwing the girl off his lap and knocking over his chair. "Cumee O'Cahan! Do you come to pay homage to the new King of Tirowen? Or, mayhap to offer me your beautiful daughter as a prize?"

"Neither," said Lord Cumee with firm emphasis.

Angus ground his teeth hearing Domnall speak so blithely of Lady Áine.

"Why ever not?" asked Domnall, his tone dripping sarcasm. "As you can plainly see," he swept his hand in a wide gesture around the tavern crowded with his men, "we are celebrating this day's victory and Tirowen's new king." The wide smile on his face left no doubt as to who he thought that was.

Angus was not impressed with Domnall O'Neill. The half-MacDougall was not physically imposing nor of handsome visage. A slight man with stringy dark hair, he had the eyes of a predator and the frozen scowl of a man who devised strategies to his own good, damning the consequences.

"You celebrate too soon, Domnall," said Lord Cumee, "for you do not yet know what the Earl of Ulster will have to say about this day."

"De Burgh?" Domnall laughed and was joined by his men. "What has he to say about *anything*? He sits in Lea Castle's dungeon."

"For now, mayhap. But King Edward will have the last word."

Domnall's face lost its smile and the tavern whispers suddenly quieted. A smirk slowly formed on his face and his chin jutted out. "And you would know about that as one of de Burgh's minions?"

"I know of King Edward and he will not like the great disturbance that fitz Thomas and his allies have imposed on Ireland."

Ignoring these words, Domnall cast a glance at Angus and Rob, flanking Lord Cumee. "Who are these two you bring with you?"

"Oh," said Lord Cumee, in what Angus recognized as feigned courtesy, "did I fail to introduce them? Forgive me. This warrior," he said, gesturing to Angus, "is no ordinary galloglass, if a galloglass can ever be ordinary. No, he is Angus Og Macdonald, Lord of Kintyre, whose brother Alexander, Lord of the Isles, is the King of England's agent in the Hebrides. And this knight," he said, turning to Rob, "is no ordinary knight. He is Sir Robert Bruce, Earl of Carrick, who has recently come from King Edward's court. Each is a friend of Richard de Burgh and can speak to what the English king might think of the earl's capture."

Domnall took another drink of his ale, the liquid running down his beard. "I have no love for de Burgh," he spit out, "and would not hear from his friends." Turlough had told Angus that Domnall was from an O'Neill faction that was hostile to the Normans and hated Richard de Burgh. Twice before, he had failed to take power in Ulster. On both occasions, he was deposed by the Red Earl.

"Nonetheless," said Lord Cumee, "you might wish to know that with us are nearly five hundred warriors who would assure my two friends are heard."

One of Domnall's men came to him and whispered in his ear. Domnall's gaze narrowed on Angus. "I see. Islesmen and O'Cahans.

What an interesting alliance. Well, I for one have no love for the Macdonalds. You are the enemies of my mother's kin." Shifting his gaze to Rob, he said, "Nor do I defer to any Scot who is a Norman knight."

Angus was only mildly surprised that Domnall's hatred should extend to Normans in Scotland as well as the Macdonalds. Having no words for such a rogue, Angus remained silent. Rob, likewise, said nothing but his look of disdain for the man before him was clear to all.

Lord Cumee did not rise to Domnall's baiting. Instead, he said, "I warn you, Domnall. Treat the people well if you ever think to reign over them. You have killed their much-loved king and you now have a difficult hill to climb to earn their respect." Turning to go, he paused, looking back. "Mayhap at another time, we can speak of your installment as King of Tirowen if, indeed, this is allowed to stand. But do not cast eyes toward my daughter, nor speak of her again."

Angus was gratified that Lord Cumee had put Domnall in his place concerning Lady Áine. His reminder to Domnall of the O'Cahans' hereditary role in inaugurating the Kings of Tirowen was a jab that surely hit home. Though the rebel might think otherwise, Domnall was not yet king.

Angus followed Lord Cumee and Rob out the door. Domnall's men parted to allow them a clear path to exit. Once outside, John and Duncan approached with an anxious look.

Before Angus could speak, Lord Cumee drew them aside with his chiefs. "We have enough men to take them, but Brian O'Neill's son is very young and, without an O'Neill to install in Domnall's place, the best course of action is to wait. Let us see to Brian O'Neill's burial and return to Dunseverick to await news of de Burgh."

Dunseverick Castle, northern coast of Ulster, February 1295

WINTER HAD LINGERED and the skies were rarely blue on the Ulster coast where once Áine had walked with her young son. Each day seemed to bring more rain, blurring the landscape and keeping the land from drying out.

On the rare occasions when the rain paused, Áine would walk the promontory, lifting her skirts to avoid the muddy ground. Sometimes she would ride to the villages with men from the castle guard or Dermot to see if they could help their people. Roofs had to be repaired and the women helped with the thatch. With so many chiefs and men gone, there was much to do and many mouths to feed.

One particularly dreary day, Finn, who had not left the fireplace all morning, breathed his last. She knew it was coming and yet the reality of it hit her hard. Sitting next to him on the rug in front of the fireplace, she ran her hand over his rough coat, remembering their times together. "I will miss you, dear friend."

Her son came to inquire of Finn's health. All in the castle knew he was close to death. "Is Finn all right?" he asked in his little boy voice, his dark blue eyes full of concern.

"He has left this life, Little Prince. We must lay him to rest beneath the stars and remember what a wonderful hound he was."

Tears rolled down her cheeks as she spoke. Brian looked from Finn to her. "Mama, are *you* all right?"

Though Brian had seen birds and small creatures die, the death of something or someone he loved was new to him. "I am well, Little Prince," she said, brushing his bright red hair from his forehead. "But I am sad Finn is gone. We must thank God he was ours for a time, eh?"

Brian nodded and laid his head on Finn's gray body. The sweet gesture of goodbye caused Áine's tears to fall afresh.

Later that day, the rain abated and they buried Finn on a spot where the flowers would grow in the early spring. While Brian was sent to his nap, Áine joined her brother on the castle battlements where he went each afternoon to watch for their father's return.

With their backs to the sea, they fixed their eyes on the approach from the south. Her brother's face was creased with worry.

"He will return," she encouraged, all the while trying to convince herself it was true. "If the reports are correct and Domnall O'Neill has slayed King Brian, he will not touch Father. Earl Richard would never consent to Domnall's remaining The O'Neill were he to do so."

"We've no news of the Red Earl's fate, Áine, and it has been months."

"King Edward will not allow his earl to rot in Lea Castle's dungeon."

As they were about to leave the battlements, Áine glimpsed riders in the distance. "Dermot, look! Can that be Father?"

"Yes!" said Dermot. "Thank God."

Her father rode at the head of his men and, from what Áine could see, he was uninjured and whole. Dermot ran for the stairs leading down.

Relief flowing through her, Áine followed.

In the bailey, Áine waited for her father to dismount, listening as Dermot pelted him with questions.

"Father, was there a great battle?" Dermot asked with eager interest.

"Nay, Son. When we arrived, the fighting was over and Lord Angus' men were burying the dead."

"Lord Angus was there?" she interjected.

"He was, though he and Earl Robert arrived too late to help. They had come from Tirconnell where they were told of Domnall's intent to invade Tirowen. I exchanged words with the villain while he was in the process of drinking himself to perdition to celebrate his stolen title."

By now, her father had shed his weapons and handed them to his armor bearer. Inside the castle, she bid him sit by the fire. While he and Dermot continued their conversation, she asked a servant to bring cups of hot spiced wine.

"Thank you, Áine," her father said, accepting the drink. To Dermot, he said, "Is all well here?"

"Yes, Father," replied her brother. "Except for the constant rain and the shortage of food, which is much as it was when you left. But news has come from Dunluce." Dermot handed their father the message that had arrived earlier that day.

Her father read the missive and nodded. "Some good news at least." Looking around the hall, he asked, "Áine, where is that hound of yours who is always by the fire?"

With downcast eyes, she said, "Finn is gone, Father. I buried him this day."

"I am sorry, Daughter, for I know you loved him much." He reached his open palm to her and she placed her smaller hand in it. A feeling of strength infused her when he closed his strong fingers around her hand and squeezed. There was the smell of sweat and horse about him. She did not mind.

Brian's nurse brought her son into the great hall just then and he ran to her father's open arms. "Grandfather!"

When Brian was ensconced on her father's knee, running his small hand over her father's beard, Áine asked, "Did Lord Angus sail for Kintyre?"

"Not yet. He is bringing his ships from the River Bann to White Fields Beach. Soon, he will be with us again." Her father gave her a curious look and Áine forced herself to a bland expression. She did not want to explain why her heart was gladdened at the prospect of Angus Og Macdonald's return to Dunseverick. She did not fully understand the implications herself.

"He and Sir Robert want to see what transpires with Earl Richard and Connaught before they return home," said her father. "Their skill at arms may yet be needed."

"They were not injured in Tirconnell?" she asked.

"When I last saw them, both were hale and hearty along with Lord Angus' cousin and brother. Our young chiefs survived and will return with them."

Taking Brian's hand and leading him to his nurse, she returned to her father. "You will want a bath and I must see to a meal for you and your chiefs."

"Both would be welcome," he said rising. "Come with me, Dermot, and I will tell you more of what transpired."

As the two walked to the stairs, Áine turned to her father's constable. "Have a guard posted on the promontory to watch for the ships. When they are spotted, have horses brought to White Fields Beach for Lord Angus, his companions and the young chiefs. I will give you some food for his men."

He bowed. "It shall be as you wish, my lady." It pleased Áine that her father, used to her taking care of such things, no longer thought to ask, and his men, aware of this, willingly followed her orders.

ANGUS AND HIS SHIPS sailed toward the wide beach north of Dunseverick as the sun was low beneath a dark cloud-covered sky. He could not recall the last time he had seen the sun since setting foot in Ireland.

The voyage east from the mouth of the River Bann had taken them the better part of the day, as they fought to make headway in rough seas on the Atlantic coast. Much rowing had been required and his men were tired and hungry. Angus wanted to sit before a warming fire with Áine O'Cahan, sharing enough wine to allow him to forget the endless rain and Brian O'Neill lying dead at Creeve.

"I never thought I would be so glad to see this beach," said Duncan, joining Angus and Rob in the prow. John was in the stern talking to the helmsman, who was guiding them in.

"Aye," agreed Angus. "Mayhap we will have a respite from the constant rain. The men would be happy for it." As his ship neared the sand, he looked up to see O'Cahan guards waiting with a dozen horses.

"They must have seen us as we sailed past the castle," he said to Rob. What little he knew of Áine O'Cahan told him she was the one who would have watched and thought to provide them mounts.

Once on the beach, he confirmed the lady of the castle had sent the horses as well as food. "Yes, my lord, they are here at her request," said the groom.

Angus waited until the ships were beached, the sails doused and his captains assembled around him before he addressed them. "My companions, the O'Cahan chiefs and I will ride ahead to Dunseverick. Follow when you can and set up camp near the castle as you did before. We will likely be here for a while, at least until we know what transpires concerning Richard de Burgh. We may yet be called to another battle, for I do not know the fate of Connaught. Fish and hunt as you can for other food may be scarce. We are still awaiting the return of the last ship from Tirconnell and, if God be merciful, a hundred of our men with it."

They nodded, obviously glad for a rest.

Once they were mounted, Angus, Rob, Duncan and John rode for Dunseverick Castle with the young O'Cahan chiefs. Angus drew his fur-lined cloak around him against the sharp February wind.

By the time they arrived in the bailey, the sun was a sliver of gold at the horizon beneath dark clouds billowing with the wind.

Lord Cumee met them in the great hall, welcoming him, his companions and the young chiefs back to Dunseverick. Lady Áine stood to the side, smiling up at Angus, her dark eyes alight with an inner fire.

Servants took their cloaks and Lord Cumee said, "We will dine shortly. In the meantime, join me at the fire. There is news from Dunluce."

"Gladly," said Rob, moving toward the fireplace where a large fire blazed.

"Aye, said Angus, "the sea was not accommodating and the fire is welcome."

"There is spiced wine, Lord Angus, for you and your companions," said Lady Áine. "You shall be warm in no time."

As the men took their seats around the fire and sipped the hot spiced wine that tasted to Angus of cinnamon and cloves, Lord Cumee said, "Edward has taken steps to assure the release of Earl Richard and his cousin. John fitz Thomas has been summoned to a parliament in Kilkenny a fortnight hence, and he is ordered to bring his prisoners."

CHAPTER 13

Dunseverick Castle, north coast of Ulster, March 1295

ÁINE SCANNED the great hall for her son, hoping to take him for a walk while the weather was fair. His nurse said she had left him with Nessa but while the handmaiden stood at the window, looking out on the promontory, Brian was nowhere to be seen.

"Nessa, where is Brian?"

Nessa spun around, a calculating smile on her face, one curly brown lock in the middle of her forehead. "Do you per chance refer to Lord Angus' shadow?" At Áine's puzzled look, Nessa said, "The lad is outside with the Macdonald lord, Mistress." Turning back to the window, she said, "I believe they are discussing ships. Lord Angus is carving a small model of his galley for Brian."

Áine was not surprised that Brian had joined Lord Angus outside. Ever since he had returned from Tirowen, she had observed her young son following him and his Islesmen about like a forlorn pup.

Joining her handmaiden at the window, Áine watched Brian gazing intently at Lord Angus' quick work with a knife as he sat on a bench, carving the soft wood. She could not hear all of their conversation for the wind and the distance but it was clear her son was asking many questions.

At four years of age, Brian was beginning to get freckles so the Macdonald men had taken to calling him Brian "Balloch", meaning freckled. Brian did not like being teased about the marks but he enjoyed the company of the Islesmen so he accepted the teasing as the price of their fellowship. Áine thought the emerging cluster of brown dots scattered across the bridge of her son's nose adorable. He was growing into a handsome boy, tall and straight, with a stout heart, who was eager to learn a man's ways.

It was no wonder he was attracted to the Lord of Kintyre, a man of noble presence, whose actions on the practice field had daily proven his skill with weapons. Earl Robert had remarked to her that Lord Angus had taught him much about the long axes. Her father had frequently sought Lord Angus' advice and Brian had taken notice.

"It is kind of him to take time to make a gift for Brian," Áine said to Nessa.

"If you ask me, Mistress, Lord Angus seeks to win the heart of the lad as a step to winning the heart of his mother."

Áine's cheeks warmed. Nessa had always been one to see more than others. Since Lord Angus had returned, he had paid Áine much attention but always with proper manners and deference to her as the daughter of The O'Cahan. If she had seen more in his sea blue eyes than she was willing to admit she did not dwell on it. "He is aware I do not wish to wed."

"You have told him?"

"I have."

Nessa turned back to the window and continued watching Lord Angus with Brian. "That may be dictating his approach. Angus Og Macdonald is not like Rory Maguire of Fermanagh, whose affection for you is open to all. The Lord of Kintyre is a warrior familiar with strategy in battles. His approach would be less obvious. I think he knows what he wants and has set about to get it. I suspect your father knows it, too."

Nessa had been right about Rory Maguire. Concerned about her wellbeing after the battle at Creeve, he had come to Dunseverick, arriving shortly before Lord Angus returned. He paid court to her, always the gentleman. But the grandson of the King of Fermanagh paid little attention to the handsome Lord of Kintyre or Earl Robert. Rory did not look down upon them but she was certain he did not consider them a threat to his suit. They were merely visitors from Scotland who would leave in due time.

At her father's invitation, Rory had lingered at Dunseverick. At this moment, he was in the stables looking over a new colt her father had offered him.

Áine was determined to hold her father to the bargain he had made. If she married again, it would be to a man of her choosing.

ANGUS HELD UP the small wooden galley, turning it in his hand. "Aye, she's a yare ship." He had carved the hull, oar holes, mast and sail, all from the soft wood. A child's toy but one that delighted the lad.

"Can I have it now?" Brian asked, eagerly reaching for the small replica of Angus' galley. The lad's red hair, bright in the sun, needed a trim for it fell nearly into his eyes as he stared at the toy in wonder.

He handed the wee ship to the boy. "'Tis yours, Little Prince," he said, using the byname his mother called him.

Brian held the toy with reverence. "I must show Mama and Grandfather."

"Before you go, may I ask you a question?"

The lad faced him and, holding the little galley close to his chest, nodded.

"Do you miss your hound very much?"

The lad nodded slowly. "Mama, too." Angus had seen the sadness in Lady Áine's eyes when she stared at the spot where the wolfhound, Finn, used to lie before the fire.

"Would you like another, mayhap a pup?"

This time, the nod was vigorous.

"Very well, I will see what I can do. But say nothing of this. 'Twill be our secret until I can make it happen, all right?"

The boy nodded and Angus held out his hand. "Men shake their hands to seal a bargain, an oath of honor between them. Will you shake mine?"

Clutching his new toy to his chest with one hand, Brian held out his other hand and Angus slowly shook it, not a warrior's grasp but at least the boy understood the solemn occasion of a man's oath of honor.

Brian ran back to the castle and Angus rose, turning his gaze to the sea. It was deep blue today and, floating in the canvas of blue above the sea were a few white clouds. He could just make out the shadow of Kintyre in the distance. He had not seen the sun in a long while and he was grateful for its dry warmth. Such weather might not last long and he was anxious for news. The last they had heard was that the fighting in Connaught had subsided in anticipation of the parliament at Kilkenny, which took place three days ago. Since then, they'd heard nothing.

He had been away nearly a year and could not stay much longer. He must return home to help his brother with the troubles in Scotland. In the meantime, a ride to Dunluce with Rob, Duncan and John might serve to inform them of the outcome of the Kilkenny parliament. Besides, he remembered that Dunluce had several wolfhounds.

Dunluce Castle, north coast of Ulster, March 1295

ANGUS WAS SURPRISED to see a large group of Earl Richard's men in the outer bailey as he and his companions and guard rode in. "Something must have happened for the earl's men to be here in such numbers."

The guard at the gate was smiling when he admitted them.

"Do you know why these of the earl's army are here?"

"Yes, my lord. The fighting has ceased in anticipation of the earl's release. The men you see here rode ahead with news that King Edward has made his desire known that the Earl of Ulster and his cousin are to be freed."

"That is very good news," said Angus, dismounting and handing the reins to a groom. "Who led the men here?"

"Sir Thomas de Mandeville, Seneschal of Ulster," the guard replied. "He comes to prepare for the earl's arrival. You will find him in the great hall."

Angus thanked him and, together with his companions, headed toward the massive gray stone castle. They took the narrow bridge across the chasm between the outer bailey and the stone edifice that loomed before them on the huge rock high above the sea.

Inside the great hall, they found Sir Thomas speaking with the earl's steward. The Seneschal of Ulster's fair countenance had taken on a weathered look. His wheat-colored hair was longer than when Angus had last seen him. As might be expected following weeks of fighting in the rain and living on spare rations, he was thinner and his pale skin, once reddened from the sun, lacked its former robust look.

At Angus' approach, the steward bowed to the seneschal and took his leave. Sir Thomas turned. "Greetings, Lord Angus, Earl Robert. I welcome you and your companions. Your arrival is auspicious, as we expect news of Earl Richard's release and that of his cousin, William Liath."

"By King Edward's command, or so we are told," put in Rob.

"Yes, my Lord Carrick. The king has made clear he will not tolerate John fitz Thomas' overstepping. And, for his rash actions and brutality in Kildare, the rebel will surely lose all of Connaught before this is done. Or, so one would hope."

"As he should," said Duncan. "Fitz Thomas has caused much of Ireland to rise against the king's agents and is responsible for many deaths."

Sir Thomas shook his head. "It was all so unnecessary." Then walking toward the table, he said over his shoulder, "I was just about to dine. Will you join me? Your guard as well. As you can see, there is plenty of room."

"Aye," said Angus, "and we thank you." Dunluce's great hall, bustling with nobles and men-at-arms the last time he had been there, was nearly empty save for servants and a few guards at the door. The mural that had begun the last time he was here had been completed with noble men and women dressed in bright colors and finery moving about on the large painting.

Walking toward the table, Angus' attention was drawn to the two wolfhounds sprawled in front of the fireplace. Gnawing on bones, they barely looked up.

The long table where their meeting had occurred the year before was bare save for candles that cast light on the jugs of what he presumed was ale. They took their seats and the servants set pork pastries before them, together with bowls of apples and nuts. The meal was modest by an earl's standards but sufficient to quell their hunger. These were not times for feasting with famine surging across the land and Angus was grateful that he had food. He'd had less on the road to Tirconnell. Still, Angus expected the fatted calf—if there were a fatted calf still about—would be slain when Earl Richard returned. "Is the earl's family still at Dunluce?" he asked, seeing no children about.

"Nay," said Sir Thomas, setting down his cup of ale and wiping his mouth with his sleeve. "A contingent of the earl's men escorted them to Carrickfergus shortly after the earl departed for Connaught. Lady Margaret is likely keeping her servants busy preparing a celebration now that Earl Richard will soon be home."

As they ate, they spoke of the war in the south, Sir Thomas telling them of all he and the earl's army had experienced. "We were prevailing until fitz Thomas burned Kildare and slaughtered its people, drawing us away from Connaught. The earl was taken in a brutal battle near Kildare. The rain had left the slopes slick with mud so that the horses had great difficulty in maintaining their footing." He paused to take a drink. "In addition to the earl's release, there is other news. Aed O'Connor has survived and is restored to his kingship."

"Good news, indeed." Angus then provided the seneschal with his own report. "We fought with Turlough O'Donnell in Tirconnell against his half-brother. The battles were fierce but resolved in our favor before we were called away to Tirowen." With a sigh of regret, he added, "Alas, we arrived too late to save Brian O'Neill. Domnall slayed him at Creeve."

"A tragic end to a promising young ruler," replied Sir Thomas.

"A truly unpleasant man, is Domnall," said Rob.

"I would agree with that assessment," said Sir Thomas. "Domnall has engaged in perfidy before and Earl Richard had to call him to account. I should have known if he won, he would kill Brian O'Neill."

"It seems he has no love for Earl Richard or any Norman, even one with the blood of Scots running through his veins," said Rob.

"Or Macdonalds for that matter," added Angus.

Sir Thomas shook his head as he stared into the distance. "Sir Hugh Bissett and I helped install Brian as Tirowen's king. I am sorry he is gone."

When the conversation subsided and the servants began removing the remains of the meal, Angus asked Sir Thomas, "Is the earl's huntsman about? Or, perhaps the keeper of the earl's hounds?"

"I cannot say where the huntsman is at this moment but the kennels for the hounds are near the stables. The steward can take you there. I will call for him."

Amid puzzled looks from his companions, Angus thanked Sir Thomas and got to his feet. "I have an errand I must attend to. I will check back with you before we leave for any news from Kilkenny." To his companions, he said, "Join me?"

"Why not?" said Rob. "I have never seen Dunluce's kennels."

With Duncan and John close on their heels, Angus and Rob followed the steward to the kennels. "Roger here is the keeper of the hounds," said the steward, gesturing to a young man with slight build and a head of nearly black hair. "He can show you the wolfdogs."

The kennels were circled by a wooden fence. The floor, raised above the ground, was comprised of boards covered with straw. "To keep the hounds from lying on the ground, which might make them sick," Roger explained. "Of course, the earl's favorites lie about the great hall."

"I have noticed," said Angus. "I grew up with hounds lying about in my father's castle, though they were deerhounds."

A wooden ramp led from the floor to a suspended platform at one end. "For winter," said Roger, "it is warmer there." Pointing to a large pottery bowl on suspended metal feet, he added, "We also have a brazier to heat the kennels on the coldest of days."

The kennels opened onto a large grassy area to which the hounds had free access. Bowls of water sat around. "We change them twice a day," said Roger, his expression full of pride in his caring for the earl's prized hounds.

"You are to be commended," said Angus. "All looks well-tended." Seeing a few wolfhounds in the kennels, he asked, "How many does the earl have now?"

"Five. Two are in the hall and two here. One is at Carrickfergus, the children's pet. Three males and two females."

The mention of female hounds encouraged Angus to ask, "Might you have a litter of pups on the ground?"

Rob shot him an inquisitive glance.

"We did three months ago. All the pups are spoken for save two and one of those, a female, will go to the earl."

"And the other?"

"There have been inquiries but no one has been granted the pup. I think the steward was waiting for the earl's return."

Hoping he might be close to his goal, Angus asked, "Is it possible that I might have the one not spoken for?"

"You will have to ask the steward, my lord. Is it for you? If so, I am certain he will look favorably upon your request."

"Actually, the hound would be for the son of a great lady whose wolfhound just died. The lad is Brian O'Neill, the young son of Lady Áine at Dunseverick."

"The daughter of The O'Cahan?" Roger asked excitedly.

"Aye, the very lady."

"If the wolfdog is to be a gift for the Jewel of the Roe's son, I am certain the steward will give you the pup."

"The Jewel of the Roe?" asked Angus. "I have never heard Áine O'Cahan called that."

"She is the greatest beauty of Ulster, my lord. We call her that for her beauty and far more. She is highly valued for her acts of charity by all who live along the River Roe that flows through Limavady."

Unsurprised by this information, which only confirmed what he believed about the lady's character, Angus smiled. "Well, then, might we see the pup?"

The keeper of the hounds disappeared into the grassy area in a part of the kennels not visible from where Angus and his companions stood.

While he was gone, Duncan said to Angus, "I begin to see what you are about."

"Very wise move, Angus," said Rob, "if you have an interest in the lady, which I perceive you do."

"I think my brother is clever," said John. "What lass can resist a puppy?"

Angus was considering a response when Roger returned with a large squirming mass of gray fur in his arms. The pup had ears that flopped down, big dark eyes and white on his paws and chest. A crimson collar circled his neck with gold studs marching across the wide band and a gold ring in the middle.

"A handsome fellow," said John.

Placing the pup into Angus' arms, Roger said, "He is a friendly one and smart, quick to learn."

"He must weigh three stone already!" said Angus, feeling the weight of the squirming young hound as he tried not to drop him. The pup reached his head up to sniff Angus' short beard, then swiped his pink tongue over Angus' nose, making him laugh.

"He likes you," said John.

"I will get his leash," said Roger.

"Does he have a name?" asked Angus, admiring the hound's expressive eyes.

Taking the leather leash from a peg, Roger handed it to Angus. "He is Lir, after the Irish god of the sea."

Angus chuckled. "Ah, then it was meant to be."

John stared openmouthed and Duncan rolled his eyes.

Rob laughed. "You could not want for a better reminder of the gift giver."

Ignoring his companions, Angus set the pup on the ground and attached the leash to the golden ring on his collar "Come, Lir, let us go speak to the steward."

Angus was in the process of sealing the bargain with the steward in the great hall when the castle door opened and Earl Richard and his guard strode inside. Thinner from his imprisonment and his red hair grown longer, the earl bore the marks of his long ride from the south. Dust and mud were splashed liberally onto his hosen and tunic. He did not wear the gilded belt of an earl this time. Instead, a plain leather belt held his sword.

"Earl Richard!" said Sir Thomas. "We have been anxiously awaiting news. To have you here is an answer to our prayers. Welcome back! Is your cousin with you?"

The earl removed his gloves. "William Liath will remain in Connaught for a sennight helping to set all to rights, then he will join me."

A servant brought a tray with cups of ale. Earl Richard took one and directed his attention to Angus and his companions. "Welcome to you, Lord Angus and Earl Robert, and to your companions." The earl shifted his gaze to the wolfhound pup sitting on the rushes at Angus' feet. "Is this one of mine?"

"Aye, my lord," said Angus. "Born while you were away, but not the one your hound master is saving for you. This is another meant for the son of Lady Áine O'Cahan, if you agree. Her wolfhound, Finn, died while you were gone."

The earl managed a smile. "I do agree and let the pup be my gift to you for all you have done for our cause keeping the Fitzgerald allies busy in Tirconnell and Tirowen. I want to hear about all what has transpired but, first, I must attend my bath. I stink of the road."

His steward stepped up. "All is ready for you, my lord. And the servants are attending your guard."

Angus and his companions stayed long enough to tell the earl all he wanted to know. Once the report was made, Earl Richard recounted the tale of his confinement in a dismal dungeon with little food. "'Twill not soon be forgotten."

"What now, my lord?" asked Angus.

"The king is sending John Wogan to Ireland. He is Edward's justice itinerant and an experienced resolver of disputes. He will be charged with working out a settlement between the Fitzgeralds and us."

"I imagine that will take some time," said Sir Thomas.

"Wogan is good but such resolutions are never quickly accomplished. Too, I expect the king will summon fitz Thomas to London to explain himself."

Angus exchanged a glance with Rob, recalling his friend's description of Edward's court and how the king could melt a man's heart with fear. Then, facing Earl Richard, he asked, "Is there more we can accomplish now?"

"No. You have done all I have asked. I thank the Macdonalds and you, Earl Robert, for coming to my call. I am gratified our alliance formed long ago still stands."

"Aye, it does," said Angus, thinking of the Turnberry pact he had witnessed while his father still lived. "With your permission, we would take our leave."

"By all means." Then, with a chuckle, he said, "Do not forget to take with you the pup asleep at your feet." Angus looked down to see the pup had fallen asleep with his muzzle next to Angus' toe.

Angus was in good spirits as they departed for Dunseverick. Lir rode on his lap, swathed in a blanket. John offered to take Lir up on his saddle but Angus declined. "I want him to get used to my scent."

Dunseverick Castle, north coast of Ulster, March 1295

ÁINE HAD JUST returned from a meeting of the chiefs' wives where they put together baskets of food for those who were suffering from the famine when she heard a shout from the battlements. "Riders coming!"

She hurried to the inner bailey, expecting her father and Dermot who had ridden out to survey the nearby O'Cahan lands. Then, too, Lord Angus, who had ridden out shortly thereafter, might also be returning. Twilight would soon be upon them and she was anxious to have all safe inside.

Rory Maguire and her young son left their game of chess where Rory had been describing the rules of the game to Brian and followed her outside.

Leading the troop of mounted men was Angus Og Macdonald, riding one of her father's finest horses, a dark chestnut with a glossy coat. He wore no mail and his hair fell to the shoulders of his deep blue surcoat. Asleep on his lap was a wolfhound pup that woke as Lord Angus pulled rein. Popping its head up, the pup looked around, giving all an inquisitive stare.

"Mama, Mama!" shouted Brian at her side. "Lord Angus has brought me a pup!"

The Lord of Kintyre beamed at her son. "I have indeed, Young Prince."

"Here, let me help," said Earl Robert as he dismounted and handed his reins to his squire. Reaching up, he took the pup from Lord Angus and set him on the ground.

"Give the lad the leash," said Lord Angus, dismounting and handing his reins to a groom. "The pup is his." Then to Áine, he said, "I hope you approve, my lady. The wolfhound is my gift to both of you."

Brian handed her his toy galley and dropped to his knees, hugging his new puppy, who responded enthusiastically, licking his face. "He likes me!"

"Aye, he does," said Lord Angus, watching the two of them.

"A fine gift," said Rory Maguire, rather ruefully.

Áine smiled at Lord Angus. "We have been in sore need of a hound to fill our hearts, my lord. It is gracious of you to provide one. Did you find him at Dunluce?"

"Aye. He is one of Earl Richard's pups, freely bestowed upon you at my request."

"What shall we call him?" Brian asked.

"His name is Lir," said Lord Angus.

A flicker of surprise flashed through Áine's mind. "The great sea god of the Irish myths?"

"Aye, 'twas the name the keeper of the hounds gave him."

"Most appropriate," Áine said, looking at her young son, smitten with his new pet.

Lord Angus returned her a wry smile. "I thought so."

She greeted the Earl of Carrick more formally, as she might have Earl Richard, briefly curtseying before him. Rory joined in welcoming Earl Robert back to Dunseverick.

Áine welcomed Lord Angus' cousin and brother. Then to all of them, she said, "My father and Dermot should return shortly. You have time to refresh yourselves before supper."

Brian and his new wolfhound bounded into the castle. Áine, hurrying to catch up, told her son to take him to the kitchens to be fed. That dealt with, she returned to her guests, who had just entered the hall. "Is there news of Earl Richard?"

"We have been wondering," put in Rory Maguire.

"Aye," said Lord Angus, accepting a cup of ale from a servant as they entered the hall. "He is free and has returned to Dunluce."

"Wonderful! My father will be happy to hear it. And what of fitz Thomas?"

Earl Robert said, "King Edward intends to deal with him and is sending a man to mediate a settlement between him and Earl Richard."

She wondered why they had not thought of that before. She supposed there was not time given the fitz Thomas attacks. Still, if a settlement approved by King Edward could avoid another war, it was worth trying.

"If you will excuse us, Lady Áine," said Lord Angus, "we will change for the evening meal. We all smell of horse, mud and, for me, hound." He smiled at Rory and turned to go.

While they were above stairs, Áine's father and brother returned with a good report. "Our lands will survive the storms and the famine but food, save fish and waterfowl, will be meager for a time. There is very little grain."

"The same is true in Fermanagh," said Rory, "though we have fish from our rivers and loughs."

When Lord Angus and Earl Robert joined them, her father said to Lord Angus, "I have welcome news. As we were riding past the valley where your men are camped, one of your captains stopped us to say that your last ship has just returned from Tirconnell. Those men are now camped below the castle with the others."

Lord Angus looked relieved. Mayhap he had been worried though he had said nothing. "With your permission, my lord, I will go to speak with them and join you a bit later. Rob and Duncan can tell you the news from Dunluce."

"Go," said her father. "If it were my men, I would do the same."

When Lord Angus and his brother left to tend to that task, Brian proudly brought out his new pup for his grandfather to see. "Lord Angus gave him to me, Grandfather. I have fixed him a bed by the fire."

"A good gift. I hope you thanked the lord."

Brian looked up at her father with a guilty expression.

"I thanked Lord Angus for both of us," she said. "I am sure Brian will convey his thanks in due time."

Gazing up at her father, Brian nodded.

Her father reached down to scratch the pup behind the ears. "He'll make a fine hound."

"The pup is from Dunluce," she offered.

"Dunluce produces the best," said her father.

"His name is Lir," Brian proudly announced.

"Lir, is it?" Her father smiled. "I might have known."

"The news from Dunluce is good," ventured Earl Robert. "De Burgh has been freed by the Kilkenny parliament, and has returned to Dunluce. Lord Angus, his brother and cousin and I met with him."

Duncan said, "Earl Richard anticipates John Wogan will be sent by King Edward to arbitrate a peace."

"All Ireland will welcome that," said Rory.

Her father nodded. "Some of the chiefs told Dermot and me that the earl was free but it is good to have the information confirmed. Still, I wonder what might follow. I am glad King Edward is involved though I doubt a peace will hold."

When Lord Angus returned from seeing his men, he was in good humor. "They are all safe. A few wounds but none serious. We have been fortunate."

Over supper that evening, a meal of fish tarts, rabbit stew and roasted quail, her father and the other men discussed England's drain on Ireland. "In spite of the famine, King Edward ships what grain we have to England for his men who fight his wars. He drains our coin as well, adding to the taxes he imposed years ago."

"The king will need men to fight his wars in France, Wales and mayhap even Scotland," said Earl Robert. "I expect he will draw upon Earl Richard for some of those."

"De Burgh has already resisted one such demand by the king," said her father. "An offer of high pay and the cancellation of debts owed the crown did not sway him."

Áine watched her brother for a reaction but Dermot's face was without expression. *Would he go if Earl Richard did? Would Lord Angus?* Guilt assailed her for feeling more concern for them than for Rory.

She did not have to ask her last question aloud as her father turned to the Macdonald lord. "I suppose you might be asked for your ships to transport men to Scotland if Edward were to challenge King John Balliol."

"Aye, 'tis possible," said Lord Angus. "For now, we are taken up with King Edward's affairs in the Isles. His enemies are our own." Then, with a glance at Earl Robert, he said, "I am committed to a free Scotland but not one under King John's rule." Áine was aware the Bruces had been contenders for the Scottish crown, which would put this younger Robert Bruce in line to one day be King of Scots.

After the meal, Lord Angus invited her to walk with him on the promontory. "While the rain holds off," he said. She made her apologies to the others and invited Brian to join them. He brought his pup, the two already inseparable.

The brisk wind caused Áine to draw her cloak around her. Gazing up at the moon, a bright silver orb gliding between billowing clouds, she said, "It feels like rain."

"Aye, mayhap tomorrow."

Brian and his pup ran a short way ahead. Áine watched them closely ready to call Brian back from the cliff's edge if he ventured too close. "Will you be staying at Dunseverick for a time?" she asked him, though with the war in abeyance, his return to Scotland was likely imminent.

"Nay, I must go to my brother. Alex will be anxious to have my ships and my men to add to our fleet guarding the Isles. I hope to sail at first light." He must have detected disappointment in her silence, for he added, "But I promise to return."

"You will be welcomed if you do." She would say no more. Already, she knew she would miss him as would Brian.

The next morning as Lord Angus was preparing to depart, a messenger rode in from Dunluce, carrying a missive for the Earl of Carrick. "This came to us because they thought you might be at Dunluce, my lord." Bowing before Earl Robert, he handed him the scrolled parchment.

The young earl's face paled as he read the letter. "I must return to Carrick immediately. My grandfather is dying."

"Allow me to take you, Rob" said Lord Angus. "I will send all of my ships, save the one in which I sail, to Dunyvaig on Islay while I take you to Turnberry."

The earl's gray eyes were full of gratitude. "Thank you, Angus."

"We sail within the hour," the Lord of Kintyre assured him. "You will be home tonight."

Áine rode with her brother and Brian to the beach where Lord Angus' ships rested on the sand. She sat atop her horse with Brian in front of her. Dermot was next to her astride his palfrey with Lir in his lap at Brian's insistence.

Lord Angus strode forward to meet them as his men were getting out the oars and loosing the sails. He relieved Dermot of Lir and lowered the pup to the sand. Dermot dismounted and took Brian from Áine's lap. Lord Angus helped her down.

"I wish you Godspeed, my lord." It was hard for her to say more, so she let her eyes speak the words she could not say. She hoped he would understand.

He kissed her hand and patted Brian's head, reaching down to admonish Lir to "be a good hound." The pup's tail beat rapidly against the sand in response.

She watched the ships as his men pulled at the oars, rowing them out to sea. Lord Angus stood in the bow of his galley his foot braced on a small wooden platform. His face was set toward the east, the wind blowing his hair behind him.

He looked very much as she might have pictured the mythical Lir in his ship *Wave Sweeper*, gliding across the beckoning sea that was his kingdom. Angus Og Macdonald was a man of the sea and ships, a man who loved his Isles. If she ever gave him her heart, she would one day cross those seas to live in his Isles. His people would become her people and her son would be raised a Scot.

CHAPTER 14

Dunyvaig Castle, Lagavulin Bay, Isle of Islay, February, 1296

"'TIS NOT ENOUGH for Edward to have Wales," Angus said, looking up from the letter he had just received from his friend, Rob. "It seems he would have Scotland as well."

Alex shifted his attention from the papers he had been poring over—papers that had come for him in his capacity as King Edward's bailiff in the sheriffdoms of Lorne, Ross and the Isles. In addition to having these privileged positions, formerly held by Alexander MacDougall of Argyll, King Edward had made Angus' elder brother Admiral of the Western Isles. His assignment, among others, was to hold the MacDougalls in check. "It was bound to happen," said Alex. "Edward has been signaling his intention to be Scotland's overlord for some time. So, what else does the young Robert Bruce have to say?"

Glancing at the letter, Angus said, "He and his new bride, Isabella of Mar, are sojourning at Carlisle Castle."

Alex sat back and crossed his arms. "She is a good match for him, of noble blood, an heiress to a large part of Inverness, and her father is one of the new Guardians. But why Carlisle? 'Tis in England and the

Bruce castles are in Carrick and Annandale."

"According to this, John Comyn has seized the Bruce lands and castles. With the death of Robert the Noble, King Edward made Rob's father the governor of Carlisle Castle, providing them a safe haven in England. Apparently, the king intends to make Carlisle his headquarters for the attack on King John." Angus read on and then looked up. "There is other news. Edward has promised Rob's father the crown of Scotland if Balliol abdicates."

"John very well might. Even the Scots who once supported him have lost faith in his kingship. That may be what is behind the appointment of the new panel of Guardians who are seeking help from France."

"I cannot think Edward will allow such a thing," said Angus.

"Nay, he will not, which is why the king is raising a great army to muster at Newcastle. One of these papers," Alex said, fishing for the document on his desk, "calls for me to transport a large number of fighting men from Ireland to meet King Edward in England this spring."

Angus' ears perked up. "Whose fighting men?"

"Richard de Burgh's, among other magnates. The king must have met the earl's price for de Burgh has finally agreed to go. Then, too, the settlement John Wogan is cobbling together between the de Burghs and Fitzgeralds may require it." Alex lifted his head and stared into the distance, his dark brows drawn together as if contemplating. "Do you remember James Stewart, the High Steward of Scotland, whom you met at Turnberry those many years ago?"

"Vaguely." Angus had met so many nobles and their sons the day he had first met Rob he could scarce recall but a few. The Stewart brothers, then in their twenties, would now be in their thirties. "I recall they had the look of warriors, their brown hair long and their beards short."

"Well, de Burgh has sought King Edward's permission for the marriage of his sister, Gille, to wed James Stewart."

"Ah, I see. Edward dangles a carrot before the earl, to be given only when he heeds the call to arms."

"I expect so. And the king would hope to secure James Stewart's loyalty in the bargain as well. Meantime, I am told Sir Thomas de Mandeville, one of de Burgh's staunchest allies, will join the Irish force going with the earl."

"I know Sir Thomas," said Angus, gazing out the window. His mind was not on the Norman knight he had met at Dunluce but on the fair Lady of Dunseverick. It had been nearly a year since they had said goodbye and not a day passed he did not think of her. Or dream of her. If de Burgh was gathering a large force to sail from Ireland, surely Cumee O'Cahan would contribute to their numbers.

Angus' gaze drifted through the window to the winter ground outside the castle. When he had first risen, it had been covered with a layer of frost. Even now, though the sun had melted the glistening crust, only his warm cloak and the fire that blazed in the stone fireplace kept the chill at bay. He considered the task that would likely be his, taking another, larger fleet of ships to the coast of Ulster. "Spring, you say?"

"Aye. De Burgh has access to Irish ships but he will need ours to bring to Edward a thousand men as well as the knights' warhorses. You will have to sail within a fortnight." Then with an amused expression, he added, "At least you will not have to sail with fitz Thomas."

"Fitz Thomas! Why would that name come to mind? Since the king disciplined him, I had not thought to hear it again, at least not soon."

"Because, dear brother, King Edward has summoned him to fight in Scotland as well, which, now that I think of it, might be awkward for de Burgh. The feud between the Fitzgeralds and the de Burghs may be settled for the moment but it still smolders beneath the surface."

"Aye," said Angus. "We have not seen the end of that one."

Dunseverick Castle, north coast of Ulster, March 1296

THE CALL TO ARMS had spread across the length of Ulster, summoning men to fight in Scotland with Earl Richard. In response,

Áine's father had called for O'Cahan men to go. With the effects of the famine still being felt in the land and knowing King Edward would provide his army with food, many young men were answering the call, especially those who could fight. It meant one less mouth for their families to feed. So, it was with great anticipation that Áine had watched the coast for she knew he would come.

Surely the Lord of the Isles would send his brother, Angus Og, to fetch so large a force.

The morning was sun-filled and she and Brian were walking the promontory with Lir, now a gangly pup more than a year of age. At forty-two inches and five years of age, Brian was just seven inches taller than the hound. They were a pair to behold as they walked together before her, the young master with his red hair blowing in the wind and his arm around the wolfhound's neck.

"Mama, look!" came Brian's cry as he pointed to the sails that appeared like clouds on the horizon.

Áine experienced a lightness in her chest at the glorious sight of so many galleys heading toward them. "It must be Lord Angus' fleet." She counted twenty-two galleys but it was the one in the lead with its golden pennon flying proudly from the mast that held her gaze. *He has come.*

Gray and white herring gulls soared between the cliffs and the oncoming ships, shrieking as if to announce the Lord of Kintyre had returned.

"PUT UP THE HELM!" Angus shouted the order that turned the ship toward the long stretch of flaxen sand. As the full force of the northwest wind billowed the sail, he gave the command, "Douse sail!" Satisfied the ship was slowing as it approached the coast, he smiled as the galley gently glided toward the wide beach.

Standing in the bow next to him, Duncan said, "I can guess the reason for that smile on your face."

"'Tis only pleasure at returning to this shore with the sun shining and no battle before us."

"Aye, there is that. But I say 'tis more. What of the lady, the 'Jewel of the Roe'? Do you smile for her as well?"

Angus silently acknowledged the truth of it. He longed to see her after a year's separation. He was anxious, too, to learn if she was still of a mind not to wed again. "One is always happy to greet a beauty such as Áine O'Cahan."

Duncan gave him a skeptical look as the galley's hull slid over the sand. Angus' men jumped down and pulled the ship ashore. Once on the beach, Angus gave orders to his captains to set up camp. "In the next day or two, expect a large contingent of men, some mounted. You will need to prepare to load the horses. I expect we may be required to sail from here to Dunluce for the rest. I will know more once I pay a call on Earl Richard."

Angus had planned to walk the few miles to Dunseverick Castle but, as he gathered his satchel, Dermot O'Cahan appeared on the grassy hill above the beach with one of the castle guards and four horses in tow.

Grinning, Dermot said, "You were spotted."

Angus waved. "And glad I am 'twas so!" Dermot, now in his early twenties, a few years younger than Angus, had the self-assured look of the heir to The O'Cahan, a man who did not shirk from duty. Proudly sitting atop a fine dapple-gray gelding, he wore the tunic of an Irish nobleman's son, decorated in elegant braid. His dark hair and beard were well-trimmed.

"I wasn't sure if Earl Robert might be with you so I brought four horses."

Angus said, "You could not know the Earl of Carrick is in England, serving Edward at Carlisle. With your permission, I will give the fourth horse to the head of my guard."

"He is welcome to it," said Dermot.

The ride to Dunseverick was short and the time passed quickly as Angus and Dermot rode ahead of the party, sharing their news.

"Has the peace held?" asked Angus.

"For now, only because everyone is focused on Scotland. De Burgh and fitz Thomas will both be fighting in those battles."

"Your father and sister, they are well?"

"They are, thank you. My nephew thrives, growing ever taller.

How fares your brother?"

"Somehow, he manages to sire more sons while occupied with King Edward's business. We are pressed by our enemies in Argyll. The MacDougalls have banded with the Comyns and MacRuaris to waste our lands."

"I do not envy you."

Lady Áine was standing in front of the castle door with young Brian and his wolfhound as Angus rode in. Dismounting, he handed the reins to a groom. Brian ran to Angus, bowing hurriedly before saying, "Lord Angus, see how big Lir is!"

It was not only the hound that had grown. Dermot was right. The lad was taller and more freckles dotted his fair skin. Angus scratched the top of Lir's gray head, more elongated than the pup's he had seen a year before. "Aye, the hound will be enormous."

Looking past the boy to his mother, Angus glimpsed the sun in her smile. Could it be that his longing for her had made her more beautiful than before? He left Brian to Duncan and John and crossed the courtyard to her.

Kissing her raised hand, he said, "I hope that smile is for me, my lady." He was certain she blushed. "Have I reason to hope you missed me?"

"I smile for all of Dunseverick's visitors, my lord." Mayhap she saw the disappointment in his eyes, for she added, "but particularly for the ones whose faces I have longed to see." Without waiting for him to reply, she greeted his companions, who had joined them, and called for her son. "We have prepared refreshments for you, Lord Angus. Do your men who remain with the ships require anything?"

"Nay, my lady. They will be fine. Since we had to leave room for horses, we brought meat, bread and chickens aplenty."

The large sack he had asked his guard to carry was being lifted down. "We bring grain for you." Angus was glad he'd thought of that, recalling the rain that had destroyed so many crops in Ireland.

She began walking toward the great hall. "That was very thoughtful. We will put it to good use." Angus went with her, young Brian and Lir beside him and his brother and cousin falling into step behind.

Once inside the hall, a servant accepted the sack of grain from

Angus' guard. Lady Áine took her young son by the hand and excused herself to lead Brian to a chamber off the great hall.

The boy looked back at Angus.

Angus, seeing the eagerness in the boy's eyes, said, "I will visit with you later."

A fire blazed in the great hearth, adding much-needed warmth to the cavernous chamber. The coverings had been pulled back from the windows allowing the sun's rays to fall upon the rushes that smelled of herbs, yet the stone hall would have been dimly lit and colder without the multitude of large beeswax candles that were set in iron stands.

A servant came to take their satchels and cloaks. Angus wore no mail, only a tunic and surcoat over his shirt and hosen. His cloak was fur-lined as he preferred at sea except in the summer. When he had no need to wear a helmet, he had taken to wearing a hat, particularly when calling upon noblemen. The dark brown felt cap, pointed at the front, shaded his eyes from the sun. This, too, he handed to the servant.

Seeing Lord Cumee look up from where he stood by the fire, Angus and his companions strode toward him. "The three of you are a welcome sight," said the Irish lord. A servant brought them ale and, once each had a cup in hand, Lord Cumee said, "Earl Richard will be relieved to know you have arrived. As you might imagine, now that the decision has been made to go, he is anxious to deliver his army to Edward."

"I was told there would be a thousand or more, some mounted," said Angus. "Will they all come to us here or might we need to sail to Dunluce?"

"Once we send word, there will be hundreds here within a day but some will doubtless gather at Dunluce. There is a wide beach west of the castle where you can set your ships ashore."

ÁINE HAD TAKEN Brian to his tutor, who had begun his lessons a fortnight ago. "I might have suggested waiting until he is older," the priest told her, "but the lad is bright and willing." That done, Áine went to the kitchens to advise the cook of the number of guests they would be entertaining that night. She had planned the meal just after she spotted the sails.

"Will they stay long, my lady?" asked the cook.

Áine saw the concern in her eyes. "I should think only a few days. They are here to transport the Earl of Ulster's army to England. And Lord Angus says we need not feed his men who have come with his ships. But he has brought us a gift of grain."

With the scarcity of grain, they had learned to adapt the dishes they served. While there were oats enough for the horses and grass fodder for the cattle, bread was rarely seen on the table except for Sundays. Still, the castle garden thrived so that vegetables and herbs were plentiful. The orchards produced apples and hazelnuts in season, which they shared with the people. Fish and fowl were often part of a meal. And eggs, cooked many ways, were offered at breakfast.

She had wondered if the Isles had suffered from the same storms that had destroyed crops in Ireland and the rain that followed, leading to famine. But with Lord Angus' gift of grain she thought not. Like Ireland, England had experienced a dearth of grain and other foods. Were the Isles blessed by God so as to thrive? Lord Angus had never spoken of going without though, as an even-tempered man, he was not given to complain. Whatever the conditions, she felt certain he would go to great lengths to keep his people from starving.

When she returned to the hall, her brother and father were sitting by the fire talking. Lord Angus was gone, along with his brother and cousin. Lir was lying next to her father. As she approached, the hound got to his feet, wagging his tail. Scratching his wiry head, she asked her father, "Has Lord Angus returned to his men?"

"No," said Dermot. "He has ridden to Dunluce with Duncan and John to inquire of the earl the number of men and horses he expects will muster there."

"Ah," she said, understanding. "Do you think he will return for dinner?"

Her father gave her a curious smile. "Yes, he was very specific about that. He said, 'Please tell Lady Áine that we will return for the evening meal, assuming, of course, we are invited.'"

"You told him he was invited, yes?" She was horrified that Lord Angus should have to ask.

"We told him, though I do not think wild horses would keep him away." This was followed by her father's hearty laugh.

Dermot joined in. "Aye, Sister, the man is fair gone for you."

Embarrassed, Áine frowned at their silliness. "You jest at the expense of Kintyre's lord."

"Mayhap," said her father, "though we do not like him less for the cause he gives us to tease you. 'Tis all in good fun."

Though she did not like being the source of their amusement, she could not deny the joy she felt at the return of the Scottish lord, even if she was not the reason he had come.

THE SUN WAS SETTING as Angus and his companions, their business finished at Dunluce, rode hard for Dunseverick. They crossed the wide green swath perched high above the sea that ran along the coast between the two castles. Flame-colored clouds, scattered across the sky, made for a splendid sight, one Angus appreciated after the year before when all he encountered in Ireland were dark clouds and rain.

As they approached the castle, the last rays of the sun shone on the stone edifice rendering it a glowing palace. Angus recalled the poetry of the Irish bards that spoke of a woman who lived in such an enchanted place. So fair was she that the sight of her melted men's hearts. Surely Áine O'Cahan was such a woman for she had melted his.

Racing beside him, Duncan shouted, "Are we in haste for dinner?"

By the look his cousin gave him, Angus knew he did not speak of food. "Nay, I have a grander purpose."

"As I thought," said Duncan with a grin. "Very well, we shall race with you."

John grinned. Angus' younger brother never complained about racing horses for he was a fine horseman.

They arrived with time to change for the evening meal but when Angus observed Lord Cumee standing before the fire staring into the flames and none but servants in the hall, Angus took his leave of John and Duncan, saying he would see them at dinner. His guard, too, was dismissed until the evening meal.

Crossing the hall to the O'Cahan lord, Angus said, "Might I have a word?"

"Of course. How went your visit with Earl Richard? Are his men ready?"

"Aye, they come. A day more and all will be assembled. As soon as we leave here with what men we have, we will sail to the beach west of Dunluce and from there to England. But that is not why I would speak with you."

"Oh?"

Angus studied O'Cahan's face, guessing he was entering his fifth decade. There were strands of silver in his dark hair and beard. Still, he stood strong and just as proud as when he confronted Domnall O'Neill a year ago. Angus knew this Irish lord would have the last word. "'Tis about your daughter, Lady Áine."

Lord Cumee's face took on a serious mien.

Though Angus feared a negative response, he forced himself to be direct. "I would ask for your blessing to court her and seek her hand in marriage."

A smile spread across the older man's face. "I wondered how long it would take you to broach the subject. Your eyes give you away whenever she is about."

"Aye, they might."

"You should be aware, Lord Angus, that many have sought my daughter's hand and she has accepted none. The last to go away disappointed was Rory Maguire, the grandson of the King of Fermanagh and a worthy young man."

Angus remembered the redheaded man who had stayed with the O'Cahans. He was relieved to know such a fine candidate had not been accepted.

"She is not eager to wed again," continued Lord Cumee. "Áine's first marriage was not of her choice, either in the man or the timing of it. But she was a dutiful daughter and complied with my will. You have my blessing to court her, even my encouragement. I knew your father, you see."

"I did not—"

"No, I said nothing of it as I wanted to see if the son had the father's mettle."

Angus raised his brows, waiting with trepidation for the verdict.

"He does. But it is not I you have to persuade. If Áine is to wed a second time, and I hope she does, the choice will be hers. Win her heart and you will have her hand."

"Thank you, sir," Angus said, relieved. "I could not ask for more. Doubtless I have before me a difficult task, for I know she loves her family and her home and is well content."

"If anyone can win her, 'tis you. May God go with you, my son."

With a lightness in his step, Angus hurried to his chamber to wash and change.

Since many chiefs and men would be sailing in the next day or two, he was not surprised when he returned to the hall to see that dinner would be a small affair.

Angus barely noticed the food, occupied as he was speaking with Lady Áine who dined beside him. At another time, they might have spoken of gardens and summer fairs, but instead, they talked of the war that was coming to Scotland, and of his family's decision, along with the Bruces, to swear fealty to King Edward. He told her of the Turnberry Band, sealed a decade before. "It comes down to loyalties forged in the fire of mutual interests and to siding with friends against long ago enemies."

"I see," she said, her lovely brown eyes full of understanding. "It is not so different in Ireland. But is not a Scotland ruled by her own king free of England something to be sought?"

"Aye and I believe it will come. But King John is weak and the nobles do not respect him. He never should have been king. Like Scotland's nobles, King Edward holds John in low regard. Yet John defies England's king, a grave mistake. Once he is gone, Edward will look again to the Bruces. At least that is the hope. Until then, we serve Edward against our enemies, the MacDougalls of Argyll and the Comyns, the Earl of Buchan and the Lord of Badenoch."

As dinner drew to an end and hazelnut tarts appeared, Angus said to her, "Will you walk with me on the promontory? There may be stars to see tonight."

"I would like that. Brian will be sleeping but Lir may join us."

Angus returned her a smile. "I am fond of the hound."

"Like the man who gave him to us, Lir is good company. And he's been known to take down a wolf."

"If there be wolves about, I am glad you and Brian have the hound."

Her eyes sparkled in the candlelight and the flames reflected in her silken hair as she said, "There will be more to see tonight than stars. Since it is clear, the lights in the north should appear."

"We have the lights in the Isles, too. I should like to see them with you."

Making his apologies to Lord Cumee and Dermot and leaving his brother and cousin to wonder what he was about, Angus accepted their cloaks from a servant and escorted Lady Áine to the door leading to the promontory. Lir fell into step behind them. Angus' head guard, who had finished his meal, took up a stance with the O'Cahan guards at the door.

They stepped into the chill night air. Across the expanse of sky, a multitude of silver stars flickered like diamond dust scattered on black velvet. A nearly full moon hovered above them. Between sky and sea, bands of violet and green light danced on the horizon, like waving curtains of colored fire. Angus had observed the unusual moving lights before but this display was striking; even the moon did not dull the effect. Angus said, "Some believe the lights are harbingers of war."

"I wonder if that is because war seems always near." Her voice held a note of sadness.

He took her hand and, placing it between his hands, turned toward her. Her delicate skin felt cold to the touch; his hands were warm. "I know you have suffered from the wars here in Ireland, my lady. You have lived through them. And I know, too, that you love your home. Much is at stake for Scotland in this coming war. We Islesmen were long free of any crown but now that we must acknowledge one, I would have it be Scotland's. But the country must be led by a strong and wise King of Scots."

"Then I fear for you, my lord." Her hand slipped from his as she took a few steps forward. Lir had gone ahead, scouting the promontory.

Angus joined her. "It will not be an easy road but I cannot avoid it, my lady, nor would I." He would not speak of their future together until he could be certain he had a future and she wanted to share it. Knowing she was devout, a request for her prayers would not go amiss. "Will you pray for me while I am about the business of war?"

She inclined her head toward him. "I will."

"Am I correct in thinking you have a choice and it is not merely whom to wed but whether to wed at all?"

"That is so."

"Then I see my task is to convince you that a life with me would not take from what you have."

She cast him a glance. "You are insightful, my lord."

"In this path, I tread carefully, yet I must ask, will you wait for my return?" Angus held his breath, for her answer would tell him much.

There was silence for a moment as she gazed into the brilliant star-studded sky. Then, turning to him, she said, "I do not believe I can do otherwise, my lord."

Her reply did not tell him all he would have liked to know, but if she could not fail to hope for his return, then mayhap he already had a place in her heart. "That being the case, my lady, might we begin with you calling me by my given name?"

She turned to face him, the moonlight shining in her eyes. "Angus." On her lips, it sounded like a prayer.

He reached for her hands. This time, they were warm. "Áine." He leaned forward, slowly, to give her time to refuse if she were unwilling. When their lips touched, she yielded to his kiss. Letting go of her hands, he drew her close, holding her shoulders as their bodies fit together beneath their cloaks.

The kiss continued, their breaths mingling. Angus had never tasted anything so sweet or so tempting. His heart pounded in his chest urging him on but, not wishing to overwhelm her, he held his desire in check. Ending the kiss, he pressed his lips to her forehead and inhaled her scent. She smelled of spring flowers like those blossoming on the cliffs. "Know that your face is ever before me," he said into her hair.

THE NEXT AFTERNOON, under gray skies, Áine and her brother watched from the rise above White Fields Beach as Lord Angus and his men loaded ten horses onto the ships, leading them one by one up the gangplank laid through the opening in the gunwale. Brian, seated in front of Dermot, stared in fascination. Lir, who had trotted behind, sat next to them on the sand.

The Islesmen had adapted the galleys for their task by adding wooden stalls, mangers for fodder and slings for the horses' protection should they encounter rough seas on the sail to England.

Angus' men carried out his orders without question, working with him as a team. He checked all before he gave his approval. She imagined his attention to detail might be the same when he led men into battle.

Finally, when all was ready, Angus came to bid her goodbye. He lifted her from the saddle and, with her feet on the ground, she looked up to meet his intense blue gaze. The brisk wind swept her cloak and her long hair behind her. Her chest ached to think what could befall him.

"My lady," he said. "We sail for Dunluce and then to England."

She laid her hand on Lir's head, for he had come to sit beside her. "I hope you will not long be away."

Gazing into her eyes, he said, "You have my heart, Áine. I cannot stay away."

He reached for her hands and pressed a kiss to her fingers. With a wave to Dermot and Brian, he turned to go. A depression settled upon her. As before, she had wished him Godspeed but this time was different. This time, he was taking a part of her with him.

She rode back to Dunseverick with Dermot and Brian. They arrived in time to see the Lord of Kintyre's ships pass in front of the castle, sailing west. She pressed her fingers to her lips, still feeling his mouth upon hers as if it were imprinted on her skin.

What if he did not return? She had to consider the possibility. He had told her of his desire to be a part of a free Scotland. He had told her he was going to war. She knew he would not always fight with the might of King Edward behind him, but rather, he would have to face that might. She had already lost one husband to the sword. Would a sword claim this man, too? Did she have a choice when her heart longed to be with Angus as it had never longed to be with another man?

She watched the galleys' sails slip from sight like a dream fading at first light, leaving the memory of his kiss her only keepsake.

Dunaverty Castle, Kintyre Peninsula, May 1296

BY THE TIME ANGUS had safely deposited de Burgh's Irish forces in England and returned to Dunaverty, it was April. Duncan and John had committed to stay with Angus to help keep the Isles in King Edward's peace. Since then, at Alex's bidding, Angus had taken a fleet of ships north on a few occasions to hold in check the MacDougalls and their allies, the Comyns and MacRuaris, all related by blood or marriage and committed to a common evil purpose.

The MacRuaris had continued to attack the Isles of Harris, Lewis and Skye. Angus believed it was no longer for pillage. Using war as an excuse, they now fought to add to their territory.

Hungry for news from the mainland, he was overjoyed to receive the messenger who arrived with a letter from Rob.

"Do not keep us in suspense," said Duncan, as he and John watched him unfold the parchment.

"Aye, Brother," said John, "what news of Scotland?"

Angus scanned the letter before responding. "Much has happened. King Edward's army, gathered first at Newcastle, marched north toward the River Tweed. De Burgh's Irish forces joined the king at Roxburgh. While that was happening, at the end of March, Balliol's army, led by John Comyn, Earl of Buchan, besieged Carlisle Castle."

"Aye, he would," said John. "Comyn is the power behind Balliol."

Angus said, "The Earl of Buchan's cousin, John the Red Comyn, was among the magnates participating in the attack. Let me read you what Rob has written."

It was not so much an attack on the English as an attack on the Bruces. We were able to successfully fight them off due, in part, to the fierce determination of the villagers and Carlisle's women, who dropped boiling oil and stones from the ramparts. Lacking siege equipment, the Comyn forces hied off to Annandale, one of our holdings that King John gave to the Comyns. From there, they rampaged across the countryside, burning homes and massacring the people.

A few days later, on Good Friday, King Edward attacked Berwick after the town refused to surrender and the people taunted him from the city's walls. That was unwise. We are told there was a great slaughter. Edward spared no one, slaying men, women and children. Blood ran in the streets for two days.

"I have seen battle, as have you," said Duncan, "but I have never seen such a slaughter. Even bairns killed without mercy. I can only imagine the horror of it."

"Aye, there has been savagery on both sides." Then reading on, Angus said,

In a gesture that surely lacked substance, King John then sent a message of defiance to Edward, renouncing his homage and fealty he claimed was extorted from him. Incensed, Edward pursued the Scots north to Dunbar where he had a great victory and captured many nobles, knights and men-at-arms. You will be interested to know that the Comyns were among them. Cowardly King John did not deign to make an appearance. I daresay, he will not be king much longer.

Angus looked up from the letter. "I would like to believe with the Comyns in Edward's gaol we will have less trouble here in the Isles but, alas, I fear otherwise. Edward will undoubtedly settle with them for their services. The MacRuaris, who remain at large, are no more than freebooters who will continue to raid. The MacDougalls, even should they swear fealty to Edward, will doubtless ignore their oath and continue to attack Macdonald lands to harass and destroy. Miscreants all of them."

"King Edward does not trust them else he would not have given your brother, Alex, so great a role in the west," said Duncan.

"Aye," said Angus. "So, I had best see what Alex would have me do."

Duncan shot a look at John and, receiving a nod, said, "We will go with you."

Angus was about to put away the letter when he happened to glance down and saw there was a bit he had yet to read. "Rob has added a postscript." Reading it to himself, he smiled. "You will want to hear this."

> *I cannot end this without telling you of my joy with Isabella. Her father might have arranged our marriage but it is a love match for us. Wish us happy for Isabella believes she is with child, due at year's end.*

"This calls for a toast to Earl Robert and his bride," said John.

Duncan flicked his golden hair out of his eyes and, with a hint of a smile, said, "Let us indulge in some of that mead I brought from Saddell we have yet to open."

"Aye," agreed Angus. "One drink before we sail to Islay."

CHAPTER 15

Dunyvaig Castle, Isle of Islay, August 1296

ANGUS HAD JUST returned from Morvern where, at Alex's request, he and John had retrieved their mother from Ardtornish Castle. "She will be safer on Islay away from the fray," his eldest brother explained, "and with another child due soon, Juliana will welcome her presence."

After the Scots' defeat at Dunbar, and the capture of a hundred Scottish nobles, there had been little resistance to Edward's rule except in the west. There, Alexander MacDougall, Lord of Lorne, despite having sworn allegiance to King Edward, continued his attacks on the Macdonald holdings, often joined by his allies, the Comyns and MacRuairis.

Angus, his brothers and cousin, Duncan, along with Alex's constable and senior captains, had gathered this afternoon around a long table in Dunyvaig's great hall to discuss the situation. The day was warm and the fireplace cold but candles were set about to add to the light filtering in through the narrow windows open to the breeze.

Since he had personally observed the situation on Mull and Skye, the men turned to Angus, awaiting his report. He also had Duncan's report from Harris and Lewis where he had met with the chiefs there. "The situation is dire in places," Angus began. "The MacDougalls and the MacRuaris have split their forces, attacking separately and sparing no one. We need more men to counter their attacks in the north."

Alex sat back, the flickering candle revealing his frown. "I have just received word from the Earl of Ulster that John Balliol has abdicated, which is good news and expected. King Edward has him in custody, bound for the Tower of London. As a result, Earl Richard will be leaving Scotland. He begs transport for his army back to Ireland."

"The two goals are not incompatible," said Angus. "We need men and de Burgh has them, freed from their commitment. Some of the Red Earl's army will surely be willing to serve the Macdonalds, provided we pay them. And, of course, we will transport them home when Edward's peace is restored."

"Aye," said Alex, leaning forward. "Edward pays us a sufficient amount to cover their pay, although he is late with his last payment. I found it necessary to compose a letter to him about the matter. I have also asked him to order the nobles in Argyll and Ross to aid us in our struggle against the MacDougalls, else we will find ourselves taking fire from that quarter."

The constable spoke up. "My lord, word has just arrived of a battle in Argyll between John MacDougall, Alexander's son, and the Campbells of Loch Awe. If the report be true, Sir Colin Mor, chief of the Campbells, was killed, shot through with an arrow."

Low groans sounded around the table, as if the men had received the blow themselves, for Sir Colin was known to many and respected by all.

"Sir Colin is dead?" asked Alex, a dark shadow crossing his face. The constable's expression was solemn, his eyes downcast. "To lose our grandfather in that manner is a travesty. Our mother will be devastated to learn her father has been killed. It was only a short while ago he attended the marriage of Richard de Burgh's sister."

"Grandfather..." muttered Angus, remembering the man of great bearing who, in a playful mood, had tossed him into the air when he was just a small lad. "How cruel a fate to be brought down by a wretched MacDougall."

Alex nodded. "'Tis one more sin to add to their account." He thanked his constable for the report, though it was sad news. "We can do nothing about it now. But there will come a time when vengeance will be ours."

"All the more reason to add to our numbers," said Angus. "Assuming you agree, Alex, I can take part of the fleet north to retrieve de Burgh and his army. At the same time, I can recruit as many Irishmen to our cause as are willing. Mayhap we can hold the Comyns and MacRuaris at bay and put a dent in the MacDougall strength."

Alex nodded. "Aye, see it done."

"What of me?" inquired John. "Am I to go with Angus?"

"Nay, John, not yet. While I am certain Angus would welcome your sword, King Edward has an assignment that would be perfect for your other skills. More, 'twould serve you in good stead to please the English king. While you are accomplishing that, you will have the chance to learn how to manage things at Dunyvaig. One day, you will have your own castle."

Angus nodded to his younger brother. "'Tis a good thing Alex suggests. There will be more battles to come and a Macdonald must learn to do more than fight. 'Sides, Duncan can go with me."

Duncan's smile was wide. "I will gladly go as I love a good fight and my father has already trained me to castle accounts at Saddell."

"What is the task?" asked John, his expression skeptical.

"Duties similar to those of an exchequer, the receipt and disbursement of monies for which we account to the Lordship and to King Edward."

"These are important duties?" John asked.

"Aye," said Alex, "very important, especially now when Edward is short of funds for his many campaigns."

The next day, under a blue sky white with clouds, Angus and Duncan sailed north with a fleet of twenty-five galleys, to meet Richard de Burgh on the western coast of Ross. They were cheered to find so many of the Irishmen ready to take up the Macdonald cause.

Better to fight for a Macdonald, they told Angus, than for an English king.

Awaiting Angus was unexpected news delivered by the Red Earl. Robert Bruce, the younger, acting independently of his father, had shifted his allegiance from King Edward to a rebel named William Wallace, fighting the English from Selkirk Forest. "The common folk follow him as do the retainers of many nobles," said de Burgh. Sir William Douglas and Robert Wishart, Bishop of Glasgow, have joined him. Wallace's numbers grow but I had not thought the Earl of Carrick among them until now. It may be that the young Robert was disillusioned at learning King Edward would not grant his father the crown."

"Aye, he would be." Angus considered what more might have led to this. "When word came that Edward had carted off the treasure, jewels, plate and regalia of Scotland's kings, even the stone upon which our kings are enthroned, I wondered how long Rob would serve such a man." Angus had wondered the same for his own family. As he thought more on it, he realized that if his friend had truly risen against King Edward that would change all.

Angus sent Earl Richard and the part of the army that wished to go back to Ireland south in some of his galleys. Bidding them Godspeed, he set out after his enemies, his ships loaded with Irish warriors.

Not content to fight his own battles, Alexander MacDougall, released by King Edward, was urging on the MacRuairis, who now engaged in what Angus considered mere piracy. Led by Ruairi, chief of the MacRuairis, they had burned all of the Macdonald ships they could find, including some under the protection of the Church. This Angus discovered as he stopped to meet with his chiefs in the north. Outraged, he donned his mail and helmet and set out, fully armored, in a blazing fury to hit the MacRuairis with his full strength.

Spotting the enemy galleys, he shouted to his captains within earshot, "Surround them!" He ordered his archers to the ready. The orders were echoed to his other captains. "Stay low until I give the order to attack."

Though evenly matched in the number of galleys, Angus had

more men and his archers were the best in the Isles. Upon his order, they rose and loosed their arrows on the MacRuairi galleys, which were still readying their attack. At close range, many fell. Then, with shouted war cries, his men jumped the gunwales to engage the enemy.

The clash of swords and men's cries rent the air.

From the deck of his ship, Angus searched for and sighted the MacRuairi chief in the stern of his galley. With Duncan on his heels and his galloglass guard around him, Angus pulled his sword from his scabbard. The slither of steel sounded a warning as he launched himself onto Ruairi's galley.

He cut down two men who veered toward him. Leaving his sword in the heart of the second man, Angus drew his long dagger and raced to where the MacRuairi chief stood.

Ruairi's eyes narrowed on Angus as he lifted his sword to strike but the press of struggling men fouled his swing. The blow missed and Angus kicked the sword from the chief's hand. Too late, Ruairi reached for the dagger at his hip. Angus yanked him into a head lock, his silver blade against Ruairi's throat, his hand blocking access to the sheathed dagger.

Duncan relieved Ruairi of his dagger, adding it to the pile of confiscated weapons accumulating on the deck, and tied the MacRuairi chief's hands behind him.

When this was done, Angus faced Ruairi. "Order your men to drop their weapons or I shall take your head!"

Ruairi grunted the order.

"Louder! So all your men may hear," said Angus.

Ruairi's eyes were full of rebellion but he repeated the order in a louder voice.

The clash of weapons gradually ceased. Men clenched in combat stepped apart, panting, their arms falling to their sides in fatigue. Blades dropped to the deck as Ruairi's men surrendered. Angus' Irishmen gathered the weapons while his galloglass stood guard.

"I'll not grant your freedom," Angus told Ruairi, "until you acknowledge the authority of King Edward and Alexander Macdonald as his man in the Isles."

Stern-faced and angry at his defeat, the dark-haired Ruairi nodded his agreement. Captured and without a weapon, he gave his oath.

As his fleet sailed away, Angus breathed a sigh of relief, thinking at least the MacRuairis had been dealt with. The goal had been to bring them into King Edward's peace. He should have known better. Ruairi had brothers, one of which was Lachlan, a ruthless, unprincipled man, no better than a freebooter. It was Lachlan who had led much of the plundering that had taken place. Shortly after dealing with Ruairi, word reached Angus that Lachlan's plundering continued despite his brother's oath as the MacRuairi chief.

With the long days of the end of August to aid him, Angus chased Lachlan relentlessly until his galleys were cornered in a small bay where Angus used the same tactics to encircle his ships. With his archers keeping the MacRuairis' swords at their sides, Angus forced Lachlan's obeisance by taking his son hostage. That done, Angus was about to return to Islay when Ruairi, the MacRuairi chief, forgetting the oath he had given, apparently at Lachlan's instigation, attacked the Isle of Skye.

Angus had had enough. Sending one ship south to retrieve his brothers and their galleys still at Dunyvaig, he vowed to Duncan, "If the MacRuairis will not act honorably, we will send their galleys to the bottom of the sea."

"They have left us little choice," agreed his cousin, his fair face red with frustration.

Two days' later, Alex and John arrived, each at the helm of a galley and accompanied by several more, many galloglass among the crews. Conferring together at Ardtornish, Angus expressed his indignation at so dishonorable a foe. "We must pursue them, whether by sea or by land, until we have struck them a final blow from which they will not recover."

"Agreed," said Alex. "We will take the head of the snake." So, a plan was devised by which they aimed their forces at Ruairi, the chief. This time, the villain retreated to Scotland's western coast in Argyll where, doubtless, he hoped to find refuge with the MacDougalls.

The chase continued for some weeks but finally they were able to capture Ruairi along with his sons. They imprisoned them in one of the Macdonald holdings on the mainland where Angus intended they would remain for the present.

By September, King Edward's mistrust of the MacDougalls had grown such that he ordered Alexander, Earl of Menteith, to take possession of the castles and lands belonging to Alexander MacDougall and his son, John, the one responsible for Sir Colin's death. At least their fortresses, of which there were many, would not be used against the Macdonalds.

Angus remembered the Earl of Menteith and his brother from the meeting at Turnberry when the pact was sealed a decade ago. Much had happened since that fateful day. He wondered if the nobles who pressed their seals to the document had any idea where that alliance would lead them.

In December, as they were about to celebrate Christmas, Angus' mother took sick and, not long after, died. With her children and grandchildren mourning her death, a pall was cast upon the season.

Dunseverick Castle, north coast of Ulster, spring 1297

NEWS REACHED Áine that Earl Richard had returned with only some of his army and that the rest remained with Angus. She wondered what could have happened. She did not ponder long. One of the returning galleys carried a messenger who rode from Dunluce to Dunseverick, asking for her.

Bowing before her and her father, he said, "Lord Angus has retained many of the Irishmen to fight for the Macdonalds. He needed them and they were willing. He wanted you to know they will be paid for their services."

"Whom do they fight?" she asked.

"The MacDougalls, the MacRuairis and the Comyns, who are allied together and ravaging Macdonald lands."

"It sounds like more a feud than a war," she said.

"Aye, my lady. But King Edward wants peace and trusts the Lord of the Isles to restore it. Thus far, Lord Angus and his brothers have met with success. The MacRuairi chief and his sons are in prison."

The messenger turned as if to go and then turned back. "Lord Angus did not ask me to convey this news but I thought you would want to know. His mother, Lady Helen, died at the end of the year."

It had been more than a year since she had seen Angus. She had known he had gone to war. That he lived caused her spirits to rise. That he had lost the mother he loved only three years after his father died saddened her.

The memory of Angus had not faded, but life had gone on as it always did, taken up with affairs in Ulster. The seasons brought planting and harvest, the tending of cattle and sheep and fishermen harvesting the bounty of the sea. While the effects of the famine remained in some places in Ireland, in O'Cahan territory there was enough food and good hunting for hare, deer and fox.

Dermot had quickly become a strong soldier and participated in the hunts when he was not with the O'Cahan guards on the practice field. Brian was now a handsome lad of six. Lir, his constant companion, was fully grown and huge in size. In the common things of life, Áine found contentment though her mind wandered often to the blue-eyed Macdonald whose kiss she remembered.

"Will Lord Angus be transporting the men back?" she asked the messenger.

"Yes, my lady. Though he could not say when, he believed it would be soon."

Dunyvaig Castle, Isle of Islay, end of August 1297

ANGUS' FLEET LAY beached on the sands of Lagavulin Bay, his Irish warriors enjoying the summer eve and a rest from their days taking turns at the oars after fighting the MacRuairis. All things considered, the outcome was a victory. They had lost but a few men and the wounded were recovering, the Macdonald physicians attending them.

Outside the castle, he stood with his brothers and Duncan, gazing into the flame-colored sky left behind after the sun deserted its post. A fledgling sea eagle, its brown and white plumage on display, soared through the sky just offshore.

While he was away, a letter had arrived from his friend, Rob. The news was sad, telling of Rob's wife dying in childbed at the end of last year, though the girl child born to her had survived. "He has named her Marjorie after his mother," he told his brothers and Duncan.

"Does he still fight with William Wallace and the rebels?" asked Alex.

"Aye, he does," replied Angus. "They are now joined by Sir Andrew Moray, a powerful lord in the north of Scotland, and Sir Roger Kirkpatrick, cousin to both Wallace and Bruce, is with them."

"Did the young Bruce say why he has left Edward?" inquired Alex.

Angus quoted from the letter, "I must join my own people and the nation in which I was born." Angus stared into the sunset wondering how long it would be before the Macdonalds joined Robert Bruce in what would surely be a quest for the crown.

News had reached Angus' brother, as Admiral of the Western Isles, of a disturbing development. "Now that King Edward has released the Comyns, including John, Earl of Buchan, and the two John Comyns of Badenoch," said Alex, "I am told by my spies they are building two massive war galleys at Inverlochy Castle, aided by Alexander MacDougall, who Edward has also released from prison."

"'Tis Edward's policy to release his prisoners in exchange for their vows of fealty," said Angus. "The Comyns and MacDougalls would take advantage."

"And to build such galleys at the southern end of the Great Glen," said Duncan, "will be a problem for us."

Angus nodded. "We cannot allow them to set out to sea."

"Aye," said Alex, "'tis a challenge to our naval supremacy. They must be captured if possible. But there is more. Tormod Macleod sent word that Alexander MacDougall has gone on another rampage, attacking Skye and Lewis."

Much as Angus wanted to be a part of the battles looming in the north, he had to return his loyal Irishmen home. Awaiting him there, he hoped, would be a winsome Irish lass who still remembered his face. He had seen hers and her beautiful brown eyes often enough in his dreams. "I must sail south."

"Aye, Brother, I am aware and would not bid you stay." Alex

grinned. "'Tis the O'Cahan's daughter I'm told has enchanted you."

Duncan and John exchanged a knowing smile.

Angus heaved a shrug. "I suppose 'tis too late to deny it."

"No need to worry," said Alex. "Allow me the pleasure of seeing to the Comyn war galleys. If I cannot capture them, I will burn them to the waterline."

"May I go with you?" John asked Alex. Angus was proud of his younger brother, now fully a man and a good fighter, who had proven himself in the battle to take down the MacRuairi chief.

"Aye, you may and welcome you are," said Alex.

Thus, Angus and Duncan sailed south while Alex and John took the remainder of the fleet north.

Dunluce Castle, north coast of Ulster, September 1297

BEFORE HE LEFT Dunyvaig, news had reached Angus of the victory of William Wallace and Sir Andrew Moray at Stirling Bridge. Though vastly outnumbered, they had triumphed over the English forces led by John de Warenne, Earl of Surrey. This was the subject of the conversation as Angus sailed with his cousin to Ulster.

From where he stood at the mast, Duncan shouted over the wind, "They say that five thousand foot and a hundred cavalry perished beneath the Scots' swords."

Angus had no knowledge of how many Scots had died. He was desperate for news of his friend, Rob. All Angus knew was that Wallace lived and had been made the sole Guardian of Scotland.

On the wide beach west of Dunluce, the wind was fierce and the skies overhead threatened rain as Angus' galleys disgorged their Irish warriors. They were full of tales of their mighty deeds and pleased to be home to tell them. Angus was anxious to see Áine but before he could set out for Dunseverick, he had to speak with Richard de Burgh.

"I expect we will spend the night at Dunluce," he told Duncan, "so the men might as well set up camp here." To his captains, who had gathered around them, he said, "If the men would seek out the practice yard at Dunluce, just send me word so I will know you are close. If you leave the beach, post guards for the galleys. I am uncertain if Ulster is fully at peace. For now, I'll take only my personal guard with me."

De Burgh was happy to see him. Reaching out his hand to Angus in welcome, he said, "Finally, you return and with the look of a man who has won over his enemies."

"Aye, though it took longer than it should, and Alex still battles the Comyns."

De Burgh welcomed Duncan and bid them both sit. Wine was poured by a servant and Angus accepted the goblet with thanks, his throat as dry as dirt. "Have you news of Robert Bruce?" he asked, wiping his mouth with the back of his hand.

"He fights with the Scots; I know that. But he was not at Stirling Bridge, or so my spies tell me. Encouraged by Bishop Wishart, the youngest Bruce raised the standard of revolt at Irvine. He was with James Stewart, the Macduff of Fife and Sir William Douglas. That rising failed. Since then, he has kept away from Edward's eye. Edward himself has helped since he has been in France battling for Gascony."

"When do you expect his return?" asked Angus.

"Spring I should think. Mayhap sooner. He plans to raise an army to fight in Scotland. He wanted me to serve in Flanders."

"Will you?" asked Duncan.

"At the moment, Edward is disinclined to meet my price. When he is desperate, he will agree to my demands. Then I will go. By then it may be Scotland."

"How are things in Ireland? Does the peace hold?"

"For the moment, all is well. Turlough is still reigning in Tirconnell. Per John Wogan's settlement, John fitz Thomas will surrender his lands in Connaught to me. He was once my vassal but no longer. He will also turn over the lands he held in Ulster. In exchange, he will gain others in the south. I can live with that. Besides, fitz Thomas is currently fighting with Edward in France."

Angus was glad to hear of peace even if it was not to last.

"Will you stay the night as my guests?" de Burgh asked them. Then with a smile, he said, "I have invited the O'Cahans to dine with us."

Angus exchanged a glance with Duncan and then replied, "Aye and gladly."

Dunseverick Castle, north coast of Ulster

ÁINE'S HEART SPED at the thought she would be seeing Angus tonight. A year was so long; mayhap he would not remember her. Outside her window, the clouds were gathering their strength. "I do hope it doesn't rain."

"Wear the crimson silk," Nessa said with enthusiasm, her brown curls falling about her sweet face. "And the circlet of gold and rubies. You will look like a queen. I daresay Lord Angus will fall at your feet."

"Nonsense, Nessa. Mayhap he will barely remember me."

Nessa sighed loudly. "No man who has ever met you had difficulty in remembering you, Mistress. Certainly not this one. What was that you were reading by the Roman poet about absence and the tide growing stronger?"

"Always toward absent lovers love's tide stronger flows," Áine quoted from memory. She had read the line many times and hoped it might be true.

"And that tide has again brought him to our shore."

"You are a romantic, Nessa."

"One of us has to be. Will you take Brian with you tonight to Earl Richard's?"

"Yes. He was invited as the earl's children are in residence at Dunluce just now. Brian is excited to be seeing the Lord of Kintyre, though he was disappointed to learn Lir cannot come."

"I will make sure he looks like the prince he is."

"Thank you, Nessa. I do want him to make a good impression."

"You need have no fear of that. A winsome Irish prince with ginger hair and blue eyes? He could charm the velvet cloak off a fairy queen."

Áine lifted her gaze to the ceiling and shook her head but there was a smile on her face.

Nessa's attention had turned to the chests at the foot of Áine's bed. Digging through them, she said, "You will need your cloaks and clothes for the morrow should you be asked to stay the night. Surely the earl and his countess will extend an invitation."

"Yes, now that you speak of it. Father may want to talk to the men late into the night. While we are away, might you be seeing that handsome guard who has been paying you much attention?"

Nessa blushed. "Mayhap. Nothing I do seems to discourage him."

"Good. I like him."

An hour later, with her father, Dermot and Brian, she set off for Dunluce in her father's carriage, the guards riding behind. Áine was glad for her fur-lined cloak as the wind blew in sharp gusts, warning of a coming storm.

Áine stepped into the great hall of Dunluce, her stomach in knots. What would she see in Angus' face?

He was standing with his back to her, talking with his cousin and Earl Richard and his countess, Lady Margaret. When the others looked up, Angus turned and their eyes met. What Áine saw overwhelmed her. His blue eyes were alight with happiness, his smile wide.

Her heart leaped with joy. The tall, handsome Angus Og Macdonald had remembered her.

Striding toward her, he greeted her father and brother and then Brian, tousling his red hair. "Greetings, Young Prince." Then he bowed before Áine, reaching for her hand. "My lady," he said, pressing a warm kiss to her knuckles.

"I feared you had forgotten us," she said, trying to sound amused when, in truth, she had spoken her fear.

"Nay, I could not. Our enemies delayed my return." He draped her hand over his arm and led her to the earl. Her father and brother followed, sharing subtle laughter between them. Over his shoulder, Angus said, "Laugh if you will, but I have the prize."

"What prize?" asked innocent Brian.

"He but pays your mother a compliment," said her father.

Wine was served. When they all had a cup, the countess turned to Brian. "Would you like to see the children before dinner?"

He nodded vigorously.

She beckoned a servant. "Take young O'Neill here to the new wolfhound pups where my own children like to gather but don't let them wallow in the dirt. They are all dressed for dinner."

Brian went willingly, accepting the servant girl's hand. "There are new pups?"

Dinner was a grand affair. After so much deprivation and war, Earl Richard must have wanted to lighten all their hearts. Music filled the hall, the sounds of flute, lyre and horn bringing ancient tunes to life.

Over a meal of fish soup, roast beef in wine sauce and vegetables simmered in herbs and spices, the company conversed, telling stories from the past year. The children, sitting at the long tables set at right angles to the head table, chattered like squirrels, especially when apple tarts, the first of the season, were placed before them.

"The young prince has grown," remarked Angus sitting on Áine's right, her father on his other side. "He seems a happy child."

"He is," she said watching her son, his expression full of delight as he licked the juice from his tart and chatted with the de Burgh children.

"Does he remind you of his father?"

"Only his hair. The O'Neill was a different sort of man. Honorable but never far from battle, mostly with kin."

"That sounds like the Macdonalds. Not that we wish it that way. The peace is, unfortunately, ours to keep."

Once the meal ended, the long trestle tables were taken down and the children urged to sit in front of the dais as the earl waved in the entertainment.

TO ANGUS IT WAS like a scene from a May fair, rich with laughter, dancing and the sounds of timbrel, tabor pipe and drums. Brilliant colors flashed before his eyes as jugglers tossed gleaming balls into the air and acrobats tumbled across the carpets laid upon the stone floor. Their elaborate costumes of crimson, green, blue and gold satin and silk were like a canvas of a mad artist whose paint splashed from the brush.

The children squealed with joy.

Having just left behind battles and war, to Angus the elaborate display seemed almost dreamlike. Leaning close to Áine, he said, "Has this been going on for the year I was away?"

She laughed and her brown eyes, catching the candlelight, sparkled like diamonds. "Not like this. I do believe your arrival has inspired celebration."

"Then mayhap I should arrive more often."

"Now, that is a worthy thought."

Angus heard the words and felt a pang of guilt. "The times in which we live do not allow me long periods to spend with you. Still, I agree we need more time."

Soon thereafter, the music became more subdued and a troubadour came to stand in the center of the hall. He sang a ballad of a great Irish lord who fought and defeated the Vikings who had troubled Ireland's shores long ago. The story captivated the children, which Angus was certain had been the man's intent. The adults, too, listened with great interest.

Angus turned to Áine. "He sings of our history. My own ancestor, Somerled, was such a one."

"Since I last saw you, I have learned of your clan's beginnings. 'Tis a noble heritage with royal Irish roots."

This pleased him for he wanted her to be proud of the family he would ask her to join. In that happy thought, he leaned in to whisper, "Have you missed me?"

She turned her gaze on him. Though she said not a word, her eyes spoke loudly. *Do you need to ask?*

"And do you warm to the idea of marriage? Even marriage to a Macdonald?"

A hint of a smile played around her lovely lips. "A bit more time and seeing more of you will tell, good sir."

"Then you shall have it, Áine." Thus, he resolved to linger in Ireland for a few more days.

That night the storm hit, the heavens thundering with loud cracks and much lightning. All were persuaded to remain at Dunluce. Angus thought of his men camped on the shore, hoping the storm would quickly pass. He and his men were often soaked to the skin when a sudden rain would come upon them. At least the tents would provide cover they did not have in the galleys at sea.

The next morning, the storm had passed to reveal a fair sky and sun. Angus and Áine rode to the beach, bringing his men warm bread, sausages and apples, a bounty owing to the countess' generosity. He told his captains they would remain here for the next few days, that he would be at Dunseverick, Lord Cumee having invited him to stay. Duncan would remain at Dunluce.

In the days that followed, Angus and Áine spent much time together, walking the green hills around Dunseverick with Brian and Lir, riding to her favorite place, not far from the castle. There, a narrow river spilled over rocks into the sea creating a magnificent waterfall that roared as it met the waves.

In the evening, when Brian had gone to bed, they played chess before the fire and talked long into the night. Her father and brother left them alone much of the time. Angus was grateful, for it was during this time their friendship, even their love, deepened.

One morning, as Angus descended the stairs to break his fast, Lord Cumee said, "You seem to be making progress in your courtship of my daughter."

"It is my fervent hope, my lord, that this time together will soften her heart. She wants time and I have promised to give it to her."

"That is wise. While you are gone, I will do my part, urging her to accept your suit."

On their last day together, when Brian was occupied with his tutor, Angus accompanied Áine on a walk around the promontory. It was a cool autumn day, the wind brisk under a cloud-filled sky. She spoke of her love for the birds that made the cliffs their home, her eyes alight with gladness.

"We have many birds in the Isles," he said.

"I expect you do." Her smile was subtle.

Knowing he could put it off no longer, he said, "Áine, I must sail tomorrow. My men will be anxious to see their homes again after so long away and I must learn how my brother fared in his battles in the north. The fighting in Scotland is not over."

"I know. I am glad for the time we have had together."

Taking her by the hand, he pulled her to him, slipping his hands beneath her cloak to grasp her waist. She came willingly, soft in his arms. He kissed her, holding back none of the passion he had kept leashed before. He would show her what was between them, the promise of their future together.

When their lips parted, she hung limp in his arms. The dark pools of her eyes slowly opened as she spoke his name in a throaty whisper. "Angus."

"No matter the time I am away from you, Áine, know this: I will not change in my desire to have you by my side. Soon, I will ask the question and you must have the answer."

CHAPTER 16

Dunseverick Castle, north coast of Ulster, September 1298

ÁINE SAT BEFORE the fire, so absorbed in Angus' letter she did not hear her father enter the great hall. Not until he spoke.

"Another letter from Kintyre's lord? He sends a galley with a letter so often, 'tis like the regular courier for Earl Richard."

She nodded without looking up. "I must finish it before Brian's tutor frees him for the day." Angus had sent her letters nearly every month, telling her of the war in Scotland and his family's role as King Edward's agents in the Isles. That he would share such things with her spoke of his respect and of the kind of marriage they would have. Then there was the searing kiss he had given her before he sailed away that left a memory she could not forget. It gave rise to dreams that left the chemise in which she slept bathed in sweat.

Finally finishing the letter, she looked up. "He writes of continued battles with the MacDougalls, who are still plaguing the Isles of Skye, Lewis and Harris."

Taking the chair next to her, warming his hands in the fire's heat, her father asked, "Does he speak of affairs in the rest of Scotland?

Since de Burgh is consumed with strengthening his lands in Connaught, there has been scant news of anything else."

"He does." Re-reading the relevant part of the letter, she said, "King Edward marched his army into Scotland and defeated the rebel leader William Wallace at a place called Falkirk. Since then, Wallace has resigned as Guardian. Angus says his friend, Robert Bruce, is likely to be named a Guardian together with John Comyn, the Lord of Badenoch."

Her father sat back, shaking his head. "That will never work. The Comyns are the enemies of the Bruces. They are the enemies of the Macdonalds, too, for that matter. Worse, the Red Comyn of Badenoch is a hot-tempered man who wants power and would betray his own mother to get it."

Her father's face was lined with worry, the crevice between his dark brows deepening. His hair, too, had recently gained more gray. When he climbed the stairs to his bedchamber, he sometimes breathed heavily, which caused her to worry for his health. He was only in his fifth decade, still strong and, yet, recently, she had observed a tiredness about him that was not there before.

Glancing down at the letter, she continued, "Angus believes Wallace was betrayed at Falkirk by John Comyn, the Earl of Buchan, who, he says, left the field with his cavalry in the heat of battle." Áine was exasperated trying to understand the relationships. "Really, Father, this is all so confusing. Why would this Comyn betray a fellow Scot who is rousing the country to fight for freedom?"

"You forget the Earl of Buchan was the one who led the attack on the Bruce castle at Carlisle that began the war. I am certain it goes down badly that the young Bruce supports Wallace, whom I hear is very popular with the people. Buchan's cousin is the Red Comyn. It was his father who competed for the crown of Scotland. Moreover, the Red Comyn's mother is John Balliol's sister. With Balliol's abdication of the throne, doubtless the Comyns think to take up the cause of their family."

"Angus told me the Comyns are also allies of the MacDougalls."

"They would be," commented her father. "They are all related by marriage."

"According to Angus, after King Edward's victory at Falkirk, he set out to attack Robert Bruce but, by the time the king reached Carrick, Bruce had burned the castle at Ayr to keep it out of English hands and then disappeared. In response, the king destroyed the Bruce castle at Lochmaben in Annandale."

"I can only imagine the temper the king must have been in. How were things left?"

"It seems King Edward has departed Scotland, leaving his English garrisons to hold the country until he can return. I find it interesting that the Bruce lands were not given to Edward's followers and loyal knights, as he did the lands of other Scots. What can that mean?"

"Only one thing," said her father, his hand stroking his beard. "He intends to take the Earl of Carrick back into his peace." Chuckling, he added, "King Edward has always had a fond regard for the youngest Robert Bruce. Some say he favors him over his own son, Prince Edward."

Áine placed the letter in her lap and sat back, staring into the flames, thinking about all she had learned.

Her father interrupted her musing. "Have you thought more on whether to accept the young Macdonald's suit?"

She nodded. The answer came easily for she'd had much time to reflect upon it. "I would be hard-pressed to reject his suit, Father, as my love for him grows."

"He is much like his father, the great Angus Mor, a man of principles, wisdom and courage. Young Angus will hold close those he loves and protect you with his life. Of that, I have no doubt."

"I know Angus to be a good man but I worry about his being in constant danger. Were I to wed him, would I lose him to Scotland's constant wars?"

"You cannot let the times in which we live dictate your choice of a husband. No one lives forever, Áine. My own time, I feel, grows short." She opened her mouth to protest but he held up a hand. "I would see you in your own home surrounded by your children when that time comes. Your brother will always give you a home here, but he will marry one day and his wife will be the lady of Dunseverick, not you. Kintyre's lord is a good man and his heart for you is clear to all. You must not forget that Angus can protect Brian, who will one day be seen as a possible heir to the kingship of Tirowen and therefore a threat to those who would have it for their own."

Her father was right. She could not stay in her comfortable nest when the world around her was changing, and she must think of Brian. She had come to love Angus and would stand with him. He would protect both her and Brian. "Then it is well that my heart belongs to him."

Dunyvaig Castle, Isle of Islay, Spring 1299

ANGUS HAD SPENT the last year with his brothers and Duncan, keeping King Edward's peace in Argyll and the Isles. Mostly, this came down to fighting the MacDougalls, who were a slippery lot. They could retreat into the hills of Argyll to one of their holdings, disappearing for weeks, only to reappear in galleys supplied by the Comyns to attack an isle or a chief under the Macdonalds' protection.

The Isle of Mull was ever in contention. How the MacDougall's ravaging of the Macdonald Isles furthered Scotland's war for freedom from England, Angus could not say.

"If the reports from the chiefs in the north be true," said Angus, breaking his fast in Dunyvaig's great hall with Alex, John and Duncan, "Alexander MacDougall and his minions have vanished into the mist yet again."

Duncan smirked. "Mayhap he celebrates King Edward's pending marriage to the King of France's half-sister."

"Hardly that," said Alex, "but he may be taking advantage of the respite Edward's absence will bring."

"I should think Edward's young bride, who is more than forty years his junior, will keep him well occupied and out of Scotland this summer," replied Duncan with a mocking smile.

John grinned at the suggestion.

Angus nodded. "A lull in the fighting while Edward remains in England will be welcomed by all."

"Which leaves Alexander MacDougall free to poke his nose in

other places," put in Alex. "I might as well use this opportunity to speak with Earl Richard. If he plans to join Edward's autumn campaign in Scotland, he will want our ships for transport."

"What would you say to leaving John and Duncan here to manage the lordship and keep watch for the MacDougalls while you and I sail to Ulster?" asked Angus. "Assuming they are willing," he added with a nod in their direction. "I could put you in at Dunluce's shore while I go on to Dunseverick. It is time I took a bride."

Smiles all around greeted this statement.

"An excellent idea," said Alex with enthusiasm. "I will let Juliana know. We have servants aplenty to help with our growing brood of sons, so she should not mind my absence."

Angus nearly choked on the piece of bread he was swallowing. "Mind? Juliana has given you a son nearly every year you have been wed. More like, she will welcome the time apart!"

Duncan and John laughed.

Alex reached out and cuffed Angus on the back of his head. "Very well, we will sail tomorrow." Directing his attention to Duncan and John, he asked, "Are you willing to manage things here at Dunyvaig?"

"Aye," they said in unison.

Then, to Angus, he offered, "If she deigns to wed you, your O'Cahan bride should bring you a fine dowry."

"I have thought some on that subject," said Angus. "Should she agree to marry me, I have a proposal for Lord Cumee. You would be surprised if you knew what I intend to ask for. 'Tis neither gold nor land."

The beach at Dunluce Castle on the coast of Ulster

THE VOYAGE SOUTH from Islay to Ulster was short and, though the dark blue sea was wind-tossed and the spring air chilled, the sky above was a clear blue. Angus watched as the galley neared the cliffs, the beach was rock-filled and treacherous in approach. High up on the clifftop, amidst the carpet of green, he could see a profusion of yellow and gold wildflowers.

The experienced captain made short work of beaching the Lord of the Isles' large galley. Joining his brother in the stern, Angus prepared to bid Alex good day. Offering his forearm, which Alex grasped, Angus said, "May your negotiations with de Burgh go well. Send word to Dunseverick when you are ready for me to return."

His dark hair whipped by the wind, Alex replied, "Do not expect me to summon you before tomorrow at the earliest. I am hoping Earl Richard will lend us some of his fine horses to hunt this afternoon so that we may dine on venison this eve."

Angus laughed. "'Tis a good plan though the presence of your bows and arrows will announce your intent before you can ask."

"Aye, mayhap, but de Burgh is a generous host so he will not mind." Then, fixing Angus with a steady gaze, he said, "May God grant you the answer from your lady you are hoping for."

"Her letters have given me hope." In truth, Angus was anxious to have her answer and prayed it would be the one he could not live without. For some time, he had imagined his future only with the beautiful Áine O'Cahan.

Shifting his bow to his back, Alex climbed over the gunwale to the rock-strewn beach. The dozen men comprising his guard and favored men, who would remain with him at Dunluce, lifted their bows and arrows and followed suit. This being a social visit, they wore tunics and cloaks but no mail.

Angus shouted, "Godspeed," and waved as his brother and his men took the winding path up to the castle. Then he ordered the shore detail to push the galley back into the water. Once done, they clambered aboard and the crew set to work, rowing for Dunseverick. Angus turned his mind to the narrow shingle shore awaiting them and the lady who was never far from his thoughts.

ÁINE HAD BEEN TOLD by a guard that a galley had arrived at Dunseverick. With her excitement rising, she hurried to the promontory to gaze down at the shingle far below, her long hair blowing behind her. Brian, freed from his tutor to greet the arriving visitors, had joined her, his wolfhound beside him.

The Galley of the Isles pennant of the Lord of the Isles flew from the mast. For a moment, she wondered if Angus' brother had come to see her father. But then she spotted Angus' light brown head turned to blazing copper by the sun. He waved to her from the galley's deck.

She raised her hand in greeting. "'Tis the Lord of Kintyre!"

Hearing this, Brian waved enthusiastically.

Her heart pounded in her chest as she waited for Angus to ascend to the promontory. Brian ran ahead with Lir to meet him. Angus reached the top and bent to speak to her son who went on to meet Angus' men.

Angus strode toward her. Without a word, he took her into his arms and swung her around.

"Put me down! What will your men think?"

He laughed. "My guard will be relieved. The crew will think their lord's brother is daft with love for his lass." Setting her feet on the ground, his blue eyes looked long into hers. "My beautiful Áine, I have come to pose the question. Will you be my wife? I cannot wait a minute longer to know if you are to be mine. Tell me, what is your answer?"

Smiling with joy, she said, "Yes, Angus. My answer is yes."

"Then I am the happiest of men." He kissed her soundly and she enthusiastically returned his kiss. He turned to his men who had arrived on the promontory. Standing with them was Brian, staring open-mouth. Angus called, "The lady will marry me!"

Cheers went up from his crew, making Áine's cheeks heat to know they had been watching them all this while.

Taking her hand, Angus said, "Come, we'd best tell your father and brother the good news."

"What good news?" inquired Brian who had left Angus' crew to join them.

"Did you not hear? Your mother has agreed to be my wife."

"Oh, that. Yes, I heard."

"That means, Little Prince, that I am to become your father. Does that please you?"

Brian's young face lit with happiness. "Yes! Does that mean we will go to live with you?"

"Aye, but we will visit your grandfather and uncle often."

"Why do you sail your brother's galley?" she asked Angus as they walked to the castle.

"Alex is at Dunluce where I will retrieve him in a day or two. He discusses with Earl Richard his next transport to Scotland in the service of King Edward."

Seeing his men waiting at the edge of the promontory, she said, "Have your men join us in the castle. We will see them fed and given lodging for the night. They might as well be a part of what will certainly be a celebration."

Angus beckoned the crew and told them to follow.

Inside the great hall, a fire burned steadily. Áine's father and brother faced them with expectant gazes. "Am I to be the father-in-law of Kintyre's lord?" asked her father.

"Aye," said Angus, "and happy I am to convey the news that Áine has agreed to become my wife."

"Is it not wonderful?" said Brian, his blue eyes large as he looked up at his grandfather. "I am to live in his castle."

"The Macdonalds have many castles," replied Dermot, who then congratulated Angus.

Áine spoke to her father's steward about providing lodging for Angus' crew. "They can join us for the evening meal." She relayed this to the captain and he acknowledged her words with a nod as he and the crew followed the steward.

Returning to Angus where he stood with her father, brother and Brian, she heard her father say, "You can be wed in Ireland, should you choose. Dungiven Priory is ours and has a small but lovely church."

The four turned their eyes upon her.

Taking Angus' hand, she gave him a teasing grin. "I care not where we are wed, only that we are wed in a church."

"Very well," said her father. "Let us toast to this grand occasion and then we can discuss the dowry." Áine sent Brian back to his tutor and stayed with the men long enough to toast the wine to her future with Angus. A peace settled about her now that the decision had been made. She was certain this was God's will for her.

ANGUS HAD GIVEN MUCH thought to Áine's dowry. Seated before the fire, facing Lord Cumee, who was attired in a tunic of fine green woolen, Angus broached the subject. "I have enough lands and gold, my lord, so I would ask neither for Áine's dowry. You have something I value far more, something the Lordship and the Isles need, something we will welcome with open arms."

The O'Cahan returned him a puzzled look, the wisdom of his years reflected in his lined face. "What could that be?"

"Men. Men of an age with me to make their home in the Isles and build a future there. I will give them land to farm and raise cattle, to fish and pursue their crafts. I will also equip them with arms and train them, if need be. Though I have fought often enough with them to know they are valiant warriors who will heed my call in a time of war."

Angus could see the idea intrigued the older lord as he pondered the request. Finally, he said, "'Tis a wise thing you ask. How many men?"

Angus did not hesitate. "At least a thousand. I would ask they include young chiefs who will marry the daughters of the chiefs of the lordship. All should be volunteers. Do you think you can raise that many?"

"We will see," said Lord Cumee, stroking his beard. "We will see."

Angus and Áine, accompanied by Brian and the hound, Lir, were walking the promontory that afternoon. When Brian and Lir went ahead, Angus described the dowry he had sought.

"You asked for *men*?" she said, incredulous.

"Aye. We have many men in the Isles but still there are some isles with few families on them and chiefs with beautiful daughters in need of husbands. Aside from that, I need men in this time of war to stand with me, men who will defend our Isles as their own. What do you think of it?"

She smiled, shaking her head, he hoped in wonder. "I think it very clever of you. And I rather like the idea of so many Irishmen joining me in your Isles."

Brian ran back to ask, "What castle shall be our home?"

"Well, Young Prince," began Angus, tousling his patch of red hair, "as your uncle said, the lordship has many castles from the tip of Kintyre to Skye in the north. My favorite is Dunaverty on Kintyre. You can see it from here." He pointed toward the shadow of land on the eastern horizon.

Brian shaded his eyes. "Oh, 'tis not far."

"No, and your mother may favor it for that reason." He glanced at Áine. "My brother, as Lord of the Isles, lives on Islay, the seat of the lordship. That isle is also close."

"If Dunaverty is your favorite, I think we should live there," said Brian.

Angus shared a smile with Áine. "I see your mother has raised a young diplomat."

As the afternoon wore on, clouds began to gather. A sudden chill in the air had Angus suggesting they return to the castle. They were headed back when Conall, the captain of his brother's crew, came running from the castle, breathless. "My lord, you are wanted on a most urgent matter." Casting a glance at Áine and Brian, the captain added, "It might be best if you came alone."

Angus could tell from the man's demeanor the matter was serious. He turned to Áine. "I will join you when I know more of this."

She nodded and took Brian's hand. Angus hurried behind the captain into the great hall where Lord Cumee met him and quickly ushered him into a small chamber where a man stood with his back to the door.

As Angus and Lord Cumee entered, the man turned. Blood ran from his head, down the side of his face and onto his tunic. The dark red stain had dried, making it difficult to tell how many wounds he had but Angus recognized him as one of his brother's personal guards. "What has happened?"

"My lord, we were ambushed while hunting. Some were cut down before they could draw their swords. Your brother, Lord Alexander—"

The guard's speech failed him. He appeared near collapse.

"What of my brother!" demanded Angus.

Haltingly, the man tried again. "He…he is dead, my lord."

"Dead? Alexander is dead?" Angus felt the blow to his gut as his body suddenly stiffened. Dazed, he tried to take in the words but his mind reeled. "No, it cannot be true. I was just with him this morning. Surely you speak of another."

"'Tis my shame, my lord, that I could not save him."

"I will not believe this until I see him for myself."

"It was the MacDougalls, my lord, led by Alexander MacDougall. He was the one who killed your brother. I saw it happen but I was too far away to reach him before I was struck down."

Trying to imagine the scene of death, rage swelled inside Angus. "Where did this happen?"

"South of Dunluce…in the woods east of the River Bann." Angus knew the woods. He had been there before when on his way to rescue Brian O'Neill, the King of Tirowen, unaware he was dead.

Angus forced his mind to work. "Who else lives?"

"No one, my lord. 'Tis certain the MacDougalls thought me dead. When I awakened, I was surrounded by the bodies of my fellow guards."

The man was swaying on his feet. Angus guided him to a chair and bade him sit. Turning to Lord Cumee, he said, "Can you ask your physician to tend his wounds?"

"Of course." Opening the door O'Cahan summoned a servant to fetch the physician.

Angus' fury boiled over. "The MacDougalls are in Ireland! Surely the devils did not follow us here. We saw no sign—"

"They did not know Lord Alexander was here," said the wounded guard. "I heard one of them say how fortuitous it was they had come to see Domnall O'Neill on a matter of business at the very time The Macdonald was in Ulster."

Lord Cumee put in, "Domnall's mother is a MacDougall. He would harbor them."

"They must have happened upon us and seized the opportunity for treachery," said the wounded guard. In halting words, he stared straight ahead and added, "'Twas murder, not battle."

With a heavy sigh, Angus dropped his head into his hands seeing his brother's face as they had said goodbye that morning, the smile he would never see again. Had he but known it would be the last time they would grasp hands in friendship… "Oh, Alex."

Angus felt Lord Cumee's hand on his shoulder. "You can take my horses."

Raising his head, seeing the O'Cahan lord through unshed tears, Angus said, "Aye, I must see my brother and find the bastard MacDougall. I will have justice; I will have my revenge. Tell Áine—"

"Do not worry. I will see to my daughter. Go and do as you must. My guard will ride with you."

"Let me go, too," said the wounded guard trying to rise.

"Nay," said Angus. "'Tis enough you brought me the news. Recover from your wounds and then, if you've a mind, you can join my guard."

The man sank back into the chair as the physician arrived. "Thank you, my lord."

Angus and the crew, mounted on O'Cahan horses, accompanied by Lord Cumee's guard, galloped for Dunluce, pausing there only to confer with Earl Richard. The earl expressed his deep sympathy and added his own fighting men to Angus' retinue, now fifty in number. "I have dispatched carts to retrieve the bodies. We will prepare Alexander for burial. I assume you will want to take him to Iona."

"Aye," said Angus. He could not think of that now but, upon his return, he knew he must.

As he rode south toward the woods where his brother had fallen, the hoofbeats of the horses in his party pounded in his ears. The Mackay seer's prophecy flashed in his mind. *A king will rule with uneasy scepter. Scotland will be imperiled as chief attacks chief. Treachery will abound as ancient conflicts are renewed and a foreign ruler will slaughter many. Two chiefs will die before a new one rises with a new king. Only then will Scotland know peace.*

He understood for the first time. The seer had meant two Macdonald chiefs would die, two Lords of the Isles, first his father, Angus Mor, and then his brother, Alexander. John Balliol's scepter had ever been uneasy; Scottish barons had attacked Scottish barons; Edward had slaughtered all in Berwick; and treachery abounded everywhere. All this had happened as the seer predicted. All save the last. A new king had yet to rise.

They searched the woods where Alex had fallen and came across the scene of a bloody slaughter, the bodies of Alex's men strewn about the grass. Earl Richard's men, dispatched from the castle with a cart and traveling at a slower pace, arrived and hastened to their grisly task.

Angus found his brother and kneeled beside him, gently running his hand over the fixed eyes to close them. The MacDougall's sword had pierced his unmailed chest. Tears welled in Angus' eyes as he remembered the older brother who had led the way to manhood. A leader of clans, a respected nobleman and a much-loved husband and father. No more would he smile in this world for he had gone on to the next.

"I will see you avenged, Alex, and I will care for your family."

Angus lifted his brother into the cart and helped Earl Richard's men to cover the body with a white linen cloth they had brought for that purpose. Then he returned to the spot where his brother had fallen for he had noticed when lifting Alex that his sword—their father's sword—had been trapped beneath Alex's body. The silvered blade was clean of any blood. He picked it up and put it in the cart with his brother.

Leaving the woods, Angus and his band of fifty warriors tracked the horses that had fled the scene, riding west to Tirowen. The trail led them to a clearing and the armed camp of Domnall O'Neill. Angus slowly walked his horse past the warriors milling about, searching for any sign of blood or battle on their tunics.

The O'Neill's men standing around spoke no challenge but their eyes followed Angus and his men through the camp.

At the door of the manor in the camp's center Angus shouted, "Domnall O'Neill, come out! I would speak with you!"

The door opened and two burly guards stepped out to flank the door followed by the half-MacDougall King of Tirowen. He was not much different that Angus remembered, though better attired in a tunic of Irish royalty embroidered in silver, this one bearing no splashes of blood. Slight in body with thin brown hair, Domnall's small eyes narrowed with suspicion as he looked up at Angus, his dark gaze full of malice. On Domnall's face, a smug smile emerged. "Ah, I know you."

Angus reigned in his fury. "I am Angus Og Macdonald, Lord of Kintyre. I would know the whereabouts of your kinsman, Alexander MacDougall."

"Now, why would I know where the Lord of Lorne and Argyll is? This is Ireland, not Scotland." He exchanged a smile with the two guards.

"MacDougall was here and well you know it, for he has murdered my brother, Alexander, Lord of the Isles, in yon woods. Where is he?"

"Even if I knew, why should I tell you?"

Angus gritted his teeth. "You might notice I come with Earl Richard's men as well as Lord Cumee's and my own Islesmen, each a galloglass." He glanced behind him, comforted by his men's stern countenances and their hands tightly gripping their axes. Turning back to O'Neill, he said, "Should you refuse to answer, the earl, by whose grace you remain King of Tirowen, has the power to take the lands you now hold. And, should you need convincing, I can raise three thousand Islemen within a sennight to descend upon you. You would not survive."

The smile disappeared from Domnall's face yet he hesitated.

"Christ on the cross, O'Neill! The man has rendered his own daughter a widow and his grandsons fatherless! His hands are red with innocent blood."

Domnall shrugged. "Very well. I tell you nothing you could not learn yourself. The Lord of Lorne and Argyll sailed from Ulster's shores more than an hour ago. To where, I know not."

Angus glared at the pitiful excuse for a king, who like his MacDougall relations, had killed for ambition. "You had best not be involved in this plot against my brother. If I find it is otherwise, I will be back. God's judgment on you!" He began to turn his horse and then reconsidered. "As for Alexander MacDougall, he will die by my hand or, if God so wills, by the hand of another. But this I promise you—for his treachery, he will die in disgrace and landless."

Angus wheeled his horse toward Dunluce, the horse's hooves kicking up dirt as he galloped through the camp. The men with him spurred their horses to follow, causing all they encountered to scatter before the furious Macdonald lord and his men.

ÁINE'S FATHER HAD told her of the murder of Angus' elder brother. All at Dunseverick were shocked. Alexander Macdonald was a man widely respected in Ulster and loved by all who knew him. To ambush and slay such a lord was a grave sin.

Her head bent in sorrow, Áine thought of Angus and how he must be suffering. She prayed God would give him strength.

Wanting to meet Angus alone in the bailey when he returned, she asked Nessa to keep Brian occupied. Kintyre's lord arrived ahead of his men, who trailed behind, as if they were allowing him space to grieve alone. He dismounted and she walked to meet him. He was visibly shaken and beneath his eyes dark shadows rested as though he was worse for the tears he had not allowed himself to shed.

His men walked their horses into the bailey. The captain, mayhap wanting to give Angus and Áine privacy, nodded to her before dismounting and urging the men into the castle.

When the stable lads had taken away the horses, Áine rested her head on Angus' chest, hoping her nearness would bring him comfort. His thudding heart was a solace. "My love..." she said.

"He is gone," Angus replied in a strained whisper. "My brother is gone."

Raising her head, she met his stunned gaze.

"How can I tell Juliana?" he asked. "Or Alex's young sons?"

"I will stand by you, Angus. I will help you tell them."

"Is not the timing ironic? 'Tis the happiest and the saddest of days."

"I know, my love. Come," she said, turning him toward the castle, "my father and brother wait within and you could do with some wine."

Slowly, they walked to the castle door, his arm around her shoulders.

THE RED WINE offered Angus fortified him but the ache in his heart and the heaviness in his head remained. At the meal that followed attended by only Lord Cumee, Dermot and Áine, Angus ate nothing save bread.

"What will you do now?" asked Dermot.

Angus desperately wanted to hunt down the murderous MacDougall but he had responsibilities that had to be seen to first. "Tomorrow, as the sun rises, I must sail to Dunluce to retrieve my brother's body. Earl Richard's physician has prepared it for burial. Along with Alex, I must retrieve the bodies of his men to return them to Islay. From there I will sail to Iona to lay Alexander to rest in St. Oran's Chapel where all the Lords of the Isles have been buried since Somerled."

"Mayhap we should postpone the wedding," Áine offered.

"Nay," said Angus. "I have waited years to make you mine. If you are willing, my love, I would have you by my side. After the burial, we can be wed in the abbey church at Iona. The chiefs will be there for Alex's burial and will want to attend. Then all will return to Islay for the naming of the new chief. In these uncertain times, with treachery all around us, the lordship cannot be long without a proper leader."

Áine stared at him. On her face he read a sudden realization and a sudden dread as her eyes filled with tears. "It will be you. You will be the new Lord of the Isles."

The seer's words drifted through his mind as he thought of an answer she might understand. *Two chiefs will die before a new one rises.* "Aye, 'tis likely, but that is for the Council of the Isles to decide. Our law provides that the chieftainship descends to the most worthy of the same blood, brothers preferred, and, of those, the most senior who is 'king fit'. Alex's sons are too young to take on such responsibility but, even were they of age, the nobility of the mother would be of concern. Since the mother of Alex's sons is a MacDougall—our enemy—none of them could qualify to become chief."

Áine placed her hand on her chest as if holding in her feelings; her lips parted. "His love for her must have been great to take her as his wife knowing any sons she gave him could never become chief."

"Aye, he loved her much," said Angus, remembering their disagreement when Alex insisted he would court Juliana. "I argued against his pursuit of her but he was determined." Then, looking into her eyes, he said, "Now I understand."

"You may not realize it, my son," interjected Lord Cumee, "but I believe it is clear to all. Though you are yet in your twenties, you have already displayed the qualities that show you to be 'king fit', as you say. In a time of grief beyond enduring, your steady hand is on the tiller. The chiefs of the lordship will not fail to see it. Even had they another to consider, their choice would be you."

"I agree with Father," said Áine, "but I worry that becoming chief will make you a target of the MacDougalls' wrath."

Angus nodded for he could not deny the truth of it. "Aye, that, too, is likely, but 'twas always true." With a sinking feeling, he asked, "Does the possibility change your mind about marrying me?"

She reached for his hand. "No. If you can be brave, so can I. My love is constant. I will go with you to Iona and become your wife."

He smiled at her through the veil of tears. He had lost a brother, his right arm, but he would soon gain a virtuous woman as his bride to stand by him the rest of his life. A gift of God at a time of great sorrow.

"It would be best," said her father, "if Dermot sailed with you and Áine. I will stay behind with Brian. My old bones are best left on land and Brian is too young for the solemnity required for the burial of a Lord of the Isles. 'Sides," he said, attempting a smile, "I must see to my daughter's dowry for such an army will take time to assemble."

"You would miss the wedding?" Áine asked her father.

Lord Cumee reached out and patted her hand. "We will celebrate upon your return, Daughter. That, too, I shall arrange, if you allow."

"Of course, Father." She reached up to kiss his cheek.

Once Áine had agreed to go with him, Angus listened, content. He would allow her father to handle the rest. "What about you, Dermot?" he said to her brother. "Will you accompany your sister north to Iona? She will need a chaperone and her handmaid alone might not suffice. Too, the chiefs will want to meet you."

"I will go, and gladly," said Dermot, now fully a man and heir to The O'Cahan. "But you will have to bribe Brian to stay, mayhap with a new pony."

Angus nodded. "The Young Prince shall have a horse fit for a king."

CHAPTER 17

The sea between Islay and Iona, May 1299

TO ÁINE, WHO in all her twenty-five years, had rarely been out of Ireland, it felt strange to be sailing on Angus' galley headed for the Isle of Iona, even more so because the ship carried his brother's body. The atmosphere, despite the sun-filled day, was understandably somber, for all were in mourning.

They had first gone to Islay, where Áine met Angus' sister-in-law, Juliana, who was lost in grief over the death of her husband. As Áine had promised Angus, she remained by his side while he told his family the terrible news.

Juliana had collapsed. Revived, she was distraught at the slaying of her husband. When told who had slain him, she was in shock, screaming, "Nay, nay, it cannot be!" Hours later, the truth sank in. Juliana was stricken with guilt for her father's betrayal.

Based on what Áine had heard, she considered Alexander MacDougall as bad a seed as his daughter, Juliana, was good. He had never given her husband the promised dowry of Lismore Isle, bringing shame to his daughter. Worse, he had burned and pillaged the lordship's lands. Finally, in an act of violent treachery, he had rendered his daughter a widow and Alexander Macdonald's six young sons fatherless. The eldest, Ranald, was but seven years.

Áine knew the grief of widowhood arrived at through violent means though it had been many years since her first husband had been slain by Domnall O'Neill to gain the kingship of Tirowen. She had been an innocent when she agreed to the marriage her father arranged with a man more than twice her age. It was different with Angus. She had made him wait until she was sure. Now her heart sang only for him. Were he to be slain, she would experience grief beyond any she had known.

In the few days they had spent on Islay, Juliana had been kind to her, welcoming her into the family that would soon be hers. "I know what it is like to leave all to marry the man you love."

In turn, Áine tried to comfort Alexander's widow as best she could. "For the sake of my son, Brian, who was then a babe, I endured the loss and went on. Do not despair, Juliana. God has given you six beautiful boys who will be a comfort to you. Raise them to revere the father they knew but a short while as I have raised Brian to revere the father he never knew." Juliana's young sons had been left on Islay, watched over by servants, for the time she would be on Iona. The two women traveled only with each other and their handmaidens for female company.

Áine had persuaded Angus to say nothing of their plans to wed on Iona until the burial was concluded. "Then, mayhap the hearts of the family can be turned to happier thoughts."

"Aye," he said. "You do this for Juliana. 'Tis a kindness I did not think of."

Now, as they sailed north, Áine stood in the bow watching Angus conversing in the stern with John, Duncan and Dermot. Nessa was speaking with the captain in midship. Breaking off from that conversation, Nessa carefully wended her way along the deck, avoiding both the oarsmen and the sheathed body, to join Áine. "Mistress, see that isle off the starboard?" her handmaiden said, pointing.

Áine smiled at Nessa's use of the new word she had learned since they boarded the galley at Dunluce. Tugging the hood of her cloak forward to shield her eyes from the sun, Áine gazed east.

"The captain says we are halfway to Iona. That is the Isle of Colonsay and beyond it, the Isle of Jura. We are to stop on Colonsay to let the crew rest."

Tired of gripping the rail and bracing her legs on the moving deck, Áine said, "I would love to sit on the beach for a while."

"The captain says the isle has a fine one." Áine glanced at the handsome captain, a tall Islesman with powerful shoulders, not unlike Angus in stature. Nessa would do well in the Isles with many such men to choose from should she wish to marry.

"He is somehow familiar," Áine said.

"You would have seen him before this, Mistress," said Nessa, gazing at the man who had the body of a seasoned warrior and the manner of one used to giving commands. "He was captain of Lord Alexander's galley and now serves Lord Angus. He is a widower."

Just then, Áine saw Angus leave his companions and, with the ease of a practiced seaman, glided along the deck to her. Nessa curtseyed and made her way to stand by Juliana's young handmaiden, the two dark heads leaning close to be heard above the wind.

"How are you holding up, my love?"

"'Tis not me you must worry about." Áine looked toward midship where his sister-in-law sat on a chest staring beyond the nearest oarsman to the sea. "'Tis her."

"I am giving Juliana privacy while I can," he said. "At Iona, she will be surrounded by chiefs and their wives and well-wishing monks."

"Juliana blames herself for bringing her father's perfidy upon the Macdonalds," said Áine. "I think she even blames herself for Alexander's death."

"'Tis no fault of hers," Angus replied. He took Áine's hand and his strength passed into her. "There was only love between Juliana and Alex. The MacDougalls have been our enemies for a long while."

Áine nodded. "'Tis sad when kinsmen engage in war."

"Aye, how well we both know it."

"And you," she said, noticing the lines etched in his face. "How do you fare?"

She heard his deep, pained breath as he closed his eyes. "I am as I must be in these perilous times. No matter how I feel, 'tis strength I must show to keep the clans united."

When he opened his eyes, she fixed him with an intense gaze. "Angus, no one expects you to set aside your grief for Alex's death. He was your brother."

He nodded. "Aye, and so much more."

A short while later, they sailed into a bay with pale blue-green waters that Angus called Kiloran. There, he beached the galley on a wide crescent of golden sand. Several galleys already rested there. Draped around the edges of the wide beach like a shawl was a swath of verdant green decorated with wildflowers.

Angus helped her down from the ship while his brother assisted Juliana. Duncan and Dermot helped Nessa and Juliana's handmaiden to the sand.

"I spent some time here before," said Angus, "and it left me with pleasant memories. 'Tis home to the Macduffies, loyal recordkeepers to the Macdonalds. Malcolm, their chief, may have gone on to Iona." Casting his gaze toward the line of galleys, he said, "I do not see his galley. I am certain the news of Alex's death has reached here by now and the chiefs have begun to gather. But, if not, he can sail with us."

As it turned out, the Macduffie chief was already at Iona but his servants came to the beach to welcome them, bringing ale, bread, dried fish and fruit for the crew lounging on the sand.

Angus led Áine to a deserted patch of beach sheltered by vegetation and bid her sit on a rock. "There is something I have been remiss in telling you, and I must do so before we are wed."

Anxious at his words, Áine looked into his earnest blue eyes. His reddish-gold hair blew back from his face revealing his chiseled features, a warrior's bold face. "What is it?"

A sigh escaped his lips. "I have a natural son in Glen Coe. He is about Brian's age."

Questions flooded her mind. "The child of your mistress?"

"Nay. There have been no mistresses. The lad was the product of an encounter of only one night, but the lass believes the child is mine and I have never said otherwise."

Mindful that he might soon be Lord of the Isles, she asked, "If he is your firstborn, is he your heir?"

"Nay. No illegitimate son may be the heir. Not since the meeting at Turnberry Castle some thirteen years ago when my father made clear Alex was his lawful, that is to say, legitimate born heir. Still, I have provided for my natural son, arranging for him to foster with a friendly clan in Lochaber. It is there, north of Ardnamurchan, where he will be tutored. And, when he is grown, I will bestow lands upon him."

She waited to see if he would say more. When he did not, she said, "I do not fault you for a young man's indiscretion but I am glad the boy will not take the place of a son God may give you and me."

"Aye." He bent down and kissed her forehead. "My heir will be the child of our love."

ANGUS WAS GLAD Áine had accepted the boy whose mother still lived in Glen Coe, unmarried as far as Angus was aware. The lad, who went by the name Iain Macdonald, was, according to all reports, a fine boy.

Hearing his name shouted down the beach, Angus turned to see his captain gesturing to him. He offered his hand to assist Áine in rising but she declined. "I would sit for a while, if I may."

"Of course," he said. "You have your cloak to keep you from the wind and the flowers around you for cheerful company."

"And more besides," she said, looking out to sea.

When he reached his captain, Angus glanced back to see Áine surrounded by shore birds as if holding court. Higher up on the rocks, shags were keeping watch, their dark plumage silhouetted against the stone. It seemed word had gone forth that their patroness had arrived in the Isles. Amused, he turned back to his captain.

"The Macduffies have invited us to stay, my lord, but we can cover the eighteen miles to Iona by the evening meal if that be your decision."

"Since the days are long, let us thank the Macduffies and continue on. I want to see my brother's body in the custody of the monks, the sooner for them to begin their prayers and chanting."

As they sailed to Iona, Angus stood in the stern, his gaze reaching over the body draped with oilcloth to where Áine stood with Juliana in the bow. Without turning, he said to his brother and cousin, "When we get to Iona, find a chief's wife who is caring—a widow might be best—and ask her to take Juliana under her wing. Lady Áine is doing her best to be a comfort, but she and Dermot will be experiencing the burial ritual for the first time and may be distracted with questions for you."

"I will keep watch over Juliana and find a widow to comfort her, as you suggest," said Duncan. "With the recent attacks in the north, I believe there are new widows among the women."

"We need to find one who will not judge Juliana for her father's evil deed."

Turning to his brother, he said, "Can you make sure the crew delivers the wine and cheese we have brought from Islay to the monks?"

"Aye, Brother," said John. "I will see to it." More often than not, Angus reflected, it was John who now stood at his right hand, always eager to help. Duncan had his own business to attend to at Saddell.

Angus thanked them, glad he had their support at so critical a time. Staring at the sea, whipped to white peaks by the wind, he recalled Lord Cumee's words telling him his hand was on the tiller. If it were true, Angus was sailing into rough seas. He could not dwell on his sorrow for Alex's loss or his desire for revenge. He must rise to take his place as the Council would dictate. Though the decision had yet to be made, he was the natural choice, the one they would see as the next chief. Already he could feel the weight of the impending responsibility descending upon his shoulders. Had not Alexander felt the same when their father died?

The Isle of Iona, May 1299

THE WHITE SAND beach of Iona, coming into view fascinated Áine. In Ulster, the beaches were golden and the water dark blue. Iona's beach was pristine white and the waters close to shore a pale blue-green, sparkling like a gemstone.

On the shore, a magnificent abbey and church, hewn out of red stone, loomed before them, a great edifice for so small an isle. Angus had told her it was the spiritual center of the lordship. But she knew from her father that before it was a part of the Kingdom of the Isles, Iona was Irish, for it was the place where Columba brought his monks and created the Book of Kells, the beautifully illuminated manuscript of the four Gospels in Latin. It seemed fitting that she and Angus were to be married here.

As a young girl, she had learned about the Irish prince who had left Ireland in self-exile to go north and settle a community of monks. Columba's attachment to Iona was strong, and his prophecy of the isle's future reflected that tie.

In Iona of my heart, Iona of my love,
Instead of monks' voices shall be lowing of cattle,
But ere the world come to an end,
Iona shall be as it was.

The shore rushed up to meet them. The seals, basking on the rocks, hardly took notice. Mayhap, thought Áine, they were bored by the many people who had already come to honor Lord Alexander, for she counted a dozen galleys lined up on the beach. Colorful pennons waved from the masts announcing which chiefs had arrived.

"Once the galley is secure," said Angus, helping her down from the ship, "my guards will carry Alexander's body to the chapel where the monks will continuously chant prayers, awaiting the burial."

The wind blew more fiercely here, bending the long grass to the rocky ground. It whipped Áine's cloak behind her before she gathered it close. "I am glad it is May," she said to Juliana, who had followed her to the beach. "Even if the wind is cold, we have flowers and sun."

Juliana looked around her as if rousing from a stupor. Above the tide line, silverweed, with its pretty yellow flowers and silver-backed leaves, bloomed in abundance. Shorebirds danced with the small waves lapping at the shore. "The isle is beautiful," said Alexander's widow. "The primroses and hyacinths were not seen when I was last here. For Angus Mor's burial, there was snow."

Áine took Juliana's arm and, together, they followed the men as they walked ahead toward what looked to be a nunnery. On either side of the path, yellow flowers bloomed in abundance. "Think of the flowers as God's gift to the memory of Lord Alexander," said Áine, trying to be cheerful.

"I would be happier with God today if He had spared my husband."

"I understand," said Áine. "I, too, asked God why He did not spare mine. My first marriage was not a love match, as was yours, but Niall O'Neill was good to me. His murder, which I witnessed, came as a harsh blow. I will never forget it."

Juliana blanched and her hand covered her mouth as she turned to face Áine. "Thank God I was spared that. I could not have borne it."

Áine studied her soon-to-be sister-in-law's face and her long nut-brown hair that fell in waves beneath her hood. Even with her skin gone pale and her tear-stained, grief-stricken countenance, Juliana was a beautiful woman. "You are only a few years older than I am, Juliana. Life is not over for you."

Áine felt Juliana's sigh through the wool of their cloaks. "It seems that way. But then I am reminded, for the sake of my sons, I must go on."

"Just remember, you do not face the future alone," Áine encouraged.

Like the abbey and church she had seen from the sea, the nunnery was built of red stone, a sculpted edifice. "The history of this place is a long one," said Angus, dropping back to walk beside Áine. "Somerled built the chapel, where Alex's body will lie. Somerled's son, Ranald, built the abbey and the church. The abbey is Benedictine but the convent is Augustinian."

"The convents in Ireland are Augustinian," said Áine.

"Aye, I have seen them. The nunnery will provide good shelter for you two and your handmaidens while we are here. The nuns, many of whom are from noble families, keep a guest chamber that is well-appointed. Since it is spring, some families may prefer to set up tents on the grass but the nights may be cold and the wind never ceases."

They arrived at the nunnery door where the black-robed abbess welcomed them. Putting her arm around Juliana, who looked about to collapse, the abbess guided Alexander's widow inside. Nessa glanced back at Áine as she followed with Juliana's handmaiden.

Duncan, John and Dermot turned to go but Angus stayed behind with Áine. "We will give you time to get settled," he told her. "I will return in a few hours to accompany you to the evening meal. I hope to speak to the abbot about our nuptials before then."

Áine looked at Angus, feeling only pride. His heart was broken yet he carried on as the chief she expected he would soon become. "We can all use a brief rest."

ANGUS AND HIS three companions took the stone path that was part of *Sràid nam Marbh,* the Street of the Dead, leading from the nunnery across the windswept grass to the abbey. With the blue waters of the sound on his right and the abbey ahead, Angus remembered the other occasions he had visited the isle. Often, they were sad ones. He warmed at the thought of marrying Áine in the abbey church, for once the burial was finished they could turn to happier events.

Since Dermot had never been to Iona, as they passed the small stone chapel, Angus described what they were seeing. "That is St. Oran's Chapel, the burial chamber of the Lords of the Isles, where Alex's body will lie in state for eight days. Beside it, where all the gravestones stand, is the ancient graveyard of *Reilig Odhrain*, where isle chieftains are buried along with many Norse, Scottish and even Irish kings."

"A humble place for its significance," remarked Áine's brother.

"Aye, 'tis the oldest and most sacred place on Iona," said Angus. Then, with a glance in Dermot's direction, he pointed out, "One of the first abbots was Irish."

Duncan explained to Dermot the tall carved crosses that stood before the chapel and the abbey. "Each is dedicated to a saint." As Duncan continued his explanation, Angus took John with him to speak to the chiefs who stood by the tents that dotted the landscape near shore.

Crossing the grass, he greeted Tormod Macleod, the aging chief of the Macleods. His silver-laced fair hair blew behind him, leaving his lined face and nearly white beard on full display.

"Thank you for coming, my friend," Angus said, grasping Tormod's forearm.

"You had to know I'd be here. Alexander was a loyal friend as well as our lord. He did much to fend off the MacDougalls and their allies."

"Are your sons here?" Angus asked, looking around.

"Malcolm is here but the others remained behind to defend our lands on Harris, Lewis and Skye against the Comyns and MacRuairis. They do not pause for our burials except to celebrate."

Anger rose within Angus to think the MacDougalls were celebrating the murder of his brother. Before he could say anything, Malise, chief of the Macleans, whose dark hair had long ago turned gray, and his son, another Malcolm, approached.

"'Tis a tragic happening that brings us together in an untimely burial," said Malise. "We are torn in spirit at losing Alexander. My clan and castle at Duart are at your disposal for however we may help. Revenge must be had and we are willing to partake in it."

"It heartens me to know you stand with us," said Angus. They would expect him to seek justice for his brother and he would not shrink from the task.

"As well," continued Malise, "we would see you take your proper role as the next Lord of the Isles. None, save you, can carry the Macdonald torch."

Angus thanked Malise for his confidence and he and John strode ahead to rejoin Duncan and Dermot.

On the way, John said, "I would be to you what you were to Alex. I would fight by your side."

Angus laid his arm over the shoulder of his younger brother. "You are ever a strong right arm to me."

They rejoined their companions and walked to the abbey where they were met by the gaunt, black-robed Abbot Fionnlagh. He was much as Angus remembered him except for the lines in his face that spoke of the years that had passed and the silver strands that were threaded through his brown-tonsured hair.

Angus inclined his head to the abbot. "My guard has carried Alexander's body to the chapel."

"The monks and I have already commenced praying for Alexander's soul and for you, Lord Angus. I will make sure they go now to stand vigil for Alexander."

Angus introduced Dermot. The abbot already knew Angus' brother and cousin.

"An O'Cahan from Ulster?" the abbot asked Dermot.

"Yes, here with my sister, Áine."

Angus shifted his gaze to the abbot. "There is a matter about which I would speak to you, if you have a moment."

"Of course," said the abbot and motioned Angus to one side as the others entered the abbey to be welcomed by the chiefs and their families.

"The sister of Dermot O'Cahan is my betrothed," said Angus. "If you agree, when Alexander has been properly laid to rest, we would have you wed us in the abbey church."

"Of course," said the abbot. "I am glad to hear of your decision to marry. 'Tis more important now than ever." Angus understood the abbot spoke of the lordship's succession and the need for an heir.

"I would invite all the chiefs and their families to join with us in what may be one of the few causes for celebration for some time."

The abbot nodded. "It would be good to have your marriage blessed with the chiefs of the lordship present to observe the day. The Bishop of the Isles is here for the burial and may decide to stay for the wedding since he will go on to Islay for the installation of the new chief."

"There is also the matter of Alexander's grave slab," said Angus. "With your permission, I will order it from one of Iona's stonemasons."

"I have already advised our finest craftsman to expect you."

"I trust they can manage two rings?"

With an amused look, the abbot said, "They are very good at

working in gold as you well know."

Angus thanked the abbot and entered the abbey. Several chiefs came to meet him, including Malcolm Macduffie of Colonsay and his son, Gilchrist, both warriors as well as known scholars.

Angus reacquainted the red-haired Macduffies with his brother and cousin and then introduced Dermot O'Cahan. "The brother of Lady Áine O'Cahan, who travels with him. We stopped on Colonsay on our way here and your servants were most gracious."

"Ah," said Malcolm, "that is good. I hastened here not knowing if Lord Alexander's body had yet arrived. 'Tis a horrible deed the MacDougall has done. Only treachery could have felled our Alexander."

"Aye," said Angus, his eyes downcast. "'Twas an ambush—murder—not battle," he said, recalling the words of the wounded guard who had brought him the news. "Thanks be to God, my brother has left six sons to carry on his name."

Malcolm Macduffie placed a hand on Angus' shoulder. "I and the other chiefs stand with you and your family, my son. We are ready to see justice done."

By the time Angus and his companions had made the rounds of the chiefs and changed their clothing, it was time to go to the chapel to pay his respects to his brother. Outside the abbey, the setting sun cast its golden light over the tall carved crosses and stone slabs that marked the graves in the ancient *Reilig Odhrain*.

In the small chapel, black-robed monks stood like sentinels on either side of the body chanting, their voices echoing off the stone walls that were covered in whitewashed plaster with paintings of the saints.

Alex's body, wrapped in white winding cloth at Dunluce, had been draped with an ivory silk pall on which was appliquéd a long-shafted Celtic ringed cross in golden fabric much like that which covered the body of Angus Mor.

Candles flickered on the wooden frame suspended above the body and on the linen-draped altar, the flames drawing the air upward. Angus had seen it all before with his father's burial, the ritual preserved as if years had not passed between the two deaths. Seeing all again, the reality of Alex's death overcame him, causing the hole in his heart to grow larger as he thought of life without his brother. He had not expected Alex to die so young. In truth, he had not expected Alex to die at all.

Angus lingered for a few somber moments, praying. Then he and his companions crossed themselves and left, passing St. Oran's cross as they followed the ancient rock path to the nunnery.

Dermot was the first to speak. "A moving tribute," he said, speaking over the wind.

"'Tis only the beginning of the burial," said Duncan. "A sennight remains for all the chiefs to arrive and for the preparations to be made by the monks."

John walked ahead describing the burial ceremony to Dermot.

Duncan fell back in step with Angus. "Imagine what the chiefs—and particularly their sons—will think when they meet Lady Áine. Hearing nothing of your pending marriage, they will think she is available."

"Aye, I am aware. I have taken from Ireland a great jewel and no man will fail to observe it. But they will soon know she is mine."

"That brings to mind an old saying," said Duncan. "A man who weds a beautiful woman is like one who builds his castle on the edge of a wilderness. It must be constantly defended."

Angus gave his cousin an incredulous look and shook his head. "Advice I did not need, Cousin."

"ARE YOU CERTAIN you would wear the violet tonight?" asked Nessa, frowning, as she helped Áine to don the velvet gown she had selected to meet the chiefs. "You have other, more alluring gowns."

"I wish Angus to be proud of his betrothed, Nessa, so I must dress to be worthy of him. But I walk a narrow path as I do not wish to draw undue attention. The violet is dark and the bodice modest enough none will think me other than a lord's daughter." Áine had chosen the gown knowing this evening was critical to her acceptance. She was meeting the lordship's chiefs at a time of deep mourning. "I must show my respect for their grief."

"I suppose that is wise, but for your wedding, I have saved the golden silk gown that sparkles like a jewel. You will wear it?"

Áine returned her loyal handmaiden a look of fond acceptance. "I will."

Nessa slipped Áine's fur-lined cloak about her shoulders as a nun came to tell her the Lord of Kintyre and his companions were calling for her and Juliana.

Walking the corridor of the nunnery with Alexander's widow, Áine said, "You slept, yes?"

At Juliana's nod, Áine said, "You are better for it; your eyes are clear and your skin again has a lovely color. Hold your head high, Juliana. After all, you were Alexander's choice over all the maidens in Scotland."

Juliana smiled at Áine as they reached the door. "You are good for me, Áine, and I suspect you are good for Angus as well."

The nun who had gone before them held the lantern high as they reached the entry where Angus, his cousin, brother and Dermot waited, all in finest attire with elegant woolen cloaks. Angus had donned his hat he wore infrequently. Behind them, the sun had set and the sky had turned lavender and deep rose beneath the high gray clouds. A few stars were already making an appearance, hinting of the night to come.

Duncan offered his arm to Juliana and, with John on Juliana's other side, the three of them walked ahead to the abbey.

Angus watched them go and then turned to Áine and Dermot. To her, he said, "You look lovely. So that you are aware, I have introduced your brother to the chiefs, their wives and their sons." With a nod to Dermot, he added, "He was graciously accepted. Tonight, we will dine together with the same group. As is our custom, we will remember Alexander and his great deeds. The chiefs will praise him, recalling stories of his exploits, some oddly humorous. 'Tis our way. But first, I will introduce you to all."

Áine took her bottom lip between her teeth and lifted her hood over her head. Then, taking her own advice, she drew a steadying breath and raised her head. She had played hostess to her father's many chiefs and though these of the lordship were new to her, she hoped they would soon become her friends. Still, the walk to the abbey was not long enough to still her anxious heart.

From the darkness around them and no moon to be seen, they emerged into the brightly lit warmth of the abbey with its blazing fire, candles and torches and the sound of many conversations.

She was pleased to see Juliana was being comforted by the other women expressing their sympathy.

Angus took Áine's cloak from her and handed it to a servant. Her long hair tumbled below her shoulders. Suddenly, Áine felt the eyes of all upon her. Angus gave her shoulder a comforting squeeze. "Worry not, they will love you."

She smiled at him. "You will not leave me?"

"Not for a minute." With an amused look, he added, "There are wolves about."

Her betrothed did not wait for the introductions. Instead, he said in a loud voice, "I come to honor my brother, fallen with his companions at the hand of our enemy, and I bring with me two whose presence is a great comfort both to me and to Lady Juliana. Meet Lady Áine O'Cahan, daughter of the Chief of the Name of O'Cahan, Lord of Ciannacht in Ulster and friend to Earl Richard de Burgh. Her brother, Dermot O'Cahan, you have already met. Please welcome them for they come to pay their respects to Alexander."

Despite the somber occasion and the subdued emotions of the gathered assembly, there were smiles on every face. Áine let out a breath and returned their smiles.

Angus introduced Tormod Macleod to her, the aging chief from Skye. He bowed before her. "My lady." By his side was his son Malcolm, also fair-haired, who she judged to be in his third decade. He stared at her, open-mouthed.

After that, Áine was surrounded with well-wishers, including Abbot Fionnlagh and Mark, the Bishop of the Isles, the latter having come for the burial. They spoke of her father's endowing the abbey at Dungiven. "Your father's generosity to the Church is not unknown to me," said the aged bishop. "I am from Galloway, a short voyage to Ulster."

ANGUS LEFT Áine with one of the chief's wives as Duncan drew him aside and whispered in his ear. "Did you notice the gaping mouths of the chiefs' sons when you removed Lady Áine's cloak? Like an amethyst jewel, she emerged sparkling, leaving them speechless. It was worth every fish in Kiloran Bay to see it."

"I noticed," said Angus.

Duncan laughed, a honey curl falling over his green eyes. "I see the defense of the frontier castle has begun. As long as you are at it, you might keep watch on both Malcolm Macleod and Gilchrist Macduffie. Those sons of chiefs cannot take their eyes off her."

Angus frowned as he cast his gaze to where the two chiefs' sons stood and saw it was true. Reclaiming Áine's arm, he wished the wife of the Macleod chief a good eve and escorted Áine into dinner.

As he had expected, the evening meal was a celebration of Alex's life. For Angus, it became a bittersweet retelling of his eldest brother's acts of valor, his wisdom in matters of state, his kindnesses to the clans and his leadership in time of war. Juliana sobbed through most of it, comforted by the women. At the end, Angus felt drained, wrung out like a wet cloth. Juliana had to be led back to the nunnery by Áine and some of the other women.

Each day thereafter, he saved time from his conversations with the chiefs about matters concerning the lordship to pray with the monks in the chapel and to take walks with Áine. On the few days it rained, a rainbow always followed, the splendid sight causing Áine to remark, "So many rainbows!"

One afternoon as they sat on rocks on the beach, he spotted a pair of dolphins playing in the waters offshore. "Look!" he said. "They are jumping from the water."

"I could watch them all day."

On another day, Áine pointed out the isle's birds, keeping—he thought deliberately—his mind off war and death. "See that one?" she said, pointing. "He is an oystercatcher, very well dressed with his red beak and black and white feathers. He and his friends are looking for mollusks. And that gray one over there," again she pointed, "the one with the black head and long tail feathers. He is an Arctic tern. They like to eat sand eels."

Seeing no one around them, he leaned toward her, placing a kiss on her soft lips. "How is it you are so newly arrived in the Isles yet you know all the birds better than I, even their preferred foods?"

Smiling, she said, "Some of them are known to me and others I have studied while you are busy with the chiefs, so I have learned their habits. I also asked Gilchrist Macduffie for their names and he was most accommodating."

"Aye, I imagine he was."

A SENNIGHT PASSED and, during that time, Áine came to know the senior women of the lordship, who were staunch supporters of the Macdonalds. None of their families had paid homage to King John Balliol. "'Twould not be the first time the Kingdom of the Isles has stood alone," said Fiona Macleod, wife of the Macleod chief. "We have no love for King Edward but we like our enemies not at all."

Out of Juliana's hearing, the women spoke often to Áine of the despicable MacDougalls who had slain the Lord of the Isles. They liked Juliana but regretted her parentage. The chiefs' wives were surprised to learn Áine was a widow with a young son as she wore no veil. "In Ireland," she told them, "married women prefer to leave their long hair uncovered." They were also curious as to how Áine was so young a widow. So, she told them. "The death of my first husband, who was the King of Tirowen, was not unlike that of Alexander Macdonald—murder at the hand of a kinsman."

The women nodded, their expressions grave.

Finally, the day came for the burial. Áine waited in the crowded abbey church with Juliana for the body to be brought from the chapel for the Requiem Mass. Her gaze lifted to the paintings on the whitewashed plaster walls where the lives of saints were depicted. How could they ever forget the history when the images were all around them?

Angus, John, Duncan and Dermot had gone to the chapel to attend to the somber task of bringing the body to the church. Angus had told her the Mass that preceded the burial would be presided over by both Abbot Fionnlagh and Mark, the Bishop of the Isles.

As the bells in the church tower rang out, Angus and the men carried in the body on a bier and placed it on a decorated wooden framework set before the altar. The monks who followed chanted as they walked to where candles burned steadily on the altar. Behind the altar, shafts of golden light piercing the tall arched windows fell upon the silk ivory pall draped over the body. High above the gathered assembly, the arched wooden ceiling drew Áine's gaze.

The music and the prayers were beautiful. Once Mass had finished, the body was carried on the bier back to the abbey. This time, the bishop, in his mitre and vestments of crimson and white, walked beside the black-robed abbot and ahead of the others. The sun on the yellow flowers on either side of the path lit the way. Angus with his tearful sister-in-law followed. Juliana needed his strong arm to lean on.

Duncan and John went next. Áine followed with her brother.

Behind the family, the chiefs and their wives walked in solemn procession.

The chapel was too small to allow all to enter. Those left outside hovered close to the arched doorway, watching.

The monks, who had been chanting their ethereal songs as the family entered, fell silent. Only the sound of Juliana weeping along with some of the other women could be heard.

Abbot Fionnlagh took his position before the altar beside the Bishop of the Isles, who held the crucifix as he spoke of Alexander Macdonald and led them in prayer.

Áine did not wish to think of the shortness of Alexander's life or his untimely death. She did not want to think that Angus, too, risked his life more often than she knew. But she could not avoid these thoughts when the long grave slabs of the prior Lords of the Isles were before her, set into the paved floor. One, freshly carved, leaned against the side wall. The carving displayed a sword and a foliated cross decorated with leaves and interlocking circles. *It must be the one for Alexander.*

The bishop's prayer ended and he called Angus forward. As Duncan explained to Áine in a whisper, as the heir, it was Angus' duty to remove the bones of his father, Angus Mor, from the tomb that had been opened the day before by the monks. Angus Mor's grave slab would be moved to a new place in the chapel, his final resting place.

A bard began to chant the long ancestry of the Lords of the Isles accompanied by a harpist she had not noticed before. The chant continued as, generation by generation, the history of the lordship was recalled, from Alexander back to the ancient Conn of a Hundred Battles, whose kingdom had been based at Dunseverick. Áine realized the Macdonald linage was, in part, her own, for Angus and she had that royal Irish ancestor in common.

When the bard finished, Angus lifted his brother's body, draped only in the white winding sheet, and gently lowered it into the grave previously occupied by the bones of Angus Mor.

"It may seem an odd custom to you," whispered Duncan, "but it signifies that at a lord's burial there is a trinity: father, son and, sadly, a brother this time. The ritual transition emphasizes that the lordship is a continuous living entity in full communion with God and the Church."

The new grave slab was rolled into place on what looked to Áine like oars. With that completed, the monks' chants rose once more, their ethereal voices filling the chapel. Finally, the abbot said a last prayer for the soul of Alexander.

Angus returned to her side and took her hand. Though his eyes were dry, his expression spoke of his heartache and loss.

She squeezed his hand. "He is with God now, my love."

"Aye. That is a comfort."

That night, they dined in the abbey with the chiefs and the monks on a meal of salmon, lamb and roast beef. Áine urged Juliana to eat. "You must keep up your strength for your boys." They drank the wine Angus and others had brought and grew merry after the sorrows of the day.

When the trenchers were cleared and sweetmeats appeared, Malise, the aging Maclean chief, rose from his chair, drawing up to his full height. "We sail from here to Islay and the Council meeting where we install the next Lord of the Isles. But as you are thinking, consider this. Can there be a better man to lead us than Angus Og? We have observed him for many years as he has stood by his father and his elder brother. Often, he has fought our enemies, risking his own life to save us and our lands. Angus is a man of courage. He must be the one to lead us. There can be no other."

Others rose to echo The Maclean's comments. Áine marveled at the overwhelming support for her betrothed.

Finally, Angus rose. "As the Maclean chief correctly notes, the Council's decision will be made at Finlaggan. However, before we sail for Islay, I would invite you to stay on Iona another day for a special ceremony. God has been gracious to me, for Lady Áine O'Cahan has consented to become my wife and Abbot Fionnlagh has agreed to marry us tomorrow in the abbey church."

Smiles appeared on every face. Many shouts of "Aye" rose into the air.

From the crowded hall, the aged Macleod chief shouted to Angus, "'Tis obvious you have plucked the fairest flower of Ireland."

Áine felt her cheeks warm at his words.

"Having met her," the Macleod chief continued, "we approve."

Áine looked up at Angus, smiling down at her, and sighed with relief.

CHAPTER 18

IT HAD RAINED during the night and Áine wanted to avoid exposing her wedding finery to the wet grass and muddy rocks, so Angus had thoughtfully arranged for her to change in the abbey in the same chamber where they would spend their wedding night.

Juliana and Nessa took the long walk with her to the abbey. The day was sunny and cool as they left the nunnery. Pale blue flowers growing amidst the short grass made for a pretty picture. Further on, Áine spotted rosy sea thrift flowers blooming among the rocks on the white sand beach off to her right. *How lovely it is to be wed in spring.*

Once in the abbey, Juliana decided to wait to welcome the *canonica*, the women who lived in the nunnery without having taken vows. Many were from the noble families of the lordship and had expressed a desire to attend the wedding.

Nessa went with Áine to help her dress, expressing her excitement to be a part of this day so long in coming. "'Tis not just today, Mistress, but your new life. It will be such an adventure!"

"Doubtless, you are correct," said Áine. She had lived through tragedy but she had not had much adventure. She was certain life as

Angus' wife would provide a wealth of it.

The bedchamber to which Áine was shown must have been one the monks reserved for visiting lords, so opulent were the furnishings. The walls were graced with beautiful tapestries, one depicting the Irish prince, Columba. A woven carpet in red and blue adorned the stone floor. The bed covering and bed curtains were of crimson velvet. White ermine furs were laid across the bed's foot for added warmth.

A long narrow arched window invited in the afternoon sun. For warmth, a fire burned steadily in the fireplace. As well, a profusion of beeswax candles were arrayed on the stone mantel and bedside table.

Nessa carefully unfolded the gown of golden silk and laid it across the large bed. "See how the firelight shimmers in the silk?"

Áine stared not at the gown but at the bed beneath it, wondering what this night would bring. Certainly, it would not be like her first wedding night, which had been a painful introduction to the ways of a man with a maiden, although the instructor had been kind. This night, she hoped, would be a feast of love for two who had waited years to become one.

"I brought the circlet of gold your mother wore at her marriage to Lord Cumee," said Nessa, proudly holding out the bejeweled band that fitted Áine's head perfectly. Small rubies, emeralds and sapphires sparkled from the gold. "You will look like a queen."

"I only hope Angus will find me so." Today, she thought not of pleasing the chiefs and their wives; she thought only of pleasing Angus.

Nessa turned a bewildered gaze upon her as she helped her into the gown. "Mistress, you have only to look at the man when his eyes are upon you to know he is enthralled. Why, you could wear rags and he'd not complain."

Juliana peeked her head in the door. "It is time. Angus is coming."

A few minutes later, fully dressed, her long dark hair brushed to a gloss and secured by the golden circlet, Áine stepped through the door. There stood Angus, beaming. His hair and beard, with bronze and copper amid the light brown strands, had been finely trimmed. Blue silk, the color of his eyes, embraced his broad shoulders and body. Circling his waist was a gilded belt holding his sword and dagger. Áine smiled inwardly. She was marrying a warrior so she could hardly expect him to forgo his weapons just because it was their wedding day.

His gaze roved over her, a look of approval on his face. For a moment, he just stared. Then he offered her his hand. "Come, my beautiful bride, Abbot Fionnlagh waits at the altar to hear our vows and bless our marriage. And, Nessa, you will not be needed by your mistress tonight. Enjoy yourself."

Áine took his hand and felt destiny leading, as if her whole life had been lived for this moment and what would come after. She did not think it possible to love Angus more, so full was her heart. Here was the man she had longed for as a girl. Here was the man God was giving her after so many years.

Hand in hand, they walked the decorated corridor with its painted tiles and arches. In the distance, she could hear the monks chanting their liturgical music. As she and Angus entered the church near the altar, the music faded and all eyes turned upon them.

Crowded into the abbey church were chiefs and their wives, the noblewomen from the nunnery, monks and the guards and men in the service of the lordship.

The lean, black-robed abbot stood before the altar, his back to the arched windows. His kind face was alight with pleasure at his task as he beckoned Áine and Angus to him. She took her place in front of the abbot on Angus' left.

The abbot cleared his throat. "Angus, son of Angus Mor Macdonald, and Áine, daughter of Cumee O'Cahan, you have come before these who are gathered to affirm your commitment to each other and to make your sacred vows before God."

Áine listened as the abbot began reciting the familiar vows they would repeat, simple words promising to love and honor. Words had been added. For Angus, the words were "to guard" and, for her, the words "to obey". She was quick to repeat them and speak "I will" at the proper time. Angus' eager acceptance of her as his wife made her smile.

Once their vows were spoken, Angus brought forth two rings

from a small velvet pouch at his waist and gave them to the abbot, who blessed them and handed them back. Angus slipped a circle of gold carved with Celtic knots onto her finger. In the center was a round emerald. His own ring that he gave her to place on his finger was like it but without the stone.

Angus had told her that among the Iona monks were superb craftsmen in metal. Looking at her finger, she smiled for the ring's design reminded her both of Ireland and the carved crosses on Iona.

Finally, the abbot prayed, asking God's blessing upon their marriage and for their union to be fruitful.

Angus kissed her, whispering before their lips touched, "It will be."

His lips were warm on hers, sealing their vows before God and their friends, promising a life together. Lifting his head, his blue eyes fixed her with a steady gaze before turning with her to greet their guests.

The first to rush toward them were the women who embraced Áine.

ANGUS TURNED TOWARD his companions though his heart's desire was to escape with his bride to the bedchamber prepared for them. He had examined the chamber that morning before sending for Áine to assure all was ready.

"You are the envy of every man here," said Duncan. "I expect you missed the groans from Malcolm Macleod and Gilchrist Macduffie when you announced you were to marry Lady Áine."

"Mayhap I just ignored them."

"Lady Áine is a golden vision," said John, "like something out of a dream I never had."

Duncan chuckled. "True for us both."

Seeing Áine engulfed by the women, Angus decided it was time to reclaim his bride. The crowd parted as he strode toward her. Taking her hand, they were swept away on the tide of chiefs, their wives and their sons carrying them to the banquet set for them in the abbey.

At the head table, Angus and Áine were flanked by the abbot and the bishop with Juliana, Duncan, Dermot and John taking up the other seats. On the tables before them was a feast of venison, fish and roast fowl with vegetables from the monks' gardens and hot loaves of bread, butter and honey.

The bishop looked out at the tables crowded with the leaders of the lordship and their families. "After so much grief, they needed a cause for joy."

Pitchers of mead appeared on the tables. "The monks have contributed the mead made from Iona's wildflower honey," said the abbot.

The mead was of very high quality and sweet to the tongue. "'Tis very good," said Angus. "Thank you for your generosity and my compliments to the monks who have made all this possible."

The minstrels Angus had sent for from the Isle of Mull had arrived a few days before and were adding their lively music to the celebration.

Turning to his bride, he asked, "Are you happy, my love?"

Her brown eyes sparkled. "Oh, yes. It is as if a cloud has lifted and the sun now shines full."

Angus knew the cloud would not fully pass until the MacDougalls were dealt with and the war ended but he would enjoy this day for all it meant.

After a few hours of frivolity and many toasts, he took Áine's hand and raised her from her chair. The music stopped. "It is not that we do not love you," said Angus. "We do. But, as you can understand, my bride and I want to be alone. Enjoy yourselves for the day is young." With that, he escorted her from the boisterous crowd.

BECAUSE THEY WERE in the abbey and leaders of the Church were present, while laughter and cheers followed their departure, there were no ribald jokes and no unseemly comments, for which Áine was grateful. Still, the eyes of all were upon them as they took their leave.

In their bedchamber, warmed by the fire, Áine's gaze drifted to the crimson bed. The cover had been turned back, revealing fine white linen sheets. A sprig of yellow flowers lay upon each pillow.

Angus took off his sword belt and dagger and set them aside. Then he pulled his tunic over his head and kicked off his leather shoes.

Áine was suddenly nervous as she faced him, trying to keep her eyes fixed on his face. Her hands fidgeted in front of her as she looked down. "It has been years since—"

"For me as well," he said, coming to her and placing his hands on her shoulders. In the firelight, his skin glowed. "There is nothing for it," he said, removing his linen shirt, braies and hosen. "We must begin anew. Our only memories will be the ones we make tonight and hereafter."

His mouth was soft and warm; hers was seeking and hungrier than she knew. His lips found the cool skin at her neck, lighting a flame as they descended to her bared shoulders. His beard tickled her skin, causing her to shiver.

Gently, he pulled at her laces and she felt the golden silk fall away. He lifted her chemise from her and she felt the fire's warmth on her bare skin.

"You are lovely as I imagined you would be. Come, my dove, let us away to our nest where a night of love awaits us."

Áine eagerly went. Never before had she known the shared passion that followed. Never before had she felt so treasured, so loved. Angus did not hurry though she was sure he wanted to. As if he were stoking a fire, carefully coaxing the flames, he drew the want of him from her until she could not bear to be separated. When at last they came together, it was a joining of their souls as well as their bodies.

Hours later when they had slept for a while, her eyes opened to see his face next to hers on the pillow. His eyes were closed and his arm lay heavy across her. The fire's dying embers cast the room in dim light.

In sleep, the lines of stress he had borne with such courage had vanished. He was a powerful warrior in repose with supple skin over hard muscle earned on his ships and in battle. She ran her fingers over his face, moving aside the errant strands of his hair that impeded her view.

So, this is what love looks like.

His eyes still closed, Angus smiled. "You are awake?" When she didn't answer, he pulled her to him, his warm chest searing her breasts. "Then you have energy for more."

She laughed and was soon swept away by his kisses.

The next time she woke, sated and happy, sunlight filtered in through the narrow window. Angus lay on his back, awake and staring up at the ceiling.

"What are you thinking?" she asked him.

"Of what must follow." Some of the lines had returned to his face and she knew he thought of the war, the new role he must assume for his people and his pursuit of his brother's killer.

"At least we had last night," she said. And then with a mischievous grin, she added, "A memory worthy of its making."

He turned his face toward her, his hand reaching out to cup the side of her face. His expression was full of love. "Aye, and there will be more like it."

The sheet fell to her waist as she rose on one elbow, her long hair falling to cover her breasts. "Whatever comes, Angus, we now face it together."

ANGUS KNEW THEY could not linger overlong in their love nest though that would have been his choice. They must sail to Islay where he would accept the burden of the lordship should that be the wish of the Council. With a resigned sigh, he rose from the bed and donned the clothes he'd had a servant bring to the chamber the day before.

He glanced back to where his bride slept, her hand tucked under her chin, her long dark hair strewn across the pillow. Silken hair he had run his fingers through during their lovemaking. With skin like cream and delicate curves, her beauty was more than he could have hoped for and her kind heart, a special gift. Leaning over the bed, he kissed her awake. "I'll send Nessa to help you dress. Once we have broken our fast, we sail to Islay."

It was with the greatest reluctance he strode to the door. Nessa was waiting outside their chamber. "Your mistress is awake."

In the main chamber where they had dined the night before, Angus was greeted with knowing smiles by the chiefs, who were breaking their fast with their sons. Their wives, who were yet to arrive, he assumed were overseeing the packing.

"He looks none the worse for wear," said Tormod Macleod, giving Angus a long perusal.

"I am not so sure," said Maolmuire, the battle-hardened chief of the MacMillans whose black hair this morning was disheveled. Then with a hearty laugh, he joked, "Are those not circles under his eyes from lack of sleep?"

"Aye," chimed in Malise, the Maclean chief, nudging his son Malcolm with his elbow, "but a lack of sleep that left him invigorated."

Much laughter followed as Angus took his place on one side of the long table, reaching for a piece of salmon and some bread to go with his ale.

"Do not torment the lad," said Malcolm Macduffie, "else he may sail to Dunaverty instead of Islay."

"Oh, right," put in John MacNicol of Lewis, a man of fair countenance like the Macleod chief. "You do sail for Finlaggan?" he asked Angus.

"Aye," said Angus, resigned. "I cannot escape but you sorely tempt me." A few more jests were bantered about before Angus asked, "Are the abbot and bishop here?"

"The abbot, yes," said Tormod. "He was just asking when we might depart. The bishop has sailed for Islay. Something about needing to ready his chamber before the horde arrives."

"Will all of you come?" Angus asked the dozen men at the table dining on kippers, salmon, bread, cheese and berries. Knowing the northern chiefs would be concerned about attacks by the MacDougalls, the Comyns and the MacRuairis, he expected some might not.

"All will come," said the Macduffie chief. "We do not install a new chief every day, war or no. But some of us will stop on the way south to add a bard or family member to our party. And mayhap a horse or a hound. After all, the usual pursuits will be observed."

"Thank you," Angus said. "I would have the clans united now. And I have something of a surprise for them." He thought of the dowry and hoped it would please the leadership as it pleased him.

Just then, Duncan stumbled into the hall with John and Dermot in tow and took their place at the table.

"You must have enjoyed the monks' mead," Angus said to them with a smile, for all looked as if they'd had a restless night.

"Aye," said John, rubbing his forehead as if it pained him. Reaching for a crust of bread and a goblet of ale, he added, "'Twas most excellent mead."

The wives began to stream in. Angus was relieved to see Juliana among them, looking as if she had slept well. "Should I go to Áine?" she asked.

"Nay," replied Angus. "Her handmaiden is with her. She will join us shortly."

Which Áine did, smiling at all as she entered.

"Now there's a happy lass," said Maolmuire. "Good morning to you, my lady."

"Good morning," said Áine, blushing as she took her place next to Angus.

He reached over to kiss her temple. "My love, beware the chiefs. They would tease your husband without mercy this morning."

She fixed him with an enticing gaze. "And do you take the teasing well, my lord?"

"Aye. All in good fun."

An hour later, Angus had thanked the monks and the nuns for their hospitality and aid in the burial of his brother. He did not worry for their sustenance as the Macdonalds had gifted them fertile lands on other isles that produced a fair income. To that, the clan added all they bestowed upon the church and abbey at Iona.

Bidding good day to Abbot Fionnlagh, Angus sailed for Islay.

He had warned his servants and the men he left on Islay to be ready for him and the chiefs at Finlaggan.

A day later, they arrived at Loch Indaal, the sea loch on the south coast of Islay whose beach could hold more than a hundred galleys. Met by his men with horses, they rode the few miles from the beached ships to Loch Finlaggan. Six years ago, his brother had been installed here as the Macdonald chief with much gaiety. He expected this would be different given it was murder that led to the need for a new chief and they were still in a time of war. But the Macduffie chief had been correct in his forecast. Over the next two days, all the clans arrived to honor the tradition.

The chiefs, who made up the Council, met in the chamber reserved for them on the smallest isle in the lake, Eilean na Comhairle. Tormod Macleod again made his speech endorsing Angus and, without dissent, Angus was confirmed as their choice to lead the clans.

The installation ceremony, presided over by Mark, the Bishop of the Isles, in his official vestments, mitre and ring, was the same one by which Angus' brother, Alexander, had been made the Lord of the Isles. At the end of it, the bishop placed in Angus' hands the same sword that had belonged to both Alexander and their father. By that, all understood Angus had agreed to protect the lordship from its enemies.

With the ceremony concluded and prayers said for the new lord's success, Angus was pronounced Angus of Islay—the designation signifying the Macdonald chief—and Lord of the Isles.

The afternoon was given to celebration and the music of bards. The women enjoyed each other's company and that of their new lady. The men hunted with horse and hound for the red deer. The good weather prevailed as if God were smiling on this day.

At the meal that evening, with Áine at his side, Angus rose to thank the chiefs. "I am grateful for your trust in me and will, with God's help, lead you in the right path for Scotland and the lordship." Looking down at Áine, whose winsome brown eyes met his gaze, he said, "You have met my bride, Áine, daughter of The O'Cahan. What you may not know is that she comes to me with a rich dowry. Not one of gold or lands or cattle but of something we need far more: worthy men to bring their skills and fighting prowess to our Isles. My lady's dowry is more than a thousand men from The O'Cahan's finest who have volunteered to come to the Isles with their lady."

Mouths dropped open. Some faces looked puzzled, but on the faces of many were smiles.

"We have a canny new chief!" shouted Malcolm Macduffie.

"Aye," said Tormod Macleod. "Who would have thought so young a chief would have so much foresight and wisdom? We do need men and we have room for them."

Angus was grateful most approved.

"What will you do with so many?" asked one chief.

"I would settle them in your lands and mine," said Angus. "I ask any of you willing to take some of the Irishmen to let me know. Among them will be young chiefs who have consented to marry your daughters. Having fought with these men, I can assure you they are worthy men of good character. And there will undoubtedly be craftsmen and those skilled in the healing arts."

Before the day was done, Duncan and John, meeting the chiefs, had made a list of the destinations for the Irishmen.

Later, when he and Áine were alone in their chamber, he said, "I hope your father is able to deliver on his promise, my love, else the chiefs will doubt my bargains in the future."

She laughed. "Oh, you need not worry, Husband. If my father made you a promise, he will keep it. The only question is, do you have enough galleys to transport them?"

"Aye, a good point. I will see to it. Some of the chiefs, who take many Irishmen, will lend me their galleys."

They stayed at Finlaggan for only a few days. During that time, they spoke again of the lordship's beginnings, of Somerled's vision for a Kingdom of the Isles, independent of the surrounding countries. "For better or worse, we are a part of Scotland now. Scotland's future is ours."

"Yet the lordship serves the English king?"

"For now, aye, because our enemies are arrayed on the other side and Scotland has no true king."

After that, they sailed to Dunyvaig on the other side of the isle in order to bring Juliana home to her sons and gather a fleet to sail to Ireland.

Duncan, John and Dermot remained with Angus and agreed to sail with him and Áine to Ulster. "You can help me in our task," he told the three men. "We must sail a fleet of galleys with room for a thousand men who we will then transport to the Isles where they will make their homes."

They agreed with eager nods. "It may take more than one trip to get them all," said John.

"Aye," agreed Angus. "We will see how many Lord Cumee is able to gather."

Dermot said, "I know the men and can help make sure the right ones go to the places assigned by the chiefs."

"I have an additional request of you, Dermot. When I left young Brian behind, I promised he would have a horse fit for a king. Can I take you first to Dunluce to procure such a horse and ask you to ride it to Dunseverick?"

"Of course," said Dermot. "But the horse must be chosen with his age in mind. He is but nine years."

"Aye, no stallion," said Angus, bemused. "I recall seeing a beautiful young dapple-gray mare when I was once at Dunluce. She is young but trained and spirited. I remember her because she is named Enbarr. The stable boy said it is the name of the horse belonging to Lir, the mythical sea god Brian's wolfhound is named for. If the earl is willing to sell her, that would be my choice. And young Brian will have a horse to match his hound."

Dermot nodded, smiling. "I like that idea and think Brian will, too. I would be pleased to do that for my nephew and for you, brother-in-law. As long as I am there, I can bring any news from the Red Earl."

The next day, Angus, Áine and his companions sailed from Lagavulin Bay with twenty-five galleys bound for the northern coast of Ulster. Angus let Dermot off at the rocky shore of Dunluce and then sailed on to Dunseverick, beaching the galleys at White Fields Bay east of the castle. They arrived at Dunseverick just as the sun reached its zenith. Lord Cumee had sent horses to the beach so Angus and his companions could ride to the castle.

In the bailey, Lord Cumee welcomed them and embraced his daughter. "So, you're a married woman now."

"Yes, Father, and a happy one."

Lord Cumee gave Angus an approving glance. "We've a celebration planned for you. I will call the chiefs to attend this eve. Your crews will have food to sustain them. Meantime, tomorrow I would show you Áine's dowry."

"I trust I will need all the galleys I have brought," said Angus.

Lord Cumee chuckled as he began to walk to the castle door. "I watched as you sailed by Dunseverick. I think you will need more!"

Inside the great hall, Angus, Áine, John and Duncan were offered ale and a midday meal of fish, bread and fruit.

Brian, set free from his tutor, ran into the hall, his red hair askew. His freckles prominent and his dark blue eyes like the waters of the Atlantic, he exclaimed, "Mother!" as he ran to kiss Áine. Then, seeing Angus, he said, "Lord Angus. Are you my father yet?"

Angus laughed. "Aye, Young Prince. Your mother is my wife. Come sit with us and eat."

Brian climbed onto the bench. "Grandfather said you would have a surprise for me since I had to stay home."

"I do," said Angus. Glancing at Lord Cumee, he added, "It will come later today with your Uncle Dermot."

Lord Cumee shook his head. "He has pestered me every day you were gone, asking when you would return and when his surprise would arrive."

Brian looked down at the plate set before him. "I suppose I can wait."

"I am proud of you," Angus said to the boy. Then, with his eyes fixed on his bride, he said, "Good things come to those who are willing to wait."

ÁINE WAS GLAD to be home yet Dunseverick—and Ulster for that matter—no longer felt like her home, only that of her family. Her home was now in the Isles, at Dunaverty or Dunyvaig or any other of Angus' many castles. Barring the effects of war, that meant a lot of sailing, at least until the babes started arriving. She would have Brian with her but her father and brother would remain in Ireland. The thought made her wistful as she gazed out the window in the bedchamber she now shared with Angus. The sun was low in the sky but had not yet set. June was the month of long days.

"I have much to do to make Dunaverty, your choice of residence, a home," she told Angus as they dressed for the dinner that was to be a celebration of their wedding.

"Since my mother died, except for what Juliana has done at Dunyvaig, we have not added to the furnishings of any castles," said Angus. "My sisters are older and married so you will have a free hand. Mayhap you might enlist Juliana's help. It would give her a purpose beyond her sons, who have nursemaids, and make her feel useful to us."

"Oh, that is a splendid thought. I will. It would be good to have her advice." Áine had released Nessa for the evening, so she turned her back to Angus for him to tighten her laces. "Shall we begin with Dunaverty?"

"Aye, but first I must distribute your dowry to the Isles and see to their military training if needed. Why not come with me as I do? It would give you a chance to see more of our lands and with many galleys and many men, you would be safe." He pulled the laces tight, tied them off, and kissed the back of her neck.

"Yes, I would like that. Can we take Brian?"

She heard him chuckle before he said, "I expect we'd better." Again, he kissed her neck, his beard tickling her tender skin. She turned in his arms. "You could keep kissing me but then we might not attend the celebration."

He let out a sigh. "Very well. Like Brian, I suppose I will have to wait."

BEFORE THE DINNER began and the chiefs and their wives arrived, Dermot appeared in the bailey riding a dapple-gray mare. Angus was there to meet him.

"Earl Richard is coming to the dinner this eve," he said, dismounting. "He says he has news for you. And the mare is his gift; he would take no coin for her."

Brian burst through the castle door with Lir at his side and ran to his uncle. Eyes wide, he asked, "Is this my surprise?"

"Aye," said Angus. "Her color is like Lir's, and her name is Enbarr, the name of the horse the mythical Lir rode. What do you think?"

Brian gazed up at the fine horse proudly tossing her head, causing her silver-gray mane to flash with the golden light of the setting sun. Her body was, indeed, mottled like Lir's coat. "She is beautiful! Can I ride her now?"

"Patience, Little Prince," said Angus. "Let her settle in and, tomorrow morning, I will ride with you."

Brian heaved a sigh. "All right." He followed the groom as he led the horse to the stable.

"You do realize he will want to sleep in the stable tonight," said Dermot.

Angus watched the boy walking away, one hand on his new horse as he fired questions at the groom. "Aye. I spent one cold night in the stable with my first horse. It will not hurt him."

ÁINE WAS THRILLED to see so many in the great hall that night to celebrate her marriage to Angus. The long days of early summer made travel easier and the last few days had brought no rain. In addition to the O'Cahan chiefs and their wives, and their elder sons and daughters, Norman nobles had come. The Red Earl and his countess, the fair Lady Margaret, were joined by Sir Hugh Bisset, Lord of the Glens of Antrim, who was kin to Angus.

Áine wondered if they all wanted another look at the middle son of Angus Mor Macdonald, who was now Lord of the Isles. If they had heard of her dowry, which doubtless they had, they also knew he would soon sail from Ireland, taking with him more than a thousand of Ulster's men.

For the evening, Áine had chosen an emerald silk gown and the same circlet of gold with its sparkling jewels she had worn at her wedding. "'Tis fitting for the Lady of the Isles to wear it," Nessa had said as she handed the golden chaplet to Áine.

Brian was allowed to attend since the Red Earl and his wife had brought some of their children who were old enough to attend yet not married. The oldest of them was Elizabeth who was fifteen and fair like her mother. The rambunctious child Áine had once known had grown into a beautiful poised young woman. Áine remembered herself at that age, soon to be betrothed to a much older man. She wondered to whom the Red Earl would give this lovely daughter.

Minstrels played as the assembled guests took their seats. Next to Earl Richard, Áine's father had placed Angus, so that the earl might have a chance to talk with him. Sitting on Angus' other side, even with the din of conversations, Áine would be able to hear the two men converse. She was anxious to know of affairs in Scotland that affected her husband.

On her father's other side sat Lady Margaret and Sir Hugh.

As the wine was poured, Earl Richard turned to Angus. "I am sorry for the loss of your brother. Such a terrible deed will not be forgotten. You will seek justice, I presume?"

"Aye. I have some duties that I must see to first, and then I will seek permission from King Edward to hunt The MacDougall."

"He will grant it."

Áine could see by the look of determination on her husband's face that he would hunt The MacDougall with or without Edward's permission.

"You may not have heard since you were at Iona," said Earl Richard, "but a Council of the Scots was recently held at Peebles in the Selkirk forest. Bruce and Comyn, as Guardians of Scotland, were charged with leading the war against Edward. Apparently, they argued over the disposition of William Wallace's lands while he is in France soliciting support from King Phillip. Bruce sided with Wallace and Comyn turned on Bruce, seizing him by the throat."

"John Comyn is a hothead," said Angus. "But how did you know this?"

"We have a spy among the Scottish Council. Bruce and Comyn had to be separated by the others who were there. That led to Bishop Lamberton being named a third Guardian. Is it always so in Scotland that a bishop is needed to keep the peace among its leaders?" With that, the earl broke out in laughter.

At Áine's side, Angus remained silent and pensive.

"I know the Earl of Carrick is your friend," said Earl Richard, "but Edward will, doubtless, laugh when he hears of it."

"When do you expect Edward to return to Scotland?" asked Angus.

Earl Richard paused, as if in thought. "He has ordered his army to muster at York on the 12th of November."

"A winter campaign?" asked Angus, surprised.

"Edward conquered Wales in winter, why not Scotland?"

"Will you go?" Angus asked the earl.

"The king has yet to meet my demands and there is work for me here in Ireland as I am the deputy for John Wogan while the justiciar is in Scotland securing the supplies for the king's army. Oh, and there was another bit of information that came from the meeting at Peebles."

Áine studied her husband's face. Angus raised his brows but remained silent.

"Apparently, a letter came from beyond the Firth of Forth, recounting how Sir Alexander Comyn and Lachlan MacRuairi were devastating the districts they were in, attacking the people of Scotland."

Angus said, "I need no spy to tell me that. I have witnessed it myself."

"The Council was none too pleased and Comyn was dispatched to rein in his relations."

At that point, Áine's father must have heard enough about the war. He rose from his chair. "Lift your goblets to Lady Áine and Lord Angus who have just been wed on Iona. They begin their life together, uniting the O'Cahans and the Macdonalds—Ulster and the Isles!"

Benches and chairs slid over the stone floor as all rose from their seats, goblets raised. "To Lady Áine and Lord Angus!"

Earl Richard shouted, "To health and long life!" The toast was echoed around the hall.

"May God bless them with many children!" cried one of the chiefs. The toast was followed with shouts of "Many children!" and that was followed by a few pithy comments shared about the hall.

Áine shifted her gaze to where Brian sat with the de Burgh children. He looked puzzled as if he had never considered the marriage would bring him siblings, competitors for her love. She would have to assure him that, as the older brother, he would have great responsibility and power that must be wielded carefully and with grace.

"May you know only happiness!" said one chief, lifting his goblet high.

More rounds of toasting followed as they were showered with blessings. Áine's soul overflowed with joy to hear them.

Angus put his arm around her, drawing her close. They had not returned to their seats since the first toast. "My beautiful bride and I thank you!"

MUSIC AND DANCING followed the toasts. Angus led his bride in a circular dance in the Irish tradition. She laughed, happiness on her face, as her hair flung out behind her. After a few dances, he gave her into the hands of waiting admirers while he went in pursuit of information and allies.

"I don't suppose you know of the whereabouts of Alexander MacDougall?" he asked the Lord of the Glens of Antrim.

The elder statesman's bushy dark brows rose above his narrow eyes and his hand pulled on his short graying beard. "No, but then I've not asked. I imagine you seek revenge."

"Vengeance, aye, but also justice, Sir Hugh. I would welcome your assistance in hunting the man down."

"I will gladly help. And John MacSween of Knapdale, who is among your guests tonight, may be interested in joining the hunt. He has no love for the MacDougalls and has been serving Edward in the hope the king will grant his request to regain Castle Sween. I believe King Edward will look favorably upon his request."

"Thank you," said Angus. "I will speak to MacSween. If I could, I would leave tomorrow to hunt The MacDougall but I have another task that must be seen to first."

Sir Hugh looked disbelieving. "What could be more important than avenging your brother's murder?"

"'Tis a matter of some urgency. I must settle over a thousand Irishmen in the Isles. My bride's dowry."

"Ah, yes, I had heard something of that. I thought it might be just a tale told over too much ale."

"Nay, 'tis truth."

The next morning, after his ride with young Brian and his new horse, Angus kissed his bride and wished her a good day as he rode east from Dunseverick with Lord Cumee and their combined, well-armed guard. Passing Coleraine, they arrived at Limavady on the River Roe at noon. Lord Cumee had told Angus the men of the dowry, who called themselves "Áine's Army", would be waiting there to be introduced to their new lord.

From where he sat atop his horse, Angus' gaze stretched far ahead, seeing rows and rows of men. Their clothing and weapons told him some were galloglass. Others were young chiefs—some he recognized. And still others were craftsmen, cattlemen, farmers and fishermen.

Lord Cumee said, "As you requested, they are all volunteers." Chuckling, he added, "The task of recruiting young men to follow Angus Og Macdonald, the new Lord of the Isles, was easier than I had thought. It seems you have garnered much respect in your time in Ireland. Then, too, you should know half of them are in love with my daughter."

"Aye, 'tis the same wherever we go. How many are there?"

"One hundred and forty from each of the ten surnames of my people, including twenty-four young chiefs, willing to marry the daughters of your chiefs. Come, I will introduce them." They dismounted and walked forward. Lord Cumee waved the men forward, calling out each surname as they passed in review, bowing before Angus and Lord Cumee at they did.

"The Munroes," began Lord Cumee, "so-named because they come from the innermost Roe-water in Derry. Almost all are redheads and fierce fighters. Next are the Roses of Kilraack, the Fearns, the Dingwalls, the MacBeths of the tribe of O'Neill, who are skilled physicians, the O'Docharties, the MacGees, associated with the O'Neills, the MacPhersons, the MacColms, and the O'Rourkes."

Angus was pleased. More than that, he was overwhelmed. "I am pleased beyond measure," he said to Lord Cumee. "You have given me men to fill my Isles, men to raise sons who will defend the lordship after them. In turn, I will give them land to call their own and training to be warriors for those who do not yet have those skills, for one must always be ready to defend one's own."

"They are eager and will serve you well."

"Is there a bard among them?" asked Angus.

"I believe so, yes. A MacMhurich poet, as I recall. Have you a need?"

"We have our Scots bards but I would have one for Áine to grace my hall, one who is knowledgeable in the Irish poems, songs and history."

Lord Cumee smiled. "My daughter will like that. You are wise."

When the introductions were concluded, Angus stood on a rock to be heard by all and said in his loudest voice, "You honor my bride and me. Know that we are anxious to have you among us, and my chiefs are ready to welcome you to the Isles where you will have land and pride in your new life. My ships are at the coast at White Fields Beach to carry you to your new homes. Say your goodbyes today for we sail at noon tomorrow. If any have horses they wish to take, let me know and we will make provision for them. Hounds are welcome, too."

During dinner at Dunseverick, Angus consulted with John, Duncan and Dermot on the list they had created for where the Irishmen would go. Some chiefs had made special requests for physicians, smiths, and carpenters. Others, faced with constant threats from the clan's enemies, had requested trained soldiers. All these requests were accommodated with more left to be settled as Angus saw fit.

"As for me," said Angus, "I would have fifty galloglass, if you can find them among the Irishmen. They will help train the others, for I intend to see them all made warriors, no matter they be farmers or smiths or fishermen when they come to us. Oh, and Lord Cumee assured me there would be a bard among them. The bard will live wherever Áine and I make our home so that his music and poems will fill our hall."

That night, Angus wrote his friend, Rob, a letter that he would have delivered by a trusted messenger, letting the Earl of Carrick know all that had transpired, though he suspected word of Alexander's murder at the hands of the MacDougalls was already widely known. As Angus came to the end of the letter, he wrote,

> *There is an English spy in your Council whose name I do not know. Be careful what you say of your plans for nothing is secret in those meetings that is not known to Edward.*

CHAPTER 19

Dunaverty Castle, Kintyre Peninsula

IN THE MONTHS following their marriage, Áine sailed with Angus and his fleet, visiting the Isles, as he transported the Irishmen to their new homes. It was a joyful time, getting to see more of his Isles and meeting his people who were gracious to her. Seeing her own kinsmen pleased at the Isles that would become their home made her heart beat proudly.

Save for the ill effects of war that had inflicted deaths, burned dwellings, and damage to their churches, the people of the Isles were a happy, industrious lot, who took pride in their skills, their farms, their galleys and their families.

During this time, she observed a change in her new husband. Not in his love for her, which remained steadfast, but in the responsibility he accepted, as easily as an invitation to dinner, and his manner toward his men and the chiefs of the lordship.

He was more observant, more focused, more careful. Oft times, more intense. Where he must have once looked to his elder brother, he now looked to no man save himself. He sought advice from his constables, his cousin, Duncan, his younger brother, John, and, importantly, the chiefs, but always in the end, the decisions were his, the weight of them borne by him alone. She had married a man of consequence who was respected by all.

John, who still did work for King Edward, as a kind of exchequer, became Angus' new confidante. This was particularly so when Duncan was at Saddell, which he now managed for his family. And sometimes Duncan was away on his own business. She had heard him tell Angus that he was pursuing one of the chiefs' daughters. "I must secure one for myself while some are still unwed, else your Irish chiefs will have them all spoken for!"

Even when it came to dealing with King Edward, who now recognized Angus as the Admiral of the Western Isles, as he had once recognized Alexander, Angus drafted his requests for authority in carefully neutral, sometimes eloquent, terms. The authority Angus requested was always granted him.

Angus seemed to grow in stature, and Áine was not the only one to remark upon the change.

"He is like sharpened steel," said his brother, John, to Duncan as they looked down upon the beach from the battlements where Angus was wielding his sword in practice with his guards. "Never have I seen him fight like this, so focused, so strong."

"Aye," said Duncan. "He worries for the future and is possessed with the need to be ready. The men sense it and admire him. Once, they followed Alexander. Now, they follow Angus, moving quickly to obey his orders."

It seemed to Áine there were many orders, as if Angus felt the time was short for all he envisioned. In good weather and bad, he dispatched his galloglass to all the Isles to assess the fighting skills of the Irishmen he had placed in various parts of the kingdom and to teach them strategy and techniques. But it was not just the Irishmen who were to be trained, some of whom Angus told her had come to him already skilled. Angus had told the chiefs he intended to see all Islesmen trained for battle with sword, axe and bow, including men whose occupations did not often see them in battle. Farmers, keepers of cattle, fishermen, smiths, carpenters, masons, administrators and seneschals would learn the basic skills.

He had told her he sent one of his best galloglass warriors to Glen Coe to see that Iain MacDonald was trained. She respected his provision for his natural son, even in this.

Angus also sent messengers to their best smiths to enlist them in making the finest weapons—swords, axes, spears and daggers. Archers were to have a ready supply of arrows.

"We will not always fight for England's king," he told her. "One day, we will fight for our own, and we must be ready."

She never asked him how he knew this or why his voice had an urgent tone to it. The look in his eyes and the set of his jaw spoke of its certainty.

In the spring of 1300, a year after their wedding, Áine gave birth to their first child, a son. They named him Alexander for the brother who had been so cruelly slain. "He has your dark hair and my blue eyes," Angus said as he stared into the face of the bairn, "a mixture of us both."

It amused Áine to see the powerful Lord of the Isles tenderly hold his young son, speaking to him as if he were already grown. Brian, listening to every word, sometimes gave his opinion and the two of them discussed the new addition to the family.

"I have asked Lir to guard my new brother, at least until he is trained," said Brian.

"The hound appears to have accepted your request," said Angus, looking at the wolfhound, "for he stays close to young Alexander."

Angus was a devoted father. From the beginning, Brian idolized him and she was sure that young Alexander would follow suit.

Áine had come to know her Macdonald husband well. Thus, she knew that despite his care for his family and the people of the lordship and his concern for Scotland's future, Angus never forgot the justice he sought for the MacDougalls' treachery. His need for retribution, though sometimes left unspoken, lay just beneath the surface. She could see it in his eyes as he gazed east toward Argyll and Lorne.

Dunaverty Castle, Kintyre Peninsula

IN AUGUST of that same year, Angus received a letter from his friend, Rob, telling him of his resignation the previous May as a Guardian of the Realm. He gave as his reason his continuing quarrels with John "the Red" Comyn, but Angus wondered if there was more to it.

> *As you are likely aware, Edward has changed his battle strategy. He now aims his army at the southwest of Scotland where we have repeatedly attacked his garrisons with much success.*
>
> *In July, the king captured the castle of Caerlaverock, just across the border, which we had been using to make life miserable for the English. While we had some victories—Edward lost much of his army as he moved north—I have lost both my castles at Ayr and Turnberry to the English. A hard blow.*

Angus had heard of Edward's losses and his difficulty in raising the numbers of fighting men he demanded from his nobles. With mounting losses and the dressing down he received from Pope Boniface for his "outrages of justice" in Scotland, at summer's end, Longshanks dismissed his army and sailed back to England.

At the beginning of the new year, 1301, Edward admitted to his parliament what everyone knew. He was without money to continue the war with Scotland or implement his plan for two armies—one led by Edward and one by his son, the newly invested Prince of Wales. Each would take a separate route north, meeting at Stirling Castle, which was still in the hands of the Scots. From there, they planned to march north, leaving the Scots nowhere to run.

In an attempt to add to his army, the king ordered John Wogan, justiciar of Ireland, to assemble a great force, the payment for which would be the forgiveness of debts owed the crown. Many Irish nobles responded, adding nearly seven hundred horse and sixteen hundred foot soldiers to Edward's command.

Angus noted with interest that Richard de Burgh, Earl of Ulster, contributed men but did not go himself, for Edward had yet to meet his price. Still, Angus made available his galleys to transport the fighting force across the Irish Sea.

Months later, Angus decided he could wait no longer to pursue Alexander MacDougall, who was fighting with his brother-in-law, the Red Comyn, against King Edward.

In October, Angus petitioned the king. In his statement to Edward, he avoided committing himself to any opinion, either favorable or adverse, as to the fidelity of the Lord of Argyll and Lorne. He humbly requested the king, if he believed in Lorne's loyalty, to order Alexander MacDougall to assist Angus and Sir Hugh Bissett in the reduction of the country. Failing that, Angus asked for written instructions that they may, with Divine help, be able to overcome MacDougall and all other enemies of the king throughout the Western Isles.

When Edward finally agreed, he also conveyed his approval of Angus' request to allow the MacRuairi brothers, who were still in Angus' custody, to return to the king's favor and receive back their lands. After their rebellion, they had repented and were now participating in Angus' military operations for the king.

It would be another month before Angus could turn to his own expedition as the Irish who had been fighting for King Edward had to be transported back home in his role as Admiral of the Western Isles.

At the onset of winter in that same year, Angus contacted the two men who had earlier committed their resources to aid him in tracking down Alexander MacDougall: Sir Hugh Bissett, Angus' brother-in-law, and John MacSween, Lord of Knapdale.

"The distances are such," he explained to Áine, as she bounced young Alexander on her knee, "that I will be able to return to Dunaverty often enough to keep your bed warm."

With a laugh, she said, "You have done very well thus far, Husband." Áine was already expecting another child. He wanted to be home for the birth but she made no demands in that regard for which he loved her the more. The burden of the lordship and all he had set in motion for its defense and administration, as well as King Edward's business in the Isles and Angus' own need to see the MacDougalls brought to justice, were keeping him well occupied.

Before he could leave on his mission, he had one last task to accomplish: a fostering for Brian, who was now ten. "Should we think of the Isles or Ulster?" he asked Áine.

"For a young prince of Ireland, I should think Ulster, mayhap an O'Neill family. He can be trained in skill at arms at Dungiven Priory where Dermot was trained. Too, my brother can look in on him from time to time. As the adopted son of the Lord of the Isles, he will not be ill-treated."

So, a message was sent to her brother. When the galley came a week later, arriving at Dunaverty under a dark, cloud-filled sky, Dermot stood in the stern, his fur-lined cloak wrapped tightly about him, his countenance grim.

"I bring sad news," he told Angus and Áine as he climbed down to the sand where they had come to meet him. Looking at his sister, Dermot said, "Father has passed from this life. It was his heart, I fear. His death came suddenly. There was no time to send for you."

Áine uttered a gasp and covered her mouth with her hand, turning her grief-filled gaze to Angus.

Taking her into his arms, he pressed her head to his chest. "He will be greatly mourned, for he was much loved. I will miss him sorely. As you would remind me, my love, your father is with God and His angels."

"I cannot believe he is gone and I was not there," said Áine.

"It was the same with my father," said Angus.

Áine lifted her tear-filled eyes to Angus. "I would like to sail with Brian and my brother to attend my father's burial. Alexander will be well tended by his nurse while I am away."

Dermot said, "That is why I came myself, to accompany my sister as well as my nephew."

"Aye," said Angus to his wife. "You must go. I would go if I could but I expect Sir Hugh's ships any day." Facing Dermot, his brown hair and eyes so like his sister's, Angus said, "I will send men to guard my wife and young Brian. You are now The O'Cahan, not only the leader of your people, my brother-in-law and my friend, but also, my ally. If ever you have a need, the Macdonalds stand with you as we did your father."

The offer was not an idle one or one without great force behind it, as Dermot well knew, for Angus now commanded the Western Isles for King Edward and thousands of Islesmen of the lordship.

Dermot thanked him. "Your bond and friendship mean much."

The next day, Angus kissed Áine and hugged Brian before mother and son climbed into the galley that would take them to Ulster. "I am sorry to spend Christmas apart," he told them.

"There will be others," Áine replied. Her voice sounded flat as if robbed of its usual life by her grief. Áine's handmaiden, Nessa, had accompanied her mistress and now stood close by her side.

Áine's son Brian by The O'Neill, who Angus still called "Young Prince", had grown somber with the news of his grandfather's passing. But he was doing his best to remain stoic. In his cinnamon-colored tunic and dark brown cloak, he held Lir's leash tightly. The mare, Enbarr, had quieted in her sling under the groom's soothing hand.

Angus wished them Godspeed and waved as they sailed from Dunaverty Bay under a brooding sky, the clouds heavy with rain. Áine stood in the bow, one end of her fur-lined cloak wrapped around Brian's shoulders as she lifted her hand in farewell. Though the sailing would be short, it would be cold and the wind at this time of year could be fierce but there was no hope for it. None would delay the voyage.

In the next few days, at Angus' request, his brother, John, arrived from Dunyvaig on Islay, and Duncan rode down from Saddell farther up the Kintyre Peninsula. It was agreed that while Angus was away, John would remain at Dunaverty. "My lady wife has sailed for Ulster with her brother to bury her father," Angus told him. "Young Brian is with her as he will begin his fostering with the O'Neills. My son, Alexander, still a bairn, is here with his nurse. Send word when Lady Áine has returned."

"And you?" John asked.

"Duncan and I will be with Bissett and MacSween in the Firth of Clyde, hunting MacDougalls."

A day later, Sir Hugh and John MacSween sailed into Dunaverty Bay. At dinner in the great hall, before a blazing fire, they discussed strategy, for the MacDougalls were wily and must be approached carefully.

At first light on the following morning, they sailed east. Angus added his galleys to those of his partners. Their destination was the Isle of Bute, where Alexander MacDougall was rumored to be.

The snow-covered peaks on the Isle of Arran rose in dramatic fashion as they rounded the isle's eastern coast. Once in the Firth of Clyde, they were surprised to find the waters of the firth choked with the English fleet.

"If the MacDougalls were ever here, they no longer are," said Duncan.

Upon inquiry, Angus learned that the English fleet awaited King Edward who was expected to return shortly from Falkirk. "His Majesty is in a jubilant mood," said one of his captains. "His young wife has given him another son, Prince Edward is with his father, and Sir Robert Bruce has submitted to the English garrison at Lochmaben Castle."

Taken aback, Angus asked. "Is Sir Robert yet there?"

"I believe so. He waits for the king."

Turning to Duncan, Angus said, "Since the MacDougalls are nowhere in sight, I would go to Rob. I must know what has led to this turn of events."

"Aye," said Duncan. "Go. I will stay with the galleys. Sir Hugh will wait for you to rejoin us." Glancing over to the lead galley of the Lord of the Glens of Antrim, Duncan said, "Just now, he appears to be enjoying the wine the king's captains are handing out in celebration."

"A week's delay will not matter if you and the men are content to remain here," said Angus. "I would take only my guard."

Angus borrowed some horses for the trip east. "I know you expected a battle on water," he said to the captain of his guard. "I do hope a ride to Lochmaben Castle will be sufficient adventure for now."

His captain chuckled. "Anywhere my lord leads, we follow."

With that, Angus took to the road that was covered with snow. Two days later, they arrived at Lochmaben Castle in Annandale, once the seat of the Bruces and now garrisoned by the English.

Angus announced himself as "King Edward's Admiral of the Western Isles here to see the Earl of Carrick", which gave him and his guard entrance at the wooden palisade.

In the castle, Angus strode into the great hall, leaving his guard just inside the door where they were offered ale by a servant.

He spotted his friend pouring wine into two goblets as he stood next to a table. "I heard you had come," said Rob.

Angus crossed the room to hug him. "It's been too long. Letters are but poor excuses for a meeting of good friends." Reaching for the goblet of wine Rob poured for him, Angus studied his friend. His face was still that of a young man, of an age with Angus, but there were signs of weariness about his eyes. The auburn hair Angus had first glimpsed when they were but youths had darkened and grown longer. He was dressed for battle, not Longshanks' court. "You have the look of one who has had to make hard decisions."

Rob's eyes roved over Angus' fine tunic, his eyes pausing on the gilded belt and jeweled pin Angus wore at his left shoulder. "As do you, Lord of the Isles."

"Aye, the reason for my new title is a sad tale of treachery." He took a long drink of his wine.

"I have heard. I am sorry for the loss of your brother. He was a good man and should not have died at the hands of kin turned betrayer." Taking a drink of his wine, Rob said, "I have also heard you have taken a bride." With a teasing look in his eyes, he said, "One so lovely they call her the Jewel of the Roe, as I recall. Is it true? You have won the hand of the beautiful Áine O'Cahan?"

"Aye, 'tis true," said Angus, unable to resist a smile. "I thank the Good Lord every day for His favor in giving her to me. I have a young son, too. Alexander."

Rob's face broke out in a wide smile. "Congratulations! That calls for more wine." He lifted the flagon and refilled their goblets.

"Enough of my news. I came not only to greet an old friend but to understand what has prompted your submission to King Edward. Not that I am complaining," he quickly added. "I am glad we now fight on the same side."

Rob heaved a sigh. "Come, bring your wine and let us sit by the fire, and I will tell you." Angus removed his cloak and took the offered chair before the fire, stretching one hand toward the warmth. Once seated, Rob said, "The decision has been a long time in coming. As you might have heard, John Balliol has been released from papal custody and is at large in northern France. Rumor has it he is raising an army and intends to return to Scotland to reclaim his kingdom. Wallace's efforts to garner French support are apparently succeeding.

"For some, that might be a cause for celebration. The Comyns, as you might expect, see in this the return of their lost leader in whose name they have been fighting. But for me and my people, it is the end of a long road. As I said in my letter, I resigned as a Guardian. It was not because of the spy you warned me of. I could no longer stomach Comyn's wretched temper. Last summer, as I wrote you, my lands were again wasted by the English and my castles occupied by English troops as they are now. The prospect of Balliol's restoration accompanied by French troops proved the final straw."

Angus could hear the fatigue in his friend's voice. "And what will King Edward do for his lost sheep returned to the fold?"

"The king has promised to preserve my inheritance, so that I need not fear my lands or title being seized by the French. He also gives me vague assurance that my rights to the Scottish crown will be preserved."

"Do you think Edward will allow a Scot to rule in Scotland?"

"Only time will tell." He lifted his goblet to his lips and then set it on the small table between them. "There is more. By Edward's order, I am to wed Elizabeth de Burgh, daughter of Ulster's earl."

Angus remembered the fair-haired beauty he had seen at Dunseverick. "The young child with golden curls we teased at Dunluce so long ago is now a great beauty. She came to my wedding celebration with her father."

Rob nodded. "She is still young but old enough, it seems, to wed."

"Do you know her?"

"I saw her at Edward's court in the last days I served the king. But I do not know her well. The marriage is Edward's idea."

Angus thought of the Turnberry Band, the alliance made long ago with Richard de Burgh, the Bruces, the Macdonalds and other nobles.

"I see how it fits into Edward's plans. He has never been able to convince Earl Richard to join his Scottish campaigns. Now, in one move, the king would bind the Earl of Carrick to his Earl of Ulster. How can Earl Richard refuse the summons when next it comes? How can you?"

"I cannot. The king and his son winter at Linlithgow but he would use me in his next campaign to help him conquer Scotland." Rob turned his goblet in his hands, staring at the dark red liquid. "I had more to be concerned about than my estates, Angus. Like my grandfather, Robert the Noble, and my father after him, I could not serve a King of Scots named John Balliol, who is aligned with the Comyns."

"Nor could I," said Angus, tossing back the rest of his wine. He leaned in, speaking in a low voice so no castle guards could hear. "But if ever there were a King of Scots named Robert, him I would serve."

Rob paused, a sigh of resignation escaping his lips. "I thank you, my friend, but you merely remind me of the old proverb that says hope deferred makes the heart sick."

"Aye," said Angus, "but does it not also say that a desire fulfilled is a tree of life? The story is not yet written, my friend. Hope may be deferred but 'tis not lost. As long as there is a delay, you might as well have a bride worthy of a king. The fair Elizabeth, as I recall, was something of a minx as a child but now she looks like a queen."

"She does," said Rob, a small smile playing about his mouth. "I have no objection to Edward's choice, no matter he brings us together for his own purposes. How long can you stay?"

Angus sat back in his chair. "Only this day. Tomorrow, I must return to the coast where my galleys and those of Hugh Bissett and John MacSween of Knapdale await me. We have permission from Edward to hunt The MacDougall who killed my brother, Alexander. We were interrupted by the amassing of the English fleet off Bute and the news of your submission to Edward."

"Well, then you have time for a meal and a game of chess. I may be watched by Edward's garrison, who do not trust me, but at least I am well fed."

Dunseverick Castle, the north coast of Ulster, 1301

THE SKY POURED forth rain as Áine and her brother reached Ulster's coast and began the long climb to the castle. At her side, Brian was silent and stern as he led Lir up the winding path. Nessa followed. She, too, was unusually subdued. From time to time, Brian glanced back to see the crew unloading his dapple-gray mare.

Cold and wet despite her cloak, grief settled over Áine like an untimely frost, turning her body and mind numb. For most of her life the one solid rock she had clung to was her father. When all else had been taken from her, he remained. Now he was gone, and she had not even been with him when he died. Had he looked for her in his last moments and found her missing?

Servants who had known her since her youth rushed to greet them. They took their sodden cloaks, pressed goblets of hot spiced wine into their cold hands and urged them close to the fire where they huddled in front of the flames.

"We have delayed the burial until you arrived, my lord," said her father's—now Dermot's—constable. "The Earl of Ulster has sent word he will attend the burial. Even The O'Neill has sent a message saying he will come to Dungiven Priory to honor your father." Richard de Burgh had not removed the man who killed Brian O'Neill but watched him closely.

"Tomorrow would be good if the abbot can be ready," said Dermot.

"I will see it done," said the constable.

Áine shivered. She could not seem to get warm. "As long as we are here," she said to her brother, "we should find one of the O'Neill chiefs to foster Brian."

Dermot gave his nephew an encouraging smile. Her son had been standing next to Dermot's chair staring at the fire, fixated on the flames. Drawing him in for a hug, her brother said, "I have a good O'Neill family in mind. With that ginger hair, young Brian here will fit in like one of their own." To Brian, he said, "I fostered with the de Burghs. It is a time of new friendships and learning many things you will need as you become a man. Just think, you will return to The

Macdonald with much to show him."

"He will not forget me?" said Brian anxiously, revealing what Áine knew to be her son's fear.

"Nay. 'Tis not possible. Lord Angus will be proud of you."

Brian seemed comforted by Dermot's words. Áine would miss her son but she knew this was important to his future. He was an Irish prince and needed to know his own people. One day, he might rule them as King of Tirowen.

The rain continued as the burial proceeded the next day. The ceremony reminded Áine of the burial of Alexander Macdonald, which had also been a somber affair. The monks chanted their songs as the people filed into the priory church built by the O'Cahans out of Ireland's rocks.

The black-robed abbot, who knew her father well, officiated, recalling the great deeds of the O'Cahan lord who had provided wisdom for his people for decades. As the senior subking to The O'Neill, her father had been held in high regard by Norman nobility. Earl Richard had come to pay her father honor in death as he befriended him in life. That meant much to Áine, for her heart was rent by so great a loss.

The words spoken by the abbot over her father's body were comforting:

Our Lord keepeth thee. Our Lord is thy protection.
By day the sun shall not burn thee, nor the moon by night.
Our Lord keepeth thee from all evil. Let our Lord keep thy soul.
Our Lord keepeth thy coming in and thy going out from henceforth, now and forever.
Eternal rest give unto Your servant, O Lord, and let Your perpetual light shine on him.

When the last prayer was said and her father had been laid to rest in the new tomb provided for him inside the church, they thanked those who had come and rode back to Dunseverick.

Áine began to feel fevered and unwell as they arrived at the inner bailey. The feeling persisted as she climbed the stairs to her bedchamber with Nessa. It was then the cramps began. She gripped her belly, bending over with the pain. A warm liquid flowed down her leg and one look told her it was blood. A moan escaped her lips.

"What is it, Mistress?" Nessa asked, alarmed.

"The babe," said Áine between stabs of pain. "It is the babe," she said in a harsh whisper as she doubled over in pain.

Nessa hastened to remove Áine's gown and turned down the bedcovers, placing a drying cloth over the sheet. "Mayhap not. Get into bed and I will call the physician."

Áine did as Nessa bid her, her handmaiden helping her as the pain continued. She hoped she was wrong. But the bright red blood flowing onto the cloth and the clots passing from her womb told her she was right. She was only a few months gone with child, not enough to show, but the bond between mother and child was already strong. She longed for the comfort Angus would bring yet she was glad he was not here to see this.

The physician, when he came, was not encouraging. The older man had served her family for decades, tending her scrapes and scratches as a child. "You have had two healthy children, my lady. A small amount of blood and the child can survive. But there is much here. I do not wish to give unwarranted hope." To Nessa, he said, "Clean up your mistress and give her honeyed wine to drink. She will not be hungry. Rest is what she needs but stay with her. If the babe is not to live, it will eventually pass from her body but that can take some time."

"I will not leave her," said Nessa, her brown eyes full of concern. "Can you send a servant up?"

He nodded. "I will look in on her tomorrow. Call me before that if need be."

When the servant appeared, Nessa issued instructions for the fire to be kept burning and the honeyed wine to be brought. Beyond that, the servant was asked to bring hot broth for Áine's supper and a pallet for Nessa to sleep on so she could stay in the bedchamber. "The mistress needs to rest. It has been a trying few days and I do not wish to leave her." Áine admired Nessa's discretion, for if the babe lived, none need know of the crisis once past.

Áine waited until a cramp subsided and then she told the servant,

"Please tell my son that I am tired from the travel and the burial. He can see me tomorrow." When the servant left, Áine said to Nessa, "Thank you for your kindness. As for Brian, say nothing of this should he inquire. It will be days before he goes to the O'Neills. Mayhap I will be up by then."

"Do not worry, Mistress. I will see to the lad and to you."

The next day, the physician came and went. "Stay in bed this day" were his only words.

Brian came, too. He held her hand and listened to Nessa's encouraging words. "She will be well very soon."

"My uncle wants me to meet my foster family so I might be gone for a day or two," Brian said. "Is that all right?"

"Yes, Little Prince. It is as it should be. This is a chief your uncle knows well. His family has flame-colored hair, just like you. I will be here when you return."

The following day, the tiny child passed from her womb, miniature in size but recognizable as a male, a son.

Áine had known there was no longer a child growing in her womb. Her breasts were no longer tender; she had no nausea. But it was only when she was sure the child was dead that the tears began to flow. "This is all my fault," said Áine, speaking her thought aloud to her handmaiden. "I should have taken more care."

"Nay, Mistress, do not blame yourself. You were never overcautious before and delivered two healthy babes. It may be this one was intended for Heaven before he was born. There will be others."

"What will Angus say when he learns I have lost him a son?"

Almost chiding, Nessa said, "He will thank God the wife of his heart is healing and will soon be as she was."

When Brian returned from the O'Neills, Áine was sitting before the fire in the great hall to greet him. Excitement for his fostering sparkled in his dark blue eyes. "They have a female wolfhound," said Brian, "and have promised me that if Lir and she mate, I can have my choice of pups!"

Dermot joined them. "The meeting went well. I think 'tis a good match."

Áine was already feeling the loss. "When do you take him to

them?"

"Tomorrow. Brian only returned to Dunseverick to say goodbye and spend the evening with you."

Running her hand over her son's red curls, Áine leaned forward to kiss his forehead. "I will miss you but your uncle will give us reports. As your writing skills improve, you must write your father and me of all you are learning."

"I promise," said Brian, his face a picture of sincerity.

The next day before Dermot and Brian departed, Áine told her brother, "It is time I left as well."

"To Dunaverty?" he asked. "I will have my galley take you."

"Angus will not have returned this soon. I have a mind to pay Juliana a short visit on Islay to recover from all that has passed." She did not tell her brother of the babe or his passing.

"Very well. I will send a message to Dunaverty so that should your husband return before you, he will know where to find you, else Angus will kill me."

Áine laughed, the first time she had done so since coming to Ulster. "Or, he might kill us both."

After Brian had gone to his foster home the next morning, with the men Angus had appointed to guard her, Áine and Nessa sailed to Islay under a blue sky covered with billowing white clouds. From the deck of the galley, Áine looked back at the home of her youth, the place where her third son was buried. The first of spring's flowers appeared on the crest of the green hills, the same flowers that decorated his small grave.

With a sigh, she turned to face north. On the horizon, she could just make out Islay, the seat of the Macdonald lordship.

BATTLING SNOW AND ICE, Angus and his guard had returned to the coast in time for Christmas. His ships were still anchored in the Firth of Clyde along with those of Edward's fleet. Wind blowing off the snow chilled the air and made for a bleak celebration in the churches and towns on Bute.

Angus longed to be with his wife but the consensus was they should linger, awaiting news of The MacDougall and King Edward.

Finally, news reached them that, in January, at the insistence of the French, Edward had agreed to a truce with the Scots and, thereafter, left Scotland.

Sir Hugh suggested they leave off their search for two months and reconvene in spring when the weather would have improved. Disappointed their hunt had not been successful, nevertheless, Angus agreed. "Mayhap, in the interim, our intelligence will flush quarry from Argyll's woods."

"Aye," said John MacSween. "The MacDougall cannot hide from us or King Edward forever."

The voyage home to Kintyre was, even in the winter, no more than a day's travel. Sighting the castle high on the promontory, Angus experienced an eager anticipation. Soon, he would be in the arms of his wife.

When he arrived on Dunaverty's shore and she was not there to greet him, he asked John, "Where is Áine?"

"She went from Ulster to Islay to recover at Dunyvaig with Juliana."

Confused, Angus said, "Recover from what?"

"The message from Dermot did not say."

The next morning, after responding to messages from his constables and chiefs, Angus gave instructions to John and Duncan, who he would leave at Dunaverty, and prepared to sail. He kissed his young son and gave him into the care of his nurse. "I do not know how long Lady Áine and I will be on Islay. If anything untoward happens, my brother can get word to me."

Anxious that Áine should be unwell and in need of Juliana, Angus sailed with all dispatch. He did not then think of the bairn that grew in her womb. But he did the minute he glimpsed Juliana's face.

She met him where he beached his galley in Lagavulin Bay, a short walk from the castle. "'Tis the bairn, Angus. Áine lost the bairn in Ireland." He was about to go in search of her when Juliana added, "She blames herself. The child was a son."

"Where is she?"

"On the far side of the great hall, staring out to sea, watching the birds. An unusual number have gathered just outside the window."

"Aye, her birds would have come."

"Her birds?"

He shook his head. "'Tis nothing."

As he took a step to leave, Juliana said, "Angus, Áine needs you. She worries you might hold her to account."

Angus turned to meet the concerned gaze of his brother's widow.

"Nay, I do not blame Áine. I never would. I only want to comfort her, to see her well. Take care of my men, will you? I go to her."

He found Áine as Juliana had said, sitting alone, wrapped in her cloak.

"My love," he said as he came up behind her.

"Angus!" she cried, turning at his voice. "I have lost your son."

He lifted her from the chair into his arms and kissed her. "Nay, my love. You have given me a son, Alexander, and you will give me more children. A healthy birth is not always certain."

Casting her gaze down, she said, "I just never thought it would happen to me. But my father's death, the burial. I did not realize how it all affected me."

"We have each other and our two sons. God has chosen to take this one early but there will be others. You must believe it."

"When I hear you speak, I do, Angus."

With his arm around her, he guided her to the fire and called for spiced wine. "You will be pleased to know I have a reprieve for a time. King Edward has agreed to a truce in his war with Scotland."

"Did you find the MacDougalls?"

"Nay. They have hidden themselves in the wilds of Argyll. Did Brian find a fostering with the O'Neills?"

"He did and seems quite happy about it. Did you see Alexander?"

"Aye. He is walking and keeping his nurse busy."

A storm blew into Lagavulin Bay the next morning, bringing much rain to the isle. Angus and Áine stayed at Dunyvaig for the next week, enjoying time with each other and Juliana and their young nephews.

One morning when he caught Juliana alone, he expressed his thanks to her for her kindness to his wife. "'Twas a great compliment to you, my lady, that in my absence, Áine came to you for comfort."

"I was happy to be there for her," replied Juliana. "I have not forgotten how she comforted me."

CHAPTER 20

Dunaverty Castle, Kintyre Peninsula

IN MARCH of 1302, Angus received word that King Edward, short of manpower and willing to make concessions, had finally met Richard de Burgh's price. In exchange for canceling his debts to the Dublin exchequer of £16,000, the Red Earl agreed to lead an Irish force in the king's next Scottish campaign.

Ulster's earl then called upon Angus, asking for ships to help transport the hundreds of horses and thousands of men that would accompany him to Scotland. In his capacity as Admiral of the Western Isles for King Edward, Angus agreed.

Meantime, life continued as Angus, Sir Hugh Bissett and John MacSween once again pursued the MacDougalls. While Alexander MacDougall no longer pillaged the Isles, Angus was not satisfied. He wanted justice and, with that in mind, he and his partners drove them from the sea back into Lorne and Argyll.

As the business of King Edward and the lordship allowed, Angus returned home to Áine and his young son. He treasured those times of peace in a world preparing for war.

That autumn, Angus received a letter from Rob telling him of his summer wedding and his orders from Edward to turn out men to fight in the upcoming Scottish campaign.

I wish you could have been there, Angus. Elizabeth and I were married at my father's manor of Writtle, near Chelmsford in Essex by the Archbishop of Canterbury. My bride, as you would expect, was beautiful, led to the altar by her father, Richard de Burgh. A lavish buffet followed with garlands of flowers everywhere. Many English earls and knights attended. It was like the times before when I was at King Edward's court, lavish in its pageantry and decoration.

The Scots may consider me a traitor for my time with the English, but I consider the blood that will be shed in my serving Edward may save my country. If the crown can be passed to a certain Scot with Edward's blessing, how much better that would be. You encouraged me not to lose hope.

De Burgh told me he has agreed to lead an Irish force in Edward's campaign next year—some four thousand strong, mayhap more. I, too, have been ordered to produce foot soldiers—two thousand of them—and as many cavalry as can be mustered from Carrick. "Bring all you owe and more besides" were Longshanks' words.

The campaign will begin next spring. This time, I fight against John Comyn and the MacDougalls, which I trust does not displease you.

I hope your hunt goes well.

In November, when the truce between England and Scotland expired, King Edward delayed sending his army into Scotland. It was not until May of the following year, 1303, that Angus thought he had discerned the reason.

King Philip of France—due almost certainly to his difficulties with revolt at home and the pope—deserted the Scots and signed a peace agreement with Edward. All of Wallace's noble efforts at the French court and in Rome had, after initial success, come to naught.

Angus did not know Wallace, the Scottish knight who Edward

considered the chief of the rebels, but he admired his courage.

Edward was now free to march upon Scotland without consideration for either France or Rome. As he had planned, Edward advanced north, taking the eastern route. His son, Prince Edward, moved north along the western route. However, the prince was checked at several points by Wallace, launching skirmishes out of the forest of Selkirk.

John "the Red" Comyn led a Scottish force in the north but he could not prevail against Edward's overwhelming numbers. The king's army, numbering more than nine thousand, swept north, past Stirling Castle whose Scottish garrison Edward considered too small to bother with, and decimated all in his path.

Like devouring locusts, his soldiers burned everything—hamlets and towns and granges and barns, both full and empty. Angus shuddered to think of the people in Edward's path.

Eventually, the king marched into the Red Comyn's lands of Badenoch that, until now, had been spared Edward's wrath.

When the Irish fleet sailed in August, it was said to be the largest naval force that had ever sailed from Ireland. Angus was proud of the Islesmen who stood at the helm of half the 173 ships and the oarsmen who labored to move the galleys across the Irish Sea.

Watching from the ramparts of Dunaverty Castle as the huge fleet passed in front of him on its way to Scotland's coast, he remarked to Duncan and John, "I am relieved our Islesmen do not fight this time, either for Comyn or Edward, but there will come a time when they will fight and, when that time comes, I will lead them."

"And I will be with you," said Duncan.

"I as well," said John.

Placing a hand on their shoulders, Angus said, "I am stronger for you both. Your counsel and your friendship mean much."

Angus had another reason to be glad he could remain at home. Áine was again with child and he wanted to be with her when her time came. She fretted much over this next birth because she had lost the last babe.

He followed closely the war in Scotland, receiving regular messages from his contacts. Thus, Angus learned that in the southwest of Scotland, de Burgh's Irish army had begun capturing castles. Rob, sent by Edward to meet the Irish force, was relieving Carlisle and the English garrisons in Dumfries and Galloway that had been on the verge of collapse.

Angus also received the welcome news that at the end of September, Edward had laid siege to the Red Comyn's castle at Lochindorb in Badenoch, and, by October, the castle had fallen. Edward celebrated with a hunt on the surrounding moors before deciding to spend the winter in Dunfermline.

By February of 1304, Edward had prevailed against all save Wallace and the MacDougalls. The leading Scots had surrendered to the king, including John Comyn. The terms of surrender with the Red Comyn as a Guardian of the Realm—a position he was soon to resign as there would be no need—were negotiated by Richard de Burgh.

In late March, Áine gave birth to another child, a girl they named Finvola who, like her brother, Alexander, had her mother's dark hair and Angus' blue eyes. Angus was there for the birth, which was celebrated everywhere in the lordship.

"Do you mind the babe is a girl?" Áine asked Angus as they watched the babe sleeping.

"Nay. I am glad we have a lass this time. I can always give her in marriage to some wealthy lord," he teased. "'Twould make for a rich alliance."

"I should have known that is all her father would think of," Áine said with a look of amusement. "But you might be surprised to find you are reluctant to give her at all."

Angus laughed, inwardly admitting the truth of it. "Aye. She is comely and I am already charmed by her."

It was that same spring when Edward, with his army dwindling—through desertion as much as battle—to one thousand men, turned his attention at last to Stirling Castle.

The ancient stronghold had inaccessible cliffs on three sides so that the garrison of fifty men under the command of Sir William Oliphant held out for three months against Edward's guns and trebuchets. Starving, the garrison sought to surrender. Edward refused. Instead, he lobbed huge round boulders into the castle's 12-foot thick walls using his giant trebuchet he dubbed "War Wolf".

Only after he destroyed the castle did the king permit the garrison to submit. But for the pleading of his English commanders, impressed by the garrison's courage, did Edward allow them to live.

Hearing that his friend, Rob, had been in charge of the English guns that battered Stirling's walls, Angus believed Rob was one who argued for the lives of the garrison. "It must have been hard for Rob, who loves his country, to have witnessed Edward's cruelty to those fifty men," he said to his brother. "After all, unlike his father, Rob is as much a Celt as a Norman."

"Aye," said John. "From what you have told me, his return to Edward made sense but I wonder how long he will continue to serve the English king."

"It will not be for always," said Angus. "And once Rob leaves Edward's service, so will I." The prophecy's words, spoken long ago, had never left him. There would be "a new king" and he believed that king would be Robert Bruce.

The day after the fall of Stirling, Edward dispatched John Comyn, along with three other Scottish nobles, all of whom now served the English king, to hunt down William Wallace. The brave patriot, who still carried on the fight for Scotland's freedom, was at large and refused to pay Edward homage.

By now, it was clear to all that John Balliol would never return to Scotland. With the country under Edward's control, de Burgh's Irish force returned home. As Admiral of the Western Isles, Angus' ships participated in seeing them back to Ireland's shores.

King Edward ruled everywhere except the Highlands and the Isles. Angus, by his own choice, continued to serve the English king, but Edward did not rule in the Isles.

While the MacDougalls, hiding in the Highlands, had yet to submit to Edward, Angus believed they could not hold out for long. He and his Islesmen kept the pressure on them from the west even as Edward's men pursued them from the east.

In April, 1304, on his way to Lochmaben to reclaim his lands from the victorious king, Rob's father, Robert Bruce VI, died. Angus went to be with his friend and to learn of his intentions now that he had inherited the Bruce claim to the Scottish throne.

The ride east this time was unlike the last. Beneath fair skies, wildflowers bloomed amid blades of grass and heather covered the hillsides. Sunlight filtered through the trees, dappling the ground with light. The air was fragrant with the season and the land appeared refreshed, as if war had not seen its ruin. A flock of sparrows, flushed from the trees by the sound of their horses, sped in front of him, reminding him of Áine.

He arrived at Lochmaben to learn the burial of Rob's father had already taken place in Cumberland and the Earl of Carrick had returned. Angus removed his hat and strode into the great hall where he had met Rob before.

His friend looked up as Angus entered. The earl wore the garments of his rank, a fine woolen tunic and a gilded belt holding his sword and dagger. His dark auburn hair had been well groomed, yet his brow was furrowed and his face bore the look of sorrow.

Angus embraced him. Pulling back, he said, "I am sorry for your father's passing."

"It was not unexpected. He lived to see my return to Edward, which pleased him. He was, after all, a Norman loyal to Longshanks."

"So, you are not only the Earl of Carrick, but now Lord of Annandale."

"And the head of a large family," Rob said. "In addition to Elizabeth and my daughter, Marjorie, there are my four brothers to consider, Edward, Alexander, Thomas and Nigel. And my sisters and nephews. Their futures weigh heavily. Alexander has only recently been named Dean of Glasgow, an honor for a scholarly clergyman."

At Rob's suggestion, they walked outside the castle where they could not be overheard. Angus asked, "What of your relationship with the king?"

Rob heaved a sigh. "He has made me Sheriff of Lanarkshire and constable of Ayr Castle. In truth, though Edward would bestow titles upon me and, in time, restore my lands, he does not trust me. Moreover, despite his words in times past suggesting otherwise, I now see he has no intention of allowing a Scot to rule the people of Scotland, even as a vassal king. He has spent too much of the crown's money and spilled too much English blood to consider such a possibility. Aside from that, Edward likes being king of all. Did you know they call him the Hammer of the Scots?"

Angus frowned. "Aye. I had heard that."

"He relishes the nickname. I think, in some twisted way, he views his cruelty as strength."

Angus was not unmindful of the worry in his friend's face, the heavy weight he carried for the safety of the many who depended upon him and the frustration he was experiencing for what—it was now clear—would never come to be under Edward's reign. "What will you do?"

"I must care for my family while I look to my destiny," said Rob, as he gazed out on the blue waters of the loch in front of the castle, the sun reflecting on the ripples. "However it ends, I cannot continue to serve Edward. Though I have lands in England, my home is here in Scotland. These are my people." Facing Angus, he said, "To that end, I intend to meet with William Lamberton, Bishop of St. Andrews, the friend of Wallace, who is also my friend. I must have the bishop's support if I am to pursue the crown and Scotland's independence."

"Bishop Lamberton would change his allegiance from Edward?"

"He already has but it is not known. I suspect Edward, having said nothing further about my claim to the Scottish crown, hopes my ambition will fade into the background as my father's did. But I have not forgotten, and I am not my father. The king is old and often unwell. I can wait for him to pass. His son has neither his strength nor his determination."

"Meantime?"

"Meantime, I will assist Edward's new government of Scotland. He has made his nephew, the Earl of Richmond, head of all. Justices are to be appointed in pairs, one English and one Scottish. A Council will be formed to advise the earl, including Bishop Lamberton, John Comyn and me."

"You are again paired with Comyn?" Angus asked, disbelieving, for he remembered the time when the hot-tempered Comyn had grabbed Rob by the throat.

"It would seem so. But for all the apparent participation by Scots, it is Edward who holds the real power." For a moment, Rob was silent, and then he asked, "What of you?"

"As long as the king seeks capture of The MacDougall, I will continue to serve him as Admiral of the Western Isles. After that, we will see."

"And how is that young son of yours?"

"Alexander thrives. He now has a sister, wee Finvola. Prettiest lass I have seen, apart from her mother. And you? How is that fair bride you have taken?"

"She has seen little of me since we were wed. Edward's many tasks have kept me busy. Her letters express her love and understanding. Her love humbles me and, for her steadfast support and her care of Marjorie, I am grateful." Rob met Angus' steady gaze. "I have come to love Elizabeth and I need her. When I leave here, I will return to Edward's court to fetch her and Marjorie back to Scotland."

IN AUGUST OF the next year, 1305, William Wallace was betrayed by a servant and captured near Glasgow by Sir John Menteith. Edward had offered a huge reward for Wallace who, for years, had been the most hunted man in Scotland. When Angus heard of what Edward had done to him, he and all in the Isles were appalled.

In an act that could only represent King Edward's hatred for the man who had oft defeated him—the symbol of Scottish pride—Wallace had been treated in a most heinous manner.

It took a fortnight following his capture for the English to bring Wallace to London. During that time, he was forced to ride with his legs bound beneath his horse. The day after his arrival in London, the English held a trial that was no true trial at all. The result was foregone and Wallace was permitted no defense. Sentenced to death, he was dragged by his ankles for four miles through the streets to the place of his execution in Smithfield.

There, he was hanged to the point of death but not allowed to die. Cut down, he was unmanned and disemboweled. The executioner then burned his intestines before him so that would be the last thing he would have smelled. Following this, Wallace was beheaded and his body quartered.

The head and the body parts were dipped in tar to preserve them. His head was displayed on a pike on London Bridge, and the four quarters of his mutilated body separately displayed in Newcastle, Berwick, Stirling, and Perth. Angus shuddered as he remembered that he and Wallace shared the same birth year.

Angus decided it was time to prepare the Isles for what was coming. Though he had laid the groundwork with Áine's Irish army in training and weapons, now he would do more. With Duncan and John, he set out in two galleys full of galloglass to assess the fighting skills of his Irish settlers and the Islesmen. He was not disappointed, for he found the men trained and their weapons fashioned from good steel. Arrows, too, had been laid aside in great numbers. Satisfied, Angus provisioned his castles should the Islesmen be away for some time from their homes and unable to tend their crops.

In autumn, the efforts of Angus and his partners in the hunt for the MacDougalls finally paid off. Alexander MacDougall was taken and submitted to Edward, which at first caused Angus to rejoice. But when no royal censure was forthcoming, nor any punishment for the murder of Angus' brother or for the decimation of Macdonald lands, it was a turning point for Angus and the chiefs of the lordship. Henceforth, they would look to their own interests, and those of Scotland, and not those of the English king. "I will yet have justice from MacDougall no matter it takes years," he told Duncan and John.

Angus quickly penned a letter to Rob before sending word to the clans for the Council of the Isles to convene at Finlaggan.

To Sir Robert Bruce from Angus Og Macdonald, Lord of the Isles,

The hunt for Alexander MacDougall produced his submission to Edward. However, there was no forfeiture or any punishment for his clan's treachery. This leaves me free to follow my conscience and my heart. I will soon meet with the Council of the Isles to advise the chiefs. When the time comes, the lordship is ready to stand with you.

At the Council meeting, Angus told the chiefs all that had happened and what he believed was coming. "This time, we will not fight for England's king," he said, "but for Scotland and the Isles." That evoked cheers from the chiefs, who had only fought for the English king because he fought against the enemies of the Macdonald lordship.

Angus did not tell the chiefs of the "new king" prophesied by the seer of the Rhinns of Islay. He only told them to be watchful and prepared, for the enemies of the Bruces and Macdonalds now served King Edward.

In late autumn, while Angus and Áine lingered on Islay, Áine gave birth to another daughter. The bairn came early but was delivered healthy. They named her Mary, for Angus' eldest sister and the mother of the Savior. Little Mary's eyes, at first as blue as his own, soon turned to her mother's rich brown. Like her sister, Angus thought her lovely.

Áine, who had prayed for a son, was disappointed. "Oh, Angus, I had so hoped to give you a son this time."

"You are not yet thirty," he told his wife. "There is time for another lad. Mayhap God did not answer you, 'Nay', my love, only 'Nay yet'."

Angus was not worried. Though more sons were desired and he would do his best to produce them, he had Alexander, an intelligent, strong and handsome lad. The boy, only five years, kept Angus' guards busy with his quick mind and fascination with their weapons. Angus finally had to give him a small wooden sword so he could play at mimicking the guards' skill. Whenever they visited Juliana and her lively sons, it was always a tussle to see which boy would prevail.

As Christmas neared, Brian returned from his fostering with the O'Neills. Angus and Áine welcomed him into their arms and back into their growing family.

A child had gone to Ulster. A young man of fifteen, tall and lithe, returned, his red hair darkened and on his chin the beginnings of a beard. The sword at his side was that of a warrior, a long blade of sharpened steel.

Accompanying Brian was Enbarr, his mare, and a different wolfhound. "Sadly, Lir died just before I left Ulster but I have his daughter." Standing beside him was a gangly hound that looked very much like Lir when he was young, his gray fur trimmed in white. "I wrote you about Fand," he said. "She is Lir's daughter and still a pup."

"I remember," said Angus. "A lovely hound she is, too."

"I am giving her to Mother," he said shifting his gaze to Áine, who stepped forward to stroke the head of the young hound. "To replace her wolfhound that died."

Angus thought the gift a grand idea, not only for the company but for protection when he was away. "Aye, 'tis a worthy gift."

"I thank you, Son," said Áine. "She is very noble looking, and her name is familiar."

"In the Irish myths, Fand is the wife of Lir."

And so Fand, too, became a part of the family.

Alexander was thrilled that his older brother had returned and announced he, too, would like his own wolfhound. Everyone laughed but Angus made a mental note to see it done.

Brian approved of his young sibling, who was eager to show him how well he could brandish about his wooden sword. "He has grown so!" remarked Brian.

Áine laughed. "So have you!"

As for his young sisters, Brian paid them little attention. They were yet too small for their beauty to be admired. But when grown, all in the Isles would be beguiled by them as they were with their mother. Both Brian and Alexander would have to guard their sisters from many suitors.

They celebrated Christmas and the days to Epiphany at Dunyvaig with Mass and music and feasting. Angus' brother, John, and cousin, Duncan, attended, along with Juliana and her brood of sons. Some of the Irishmen had settled on Islay, becoming a part of Angus' crews, and they happily joined in the celebrations.

After Christmas, a letter arrived from Rob, telling Angus he had returned to Scotland.

> *I was in London to witness the torture, trial and brutal treatment of Wallace. It was all I could do not to retch. Cruelty unmeasured. I am glad I had nothing to do with his betrayal or capture.*
>
> *He was brave to the end, Angus. At his trial, when accused of*

treason, speaking of Edward, he said, "I cannot be a traitor, for I owe him no allegiance. He is not my sovereign; he never received my homage; and whilst life is in this persecuted body, he never shall receive it."

All of Scotland mourns him and, because of the manner in which his death was accomplished, the hatred for Edward grows. The king committed a grave error when he made a martyr of noble Wallace.

I would have gladly fought with Wallace for Scotland's freedom. Now, I must take up the torch and proceed without him. At the time of his capture, Wallace had in his possession letters from me. It is too late now to worry what the king might make of them.

Meantime, word of my pact with Bishop Lamberton became the subject of suspicion while I was still in London. As winter approached and Edward's health seemed to fail, in the hope of uniting Scotland, I met with John Comyn.

I proposed that he and I should enter into an understanding by which he would support my claim to the throne and receive my lands as compensation or, conversely, I his. He agreed and decided in favor of supporting my kingship and receiving my lands. The agreement was reduced to writing by Lamberton and his clerics. Two copies were made, signed and sealed.

I should never have trusted Comyn. I thought he would put Scotland above his own ambition. I was wrong. Despite his choice of my lands, I now believe he covets the crown for himself and was willing to betray me to get it.

Apparently, he revealed the sense of our agreement to Edward. At the time, I was at the English court. Unbeknownst to me, Edward gave orders to arrest me for treason. I was saved by Sir Ralph Monthermer, Earl of Gloucester, who sent me a warning. With thoughts of Wallace's fate in my mind, I fled into the night with my squire.

Riding north to Lochmaben, we encountered Comyn's servant on his way to London with the written evidence of my agreement with Comyn and instructions to present the writing to the king. It was damning because, by its terms, I was to be king. Needless to say, that document will never be delivered.

I have arranged to meet Comyn in Dumfries where I intend to confront him with his betrayal. The time is coming, Angus, when I will need that support you offered.

Angus was shocked to see how badly things had deteriorated and how quickly. But, as he thought about it, he decided it was inevitable. His friend could not remain in Edward's service and fight for Scotland's freedom. Angus could have told him Comyn would never have served a Bruce king. There was one advantage to what had happened. There was no longer any reason for Rob to hide his true intention.

A month went by and Angus had no word from Rob, yet he knew instinctively his friend was preparing to take the crown, winning Scots to his side and recruiting Scottish nobles to the cause of Scotland's freedom.

Dunaverty Castle, Kintyre Peninsula, February 1306

"HE DID WHAT?" Angus blurted out when Duncan brought news of John Comyn's murder at the hands of Robert Bruce. Knowing his friend had planned to confront Comyn with his betrayal, Angus was unsurprised the two had come to blows. *But murder?*

"Murder is what they are calling it," Duncan repeated, as they gathered around the fire against the cold. "And not just the Red Comyn but his uncle who attacked Bruce and was slain by Bruce's brother-in-law, Sir Christopher Seaton."

Angus' cousin had received the news at Saddell where it had traveled like wildfire from Dumfries.

"Worse than the murder was the place it occurred," said Duncan. "On sacred ground, at the altar of the Greyfriars Church in Dumfries."

"If that is where they met and the deed was done," said Angus, "it could not have been murder. Nor could Comyn's death in a church have been planned. Rob is deeply religious and would never intentionally defile the house of God."

Angus believed there was no way to contact Rob for he had become an outlaw and would be on the run. But a few days later, as he and Áine were breaking their fast, a message came telling Angus that Bishop Wishart in Glasgow had granted Robert Bruce absolution and was planning on installing him as King of Scots. Apparently, the bishop had hidden from King Edward the royal robes when he pillaged Scotland. Angus wondered if Abbot Henry of Scone had hidden the true Stone of Destiny as well. The stone seat at Scone Abbey had long been the place where Kings of Scots were enthroned.

"My God," said Angus, a lump forming in his throat as he looked up from the page to meet Áine's expectant gaze. "It has finally begun." Emotion welled up inside him. "He has taken the only path left open to him, though circumstances have forced a change in timing." At Áine's confused look, he said, "Rob is to be King of Scots."

She was silent for a moment, her expression pensive. Then she said, "Another war…" Her voice trailed off.

"Aye. Edward will never accept this. But then, one could have guessed this would happen when Edward ignored Rob's rightful claim to the throne."

"Will all of Scotland support him?"

"Half the nobles will, but the other half and the common people will distrust one who, like me, has served the English king. The Comyns and the MacDougalls, allied together, will fight against him. They have already turned to Edward's side. Rob will have to earn the country's loyalty. It will not be easy."

News of Rob and his followers continued to reach Angus. They were taking castles on the western seaboard, likely to preserve access to supplies from the Firth of Clyde. Ayr, Inverkip and Rothesay had fallen into their hands, the latter castle in what was described to Angus as a daring attack from the sea.

He and Áine were standing on the castle's battlement gazing east toward Turnberry when the news reached them. With anxious eyes, Áine asked, "Will you go?"

"Aye. And not only me. Our chiefs and our Islesmen, including your Irish army, will all fight for Robert Bruce. This is what we have wanted for a very long time, what I have been preparing for, and what my father agreed to at Turnberry long ago. We will support The Bruce and stand by him until his enemies and ours are vanquished.

Our honor, having been pledged, demands nothing less." He took her in his arms and, seeing her pained expression, said, "Ah, love, do not fret. Only pray we succeed. Our cause is noble and just."

"I know," she said, "it is just—"

"Do you recall the prophecy I told you about, that a new chief would rise with a new king, and then Scotland would know peace?"

"I remember."

"I believe I am that chief, Áine, and Rob is that king."

Looking up at him, she said, "I will pray that you and our new king succeed. And I will do whatever I can to help, for peace is what all mothers want."

On the 25th of March, six weeks after Comyn's death, Angus' friend was created Robert I, King of Scots. In the same ceremony, Elizabeth de Burgh was crowned Queen of Scots.

It was said that Bishop Wishart brought out the royal robes he had kept hidden from Edward to put on the new king. Though Edward had taken the rightful crown, a circlet of gold had been fashioned for the day and was set upon Rob's head by Isabella, Countess of Buchan, in defiance of her husband, a Comyn. As a MacDuff and the sister of the young Earl of Fife, who was held hostage in England, it was hers to do, for it was the hereditary role of the MacDuffs to crown the Scottish kings.

Bishop Lamberton had apparently reached Scone two days later on Palm Sunday in time to celebrate High Mass for the new king.

In April, when signs of spring were everywhere, Angus dispatched galleys to all the chiefs in the lordship, letting them know what had transpired should they not have received the news. It was time, he told them in his message, to celebrate their new king, a friend to the lordship, and to prepare for the war that he had warned them would come. "We will raise our banners and our swords for our true king, Robert Bruce!"

Having heard The Maclean of Duart Castle had a litter of wolfhound pups, he asked the captain of the galley going to Mull to bring back a pup for Alexander. They named the gray ball of fur that returned "Cormac" and six-year-old Alexander and his hound soon became inseparable.

Because of his former service for England's king, Angus received news in late June that Edward had sent Aymer de Valence, brother-in-law to John Comyn, north with a force of three thousand men. Their orders were to lay waste the land and to capture or kill Robert Bruce. Pursuant to Edward's instructions, they hunted the new Scottish king under the dragon banner that announced they were freed of any bounds of chivalry. Even Bruce's women could be assaulted or killed. It was well Angus received no orders for he would not have obeyed them.

As de Valence traveled north, his force grew to six thousand men. King Robert had gathered to himself the lesser number of four thousand. In contempt for the knightly code, de Valence betrayed a challenge he had accepted from Scotland's new king to meet him on the field of battle. Instead, the English knight attacked at night near Methven where Rob and his force were camped. Chaos ensued as the camp was roused. The English did not capture King Robert or the women with him, including Queen Elizabeth. They escaped into the night with two hundred followers. Those who did not manage to escape were slain, receiving no mercy at the hands of the English.

From the Scots, Angus received word that, in August, Rob and his men were heading west when he was ambushed at Dal Righ by John MacDougall of Lorne, the son of Alexander MacDougall, who murdered Angus' brother. Rob was able to escape only by valiant efforts that left many dead and wounded.

"He is coming here," Angus told Duncan and John.

"How do you know?" asked Duncan.

"He was heading west when he was attacked by the MacDougalls. He knows I will give him shelter. In truth, I will give him more—the strength of the Isles will be his. I am certain he will come to us. All is not yet lost."

In September, Duncan sent a message to Angus by a fast rider from Saddell:

He is here. I will bring him and the few others to you by galley. Two are wounded, one badly.

When a galley flying Duncan's MacAlasdair pennon appeared off

Dunaverty the next day, Angus told Áine to prepare to receive the king. With John, he descended the headland to the beach where a cold wind greeted them.

The man who climbed down from the galley appeared the same as before only thinner in a misfitting tunic and without his sword or mail. His dark auburn hair had grown longer and his only weapon was a dagger at his side. As he came closer, Angus could see his haggard visage and the haunting look in his eyes.

"My lord king," Angus said, bowing. Then, straightening, he smiled. "I've been waiting for you."

Because his friend was now King of Scots, Angus did not feel free to embrace him as he had before. Rob must have sensed his hesitation for he strode to Angus and threw his arms around him. "Angus! My friend. How glad I am to see you. And you may call me Rob, save when the formal address might be important."

"My brother, John," said Angus, gesturing to the man standing with him.

"I would have known it by his appearance, his likeness is yours."

The king held out his hand and John grasped it. "Your Grace."

Seeing only a few others jumping down from the galley to join Duncan on the beach, Angus asked, "Are there more coming?"

Rob dropped his gaze. "Alas, these few are all I have left of my army, Angus. Aymer de Valence attacked us at night at Methven. Only two hundred escaped with me and most of them fell before the MacDougalls. We were heavily armored and awkward on our horses against their axes. We barely got away with our lives. I feared for the women, so we gave them our horses and sent them to safety. Elizabeth, Marjorie, Isabella, the Countess of Buchan, and my sisters, Christian and Mary went to Kildrummie Castle with my brother, Nigel, and two knights, Sir Alexander Lindsay and Sir Robert Boyd. After that, we abandoned our plate and mail armor and our swords and set off on foot, with our daggers, traveling light.

"If it had not been for Malcolm, Earl of Lennox, who escaped Methven after us," Rob continued, "we would not be here today. He came upon us as winter approached, trudging across his lands, exhausted, freezing and near starving, too afraid to light a fire to cook what meat we had. Lennox thought we were poachers."

"Where is Lennox now?"

"I do not know. He was to follow us in his galley but we have not seen him."

Angus could see Rob was haunted by the memory of the friends he had lost; it was tearing at his soul. "Do not despair. You are in the Isles now. There are thousands here who will fight for you."

Rob nodded. "I had hoped it might be so."

Seeing the others coming toward them, Angus said, "You met my cousin, Duncan, at Saddell. Might John and I meet those who came with you?"

The king turned to the men approaching with Duncan but spoke to Angus. "Sir Gilbert Haye, who was with me at the siege of Stirling. He was captain of my guard at Methven, which may explain how I survived."

Sir Gilbert dipped his head of dark hair. His face revealed a man of many battles, stern and lightly scarred.

"And Sir Neil Campbell," said the king, "who I think is known to you. Both were with me at Scone. Also with me are my brothers, Sir Thomas, Sir Edward and Alexander, Dean of Glasgow." Then to those he had named, the king said, "My good friend, Angus Og Macdonald, Lord of the Isles, and his brother, John."

Angus and John shook each man's hand. To the dark-haired Sir Neil Campbell, Angus said. "Aye, we know you, Cousin." Turning to the king, Angus said, "As he may have told you, his father and my grandfather were one and the same man, a noble lord until a wretched Comyn's arrow slayed him."

The men with Rob appeared as weary from their battles and travels as did the king. Sir Gilbert had one arm in a sling and the others, while whole, were bruised with cuts, likely from their time in the wilds of Argyll.

The king looked back to the galley where a man was being helped onto the stretcher that Angus' guards had brought to the beach. "Young James Douglas was Lamberton's squire. He came to me with a message from the bishop when I was on my way to Scone and stayed, declaring his allegiance to me. He is the son of the brave Sir

William Douglas who fought with Wallace and died in Edward's prison. Jamie understandably wants the Douglas lands back, which Edward denied him. Since I became king, he has made himself indispensable. After Methven, his hunting and fishing kept us in food. He was wounded defending me in the MacDougall ambush at Dal Righ."

"He sounds like a good man," said Angus. "I had heard about what happened at Dal Righ. I am sorry."

"We lost many good men, most all of those who had fled with us from Methven," said Rob. "I insisted Jamie be carried on the stretcher. Thank you for thinking of it. As you might imagine, 'twas much to his dislike."

"The climb to the castle is not a small one," put in John. "He will be glad for it."

As the stretcher drew closer, Angus could see the black-haired, bearded Douglas had a thin youthful face. A white bandage circled his head. His eyes were closed against the pain revealed by his grimace. A blanket had been draped over his still form for the cold day.

Angus said, "My men will see him safely to the castle." Then, turning to Rob and those with him, in a louder voice, he said, "Come. My lady is eager to welcome you to our hall where the warmth of a fire and a feast await."

CHAPTER 21

Dunaverty Castle, Kintyre Peninsula, late September 1306

EXCITEMENT GREW within Áine as she attended to the tasks for the men who would soon arrive at Dunaverty. Since the messenger had come early that day, telling them to watch for a galley from Saddell, she had known they would be entertaining the new king that night.

Áine remembered the handsome young man near in age to Angus, who she had first met at Dunseverick. Then, he was Sir Robert, Earl of Carrick. Now he was the King of Scots. For that reason, she had donned one of her best gowns. The azure blue velvet, its fitted bodice trimmed in rows of brilliant seed pearls, shimmered in the fire's light.

She had kept her husband's steward busy all morning directing the servants who were preparing chambers and setting out clothing. The cook had begun the meal they would serve to the king. As a final check, she had asked her handmaiden to see that all had been done properly. At midday, Nessa appeared to say, "It is done, Mistress. All is ready and the children will be kept occupied."

"Thank you, Nessa. Brian is now a man so I expect him to join us for dinner but can you ask him to keep from the hall until then? I do not know what condition the king and his men will be in and I would see to their needs before they encounter a youth's adoration."

"He will understand." Nessa said as she briefly curtseyed and left.

Áine sighed as she gazed about her, pleased with all she saw. The hall was redolent of roasting beef, herbs and fresh-baked bread. Soon, the cook would be baking apple tarts spiced with cinnamon that Áine had requested. The candles were lit and the fire, well-stoked, was flanked by cushioned chairs.

A servant was just pouring the wine when the door opened. In strode Angus, John and Duncan with a half-dozen men. Behind them, a black-haired man was carried on a stretcher by two of Angus' guards.

She recognized Robert Bruce despite his unkempt auburn hair, his too-long beard and his worn clothing that spoke nothing of royalty. Dropping into a deep curtsey, she said, "My lord king, welcome to Dunaverty."

To his companions, the king said, "Meet the Jewel of the Roe, as the beautiful Lady Áine is known in Ulster."

The men smiled broadly and bowed before her, echoing the words, "My lady." At that point, the man on the stretcher insisted he be allowed to stand and was helped to his feet by the guards.

Angus, who had never become accustomed to the attention she received from other men, came to stand next to her, draping his arm possessively around her shoulder. "My wife, gentlemen."

The man who had risen from the stretcher said, "Sounds like a warning."

Inwardly, Áine smiled.

Angus turned to her. "Áine, the man who just spoke is James Douglas, the Lord of Douglas since his father's death, though his lands have yet to be restored to him. He was wounded in service of the king. Is our physician available to attend him?"

Áine nodded. "Conor MacBeth is waiting in the small chamber just off the hall."

Angus said to the king, "The MacBeth is well-trained and skilled."

James Douglas inclined his head. "You have my thanks." And then, with a smirk, he added, "All I have had until now to tend my wounds are the rough hands of the king's knights."

"Impudent ungrateful lad!" said one of the knights but not in bad humor thought Áine. And, with that, a guard helped the young Douglas make his way to the room where the physician waited. The warrior's limp told her his leg bore a wound as well as his head that was wrapped in a white bandage.

Áine sent a servant after them with two goblets of wine.

King Robert then introduced the rest of the men. "My lady, may I introduce Sir Gilbert Haye, who commented on young Douglas' ingratitude. Next to him is the dark-haired Sir Neil Campbell, a cousin of your husband's. And, finally, my brothers, Alexander, Dean of Glasgow, and Sir Thomas and Sir Edward. My other brother, Sir Nigel, has taken my queen, Elizabeth, my daughter, Marjorie, my sisters and the Countess of Buchan to safety."

Áine smiled at the men. Though their clothing was in tatters, their stance spoke of their knightly training and the pride they had in serving the new King of Scots. The king's brothers had the look of him, the same noble carriage and bold features. To the king, she said, "I am sorry that your queen and the other ladies could not be with us. I have not seen Elizabeth since our last meeting in Ulster."

"The first time I met Elizabeth, she was but a young lass," King Robert said with a smile.

Angus nodded. "Aye, 'twas a less complicated world."

Áine asked a servant to pass a tray of wine to the king and his men. When each had taken a drink, she said, "As soon as you are ready, my king, I would have you and your men shown to your chambers where you can freshen up ere we dine." Noticing the dark-haired Sir Gilbert's arm was in a sling, she said, "If you would like to have the physician replace your bandage and check your wound, Sir Gilbert, I can send him to you."

"Thank you, my lady" said the knight.

King Robert turned to Angus. "As for freshening up, we have only the unkempt clothing we are wearing so there is little to refresh but our persons."

Angus returned the king a knowing smile. "My lady took great pleasure in planning for this hour. In each of your chambers, you will find a fire burning, water for washing and suitable attire for your persons—hosen, tunics, surcoats, cloaks and soft leather shoes. Baths can be quickly had as well. I will supply you with mail, sword belts and weapons. As you know, my galloglass are well-armed."

The king laughed. "Ah, Angus. You and your lady are ever generous. I promise we will make use of it all." The king looked around and added in an amused tone, "I wager somewhere in this castle you have hidden an army, too."

"Hidden, yes," Angus said. "But not in my hall. The army lies in the Isles. Did you know that Áine's dowry was over a thousand Irishmen, among them two dozen young chiefs? The MacBeth physician who tends young Douglas is one of Áine's army."

King Robert smiled at Áine. "I did not know of so rich a dowry but it seems fitting for Lord Cumee O'Cahan's daughter."

"My galloglass have been training all in the Isles to be ready for war," said Angus. "Our chiefs and our people stand ready to support their new king."

The king's men smiled and nodded to each other.

Robert Bruce said, "I am humbled by your words, Angus."

"Best take him up on his offer," said Sir Neil Campbell. "The Macdonalds are a fearsome lot, and Angus commands thousands more than his Irishmen."

"I experienced their fighting skill firsthand when Angus and I fought together in Ireland," said the king. Then, placing his goblet on the tray the servant held out to him, he said to Áine, "We are ready, my lady, lead on."

LATER THAT EVENING when Rob and his men had been freshly clothed and fed and the hall had grown quiet, Angus sat with the king alone by the fire. "Can you speak of what happened at Greyfriars?"

Rob took a deep breath and let it out. "It was not murder."

"I never thought it was. But, if you tell me what happened, I can speak truth when my chiefs ask."

Rob stared into the fire as if seeing again the scene in the stone church in Dumfries. "You knew I intended to confront him."

"Aye."

"When I learned he was at his castle at Dalswinton in Dumfries, an hour's ride from Lochmaben where I had fled when I left London, I sent him word to meet me at Greyfriars Church. He must have been surprised that I was in Scotland since he would have expected me to be Edward's prisoner, but he made no sign of it. At first, all was affable between us. But when I spoke of his betrayal, he became angry, denying it strenuously. Until I showed him the copy of our agreement that bore his seal, the one carried by his messenger to King Edward. Since I had both his copy and mine, he knew he was caught. I will never forget the look in his eyes, like that of a wild animal when cornered.

"Both of us drew our daggers but I struck the first blow. Comyn fell, wounded. His uncle rushed in and attacked me. Christopher Seaton, my sister Christian's husband, came behind him and defended me. We got away and, as we left the church, Roger Kirkpatrick, waiting outside, asked what had happened. When I told him I might have killed the Red Comyn, he said, 'I will make sure', and hastened into the church."

"'Tis the place that is most troubling," said Angus. "Were it not for that, it would be a fair fight the Comyns lost."

Rob nodded. "Now, it is sacrilegious murder in the eyes of the Church. Even with Bishop Wishart's absolving me, I can still be excommunicated by the pope."

"He may well do. But that is hardly a concern if you prevail as King of Scots. Popes are men and, like all men, have been known to change their minds. Too, our Celtic clerics would remind you it is God who absolves us of sin and He has forgiven you. King Edward is the one we must fear for he will use this as an excuse to annihilate all who support you."

"He has already given the command that the knights and lords who support me are to receive the same fate as Wallace. Did you know that de Valence attacked us at Methven under the dragon banner?"

"I had heard that. It is something Edward would do."

Rob bent his head, his eyes closed. "Many of my followers fell to English swords. The guilt of their blood is ever with me."

Angus could not allow his friend to wallow in remorse. "Edward would have come against you had Comyn never been killed. And the Comyns and their allies, the MacDougalls, would have fought with England's king then as they do now. You stand for a free Scotland, Rob. Edward will hear nothing of our freedom. Your reign may not have begun as you wished but your cause is just and I believe you will prevail."

Rob met Angus' unwavering gaze. "You sound so sure."

"Aye. I am."

"You would risk all to stand by me?"

Angus smiled, for he had committed himself and his Isles long ago. There was no turning back now. "Aye. I will, and gladly. What is worth living for, Rob, if not something worth dying for?"

In the king's eyes there were tears.

The next day just before noon, as the sky darkened, threatening rain, a galley sailed into Dunaverty Bay. The red and white pennon flying from its mast told Angus who was onboard. The guard on the battlement shouted, "Ship approaching!"

"It is Lennox," said Rob, standing next to Angus on the parapet, watching the galley head for shore.

"Shall we go down to the beach to meet him?" asked Angus.

"For all he has done for me, that is a smallest gesture I can give him when I owe him so much more," said Rob.

On the beach, Earl Malcolm waited, hands on hips, as he watched them descending the headland.

Once Angus reached the sand, he welcomed the tall, blond earl. "I am Angus Og, Lord of the Isles. Welcome to Dunaverty."

"Aye," said Lennox, reaching out his hand, "I know of you, Angus Og, son of Angus Mor Macdonald. My father and yours were friends."

Before Angus could reply, Rob said to the earl, "What kept you, Malcolm? I thought you were right behind us."

"I was, Sire, but the MacDougalls gave chase in their galleys and nearly caught us. I had to throw all my goods overboard to distract them. It worked, as they slowed to gather their prizes from the water. Still, I do not think we have long until Edward's men will find us here. A day, two at most."

"A night's food and rest will do you good," said Angus. "We can sail tomorrow for a safer harbor. Meantime, enjoy our hospitality while I send for warriors to accompany us on our voyage."

ÁINE LISTENED THAT night at dinner as the men discussed where they might take the king.

"We've many Isles where one can hide," said Angus to Rob, "where you can plan your return. Trouble is, the strongest of our castles are close to Lorne and Argyll. And the outer Isles are inconvenient for your purpose."

Áine had an idea and, while she would not often interject comments when the men were hard at discussion, she did now. "Angus, would you consider a suggestion?"

"Aye. What are you thinking?"

Aware that all eyes were upon her, she said, "When I thought of what you seek, a convenient isle close to friendly territory with resources and options for quick escape, where men willing to fight for King Robert could be had, one island came to mind." She paused to read their expressions and then said, "Rathlin."

"Off the Ulster coast?" asked the king.

"Yes, my lord. You can see the island from here. It is but eleven miles from Dunaverty. The island itself is only six miles long but there is a well-tended castle and beaches for many galleys. My family's castle at Dunseverick on Ulster's coast is just a few miles across the Sea of Moyle. The O'Cahans would provide men and resources for you, as would the O'Neills."

"I know Ulster and I know of the island," said the king. "A definite possibility."

"My son, Brian," said Áine, gesturing to where Brian sat not far away, "is an O'Neill himself, the son of my first husband, then the King of Tirowen. Until recently, Brian fostered with the O'Neills in Ulster."

"What of the Earl of Ulster who is Edward's man?" asked Sir Gilbert. "He would be close, too."

"Yes, but he is my father-in-law," said the king. "He may be loyal to Edward but he would do nothing to harm the husband of his daughter who is now my queen."

"And the castle on Rathlin?" asked the James Douglas. "Whose is it? How great a fortification?"

"'Tis a great fortress and the master is Sir Hugh Bissett," said Angus, "Lord of the Glens of Antrim and my brother-in-law. He helped me hunt the MacDougalls not long ago. I believe he would give us welcome or at least turn a blind eye."

"As a youth, I fostered with the Bissetts," said Sir Edward. "They will not turn us away even if it means opposing Longshanks."

"Then it is agreed," said King Robert. "With Angus' help, we are for Rathlin."

AT MID-MORNING the next day, three galleys laden with men, weapons and supplies, appeared off Dunaverty's shore. John, who had been watching for them, brought the news to Angus. They flew no banner as they had been instructed. Angus, John and Duncan went to the parapet to observe their landing.

Rob came up behind them. "Whose are they?"

"Your escort," said Angus. "Islesmen, including some of my galloglass, who will accompany us to Rathlin, prepared to fight."

"There must be a hundred in each galley," said the king.

"Aye, three hundred was my order and three hundred have come," said Angus. "Lennox can fill his empty galley with supplies and more. You can sail in my ship with your small group and my family. Every member of my crew is a galloglass."

"How did I never know of your reach?" asked the king.

Duncan and John exchanged a smile.

"My eldest brother was Lord of the Isles when you and I last fought together," said Angus. "He commanded the fleet of the Isles and led the chiefs. Now, they are mine to command, my responsibility to lead. But were Alex alive today, the result would be the same.

Though Alex served Edward for a time, as did we all, he was ever loyal to the Bruces."

Angus had told Áine the evening before to be ready to sail the next day with their children, Alexander's tutor, the nursemaids who attended the two younger ones, the physician, their Irish bard, and the servants she would need at Rathlin. He also told her she should take any clothes and jewels she did not want to fall into the hands of the English. Meanwhile, he arranged to take all the spare weapons, and the barrels of wine and rounds of cheese in his cellar and enough food for many days.

Duncan's galley was sent home to Saddell with Angus' hawks and the horses they would leave behind. As Angus had anticipated, the Earl of Lennox made his galley available to carry supplies, the two wolfhounds and the few horses they would take with them, including Brian's dapple-gray mare, Enbarr.

At noon, as they made ready to sail, Angus called his seneschal to him. "The English will come, mayhap with siege equipment. Under whose command, I know not. Do not resist them. Keep the bridge and gate open. Welcome them as guests. When they ask where I am, tell them 'Lord Angus has sailed, as he often does, to the Isles.' Since you do not know where I am going, you cannot tell him. Are we agreed?"

"Aye, my lord. If they throw us out, I will come to Islay. If they allow us to remain, we will be here when you return."

Angus was taking his personal guard with him and left only ten men-at-arms garrisoning the castle. He hoped it would make the English less suspicious but, more likely, word had already spread that the Lord of the Isles harbored the outlaw, Robert Bruce.

A strong current bore the galleys southeast the few miles to Rathlin. At times, the waves rose so high around the ships that Angus lost sight of one as it slipped into a trough only to rise again, doused in cold sea spray. The wind, blowing strong and fair, swept them along as the fate of the Scottish nation and her king were entrusted to the waves.

The rain held off until they reached Rathlin's coast. Angus was eager to unload the galleys and settle his family and the men in the warmth of a castle where, he hoped, fires were kept burning against the cold winter.

As they beached the five galleys, the island's residents, who had initially gathered, fled as hundreds of warriors were disgorged from the ships.

"To them it appears an invasion," said Duncan.

"Aye," said Angus, looking back to see his three hundred warriors climbing down to the sand.

The islanders who remained, rugged men of the land and the sea, stood their ground and turned hostile looks upon them. Angus was about to go to them when Áine said to the king, "Allow me, my lord. I know these people."

"Only if I accompany you," Angus insisted.

Angus followed close on her heels as his wife went forward to meet the boldest of the Rathlin residents. The man was of middle years, his broad-shouldered frame muscular and his face weathered. His dark hair was streaked with gray and his beard was the color of dull steel. His furrowed brow gave him a stubborn look.

"I am Áine O'Cahan," Áine said in a loud voice, "sister of Dermot O'Cahan, who is known to you as the master of Dunseverick Castle. This man," she said, gesturing to Angus, "is my husband, Angus Og Macdonald, Lord of the Isles, who is kin to your master, Sir Hugh Bissett. We come in peace with a very important passenger, the King of Scots, Robert Bruce."

Angus wondered if it was wise to speak of their infamous guest, but Áine's judgment had been correct, for the man's dour expression suddenly turned into a wide smile. He beckoned the people from their hiding places and they came slowly forward. "The king is here?" he asked.

"Aye," said Angus, "and in need of a place to rest for a while. Will you welcome him?"

"Indeed, yes!" said the man, as whispers spread to all the others now gathered around Angus and Áine to stare beyond them to Robert Bruce.

Angus waved the king forward, and he strode to them, flanked by his brothers. "Allow me to introduce you to the King of Scots, who was once known to you as the Earl of Carrick, having spent much time in Ulster. His brother, Sir Edward, who comes also, fostered with the Bissetts. The others with him are his brothers, Alexander and Sir Thomas."

The Rathlin leader bowed before the king. "My lord, I am Daniel Black. You are welcome here."

"May God bless you," said Scotland's new king. "Your kindness will not be forgotten."

Angus asked the Rathlin leader, "Is Sir Hugh in residence?"

"Nay, my lord."

"I would send word to him if you can take my message without anyone knowing. And I would ask you to say nothing of the island's royal guest."

The man inclined his head. "It will be as you wish."

In the days that followed, Angus sent word to Sir Hugh that he was "borrowing Rathlin's castle for a time and hoped that was acceptable." He was told the message had been received and that Sir Hugh agreed with the proposal. Sir Hugh would learn in time that King Robert was on Rathlin if he did not know already. Angus counted on their kinship and their friendship to keep the English dogs away.

Angus put Duncan in charge of the three hundred men they had brought to Rathlin. The warriors quickly went to work building quarters for their lodging as the castle's great hall could not contain the whole of them comfortably. The shelter would serve for the winter to keep them from the near constant rain and the wind that could chill a man's bones.

Angus' family and the king and his companions settled into the castle at Rathlin. Set on the rocky coast, the large stone edifice looked across the blue sea toward Kintyre just visible on the horizon.

Angus sent word to Áine's brother, Dermot, who came from Dunseverick to visit. Dermot's nephews, Brian and Alexander, were delighted to see him. He remembered the wolfhound, Fand, and remarked at how she had grown. Alexander's hound, Cormac, was new and the boy was proud to introduce him to Dermot.

"It is plain to see they are enjoying themselves with the warriors who serve Scotland's king," Dermot said to Angus.

"Aye. To them, this is a grand time."

Angus often spotted Rob watching the Macdonald children with longing in his eyes. "I miss Elizabeth and Marjorie," he confessed to Angus soon after they arrived. "I hope they are on their way to Orkney by now with my sisters and Countess Isabella."

In the evening, they enjoyed each other's fellowship, entertained by Angus' Irish bard who had composed a tribute to King Robert and his trusted ally, the Lord of the Isles. When the bard concluded, they discussed the strategy for re-engaging with King Edward.

"We've a kingdom to take back," said Lennox. "'Tis well we were at it."

"We cannot fight as we have before," said the king, "in the open, arrayed for battle. We do not have the numbers, not even with Angus' men."

Angus agreed. "For the now, a 'secret war' would be more effective, like we fight in the Highlands. Give no warning, strike hard, and then retreat into the woods."

"'Twas Wallace's strategy before Falkirk," said Neil Campbell. "And it worked."

"We should burn every castle the English can otherwise use," said the fiery young Douglas, now fully recovered, "my own stronghold among them."

"And mine," added the king. "We should begin in Carrick, for I know the land."

The strategy having been agreed to, it was only a matter of waiting for spring. But in February of 1307, Sir Robert Boyd, who had been one of the knights sent to Kildrummie with the Bruce women, arrived on Rathlin, haggard and dripping water from the rain that fell hard that day.

The knight dropped to one knee before the king, who rose from his chair near a window in the great hall where he was meeting with his men. "My lord king, please forgive my appearance. A fisherman brought me."

"Sir Robert, why are you here?" asked the king, lines of worry cut into his face.

Rising, Sir Robert said, "I have been a prisoner of the English for nearly six months. I only escaped recently. Hearing that Edward was searching for you in Ireland and the Isles, and knowing of your ties to Ulster, I thought to come here."

Rob's countenance was grave, as was Angus', for both knew the story could not end well. Boyd had been a trusted ally of Wallace and was faithful to Robert Bruce. Nothing short of tragedy would separate him from his duty.

The men the king had brought with him gathered around to hear what news Boyd had to convey. Áine handed the sodden knight a goblet of hot spiced wine. "Thank you, my lady," he said, before Angus introduced himself and his wife.

"What happened at Kildrummie?" asked the king, his eyes narrowed on his knight. Angus could see it was only by tremendous restraint Rob was holding his passions in check.

Sir Neil Campbell stood watching intently, reminding Angus the knight was married to the king's younger sister, Mary, who had gone to Kildrummie.

"We were betrayed by a blacksmith and the castle was breached by Prince Edward. Sir Alexander and I fled with the queen and the other women to St. Duthac's Chapel at Tain in Ross, where we sought sanctuary. You would have been proud of the queen, Sire. When the Earl of Ross breached sanctuary to seize us, she accused him of cowardice. She said he was more afraid of Edward's wrath than of God's."

With a pained look, the king said, "They did not harm her for her brave words?"

"No, they did not harm any of the women but led us all away."

"What of my brother, Nigel?"

Sir Robert dropped his gaze. "He stayed with the garrison at Kildrummie, my lord, to mount a defense. He was captured. All tell of a traitor's death at Berwick."

Angus did not need an explanation. It was Wallace's death. The look of horror in Rob's eyes told him his friend was thinking the same.

Rob dropped his head into his hands. He did not weep but a ragged gasp sounded from his throat. His three brothers gathered round him, Edward's hand on his shoulder.

Raising his head, Rob asked anxiously, "What of Elizabeth and the ladies?"

"In London, I heard the queen was initially confined at Burstwick but she is often moved, doubtless to prevent a rescue. Her father, the Red Earl, intervened on her behalf so that she is provided servants. Since King Edward arranged your marriage, he can hardly hold it against her. I'm told your sister, Christian, was sent to a convent as was your daughter, Marjorie."

"Better a convent than prison," said Sir Neil.

To be alone without comfort of family at so young an age must have been terrifying, for Angus remembered Marjorie was only twelve.

"And the other two?" asked the king, by now his face a mask of grief.

"My wife?" asked Sir Neil.

"Edward was beyond cruel, my lords. He has ordered a savage treatment. They are confined in cages, Isabella MacDuff in one of the towers of Berwick Castle and Mary at Roxburgh Castle."

"A cage?" exclaimed Sir Neil. "My wife, Mary, is in a cage?" Neil Campbell clenched his fists, his knuckles white with his rage.

The king looked at Neil Campbell's anguished face. At that point, Angus could see that Rob's grief was beyond his ability to contain. The king rose and screamed, "Only a devil could treat women so!" Dropping into his chair, he said, "And Christopher Seaton, what will he say when he hears I did not protect Christian from Edward's wrath?"

Angus glanced at Sir Robert Boyd, knowing something was not being said. "What of Sir Christopher?" he asked the knight. "Do you know something?"

With a sheepish look, Sir Robert faced the king, "Seaton escaped Methven, my king, and took shelter in his castle at Loch Troon. But he was betrayed and captured along with the standard bearer, Sir Alexander Scrymgeour. They were hanged and beheaded by Edward's man, de Valence. The Earl of Atholl, King Edward's own cousin, was captured trying to escape from Methven and hanged in

London. This shocked even the English, for no earl has been hanged in more than two hundred years. Others were hanged at Newcastle along with Sir Christopher's brother, Alexander."

The king's voice, weak with strain, betrayed his despair. "So, loyal men and dear friends are gone from this life and Edward shows no mercy, even to women. My sister, Christian, made a widow, and confined to a nunnery while Mary is kept in a cage for all to mock."

Seeing Sir Robert hesitate, Angus asked, "Is there more?"

The knight nodded. "Bishops Wishart and Lamberton and Abbot Henry of Scone were captured by de Valence and sent south in chains. On my way here, I heard they are now in prison."

Tears rolled down the king's cheeks as his eyes closed. "It is more than I can bear. Leave me."

And all did.

Hours later, Angus stood with John and some of the king's men while Duncan had gone to check on the food supply for the warriors they had brought to Rathlin. The only sound in the hall was the crackling of the logs on the fire and the rain beating against the windows. The king had refused all food.

Áine approached Angus. "He must have some refreshment for he has been sitting in silence all day staring through the rain to the sea. At least let me take him some spiced wine and his cloak."

Angus was not inclined to disturb his friend, who was lost in grief, but he would trust Áine. "You can try, my love."

ÁINE GATHERED THE woolen cloak and a goblet of hot spiced wine and crossed the great hall to where the king sat. His head was bent over his folded hands held close to his face. Áine thought she heard a whispered prayer before he looked up. His eyes were red and his skin pale.

"Forgive me, my lord, I did not know you were praying. I brought you some hot wine and your cloak." She handed him first the goblet, which he wrapped his hands around, and then she draped his cloak over his shoulders. "It is cold in this part of the hall so far from the fire."

The king stared out the window. There was still light upon the sea but the sun had set and the rain poured down as it had all day. It would soon be dark. "I have tried to pray," he said, "but I fear God has forsaken me."

She took the chair across from him. "No, my king, God has not forsaken you. Rather, I think He may be testing you and preparing you to be a king after His heart."

The king turned to her with a questioning look.

Seeing he was willing to listen, Áine said, "As I have thought of all you have been through, I am reminded of another king, one anointed by God, as you were, who was hunted for years by a ruthless king who sought his death, just as you are hunted by ruthless King Edward, who seeks yours."

"What king was that?"

"I am sure you learned of him as a lad. King David of the Scriptures was Israel's greatest king yet his path to the throne was not an easy one. He fled so fast in the face of King Saul's fury, he had nothing, not even food."

"Yes, now I remember."

"At his lowest point, when David was alone and living in a cave, he made God his refuge. He had come to the point where God could begin to shape him into the king he would become. God brought men to David, those in debt and distress, broken men who were discontent. He and his men lived in caves in the wilderness, surviving on what food they could forage, what beasts they could hunt."

The king said, "Before I came here, we lived in the wilderness, cold and hungry."

She nodded for she had heard from Angus of the king's plight. "It was at that point David's kingship began. His mighty men of valor the Scripture speaks of rose from the men God brought to him. Years later, in a great battle, King Saul and his sons were slain and David finally was recognized as king. It occurred to me, my lord, this may be your story, too."

King Robert gazed intently into her eyes, his nod acknowledging all she had said.

"You have lost much. David lost his closest friend, Jonathan, and many of his allies. He lost his wife for a time, a marriage arranged by

King Saul, as yours was arranged by King Edward. Many of your friends have fallen to Edward's wrath. And you have lost family, your brother, Nigel, killed and your wife, daughter and sisters taken from you."

Grief hung over the king like a dark cloud. She must give him something to encourage him to go forward. "Why, I asked myself, did God allow David to remain on the run all those years, living in caves in the wilderness, hunted by an evil king, when He could have secured the throne for David years before?"

"Did you find an answer?" asked King Robert.

"Mayhap I did, for it was during those years David was tested and taught many lessons. Like you, he was already a great warrior, but now he had to learn to be a great leader of God's people. Where he had once led thousands of trained warriors in battle, just as you did, now he led small bands of rough, broken men. David learned to show mercy. Most of all, he learned the faithfulness and power of God. In his darkest hour, he made the decision to trust God, and the Scripture says that God delivered David from all his enemies. He will deliver you, too, my king. You have only to trust Him."

The king let out a sigh and Áine saw the tension fall from his shoulders. "You think so?"

"I do. From this point on, my king, you begin anew. Trust God to lead you, and I will pray that your wife, daughter and sisters are restored to you."

She rose to leave, and the king took her hand and kissed it. "Thank you, my lady. You have given me hope where I had none."

That night, King Robert joined Áine and Angus, along with the king's companions at the table for supper. The king ate little. Áine was pleased to see he ate at all.

During the somber meal, the hushed conversations respected their shared grief. In the flickering light of a candle, the king leaned close to Angus, allowing Áine, who sat next to her husband, to hear the king's words. "I knew you married a beautiful woman," he said. "Her reasons for choosing Rathlin as our refuge told me she is wise. When she faced the hostile islanders, I realized she is also brave. But only today did I discover you married a saint."

CHAPTER 22

Rathlin Island off the coast of Ulster, March 1307

SPRING ARRIVED on Rathlin, with nesting birds and a profusion of wildflowers on the verdant hillsides. Although the air remained cold, the clouds often parted to allow the sun's rays to reach the flowers.

As the weather began to improve, Angus observed the men growing restless. Not only his own men, but those attached to the king as well. Now that winter was ending, they wanted action. Hunting and vigorous practice sessions with sword, spear and bow helped some, yet Angus knew this would not satisfy for long.

Angus' brother, John, had improved in the fighting skills Angus had taught him and could now match his skills with any Isleman. Angus kept his own skills honed in practice bouts with the king, Sir Robert Boyd and the young James Douglas, who was very fast with his sword. But all this practice served merely as a prelude for war. The time had come for the king to move forward with his plans to take back his kingdom.

In conversation one evening, King Robert reminded Angus that, through his first wife, Isabella of Mar, he was related to Christina of

Garmoran, heiress to the MacRuairi lands.

"The MacRuairis hold lands in Moidart and Lochaber as well as a number of small isles," Angus told him. "Christina is the heiress. Her illegitimate half-brothers once sailed with me when I served King Edward. I am certain they would much prefer to serve you."

"Might she help us?" asked the king.

"Aye. I expect Christina would contribute men as well as ships to your cause. I can take you to her at Castle Tioram. On the way back, we can gather more to your cause."

The king nodded. "A worthy idea. Let us sail to my kinswoman."

Sir Edward, who had been listening, said, "While you sail north, Robert, I would take our brothers to Ulster where our friend, Malcolm McQuillan, dwells next to Coleraine in Tirowen. There, I am confident we can raise more recruits."

"My stepson, Brian, would want to go with you," put in Angus, "and he might be of help with the O'Neills."

"He is welcome to come," said Edward Bruce agreeably.

The next day, Angus, the king and two of his knights sailed north, while Edward Bruce and the other Bruce brothers sailed the short distance south to Ulster. They took along the horses and Angus' stepson, Brian, who was proud to be included.

The Earl of Lennox, Duncan and John thought it best if they remained on Rathlin with the bulk of their warriors.

Angus felt the chill of the air as they sailed north to Castle Tioram in Moidart. It rained often but the rain sometimes brought them rainbows, which cheered all.

Christina MacRuairi welcomed them to her lands and expressed her eagerness to help King Robert. She contributed three galleys and fighting men to sail them. "You are kin, my lord," she said to the king. "Of course, I will help." She offered more resources, too, should the king have need of them. "Lord Angus can send word."

By early April, they returned to Rathlin with a fleet of galleys and a small army of Islesmen who were committed to the king's efforts to free Scotland from the English. It was not all Angus could have raised but he believed it was enough for now.

About the same time, the king's brothers returned from Ireland with hundreds of recruits and the Irish nobleman, Malcolm McQuillan, and Sir Reginald Crawford, both of whom had served King Edward but had since given their loyalty to King Robert.

With Fand, the wolfhound that had been Brian's gift, at her side, Áine greeted her son. "It is good to have you with us again."

All the Irishmen who came to Rathlin lamented King Edward's atrocities and were anxious to be part of removing the English from Scotland and Ireland. To the Irish of Ulster, the Scots in the Isles and Gaelic Carrick were considered kin.

The Earl of Lennox and the knights who had traveled with Robert Bruce anxiously expressed their desire to be about the business of securing King Robert's throne. To their many questions, the king promised, "We will leave soon."

The passionate young James Douglas was more anxious than most to move forward without further delay. He spoke his mind that night as they dined on a dinner of the island's hares and fish caught offshore. "We are nothing but a burden to the islanders when there are castles to be burned and Englishmen to be put to the sword. 'Tis time to act!"

Angus shared a look with Áine who listened but did not speak.

"Where would you go?" asked the king.

"To Brodick Castle on the east coast of Arran in the Firth of Clyde, my lord. 'Tis garrisoned by the English and known to me—a rich prize."

"If you send Jamie," said Sir Robert Boyd, "send me with him. I know the castle well. It is in the keeping of Sir John Hastings, an Englishman loyal to Edward but with estates in Scotland. You will recall he was a competitor for the crown when Edward unwisely picked John Balliol."

King Robert nodded. "Very well, go. Take a galley and a small party of warriors and attempt the surprise of Brodick. Send word when you have arrived and, depending on your assessment, I will follow with more ships and men."

Angus believed the king was being careful in this next move after losing so much so soon following his coronation.

When Douglas and Boyd sailed for Arran, Angus decided the time had come for him to take Áine and his children to safety. "Come with me to Islay," he bid the king, "where I keep most of my fleet. We can be back in three days' time."

The king agreed and, the next morning, they departed the island in Angus' galley with a second ship following. As before, he left Duncan in charge of the men at Rathlin but took John with him. Áine, their four children, her handmaiden, and the servants who had accompanied them from Dunaverty, sailed for Islay.

During the crossing, Áine came to Angus where he stood in the bow of the ship with his foot braced on the small platform. "My only regret at leaving Rathlin," she said, "is that the puffins have only just arrived and they are among my favorites."

"Birds, you mean?" said Angus, distracted by something on the horizon.

"Of course. Do you know of any other puffins?"

Angus chuckled and turned back to her. "Well, no, now that you speak of it." Then pulling her close and kissing her forehead, he said, "Can you not think of another reason you will miss Rathlin?"

"Well, there were the nights with you. I will miss those terribly. Once you have taken me and the children to Islay, you will leave with the king, yes?"

"Aye."

Her beautiful eyes sparkled with unshed tears. "Then I will not see you for some time."

Angus did not answer for they both knew they would soon be parted, and he could not say when, or if, she would see him again. Instead, ignoring the men at the oars, he kissed her.

When the kiss ended, she gazed toward the stern. "Angus, have you noticed the growing affection between your captain and my handmaiden?"

Angus turned to see his captain in the stern and his wife's handmaiden next to him, laughing.

"It has been going on for longer than you might realize. They have only grown closer on Rathlin. I must ask you, is he honorable concerning women?"

"Aye. Conall was captain of my brother's galley before mine. He is a seasoned warrior and a good seaman. He was married but his wife died three years ago in childbed."

"Well, as you might observe, Nessa is taken with him. She would make him an excellent wife. Since they both serve us, a marriage between them would be convenient for all. Might you mention the thought to him?"

"If it pleases you, my love, I will."

His wife smiled and the sun rose in her eyes. "Thank you. Just remember when you speak of it that it was *your* idea."

He laughed. "Aye, I shall remember." Many of her ideas had become his own.

White clouds flitted across the blue sky as Angus' galley transported them from Rathlin to Dunyvaig. They did not put in at Lagavulin Bay, where Angus' large fleet lay, but headed for the rocky shore in front of the castle. The gray seals lazing on the rocks barely noticed.

They beached the two galleys and began the walk to the castle. The crews helped the children and their nurses over the rocky shore along with all else they had brought. Young Alexander raced to the castle, eager to see his cousins. Brian walked with the king's knights. Angus and John, striding beside the king, followed Áine and her handmaiden up to the tall stone tower that looked south to Rathlin and east to Kintyre.

At the door of the castle, Angus' sister-in-law welcomed them.

"Juliana," said Angus, "I come with our new lord. Greet Robert Bruce, King of Scots."

Alex's widow smiled her delight and curtseyed before the king. "Welcome, my lord king."

Just then, her sons burst into the great hall like a pack of wild dogs, followed by Angus' son, Alexander.

Juliana's sons, apparently schooled beforehand, came to a sudden halt and bowed before the king. Rising, one said, "Are you really the King of Scots?"

Rob said, "Crowned king, aye, but I have yet to secure my kingdom."

The boy, too young to understand, looked up, confused.

"Are some of them missing?" Angus asked Juliana. "I seem to recall I have six nephews but I count only four."

"The two oldest are fostering in Ireland," said Juliana. "They are determined to join the galloglass." Alex's boys were an unruly bunch, kept in line by Angus' constable on Islay, who reminded them often they were the sons of Alexander Macdonald and grandsons of Angus Mor, and must behave as such. They would make exceptional galloglass; of that Angus had no doubt.

"Time has sped away," said Angus. "I did not know they had reached that age." Glancing at the king, he said, "It will happen to you again one day, my king, when the queen has given you sons." Then to Juliana, he explained, "We are only here for two nights to bring Áine and the children to Islay for safety. I expect by now Dunaverty has been overrun with English."

Juliana embraced Áine, and said to Angus, "Well, then 'tis good you have brought them here where the fleet is based. Should Dunyvaig ever be in danger, there is always Finlaggan."

"Aye," agreed Angus. Turning to his friend, Rob, he said, "Finlaggan is in the middle of the isle, the true heart of the lordship. 'Tis an island within an isle. The Council of the Isles meets there."

The crews of the two galleys carried the chests and supplies into the castle.

The next day, Angus sent John to the captains of the galleys in Lagavulin Bay to request their presence in the castle where he intended to introduce them to the king.

As they waited in Dunyvaig's great hall for the men to appear, Angus said to his friend, "If you mean to join Douglas and Boyd on Arran, we had best take ships and warriors with us to accomplish your purposes. In addition to the galleys we left on Rathlin, I propose to add more."

The king nodded in agreement. "De Valence has a great force, and the castles the English hold are fully garrisoned."

The captains who agreed to go with Angus were eager to sail and asked only for that day to supply the ships and bid their families goodbye. "How long might we be away on the king's business?" asked one.

Angus told them what he knew. "As long as it takes to secure King Robert's throne, though I expect we will be able to come home from time to time. Some of you will go now while others will stay to go in the future."

Before the sun had set on the horizon, a message arrived on Islay for Angus from his seneschal at Dunaverty.

> *I trust this has found you through the circuitous route I was required to use. The English did, indeed, arrive at Dunaverty and have taken the castle. As our local people were reluctant to supply them with provisions, King Edward ordered his man, Sir John Menteith, to compel them, which he did.*
>
> *The English king has made John MacDougall of Argyll his "Admiral of the West Coast", and dispatched Sir Hugh Bissett to join Menteith to hunt Robert Bruce and his abettors.*
>
> *Take heart, my lord. Wherever you are, you remain hidden with your valuable cargo.*

Angus shared the message with the king, his companions and John. "So," he said to Rob, "you are hunted but not found and Bissett has not betrayed us." With a smile, he added, "What title King Edward gives to the MacDougall's son is merely temporary."

The king looked up from the missive and smiled. "Your lady's prayers are answered."

"Aye. It would seem so. We remain undiscovered."

The farewell the following day was a tearful one for all involved. In Lagavulin Bay, the wives and children of Angus' captains hugged the men they would not see again for some time. As for Angus, he and Áine had parted before when he had sailed to battles for King Edward, but this time would be different, for he was leaving for a war of less certain outcome in which the stakes for both the lordship and Scotland were too great to fail.

"I will come to you as often as I can," he told Áine as he bent his head to her where they stood on the shore next to his galley. "When I cannot come, I will send news."

Her beautiful, tear-filled eyes gazed back at him. "I will continue to ask God to protect you and King Robert and give you victory over your enemies."

Angus' captain, Conall, parted from Nessa, Áine's handmaiden, with whispered words and a quick kiss. When she brushed her brown curls from her face, Angus could see tears flowing unimpeded down her cheeks.

Áine and Nessa stood on the shore next to Juliana and the children. Brian looked on as Angus' crew made ready to sail. He had wanted to go but Angus did not give his permission. "There will come a time in the next few years when you will go with me," said Angus. "See that your skills are perfected and approved by my constable while I am gone. When I return, I will test you myself to see if you are ready."

Standing straight as a mast, Brian nodded. "I will be ready, sir."

As the crew pulled at the oars, taking the ship out to sea, he heard Áine shout, "Godspeed!"

Angus led his fleet of ships south to Rathlin. They would sail from there to the Isle of Arran near Scotland's mainland.

A few days later, a fisherman brought King Robert a message from James Douglas.

To Robert, King of Scots, from his liegeman, James Douglas,

We came ashore at dawn, having sailed through the night from Kintyre to avoid the English. Wet and hungry, we were pleased to see three ships loaded with goods had arrived at Brodick the night before and were anchored in the bay.

We waited and, the next morning, soldiers and sailors from the garrison came to unload the cargo. We set upon them and seized the spoil, a rich harvest of clothing, food, wine and arms. No one from the castle came to their rescue or to interfere with us. Instead, they closed the gates where they remain.

Come to Arran! We have taken up a position in a narrow pass and will keep watch for you. When you arrive, we will send one to lead you to us.

"So, it begins," the king said, handing the message to Angus.

He read it and handed it back. "All to the good. The men are ready."

Thus, it was that ten days after James Douglas and Sir Robert Boyd had left Rathlin, Angus, Duncan, John and the king and his companions arrived on Arran with over thirty galleys and more than a thousand men from the Isles and Ireland.

Shortly after they beached the ships on Arran's eastern shore, a peasant woman of middle years appeared. One of Angus' captains brought her to him where he stood next to the king.

Her appearance was well-ordered, her tunic simple and her dark hair confined with a scarf. In a clear voice, she said, "I was sent by one called Douglas to lead you to him."

The captain who had brought her to Angus said, "She asked for you, Lord Angus."

He shared a glance with the king. It made sense that Douglas would not reveal to the woman that the King of Scots, hunted by King Edward, waited on the beach. The temptation to the riches gained from a betrayal would be too great. Thankfully, there was nothing in the king's clothing to speak of royalty.

Angus said to the woman, "You go ahead and we will follow. When we are close, let us know."

Leaving most of the men at the shore to guard the galleys, Angus and the king followed the woman into the forest, thick with pine, birch and whitebeam. Close on their heels were Duncan, John, the king's brothers and his knights.

They trod in the woman's steps over the damp ground surrounded by trees. In the occasional parting of branches, sunlight dappled the forest floor with golden light that illuminated the yellow gorse and the white snow drops that had only just bloomed.

Some distance on, they came to the mouth of a woody glen. The woman stopped and turned to them. "He is just ahead, my lord."

Angus had noted the king carried a horn at his side such as one might use in battle, but not until now did he use it.

Rob raised his horn to his lips and blew a loud cry that echoed through the woods. A moment of silence passed and he blew another.

Minutes later, James Douglas and Sir Robert Boyd appeared, smiling broadly. Once the woman had been paid and dismissed, Douglas said to Boyd, "I told you it was the king. I know that blast."

"With your permission, Sire," said Sir Robert, addressing the king, "we will show you where we have hidden the booty we took from the English. The crew of the galley stands guard."

They arrived at a pile of boxes, barrels and chests, some of which had been opened to reveal their contents. Silk and velvet fabric, silver goblets, wheels of cheese and barrels of ale and wine were among the offerings, along with daggers and other weapons.

The king surveyed all with a look of pleasure. "A rich bounty, indeed. Has anyone emerged from the castle to try and re-claim it?"

"No one, my lord," said Sir Robert.

The king raised his head and gazed toward the south. "The earldom of Carrick lies but twenty-five miles to the southeast. My birthplace of Turnberry is there on the coast. I would send a spy to see how it fares, who holds it and if the people are well disposed toward me."

"Cuthbert, who is one of my crew," said Angus, "is an excellent man for that kind of assignment. He knows the area and can move like a cat."

Once the seized goods had been carried to the galleys, Cuthbert was found and the king gave him his instructions. "Spy out the country around Turnberry. If the people have goodwill for me, light a fire from Turnberry Head in the evening at seven of the clock. Once we see it, we will come."

Angus sailed the galleys to the south end of Arran where they would be able to see a fire lit at Turnberry Castle across the Firth of Clyde.

Meantime, at their request, the king dispatched his brothers, Thomas and Alexander, with the Irish lord, Malcolm McQuillan, Sir Reginald Crawford and hundreds of Irish kerns from Ulster to Loch Ryan in Galloway. They sailed south in eighteen galleys. From Galloway, they were to attack the main supply route through Ayrshire in order to hinder any retaliation from the king's attack on Carrick.

"I know the route well," said Sir Reginald. Like many of them, he had once served King Edward but now pledged his loyalty to the new

King of Scots.

Still on Arran, Angus and the others waited three days before the watch spotted a fire near Turnberry.

"The fire!" exclaimed the king. "'Tis Cuthbert's signal."

Sailing from Arran, they rowed all night, steering for the fire hoping for an exuberant welcome.

They arrived before dawn to find Cuthbert pacing on the shore, beside himself with fear. "I did not light the fire, my king. 'Twas lit by the farmers burning heather and gorse in their pastures. I could not put it out so I have waited in fear for your coming."

With furrowed brows, the king asked, "What did you find?"

"In truth, what I found was not encouraging. Percy has the castle with three hundred in his garrison, though most are not quartered behind its walls. As for the people, they are indifferent if not hostile to us. They fear Edward more than they love you."

Angus exchanged a look with Rob, seeing disappointment and concern in the king's expression. It mirrored his own. The knights gathered around Angus and the king to discuss what should be done.

Edward Bruce, clearly impatient, spoke first. "I am tired of all this seafaring. I would risk our fortune on land. We should attack now."

Others urged caution but all recognized that the hundreds of warriors they had brought to Arran would resist any further delay. Angus knew that his Islesmen, among whom were many galloglass, would not care about the local population's sentiment.

Lennox said, "We are here with all of these men, eager to fight. Why not strike now?"

Cuthbert said, "My lord king, most of Percy's men are lodged in the town or housed in barracks outside the castle. Those could be taken more easily."

Angus met the king's inquiring gaze. "I am not opposed to striking now while we still have the cloak of darkness. My Islesmen are ready."

"Very well," said King Robert, disappointment clear on his face for Turnberry was his true home. "We will not attempt the castle. We will make our target the hundreds of English outside."

Angus knew Rob regretted the attack on the unsuspecting garrison. It had been the tactic of de Valence at Methven and was against the code of chivalry, but at Rathlin they had committed themselves to a different way of fighting. Different for Robert Bruce, but long known to Angus, his Islesmen and the Highlanders—one practiced by Wallace.

The king gave the signal to move out. Angus, the knights and the Islesmen followed him, treading silently through the darkened forest. John and Duncan flanked Angus and the king. Not a scabbard rattled. Not a word was spoken. Wearing deerskin on their feet, their steps made no sound as they crept closer to the English barracks.

The king came to a halt and, with a wild war cry, rushed forward with Angus, his islesmen and the king's knights. They fell upon the English, who were cut down as they struggled from sleep. Some roused to fight only to meet their end at fierce Scottish blades and fiercer axes.

Percy did not rouse from the castle while the battle raged outside its stone walls. Angus guessed that, in the dark, Percy feared what might be a large force he could not see.

In a short time, the muffled sounds of battle silenced and the air was still. Angus wiped his axe on an enemy's tunic and, as light dawned, surveyed the area in front of him. Many bodies lay on the ground. He recognized none.

Angus glimpsed the king, standing not far away. He appeared whole and unharmed, splatters of blood from his encounters with English the only stains on his surcoat. Joining him, Angus asked, "Is it possible we have won without casualties on our side?"

The king smiled and slowly nodded. "Unless my knights tell me otherwise, it would appear so."

In truth, they had won a great victory. Not one of their men had been wounded beyond scratches and cuts that would heal. They collected all the weapons and armor they could carry and the spoil that was now theirs, including Percy's warhorses, and disappeared into the forested Carrick hills.

Angus dispatched Cuthbert and another spy to learn of the countryside around them. Days later, the spies returned with a report of the knowledge they had gained.

Angus was with the king when Cuthbert said, "News has spread of your victory, my lord. It has awakened your enemies, both English and Scottish, who surround you. To the north, John MacDougall of Lorne, son of Alexander, awaits; to the south in Galloway, where your brothers have gone, Dungal MacDouall leads his Galwegians; and to the east, Aymer de Valence and John Botetourt stand fast. All serve King Edward."

Angus let out a breath. He knew the king worried for his brothers. Since coming to Carrick, they had heard nothing of Thomas and Alexander's expedition to Galloway.

"If MacDouall still holds Galloway," said the king, "then my brothers must have failed."

Angus said nothing for he had felt a foreboding for some time at the silence coming from Galloway. "With your agreement," said Angus, "I will keep my men on constant move, no two nights in one place, and set guards all around the camp. We will not be surprised."

"A good idea, Angus. See it done. Though the woods are dense and will provide us cover, at least for a time, we are trapped here. I would not again be attacked at night like we were at Methven."

Angus gave the orders so that they would be aware of anything moving around them. A wolf in passing, be he animal or man, would be noticed. Since the men had to hunt far and wide to feed so many, it was rare all were in camp at the same time.

The weather improved as the weeks passed so it was not a burden to be outside except when it rained, which was often enough for them to oil their cloaks.

As news of Robert Bruce's return spread around the countryside, men came to him—poor men, broken men and valiant warriors stricken with a passion to free Scotland from England's yoke. As Angus and the king observed the new men in camp, King Robert said, "It is just as Lady Áine told me."

"My wife spoke of this day? These men?"

"Not exactly. She spoke of another king who walked through deep valleys, hunted as I am, one to whom God brought men like these to stand with him. She spoke of King David of Israel."

"Ah, I see. Yes, she mentioned that. My lady knows the Scriptures."

On another day, into their camp, accompanied by some of Angus' guards, came a woman known to the king, a former mistress of the Earl of Carrick named Christian. Her tunic was a simple woolen one and her cloak dark green, blending with the woods around them. "I have brought men and supplies," she said.

"Bless you, my lady," replied Robert Bruce.

She glanced at Angus and then at the king's companions before saying, "I also bring sad news, for which you may curse me."

"What news?" the king asked, his expression turning grave.

"'Tis your brothers, Thomas and Alexander. They sailed into Loch Ryan where their galleys and Irish kerns were quickly overwhelmed by forces under Dungal MacDouall, a friend of the Balliols and the Comyns. I am told only two galleys escaped. MacDouall executed Lord McQuillan."

"And my brothers?" asked the king. His face told Angus his friend dreaded what he would hear next.

She paused and then said, "All the leaders were taken. Your brothers were badly wounded, my lord. Along with Sir Reginald, they were sent to Carlisle and presented to King Edward who has come north in pursuit of you." In a final rush of words, she added, "He executed all three and set their heads on the gates of the castle."

The king turned away and said under his breath, "Three of my four brothers dead, my dear ones lost and their blood on my hands."

Angus laid his hand on Rob's shoulder. "Courage, my king. They willingly accepted the risk and would not regret so noble a death as to die for you and Scotland."

To Angus' great relief, James Douglas returned the next day with news that cheered all. Alight with excitement of his victory, the young man with wild black hair eagerly told the king his news. "Douglas Castle, under the command of Sir Robert Clifford, was crawling with English when we arrived. Being few in number, we had to be clever.

"As Palm Sunday was approaching, my men and I planned a surprise. When the garrison of thirty men left the castle for St. Bride's Church a mile away, we disguised ourselves as local peasants and hid among the congregation.

"In the church, I raised my war cry, 'A Douglas'. Hearing it, my men and the locals who were with us killed twenty soldiers and took ten prisoners. At the castle, we found only the cook, the steward and a few others so we barred the gates. A banquet had been prepared for Edward's men. Hungry as we were, my men and I invited in the servants and sat down to dine. We ate what we could and piled the rest in the cellar along with the grain and wine we could not carry and set it afire to which we added our ten dead prisoners.

"The castle burned to the ground, thus depriving the English of my stronghold. After that, we took to the hills, avoiding pursuit by Sir Robert Clifford, who managed to escape, being elsewhere at the time."

When Douglas appeared disappointed at the king's lukewarm smile in response, Angus took the young warrior aside and explained recent events. Douglas turned somber at hearing of the deaths of the king's brothers. "How could they kill Alexander? He was the Dean of Glasgow, a churchman!"

"Apparently, Edward overlooked such niceties for Alexander's relationship to the king."

Douglas frowned, his black brows drawing together. "Aye, he would, the bastard."

At a time when the king was surrounded by enemies and his mood at its lowest ebb, the guards Angus had ranged around the camp proved their worth, bringing news of an approaching force.

"How many?" inquired Angus in the presence of the king.

"About two hundred on horseback. Their speech is that of the Galwegians," said the guard. "I warrant they are MacDoualls."

King Robert said, "So, they think to come for the two remaining Bruce brothers. Where are they?"

"Approaching the riverside path, my lord." The nearby river provided fresh water for King Robert's forces so they were very familiar with its twists and turns.

Calling for Sir Gilbert Haye, who had assumed the role of constable, the king said, "We will go to the riverbank. There is a narrow ford there where the water is shallow. They will surely be forced to use it."

Angus and the knights followed the king and Sir Gilbert with a large force. As they neared the river, they could hear men and horses moving on the other side, their dark outlines stark in the moonlight.

Rob ordered Sir Gilbert, Angus and the others to stay back and went to the riverside alone to wait for the MacDoualls.

Angus' right hand nervously clutched the hilt of his sword while his left hand gripped his dagger. His sparth axe he had left in camp. With his heart hammering in his chest, he peered through the darkness lit only by the moon reflecting off the water.

Pausing on the other side of the river, the MacDoualls appeared to stare at the lone figure standing on the riverbank.

Suddenly, with a shout, they raced forward toward King Robert.

"What is he doing?" shouted Sir Robert Boyd. "They will kill him!"

The king's knights leaned forward to move. Angus held out his hand. "Wait! The king knows what he is about."

Forced to cross the river at the narrow ford, the MacDoualls moved forward one by one, giving King Robert time to cut them down as they approached him. After several had fallen to his sword, the king yelled to Sir Gilbert and the others to join him. "Come!"

Angus rushed forward into the fight to stand at the king's right, slashing with both his sword and his dagger, felling the king's enemies.

The single column of MacDoualls were now in disarray. Those they did not kill fled up the bank and back to whence they had come. Later, upon reflection, Angus understood why the king had done what he did, facing the MacDoualls alone. It was not only to entice them into a trap but to have his singular revenge for the death of his brothers. 'Twas a victory the king sorely needed, though a small one, for those faithful to him.

All celebrated.

By April, Angus had moved with his Islesmen and the king to Glen Trool, a narrow valley in the heart of Galloway's forests, with the beautiful waters of Loch Trool at its head. Word reached them there that King Edward's general, Aymer de Valence, knew of their location and was headed their way with fifteen hundred heavy cavalry.

Sitting on the hillside overlooking the dark waters of the loch below, eating the remains of the pike fish they had caught that morning, they discussed the possibilities. Angus pointed to the southern side of the glen at the eastern end of the loch. Above, a golden eagle soared into the blue sky. Angus followed its flight for a moment and then returned his attention to the far side of the loch. "See that track running between the mountain top and the marshy ground below?"

"Yes," said the king. "I see it."

"That will be where de Valence will enter. The track is too narrow for warhorses to charge, so he will be hemmed in and restricted. If we were to place our forces above that track, we could pelt them with rocks, forcing them down to the marshes at the loch's edge where their warhorses laden down with armor will not gain a footing."

The king looked to where Angus pointed. "I can see how it would happen and I believe it would work. Disabled by the rocks and mayhap arrows to follow, and forced to the water's edge, de Valence's warhorses would struggle to stand."

"Aye. And we would follow them down with our swords and spears. It would be a rout."

The king slapped Angus on the back. "Brilliant!"

"You would have thought of it, Rob, had you not been busy eating that last fish."

Days later, when the king's spy brought word of de Valence's approach, Bruce led the men in prayer, as he always did before a battle, and positioned them on the crags and steep slopes above the southeast corner of the loch. There, they waited, aligned with huge granite rocks, like a broken wall strung across the hillside.

The lookout came running to the king. "My lord, Aymer de Valence's troops have left their horses at a farm and are advancing on foot."

"This calls for an adjustment," said the king to Angus. "I will leave a third of the men on the hillside and position the rest out of sight at the end of the loch." Angus' brother, John, and his cousin, Duncan, were among those stationed on the hillside. Angus, Sir Edward and the king retired to the opposite slope with a few of his knights where they could watch and the king could control the battle.

De Valence led his men into the valley. Even on foot, they could not retain their formations and soon became ragged columns of single file. Strung out across the slope in disarray, they were ripe for the king's plan.

Robert Bruce blew three blasts on his horn, the clear sharp sound ringing across the water. In response, the Islesmen and Highlanders sent huge rocks rolling down the hillside.

With loud cries, the English troops scattered. Some were struck and rolled into the loch where they drowned. Others were killed outright.

The king gave the signal for the archers to rain arrows on de Valence's men. Some fell with those volleys. After that, Bruce's warriors advanced with swords, spears, axes and daggers.

The helmeted English soldiers were now in full retreat. With their swords flapping and their boots slipping, they fled across the hillside overrun by King Robert's army.

A great slaughter ensued. Only those in the rear escaped. One of them was the humiliated Aymer de Valence.

"It would seem," Angus said to the king later that day as his knights and his brother, Sir Edward, gathered around him, "God is with us."

"The prayers of our wives follow us," said the king.

Angus had often observed the king's gray eyes filled with longing, doubtless for his queen, as he stared into the distance. This was one of those times. "'Tis a great comfort."

With this victory and news of Douglas' triumph, the reputation of Angus' friend as the successor to Wallace had grown. The army of Robert the Bruce doubled in size. Scots who had held back out of fear of King Edward now came forward to join the fight.

The king smiled more than he had in months.

In discussions with Angus and the knights, the king decided to move the army west to Ayr. Before they reached the coastal town, however, they learned that an angry King Edward had ordered Aymer de Valence to return north to attack King Robert's army and complete the job he had left undone.

Accordingly, they made plans.

In May, King Robert moved his army to a place known to him called Loudoun Hill where a massive plug, the remnant of an ancient volcano, rose from the plains. There, they set a trap.

Angus knew from their spies that de Valence had replenished his forces, which now numbered three thousand to King Robert's thousand. For the trap to work, the English had to take the bait offered—one that would be hard to refuse.

When the English came across some of King Robert's men fleeing on horses toward Loudoun Hill, de Valence's men charged after them.

The only clear path lay to the south of the big rock. On either side was boggy terrain covered by streams and burns. Plunging ahead, de Valence's army fell into grass-covered ditches, for the entire path had been pitted with traps, which the Scots knew how to avoid but the English did not.

De Valence's army, thrown into confusion, struggled to move forward. Horses screamed in protest as they went down throwing their riders to the ground.

From the back of Loudoun Hill, King Robert's men came running on foot with spears, swords and axes, shouting their war cries.

To forestall an English retreat, the king had ordered Angus and the light horse to the rear.

Penned in between King Robert's two forces, de Valence managed to escape though most of his men did not. Twice now, with greater numbers, he had been humiliated by the Scots.

"A fitting revenge for de Valence's treachery at Methven," Angus told the king at the end of the day as they sat eating before an open fire.

"It cannot give me back my friends and family lost to Edward's gibbet, but this proves Edward cannot easily dismiss either me or our determination to gain Scotland's freedom."

With renewed strength, King Robert and his army attacked a force under Sir Ralph Monthermer, Earl of Gloucester, pursuing him to Ayr Castle on the coast. Angus thought it ironic that Robert Bruce would soon face in battle the same man who had saved his life with a warning to flee Edward's court when the Red Comyn had disclosed their pact. But, before the two could meet on the field of battle, fresh English troops arrived and King Robert drew off.

From the beach at Ayr later that day, Angus could see the dark shadow of Arran across the Firth of Clyde, silhouetted against a cloud-studded vermilion sky. Thinking of Kintyre and Islay that lay farther west, while it was still light, Angus wrote a letter to Áine he would send the next day by messenger with other letters his men had written.

From Angus Og to his dearest Áine,

It is cold tonight at water's edge where we are camped, but I am warmed by the thought of you and home. I see your face, so dear to me, your expressive brown eyes that say more than your words, and your silken hair I long to touch. I can almost feel your skin beneath my fingers.

Lest you wonder, I do not forget all that is between us.

The king has lost much but has gained ground. Mayhap you have heard of his successes at Glen Trool and Loudoun Hill and Douglas' destruction of the English garrison at Douglas Castle.

King Robert is clever and fights as much with his wits as with his sword, always using the land to his advantage. The tales of his victories, both small and great, grow as they are told and retold. You would smile at some we hear. He remembers your story of Israel's King David and is encouraged by your prayers.

The people now see him as their leader and are coming in great numbers. We are full of hope for Scotland.

I am well, as are John and Duncan. They fight with the king's army and distinguish themselves. You may tell your handmaiden that my captain remains unwounded.

Give my love to our children and to Juliana and our nephews. I cannot say when I can come to you. It depends on the fortunes of our king.

I will ask the messenger to wait for a reply should you have any.

My love is ever yours.

CHAPTER 23

Ayrshire, Scotland, July 1307

IN THEIR CAMP on Scotland's southwestern coast near the town of Ayr, Angus received word that King Edward, frustrated at the lack of results from his generals—specifically, Aymer de Valence—decided to lead the English army north himself.

Rising from his sickbed, where rumor had him off and on for months, the aging and unwell Edward set out from Carlisle. His progress was sufficiently slow that Angus' spy, Cuthbert, could follow it closely.

Days later, Cuthbert returned to camp with the startling news that England's king had fallen from his horse and lay near death at Burgh-on-Sands.

Angus shared a smile with his friend, King Robert. Around them, there were many smiles on the faces of his army.

"You were hoping Edward would pass from this life, that you might claim the throne without his interference," Angus said to his friend. "The event came later than you might have wanted, but at least it has finally come."

"None too soon," said Robert Bruce. "Edward's son has his father's penchant for cruelty, but he lacks Longshanks' shrewdness in battle or his determination to win at all costs."

On the 7th of July, cursing Scotland with his last breath, or so it was said, King Edward died three miles from Carlisle, never having reached Scotland. When the news arrived at King Robert's camp, all celebrated.

"Where will you go now that much of the southwest is yours?" Angus asked his friend.

"Since de Valence has returned to Ayrshire and James Douglas has gone back to Douglasdale with plans to move on to Selkirk, I think I will take the rest of the men to Galloway to deal the MacDoualls a final blow."

"A worthy target for the devastation they dealt your brothers and their Irish allies. And then?"

"If all goes well in Galloway, I would head toward the Great Glen where the Comyns and MacDougalls hide, along with the Earl of Ross who betrayed my queen and defiled a church's sanctuary."

"If you but give me a few weeks to see some of my Islesmen home and come with fresh galleys and fresh Islesmen, I would join you there."

Rob smiled. "I suppose I can allow my good friend a brief respite. Come to me at the beginning of September. I would go up the Great Glen with you."

"Aye," said Angus. "'Tis a plan. I will anchor my galleys off the north end of Lismore Isle and wait for you at Port Appin. The isle was to be Juliana's dowry when she married my brother, Alexander, but the MacDougalls refused to keep the bargain. It is time I claimed it. If you need me before then, send word to Islay."

They parted as good friends with a strong handshake and an understanding of their future plans.

Angus allowed any of his men who desired to stay to remain with the king. Those who wanted to go home to see to their families, crops and cattle were told they may return with Angus. Since Ayr was not far from where he had hidden his galleys, he was soon sailing west for Dunyvaig, his heart eager for the sight of Áine.

Dunyvaig Castle, Isle of Islay, end of July 1307

ÁINE HAD CARRIED her husband's letter with her since the day a fisherman brought it to Dunyvaig. She had read the words so many times the parchment was now ragged in her hand. Standing with Fand on the summer grass in front of the castle, the wind blowing her hair behind her, she read the message again.

Angus invited a reply and she had sent one, assuring him she and the children were well and that she prayed for him and the king each day. She hoped he had received it. She did not want him to worry for them while he was gone.

It had been months since she'd seen Angus' face or felt his touch or heard his laughter. Her heart ached for want of him.

News filtered to the Isles, so she and Juliana and the men Angus had left behind to guard his realm could follow the war raging in the east. Thus, she knew that King Edward died while leading a great army north to fight Robert Bruce. She took it as a sign of God's protection of both the new king and her husband that the one they called Longshanks died on English soil, never reaching Scotland.

Clutching the letter to her breast, she bowed her head and asked God that King Edward's son would fail in the war he would continue. "Lord, let King Robert and Angus prevail."

Looking up, a flock of geese crossed the sky in front of her. She gazed past them, looking southeast toward Carrick, shielding her eyes from the noonday sun. At first, she thought the puff of white on the horizon might be a cloud but, as she continued to watch, it grew and she realized it was a sail. More than one sail. It was a fleet of galleys! Tears filled her eyes. *Angus. Could it be Angus?*

Juliana came running from the castle. "Áine, do you see? The lead galley flies the Lord of the Isles' banner."

Áine nodded, tears spilling from her eyes. "Yes, I see it. Angus has returned."

Before the galleys entered Lagavulin Bay, a crowd had gathered on the grass-covered headland to await the returning warriors. Angus' constable and some of the guards strode toward the ships. The families of the crews were already making their way to the wide beach where the galleys were being dragged up to higher ground.

In front of Áine stood Brian, now a tall sixteen, and Alexander, a sturdy seven-year-old, with the two wolfhounds, Fand and Cormac. Juliana's boys, in between Áine's sons in age, gamboled not far away. The nurses for Finvola and Mary, age three and two, took them by the hand. Nessa, who suddenly appeared at Áine's side, shielded her eyes and stared intently at the lead galley.

Áine watched Angus, studying his walk, his manner. She detected no limp, no change in his stride. *Thank God.*

Casting her gaze over the women who waited on the beach some distance away, Áine said, "He speaks with the families. Likely, some of the men who went with him have not returned."

Nessa said, "'Tis always a sad day when sons do not come home to their parents and fathers do not return to their children, Mistress, but you cannot keep men from war."

"Not this war in any event," replied Áine, for she knew the war for Scotland's independence was embraced by the Macdonalds and all in the Isles.

They began to walk toward the beach where the galleys disgorged their crews. The boys ran ahead.

"Angus and I must comfort the families who have lost sons and husbands," she said, dreading the task but understanding its importance.

"Look, Mistress!" exclaimed Nessa. "Lord Angus' captain is there on the beach."

Áine smiled at her handmaiden. "From here, Conall looks to be unharmed."

Nessa's face lit with happiness. "Lord Angus, too, Mistress."

"Go to your captain," said Áine. "His eyes are searching for you."

Nessa acknowledged Áine's words with a smile and hurried toward the beach.

Áine watched as Angus paused in his stride up the beach to speak to some of the families. After that, he proceeded on toward the castle. Nearing where Áine waited, the smallest of their children, their two daughters, let go of their nurses' hands and bounded into his arms. Angus dropped his satchel and hugged them. Then, looking up, he caught sight of Áine, drawing closer.

She drank in the sight of him, full of life, full of health. His blue eyes shone brilliant against his sun-browned skin. His hair and short beard were streaked with lighter strands. She could see no visible scars.

He said not a word, but gave their daughters back to the care of their nurses and strode to where Áine stood, taking her in his arms. In front of his people and his sons, he kissed her. "A year is too long to be away from you, my love. Come, let us have some time to ourselves."

Áine took his hand. He picked up his satchel and led her toward the castle. Questions flitted through her mind but, seeing how tired he was, she did not speak them.

On the way to the castle, Brian and Alexander came to walk alongside them with their cousins. Their looks of admiration told her the Lord of the Isles was a great man in their eyes.

"Will you tell us the stories of your battles?" asked Brian as Alexander looked on expectantly.

"Aye," said Angus, stooping to hug Alexander and then, rising, tousling Brian's red hair and smiling at his nephews. "I will tell you all the stories but, first, I need time with Lady Áine."

The children made way for them and he and Áine walked on. "What were you saying to the people?" Áine asked him.

"I gave my men the choice to stay with the king or return with me. The unmarried ones decided to stay. I assured their families they are well. Sadly, a few men were killed in battle. I spoke to those who had families. Never a pleasant task."

"Only a few?"

"Aye. We have done well, considering we were always outnumbered by many hundreds if not thousands."

He met her worried gaze. "The king's army grows with his reputation for courage in battle. Soon, Rob's men will number in the thousands, too."

They arrived at their chamber to find a thoughtful servant left them a tray of food and a flagon of wine. "Are you hungry?" she asked.

"Aye. But not for food."

A hot bath awaited him and he began to shed his surcoat. She helped him with his mail and tunic. "I will be quick about this," he said with a grin.

He sank into the steaming water and she reached for a cloth and soap to scrub his back and shoulders.

He lifted her hand from the edge of the tub and kissed her palm. "I have sorely missed you, Wife."

"And I you. I must ask, are King Robert's closest knights still with him?"

"Aye."

"The young James Douglas as well?"

"Aye, Jamie, too. He is a fierce fighter. The English fear him." He told her what had happened at Douglas Castle when James Douglas took the garrison and burned his own keep.

Áine thought of their home at Dunaverty and the other castles her husband controlled. "It must have been a hard task to burn his family's castle."

"Many castles will be sacrificed to keep them out of English hands," said Angus. "Douglas was determined to do it. In time, under King Robert, they can be rebuilt."

Minutes later, he rose from the water and she handed him a drying cloth. As he dried his body, she noticed his muscles, filled out with his days of fighting. There were a few new scars, thin lines across his shoulders. Otherwise, his body was the same as she remembered. "I am glad to see you have returned to me whole."

"A few scratches early on but they have healed." He turned her around and reached for her laces. In joyful anticipation of what was to come, her body was already responding.

He kissed the back of her neck, sending chills through her. Lifting her gown over her head, he turned her to face him, his gaze roving over her form covered only by her linen chemise. He led her not to the bed but to the furs in front of the fireplace where a small fire burned. "I am used to sleeping on the ground but not upon furs beside the fire. To be with you here like this has been a dream I conjured at will most nights."

The thick fur cradled her as she welcomed him into her arms, running her fingers through his damp hair. "I love you, Angus Macdonald."

"And I you, my Irish lass." His lips on her breasts had her melting into the furs.

Eventually, they found their way to the bed where they took their fill of each other and lay entangled for a long while. She rested her head on his shoulder.

"I suppose my constable and steward would have words with me," he said, "yet I find it hard to rise from this bed and the loveliest woman in the Isles. The king's men still speak of your beauty. 'Tis most annoying."

She laughed. "Jealousy becomes you." Áine knew she was being selfish to keep him so long from his men anxious to meet with him concerning the business of the Isles as well as the war. Eventually, she would have to let him go. "Some of the chiefs have paid me a visit in your absence. They would speak to you about the war and other matters. Will you call a meeting of the Council before you rejoin the king?"

"It might be prudent," he said, kissing her forehead. "I would ask them to join me when I sail in a month."

"So soon you would go?"

"The king has need of my warriors and galloglass for he would pursue our enemies, the Comyns and MacDougalls." Then, pulling her into his arms, he whispered into her hair, "At least we have this time."

"Before you sail, we might have a wedding to attend."

"Really? Whose?"

"Did you not notice how your captain embraced Nessa on the beach? I assume you spoke to him and he is willing, if not eager, to take her as his bride."

"Oh, aye. Conall is willing. It would be a happy event ere we sail."

They rose and donned fresh clothing. Angus asked if she wanted to attend his meeting with his men. Because she desired to know of the plans that would see her husband again in battle, she nodded and followed him down to the great hall. There, a group awaited him:

John, Duncan, his constable, the Dunyvaig steward, Angus' guards and the leaders of his men still on Islay.

ANGUS RECEIVED THE reports from the men left in charge, which assured him that, except for Dunaverty, the rest of their castles and the Isles had escaped raids by their enemies during his absence. "Lachlan MacRuairi holds the Comyns in check on the north coast," said his constable.

In turn, Angus apprised them of the war in the southwest, of King Robert's loss of two more brothers and how the king's army grew with his successes. "With these battles behind us and King Edward's death, I was able to return to the Isles. But I can stay only a month. Scotland's fate remains at issue. When he resolves matters in England, the new King Edward will turn his attention to Scotland. Meantime, King Robert must see to his Scottish enemies." Then, passing his gaze over each of the men assembled, he said, "When I return to the king, I will take more men and ships. Some of you can go with me.

"Then there is another matter. Before his death, King Edward ordered Sir Hugh Bissett to gather a fleet in Ireland and sail to the Isles to hunt King Robert and his abettors, which, of course, includes us. Thankfully, Sir Hugh failed in that effort, in part, I believe for his lack of enthusiasm for the task. Still, we should patrol the waters of the Irish Sea from the Isle of Man north and the waters between Ulster and Scotland.

"The merchants who sail past Galloway and the Ayrshire coast on their way to supply English soldiers are lightly-crewed and easily taken. In this manner, we can deprive the English of their provisions while enriching King Robert's army."

"With your permission, my lord," said one of his captains, "I would take four galleys and see to that task."

"Very well," said Angus, pleased.

"How might we help you support King Robert?" asked his constable.

"Before Robert Bruce can face the young King Edward," said Angus, "he must deal with the Comyns and the MacDougalls, who now serve the English."

"Our enemies," said the constable, nodding.

"Aye. They have changed sides with the rise of Robert Bruce, as have we. For such a fight, we will need more warriors. Unlike the English, who do not fight like Highlanders, and thus can be deceived, the Comyns and MacDougalls know well both our Scottish lands and our methods of striking fast with stealth and then retreating into the mist. What they do not have is the power of a hundred galleys and our many galloglass. They have some, I grant you, but not as many."

"What would you have us do?" asked his constable.

"Pay a visit to our shipwright on Islay to ask what he needs to increase the number of galleys he can build."

"I will gladly see to that," said his constable. "I can do it and still command the galloglass here."

"If you call upon the chiefs as you sail north," said Áine to Angus, "you could speak to them about their fleets and men to fight for King Robert without the need for a Council meeting."

"Aye, a good idea. The MacNeils of Barra and the Macleods of Skye come to mind as builders of galleys. The MacRuairis of Garmoran build them as well." Then, with a smile for his wife, he added, "After all, my lady, your Irishmen did not come with their own ships nor did I expect them to, but we must have ships for them when we summon them to war."

"We will need more armor and weapons," said one of his galloglass captains.

"Aye," agreed Angus. "We had best check the status of our armories, and you would be the man to do it. We confiscated some weapons from the English as booty but those were needed by King Robert's growing army."

The galloglass captain inclined his head. "I will see it done, my lord."

Áine said, "The women can help with supplies. Not just food but bandages and clothing. You will need fur-lined cloaks and those that are oiled for the rain. Leather ankle boots wear out on rough terrain. I could secure the supplies you will need. I am sure Juliana would help. If you agree, I would go with you on your voyage to the chiefs. As you call upon them, I can call upon their wives."

"Another good idea." Angus was proud of Áine. In her, he had more than a beautiful wife who had given him his heir. She was a partner who did not begrudge his going to war.

Angus remained on Islay long enough to reacquaint himself with his children, to see his captains and crews rested and the dead remembered with special Masses.

He tested Brian's fighting skills that assured Angus his adopted son was ready to have those skills tested in battle. Then, with Áine and Brian and his brother, John, he sailed north, taking two galleys with fresh crews and armed warriors.

Duncan agreed to remain on Islay to coordinate with the chiefs, to attend to the rest of the fleet and send out scouts for reports. Juliana continued in her role to work with the Dunyvaig steward and servants in overseeing the household.

THE DAY WAS FAIR when they set out from Dunyvaig. Áine's spirits rose as the galley skimmed over the sun-kissed water, a deep blue today. Overhead, hung a cloud-studded sky.

The men pulled hard at the oars as they passed the Isle of Jura and raised the sail. Behind them, in the two following galleys, she glimpsed the sun reflecting off the crews' silvered weapons.

Gulls followed them for some while, screeching overhead. When the gulls left them, dolphins swam alongside the galley to the delight of the crew.

Angus had told her they would sail first to Colonsay, then to Mull, Morvern, Moidart, Skye and Barra. From there, they would return to Islay. Having sailed these waters before with Angus, she looked forward to the familiar shores.

This place of blue sea and lochs and great glens, though not the place she had imagined she would spend her life, had become her home; and the man who stood tall in the prow, his face set toward the north, was the much-loved father of her children. Except for the lines around his eyes where he laughed and squinted in the sun, he had changed little since she had first met him. At thirty-four he was as handsome as that day he first came to Dunseverick, mayhap more so, for now she saw him through the eyes of love.

"You worry for my brother," said John, coming up to her where she sat midship.

"It is so obvious?"

"Aye, to me. I have come to read your face and discern your thoughts, particularly when you watch my brother. You need not worry. Angus takes risks but not before considering them carefully. Like Robert Bruce, my brother is a man of strategy. The two rarely disagree. In the battles to come, Angus' knowledge of our enemies and our galloglass under his command will be crucial to the king's success."

Áine looked at the man beside her, so like Angus in appearance a stranger might confuse one for the other. But their manner was different. John was quieter, less apt to assume command. "Does he watch out for you or you him?" she asked with a smile.

"Aye."

She chuckled. "I suppose it is best you allow him to think he is your protector."

"Since Alex's death at the hands of the MacDougalls, Angus keeps me close, always arranging my position in battle near his. I feel the same about him. We are the only sons of Angus Mor left. It is much like Robert Bruce's treatment of his one remaining brother, Sir Edward."

Áine thought again of King David of Israel and the story she had told Robert Bruce. David had lost his friend, Jonathan, who was closer than a brother. How lonely David must have been. "I understand," she said. "I am glad Angus has you with him."

"Have you ever seen Angus fight?" John asked her.

An image of him on the practice field came to her. "Only in practice bouts with his men."

"In those, he holds back his full strength, but in battle, he is near invincible. His sparth axe is a blur as it carves into flesh. His sword and his dagger, when he resorts to them, are deadly. He has fought with the galloglass since he was fourteen. And, for a man his size, he is fast. There is a reason King Robert places Angus on his right, for once he is there, the king never fears an enemy coming at his most vulnerable side."

The Isle of Colonsay loomed ahead. Áine rose to watch the Bay of Kiloran come into view. She remembered sitting on that same crescent beach listening to Angus tell her of his natural son in Glen Coe. She wondered about the lad who was of an age with her own son, both old enough to join their father in battle. Brian, standing near Angus in the prow, would want to go. Would this son in Glen Coe do the same?

Gilchrist Macduffie, came to meet them as they beached the ships in the wide crescent bay. When it began raining, he invited them into the castle where they shared tankards of ale and a light repast. Gilchrist had become chief of the Macduffies since his father, Malcolm, died the year before.

Gilchrist's first question to Angus concerned the war. "How goes it with the new king? Does he prevail?"

"Aye," said Angus, "though the war is far from over. I have come to ask for your support, for the next battles will concern our enemies, the MacDougalls and Comyns. My plan is to sail up Loch Linnhe and meet King Robert to advance up the Great Glen."

"We will gladly supply men and galleys for that venture," said Gilchrist. "I shall go myself. In Robert Bruce, we finally have a worthy King of Scots."

"I take pleasure in thinking of you leading the Macduffie galleys," said Angus. "Since you keep our records, you would be an asset to me to account for our supplies and our needs for such an undertaking."

"You must tell me how Bruce's being crowned king began, as your earlier messages were general in nature."

"Aye, I will," replied Angus.

Sometime later, Áine observed Angus and Gilchrist speaking away from the hearing of others. She assumed Angus was explaining what happened at Greyfriars Church and the Red Comyn's betrayal. Since King Robert had subsequently been excommunicated, the Macduffies should know the truth.

As they made ready to sail, Angus said to the Colonsay chief, "If you remain of a mind to join me, come to Dunyvaig at the end of

August. We will sail from there."

"I will be there," said Gilchrist.

Next, they beached the galleys at Duart Castle on Mull. Áine remembered Malcolm Maclean, whom she met on Iona. He had succeeded his father, Malise, who died the year after she and Angus were wed.

Malcolm welcomed them into his castle where they stayed the night. He had taken a wife, a pleasant woman from a neighboring clan. Áine was pleased to tell her of the effort to gather provisions for the men.

Because the Comyns and MacDougalls had plundered their lands, the Macleans were anxious to join the fight. "Aye, my men and I will meet you at Dunyvaig," said Malcolm when Angus asked about joining him. "All here want to see justice done."

On the other isles, they also met with success. Christina MacRuairi at Castle Tioram, who had already provided ships and warriors to accompany King Robert to Arran, agreed to send more.

Over a dinner of roast beef and salmon, Christina informed Angus, "I will lead the MacRuairi men myself." Turning to Áine, she said, "Give me your list of needed supplies, my lady, and when my men and I sail to Islay, we will bring with us the items you request."

Surprised that Christina of Garmoran would fight with the men, Áine inquired of John how this came to be. "With her fierce half-brothers, she has had to fight to maintain her stature as the MacRuairi heir. These battles ahead will not be her first."

They left Moidart and sailed north to Skye. It rained off and on, making Áine grateful for her oiled cloak. Because it was high summer, the air was warm and they were soon dry. The rainbows that followed them were sufficient compensation for the discomfort.

At Dunvegan, Tormod Macleod gave them a hearty welcome. "Lord Angus, I see you have brought your lovely lady."

Since she had last seen him at Iona, Tormod's son, Malcolm, tall and fair like his father, married a Campbell woman and fathered a son. He appeared well content with his new family.

Malcolm's wife asked Áine, "Is it true that Sir Neil, the Campbell chief, is one of King Robert's knights?"

"He is and has been with him from before Rathlin."

Áine listened as Angus explained King Edward's cruelty. "Such noble men were unworthy of the deaths they received at the hands of the English, but then Edward, the first of that name, was that kind of king. He treated the Welsh nobles no differently."

They discussed the need for more galleys, and Angus asked, "Can your shipbuilders supply more?"

"Aye," said Tormod, "with enough wood. We've a croft at Colbost across Loch Dunvegan where the building takes place."

"I can supply oak and sawn boards from Ireland," said Angus.

After that, they struck a bargain for ten more galleys. Then, Angus placed before the chief the opportunity to send men with him when he returned to King Robert. "The next battles will be crucial. Will you sail with us?"

"Aye," said Tormod with a glance at his son. "The Macleods will accompany you. My son, Malcolm, will lead them."

Malcolm, his blond hair framing his blue eyes, nodded. "We could hardly refrain. The Comyns and MacDougalls plundered and burned Skye. I will speak to my brother, Torquil, on Lewis. I am certain he will go as well."

Áine observed her husband's pleasure at all he accomplished. As they rose from the table, Angus reminded them that Robert Bruce had also been attacked by the MacDougalls of Lorne and Argyll. "They killed many of his men who escaped the slaughter at Methven. 'Twill be good to have the lordship united as we help our new king defeat our common enemies."

That night, they dined on roast goose glazed with honey, accompanied by stewed beans from the castle gardens fried with garlic and onions. Since barnacle geese would begin arriving on Islay in September, Áine made a note to ask Malcolm's wife for the ingredients for the splendid glaze.

As they lingered over dinner, Tormod and Angus discussed the war.

"'Twas good timing for the English king to die when he did," said Tormod.

"Aye," said Angus. "But his son will continue the fight with his

English nobles and knights, aided by our Scots enemies. That is why King Robert must defeat the Comyns and MacDougalls, else they will be attacking from the rear as the English attack from the front."

"You'll not get an argument from the Macleods," said Malcolm. "Nor any other clan of the lordship, I wager. It is time we rid the Isles of the varmints."

"Will you call for signal fires?" asked Tormod.

"Not yet," said Angus, "but you are right to ask. I envision a time when we will need them to call the lordship and summon all our galleys. For now, I am not asking for every man or every galley, only enough to see the task before us done. Others must stay to protect the women and children, to bring in the harvest, to sow the seed in spring and tend the cattle."

"Very well," said Tormod as the others leaned in to listen. "I agree with your plan. We shall do as you ask and meet you in Lagavulin Bay at the end of August."

Áine's husband reached across the table to shake Tormod's hand. "Thank you, my friend."

At each of the places they stopped on their voyage, Áine spoke to the women, telling them what Angus and the men would need. "We do not know how long they will be gone," she said, "so they must have supplies enough to replace what they have now."

The women understood and were happy to provide for their menfolk.

On Barra, Áine had learned more about the building of the galleys. Neill MacNeil, the clan chief, and his son, Neill Og, entertained them in Kisimul Castle. In an unusual arrangement, the castle had its great hall on the top floor of the keep. Áine liked the view where she could see many shorebirds, but the climb up the stairs on the outside of the castle would be treacherous in icy winters.

"Our shipbuilding is active now since we have good weather," said the dark-haired MacNeil chief. He was not as tall as the Macleods or Angus but he had a warrior's build.

At Angus' request, Neill took them to where three galleys lay alongside each other near the beach, half-finished. The pounding of hammers sounded in the clear air as men, stripped to the waist, were working under the noonday sun. "When these are completed," said Neill, "we can begin three more."

"Good," replied Angus. "The battles I spoke of will take place in autumn. Doubtless, they will be followed by more. Any galleys and men you can add to our numbers will be appreciated."

The sky overhead was a blue canopy over a calm sea that morning as they left Colonsay where they stopped for the night.

On the voyage south, as they neared Islay, John came to speak to Áine. "What did you learn in the conversations you heard?" he asked.

She thought for a moment before answering. "They are united in their desire to go with Angus when he returns to King Robert."

"Aye. You heard the chiefs, young and old, speak their reasons for going, but what was left unspoken is just as important."

"What would that be?" asked Áine.

"The chiefs see Angus' commitment to the king and his confidence in Robert Bruce even though he fights the might of England. To a man, the chiefs trust Angus and will follow him into battle."

She remembered the look in their eyes as the chiefs spoke with her husband about the war. It was one of admiration and respect. Their laughter, as they joked with him over the evening meals, told her the chiefs liked him. "Yes, I see what you mean."

"It is important now for them to trust him but it will be even more critical in the future when England brings its might against the Scots king and the entire lordship is at risk."

Áine nodded, suddenly realizing how much Angus risked for the sake of the new king. If Robert Bruce lost, so would Angus and the lordship. "I have never considered they might lose," she said. "I believe God is with them."

"'Tis odd you should say that," said John with a pensive look. "One of King Robert's priests said the same and remarked that the Scots people believe it as well. That, and the king's courage, is why they are coming to him in great numbers."

Near the end of August, they returned to Lagavulin Bay and beached the galleys alongside those that had remained behind.

There was only a brief time left for Áine to spend with Angus and she meant to make the most of it. Too, she had a wedding to plan with Nessa.

SEVERAL DAYS BEFORE Angus planned to leave to join the king, Conall, his captain, and Nessa, Áine's handmaiden, were wed. The weather being unusually fair and warm, once Mass was said in the chapel, the wedding guests dined on a feast held outside on the grass.

All of Angus' captains and a good part of his men and their wives who lived on the isle came to share the happy day with one of their own. The chiefs from the distant isles began to arrive and happily joined in the celebration.

Angus knew he must make a decision concerning Brian. At sixteen, he was older than Angus when he first joined his father, Angus Mor, in battle. The lad possessed the requisite skills, but he was young and his sword yet to be blooded.

Angus stood with his wife, watching the dancing. Conall and Nessa were in the center, laughing as they twirled around to the sound of the pipe and drum. "They look so happy," observed Áine. "I have never seen Nessa so pretty."

"Aye. And Conall is fair smitten. After today, they will have a few days to drink their mead together before we sail."

"They would hope for more time, of course," said Áine, "but 'tis enough so that they will not be strangers."

Angus laughed. "Nay, not strangers. I have asked the steward to give them a chamber in the castle."

"That was thoughtful, Angus. I will have the servants prepare it for them."

Standing apart from the others where he and Áine could not be overheard, he raised the issue of Brian. "He wants to go with me when I sail. What do you think? Should I take him?"

Áine turned her lovely eyes on him. "The mother in me says 'No', but the wife of the Lord of the Isles says 'Yes'. He would be very disappointed to be left behind again. Can you protect him?"

"I can keep him between John and me in battle as Alex once kept John between him and me. At least that is how it begins. How it ends is not a sure thing. We must take the risk if we are to see him become the man he wants to be."

"Very well," she said, letting out a sigh. "Take him with you. If he is ever to seek the kingship of Tirowen, he must be a warrior as well as a leader of men."

Angus put his arm around her and drew her close. She laid her head on his shoulder. "It will be all right, my love." He only hoped it would be so.

"Since I was a young girl, I have known the world is not a place of peace, at least never for very long. Battles among the O'Neills and their kin were frequent as I grew up. And then there were the battles you fought for the Earl in Ulster. 'Tis no different now."

"Except that now we fight for Scotland's freedom and our rightful king. The seer of Rhinns promised peace after that."

"I pray it comes soon."

CHAPTER 24

Loch Linnhe, Argyll, September 1307

FROM THE DECK of his galley on Loch Linnhe, where he awaited King Robert, Angus gazed at his fleet of twenty galleys spread over the loch's deep blue waters. The men were still in their mail, their hair tied back or braided clear of their smiling faces, brown from the sun. Victory over the MacDougalls on Lismore, the isle that should have been Macdonald territory since Alex's wedding to Juliana, was theirs.

Now, all was quiet. In the distance, white clouds rested on the tops of the brown Grampian Mountains that lay between loch and sky. On either side of the loch, tree-lined slopes descended to the shore.

They had not been waiting long when a small boat put out from the eastern shore, causing ripples in the calm water as two men pulled at the oars and a third sat in the stern. Angus recognized the king and strode to the gunwale to welcome him aboard.

Someone had made him a surcoat of yellow on which Scotland's crimson lion rampant was proudly displayed. A banner with the same royal lion rampant had been given to his friend by Bishop Wishart when he absolved him of Comyn's death. It was fitting the king should wear the royal symbol on his chest.

Angus offered his hand to help the king aboard. Duncan, John and Brian joined in welcoming him. After they exchanged greetings, Angus asked, "How goes the fight?"

"Well enough," said the king. He removed his helmet, circled by a golden crown, shaking free his auburn hair. "We sent the MacDoualls fleeing from Galloway across the border into Cumbria. Unfortunately, Dungal MacDouall escaped and still lives. But we did manage to take back Turnberry Castle, a most satisfying day.

"I have left Jamie Douglas in command of the southwest where he thrives." With a smile, he added, "The English continue to fear him and call him 'the Black Douglas'. When he moved on to Jedburgh, I moved north."

"Who is with you now?" Angus asked.

"All whom you know. My brother, Edward, Sir Neil Campbell, Sir Gilbert Haye, Sir Robert Boyd and Malcolm, Earl of Lennox. The brother and son of Simon Fraser, who died the death of Wallace at King Edward's hands, have joined us as well, along with their military retainers. Oh, and I now have a thousand men."

"Ha!" Angus smiled. "You have been busy, my friend, meeting with much success. I have had a minor success in taking Lismore. Except for Andrew, Bishop of Argyll, who we left in his castle, we sent the MacDougalls running for the mainland and installed our own garrison to hold the former MacDougall castle at Achanduin. Beyond that, as you see," Angus gestured to the fleet before him, "I bring many galleys, several commanded by chiefs of the lordship. All are loyal to you.

"Christina of Garmoran, whom you met, is in the MacRuairi galley just there," Angus said, pointing to the galley flying her pennon. From the deck, a woman with her dark hair confined at her nape waved. "We have many more galleys than you see here, Rob, and I am keeping the shipwrights well occupied in constructing others. I thought these one thousand trained warriors and galloglass might do the job you have in mind."

The king's smile widened. "You have done well, Angus."

"I would do more. What is your plan for our enemies, Rob?"

"To squeeze the MacDougalls between your galleys attacking from the water, and my army attacking from the land. I do not want them at my back when I go after the Comyns and the Earl of Ross."

"Where are they?" Angus asked.

"My scouts tell me they are halfway up the loch on the east side in the woods. A day's march for my men. I propose to chase them west to you so that, in two days' time, you could intercept them on the loch's shore."

"Aye. We will be there."

A day later, Angus' galleys were arrayed along the bank of the loch at the location the king had indicated. In the afternoon, Angus ordered his galloglass onto the shore, a fierce wall of resistance to any MacDougall who would be running toward the loch and galleys that were no longer waiting for them as Angus had ordered them moved.

Crouched in front of the galloglass were his archers, their bows ready.

As King Robert had anticipated, soon, a large body of armed men came rushing toward them from the woods. Abruptly, they halted. In front of them, the Lord of the Isles, his galleys, galloglass and archers. Behind the fleeing MacDougalls, Robert Bruce and his army of Highlanders in pursuit.

Their defeat being imminent, the MacDougalls dropped their weapons.

John MacDougall of Lorne, Alexander's son, acted as spokesman. "I would seek a truce."

The king strode to stand next to Angus, meeting his steady gaze and slight nod.

"Very well," said King Robert, "a truce will be granted you until June of next year on the condition you do not attack us during that time or assist the Comyns or the Earl of Ross. I will also require tribute."

The MacDougall agreed and tribute in the form of weapons and foodstuffs was paid so that without a sword being raised, King Robert had neutralized the MacDougalls, at least for the moment. Angus looked forward to the end of the truce when he could deal them the blow they deserved.

That evening, camped farther north on the shore of Loch Linnhe, Angus said to the king, "We will have to face that evil lot again. I expect John of Lorne has already dispatched a rider to the young King Edward asking for reinforcements."

"Doubtless you are correct. If English aid arrives, the MacDougalls will end the truce. But we will be stronger when we next face them, and I will have dealt with the Earl of Ross and the Comyns, so there will be no Scots to come to their aid." And then, with a smile, he added, "I am told we have friends in the lands north of here who will add to our numbers."

In October, declining Angus' offer to sail with him, the king marched his army north to Inverlochy at the southern end of the Great Glen where Angus would meet him.

The great stone fortress, built by the Red Comyns of Badenoch and Lochaber, was set on the River Lochy. It was the first of three targets Angus and King Robert had agreed upon.

Surrounded by a moat on three sides, the castle also had the natural defensive advantage of backing up to the river. To those natural defenses had been added a curtain wall of black rock nearly nine feet thick and twenty-five feet tall. Round towers rose on each corner, the largest serving as the keep. The walls were topped with a parapet from which flew the Comyns' banner of three golden stalks of sallow on a field of red.

"I will make no truce here," said King Robert to his knights and captains. "This is the seat of the one who betrayed me to the old King Edward. I have paid the price for that once and will not do so again."

"'Tis formidable," whispered John to Angus from where they observed in the woods some distance away.

"Aye," agreed Angus, "but the king will take it with our greater numbers. We have nearly two thousand while the Comyns cannot have but a few hundred behind their walls. And they do not know of our coming. Keep Brian between us as we fight. I will be on the king's right."

Standing with them, Duncan said, "I will guard your backs."

Angus dispatched a small contingent of galloglass that managed to kill the guards at the southern entrance to the castle, taking the Comyns by surprise. With access granted, King Robert's army of men had only to race inside and meet the enemy, most of which were unprepared for battle.

After a morning's hard fighting, they had captured Inverlochy Castle. Many Comyns had been killed, causing Sir Neil Campbell to remark, "We have all but obliterated the clan."

"Do not forget," said Angus, gazing at the bodies scattered on the grass in the castle's grass-covered bailey, "we have the Comyns of Buchan yet to deal with. They still live and also serve King Edward, the second of that name."

"We will deal with them after the Earl of Ross," said King Robert. To his captains, he ordered, "Gather the weapons and the gold, if there be any. Then remove all the food stores we can carry or load into the Lord of the Isles' ships. When that is done, burn everything that responds to a flame. We will leave no enemy castles to be reclaimed by King Edward when he finally turns his attention to Scotland."

Angus watched the flames leap from the roofs. It was the right strategy. They would have no time to besiege castles retaken by the English and fortified with large garrisons.

Everything in the castle, not only the wooden roofs, but also the beams, doors and furniture, was set afire. Only the huge stones in the walls and towers that would not burn were left standing, open to the elements.

Brian had done well fighting between Angus and John, defeating the enemy Comyns he encountered. "You have weathered your first battle," Angus said to his adopted son, noting with approval his blooded sword. Patting him on the back, Angus said, "And you managed to come through it with only a few scratches."

John laughed and turned to Brian. "That's my brother's way of saying, if we were in a tavern, you'd be buying the ale."

Brian smiled, his freckles vivid on his sunburned face. "I would gladly buy you ale, but since the Comyns have furnished us with a generous supply, I can at least pour."

As the air began to fill with smoke, Angus took Duncan aside and thanked him. "Knowing you guarded Brian and my brother gave me freedom to look to the king."

"My privilege," said the golden-haired Duncan, who had stood beside Angus for years, more a brother than a cousin.

That evening, the rain held off and they shared a meal around an open fire, courtesy of the Comyn larders. With the light of the fire illuminating his bold features and dark auburn hair, the king addressed his inner circle. "Now to the Earl of Ross who holds Urquhart Castle for King Edward."

"His mother was a Comyn," said the Earl of Lennox.

"Aye," said Angus, "which explains his loyalties. She was the daughter of the Earl of Buchan, the Comyn we have yet to face."

"Ross' fortress lies at the north end of Loch Ness," said Lennox. "With so great an army, it will take at least a sennight's march to cover the fifty miles."

The king nodded. "Long marches cannot be avoided."

Angus said, "I will leave my ships here and join you on the march. We can bring the wounded aboard for one of my physicians to attend."

The next morning as the gray clouds drizzled rain, Angus' men took the wounded aboard his galleys. When King Robert began his march north, Angus and most of his men joined him. The rest he left to guard the ships and the wounded.

As autumn deepened, the weather changed. It grew colder, especially at night, and the days often brought rain. The leaves turned to brilliant shades of red, gold and yellow, blazing across the glens and reflected in the streams. At night, the men built fires to keep warm and when the rain required, erected tents for shelter.

Over the evening meals, he and his captains, along with Christina MacRuairi, and his other companions, gathered to consider what lay ahead.

"The king may rightly deal the Earl of Ross the same end as the Comyns at Inverlochy," said Duncan when the question was asked.

"For a breach of sanctuary to seize Queen Elizabeth, he deserves no less," said one of Angus' captains, a galloglass who was very protective of his own wife.

Christina said, "My half-brother, Lachlan, attacks the Earl of Ross in the west where his lands meet the sea. When King Robert attacks from the south and east, the earl will be left with nowhere to run."

"The earl will know that," said Angus. "Facing the king's thousands, he might surrender before Urquhart is taken."

The speculation went on into the night until the men, tired of talking, found their beds.

More than a sennight later, the king's army arrived just south of Urquhart Castle. By then, their numbers had doubled as Highlanders, loyal to the king, joined the cause.

Angus stood with the king, his knights and his brother surveying their army. "Your march has gained you more men," said Angus, smiling at his friend.

"So it has." Not all were armed warriors but all were willing to fight. "Think, Angus, thousands of Scots now recognize me as their true king and we have only begun!"

Rob appeared well pleased with his larger army and new followers but Angus saw past the king's smile to the lines of fatigue in his friend's face and his gray color. When the king turned aside to speak to some of his men, Angus said to the king's brother, "He looks tired. Has he had any sleep?" Then taking a good look at Sir Edward, he asked, "Have any of you?" Angus, too, was weary after so many days marching through the woods and over rough terrain.

"Not as you'd notice," said Sir Edward. "As you have experienced, Robert plunges forward, driving his men hard and himself harder, inspiring all who come to him. It is like trying to hold back a stallion eager to race. It was all I could do to persuade him to give the men a few hours of sleep at night."

Angus shook his head. "He cannot keep up such a pace."

"You tell him that. I have tried."

Angus joined the king and a few of his knights to walk farther on until they could see the castle looming over Loch Ness. The place had been used as a fortified site for hundreds of years, protecting the lowlands of Moray against assault from the west. From Urquhart, too, timber, cattle hides and other materials were transported to the markets of Inverness at the top of the glen and beyond.

Set on a promontory, jutting into the loch, the castle was protected on the landward side by a deep ditch as well as tall, stone battlements. A bridge led over the ditch to a gate and round tower guarding it. The castle grounds were so large as to resemble a walled village strung out along the loch's shore.

"If you agree," Angus said to King Robert, "I would have my men take their stand between the loch and the castle just out of arrow range. That leaves your army on the earl's more vulnerable, land side. The Earl of Ross will see he is surrounded by thousands."

"I agree," said the king. "He might as well know what he is up against."

Once Angus' men were in place, he came to the king to see what his wishes were. King Robert told him he was just about to order the siege to commence. As they spoke, a shout came from the gatehouse next to the drawbridge. "His lordship, the Earl of Ross, would speak to Robert Bruce!"

The king stepped forward with Sir Edward on his left and Angus on his right. Behind them were Sir Gilbert Haye, Sir Neil Campbell, Sir Robert Boyd and Malcolm, Earl of Lennox.

"Sir Robert!" shouted the dark-haired Earl of Ross. His long thin face was pale, speaking of weariness.

"That is King Robert to you!" shouted back Sir Edward.

"Pardon me," said the earl, "King Robert, I would save my garrison and the people here a siege. Will you grant me a truce?"

"For the man who handed over the queen and the king's daughter and sisters to King Edward's cruelty?" shouted Sir Edward.

The Earl of Ross was silent for a moment. Then he said, "I beg your forgiveness, lord king, for such a sin."

Angus leaned toward the king. "Rob, with your thousands and my men, you can take the castle if that be your wish."

His friend nodded. "It is in my heart to do so for the wrong he did to Elizabeth and Marjorie and my sisters, as well as Isabella MacDuff. The women suffer to this day because of him."

"Yet you hesitate," said Angus.

The king's brother looked on with a confused expression. "Why?"

King Robert heaved a sigh. "Something your lady said to me, Angus, comes to mind. Mayhap 'tis from God. She told me one of the things King David learned in the years he was hunted by King Saul was mercy. Yes, we could take this castle and kill all. Justice, if not vengeance, calls for such action. Yet, if I grant the earl a truce, I may gain more."

Angus nodded. "Aye. At the end of the truce, you could possibly gain his allegiance and his territories of Caithness, Sutherland and Ross to add to your growing kingdom."

"Just so," said the king. Walking a few steps ahead, he shouted to where the Earl of Ross stood on the battlement, "You shall be granted clemency if you surrender peacefully. A truce shall remain in effect between us until the first day of summer of next year. Meantime, you will raise no weapon against me or my allies."

"You have my word," shouted the Earl of Ross.

"You trust him?" asked Sir Edward with raised brows.

"Yes," said the king. "Like me, he once served the old King Edward, but he has fought for the Scots and is, himself, a Scot. I would have him in my kingdom if I could. William will keep to his oath, though he will likely send word to King Edward, asking for aid to end the truce. Meantime, our support grows."

When the business at Urquhart was done, they departed for Inverness. The castle lay a day's march north at the most northerly point of the Great Glen on the River Ness, and was the third castle the king had set out to capture, raze or otherwise render harmless.

Rob had told him this castle, held by the English, would be granted no truce.

As the combined army assembled, a surprise visitor joined them. David Murray, Bishop of Moray, arrived with a large party of men to welcome King Robert. "I have been waiting for you, my king," said the bishop. "You asked me to raise support and I have."

"Bless you," said the king, looking beyond the bishop to the large body of men behind him.

"I should be blessing you, my lord. And I shall. In any event, we are ready to take the castle with you."

King Robert smiled. "I believed the men of Moray to be of independent minds. You have proven me correct."

The king still looked weary to Angus, yet he could see his friend was pleased to have a bishop with him since Bishops Wishart and Lamberton were still held prisoners by the English.

"If you remain of a mind to bless us, Lord Bishop," said the king, "I would ask you to lead us in prayer for the battle."

With heads bowed, Bishop Murray led them in prayer and blessed the king and his army.

In a matter of days, Inverness Castle fell to King Robert and his army of thousands of which Angus and his Islesmen were a part. Once the castle was taken, the battlements were razed to the ground. As with Inverlochy, King Robert ordered all that remained, save the booty they removed, be burned.

They had successfully dealt with the three strongholds of the English. Fresh from victory, they headed eastward to destroy Nairn Castle, a tower on a peninsula of extraordinary height. That done, the king turned his attention to the major enemy: John Comyn, Earl of Buchan, cousin to the dead "Red Comyn".

Angus and his men remained with the king, again proceeding over land. As they headed east toward Buchan, north of Aberdeen, the oncoming winter hit them full force, pelting them with rain and snow. Angus was grateful for Áine's foresight that kept him and his men in warm cloaks and dry ankle boots, for they had a fire's warmth only at night.

Reaching Inverurie, King Robert suddenly fell ill. He could neither drink nor eat and the medicine Angus' physician offered seemed to have no effect.

What Angus had feared has transpired. The king had exhausted himself, and the worsening weather did not help. Robert Bruce was strong—only thirty-three, a year younger than Angus—but he had demanded more of himself in a short amount of time than one could expect of mortal men. Aside from all the marching in bad weather, he had the burden of command and the worry for his kingdom.

When the king showed no improvement, his brother, Sir Edward, took charge. They carried the king on a litter, laid with furs to keep him warm, and took him to Slioch, a few miles north of Inverurie.

There, his army found shelter in a dense wood.

They were in Buchan's territory, well-hidden, but encircled by the earl's forces. Buchan's men could not see them. Frustrated, they fired arrows randomly into the trees. Angus' archers fired back. "My men are the best archers in Argyll and the Isles," said Angus to Sir Edward. "They will inflict sufficient damage to hold back Buchan."

It was Christmas Day and the ground frozen with snow. King Robert, though weak, was able to give his thoughts on strategy. "Move the men every few days so Buchan is kept guessing as to our location." The strategy worked, anointed as it was with Bishop Murray's prayers for their safety. Buchan finally gave up and retired to his hearth fires.

"Buchan's scouts may have alerted him to the king's condition," said the Earl of Lennox to Angus as they warmed their hands in front of a fire. "In that event, they may be waiting for him to expire."

As Lennox walked away, Angus' brother joined him. "The king's army grows restless, Angus. Provisions are low and some wonder if the king will survive. Something must be done else there is a risk of desertion."

"Aye," said Angus. "I have seen the king's men whispering among themselves. I will speak to Sir Edward." Angus conferred with the king's brother, telling him what they both knew. "We cannot stay here."

"Sir Robert Boyd just told me the same. I agree. Our situation is not good and it seems the men will not fight with the king as he is. I have been thinking we should retreat to the Strathbogie Hills and hope Buchan does not attack while we are on the move."

"My galloglass and I," said Angus, "together with the king's knights, will cover the king."

Thus agreed, the king's army moved out in full view of the enemy, marching slowly in fighting order with the king on a litter in the center. Buchan's archers fired at them but with little enthusiasm, the ground being covered with snow. More of Buchan's men fell to the king's arrows than Bruce's men to Buchan's.

To everyone's surprise, they reached Strathbogie without a battle. There, they rested for the worst of the winter.

With the turning of the year, the king began to improve, lifting everyone's spirits. Angus composed a letter to Áine but had no way to get it to her just now. It spoke of his love for her. "I can scarce look at one of your birds without thinking of you, my love. Your face is ever before me."

As the king continued to improve, they moved him to the village of Inverurie, preferring the risk of being attacked in the plains to the certainty of starvation in the hills. Buchan, for whatever reason, did not pursue them. "He may be gathering forces to attack in the spring," speculated Sir Gilbert.

"Let us hope he has difficulty recruiting men to the Buchan cause with King Robert's popularity growing among the people," suggested Lennox.

During this time, Bishop Murray brought them news of Queen Elizabeth. "She is being held in Yorkshire at Burstwick in Holderness," he told Sir Edward in Angus' presence. "Should we tell the king?"

"It might comfort him to know she is safe," said the king's brother, "yet there remains the issue of his daughter, our sisters and Isabella MacDuff, Buchan's countess he abandoned, for her crowning Robert king. Mayhap it would be best to say nothing."

Angus, too, wondered what was best. He knew the king missed his wife with every passing day, but the news would be only slightly encouraging. And it would remind him of the others whose fates were less certain. Thus, he finally agreed they should say nothing unless the king asked.

As the snows melted and spring approached, King Robert continued to grow stronger, though he still could not gain his saddle without help. When told that John Comyn, the Earl of Buchan, had amassed a great force only five miles northeast of Inverurie, including English soldiers under Sir John Mowbray, Angus and John went to the king to confer with him on how Buchan should be dealt with.

They entered the small cottage to hear Sir Edward telling the king that Sir David Brechin, a knight in King Edward's service whose mother was a Comyn, had attacked a detachment of Bruce's men on the outskirts of the village.

The king struggled to stand. Angus could see his friend was determined and moved to help him. The knights watched, sharing looks of concern.

King Robert said, "I will lead the men myself. Help me with my armor."

The king's servants moved quickly to assist him into his mail and then handed him his weapons, sword, dagger and small axe.

"But Robert," said his brother, "you are not yet fully recovered. You can only sit a horse with help."

With one arm holding on to Angus, the king slid his sword into its scabbard. "I am aware of my weakness and that Buchan thinks I am too ill to lead the men. I must prove him wrong and gain the advantage."

"'Tis true, my lord," said Angus, "if John Comyn believes the rumors, he thinks you on your deathbed and has so informed his army. If you can manage to show yourself, your reputation of courage in battle will speak strength to your men and fear to the enemy."

The king braced himself on a table. "Of what does their army consist?"

Sir Robert Boyd said, "Like our own, some cavalry but mostly foot soldiers, more than a thousand. The difference is that ours are patriots who believe in their king."

"It will be enough. We must ask Bishop Murray to pray for us." The bishop was summoned and the king stepped out of the door, leaning on his brother for support. The king's captains knelt and Bishop Murray prayed for them, asking for God's blessing and strength for the king.

"I will ride close on your right side," said Sir Edward, "and Sir Gilbert will be on your left. Our hands will steady you. You shall not falter."

"My brother, my stepson and I will be at your back," said Angus, "and the other knights will ride in front of you."

The king was pale but resolute as he was helped onto his horse. His army cheered to see their leader once again among them.

At Sir Edward's order, the army formed up and marched toward

Old Meldrum where the Earl of Buchan and Sir John Mowbray had drawn up on the road.

As the king appeared, his crowned helmet shone in the morning sun, as if God Himself had approved.

Buchan and his captains, with shocked expressions, began to edge back. The sight of their leaders backing away from Robert Bruce caused Buchan's army to break apart and scatter, running in all directions.

"After them!" yelled King Robert.

With shouted battle cries, the king's army charged forward. The fighting that ensued soon became a rout. Even Buchan fled, north toward his lands.

King Robert, who watched all from his horse, smiled at Angus. "So you said, so it was." To his brother, the king said, "We must destroy Buchan's lands in the northeast so there is no doubt who rules the Scots. I am not yet strong enough to do it, so I put you in charge."

"With pleasure," said Sir Edward. "I leave you in the good care of the Lord of the Isles and your knights."

During the time of the king's recovery in Inverurie, he sent men to retrieve James Douglas. "Look for him in the forest of Selkirk," he told the messengers who were to ride south. Then, to Angus, he said, "Jamie will be useful to us for what comes next."

By the time Douglas had been found and made his way north to join the king, it was late spring, and the king had recovered his strength.

Around the fire that night, Douglas described his success. "While the young King Edward married his French bride, Isabella, and argued with his barons over his too-intimate relationship with his favorite, Piers Gaveston, we were well-occupied. The tenants of Aymer de Valence joined with us, much to the disappointment of their English lord. We have taken, without much trouble, the forests of Selkirk and Jedburgh.

"One night, we came upon a contingent of English soldiers on the water of Lyne and attacked in the dark. They fled before our swords, leaving behind two prisoners of some importance: your nephew, Thomas of Strathdon, and my first cousin, Sir Alexander of Bonkill, brother of James, the High Steward."

"Well done!" said the king.

"You will have to school young Thomas," said Douglas. "He was a willing captive of the English and has accepted all their lies."

"Some time in close confinement during which we feed him the truth will change his mind," said the king, and gave the order to see it done.

"There is good news, my king," said Douglas. "Bishop Lamberton has been released and is on his way to Scotland. He had to swear fealty to the English king and pay a large sum but, being forced, I doubt it will prevent him from again serving as your good bishop."

Encouraging news also reached them from Aberdeen where citizens of the town loyal to King Robert stormed the castle and put the English garrison to the sword. A key port for trade with the Continent, gaining Aberdeen meant much to the kingdom's economic strength.

"Now we must secure the western seaboard," said King Robert, "which means it is time to deal with the MacDougalls."

Before they left the north, the king's brother, Sir Edward, passed through with news that he had plundered the lands of Buchan. "The earl and Sir John Mowbray have fled Scotland. What would you have me do next?"

Without hesitation, the king said, "I hear the MacDoualls in Galloway are regaining strength. I would see Dungal MacDouall gone and Galloway ours."

The king and his brother exchanged a knowing look before Sir Edward said, "Consider it done." Angus saw in their eyes the memory of their brothers, Alexander and Thomas, who had been captured by the MacDoualls and turned over to the old King Edward for grisly deaths. "And where are you bound now that you are yourself again?" Edward asked the king.

"To Argyll. We will retrace our steps down the Great Glen and at Inverlochy, join with Angus' fleet of galleys to deal with the MacDougalls." Glancing at Angus, the king added, "We have both lost much at their hands."

"You should know," said Douglas, "that John of Lorne has been appointed Sheriff of Argyll and the Hebrides by King Edward."

Angus snorted. "An insult to the Hebrides and the Lordship of the Isles," said Angus. "But no matter." He faced the king. "I seem to recall the truces you gave both John MacDougall of Lorne and the Earl of Ross have expired."

The king smiled. "My thought exactly."

CHAPTER 25

Argyll, Scotland, August 1308

THE WARM DAYS of late summer were upon them as Angus sailed his fleet down the waters of Loch Linnhe. To conserve his strength for the battles ahead, at Angus' urging, King Robert agreed to sail with him.

From the stern, Angus watched his friend standing in the prow talking with Sir Neil Campbell, whose lands around Loch Awe were near their destination, the place their scouts had told them the MacDougall forces were gathered.

Rob was no longer the man the MacDougalls had ambushed at Dal Righ two years before, a knight untrained in Highland warfare. Newly crowned, he had been hunted as an outlaw. Since then, he had become wise to the ways of fighting using stealth and the land itself. A battle-hardened warrior known for his courage and clever tactics, King Robert was respected in Scotland and feared by the English garrisons.

Now, he fought like a Highlander, on foot and striking fast only to retreat into the woods. In addition to his sword and dagger, the king carried an axe he used to great effect, not a long-shafted sparth axe like the one Angus wielded, but nonetheless efficient at cutting down enemies.

James Douglas and Sir Gilbert Haye had agreed to lead the king's army over land, following a path parallel to Loch Linnhe. Angus did not envy them the midges that swarmed at this time of year. Too soon, he would again experience that brand of torture himself.

In his idle moments, he thought of his wife and his isles. He wanted to be with Áine but he could not leave the king at such a time. He could, however, send his brother home to see that all was well and to assure her he lived along with her son.

Transferring the wounded to one galley, Angus sent John to Islay. "Give this letter to my lady and see that the wounded are cared for. I put you in charge of Dunyvaig and my family in my absence. If the chiefs have questions, and they may for my long absence, you can provide them answers. Encourage them with the news the king has nearly secured Scotland."

John tucked the letter into his tunic. "I will do as you ask. Doubtless, Lady Áine will ask me when she might see you. What would you have me say?"

"In truth, I do not know. We must deal with the MacDougalls and then the Earl of Ross. The king needs all of Scotland with him before he faces the English. And since Alexander MacDougall murdered our brother, this hunt is personal to our family and to the lordship."

John nodded. "Your lady will understand."

"Aye, she will. In any event, I hope to be home for Christmas."

"I will tell her. Take care, Angus." They embraced and John departed.

Earlier, Duncan had gone with Sir Edward to Galloway, taking with him Brian and some of Angus' galloglass, saying he would join them later. With Angus were the chiefs and most of the men who had come with them—all still alive, praise God. Christina MacRuairi, a woman of boundless energy, continued to lead her men with great success.

Angus beached the ships on the banks of Loch Linnhe, watched over by his men on Lismore, and headed inland with the king. As they approached MacDougall territory, King Robert sent James Douglas ahead with scouts to view the land. "Bring me back your thoughts on what they are planning."

A day later, late in the afternoon, Douglas appeared, covered in dust and mud. The day had been hot but as the afternoon descended, the air began to cool and midges swarmed beneath the trees. Offered a drink of ale, Douglas batted away the midges and accepted it gratefully. Taking a large swallow, he wiped his mouth with the back of his hand. "They think to take us again as they did at Dal Righ, my lord."

"I trust we are wiser now," said King Robert.

"So we are," replied Douglas. "They have set an ambush at the Pass of Brander where a narrow track separates Loch Awe from the heights of Ben Cruachan. From what our scouts overheard, Alexander MacDougall remains at his castle at Dunstaffnage, too old and ill to fight. His son, John, leads the MacDougall men but he, too, is ill and plans to watch the battle from a galley on Loch Awe."

Douglas picked up a stick and, smoothing a place in the dirt with his foot, he drew a few lines. "The MacDougalls—thousands of them—wait here, blocking the west end of the pass. And here," he said, pointing midway down the pass, "hidden on the slopes of the mountain, waiting to pounce as we go by."

The king studied the drawing, resting his chin in his hand. "You have done well to give us this, James."

Sir Neil Campbell said, "I know the mountain. It is possible to climb the ben from the other side and crouch unnoticed above the MacDougalls."

Douglas nodded. "It could be done."

"Then that is what we will do," said the king. "Jamie, at first light, take a group of men over the top of the ben to wait above the MacDougalls. I will lead the army across the track below. Before we cross in front of the enemy, I will signal you to strike."

Angus nodded, satisfied with the plan. Finally, he would have justice for the murder of his brother. Finally, the king would have revenge for the MacDougalls' ruthless attack at Dal Righ that left so many of his loyal men dead.

"I will lend you my archers," Angus said to Douglas. "My gallo-glass and I will stay with the king. God willing, the wretched MacDougalls will be squeezed between our two forces."

Their plans laid, the king skirted the loch on the north and, marching two abreast along the path, led his army, of which Angus and his Islemen were a part, into the pass at Brander. When they were well along, and just before they reached the place where the Mac-Dougalls hid on the mountain's slopes, King Robert sounded two blasts on his horn, the signal for Douglas to attack.

With the haunting sound of the horn still echoing off the loch, the air was suddenly filled with arrows, the dark shafts flying down the slope to hit the horrified MacDougalls. Shrieking, they tried to escape. A barrage of rocks followed, dropping more to the ground. Moans of the wounded rose from where they lay.

His heart thundering in his chest, Angus shouted his war cry and ran with the king, swiftly climbing up the slope, his axe clutched in his right hand, ready to meet the retreating enemy.

The MacDougalls, armed for battle, had failed to consider they might get closed in from both front and back. In the confusion, they ran in all directions.

Behind Angus and the king were the king's knights and Angus' chiefs and their warriors. They flooded the slope and attacked the panicked MacDougalls. Shouts filled the air as metal clashed against metal.

The MacDougalls who did not fall fled west. King Robert ordered his army after them. Angus kept pace with the king as they ran. Sparing a glance at the loch, he noticed the galley, where John of Lorne had planned to observe all, was gone.

At the west end of the pass, where the rest of the MacDougalls were waiting, the two armies met in a clash of weapons. Angus' axe dripped blood as he repeatedly struck, the red liquid splashing onto his mail and surcoat.

As Angus and the king engaged one tight knot of MacDougalls, Angus felt the flat of a sword hit his shoulder. Turning, the man raised his sword to strike but Angus' sparth axe with its long shaft struck sooner, dropping the MacDougall to the ground. A fatal gash in his neck gushed blood, the bright red liquid spreading into the grass.

They had fifteen miles to travel to reach the MacDougall castle of Dunstaffnage on the coast. Along the way, the king's army defeated the rest of the MacDougalls and plundered their lands, taking booty and driving off their cattle.

By the end of the day, exhausted, filthy and smelling of sweat and blood, they reached the coast and the massive stone fortress that stood guard at the entrance to Loch Etive. To the northwest lay Lismore Isle, just visible on the horizon.

Angus had last seen Dunstaffnage Castle the day his elder brother had married Juliana. Even then, there had been hints the MacDougalls were plotting to deprive Alex of the promised dowry.

That night, they ate well from the MacDougalls' larder. Angus exchanged smiles with his friend, the king, pleased they had defeated one of their ancient enemies.

King Robert began the siege of the castle the next day. It went on for a month until Alexander MacDougall surrendered both the castle and himself. He paid homage to King Robert, but none of the king's men were content to leave it at that. Angus would have preferred to see Alexander MacDougall dead, but it was apparent the king would show mercy to this old man. So, Angus offered a suggestion. "It would be best to hold him hostage against his son's treachery, my lord. John of Lorne escaped, and the MacDougalls cannot be trusted."

Acknowledging the truth of Angus' words, the king made Alexander MacDougall a hostage and declared the MacDougall lands forfeit. The king did not destroy Dunstaffnage. "It will be a royal castle," he declared. "I appoint as constable Sir Arthur Campbell, first cousin to Sir Neil Campbell." The king also supplied Dunstaffnage with food and provisions.

With the MacDougalls and Comyns defeated, all of Argyll paid homage to their new king.

James Douglas and Sir Robert Boyd headed south to join the king's brother in Galloway, while Angus and the king, having changed from their bloodstained tunics, headed north, up the Great Glen to Urquhart Castle and the unfinished business with William, Earl of Ross.

As the days moved into autumn, the weather remained unseasonably mild. Often there were days of sun. With the cooler nights, the men rejoiced that the midges were gone until late spring.

At the gate of Urquhart Castle, King Robert confronted the earl, demanding he surrender or endure a siege. The truce with Ross having lapsed and no help coming from the English king, who all knew was occupied with his angry barons, the earl had little choice.

"What do you intend with the one who betrayed the queen?" Angus asked his friend.

Rob sighed. "What I want to do and what I must do for the sake of Scotland are two different things." The pain in the king's eyes at the reminder of the suffering of his women told Angus he struggled with the decision to allow the earl to live.

"Ross will surrender rather than be taken if that be your choice," said Angus.

"I am counting on it," said the king, striding forward.

Leaving his sparth axe with one of his men, and gesturing the knights to follow, Angus walked at Rob's side, his sword ready should they face treachery.

The gate opened and William, Earl of Ross, humbly admitted King Robert into the castle. A man of noble blood, the earl had defeat written on his face. Word had obviously spread of Robert Bruce's successful battles against the Comyns and the MacDougalls. In a few words, the Earl of Ross, his face pale and drawn, offered his unconditional surrender.

With a stern countenance and gritted teeth, the king accepted the earl's sword, offered with shaking hands, and his oath, made on bended knee, to serve the king thereafter.

"I will stand surety for the earl," offered David Murray, Bishop of Moray, who had entered the castle behind them.

"Very well," said the king. "You may do so."

Hard as it came to show the earl mercy, Angus thought his friend's decision had been wise, for he had gained not only Ross but also Sutherland and Caithness. The whole northwest of Scotland was now under his control. Still, the mercy granted for the sake of a united Scotland left a bitter taste in the mouths of the king's inner circle, particularly Sir Neil Campbell whose wife, Mary Bruce, was still in a cage, and Sir Robert Boyd who had guarded the women when the Earl of Ross breached the Church's sanctuary. With solemn expressions, they kept silent, accepting their king's decision, yet Angus could see they liked it not.

Angus felt the need to encourage his friend. "Except for the castles yet to be freed from the English—Perth, Berwick, Edinburgh and Stirling—you are recognized in all of Scotland as the just and lawful King of Scots. You have won your country, Rob, and the hearts of her people."

The king nodded in acceptance of what his hard-fought campaign had won him. "First, I will capture the English-garrisoned castles and then we must break the back of King Edward's army."

"Aye," said Angus. "You will accomplish both."

While they had been busy in the northeast and in Argyll, Sir Edward and James Douglas arrived to announce they had brought all of Galloway into King Robert's peace.

"We have defeated the Galwegians and their English allies," said Sir Edward, his clothing showing his hard days on the road.

Angus was relieved to see Duncan and Angus' stepson, Brian O'Neill, return unscathed. Brian looked more a man than when he had left. He had grown taller and displayed a new air of confidence. His freckled face was brown from the sun and his red hair streaked with copper. On his face was a smile. "Greetings, Father…er, Lord Angus."

Sir Edward placed a hand on Brian's shoulder. "He did well, Angus, as did Duncan and your galloglass."

"Lord Angus and his galloglass trained me," said Brian, pride shining from his dark blue eyes.

"It shows," said Sir Edward with a nod in Angus' direction.

Angus offered his hand to Brian. "Well done, lad." He exchanged a glance with Duncan who must have looked after the lad.

That evening, the king's inner circle dined in Dunstaffnage on MacDougall cattle, and the king's brother gave his report of events in the south. Angus' chiefs had been invited, including Christina MacRuairi. All gathered round to hear.

"They had nearly three times our numbers," began Sir Edward, "including fifteen hundred English soldiers under Sir Ingram de Umfraville, the Scots noble whose loyalties have shifted more often than ours. Added to their numbers were the Galwegians. Though we were greatly outnumbered, I thought of our brothers, given traitors' deaths as a result of Dungal MacDouall, Lord of Galloway, and cared not they were many to our few.

"With Douglas at my side, we charged at them, screaming our war cries. I think our sheer ferocity surprised them." He smiled. "Jamie, as you know, with his black hair flying about his menacing face, can be quite frightening."

Douglas smiled widely. "I surely can."

Sir Edward continued, "The MacDoualls and their English allies fled, taking refuge behind the stone walls of the English-held Buittle Castle."

King Robert turned to his brother. "That is the castle our grandfather captured in 1286 when he thought to take the throne."

"I remember," said Edward Bruce. "'Twas a Balliol castle then." With a nod to James Douglas, who was sitting nearby, enjoying the tale immensely, the king's brother said, "'Twas Jamie who had the idea to use a heavy mist to our advantage. The mist became our cloak and allowed us to creep unseen toward the castle. We took it at night. Wallace would have been proud."

"As we attacked," said Douglas, "the MacDoualls and their English friends fled in the dark, their only light the moon when the mist dissipated. Dungal, the Galwegian chief, escaped toward England where, doubtless, he has been rewarded for his perfidy. You may be certain he will not return to Scotland anytime soon, else I will see him gone."

For the great victory that it was, the celebration that followed was subdued. Angus did not have to ask why the evening was bittersweet. The Bruces had defeated the MacDoualls, but they would rather have their beloved brothers, Thomas and Alexander, alive to celebrate the day.

At one point in the evening, the king turned aside to confer with his brother, who nodded at what was shared between them. Then, turning to James Douglas, the king said, "For your valor aiding my brother, Jamie, I give you the castle at Buittle. And Edward, for avenging our brothers, is hereafter made Lord of Galloway."

Smiles from the two named spoke their pleasure, and a chorus of voices rose to shout, "Hear, hear!"

Directing his attention to Angus and Christina, the king said, "As for the MacDougall lands, I will divide them between my friend, Angus, and my kinswoman, Christina. I will also give to Angus the Isle of Mull, formerly held in part by the MacDougalls, for your eldest son, and Lochaber, formerly Comyn territory, to be shared with the MacRuairis. "With these grants, I expect you to assist Dunstaffnage's new constable in guarding the seaways."

"Aye, and thank you, my lord," said Angus. "It shall be my pleasure to do as you say." Inclining his head toward Malcolm Maclean, Angus said, "The Macleans of Duart Castle on Mull have frequently reminded me how uncomfortable they are having the MacDougalls so near. I suspect they are relieved at the change."

The king smiled at Angus' words. "'Tis my hope the charters for these grants will be witnessed by Bishop Lamberton. Lord willing, he and Bishop Wishart will soon be restored to me."

Heads nodded at the mention of the two bishops returning to Scotland as they were loyal to the king. Meanwhile, Angus was pleased for the new lands. That two of the descendants of Somerled were to share in the lands of the third, now forfeited, was an irony not lost on him. But there was one favor he would ask. "My lord, might Glen Coe be included in my portion?"

"You may certainly have Glen Coe, Angus, but why would you ask for that?"

"For my natural son, Iain, as his inheritance. 'Tis the place of his birth, the land of his mother's people."

"Ah. I understand. One of my natural sons fights in my army. You will not be surprised to know he is called Sir Robert Bruce."

Angus chuckled, remembering what his father had once told him about the Bruces and the name Robert. For a nobleman to have offspring that were not legitimate was more common than openly admitted, thus, he was unsurprised by this news of the king's having natural sons. For himself, Angus was pleased he could offer Glen Coe to the lad called Iain MacDonald.

"In addition to a castle for Douglas and lands for you, Angus, I would knight you both." The king rose. "Kneel."

Surprised at the king's magnificent gesture, Angus kneeled beside Jamie Douglas. The king unsheathed his sword and touched each of their shoulders. "I, King Robert Bruce, do hereby dub thee Sir Angus Og Macdonald. May your courage and devotion continue to be an example to my subjects in Scotland."

When the king had finished knighting Angus, he moved on to Douglas and with gracious words, acknowledged the loyalty and strength of Douglas' courage.

The two rose to receive the congratulations of all present.

"I am humbled by this honor," said Angus. His father had been knighted as Sir Angus Mor Macdonald. Angus had never sought the honor but because this knighthood was conveyed by his friend, the king, it meant much to him.

With the onset of winter, Angus asked Rob for leave to return to the Isles. "You have an army now to take Perth and those remaining castles. Sir Edward and Sir James certainly have great enthusiasm for the battles required. It is time I see to my Isles." Then, gesturing to his chiefs gathered around, he said, "The lordship's chiefs have been long from their lands."

The king nodded. "You and your chiefs have earned this respite, my loyal friend. As for you, it is right that you should return to that beautiful wife of yours. I cannot yet return to mine, but if Lady Áine's prayers are answered, I will one day."

Angus said, "I have no doubt you will, my king. I am mindful that the English are still to be faced. You have but to send for me, and I will come with a great fleet and many warriors—all in the Isles if need be."

"I will remember," said the king. "By the bye, I am thinking of holding my first parliament in the spring at St. Andrews. Will you attend?"

"Aye, if I can," replied Angus. "If I am not able, might I send my cousin, Duncan MacAlasdair?" He glanced at Duncan, who sat silently observing. "He is like a brother to me and has faithfully fought for you and Sir Edward. It would mean much to him to attend your parliament as my representative."

The king smiled and turned his attention to Duncan. "By all means, send the cheerful Duncan. I suspect with the gloomy face of Alexander MacDougall attending—whether he wishes to or not—Duncan will be a welcome addition."

The next day, Angus and the king embraced on the shore at Dunstaffnage before Angus sailed with his fleet and the men who had fought so valiantly and lived to speak of it. Duncan and Brian stood with Angus in his galley, their smiles telling him they were happy to be going home.

Hinting of the winter to come, the weather turned cold and windy as they departed. Sailing from Loch Linnhe, Angus headed south along with the Macduffies, into white-capped waters, while Christina MacRuairi turned north toward Moidart and Castle Tioram. Malcolm Maclean sailed toward Mull and Castle Duart. The Macleods of Skye had farther to go and turned north. Other chiefs broke from the fleet as the isles they called home came into view. By the time Angus reached Islay, he had only his own galleys to beach at Lagavulin Bay.

Angus' heart swelled as he spotted Dunyvaig Castle. Too long had he been on land not surrounded by the sea. He had been gone long enough for the youngest of his children to have forgotten what he looked like. Would his daughters remember him? He thought of his chiefs, who had gone with him, who would be wondering the same of their own children.

On the battlements of Dunyvaig Castle flew the Galley of the Isles pennon pronouncing it as the seat of the Lord of the Isles. Once he drove the English from Kintyre, he would again have Dunaverty Castle but, for now, this isle and this castle were home.

Dunyvaig Castle, Isle of Islay, November 1308

ÁINE PAUSED BEFORE the window in the great hall to glance

northeast, as she did each day. She did not look for the occasional merchant ship or the galley of a chief come to call upon Angus' brother. She was looking for the white sails of a fleet. But all she saw was a flock of hooper swans in the far distance skimming over the water. The huge birds with seven-foot wingspans had come to winter on Islay. Áine frequently marveled at their pageantry of white gliding over the blue water.

It had been months since John had come to Islay with a galley full of wounded men and a letter from Angus. His words had given her hope that he and Brian would return to her with Duncan, strong and in good health. But with every day that passed, she worried.

It was the plight of women who stayed behind, tending the home fires, to pray and wonder at the fate of their men. She had kept busy, assisting John with the business of the lordship and seeing to the needs of the women whose husbands had gone to war. Each morning, she prayed for Angus, King Robert and the men who fought with them.

She was just turning back to Nessa and the task they were pursuing of overseeing the hanging of new tapestries, when her mind questioned something she had seen. The swans had been moving more slowly than usual. Walking back to the window, she stared at the emerging patches of white. As she watched, they grew larger, causing her to smile. *Not swans. Sails!*

A lump rose in her throat. "Nessa! 'Tis Angus and the fleet. It must be!"

"And Conall!" said her handmaiden, joining Áine at the window. "'Tis about time. Won't he be surprised to know he has a son?"

"A beautiful boy is your Cináed," said Áine.

"Do you think he will be pleased I named the babe for an ancient King of Scots and Picts?"

"Knowing Conall, he will be proud of the name you have chosen. Come, let us meet the galleys."

Áine issued instructions to the servants to make sure the evening meal would accommodate the returning men. Then, taking up their cloaks, the two women hurried to the beach.

Once Angus finished speaking to his captains, Áine went to him.

Nessa, who had gone with her, curtseyed to Angus before walking on to welcome her own husband.

Angus gave Áine an assessing gaze before taking her into his arms and kissing her. "Too long, Woman. I have been too long. You only grow more beautiful. This time, I do not intend to leave soon."

"Then I am happy, for I have missed you. Your children miss you. Your chiefs who remained behind miss you." They began to walk arm in arm toward the castle. "I was glad to receive your letter, to know you were well, but tell me, did we lose any men? And how goes King Robert's war?"

"Your prayers have been answered, my love. Except for the wounded I sent ahead with John, all of the men have returned, including Brian, who will be along shortly. As for your other question, King Robert has done well. He needed to defeat his Scottish enemies and he has. Most importantly, the MacDougalls and the Comyns will trouble us no more, except for the Red Comyn's son, John Comyn, and Alexander MacDougall's son, John. Both escaped to serve the English."

"That is a relief."

"Besides all that," added Angus, "the king has bestowed upon me a knighthood and more lands as the MacDougall and Comyn lands were forfeit."

"I am so glad. The king's gifts to you are well earned." Suddenly, all was right with Áine's world. Arriving at the castle door, opened for them by a guard, she said, "I have asked a meal be prepared for you and your men should they wish to join us."

Angus looked back to the beach where Conall and Nessa were slowly making their way toward them. "I imagine Conall will dine with us since he now lives in the castle. The guards who remained behind and those who want to hear the news will also attend. But those who have just returned will be happy to spend the evening with their wives and families."

Áine looked forward to the homecoming celebration but even more to their private time after. "Conall has a new son, Angus. A handsome babe named Cináed, born nine months after Conall left. Do you think he will be pleased?"

"Oh, aye. He will be bursting with pride."

SINCE IT WAS LATE when Angus brought the fleet into Lagavulin Bay and the days were shorter now, he would have rather dined with Áine in their chamber, spending the evening with her. But his wife, mindful of those who waited for him below, suggested they have supper in the hall. It was well she did, for before he could even shed his surcoat and mail, Alexander and his young sisters were knocking on the chamber door.

"Father! Let us in!"

"They are excited to see you," said Áine.

"Help me with this mail and a clean tunic."

Áine pulled the mail from him and told the children to be patient.

"Will they recognize me, do you think?" asked Angus. Not for the first time, he wondered what they would look like now.

"Alexander certainly. Finvola and Mary might have to be reminded but then they are young at four and three. Your brother, their Uncle John, reminds them often of their great father." Then with a smile, she handed him a blue tunic. "That would be you."

Shaking his head at his wife's humor, he said, "This tunic is new." He fingered the embroidered silver threads. "The handiwork is fine."

"With the time I had in the evenings, I embroidered the Celtic symbols. Now that you are home, mayhap we can spend our evenings together in the hope you will have another son."

"A son…indeed, yes." The thought pleased Angus. "In which case, Wife," he said with a knowing smile, "I will not want to linger long at the table tonight."

"Nor I, Husband."

As soon as they opened the door, Alexander stepped in and their daughters bounded into Angus' arms as he kneeled before them. "Rascals, both of you!" But he was pleased they did not shy away from him. Rising, he grasped Alexander's hand. "You have grown!"

"Aye, Father. Soon, I will be as tall as you."

Angus inwardly smiled. "Eventually."

When they finally descended the stairs with their brood in hand

and stepped into the great hall, it was to see a large crowd. Áine said, "News has spread of your return."

The men were hungry for both food and tales from the battles. It seemed their wives did not want to be excluded, so the hall was merry that night. Conall strutted around with his new son in his arms, proudly announcing to all who would listen that the lad's name was "Cináed".

"You could not have given your husband a better gift," Angus said to Nessa who stood with him and Áine, watching their guests. As Nessa went to join her husband, Angus turned to Áine. "Conall's heart, once broken, is surely mended."

"I think so. He looks happy to be home and happy to be with Nessa. In truth, she could not love him more."

Angus looked at his beautiful Áine. "Like me. A contented man."

"And much loved," she added.

The supper of venison, roasted with apples and leeks, made up for the often spare fare Angus and his Islesmen had endured on the many days they had marched with King Robert and his army through freezing cold. Their only feast had been the roast beef they had dined on at Dunstaffnage in Argyll courtesy of Alexander MacDougall.

For a while, the sounds in the hall were of men eating and women laughing. As the hall quieted, servants brought honey tarts and more wine, and the men called for stories.

"Tell us of the battles fought against the Comyns and MacDougalls," said his constable. Angus gave the privilege to Conall, his captain, to tell of the battles in Argyll and the northeast and the surrender of the Earl of Ross. Angus' captain was a good storyteller so, with grand gestures, he embellished the events to the delight of those listening. "Chased them all the way to Dunstaffnage," he finished. "After fighting all day, exhausted, we feasted on MacDougall cattle." In a somber tone, he said, "My Lord Alexander, slain by the MacDougall, would have been pleased."

It had been nearly a decade since Angus' elder brother, Alex, had passed from this life yet Angus still missed him and their evenings by the fire when he would turn to Alex for advice. In a melancholy mood, Angus said, "Conall forgot to mention that he and the

Islesmen claimed Lady Juliana's dowry of Lismore that should have been my brother's long ago."

Many cheers went up.

"Lismore is ours now," Angus continued, "and King Robert approves. He asks only that we use it and the other lands he has given me to guard the seaways."

Juliana, who had attended the dinner and was sitting on the other side of Áine, reached for her hand. "I am satisfied, for the loss of Lismore was a source of great shame to Alex and me. I am glad, too, that my father and my brother still live, though I could not mourn their loss had they died. They took Alexander from me and left our sons fatherless. Given the MacDougalls' disdain for the Bruces, I doubt they will serve King Robert for long."

"Aye," said Angus. "I believe King Robert is of the same mind. Alexander MacDougall will attend the king's parliament in March, as he must, but he will not be smiling."

Angus then suggested Duncan tell the story of his exploits with Sir Edward in Galloway. His cousin did so most eloquently, finishing, "Alas, Dungal MacDouall escaped and likely now serves the English but, then, he was always an ally of the MacDougalls."

The rest of the evening was spent enjoying their family and friends, good wine and cheese from the larder. Looking at Áine laughing with Duncan brought a feeling of contentment to his soul. He was home surrounded by his family.

As the year came to an end, Angus was thankful they had returned to Islay before the winter storms, for Christmas arrived with snow, causing all to stay close to the hearth fires.

One morning, as he lazed in bed with Áine, watching through the window as the snow fell, it came to him that the joys of this life are often defined by such moments, small bits of time carved into a memory to be remembered later when such moments were long past.

Áine turned her head on the pillow to face him. "What has you so pensive this morning, my love?"

He met her inquiring gaze. Her eyes were deep pools, drawing him in. Her dark hair fell in waves about her shoulders, her pale ivory skin luminescent in the dim light. "I was thinking of this moment, of you beside me, of our home in the Isles. Wherever I am, I shall remember it, like a glistening jewel that can be taken out and marveled at."

"A poetic thought. Teal, our Irish bard, must have left an impression last night."

He reached out his hand to run his fingers through her long locks. "Nay. 'Tis the time I have spent away from you, making our time together all the more precious."

"But you said you will not go away soon."

Hearing anxiety in her voice, he gave her an encouraging smile. "Nay. 'Tis my intention to stay until the king calls for me. He will hold his first parliament in March and I plan to send Duncan. He will do well in Rob's court with the mixed array of nobles that will be there. The king has given his approval."

With a smile on her face, she said, "Then I shall have you for a while longer."

"Aye. I must see to my Isles, especially the lands that are now part of the lordship, lands that were formerly those of our enemies. Mull is to be Alexander's when he comes of age. Too, the king has asked me to keep under observation the northern waters and help secure Dunstaffnage, now a royal castle."

"When you leave to see to your new lands," said Áine, "I would go with you."

"Aye, you could come on the voyage north. We should be safe from the MacDougalls and Comyns now, and the English king is well occupied with his own troubles."

"In which case, Brian and Alexander will want to go, too."

"And they shall."

Angus spent the winter on Islay, enjoying his family and the men who sailed in his fleet. He received the reports of merchants who regularly arrived in the Isles and of his men who were keeping a watchful eye on the Irish Sea. But he wanted to sail north to see for himself how the lordship fared.

In early March, as the earth came back to life and flowers bloomed on the rocky shores, he sent Duncan to St. Andrews on the east coast of Fife for King Robert's parliament. "Be my eyes and ears,"

Angus said as he wished his cousin Godspeed. "And write!"

Isle of Islay, spring 1309

THE CHANGE OF seasons brought new life to the isle. With the longer days and more light, Áine often walked the shores, watching the birds. The gray barnacle geese that had come by the thousands in autumn were still here but the winter sounds had gone, replaced by songs of love as the birds began to mate. At such times, they paid her little attention.

Everywhere she could hear birds singing, skylarks high above the fields, blackbirds in the castle garden, lapwings over meadows and song thrushes on branches. Offshore, black and white divers with their long, sharp beaks entranced her. Gulls, too, made an appearance each day, their cries rising in the air, especially when the fishermen returned.

With the birds nesting, and Nessa again with child, it was not surprising Áine's thoughts often turned to her desire to give Angus another son. Brian was grown and spent more time with the men. Alexander had turned nine and wanted to trail after Brian. Finvola and Mary were still watched by their nurses but they, too, were growing and sometimes joined Áine on her walks along the shore.

Reminders that time was passing.

Angus said nothing about another child, but she knew he was mindful of the need to produce a male child who could stand in Alexander's stead if need be. The Macdonalds had been prolific since the time of Somerled. The chief of each generation had produced multiple sons. She did not want to disappoint Angus.

In the time Angus had been gone, she had assumed a greater role, not just at Dunyvaig, but with the chiefs and warriors who called upon John. They would ask her advice and sometimes brought their wives who also consulted her. The Irish who had come to the Isles as her dowry often sought her opinion on where to live, where their trades were most needed and even on the women to marry.

With Angus' return, she had expected all that to change but it did not. Angus had much to do observing the waters between Islay and Skye and the English ships in the Irish Sea. He was happy to allow her a greater role than she'd had before. "The chiefs' wives—even the chiefs—and your Irishmen trust you," said Angus. "They want your advice. I see no reason to change that. After all, the king will eventually call me away again. I draw comfort from knowing my lady is respected and can stand in for me when needed." And so, they became partners in many things giving Áine great joy.

She and Angus had just returned from their voyage to the northern isles and his new lands of Mull and Lochaber when a package containing papers and a letter arrived from Duncan. Alone in their chamber, Angus read the letter to her.

From Duncan of Kintyre to my dear cousin, Angus, Lord of the Isles,

You could not have known what an adventure you sent me upon, how the nobles flock to our rightful king, including the Earl of Ross, and how Alexander MacDougall, reluctant liegeman of Bruce, sat with dour countenance, listening to all. I thoroughly enjoyed myself.

The parliament commenced on the 16th of March, but even before I arrived, a letter came from King Philip of France, affirming the alliance between France and Scotland and Robert Bruce's rightful claim to the Kingdom of Scotland. King Robert's barons drafted the reply. All this was viewed as a good sign.

The earls attending the parliament—because I know you would want the list—included Ross, Lennox, Sutherland, Fife, Menteith, Mar, Buchan and Caithness. Of the king's barons, these were present: Sir Edward Bruce, Lord of Galloway, James Stewart, the High Steward of Scotland, Hugh, son and heir of the Earl of Ross, Sir Gilbert Haye (who has been made High Constable of Scotland), Robert Keith, Marischal of Scotland, Sir James, Lord of Douglas, Sir Neil Campbell and his brother, Donald, Alexander Lindsay, Alexander Fraser, Sir Robert Boyd, and Sir Thomas Randolph, as the king's nephew is now called. Notably, and continuing the king's show of mercy, Sir John Menteith, the captor of Wallace, attended, having left England and sworn allegiance to King Robert.

William Lamberton, Bishop of St. Andrews, was enthusiastically welcomed to the assembly. Apparently, Lamberton was freed by

King Edward to negotiate a truce with King Robert but Wishart remains a prisoner. King Robert, in his response, made clear he is the king of an independent kingdom, answerable only to God. (He told me he would not make Balliol's mistake.) Thus, the truce talks ended but Lamberton stayed.

The king has me acting as scribe as well as warrior. At other times, I am but his messenger. In that regard, with this letter, I include the grants of the new lands from King Robert to you, as witnessed by Bishop Lamberton. The king tells me there will be more.

On the 17th of March, eight bishops, abbots, priors and clergy affixed their seals to a "Declaration of the Clergy" attesting to King Robert's right, by his lineage and the grace of God, to be endowed with the Kingdom of Scotland and to be King of Scots.

After this, Alexander MacDougall left for England, presumably to join his son, John. You will be most interested to know that he took with him to England Andrew, Bishop of Argyll, formerly of Lismore Isle. Mayhap you know this if you have visited your men holding Lismore for you.

Angus, King Robert has asked me to stay with him, and I think there is merit in the request. If I do, I can remain your "eyes and ears" as you desired. With your permission, I will stay until you call me to you.

I am your man, Angus, and ever will be. May the good Lord have you in his keeping.

As an additional matter, Cousin, which you may share with your lady, I would tell you there are few women at King Robert's court, but I remain alert should the opportunity present itself to take a comely wife.

Angus chuckled as he read the last line. "We did know of the Bishop of Argyll's departure from Lismore, but the news of his travels with Alexander MacDougall to England is new. There is much in this letter that is helpful, Áine. What do you think of Duncan's thought to stay with the king?"

"I think it well worth the galley that will be kept busy sailing between Islay and the coast of Scotland. You will not have to wonder what is going on, for Duncan will keep you apprised."

"Aye. My cousin does seem to have a fondness for his new position as confidante to the king. I will miss him here, but he is of more value there."

Áine smiled at her husband. "In time of war, a cheerful person is much appreciated."

CHAPTER 26

Dunyvaig Castle, Isle of Islay

THE REST OF that year passed in relative peace for Angus and his family. King Edward did not march on Scotland which, according to Duncan, allowed King Robert time to travel across the country, accepting allegiances and solidifying his rule. As Duncan advised Angus in his letter,

> *While Edward did not invade Scotland himself, he did send separate forces, led by Sir John Segrave and Sir Robert Clifford. They arrived in the English towns of Berwick and Carlisle, intending to cross the border to engage with us. But, remembering their prior unsuccessful campaigns in Scotland and foreseeing a harsh winter, they agreed to a truce with King Robert and turned back.*

"It seems Edward's barons have little enthusiasm for his ventures into Scotland," Angus told Áine.

"Doubtless they recognize he is not his father, and we can thank God for that, but his problems with his barons have little to do with us."

"Aye. They like not his infatuation with Gaveston."

Meantime, leaving John at Dunyvaig, Angus made frequent voyages with Áine, Brian and Alexander to his new lands and to call upon his chiefs. Some of Áine's Irishmen wanted lands in Lochaber and Mull, and he was able to arrange places for them. Mull was a good isle for farmers, fishermen and keepers of cattle and the Macleans were gracious hosts.

At Glen Coe, he dispatched one of his trusted men to deliver word to Sorcha MacEanruig of his gift to her son, Iain. Angus had previously arranged for Alan, Bishop of the Isles, to witness the grant. Years before, he had told Sorcha he would provide for the lad, and he had kept his word.

"She must know you are King Robert's man," said Áine when he told her what he had done. "Do you think her son will fight for him?"

"Aye. Iain is Brian's age, and the men of Glen Coe hated the MacDougalls. They would be loyal to Robert Bruce. Once they know Iain is now the Chief of Glen Coe, albeit a young one, they will rally around him."

The question of when the next battle involving the Isles would occur was frequently raised in Angus' meetings with the chiefs. He believed the time was not far off but so much depended on the English king's relationship with his barons.

"No matter when King Edward leads his army north," he said to Malcolm Maclean one evening as they dined at Duart Castle, "he will encounter a different Scotland than his father left behind years ago. The Scots are united as never before."

"We will be called to fight in that battle," acknowledged the Maclean chief. The faces of their wives reflecting the candlelight disclosed their grave appreciation for all that would mean.

"Aye," said Angus. "All of Scotland will fight then."

As autumn arrived and Angus returned to Islay, news came that Alexander MacDougall was dead. "When he left King Robert," explained Angus' constable, "he found his way to Ireland where he died of sickness."

"How fitting," remarked Áine, "that the man who killed your brother in Ireland should come to his end in the same place after losing his lands and his title. Surely that is God's justice."

Angus said, "I'd like to believe this is the end of it but his son, John, formerly of Lorne, still lives and serves the English king."

At Christmas, to Angus' great delight, Áine informed him she was with child. With one hand protectively over her belly, she said, "'Tis my hope this child will be a son."

Inwardly, Angus smiled, for he harbored the same hope. That night, they celebrated, just the two of them. In his next letter to Duncan, Angus conveyed the good news that Áine expected another child, and Alexander MacDougall was gone from this life.

In June of the following year, 1310, on a fair summer's day, Áine delivered a healthy bairn. When told of the birth, Angus came to see his wife and child. As he entered the bedchamber, Nessa exclaimed, "A son, my lord, you have another son!"

Propped up in bed with pillows, Áine's long dark hair fell in waves around her shoulders. On the floor next to the bed lay Fand, attentive to Angus and the handmaiden's every move.

After gazing at the beautiful child, Angus leaned over to kiss his wife. "Thank you, my love, for this son. His dark hair and blue eyes, should he keep them, remind me of Alexander's."

"He is much like Alexander as a babe," said Áine. "We shall have to see if they share the same temperaments."

Angus chuckled. "Oh, aye." Alexander had all the traits of a firstborn son, courageous, capable and domineering. A force to be reckoned with.

Their other children came to visit, fascinated with their young sibling. Ten-year-old Alexander furrowed his brow as he gazed at the babe in his mother's arms. "He looks awfully small."

"You were once that size," said Angus.

"He will grow," Áine assured her son.

Alexander's furrowed brow told Angus the lad was skeptical.

Angus' daughters peeked over the bed to see their new brother. "Is he ours?" asked Finvola.

"He is yours to care for and love," replied Áine. "You must take very good care of him."

Finvola's expression turned serious as she nodded to her mother.

With his wife's agreement, Angus named the child John. Thus, each of his sons was named after a beloved brother. That same afternoon, Angus' brother, John, came to see the new arrival. Angus told him, "We would like you to stand godfather to the lad."

John received the news with great humility. "There are many other names you could have chosen for the boy, and others who would gladly be the lad's godfather. I am honored you chose me. Since he is to be my namesake, I will take great care to see he is raised as you and your lady would want."

"We know you will," said Áine.

Later that summer, another letter arrived from Duncan that conveyed King Robert's request for Angus to transport food—corn, meat, and wine—as well as weapons and armor from Ulster to Scotland. Ireland had become a source of needed supplies, and Angus was only too happy to undertake this task for his friend. "The O'Cahans and O'Neills will willingly assist us," he told his brother, John, and asked him to go along. "While we are there, we can call upon Áine's brother. It has been years since I paid him a visit."

When he told Áine of the planned trip, she wanted to go, as did Brian, who had his own ties to Ireland, by his birth, his heritage and his fostering.

"Very well, we shall make the voyage as a family," said Angus. The Earl of Ulster was King Robert's father-in-law but his allegiance was to King Edward. Thus, Angus made sure his crews were armed for battle.

The crossing from Islay to Ulster, which they made at the end of August, was a short one. The weather and the sea cooperated. While his captains arranged to load the goods the O'Neills had gathered at their request, Angus, John, Áine and Brian called upon Dermot O'Cahan at Dunseverick.

Angus had learned of Dermot's marriage and the birth of a son and daughter through his letters, but he and Áine had yet to meet them. Dermot's wife was one of the granddaughters of the King of Fermanagh, a lovely redhead named Flora with clear blue eyes. Both children had the O'Cahan dark hair.

"Come into the hall and share some wine with us," said Dermot.

"I can see Brian has grown, but you must tell us of Alexander, your daughters and your new son."

Áine chuckled, her dark eyes sparkling with mirth. "My brother is already arranging a match for our Mary."

"I warn you," said Angus as they entered the hall, "our youngest girl is the stubborn one."

They had only a few hours to spend with Dermot, but it was a sweet time of reunion. As Angus expected, the war in Scotland came up early in their discussion.

"The Earl of Ulster was supposed to negotiate a truce between King Edward and Robert Bruce," said Dermot. "The earl is most willing but the truce has yet to materialize due to Edward's continuing problems with his nobles, all centered around his favorite, Piers Gaveston, who he made the Earl of Cornwall, and to whom he pays undue attention. Some say they are lovers. At the king's recent parliament at Westminster, the barons were more concerned with Gaveston than Robert Bruce. A sentence of perpetual exile was pronounced by the barons on the detested favorite, and the Archbishop of Canterbury threatened all who should receive or support him with excommunication."

"That does not bode well for Cornwall's future," said Angus.

"Will you be making other trips to Ulster for provisions?" Dermot asked.

He nodded. "At least until the English king learns of our source of supply. I trust our family ties to the Red Earl will allow my ships to anchor here for that purpose. If that is the case, we should be able to call upon you more often."

"You would be most welcome," said Dermot.

As they sailed to Scotland to deliver their cargo, Angus told Áine, "We are past time arranging a fostering for Alexander. Mayhap we should think about Dermot. It would give Alexander a tie to your birthplace. Dermot commands many warriors now, galloglass among them. He has also added lands to the O'Cahan holdings."

"The thought appeals," said Áine. "My brother would treat his nephew well. I will send Dermot a letter when we get home and see what he thinks."

As it turned out, Dermot was most receptive to his nephew's fostering at Dunseverick, and Alexander, influenced by his half-brother, Brian, was pleased with the idea. Before the summer was over, Angus made arrangements for Alexander to sail to Dunseverick.

Just over a year later, in September of 1311, King Edward led his army north into Scotland. A month after that, a letter arrived from Duncan.

To Angus, Lord of the Isles, from his cousin, Duncan,

King Edward finally managed to appease his barons. He has led an army across the border, marching from Berwick through Roxburgh and Jedburgh to Biggar in the Lowlands. There, King Edward waits. Our spies tell us he thinks King Robert will come out to meet the challenge on the open field. He can wait forever.

The Lowlands are deserted, for we are behind the Highland line and have removed all sustenance in King Edward's path.

King Robert, merciful and wanting to avoid spilling Christian blood, wrote Edward a letter seeking to meet face to face. No warm reply was received. Hence, the king has sent Sir James Douglas with foot soldiers to harass the English troops as they head west.

Sir James, to no one's surprise, relished the task.

The king sends you his congratulations on the birth of your new son. His orders, by separate message, are enclosed herein. My prayers are with you as you confront the enemy.

A separate parchment, folded and impressed with the king's seal, gave Angus a new task.

To Angus, Lord of the Isles, from Robert, King of Scots by the grace of God,

My attempts at peace with King Edward have failed, for I insisted any such discussions must recognize Scotland's independence, which he is loath to do. Thus, I must tell you that our old enemy, John MacDougall, has been named Edward's Admiral of the Western Seas. (Did you once have that title?)

As Edward marches his hungry troops west, toward the coast and the Clyde, I cannot but think he expects MacDougall to meet him at Dumbarton with ships carrying provisions. I ask you to intervene to prevent MacDougall from succeeding.

Sir John Menteith, who was Constable of Dumbarton Castle when he served Longshanks, believes the English may be headed there. It was in English hands but, as we have taken the castle, it can afford them no shelter.

Control of the western seas is yours, Angus, and since you are ever faithful, I know you will not disappoint me.

Angus immediately raised a fleet of twenty-five ships, sufficient for the purpose, for he knew well the Firth of Clyde. Each galley carried galloglass, archers and trained warriors, fully armed.

He kissed Áine goodbye on the shore. "Have no fear, my love. We fight with my men, in my ships and on my seas."

With the Galley of the Isles pennon flying from the mast, Angus and his brother sailed the fleet east from Lagavulin Bay around the southern end of Kintyre and past Arran to the Firth of Clyde. The rain was light as the golden days of early autumn lingered.

Where the Firth met the River Clyde, at a narrow point, Angus set up a blockade, his ships stretching across the waters that led to Dumbarton.

At the first sighting of a ship flying the MacDougall pennon, Angus ordered his archers to the fore. "Ready your bows!" His captains in the other galleys repeated the order to their crews. Crouching on the starboard side, the archers steadied their bows. Behind them, his galloglass stood, axes to hand, while the rest of the crew kept the ship steady.

Angus had no need to slowly announce each command to his archers. They were sufficiently experienced that he could shout the commands in rapid succession. He said them slowly on this occasion to announce to MacDougall his time to decide a course of action was short.

John MacDougall's ships, an even dozen loaded with crates and barrels, slowed, the crews shipping oars. They drifted closer.

When they were thirty feet away, Angus shouted, "Nock!" The order was carried down the line of his ships. In response, in a single move, his archers fixed their arrow shafts to the strings. Tension hung thick in the air as the MacDougall ships drifted closer.

John MacDougall, lightly armored, stood in the lead galley. "Let us pass in the name of Edward, King of England!"

Angus smiled, for he anticipated with pleasure what would be his reply. "In the name of Robert Bruce, King of Scots by God's grace, you shall not pass!"

Before the MacDougalls reached for a weapon, Angus ordered the archers to "mark" and then "draw". Their bows poised to send hundreds of arrows into the MacDougalls' galleys, John MacDougall abruptly ordered his crews to draw back out of range.

Once Angus was satisfied the threat had passed, he ordered his archers to lower their bows. He was prepared to stay as long as it took to turn the English ships around and send them home. As it turned out, he did not have to wait even a day. Hours later, MacDougall turned his ships and rowed out of sight, presumably back to the Firth of Clyde.

"Do you think they have really gone?" asked John.

"They will wait out of sight, hoping we will leave. I will send galleys to either shore to give the crews a respite, but we will not depart until we are certain they have given up. And that will require scouts. Take some men in one of the galleys to the shore and track the MacDougall galleys on foot, staying hidden in the trees. His galleys will not be moving swiftly."

Angus appointed one galley to stand watch further down the Firth so most of his men could spend the night ashore. Food was not a problem; they had brought sufficient provisions.

The next morning, John appeared with the scouts. "They are well away."

When Angus was sure the English king had been deprived of his provisions, he took his fleet home to Islay, where his men celebrated their easy victory.

At the turning of the year, another letter arrived from Duncan. Angus read a few passages to Áine:

King Robert sends his thanks for a job well done. As a result of your blocking the English ships in the west, King Edward had no choice but to retrace his steps east and cross the border back to Berwick, all the while harassed by Jamie Douglas like a midge after bared skin.

With the English in retreat, King Robert conceived a clever plan. Just before Christmas, he sent rumors about that he intended to attack the Isle of Man, which, as you know, is in English hands. In truth, he had no such intention, at least not then. He merely wanted the English ships hovering off Scotland's east coast to leave, which they promptly did, likely heading toward Man. That allowed our ships on the Continent to return and deliver much-needed food and weapons. With the food and supplies we have received from Ireland and the Continent, 'tis a happy Christmas for all.

Our spies tell us King Edward is playing cat and mouse with his nobles as he hides his favorite from those who want his head. I do not suppose that will turn out well for Gaveston but it serves our purposes to keep the English distracted. Lastly, King Robert asks you to watch the ships sailing the Irish Sea.

Dunyvaig Castle, Isle of Islay, late February, 1312

WINTER'S HARSHER WEATHER often brought wind, rain and snow to Islay. February was the coldest month. Áine did not mind, for she treasured the time with Angus the colder weather gave her. Only galleys needed for important observation of enemy-infested waters or the delivery of critical supplies and messages ventured out.

With Alexander fostering in Ulster, and her youngest son, John, often with his nurse, Áine spent part of each day with her daughters. Finvola and Mary, now seven and six, were the delight of their father, scrambling into his lap to shower him with kisses.

When the weather allowed, the young girls joined Áine on her walks along the shore to visit the birds. Fand, her wolfhound, was ever at her side.

Juliana, her sons all in Ireland, either fostering or in the employ of Irish lords as galloglass, often accompanied Áine. "'Tis very cold today," said Juliana, as they broke their fast together, "but it is clear and the sea fairly calm."

Áine nodded. "If we wear our heavy cloaks, we could take the girls on a walk. They would like that. The weather has been miserable for so long, they have rarely been outside the castle."

Áine found Angus and John in the small chamber above the hall where they often met to discuss the business of the lordship. Warmed by the fire, it was a good place to be on a cold morning. "Angus," she said. Both men looked up, two sets of blue eyes focused on her. "I just wanted to let you know, Juliana and I are taking the girls for a walk."

Angus glanced out the window. "Not too bad. Mayhap even sun today."

"We will not be long. The wildflowers have begun to bloom and some of the birds are returning." Seeing the parchments scattered on the table, she asked, "Are you two planning another trip for the king?"

"Aye," said Angus. "He is busy raiding English cattle but food is still needed for his army and he'll want weapons, of course. We will make another trip next month."

"If you need me, I will not be long." She turned to go, gathering her cloak and the girls' warmest mantles. Soon, they left the promontory and were walking along the pebbled shore, Fand following closely, sniffing at the ground.

Mary pointed to the seals lazing on the rocks near shore, absorbing what sun there was. "Look! The seals are out!"

Offshore, black and white gannets soared high into the sky only to dive sharply into the water, fishing. Mary noticed those, too, staring at their amazing feat. But Finvola was looking down at the tide pools with serious intent. She was Áine's starfish and shell finder. Picking up a shell, she held it up for Áine to see. "I shall add this one to my collection," she said, handing it to Áine.

"At their age," said Juliana, "they find joy in the small things. Would that it will always be so."

"I recall being fascinated by starfish and gulls and all the birds that lived on the cliffs at Dunseverick. Life was not so complicated then."

"Much has happened since we were that young," said Juliana. "I never expected to love a Macdonald. I do not regret it, for the years I had with Alexander were wonderful, and the Macdonalds have been good to me."

Áine draped her arm over her sister-in-law's shoulder in comfort. "I never expected to leave Ireland. Like you, I have no regrets. Angus is a good husband. And then there is you, Juliana. We are fortunate to have found a friend in each other."

"Aye, we are. If it were not for you, since I have only sons, I would not know what it is to take a walk with little girls to enchant me."

Áine squeezed Juliana's shoulder. "Someday, you will have grandchildren. Surely some will be girls." She knew Alex's widow was often lonely, even when surrounded by people, for she still loved her husband, taken from her years ago. "Does it sadden you to know your father is dead?"

"Nay. He was never a warm father. How could he love me yet kill my husband and deprive him of the promised dowry?"

Finvola found an unusual rose-colored starfish and shouted for Mary to come see it. Two dark heads bent over the tide pool, examining the find. Fand, curious, came to sniff the creature. The wolfhound's reaction reminded her of Finn, her first wolfhound, who she had loved dearly.

"I'm glad my girls have each other," said Áine. "There may come a time when they will need to rely upon their shared strength."

"They are very protective of young John," said Juliana. "He will have his sisters to look out for him."

Wildflowers were poking their heads up between the rocks, a sure sign that spring was not far off. "Angus is planning a trip to Ireland for the king next month. Why not sail with us? You can visit your sons as I visit Brian. And then we will sail from Ulster to Dumbarton to deliver the supplies."

"I would like that," said Juliana.

And so, the rest of the year passed with the lordship's galleys supplying King Robert with food and weapons from Ireland but neither Angus nor his chiefs being called to battle. Duncan's letters brought news of the king raiding into England, returning with great spoils of cattle and tribute that was exacted when he refrained from slaying men or burning houses.

Dunyvaig Castle, Isle of Islay, early May, 1313

IN MAY OF THE next year, spring bloomed on the Isle, albeit under cloudy skies. Angus stood in front of the castle, the wind driving his hair from his face as he watched three of his galleys sail into Lagavulin Bay. His brother had taken them to Dumbarton with supplies for the king. Angus strode to meet the ships on the beach only to discover when John jumped to the sand, he was not alone.

"Look who insisted I bring him back with me," said John.

"Greetings!" said Angus' golden-haired cousin.

"Duncan!" Angus exclaimed, thrilled to see him. Embracing Duncan, Angus stood back, taking a good look at the man he'd not seen for several years. Like Angus, he was just into his fourth decade. The golden hair was still golden and his green eyes were the same. Only the wrinkles at the corners of his eyes, brought on by years in the sun, had increased. Still, there was something else that was different about his cousin this time. "I sense a change in you. Is it from following the king about these past years?"

"It might be, for though I have been too long away from the sea, I have acquired new skills. King Robert crosses the border to raid English towns, sometimes for cattle, sometimes for tribute to fill his coffers. Of course, I go along." He laughed. "Someone has to account for all that booty."

"Have you come for a visit because you miss us? Or have you taken a wife mayhap? John is to wed a Campbell lass this summer."

"Aye," said Duncan with a glance toward John. "He told me as we sailed. A lucky man. As to your questions, Angus, I miss you all, but I've no wife yet. Though I've my eye on a few of the lasses whose fathers bring them to court. I came to deliver news and a request from the king. He obliged me as I have been away a long time."

"Aye, you have. Áine will be glad to see you. Come, let us get out of the wind. In the hall, I can better play host." The three of them walked toward the promontory. Angus said, "I wrote you about my new son, John, but you have yet to see him."

Duncan gazed toward the castle with the Galley of the Isles pennon fluttering above the battlements. "I have sorely missed this isle—

and your friendship, Angus. You are more my family than my own."

Angus set his hand on Duncan's shoulder. "You have always seemed like a brother to me. My home is yours."

They dined in the great hall that evening. Duncan's homecoming was celebrated by all. Angus allowed the children to join them, which delighted Duncan. "Where is your eldest, Alexander?" he asked.

"Fostering in Ireland," said Áine.

John's nurse led their youngest son, now three, into the hall to meet his cousin.

"Like Alexander at that age, a handsome lad," observed Duncan, "and watched over, I see, by your beautiful daughters. I imagine the offers for their hands are already piling up."

"Aye," said Angus. "I am beating them off."

Áine laughed. "Angus is quite determined to select only the best for his girls, which means they may marry very late."

"'Twould please me if they did," said Angus, agreeing with his wife.

Duncan returned Angus a look of amusement. "No surprise there."

When the children left the hall, Duncan shared all that had happened since his last letter. "The king is pleased with himself. He has a new treaty with Norway they are calling the Treaty of Inverness, which binds the two countries together. It is the second country after France to recognize him as the rightful King of Scots. But there is other news. He has taken Perth."

"That is quite a prize," said Angus.

"Most of the castles have been taken by Sir Edward, Sir James or the king's nephew, Sir Thomas Randolph. But the royal castle of Perth was taken in a rare bit of cunning by the king himself. I was there to experience it.

"When he first attempted a siege last November, it produced no good result. William Oliphant, Earl of Strathern, the Scot who once surrendered Stirling to the English, was in command. He's a brave soldier."

"King Robert could not have been happy about such a failure," said Angus.

"Ah, he was not. But he had a plan. In January, after having watched the castle for more than a month—in the freezing cold, mind you—the king marked the shallowest part of the moat, feigned retreat, and marched us away. A sennight later, we returned at midnight. The king ordered us to strip down to our tunics and carry only our dirks and his rope ladders. In the black of night, he led us across the moat, probing the way with his spear and wading up to his throat in the icy water. It was colder than sea splash over a gunwale in winter. A French knight, who was with us, was astounded the king would take such a risk for what the knight considered 'a wretched hamlet'."

Unsurprised at the daring exploit, for he knew the king, still, Angus had to ask, "Was there no watch to detect your advance?"

"Nay. Believing King Robert had left in defeat, they must have thought the castle and the city walls impregnable. By the time the castle woke, we were over the wall with our rope ladders. King Robert was the second man to accomplish that feat. Just imagine, Angus, me scaling castle walls with the king! In any event, we were soon in possession of the fortress and the town. After that, the garrison surrendered with little fight."

John asked, "What did the king do with the castle?"

"Since the garrison was comprised of Scots, albeit in English pay, the king gave orders against slaughter, but his men were allowed to take booty from the town. He made the Scots nobles, including Oliphant, his prisoners. The rest were allowed to withdraw. He then gave his men orders to raze the castle to the ground along with the city's walls to keep them from English hands."

Angus nodded. "I can see why Rob is pleased."

"Before the walls were down, the king moved on to Dumfries, and I went with him. You might recall that Dumfries Castle was the place King Edward's justiciars were meeting on the morning that Robert Bruce met John Comyn in Greyfriars Church two miles away. As the king reminded me, it was at Dumfries that his brother-in-law, Sir Christopher Seton, was given a traitor's death for defending Bruce when Comyn's uncle attacked him in the church. The irony of it is that the castle has been under the command of Sir Dungal MacDouall for the last two years."

"The former Lord of Galloway the king chased from Scotland?"

"Indeed, the very same. As we arrived, he was out of provisions and his garrison starving, without hope of English intervention. It was a sight to see, Angus, the MacDouall surrendering to King Robert and his brother, Sir Edward—again."

"I would have liked to be there for that, the betrayer of the king's brothers in King Robert's hand. Did he slay him?"

"You would think so for his terrible deed, but nay. He forgave MacDouall and accepted his allegiance rather than alienate his clan. The king's mercy was not appreciated, however, as MacDouall fled to England shortly thereafter."

Angus sighed. "And doubtless plays chess with his ally, John MacDougall, formerly of Lorne."

"Meanwhile," said Duncan, "Sir Edward has been sent to take Stirling Castle while the king sees to another target, one in which he requires your help and the reason he was so willing for me to come to Islay."

"I am intrigued," said Angus. "What is it?"

"The Isle of Man."

Angus grunted. "These are not just rumors put about to distract the English as before?"

Duncan shook his head. "Not this time. King Robert means to take the isle, which he considers of strategic importance."

"He is right in that, for whoever controls Man controls the Irish Sea. Our ancestor, Somerled, knew that well. I cannot speak for the entire isle but Castle Rushen will require many men for it is well defended."

"You will not believe who the English have placed in command of Castle Rushen."

Angus raised his brows expectantly. Rushen had stood in Somerled's time, a strong fortress.

"Dungal MacDouall."

"Good Christ," said Angus. "How many times does King Robert have to expel that man from Scotland?"

"More than a few, apparently. Only think! You will have your own opportunity to see Dungal MacDouall surrender."

Angus found the task at hand to be one of his liking. "When do we sail?"

"The king will come to Dunyvaig a fortnight from now in one of Campbell's galleys."

"That gives me time to add to the fleet," said Angus. "I will send some of my captains to the other isles to gather ships and men. This is one battle that should draw our Irishmen in large numbers."

By the time the king arrived on Islay, it was mid-May. Beached at Lagavulin Bay were thirty galleys, and Dunyvaig was overflowing with armed men and galloglass.

"I see you are prepared, as I expected," said King Robert, who climbed down from the galley that was beached, not in the bay, but on the shingle in front of the castle itself.

"'Tis a great adventure and a worthy cause you have called me to, Rob. I would not miss it!"

It was good to have his friend back at Dunyvaig, and that evening the hall was crowded with Angus' captains as well as the king's contingent. Many of Angus' Irishmen wanted to shake the king's hand.

Over dinner, Angus remarked to his friend, Rob, "It has been seven years since you first came here. 'Twas before you launched your campaign to take back Scotland. Think of all you have accomplished."

King Robert nodded. "I can see God's hand in it all." Looking past Angus to his wife, the king added, "He has answered your prayers, Lady Áine."

"I thank Him for that, my lord, and continue to pray for you. I ask God to give you an independent Scotland to rule and return your wife, daughter and sisters back to your arms."

"Thank you, my lady." Then, looking around the hall, he asked, "Where is your eldest son, Alexander?"

"Fostering in Ulster with my brother, Dermot O'Cahan," said Áine.

"How old is he now?"

"Thirteen," said Angus. "Next year he is due to come home. Lord

Dermot tells us his training goes well. He is good with a sword, as I knew he would be. Beyond that, from scholarly Dermot, he has learned to love reading."

"As you know, I, too, love to read," said the king. "Many a time a good book has entertained my men and me as we waited for a battle to come."

Angus laughed. "I do remember you reading to us a romance about the Saracen knight, a giant of a man named Fierabras."

"One of my favorites," said the king. "Does your son read in French?"

"We all do," said Áine.

"Well then, I shall see he has the poem from me."

"He will treasure it."

The next day, with the sun rising and King Robert and his small band of knights aboard Angus' galley, the fleet sailed to the Isle of Man.

On the 18th of May, they put in at Ramsey on the northeast shore where miles of sandy beaches made an ideal landing place. The king issued orders to the men to fan out over the isle, asserting his authority.

Returning days later, they spoke of meeting little resistance. "We have all but taken the isle," said Sir Neil Campbell.

"There is a priory I would visit on our way to Castle Rushen," the king said to Angus. "'Tis but a half-mile from the harbor at Douglas. The prioress, Lady Catherine, is also the Baroness of Douglas, and an interesting woman."

The next morning, they sailed south to Douglas Bay on the east coast of Man. Leaving most of the men with the beached ships. Angus and the king, together with his inner circle and a contingent of galloglass, walked the half-mile to the monastery of nuns.

The convent was surrounded by beautiful well-tended gardens where the elegant Lady Catherine met them. She invited the king and his inner circle to spend the night at the priory, which they decided to do.

Over a dinner of cod baked in herbed butter sauce, roast beef and very good red wine, Angus learned the prioress' thoughts on the king's claim to the isle.

"My title comes with authority over lands, revenues and people," she said, "but I must still swear fealty to the Lord of Man, which, at the moment, is Dungal MacDouall, late of Galloway. He has not been long on the isle, and I have yet to swear fealty to him." Angus had to wonder if she was delaying the oath for dislike of the man.

"He has not been here long," said King Robert, "because I have just expelled him from Dumfries Castle, another stronghold he held for the English."

The dignified Lady Catherine smiled at hearing the king's words. "Then you will understand when I tell you the only resistance you are likely to encounter on the isle will be from the English at Castle Rushen, which MacDouall commands."

"It will be my pleasure to relieve him of yet another fortress," said King Robert.

A hint of a smile played about Lady Catherine's lips. "Assuming you are successful, my lord, I will be pleased to swear fealty to you."

That brought a smile to King Robert's face, and he lifted his goblet of wine in toast to the baroness.

The next day Angus sailed his fleet the short distance to Castletown at the south end of the isle where he ordered the ships beached in the broad harbor watched over by Castle Rushen.

Built in the Norman fashion, the stone fortress had stood for hundreds of years, ruled by the Norse-Gael Kings of Man, from which the Macdonalds descended. A strong defense against invaders, its limestone keep soared more than seventy feet into the air, and was flanked by towers on each side.

They arrived as the sun was beginning to set, its golden light making the castle's thick walls seem to glow. Around the castle, the moat's waters, refreshed by the nearby river, glistened in the reflected sun.

Angus said to the king, "My ancestor, Somerled, took as his bride the Princess of Man who lived in Castle Rushen. He knew well this castle and later ruled as the King of Man."

"Then our actions reclaiming the isle for Scotland should feel like coming home. Tomorrow, at first light, with the aid of your Islesmen, we lay siege."

"Doubtless, your history with Dungal MacDouall will instruct him on how this will end," said Angus.

"I am trusting that to be the case," replied the king, "for I do not intend to lose."

The next morning, their archers applied themselves, dropping many from the battlements. The siege continued for three weeks before the king's men scaled the walls using his rope ladders. The sound of the iron portcullis being raised marked the king's victory.

Dungal MacDouall, accomplished at escape, managed to slip away in the fighting, headed, some of the captives said, for Ireland.

"This time, we will pursue him," said the king as he ordered some of his knights after MacDouall.

Angus graciously offered some of his galleys and the services of his Irishmen to sail to Ireland. "The crews of these galleys are mostly Irishmen who came to the Isles as a part of Áine's dowry. They know Ireland well."

CHAPTER 27

Dunyvaig Castle, Isle of Islay, July 1313

A MONTH AFTER the king returned to Scotland, Angus received a letter from Duncan that spoke of a dark cloud hanging over the country.

To Angus Og Macdonald, Lord of the Isles, from his cousin, Duncan MacAlasdair,

I have never seen the king in such a rage. And at his brother!

You recall that when the king sailed with you to the Isle of Man, he sent Sir Edward to capture Stirling Castle. Apparently, after expending some effort in that pursuit, Sir Edward concluded the castle's defenses were too strong to overcome and the garrison too well-supplied to starve into submission. (The king doubts the truth of that.) Nevertheless, Sir Philip Mowbray, the castle governor, put forward a challenge: he would surrender the castle if the English army did not arrive to rescue the garrison by Midsummer's Day a year hence.

Without consulting the king, Sir Edward accepted Mowbray's challenge, thus giving the English an excuse for invasion and a year to prepare for a pitched battle on an open field, something King Robert would never have agreed to.

Once his temper cooled, the king ordered all remaining castles held by the English—Linlithgow, Roxburgh and Edinburgh—to be taken and rendered useless. (The king's sister, Mary, was at Roxburgh but apparently has been moved to Newcastle.)

Sir James Douglas and the king's nephew, Thomas Randolph, now Earl of Moray, are ever in competition to please their sire. Hence, they have vowed to take all three and destroy them, all save St. Margaret's Chapel at Edinburgh Castle, which the king has allowed to stand. It grieved the king to give the orders to raze the castles but, as he told us, "They can be rebuilt."

King Robert's orders for "his friend in the Isles" are enclosed.

Inside the parchment was a small folded note bearing the king's seal;

To Angus Og Macdonald, Lord of the Isles, from Robert, King of Scots by the grace of God,

One battle more, Angus, and Scotland will be free. As I am sure Duncan has told you, I did not set this in motion nor did I choose the time, but I will choose the battlefield and train my men to use all to their advantage.

The location will be south of Stirling Castle where the Bannock Burn crosses the old Roman road coming from Falkirk. It is the road the English will be forced to take as they march north.

I will base my camp in the New Park forest, which commands the approach to Stirling from the south.

I expect King Edward will take the full year to gather his forces as he will draw from the Continent, Ireland and Wales. Now that he is reconciled to his barons, I do not doubt he will be able to raise the numbers he seeks, which are tens of thousands. However, I understand the four earls involved in Gaveston's demise—Lancaster, Warwick, Arundel and Surrey—will not accompany Edward to Scotland. My spies in Ulster tell me that my father-in-law, the Red Earl, has been summoned but is reluctant to go. One of his daughters is married to me and another daughter to the Earl of Gloucester, my cousin.

I need you now as never before, Angus, and would have you at my side as I face the English horde. Come with your Islesmen in early June.

If God be with us, we will prevail.

Angus quickly drafted a letter in response.

To Robert, King of Scots, from his friend, Angus Og Macdonald, Lord of the Isles,

Trust me to come. I have been anticipating this day and preparing for a long while. Every man in the Isles and the lands you granted me in Lochaber and Argyll, who can wield a bow, sword, spear or axe, will be summoned.

The English may have greater numbers, but we have an honorable cause and a leader whose brilliance shines in battle. It is my honor to fight at your side.

My lady and I hold fast to this truth: God is able to deliver both you and Scotland.

In August, Angus called a meeting of the Council of the Isles at Finlaggan. He invited more than just the members of the Council; he invited all the chiefs and senior men and their families, as well as Alan, Bishop of the Isles.

For a fortnight, his wife and the other leading women worked hard to assure all was made ready to receive them in that ancient meeting place. The Council had not met since Angus was pronounced Lord of the Isles in the year Alex was murdered. All were keenly aware this next gathering would be significant.

Under sun-filled skies, tents crowded the banks of the loch and brightly colored banners waved in the summer breeze. On the large isle in the loch, the atmosphere was one of gaiety, as the families had come, expecting much feasting and entertainment with bards, dancers and contests. Yet a serious undertone permeated all. Given the uncertainty of the upcoming battle, it might be the last time some would gather here.

The Council and others invited crowded into the chamber on the smaller Council Isle in the loch. After the bishop prayed for them, asking for God's guidance and blessing, Angus rose.

"We have been at war," he told them. "Now we prepare for the battle that will decide Scotland's fate. Fortunately, we have time. But then, so do the English."

Angus knew every man whose face looked back at him in somber acceptance of this truth. Some he had known since he was a lad, others for more than a decade. In years past, he had visited them in their castles and strongholds. He knew their wives and children.

He began by explaining all that had happened: King Robert's many successes; his strategy in taking the last remaining castles; and the challenge concerning Stirling, held apart as a great prize.

Then he told them of the battle they would face in the coming year.

"This will not be a battle of stealth or quick strikes from the woods. Nor will it be a battle waged from our galleys. This will be a pitched battle fought on an open field with mounted English knights and thousands of well-armed soldiers and archers.

"I have done what I can to prepare the Isles, adding fourteen hundred Irishmen to our ranks, providing galloglass to help train your warriors, assuring sufficient weapons for our armories and provisions for our castles and galleys to carry our fighting men across the sea."

Heads nodded as they remembered Angus' visits and those of his galloglass to ready an army for the Isles.

"We must continue as we have begun. I will prepare my own men as you must prepare yours. When you leave here, on every hill before every castle, prepare the *Crann Tara*, the fiery cross, ready to be lit when you see the signal fire closest to you. I will light the fire from Dunyvaig. Those on Jura will see it first.

"Watch for the fire in May of next year. When you see the flaming signal, light your own fire, sending the word north. Then sail quickly to me at Dunyvaig. We must reach King Robert in early June with provisions for a month."

Angus' voice rose with his next words.

"I am not asking for your heirs if you think it best they remain behind. I am asking for men who are free to fight—every man who can wield a bow, sword, spear or axe. This is the battle that will see our king reigns over a Scotland free of English oppression." His voice nearly a shout, he ended, "We fight for King Robert Bruce and Scotland's independence!"

The men jumped to their feet and a great roar rose into the air. Drawing his sword and holding it high, the silver-haired Malcolm Macleod shouted, "For King Robert and Scotland!"

The loud cheer was repeated again and again until the chamber walls reverberated with the sound.

Angus was the last to leave the Council building. Flanked by Duncan and John, he crossed the causeway to the larger isle where Áine waited, her expression anxious. "I heard the shouts. We all did." She glanced first at Duncan and John and then at Angus, her brown eyes inquiring. "It went well?"

Excitement still thrummed in Angus' chest. "Oh, aye. We are united as never before. Next May, I will light the fiery cross and they will come to Lagavulin Bay with thousands of men, including your Irishmen."

Duncan winked at Áine, and John bid her good day as the two men walked ahead.

"Angus," Áine said, as she took his arm and they proceeded forward, "Alexander is due to return to us next spring from his fostering."

"Aye. I have not forgotten."

"If he is here, he will want to go with you. He will be nearly fourteen and will consider himself a man."

"Aye. I have thought of that also." Angus had pondered what he should do concerning his eldest son and heir. At fourteen, Angus had fought with his father, Angus Mor, but the battle to come would be different, and Angus was not sure Alexander would be ready. Other chiefs would have the same concern, which is why he allowed them to leave their heirs behind.

"Is your main objective to assure King Robert lives to enjoy his victory or, if victory be denied him, to live to fight another day?"

"Aye. You have summarized well."

"That being the case, it occurs to me that if Alexander is with you, untested in such battles as Brian is, you will be distracted and concerned with preserving his life. But if he were to remain in Ireland for a few months longer, you would be free to think only of the king."

"My astute wife," said Angus, smiling down at her. "I cannot hold back Duncan or John. They have fought too long for King Robert and would not be denied this chance to fight for him again. Brian, too, will want to go. Nay, he will insist upon it. Should we not return, there are those who would stand with young Alexander until he is ready to assume the lordship."

Áine looked up, startled. "You will not fail to return, my love. I have asked God for your life and the life of the king. He faces a Goliath but then so did young David. He trusted God and God gave him the victory. I believe it will be the same with King Robert."

Angus stopped and turned to his wife. Her ivory skin glowed in the morning sun. "That is my hope as well."

Edward of England's foot soldiers and cavalry possessed skills that were honed in the course of many battles, whereas the Scots would have a much smaller force and only light cavalry, who were untested in pitched battles. Had King Robert not confirmed it? But Angus would not speak of that to Áine. It would only cause her to worry. Instead, he would trust in her prayers.

"And Brian?" he asked. "You are content with my thought to take him?"

She appeared to think for a moment. "You must take him, and I will ask God to protect him."

"Very well. In any event," he said, "I agree that Alexander will remain in Ireland until the end of next summer."

She looked up at him. "And you will tell him it is your idea that he do so?"

Angus chuckled, for it had become Áine's way to hide her wisdom behind his words. "Of course, my love."

As the year turned and spring arrived, a letter came from Duncan with news.

To Angus Og Macdonald, Lord of the Isles, from his cousin, Duncan

MacAlasdair,

Our spies tell us that Edward has summoned thousands of knights, more than twenty thousand foot soldiers and three thousand archers, including those from Wales. How many will heed the call is unknown. The English force is to muster by the 10th of June at Berwick. The pretext, of course, is the relief of Stirling's garrison, but the real motive is to conquer Scotland for the English Crown.

The castles that remained in English hands have been taken. Roxburgh was the first, taken in a daring night attack where Douglas concealed his men in black cloaks among a herd of cows and fooled the watch. The men were over the walls before they were discovered. Randolph, frustrated at not finding a way into Edinburgh, discovered a secret way in known only to a few, and so gained entrance. Linlithgow was taken by a farmer named Bunnock. Ordered by the English constable to bring hay to the castle, he decided to bring more—eight well-armed Scots, hidden beneath the hay. He has been well rewarded!

The king has made a few changes in title: Sir Edward has been made Earl of Carrick, and the king's nephew, Sir Thomas Randolph, Earl of Moray, has been named Lord of the Isle of Man. (Disappointing, I know, that such a prize did not go to you, but the king says he has more to give you.)

When you come to Stirling in June, King Robert will be training schiltrons south of the castle near Bannock Burn, for that is how he intends to fight. I will be there waiting, eager to join your ranks, for I have determined to fight with you and John and the Islesmen of which I am one.

Dunyvaig Castle, Isle of Islay, early June 1314

THE GALLEYS BEGAN to arrive in late May, having come in response to the fiery cross first lit by Angus and carried north, lighting the night sky above every castle from Islay to Lewis.

This afternoon, beneath an unclouded sky, Angus stood on the battlements of Dunyvaig, looking into Lagavulin Bay where nearly a hundred ships were beached on the shore in rows like a great haul of fish, waiting to be counted. Their colorful pennons waved in the breeze, and his heart raced to see it. *So many have come!*

The chiefs arrived at the castle and Angus welcomed them, thanking them for their loyalty and faithfulness. Chiefs who had long stood by the Macdonalds were among them—the Macleods, MacNeils, MacMillans, Macduffies, and Macleans. Many had sailed in new galleys, built at Angus' urging, bringing not only their own men but a thousand of his Irishmen, including the Munroes, MacPhersons and, importantly, the MacBeth physicians.

Five thousand men were camped on the shores of Islay, waiting to sail on the morrow.

As he watched the pennons wafting in the summer breeze, the end of the old prophecy came to his mind. *Two chiefs will die before a new one rises with a new king. Only then will Scotland know peace.* He had told Áine that he was the new chief and Rob was the new king. Of that, he was certain. But would they both live to see that peace? Certainly King Robert must live for there to be peace in an independent Scotland, but whether Angus would be there to see it was unclear. *God, grant I might live to see the peace that is coming.*

"So this is where you are!" said Áine, out of breath from climbing the stairs. "I have been looking for you."

He turned to see his wife, her long dark hair blowing behind her. She was as beautiful as the first day he had seen her in her father's castle. "I wanted to get a view of all the galleys. Look, Áine," he said, pointing, "never before have so many ships and so many Islesmen prepared to sail to Scotland under the Lord of the Isles banner. Is it not grand?"

She came to his side and peered over the parapet. "'Tis very grand. Alexander will be disappointed not to have seen this. Our daughters are fair impressed."

Angus nodded. "Aye, but we can take comfort in the knowledge Alexander will live to see another day and another fleet."

She laid her head on his shoulder and wrapped her arms around his waist. "Come back to me, Angus. I love you."

He drew her close and kissed her. "And I you, my love."

They clung to each other for a long moment. Angus drew

strength from her warmth, grateful to God she was in his life. Kissing the top of her head, he asked, "Why were you looking for me?"

"I came to let you know all is ready for the chiefs' dinner and suggest you wear the new surcoat I made you. The black galley flying a red pennon on gold cloth announces to all who you are. If you are captured, it will save your life for the Lord of the Isles will bring a large ransom."

"Very practical," he said with a teasing smile. "I will wear it. l am looking forward to the dinner, for I would have the chiefs know I am grateful to them. Besides, the next time we gather, there may be fewer of us in attendance."

At the dinner that followed, all in the hall were merry, toasting each other and telling tales of past battles. While Christina MacRuairi did not come herself this time, she sent a contingent of three hundred led by her half-brother, Ruairi MacRuairi, who was sworn to King Robert.

As the meal drew to a close, the notes of the harp stilled, and the bard finished his poem, a tribute to the men of the Isles. All were in a contemplative mood.

Angus rose to speak. "I am more grateful than you can know that so many of you have come. King Robert will be much encouraged." The chiefs listened intently as he continued. "Tomorrow, we sail at daybreak for the Firth of Clyde and then up the River Clyde where we will leave our galleys and head inland toward Stirling.

"In a sennight's time, we should arrive at the king's camp. I understand our spearmen will fight in schiltrons organized by the king. Those of us who carry sparth axes are not likely to wield a spear, but the king will advise us once we are there. Before you depart tonight for your bed, I have asked Alan, Bishop of the Isles, to pray for us that God may protect us and bring us home. Tomorrow, before we sail, he will pray with the men."

The tonsured bishop, wearing a plain cassock, came to stand before the chiefs. All bowed their heads as he prayed. Some of the chiefs and some of the warriors outside might be going home to Heaven rather than returning to the Isles, for death, too, was a part of life. Every warrior had to be prepared to face it.

Angus made love to Áine that night, knowing it might be the last time. He treasured her body, wanting to leave his beloved wife with a memory for the nights, however many there would be, when she would sleep alone.

On the shore the next morning, Bishop Alan prayed for the men who kneeled before him. Then, Angus kissed Áine and their children goodbye and, with his brother and Brian O'Neill at his side, turned toward his galley.

From behind him, Áine cried out. "Wait! I nearly forgot!" Handing him a sealed note, she said, "For King Robert."

Angus had no need to read it, but he was curious. "What is it?"

"Encouragement."

"From the life of King David?"

She smiled, tears welling in her eyes. "Just so."

With shouts of "Godspeed" from all who stood on the shore, the men took to the oars. Once in the sea, they shipped oars and raised the sails. To see so many galleys with colorful pennons flying from the masts was a grand sight that Angus knew he would remember for as long as he lived.

"My heart beats faster looking at all the galleys behind us," said John.

"Aye," replied Angus. "I do not expect to see such a sight again in my lifetime."

They sailed around the southern tip of Kintyre and into the Firth of Clyde. As the Firth narrowed to the River Clyde they followed it past Dumbarton.

Angus gave the order to lower the sail as they headed for shore. The men again took to the oars and soon beached the ships on the riverbank just as a light rain began to fall.

Angus knew they could reach the woods south of Stirling in one day if they marched straight through, but it would be a very long day and the men had already rowed much. In consultation with his chiefs, he decided to camp at the halfway point where they could seek shelter from the intermittent rain.

Two days later at midday, they arrived at the Torwood forest south of the Bannock Burn to find thousands of armed men overflowing the ground. Many carried long spears.

"From the activity," said John, "they appear to be training the schiltrons."

"With your permission," said Brian, "I would seek out Sir Edward."

Angus knew of Brian's friendships with the king's brother and his men, forged in their trip to Ulster and their fight in Galloway. "Aye, but come see me before bedding down for the night."

Brian eagerly nodded and left them.

Asking his captains to wait, Angus strode forward to greet King Robert, standing at the edge of the woods, surveying all. Behind Angus was his galloglass guard, their six-foot sparth axes to hand. The men standing around the king drew back at their approach, for Angus' guards were men of great strength and stature, bristling with weapons, reminding all of their reputation as those who charged the enemy with extreme aggression.

The king turned with a wide smile for Angus. "Here is a welcome sight." To the others, he said, "Now that the Lord of the Isles has finally come, our army is complete."

Douglas, who stood a short distance from the king, let his gaze pass over Angus and his guards. "I see giants again walk among us."

Angus chuckled. "Is not the cunning Black Douglas a giant among the king's men though he be of lesser height? So feared by the English that mothers tell their children to obey else the Black Douglas will get them?"

The men standing around the king laughed at Angus' words. "Aye, those be the words," said Sir Robert Boyd.

The king nodded. "If Wallace had such men as your galloglass at Falkirk, he would have won."

"Aye," said Angus. "I have brought them, but I have brought more. The Isles adds five thousand to your army, my lord."

The king looked behind Angus where his thousands of Islesmen stretched through the forest of Torwood far to the southwest. "More than any single faction and an answer to prayer."

Angus handed his friend Áine's sealed message. "When you get time."

"What is this?" asked the king.

"A message from my lady to encourage you."

King Robert broke the seal and read. When he finished, he looked up. There were tears in his eyes as he handed the message back to Angus. "You should read it."

Angus did as the king suggested, for he could see it was not long.

To Robert, King of Scots, from Áine O'Cahan, wife of Lord Angus Og Macdonald and Lady of the Isles,

My lord, as the battle for Scotland's freedom approaches, I remind you that King David was fearless, always leading the charge, raising his sword and returning with victory. Such a king are you. But one battle was different—Baalperazim. David went there, directed by the Lord, and defeated the enemy. After his victory, David said, "The Lord hath broken forth upon mine enemies, as the breakthrough of waters."

That is my prayer for you, my lord, that God will, like a flood of waters that breaks over the banks, overflow your enemies, giving you a great victory, for you have trusted Him.

When Angus finished, he gave the message back to the king who tucked it into his belt. "My lady is a remarkable woman."

"Indeed," said the king. "As for your men, have them set up camp in the New Park woods." He pointed ahead and to the left where there was a large forest of trees. "It was a hunting ground used by King Alexander and serves well to hide our forces and give them shade from the hot sun. It is about a mile from north to south and two miles from east to west."

Angus so advised his captains who greeted the king before setting out for New Park with Angus' brother and his guard. "I'll join you shortly."

Left alone with Angus, King Robert said, "My brother, Edward, is just training his schiltron." He gestured to an area of cleared land between Torwood and New Park, where a great crowd of spearmen were forming a square with their spears in layers pointed outward.

Angus scanned the warriors comprising the schiltron. The men were not altogether uniform in their appearance. While most wore padded jackets, only some overlaid them with mail and mail coifs, as Angus wore. On their heads, an occasional helmet or a bascinet reflected the sun. A rare few had gloves of plate; most wore leather gloves. In addition to the twelve foot iron-tipped spears, at their belts they carried a sword, small axe or dagger, or all three. "You would use schiltrons as Wallace did at Falkirk?" Angus was thinking they did not work so well for the warrior they all revered.

"Not exactly. These are not merely defensive and stationary as were the circular schiltrons Wallace used. Formed into a square, these will be offensive weapons, moving to attack as one. Knowing the English, King Edward will lead with his mounted knights. I am told there will be some three thousand. The schiltrons will greet them like a spear-tipped hedgehog."

Angus tried to envision the knights encountering so many spearmen locked in a tight formation.

"It is my hope to force them into the Carse," the king said, pointing to the flat, boggy area to the east of where they stood. "'Tis bounded by the Bannock Burn, the Pelstream Burn and the River Forth. Water from the hills drains into the Carse leaving pools of water even on hot days like today."

From where they stood, Angus looked across the old Roman road to the flood plain of the River Forth, the area the king called the Carse.

"Once there," the king continued, "the knights and mounted forces will be crowded together with no room to move. All the while, King Edward's foot soldiers and archers will be pressing them from behind. If our men hold together as they have been trained, the knights will not get past their spears."

"You are a knight yet you will fight on foot?"

"I have a small cavalry of five hundred light horse under the Marischal, Sir Robert Keith. I will hold them in reserve, but the rest of us will be on foot, except for Jamie Douglas who periodically rides out with some of his men on garrons acting as scouts to watch for the English. Even he will eventually lead a schiltron on foot. If we try to fight on horseback, when the enemy is stronger and better horsed, we will be in great danger. On foot, we have the advantage in the woodlands. The English knights will be disadvantaged. Attempting to move, the streams will hem them in, hopefully throwing them into confusion and into our schiltrons. At least, that is my plan."

"How will you force them into the Carse?"

"I have a few impediments in mind to keep them from any other course. In addition to those, after their long march from Falkirk, they will be wanting water for their horses and the Carse will be invitingly empty and flat."

Angus smiled at the strategy of his friend. "You have planned well, Rob."

"I have had a year to do so. I know how the English fight, having trained and fought with them. And I know this ground like the back of my hand. We will be outnumbered by two, mayhap three to one, so we must be clever. If all goes well, the land itself will fight for us."

"God, too, if you believe in Áine's prayer."

The king smiled as he stared ahead, looking east toward the Carse, mayhap seeing the great English force that would come against them. "I do."

"Where would you have me and my men?"

"You and your galloglass will be in the center of my schiltron, a reserve of the best fighters I will hold until the end. Around you will be the men of Carrick and Argyll as well as some of your Islesmen who carry spears. We may use others of your spearmen to fill in the other schiltrons. They drill daily so there is time for you to practice."

"That sounds fine. I will advise my chiefs." He started to walk away.

"Oh, Angus."

"Aye?" He turned back with raised brows.

"You will not be surprised to learn there are Scots who will fight with the English—the MacDougalls, the MacNabs and the Red Comyn's son, John."

"Aye. I expected that."

"However, you may not know that among the men of Argyll loyal to me there are those from Glen Coe. One of them is an Iain MacDonald, who has the look of you. Fights a bit like you, too," he added with a smile. "The warriors from Glen Coe will be under your command as well as your Islesmen."

Angus thanked the king for his confidence in him. With his mind reeling to think his son by Sorcha would fight among his warriors, he turned for the New Park woods where his men were setting up camp. It was time he had a conversation with this son of his.

Just before he slipped among the trees, he gazed north to see Stirling Castle in the distance. Perched high on a volcanic rock, the brooding fortress had guarded the lowest crossing point of the River Forth for more than two centuries. It was standing at the time Somerled reigned as King of the Isles.

Angus entered the woods, welcoming the shade the trees provided. Tents were everywhere like mushrooms that had sprouted overnight. He walked toward a ring of tents standing around a clearing where servants and squires were busy attending to their duties. Spotting his brother, he crossed to where John was speaking to one of the men.

The Isleman with whom John spoke inclined his head to Angus and begged his leave.

Once he had gone, John said, "I have placed your tent to the right of the king's, as directed. Together with the tents of Sir Edward, Sir James, the young Walter Stewart and Sir Thomas," he said gesturing, "they form a circle. Our chiefs are setting up their tents behind yours, and the king's army camps around all."

Angus nodded, content with the arrangement. "Let the chiefs know our men will have this afternoon to rest and acquaint themselves with the terrain. Tomorrow, we train with the schiltrons." As John turned to leave, Angus called him back. "Can you find out where the men of Glen Coe are camped?"

"Of course."

That evening, it was still daylight when Angus joined the king's inner circle in his tent. King Robert explained they were to fight in four divisions, each forming a schiltron. Using two parchments, the king showed them how the positioning of the schiltrons might change.

"Randolph will lead the vanguard, composed of men from Ross

and Moray. You will need to guard the way to Stirling, Thomas, not allowing any English to pass. My brother will lead the men from Buchan, Mar, Angus and Galloway. Because you have more experience, Jamie, I have paired you with your cousin, Walter Stewart. You two will lead the men from the borders." The king's gaze moved over his commanders, who nodded their acceptance. "My own division," said King Robert, "will take the rear, positioned on higher ground so that I can view all. It will be composed of men from Carrick, the Lowlands, Argyll and the Isles, to be led by Angus. Some of Angus' spearmen will be added to the smaller schiltrons."

"My light horse," said Sir Robert Keith, the Marischal, "is at your disposal, my lord."

"I will hold you in reserve against a need that may arise in battle," said the king.

Douglas studied the king's drawing. "We have the archers from Ettrick Forest but they do not carry the longbows of the Welsh archers."

"We will make do with what we have," said the king. "It will be enough."

Angus had no questions, having been told of the king's plans earlier in the day, but it was good to see how the king would place the schiltrons. He thought it wise for the king to pair Douglas with the young Stewart, the eldest son of James Stewart, the High Steward, who had been a signatory to the Turnberry Band. After the death of his father, Walter inherited the position of the Steward.

"As the English knights approach from the Roman road," interjected the king, pointing to his map, "they will pass through the Torwood and cross the Bannock Burn that flows between the forest of Torwood and the woods of the New Park. As they descend the burn's steep bank, they will want to spread out. We cannot allow that to happen."

"How do you intend to prevent it?" asked the king's brother.

"Tomorrow, we will begin digging trenches and pits on either side of the road, across what will be their position, to break up any mounted charge. We used it at Loudoun Hill on a smaller scale. Hopefully, Aymer de Valence, Earl of Pembroke, will not recognize the tactic. As I envision them, the pits will be a foot in diameter and as deep as a man's knee with a spiked iron caltrop at the bottom. All will be camouflaged by sod and grass, so that it will appear as it was before. Beneath the surface all along this way," he said, pointing, "will be a honeycomb of traps. The knights will not see them until they are stumbling into the pits."

"Clever," said Angus.

After the meeting with the king, Angus went to the Glen Coe tents that John had pointed out to him. There he called for the young Iain MacDonald and took him aside. "I am your father, Iain, but then I assume you know that." The blue eyes that looked back at him were the same as those of his brothers. 'Tis clear to me you are my son."

The young man smiled. "I did know and was hoping to see you here, but I also know King Robert has many duties for you. All speak of your friendship with the king."

"No duty so important I could not make time to greet my son. I should have done so earlier and not been content to remain in the background of your life."

"I have much to thank you for, Father: my fostering, my training as a warrior with that galloglass you sent me, and for Glen Coe. I never thought to have such a prize."

Angus smiled at hearing his son refer to him as Father. "I was pleased to make you Lord of Glen Coe. It is a rich glen with much beauty. Lead your people with honor and wisdom and know that you will always have an ally in me."

"I will."

"How is your mother?"

"She is well and speaks often of you, reminding me of all you have accomplished. I am proud that my father is Lord of the Isles."

It warmed Angus' heart to hear it. "I am told you are to fight in the king's schiltron where I and my Islesmen will be. Keep your men close to mine. I do not wish to lose you now that we are finally acquainted."

"I will do all you ask, Father."

Angus offered his hand and the young man grasped his forearm. "I know you will, Son."

They parted and Angus returned to his tent much in thought. Duncan was waiting for him along with Brian. He was glad to see Duncan after so long. "You look well, Cousin."

"And so I am. Assuming I survive this battle, I believe I have finally found a lass willing to marry me and make Saddell home."

Angus was pleased. "That is a bit of good work."

Brian spoke up then. "Father, might I join Sir Edward's men and fight in his schiltron?"

Angus studied the face of his stepson. At twenty-three, he was a man grown, of noble Irish lineage and a fine warrior. "I would not stand in your way if that be your choice. Is Sir Edward willing?"

"Aye, he has said so, if you agree."

"Then go with my blessing, and do all the king's brother orders that you may live and return to us."

With a wide smile and his red hair and dark blue eyes shining in the candlelight, Brian said, "Thank you!" and was gone.

A feeling of sadness came over Angus as he turned to Duncan. "I know it is inevitable he will pursue his own future, but I have raised him from a small lad and regret I cannot protect him in this battle we face. Since we are the rearguard, Brian is likely to see more action in Sir Edward's schiltron than we will see in ours."

"Do not worry, Angus. Sir Edward says Brian is one of his best."

"Aye, and I take heart from the knowledge Brian has fought with him before." Shrugging off his discomfort, Angus said, "The king informed me my natural son, Iain of Glen Coe, will be fighting in our schiltron."

"Does it please you?"

"Aye. At least I can protect him better there." Turning to another subject, he said, "I suppose you know of the king's plans for trenches and pits to be dug impairing the progress of King Edward's knights?"

"I do, and I think 'tis a good measure to frustrate a charge by the English vanguard. All will participate in digging the pits, even the king. It will take thousands of us to see the job done."

"It would seem so," said Angus. "As for the rest of the king's plans, I can fault nothing."

In the days that followed, they prepared a honeycomb of trenches and pits, laid with caltrops and then disguised, though all in King Robert's army knew where they were.

The schiltrons were exercised and inspected every day by the king. Angus was amazed at the speed at which they could move when all faced forward and ran ahead. Stationary, the men in the front would kneel, digging the end of their spears in the ground and the layers of men above them pointed their spears out, making a strong iron-tipped wall. Moving, they picked up the spears and ran quickly forward.

From reports the king had in May, they knew King Edward had assembled his army across the border at Berwick. In the middle of June, more reports flooded in as the English began their march into Scotland. The mounted knights were, as King Robert expected, in the vanguard, followed by the slower-moving foot soldiers accompanied by flocks of sheep and cattle that would be food for the troops, and carts carrying baggage and fodder. The baggage train alone was said to extend for two miles.

Hearing from their scouts that the English were coming west, taking the old Roman road, King Robert positioned his army just inside the New Park.

Randolph, Earl of Moray, with the vanguard, would be north of the king's division and south of the nearby St. Ninian's Kirk. His would be the closest division to Stirling Castle. Edward Bruce's division, in which Brian now fought, was positioned next to the Roman road and behind the pits. Douglas' division was between Edward Bruce's and Randolph's. King Robert's own division would be on the high ground at the entry to the New Park. Keith and his light horse were behind and to the right of the king. Finally, circling the New Park, the king posted a line of Ettrick archers.

"In this way," said the king, pointing to the map, "we can oppose the English advance, whether it comes from the front or the flank."

In his own division, the king could look down upon the Carse and guard the road. Angus, beside him, had a view of all.

They were ready. They had only to wait.

CHAPTER 28

The New Park forest, south of Stirling Castle, 23rd June 1314

AFTER A RESTLESS night's sleep, Angus woke at daybreak to the sounds of men stirring around him and the chorus of bird song from the trees above.

Still in the positions the king had assigned them the previous day, the men were soon called to Mass, celebrated by Maurice, Abbot of Inchaffray, and Bishop Lamberton. Clothed in dark robes, they walked between the divisions, the Abbot of Inchaffray holding high a large cross.

After Mass, King Robert dismissed those who would not be fighting, the camp followers, servants, cooks and clergy he dubbed "the small folk". He directed them to Coxet Hill east of the New Park where they could observe but be safe from the battle to come.

Sitting atop a gray palfrey, his helmet circled with a gold crown, the king rode back and forth in front of the lines, addressing the army. "We will observe the vigil of St. John as a solemn fast." All knew this meant bread and water but no one complained. They wanted God on their side. In a loud voice, the king proclaimed, "We are here to win

Scotland's freedom, not just defend Stirling Castle. If you do not come to conquer or to die, you should quit the field."

Not a man moved; not a word was uttered.

Angus and his chiefs raised their swords and shouted the words they had declared at Finlaggan. "For King Robert and Scotland!" They were immediately joined by the rest of his Islesmen and then by thousands of their fellow warriors, making clear to the king they were ready for battle.

As the sun rose over the hills, tidings came of the approach of the English army from Falkirk, ten miles away, where they had camped the night before. King Robert dispatched Keith and Douglas to lead a mounted patrol to watch for their arrival.

The sun had reached its zenith when the two knights came galloping back to report to the king, still sitting his palfrey. Angus, Thomas Randolph, Gilbert Haye, Neil Campbell and the king's brother stepped out of their divisions to approach the king and the two returning from patrol.

"Sire," said Keith. "A forest of pennons fills the horizon. The sight took my breath away. The sun reflecting from their weapons and armor was like a river of silver flowing into Scotland."

"They are formed into ten divisions," said Douglas, "thousands in each with banners of their knights going on for miles. We recognized some of the commanders. Gilbert de Clare, Earl of Gloucester, and Humphrey de Bohun, Earl of Hereford, appear to be jointly leading the vanguard of hundreds of knights in heavy armor. Hereford's nephew, Henry de Bohun rode close by his side."

The king frowned. "Gloucester is my kinsman and Hereford once my friend. If King Edward has given them a shared command of the van, he has made a grave error. For the sake of his nephew, he has undermined Hereford, the Constable and rightful leader."

No one commented on that. They all knew King Edward rewarded his favorites, no matter the dictates of military custom.

"The English army is accompanied by thousands of Welsh archers armed with longbows," said Keith.

The king faced the two, sitting on their horses across from him, his countenance stern. "Say nothing of this to the men. Such a report will only cause alarm." As if to add emphasis, he looked down at the small group standing beneath him. "Rather, tell them the English troops came on in great disorder, tired from their long march in the hot sun."

Angus agreed with this strategy. The army needed to maintain their confidence. Moreover, the army would believe it. Already, the sun had heated his mail and helmet, making him glad the king had positioned them in the New Park where the trees provided shade.

"That much is true," said Douglas. "The vanguard presses forward eagerly but the army behind them is strung out over many miles and straggling. In truth, the main army appeared to be halted while the van moved on."

Thus informed, Angus and the others returned to their schiltrons. In the rearguard, Angus gave a report, using the king's words. Duncan and John might look beyond the words to Angus' concern but they said nothing.

Scanning the men in the large schiltron, Angus searched for the young man the king had said resembled him in appearance and spotted one not far away with copper-tinged light brown hair whose stature was that of a Macdonald. Determined to keep an eye on him, Angus had asked Duncan and John the night before to do what they could to protect the lad when their division was released into the fight.

Meantime, the English vanguard under the Earls of Gloucester and Hereford emerged from the Torwood, followed by hundreds of knights and mounted men-at-arms. The young Earl of Gloucester, in his bright yellow surcoat with red chevrons, dashed through the Bannock Burn and advanced on the New Park.

Angus watched as the young earl and the English knights encountered the covered pits on either side of the road and were thrown into great disarray. Despite these difficulties, the English knights pressed on, their advance covered by a cloud of Welsh archers, who made their way where the heavy cavalry could not pass.

Sir Edward's schiltron was ready to receive them, his spearmen in staggered lines forming an impenetrable wall of steel-tipped shafts. Angus, spotting Brian's red hair beneath his helmet, prayed Edward's division would hold.

Suddenly, a detachment of English knights, numbering in the hundreds, broke off from the main group and circled around the Scottish line, skirting the woods where Randolph was posted. "Look!" Angus shouted to the king, pointing to the horsemen riding near the Forth beyond the Bannock Burn. "They are heading to Stirling Castle!"

"I see it," said the king and rode to his nephew, the Earl of Moray, shouting, "Randolph! Look! A rose has fallen from your chaplet! Thoughtless man. You have permitted Robert Clifford and Henry de Beaumont to pass!"

Randolph must have been horrified at failing to perceive what he had been warned about by the king the day before. He rushed his foot soldiers down to the path to block Clifford and de Beaumont. A terrible fight ensued with the English horsemen attempting to get past the spears of Randolph's schiltron.

Beaumont's hundreds of lances circled Randolph's schiltron. Some foolishly galloped onto the spears. At least one knight was killed and one unhorsed and taken. Under so vigorous an attack, the schiltron appeared hard-pressed to hold the formation.

Douglas, still on horseback from the morning's foray, asked King Robert's permission to go to the assistance of Randolph, but his request was refused. "You shall not move," said the king. "Let Randolph free himself as he may. I will not alter my order of battle, nor lose my vantage of ground."

"My lord!" cried Douglas, as the heavily-armed English knights closed in on Randolph's foot soldiers, "I cannot stand by and see Randolph perish when I can give him help! By your leave, I must go to his aid!"

King Robert, observing the worsening conditions, nodded his consent. "Very well, Jamie, go."

Douglas hurried off. As he and his schiltron moved nearer to Randolph, the English knights fell into confusion, some galloped off while horses rushed away riderless. The Scots held their lines amidst their dead enemies. The English knights that still remained threw swords, maces and knives at Randolph's spearmen in apparent frustration, but the hedge of steel remained unbroken.

"Halt!" Douglas shouted to his men. "Randolph has won, and we will not lessen their glory by seeking to share it."

In the hot sun, a mist of dust and heat brooded over the battlefield.

The English detachment that had attempted Stirling broke in two. Half rode for the castle and the remainder, including Clifford, returned to the main army.

Meanwhile, the English army moved out of the Torwood. Ahead of them rode the vanguard, led by Gloucester and Hereford, moving into the New Park. They were near enough to see King Robert, with his yellow surcoat bearing the rampant red lion and gold crown encircling his helmet, riding his palfrey along the front of the lines, giving last minute orders to oppose the English advance.

A knight riding ahead of the English van paused, his focus on the king. The knight wore full armor and rode a powerful destrier. Facing the king, his shield at the ready, he lowered his lance and dropped his visor, as if preparing to charge.

The men around Angus gasped in horror to see the king threatened, for he was mounted to command infantry not to defend a heavy cavalry charge. He wore only light armor and carried no weapons save a short axe.

Fearless, King Robert rode out to meet the eager knight.

Angus held his breath though he did not despair. *This must be a young knight to challenge the king hailed as one of the best knights in all of Christendom.* "Who is that knight?" he asked Sir Neil Campbell who stood with the men of Argyll in the king's division.

"'Tis Hereford's nephew, Sir Henry de Bohun. Fool that he is to challenge the champion of the Scots in single combat."

"The king risks much to allow this," put in Sir Gilbert Haye, standing by Angus.

It was too late to shout an objection. Bohun thundered toward the king, his lance poised to strike.

As they closed, Bruce swerved his agile palfrey aside to avoid the lance. It was a near miss but a miss all the same. Turning, the king stood in his stirrups, raised his axe and struck the knight with a powerful blow. The blade cleaved through his helmet to lodge deep in his skull, shattering the axe shaft.

De Bohun crashed from the saddle, dead before he hit the ground.

Cheers rose from the Scots army. Angus' heart thrilled at the king's courage and skill. Had Rob failed, Scotland's hopes would have been dashed. Instead, he had triumphed and, Scots being Scots, the men took it as an auspicious omen. How could they not fight to the death when their king, alone with only an axe, had been willing to do the same? It might have been foolish to risk so much, but its effect on the army was glorious.

Emboldened by the king's feat, Angus ordered the king's schiltron forward, forming a bristling hedge of steel-tipped pikes, against which the English vanguard, far outstripping their foot soldiers, foundered in confusion.

Gloucester's horse was killed under him. Only his troops, dragging him to safety in the thick of the fray, saved him from capture.

As Sir Edward's division emerged from the woods in support of the battling rearguard in which Angus and his Islesmen fought, the English fell back. With a great shout, the Scots surged forward.

The English horsemen turned and fled, beaten and in disorder. Trapped by the ford of the Bannock Burn, they were prevented from moving forward by the hidden pits into which they stumbled.

A slaughter ensued until the remaining English gave up their attack and retreated. King Robert recalled his men and withdrew to the safety of the wooded New Park.

Once under the protection of the trees, the king dismounted and was confronted by his angry nobles. An exasperated Sir Gilbert Haye said, "What were you thinking risking all?"

"You could have been killed!" exclaimed Malcolm, Earl of Lennox. "And where would Scotland be then?"

Sir Edward shook his head.

Sir Neil Campbell stood by, his arms crossed over his chest and his brow lowered.

It was clear to Angus the king's men had been shocked, and possibly frightened, at what had transpired.

King Robert's only reply was to complain about the loss of his favorite axe.

Angus smiled at his friend. "I would have done the same, though mayhap with not so glorious a result. You risked much, yet you have given the men cause to celebrate the courage of the kingdom's brave king and to commit their all for Scotland."

Angus returned to his chiefs and Islesmen to see how they fared. Save a few wounds of minor consequence, all were fine.

As the day waned, Angus stepped out of the woods for a brief moment, gazing east, hardly believing his eyes. The English forces, thousands both mounted and on foot, had retired to the boggy Carse.

He returned to the king and the other commanders. Entering the king's tent, he smiled at King Robert and nodded to the others, their faces cast in shadow by the candles set about. In addition to Sir Edward, the familiar faces of the men who had been with the king from the beginning greeted him: Sir Neil Campbell, Sir Robert Boyd, Malcolm, Earl of Lennox, Sir James Douglas, Sir Gilbert Haye, and Walter Stewart, only twenty-one, who had been added not long ago.

Angus said to the king, "It appears your invitation to the English to bed down on the midge-infested Carse has been accepted."

"Ah, that is good," said the king. "Now, if we can only keep them there. We have done well this day, but I must ask you all, would it be prudent to withdraw to the rugged land of Lennox? The country is too wild for the English to follow. From there we could fight as we have in the past. Or, do you think we should remain here and renew the battle on the morrow outnumbered as we are?"

Angus, along with Sir Edward and Sir Neil Campbell, urged a resumption of the battle. "We are here with a great army. Aye, it is half the English force, but the battle space is ours to control and the men are in good spirits after today's victory."

"On this terrain," said Douglas, "the English are at a disadvantage with their three thousand knights. You saw them stumble and fall onto our spears today. Why should it be different tomorrow?"

They debated the merits of the two choices for a long while. Before they reached agreement, a messenger arrived with news. "The detachment under Sir William Airth, who was guarding our supplies at Cambuskenneth Abbey, east of Stirling, has been attacked."

"By whom?" demanded the king.

"David Strathbogie, Earl of Atholl, who fights with the English. Sir William was slain along with many of his men."

King Robert tossed his brother a dark look. "It seems Strathbogie would have his revenge for your rejecting his sister after getting her with child."

The death of a good man on his hands, Sir Edward dropped his gaze and said nothing.

Night had descended when a knight, wearing a scarlet and gold surcoat with three crescents, marred with mud from the day's battle, was escorted into the tent by the king's guards.

"Who is he?" Angus asked in a whisper to Neil Campbell.

"Sir Alexander Seton, the son of Christopher Seton and the king's sister, Christian. Despite his father's loyalty to the king, Alexander sided with the English to protect his lands."

"Why are you here, Alexander?" asked the king, his gray eyes narrowing on the man before him who was the same age as Angus and the king.

"I come to swear fealty to you, lord king. And to bring you intelligence."

The king returned him a wary expression. "Continue."

"Morale is low among the English and the men are discouraged. They believe that God has been on the side of the Scots and, because of that, the English will have no success in the battle to come."

The king paused, considering.

"If you wish to take all of Scotland," Seton urged, "now is the time."

"And King Edward's leaders?" asked the king. "Are they, too, of low morale?"

"There is dissent and confusion among the leaders of Edward's army. They are unhappy with the king's haste. Gloucester urged a delay for the sake of the men, for which the king called him coward. Edward has five hundred horse attached to his person, and Aymer de Valence, the Earl of Pembroke, Sir Ingram de Umfraville and Sir Giles de Argentine guard him at all times."

"Sir Giles was with me at the Siege of Stirling Castle," said King

Robert. "And he fought the Saracens in Palestine. A very brave knight."

Seton nodded. "Aye, he is considered the third best knight in Christendom."

"My brother is counted the second," put in Sir Edward, "following Henry VII of Luxembourg, Emperor of Germany, but he died in Italy of malaria last year."

The king dismissed his brother with a sharp look. Angus knew his friend did not brag of accomplishments even when praise was deserved.

Douglas turned to Seton. "We have heard the English camp making merry tonight as if celebrating a win. How can you say they are discouraged?"

"If you crept close to the Carse," said Seton, "you would hear the foot soldiers shouting toasts to each other. But that is not for a victory they believe will be theirs. They have ransacked the supply wagons and now make merry, drowning their misgivings in drink."

As King Robert and his commanders pondered this information, Seton said, "I tell you they can be beat on the morrow, my king, with little loss and great glory."

"I thank you for the information, Alexander," said the king. "You may return to the English camp with no consequences."

"I will not return," insisted the knight. "I am here to fight for you. And here I will stay."

A small smile played about the king's mouth. The candlelight flickered over the faces of the king's men as each nodded in solemn agreement. "Then we are decided," said the king. "Since the English force is already in the Carse, our job will be to keep them there, penned in by the streams like sheep for the slaughter. Accordingly, the positions of our schiltrons will change with the dawn."

That night, Angus watched and prayed with the king and his smaller but more resolute Scots army, while the larger English force reveled, drank heartily and slept.

The next morning, Angus woke to the first bird song. He thought of his beautiful wife and asked God to let him see her again.

The sun rose into a clear blue sky, signaling to Angus the day would again be hot. Abbot Maurice of Inchaffray heard the confessions of the king and his inner circle. Angus was relieved to have his relationship with God a settled matter.

The king then commanded Mass to be heard by the army for they would need God's protection. That done, they broke their fast, and the king ordered them into their formations with all their banners displayed.

As part of the morning's ceremony the king knighted those of his army he considered had distinguished themselves on the previous day and made Walter Stewart and James Douglas, already knights, bannerets, allowing them to command their own forces on the battlefield. "You already command your own men," said the king to Angus. "I but recognize it."

King Robert then spoke to his troops, reminding them of all they had lost at the hands of the English—brothers, friends and kinsmen. "Our country's nobility has poured forth its blood in war. Those English barons you can see before you, clad in mail, are bent upon destroying me and obliterating my kingdom, nay, our whole nation. They do not believe that we can survive. They glory in their warhorses and equipment. For us, the name of the Lord must be our hope of victory in battle."

The king then ordered his four divisions out of the wooded New Park, across the Roman road that led to Stirling Castle, and down to the edge of the Carse, where they faced the English forces.

Randolph, Earl of Moray, led the vanguard; the second and third divisions behind the wings of the van were led by Sir Edward, nearest to the Bannock Burn, and young Walter Stewart and his cousin, the experienced James Douglas. The king's own division, the rearguard, in which Angus, Duncan and John would fight, was situated behind the van up on the ridge at the edge of the New Park.

"You and your Islesmen will be in the center of my spearmen," the king told Angus, "giving me a dual-armed schiltron with your large galloglass battle formation a whirlwind to be released at the right time."

Angus inclined his head. "You can do me no greater honor."

Thus, while the bulk of the Scots army had moved in three divisions down to the edge of the Carse, prepared to attack the English like a thick-set hedge, King Robert stayed with the reserve, allowing him and Angus to watch the battle unfolding below. Keith and his light horse were behind the king's schiltron just inside the New Park, and the archers, between the king's division and the other schiltrons, were to be held in reserve.

Standing in front of the Scots army, the abbot called the men to prayer. Angus and the commanders kneeled in full sight of the enemy, followed by the whole of the Scots army, thus demonstrating they were unafraid. Their souls were in the hands of God.

Facing them in the Carse, the English watched, their cavalry's armor glinting in the early morning sun, for it would be sacrilege to attack a man in prayer.

When the prayer ceased, the Scots rose to their feet, gripped their spears—and charged. Their archers now fired over the heads of the Scots, their arrows finding targets in the huge mass of English cavalry and foot before them.

The English were slow to react, surprised by what they obviously did not expect.

First to respond was the Earl of Gloucester who scrambled onto his horse and rode out ahead of his cavalry without even his surcoat. Angus only recognized the young earl and his horse from the day before.

Spurred into action by the sound of the bugle, the Earl of Hereford and his knights charged after him, straight onto the waiting spears of Sir Edward's schiltron.

The Scots vanguard received the English cavalry like a dense woodland of thistles, the great horses dashing themselves in vain against the solid and impenetrable schiltron that stood immovable against the English horse. Their spears clattered against the English armor until the hills rang with the sound.

Those behind the English vanguard pressed forward, only to fall to the dust under the spears and axes of the Scots.

With the strain on Sir Edward's division, Randolph moved to support him and drew an equally heavy attack upon himself. The king then ordered the third division under Douglas and Stewart into the fray.

The English grappled with the newcomers in stubborn conflict, until blood stood in red pools on the field.

After repeated efforts to penetrate the impenetrable wedge of Scots, Gloucester's charger was slain under him by a spear thrust forward. The earl was thrown to the ground. His men did not move to aid him to rise but stared speechless. Burdened as he was with the weight of his armor, the young earl was killed in front of the hundreds he had led into battle.

Next to Angus, King Robert inhaled sharply. "Brave, impetuous Gloucester," he muttered. "The cowardly English did nothing to help him."

Soon thereafter, Sir Robert Clifford was slain.

On the right flank of the English, the Welsh bowmen took up their position and loosed hundreds of arrows into the air. Placed behind the knights as they were, the volleys of arrows hit more of the English than the Scots. The Welsh bowmen then changed course. Working their way around to the right of Sir Edward's division, they plied their bows with such energy they began to have an effect upon Sir Edward's men. Angus searched for Brian in the schiltron but did not see him. "Rob, we must stop the English archers."

The king said, "It is time for my light horse." Shouting to Sir Robert Keith, the king commanded his five hundred armed horsemen into the battle. "Cut out the Welsh archers!"

Keith and his horsemen dashed upon the archers. A few archers got off killing shots but, having no weapons fit for a close encounter with mounted men-at-arms, the vast majority of them fled, some to be trodden down and the rest utterly dispersed.

More English cavalry quickly occupied the ground abandoned by their archers.

To support the assault of the schiltrons, the king ordered the Scots archers to pour volleys of arrows into the struggling English cavalry. "Force them back into the Carse!" Trapped and pressed between the Scots and the streams, the English were unable to assume their battle formations, and they soon became a disorganized mass.

Pushing forward, the Scots began to gain ground, trampling over the English dead and wounded. Driving home their assault with cries of "Press on! Press on!" the Scots' attack forced many in the English rear to flee back across the Bannock Burn, the wild careening of their wounded steeds making the preservation of order impossible.

In spite of this success, the schiltron of Douglas and the Steward was taking heavy casualties, leaving the left flank of the Scottish line exposed. Desperate for action, Angus turned to the king. "If the English push hard on their right, they can break out and fatally flank Randolph's and Edward's schiltrons. Douglas is too pressed to support them."

King Robert met Angus' intense gaze. "I agree. The time has come. You are my last resource, Angus. I have saved you until now. Go with your Islesmen and the Highlanders and win me this day. Capture King Edward if you can. My hope is constant in you."

Knowing the king risked everything with this last move, Angus said, "From the time we were lads, I have been bound to you by my honor. I will not fail you." Turning to Iain MacDonald standing with the men of Glen Coe, Angus shouted, "You and your men stay behind me, lad." To Duncan and John, he shouted, "Protect him!" Then, with the Galley of the Isles banner raised high, Angus shouted his war cry and swiftly led his men down the slope, his long axe to hand.

His galloglass, echoing his war cry, ran forward to meet the enemy, streaming out of the tight formation in all directions, wielding their six-foot, razor-sharp axes. Like a sharp scythe through ripe wheat, they moved over the battlefield, cutting down all before them. With them were the Highlanders of Argyll and the men of Carrick wielding their swords.

Angus and his Islesmen struck hard and fast, fighting as if in a rage. Where their blows fell full and straight, they inflicted a terrible wound no armor could stop. Charging against all they could reach, with their long sparth axes and swords, they rendered blows that cleaved helmets and heads.

The English disputed every inch of ground, but they could not stand against a force compelled by so much courage and ferocity.

Gazing ahead, Angus saw King Edward mounted on a destrier, his red surcoat with three golden leopards and golden crown calling attention to his royal person. He had not quit the field. Instead, he was rushing upon the Scots like a lion robbed of whelps, shedding the blood of many.

Angus commanded his men ahead of him to grab the English king's horse. "Take his bridle! Capture the king!"

Only King Edward's desperate wielding of his mace thwarted their efforts. Still, they used their axes to take down his horse. Angus ran to join them but before he could reach the bridle, Aymer de Valence, Earl of Pembroke, Sir Ingram de Umfraville and Sir Giles de Argentine, pulled the protesting king onto another mount and fled the battlefield, riding fast toward Stirling Castle. Hundreds of English knights rode in their wake.

James Douglas, once again on horseback, begged King Robert for leave to pursue King Edward. "Take sixty horse, no more," said the king. "We need the others for order."

Seeing their king deserting the field, the English turned to flee. Angus and his Islesmen pressed forward against the increasingly exhausted English army. The cry went up, "On them! On them! They fail. They fail."

Giles de Argentine suddenly reappeared on the field, a steel-tipped lance in his hand. "I have never run and I will not this day!"

He threw his lance with deadly accuracy. Angus, too far away to intercede, watched in horror as the lance pierced Gilchrist Macduffie of Colonsay. Undaunted, Macduffie rose against the spear that held him and swung his sword at de Argentine, striking the knight from his horse. Once on the ground, he was quickly slayed, pierced with many wounds.

Angus hurried to his dying friend, kneeling beside him to cradle his head and remove his helmet. Gilchrist's red hair fell to either side of his face. Duncan and John came to stand guard.

The Macduffie chief smiled as life ebbed from him. In a halting voice, he said, "I have well repaid his mortal thrust with my blade."

"You have done well, my friend," said Angus. "He was the third best knight in Christendom. No man could have done what you did, wounded as you are."

Duncan handed Gilchrist's sword to Angus, and he placed it in

The Macduffie's hand.

The MacDuffie chief smiled and closed his eyes, as his spirit left him. Angus crossed himself as the heart-pounding fever that had thrummed through his veins only a moment before subsided, replaced by a heaviness settling over him.

Hearing a great noise of shouting and cheers, Angus rose from the body of his dead friend to see the crowd dubbed "the small folk" emerging from behind Coxet Hill north of the New Park. Cooks, camp followers, pages, servants and clergy shouted as they waved drying cloths and sheets as makeshift banners. Wielding knives and clubs, they poured down the hill toward the field of battle.

The English who remained watched the oncoming flood of newcomers with looks of terror. "The Scots are reinforced!" one yelled before turning to flee.

Chased by the Scots, some of the English fled to the Bannock Burn, Pelstream Burn or the River Forth where those mounted and wearing armor sank beneath the waters. Others, losing their footing in the pools of blood in the Carse were quickly slain.

A roar of victory rose from the Scots when they realized they had triumphed over the might of England. Angus' spirit soared within him, so great was his joy.

Once Duncan informed Angus that Brian and Iain MacDonald lived, Angus asked him and John to see Gilchrist Macduffie's body returned to his clan. "I must find King Robert."

He found the king on the battlefield, splattered with blood and mud, but very much alive. "We have won, my king!"

"We have indeed, Angus. England is humiliated and Scotland is free. A victory due in no small part to you and your Islesmen."

The king allowed his schiltrons to disband and pursue the English foot, which they did with a vengeance. He asked his captains and knights to take as prisoners any wearing noble surcoats. "We will not treat them as the English treated us." He directed some of his men to seize the English baggage train. "It will feed our men and the people for months."

The king turned to Angus. "How many lay slain, do you think?"

"I cannot say for certain," said Angus. "Tens of thousands on the

English side. Hundreds of their knights. Half the English army at least. There were English knights who never entered the fray and some of their foot fled without fighting. On our side, mayhap only hundreds. It is owing to your training and command that held our men in order, to the land that fought for us, as you predicted, and to God that we owe this great victory."

The king nodded as he surveyed the battlefield strewn with the bodies of men and horses, the sun reflecting off weapons and armor. "I thank God for the victory."

That night, after much of the cleanup work had been accomplished, Angus and the king's men bathed upstream where the water was clear. The cooks, who had come at the end as a part of the small folk to drive the remaining English off the field, served them a great feast of roast beef, goose and mutton, washed down with fine French wine from the English baggage train.

Reports came in constantly as they ate. At one point, an English knight was led into the king's presence, bloodied from the day's fighting. Angus did not know the man but Rob did.

"Sir Ralph de Monthermer!" exclaimed the king.

Angus recalled the name. Monthermer had been the Earl of Gloucester at the time he warned Robert Bruce of King Edward's intent to arrest him. When Monthermer's wife died, by whom he held the title, the earldom passed to the young Gilbert de Clare, Earl of Gloucester, who was now dead.

The knight bowed. "I am your prisoner, my lord."

"Nay," said the king. "You shall be my guest. Sit down and join us."

A chair was offered the knight along with a cloth to wipe his face. Bewildered, he took the cloth, wiped the blood from his face, and sat.

"This man saved my life," said the king to his inner circle, who were dining with him. "He warned me that King Edward, the first of that name, was going to arrest me when Comyn betrayed my trust. Had that happened, my end would not have been pleasant. Dine with us in celebration, Sir Ralph. You shall have your freedom, and no ransom shall be required."

The knight, clearly overwhelmed, thanked the king profusely.

"You may carry back to England your king's shield he left behind with his seal. Both shall be returned though he must never use the seal again."

"I will see to it, my lord," said Monthermer.

A short time later, another English knight came to the king's tent. His white surcoat with three green parrots was splashed with dried blood. Sir Robert Boyd escorted him in, announcing, "He has voluntarily surrendered."

"Ah, Sir Marmaduke Twenge, my kinsman," said King Robert to the grizzled old knight, whose skin was like leather beneath his gray hair. "As with Sir Ralph here, you shall pay no ransom. Instead, I will send you home to England with gifts."

Clearly shocked, Sir Marmaduke thanked the king and took the seat offered him.

"Meanwhile," said the king, looking at Angus, "what think you of this ransom? It seems Robert Baston, the Carmelite Friar and poet of great repute, was brought to the battle by King Edward to compose a song of the English victory. Since the Good Lord thankfully had other plans, I have asked the friar, for his ransom, to sing a different tune, one celebrating the Scots' victory."

The Scots sitting around the table voiced their support for this ransom. "'Twill make a better tune," said Angus, to which many sounded their "Ayes".

"Then I shall read a few stanzas from his ballad," said the king, and proceeded to read.

What is truth worth? How can I sing about so much blood?
Could even tragedy bare its breast to show such cut and thud?
The names may be famous but I do not know them all.
I cannot number the humblings and tumblings of hundreds that fall.
Many are mown down, many are thrown down,
Many are drowned, many are found and bound.
Many are taken in chains for a stated ransom.
So some are rising, riding rich high and handsome.
Who were before the war poor and threadbare souls.
The battlefield is barren but piled with spoils.
Shouts and taunts and vengeful cuts and brawls—

I saw, but what can I say? A harvest I did not sow!
Guile is not my style. Justice and peace are what I would show.
Anyone who has more in store, let him write the score.
My mind is numb, my voice half-dumb, my art a blur.

"What dreary verse," remarked the king's brother.

"One must make allowances for the poet's lack of joy," said the king. "Though I would share a lament for the loss of those I once called brothers-in-arms, I cannot feel as the poet does about this day. The English invaded Scotland seeking to conquer and we but resisted. By the grace of God, we have won. Aside from that, the poet is English and has served English kings who never expected to lose."

Later that night, Angus made the rounds with Duncan and John, calling upon the lordship's chiefs and Islesmen, thanking them, and paying his respects to the men of Colonsay whose chief had died so valiantly. Being the last into the battle and fresh for the fight, the Isles had lost only a few men. He had worried about Brian in Sir Edward's schiltron, but Áine's son by The O'Neill had prevailed and was understandably proud of it.

Angus left Duncan, John and Brian to celebrate with the Islesmen and went in search of the king. On the way, he was greeted by his son, Iain, Lord of Glen Coe, who had been looking for him.

Bowing his head to Angus, the young man said, "Thank you, Father, for letting me follow you into battle and to victory. 'Twas a great honor."

Their gazes met. Both were teary-eyed. Angus reached for his son, embracing him. "I am just glad you live and now that the king assures me Morvern is mine, I will never be far away."

Angus reluctantly said goodbye before proceeding on to make inquiry of the king's whereabouts with the guards. "You can find the king at St. Ninian's Kirk."

Situated on the old Roman road just north of the New Park on the way to Stirling Castle, the gray stone kirk was centuries old. Though it was not as grand as the abbey church on Iona, Angus thought it surprisingly large for a parish church.

The heat of the day had cooled and the stars were beginning to glisten across the sky when Angus entered the musty-smelling stone building. Many wounded lined the nave, waiting to be tended. Healers were bent over some, administering aid.

He asked the first priest he found to direct him to the king. "In the curtained alcove on the left of the chancel," the priest said, gesturing. "He stands vigil over Gilbert de Clare, Earl of Gloucester."

The guard who stood beside the curtained alcove recognized Angus and, with a nod, allowed him entry.

Holding the heavy curtain aside, Angus peered into the alcove that was dimly lit by two candles set on a table against the far wall. A small window was open to the night air. In the center of the rectangular room, a body lay on a narrow table. The king stood over it with his head bowed. As Angus silently stepped inside and made the sign of the cross, the king looked up.

"Angus."

Studying the body of the knight, Angus said, "He wears his yellow surcoat with the red chevrons, unsullied by battle."

"This is a new one we found in his tent. Had he worn it today, he would have been recognized for who he was and captured for the great ransom he would have brought. He was the most prominent noble killed. Alas, in his haste, he foolishly left it behind."

For a moment, the only sound was the candles sputtering in the night breeze. When the king spoke again, his voice was a lament. "He was but a squire when I served the first King Edward as a knight. I grieve to see him lying dead at twenty-three. Always impetuous, Gloucester was brave and eager for the fight. Too eager, mayhap."

"Yet Sir Alexander Seton told us it was Gloucester who argued for delay."

"Only because his men were tired." Looking at the face of the young knight, his wounds washed free of the day's mud and blood, the king added, "He would have thought of that."

"I am sorry, Rob. You must have loved him."

The king sighed. "He was my cousin and my brother-in-law." Raising his gaze to Angus, he added, "We both married daughters of the Earl of Ulster. And, yes, I was fond of him. He was not the only one killed on the English side who was my friend. Sir Giles de

Argentine was another. His body lies in a nearby alcove. I will see the bodies of Gloucester and Clifford are returned to Berwick for burial by their own, and I will give Sir Giles a noble's burial at Edinburgh."

"You have been gracious to your enemies in your victory, Rob. All will know of it and admire you."

"I have much to be grateful for. Not only our victory but soon I will exchange our noble prisoners for my queen, my daughter and my sisters—and Bishop Wishart, who has been a prisoner of the English for the last eight years. I am told, he is unwell."

"Aye, let us hope they will be quickly returned."

A shadow crossed the king's face. "It seems Isabella MacDuff, Countess of Buchan, who risked all to crown me, has died in captivity."

Angus heaved a sigh. "A great loss to Scotland."

The king nodded his agreement. "Come, let us see what has developed in my absence."

As they returned to the camp in the New Park woods, Sir Robert Boyd met them with a rush of news. "Sire, Douglas has yet to return from his pursuit of King Edward. Your captains are taking the English baggage train in hand. There is much to be accounted for in that effort. Of the hundreds of English knights slain, those I can name besides Gloucester, de Argentine, Clifford and de Bohun, include Sir Pagan de Tybetot, William the Marshal, Sir William de Vescy, Sir William d'Eyncourt and Sir John Comyn of Badenoch, son of the Red Comyn."

At the mention of the last name, the king exchanged a glance with Sir Robert, for this meant that the Comyn claim to the throne was finally dead. "And our knights?"

"Only two, my lord, Sir William Vipont and Sir Walter Ross." Angus recalled the Earl of Ross, who had submitted to King Robert at Urquhart Castle. Sir Walter was one of his sons.

While Sir Robert was still speaking, Sir Neil Campbell approached. "A messenger arrived while you were away, my king. It seems the Earl of Hereford and other nobles escaped and headed for Carlisle. With him were the Earl of Angus, Sir John de Segrave, Sir Antony de Lucy, Sir Ingram de Umfraville, and many other knights, numbering over a hundred, as well as many foot soldiers. At Bothwell Castle, they appealed to the constable, Sir Walter Fitz Gilbert, who was holding the castle for England's king. Fitz Gilbert admitted them and quickly took them prisoners. His message to us said the castle is yours, and he asked for Sir Edward to come and retrieve his English 'guests'. Your brother has gone with a large force to bring them back."

"These will have rich ransoms, indeed," said Angus.

"Enough, mayhap, to win me my queen," said King Robert.

"There is news of Aymer de Valence," said Sir Robert. "He got away with his Welsh archers but he must have lost his last horse because Pembroke was seen running on foot."

"A fitting end to his many losses following his unchivalrous behavior at Methven," said Angus.

"At last, my brave friends who died at his hand are avenged," said the king.

That night, Angus slept soundly, exhausted from little sleep the night before and two days of fighting, though admittedly he had not fought for the entire battle as had some.

The next day, he was up with the birds and broke his fast with his chiefs before setting out to see the king. The king's brother and James Douglas had yet to return from their missions. King Robert was hearing a report from Sir Neil Campbell of the booty taken from King Edward's baggage train.

"There are one hundred and ten wagons, Sire. Beautiful horses, flocks of cattle and sheep, pigs and poultry, corn and wine in abundance, sumptuous clothing from the royal wardrobe, armor for the nobles and knights, vessels and utensils of silver and gold, and money chests with coin for the payment of the army."

"So much!" exclaimed the king. "We are rich, indeed."

"What will you do with it?" asked Sir Robert Boyd.

The king smiled. "Why, I will distribute it to my captains and the men who have fought with me for so long. That includes all of you," he said, looking at the small group that never left him. "And the coin will help pay our army and keep the realm stable."

The king was true to his word, so that the whole Scots army was enriched by the victory. Beyond that, the king said he would be distributing lands to his faithful men.

To Angus, the king said, "I trust you have no problem with my retaining and fortifying as a royal castle Tarbert at the north end of Kintyre."

"None at all," said Angus. "It will be good to have you close as you find time to visit."

"Next year," said the king, "I will come to your Isles, mayhap with my queen, to bring you the charters to the lands I intend to bestow upon you. Since your cousin, Duncan, has faithfully served me and makes his home on Kintyre at Saddell, I will see him rewarded as well. There is an abbey at Saddell whose mission I may be able to assist. Tell him, too, that I will make sure the lass he has been courting has a worthy dowry."

"I will," said Angus. Angus thanked the king and, later that morning, told Duncan of his good fortune.

"I shall see about wedding the lass as soon as I can," said his cousin.

"Well, and you might introduce her to us," said Angus.

"Aye, if you insist," said Duncan with a smile.

Late in the afternoon, Sir Philip Mowbray surrendered Stirling Castle and swore fealty to King Robert. Unbeknownst to the king, Mowbray had tried to persuade King Edward not to fight the Scots. "I watched you preparing your army and the land for battle. I knew the English would lose."

Douglas finally returned, weary from his long journey and, like his men, covered with dried blood from battle and dirt from the road. "As I reached the border of Torwood, I met Sir Lawrence de Abernethy." Douglas gestured to the man beside him. "He was coming to assist the English but, learning of the battle's end, quickly changed sides and joined me, adding his eighty men to my sixty. At Linlithgow, we came within bowshot of King Edward and his party, but lacked the force to attack them. Instead, we hung on their tail and captured or killed the stragglers."

"He did not even allow the English time to make water," said Sir Lawrence with a chuckle.

"Sounds like our Douglas," put in Angus.

"When Edward found shelter at Dunbar Castle," said Douglas, "we left off our pursuit. The English king would not admit to the castle those English who followed after him, but abandoned them to their fate. We let them go on to Berwick, but I brought back many horses."

"You did well," said the king. "I am glad you have returned to me unscathed."

Angus remained at Stirling only as long as King Robert needed him. When he was ready to go home, he asked his friend, "Do you wish Duncan to remain with you when I sail for Islay?"

"For the time being, yes. I will return him to you next year when I come. Mayhap, by then, he will have wed and you will have reclaimed Dunaverty Castle."

"My very thought," said Angus.

His friend paused and, with a pensive expression, said, "I have a request."

"Anything."

"I want you to thank Lady Áine for me. When you and your galloglass rushed onto the battlefield, I thought of her prayer that God would overflow our enemies like water breaking over a bank, giving us a great victory. Tell her it happened just that way."

CHAPTER 29

Dunyvaig Castle, Isle of Islay, early July 1314

WEEKS BEFORE, FISHERMEN had brought Áine news of a great Scots victory near Stirling. She was elated to hear her prayers had been answered, but she had received no news of Angus or the Islesmen who had gone with him. Anxiety for his safety and that of her son, Brian, hovered above her like a dark cloud.

Each day, she and Juliana and Nessa watched for sails coming from the south, for the fleet would have to round Kintyre on their way home.

It was her eldest daughter, Finvola, ten years old, who sighted them first. "Mama! Sails!

They watched from the parapet as a great number of galleys came into view, their white sails billowing in the wind against the blue sky. Áine's heart sped as she wondered if Angus would be leading them.

At the bottom of the stairs, she took her daughters by the hand. "Let us go meet the fleet!" She did not mention Angus to their daughters, for she did not yet know if he was among the returning warriors. Fand, her wolfhound, was old and rarely left the hearth these days, and Alexander's wolfhound, Cormac, was in Ulster with his master, so there were no hounds trailing them as they left the castle with Nessa and her two boys.

They walked down to the bay and waited on the shore as the galleys drew closer. Her young son, John, now four, came to join them with his nurse. Others began to gather on the shore, eager to greet the returning Islesmen. Like Áine, there were women among them who were anxious to know if their husbands had survived.

Finally, the lead ship was close enough for Áine to see who was on deck. With a great sigh of relief, she spotted Angus standing in the prow, his sun-browned face smiling as his hair blew behind him. "Your father has returned. Thank God."

The children jumped up and down with cries of happiness. They were aware their father had gone to fight with King Robert, but they knew nothing of war and its terrible consequences.

Even before the galley was beached, Angus jumped to the sand and ran to her, sweeping her into his arms and twirling her around. "A great victory is ours, my love!"

She held him tightly to her, comforted by his lean strength and his familiar scent of the sea. "Brian? Duncan? John?"

"All well." Angus turned to look back at the ship and the men pouring over the gunwale. "Brian is just there with John, and Duncan remains with the king until next year."

With her young sons in tow, Nessa hurried past them to Conall, who waved to her from the stern of Angus' ship.

Áine released Angus to their children, and he stooped to gather them into his arms. She could see from his tears he had not been certain he would return.

Many happy reunions occurred that afternoon on the beach, but there were tears, too, for some did not return. "I sent the chiefs home to their isles," said Angus, "to assure their loved ones they live. Gilchrist Macduffie was the only chief killed. His men bore his body home for burial."

Áine was saddened to learn of it. "Such a kind man."

"He was very brave at the end," said Angus. "The story will long be told among us."

Áine looked for Brian and found him with some of the Irishmen who lived on Islay. Handsome at twenty-three, he received a warm welcome from the women. "Did Brian do well?" she asked Angus.

"Oh, aye. He was with Sir Edward who received the worst of the English attacks. I am very proud of him that he wanted to fight in that schiltron."

She gazed into Angus' blue eyes. How she had missed him. "Thank you for bringing him home."

He wrapped his arm around her shoulders. "Come, my love, let us go to the castle and I will tell you more."

For the rest of the summer, Áine knew only happiness. August brought their eldest son home from Ireland. Around the fire at night, with his wolfhound, Cormac, at his feet, Alexander recounted many stories of his fostering with the O'Neills. Brian often interjected his own memories of life in Ulster. Alexander wanted to hear of the battle his father and half-brother fought near Stirling with King Robert. Though there was regret in his eyes for having missed so great a battle, Áine believed they had made the correct decision in delaying his return from Ireland.

At the beginning of autumn, Angus decided it was time to retake Dunaverty. He left Islay with a fleet of warriors who had fought valiantly at the battle now called Bannockburn. The English garrison must have fled at the sight of so many Scots determined to take what was theirs, for Angus returned in a fortnight with happy news.

"Dunaverty is ours again," he said. "It will need some repair and application of our servants' cleaning for it smells like a soldiers' barracks."

Áine could see from his expression how much it meant to have his favorite castle back in his hands. "It has been eight years since we lived at Dunaverty. Would you call it home again?"

"I asked myself the same question as we sailed to Islay. I do not think so. Islay is home now. You do not mind?"

"Not as long as we are together and our family is close."

Angus nodded. "We can visit. Besides, with the new lands the king has already given me, we will often need to be in the north. Islay is more convenient for that as well as for Finlaggan. I intend to institute courts in each of the clans with appeals heard by the Council each year at Finlaggan."

"That is a wonderful idea. I like to see the families gathered together when the Council meets. I enjoy watching the children grow."

At the turn of the year, they received a letter from Duncan with welcome news.

To Angus Og Macdonald, Lord of the Isles, from his cousin, Sir Duncan MacAlasdair,

First, I should note that King Robert has bestowed upon me a knighthood, so that I am henceforth Sir Duncan. My lady, Catherine, who became my wife at Christmas, is fond of the address. She is a Campbell and brought me lands in Glen Orchy, Argyll. You shall meet her when I come with the king.

You may have heard that last October, the king traded the Earl of Hereford and other men of rank for Queen Elizabeth, his daughter, Marjorie, now twenty, and the king's sisters. Sir Neil Campbell was beyond glad to have his wife back. The king has awarded him the lands of David Strathbogie that were forfeit. Bishop Wishart, old and infirm, has also been returned to us.

Sir Walter Stewart, the High Steward, was sent by the king to collect his family at the border. It seems that while discharging this duty, the young knight became smitten with the king's daughter and she with him. They are to be wed in early spring in Dundonald, Ayrshire, home of the Stewarts.

I do not suppose you will be surprised to learn that King Edward has forsaken the border, leaving the land undefended. Hoping to provoke the English, King Robert sent his brother, Sir Edward, Earl of Carrick, and Sir James Douglas to Northumberland, where they raided unimpeded.

The king sent letters to England, expressing his desire for a lasting peace between the two nations. A meeting took place with Sir Roger Kirkpatrick and Sir Neil Campbell attending from our side, but nothing came of it due to the refusal by the English to recognize Robert Bruce as King of Scots. In any event, King Edward is again at war with his barons, thus, the raids into the north of England will continue.

King Robert, who never seems to tire, led one of the raids himself to take back Tynedale, the lordship that once belonged to the King of Scots. It does so again.

It is the king's intention to sail to his castle at Tarbert in late May. The queen and his daughter and Walter Stewart, who will by then be her husband, will accompany him.

I look forward to seeing you and Lady Áine. This time, I will return to the west for good.

Dunaverty Castle, southern end of the Kintyre Peninsula, May 1315

A DAY'S SAIL would see them to Tarbert where they would meet with the king, but Angus stopped at Dunaverty for a few days to assure himself all was well there. His faithful seneschal, who had remained when the castle was in English hands, greeted him.

"My lord, my lady, we are happy to have you at Dunaverty. Can we hope you will stay for some while?"

"Only a few days this time," said Angus. "We are bound for Tarbert to meet with the king and queen."

The seneschal smiled. "All on Kintyre celebrated the king's victory and your return, my lord. I was never so glad to see the English leave Kintyre."

The time Angus and Áine spent at Dunaverty brought back memories of the early days of their marriage when Áine was his bride and King Robert had fled to Dunaverty for safety.

The next evening, he and Áine walked the battlements, observing the evening sky. Above them, a canopy of golden yellow illuminated all. Beneath the headland, the sea appeared as a shimmering golden cloak laid on the water. "I will never tire of this sight," he said.

"Nor I," said Áine, smiling up at him. "'Tis a fitting place for me to tell you of my news. I am with child."

He could not stop the wide grin spreading across his face. Looking down at her waist, still slim in her emerald gown, he could discern no change.

"It is early," she said. "The child will be born at Christmas."

He kissed her, a long, lingering kiss. One that he hoped conveyed his gratitude for her becoming his wife and standing by him through the long years of war. She had always been his strength.

"We can pray the peace continues for us to raise the little one," said Áine.

"Aye, a good thought."

THE SAIL UP the Kintyre Peninsula to Tarbert took only a morning. It was a fine day with sun reflecting off the water and Angus' spirits were high as he looked forward to seeing his friend, the king.

Once his galley was anchored in the harbor at Tarbert, Angus donned his hat and looked up to the grass-covered hill and the castle overlooking the bay. "It was once a stronghold granted to John Balliol by the first King Edward," he remarked to Áine. "I think it was a good choice for a western castle for King Robert. It has a ready access to the Firth of Clyde and is but a few days by land to Stirling."

On the shore, two of the king's guards were waiting to escort them up the hill to the castle. There, Duncan was standing with a beautiful woman whose coloring was like his, golden hair and fair eyes. "Lord Angus, Lady Áine, allow me to introduce you to my lady, Catherine."

The first thing Angus noticed was how young she was, somewhere in her twenties. But mayhap he only thought her young since Duncan was in his mid-forties. Smiling shyly, she said, "I am honored to meet you and your lady, Lord Angus. I have heard much about both of you from Duncan and King Robert."

"The king is here?" asked Angus, not sure his friend had arrived.

"Aye," said Duncan. "He arrived a few days ago. We are the scouts and will take you to him and the ladies."

Inside the castle, they crossed the great hall to join King Robert, Sir Walter and their ladies. Angus had not seen Elizabeth de Burgh, now Queen of Scots, since she was at Dunseverick for the celebration of his marriage to Áine. He had never met the king's daughter. Both were pleasing to look at; the queen was fair and the king's daughter dark, like her father. Queen Elizabeth was obviously with child but not very far along by his judgment.

Without removing his arm from around his queen, the king made the introductions. "Elizabeth, allow me to introduce you to Lady Áine O'Cahan, the woman who prayed us to victory and encouraged me in my darkest hour. She is the wife of this man, my faithful friend, Sir Angus Og Macdonald, Lord of the Isles."

Áine curtseyed before the queen, and Angus bowed over the queen's hand.

"I am grateful to you both for all you did for my husband," said Queen Elizabeth. "Robert is effusive in his praise for you and for your cousin, Sir Duncan."

"Thank you," said Áine, "though I take no credit. If I may say so, my queen, your beauty reminds me of your mother's as it did when last I saw you. Your mother was a very gracious woman. I admired her."

"I was in your father's castle at Dunluce once when you were there," put in Angus, "but you may not remember me." Then, with a smile, he added, "I was there with my friend, Robert Bruce."

"I was a child at the time," said the queen, "concerned with childish things." With a smile aimed at the king, she said, "and often into mischief, I am told."

"You have yet to meet my daughter, Marjorie," said the king to Angus and Áine, "but Angus knows well Sir Walter, her husband."

Angus glanced at the young woman, who looked to be the same age as her husband. "Sir Walter is a man quick to act when he finds his heart's desire."

Sir Walter blushed and looked toward his wife.

She laughed. "He is much teased for that."

Áine greeted Marjorie. "I often prayed for you and the queen to be released. I am grateful to God for answering my prayers, which were, doubtless, the prayers of many others."

Sir Walter bent over Áine's hand. "Your beauty was not exaggerated in the stories I have heard about you," said the young Steward. "Angus is, indeed, a fortunate man."

After the introductions were made, the king invited Angus and the other men to go outside with him so he could tell them of the improvements he was going to make to the castle. Angus left Áine with the women as the four men walked to the grass-covered bailey. There, the king stopped. "I intend to enlarge and fortify the castle, adding a curtain wall and towers. There exists a chapel but I want to improve it. I also thought to have a brewhouse for ale."

Angus chuckled. "Your men garrisoned here will be pleased."

"As I hope," said the king. "I also plan to build some ships. A king who rules a country surrounded on three sides by water with long lochs needs ships."

"We can help with that," said Angus.

"Good," said the king. "I thought you might. I like to think there will be days to reflect and plan, but the English and my brother's ambitions in Ireland may not leave room for that."

"Do you think you will spend much time here?" asked Angus.

"Some, however, I have a thought to build a manor house for Elizabeth and me somewhere in the west with a chapel and a garden but no stone walls."

"When might you do that?" asked Sir Walter.

"I have no date in mind but it will be done. We need a place for ourselves and our children. But before that, I must make Scotland's Church a priority. The priests and bishops stood by me, and I will see them richly rewarded."

That evening at dinner, the king asked Duncan for the papers he had brought to the meal. Taking them from Duncan, the king said, "These are the charters confirming you in certain lands you already possess and in others I am giving you for your faithful service." Handing a leather case to Angus, the king said, "In addition to those lands I have given you, Glen Coe, part of Lochaber, Morvern and the Isles of Mull and Tiree, I am confirming you in the Isles of Islay, Jura and Gigha and the Kintyre Peninsula. I also give you the Isles of Coll and Colonsay, and the mainland territories of Duror and Ardnamurchan."

"You are most generous," said Angus. Sharing a glance with Áine, an understanding passed between them. "We are overwhelmed."

"You should know I have granted the MacRuairis the lands of Lorne, forfeited by the MacDougalls, Garmoran, the remaining part of Lochaber and the North Isles."

"Christina will be pleased," said Angus.

Later that night, Angus told Áine he intended to give his brother, John, Ardnamurchan. "It has a strong castle, Mingary, that will serve him well. And the peninsula, jutting into the western sea, is not only beautiful but of strategic importance to the lordship."

"John will be delighted," said Áine. "In which case, it seems time he takes a bride."

"Aye, it is time."

The gifts King Robert rendered to Angus made the Macdonalds the most powerful clan on the northwestern seaboard. And yet, the next morning, the king told Angus, as a reward for faithfully fighting with him to win back Scotland and for his contribution at the battle of Bannockburn, he was bestowing upon Angus yet another honor. "I give the Macdonalds the honored position of the right wing of the Scots army forever."

Angus was deeply touched by the great honor bestowed upon him and his clan. "You have won the peace, Rob, and it was my privilege to fight at your side." They had both survived the long road to Scotland's freedom. Angus knew there might be skirmishes and other battles ahead, for the English would be reluctant to admit Scotland was not theirs. But there would be none like Bannockburn. The English were beaten. "If there are more battles to come, it would be my desire to fight at your side."

Angus was true to his word. For the rest of his life, he remained loyal to Robert Bruce, holding fast to the vow of honor he had made in his youth.

AUTHOR'S NOTE

In Somerled's time (the 12th century), Norway ostensibly had sovereignty over Argyll and the Isles, but the Lords of the Isles were fiercely independent and rendered only nominal allegiance to the distant Norwegian crown. Today, "the Western Isles" refers to the Outer Hebrides, but in the 13th and 14th centuries, the Western Isles included all the isles west of Scotland's mainland. Hence, Edward I made Alexander MacDonald, and his brother after him, "Admiral of the Western Isles".

After 1266 and the Treaty of Perth, following the inconclusive Battle of Largs in 1263, the Isles became subject to Scotland, and the Lords of the Isles were accepted into Scottish nobility while generally maintaining their independence. By the third quarter of the 13th century, Somerled's descendants were making marriage alliances with Scottish nobility.

At the time of my story, the kingdom forged by Somerled, as told in *Summer Warrior,* had been divided among his descendants. The northernmost territory of Garmoran, along with the isles from Eigg to the Uists, became the territory of the MacRuaris, descended from Donald's brother, Ruari. The power center of the Macdonald Lords of the Isles, including the lands of Angus Og and his brother Alexander, were Islay (pronounced Eye' la) and Kintyre though their influence was felt across a much greater area, including the lands and isles eventually bestowed upon Angus Og by his friend Robert Bruce. The MacDougalls were the senior line but eventually were eclipsed by the Macdonalds. Both the Macdonalds and the MacRuaris would support King Robert and his brother Edward Bruce, which contributed greatly to their rise in prominence.

The MacDougalls, based in Lorne and Argyll, were not just the enemies of the Macdonalds. Aligned with the Balliols and power-hungry Comyns, they were also the enemies of the Bruces, including notably, King Robert Bruce. In choosing the wrong side in the First War of Independence, the MacDougalls eventually lost all.

I chose to begin my story in 1286 with the Turnberry Band because of its significance in light of the events that followed. It is known that Angus Og was ever loyal to Robert Bruce (Robert Bruce VII, eventually King Robert I) but, as far as I could determine through considerable research, no one knows exactly when their friendship began. I imagine they might have met and Angus pledged his honor when they were young. It is more than plausible given that their fathers came together that September to discuss Scotland's fate and pledge themselves to a common purpose, including the Bruces' claim to the throne. In those times, boys of twelve and fourteen would have been given much responsibility and might have tagged along.

There was this line in *The Macdonnells of Antrim* by George Hill, written in 1873: "From the time in which Angus Og joined the party of Bruce, so early as the year 1286, his loyalty never faltered, even when the fortunes of the king became at times apparently hopeless."

There is also evidence that Robert Bruce and/or his brothers fostered with their Gaelic kin, the O'Neills, in Tirowen. (See *The MacDonald Lordship and the Bruce Dynasty, c. 1306-c. 1371* by Michael Penman, at p. 64: "As earls of Carrick and rightful lords of Upper Glenarm (Larne) the Bruces had married directly into this complicated Irish Sea world, an inheritance rendered all the more personal for the future Robert I by being fostered in childhood to Gaelic kin—probably along with his four brothers to the Carrick relatives, the O'Neills of Tyrone..."). Tyrone was the later name for *Tír Eoghain* (Anglicized to the term I have used, "Tirowen"), which was a larger territory than the modern Tyrone. If that is the case, then the young Robert might have first met the Macdonalds and the O'Cahans earlier than 1286.

Angus Og "the noble and renowned chief of the Innsigall" (the

Hebrides, or the "Isles of the Strangers") has been remembered in historical accounts as "personable, modest and affable", yet we know he was a formidable warrior. (He was several inches over six feet and would have carried many weapons and trained with the galloglass.) One historian has described the Macdonalds of that era as "the Hell's Angels of the Hebrides" likely because of the galloglass they were known for. I put that together with my research and what emerged was a fierce warrior, a skilled fighter and a leader of men, who was also well liked. Angus was staunchly loyal to his friends, including Robert Bruce, to whom Angus had bound himself by the honor of Clan Donald and never wavered.

Angus brought thousands of Islesmen to fight alongside Robert Bruce at Bannockburn, securing the new king's victory, a fact often omitted in accounts of the battle. For his valiant loyalty, King Robert honored Angus by bestowing upon him many isles and lands and giving the Macdonalds the honored position of the right flank of the Royal Scots Army—for always. The same position Angus held at Bannockburn.

Angus Og was Lord of Kintyre from his father's death in 1293 to 1299 when, at his brother, Alexander's death, he became Lord of the Isles. In researching history this far back I have seen many contradictory sources as to dates, names and even people. Some sources say Angus' brother, Alexander, died later, fighting Robert Bruce. However, from all the sources I consulted, including Ian Ross Macdonnell, author of *Clan Donald and Iona Abbey 1200-1500*, I am persuaded that is not the case. Angus' brother, Alexander, was loyal to the Bruces as were his father and younger brothers. He died in 1299 in Ireland, slain by Alexander MacDougall. From that year, Angus Og began acting as "The Macdonald" and Lord of the Isles, styling himself "Angus of Islay" the chief's designated title.

Angus Og was killed in 1318, along with his eldest son and heir, Alexander, at the Battle of Faughart in Ireland. Angus had gone there at the request of his friend, King Robert, to fight with his brother, Sir Edward, who had become King of Ireland, and the O'Neills. They had hoped to rid Ireland of the English. Many Islesmen were killed in that battle, including some from my story: Ruari MacRuari, Sir Philip Mowbray and several Stewart cadets. It must have broken Áine's heart to lose both her husband and eldest son. Her son, John, now the heir, was only eight.

Angus Og was buried at Iona in the manner of all Lords of the Isles. (You can see his grave slab on Iona today.) Eventually, he was succeeded by his younger son, John of Islay, half-brother to Brian Balloch O'Neill, Áine's son by Niall Culanach O'Neill.

The close relationship between Angus Og and his younger brother, John, came from my imagination, but I think there may be a basis for it as each appeared to have named one of their sons after the other. Angus Og gave John the province of Ardnamurchan (the peninsula north of Morvern). I have no sources that say Angus Og's brother, John, or Áine's son, Brian O'Neill, fought alongside Angus Og at Bannockburn, however, I deem it very likely.

Angus had a "natural son", Iain Fraoch ("John of the Heather"), by the daughter of Dugall MacEanruig, the "chief of Glen Coe". The historical accounts of that son's status conflict. He could not be a product of a handfasting, as some suggest, because a child born of such a union made the trial marriage permanent. Further, in the medieval era, handfasting represented the betrothal of the intended couple, not the actual marriage. Angus Og's wife was Áine O'Cahan and there is no record of another. What is true is that Angus provided for this natural son, both a fostering in Lochaber and ultimately lands in Glen Coe (today "Glencoe"), which were among the lands Angus received from a grateful King Robert. Iain was the progenitor of the MacIains of Glencoe, also known as the MacDonalds of Glencoe.

Should you be wondering, Angus Mor's younger brother, Alasdair Mor of Saddell (the father of Angus' cousin, Duncan MacAlasdair), was also an "Alexander". To make this less confusing in the midst of all the Alexanders I already had to deal with, I used another form of that name. Angus Og's elder brother, Alexander, was actually

"Alexander Og" to distinguish him from his uncle in the same way Angus Og was so named to distinguish him from his father.

Edward I, called "Longshanks" for his height (6 feet 2 inches, the same as Angus Og) was known for his arrogance, intimidating manner and his brutal conduct toward the Welsh and Scots, including William Wallace and Robert Bruce's brothers and his women. He also issued the Edict of Expulsion in 1290, by which the Jews were expelled from England. The edict remained in effect for the rest of the Middle Ages. England was poorer for it. Many Jews found refuge in Scotland, France and the Netherlands.

Robert Bruce was excommunicated by Pope Clement V in 1306 for the killing of John "the Red" Comyn, Lord of Badenoch, in Greyfriars Kirk. In 1320, thirty-nine Scottish barons and earls signed a letter to Pope John XXII, which is known today as the Declaration of Arbroath. Their letter was an appeal to the pope to lift the excommunication of King Robert and recognize him as the rightful King of Scots. Angus Og Macdonald, Lord of the Isles, would undoubtedly have been a signatory to that document had he not been killed in 1318.

Meanwhile, Edward II continued to object to a free Scotland. In 1327 he was deposed by his nobles and senior clergy. He died that September, and the tale is told of murder with a red hot iron. It wasn't until 1328 and the Treaty of Edinburgh that England gave up all claims to Scotland, and the pope lifted the excommunication. King Robert lived to see it. Finally, he had brought the Kingdom of Scotland to peace.

When I think of King Robert's last years, I think of a man full of memories, who was grateful to God for allowing him to lead a free Scotland. Scotland's hero-king died on June 7, 1329 in a manor house he built for himself at Cardross on the north shore of the Firth of Clyde, a place open to the sea lanes and the Isles, very Gaelic in nature. By then, he had lost his wife, his daughter, his brothers, his friend, Sir Angus Og Macdonald, Bishop Lamberton and Sir Walter

Stewart, the High Steward. Perhaps Sir James Douglas, who was ever faithful, and his nephew, Sir Thomas Randolph, Earl of Moray, were with him at his death. I like to think so.

As is so often the case, we know more about the men than the women they loved. And that is where fiction comes into play. What historians tell us, I have used. Otherwise, what you have is a product of my imagination.

Áine O'Cahan (pronounced "awn-ya"), sometimes called Agnes or Margaret, was from a family of Irish nobles who had long supported the O'Neills of Ulster. She would have been intimately familiar with the internecine wars within the O'Neill clan, for her first husband, Niall Culanach O'Neill, had twice been King of Tirowen. (Ireland had many kings, the equivalent of English earls.) The last reign of Niall as king began in 1286 when he was installed by Richard de Burgh, Earl of Ulster. It was during this reign that I believe he married young Áine. O'Neill expert Dr. Elizabeth Simms, author of *Gaelic Ulster in the Middle Ages*, with whom I consulted on many issues, agrees with my deduction that it was Niall Culanach who married the beautiful young Áine O'Cahan. As my story indicates, after being ousted by his cousin, Domnall O'Neill, Niall was re-installed as king in 1291 only to be murdered by that same cousin.

According to an old article I found in researching medieval Ireland, Áine was nicknamed "Finvola", an Irish name meaning "white shoulders", a reference to her great beauty. Interestingly, Áine and Angus gave this name to their first daughter. Their second daughter, Mary, who is "the stubborn one" in my story, married William, the 5th Earl of Ross and became aunt to Donald of Islay, the next Macdonald chief in this series.

Áine O'Cahan was called "the gem of the Roe" (I changed it to "jewel" in my story). The word "Roe" was a reference to the River Roe, part of O'Cahan territory. The article said she was "a beauty of her time and known and talked of in Holyrood Palace, and her fame had even reached the English Court". The same report said that

Angus Og was enamored of her. This I discovered after I had contrived my own image of the dark-haired beauty who captured Angus Og's heart. In turn, he would be her one true love.

Áine outlived her Macdonald husband by many years, leaving the Isles to her surviving Macdonald son, John of Islay, who became the next Lord of the Isles. Though she returned to Ireland to live out her days, perhaps with her brother Dermot and her son, Brian, she often visited John of Islay. John tried twice, unsuccessfully, to install his half-brother, Brian O'Neill, as King of Tirowen.

Married Irish women did not take their husband's name, so the widowed Áine would have been "the daughter of O'Cahan" when Angus met her. And, since Irish noblewomen prized their long flowing hair, according to expert Dr. Katherine Simms, they were rather lax about wearing veils.

The O'Cahans would have been familiar with the Macdonald Lords of the Isles who had long been involved in Ireland. (Angus Mor had permission to take timber from Ireland, most likely for his galleys.) In any event, since the O'Cahans and Niall O'Neill were allies of Richard de Burgh, Earl of Ulster, it was not surprising that they would have been swept up in the affairs of Scotland involving the nobles who were signatory to the Turnberry Band.

Elizabeth de Burgh, who became Robert Bruce's queen, was returned to her husband in October 1314 after eight years of captivity. She and the king had four children, three of whom survived to adulthood: two daughters, Matilda and Margaret, and David, the future King David II. Her son John died young.

The galloglass (sometimes "gallowglass") in Ireland were actually fighting men from the Hebrides and the West Highlands. An elite class of warriors, they wore knee-length chainmail over a quilted tunic or coat and carried sword, dirk/dagger, spear and long-handled sparth axe, the weapons Angus wields in my story. Sometime in the 13th century, they made their way to Ireland as mercenary warriors.

Their training was rigorous, their discipline rigid and their reputation fierce. Angus Og would have grown up surrounded by these men in his father's retinue and likely trained with them under the supervision of his father's constable, the head of the galloglass. Initially, these warriors served as personal guards to the constantly warring Irish nobility but, inevitably, they followed the chieftains into battle. By the time of Angus Og, there would be many galloglass in the army of the Lord of the Isles.

At least some of the sons of Angus Og' elder brother, Alexander, left for Ireland sometime after their father's death in 1299 to become the Macdonnell galloglass in Tirowen, Connaught and eventually Leinster. When the MacSweens were driven from Castle Sween in Argyll, they, too, found fame in Ireland as galloglass.

The ships Angus Og and the Macdonalds sailed were smaller than the larger longships of the Norsemen. Sometimes called "lymphads" or "birlinns", they came in different sizes referred to by their number of oars. A typical galley might have twenty-four oars but a chief might have a larger ship. These galleys could have two or three men on each oar so even a small galley could transport 40 to 50 warriors. The larger galleys could hold more than 100 warriors. Even then, the vessel would be small enough to maneuver around the isles. The galleys of mainland Argyll might be larger.

A note on cattle raiding in medieval Ireland and the Isles: Both the Irish and the Islesmen kept cattle. Dairy was an important part of their diet. The raiding of each other's cattle was not only common, it was a celebrated practice. Successful raids were a means of gaining prestige, and the inauguration of a regional king called for a cattle raid to mark the occasion. It was even accepted and honored under the early Christian Church with monasteries sometimes receiving a share of the cattle raided. Thus, the bard's poem celebrating Angus Mor could reasonably praise his cattle raiding in Ireland.

A note about Iona: While it is unfortunate that the literature and guidebooks written about Iona and its abbey and church do not make this clear, the medieval Iona Abbey (restored in the 20th century) is principally the legacy of the Macdonald Lords of the Isles and their abbots and bishops. Thus, Iona Abbey's church is, in all but name, Clan Donald's Cathedral of The Isles.

Because I've been asked about the chess game and why the pieces were red and white and the red made the first move, I thought to include a bit of my research that I first did for my novel, *King's Knight*. Red and white were the most popular colors for the board and pieces, although blue, black, or other colors could be substituted for red. The convention of white having the first move is a development of the 19th century. Thus, in the chess game between Angus and Rob, the chess pieces are red and white, and red moves first.

A word about the castles. My research has convinced me that Angus Og's castles, including Ardtornish, Dunyvaig and Dunaverty, to name a few, were stone by this time. So was Christina MacRuairi's Caste Tioram. The same is true of the Bruces' castles at Turnberry and Annandale and the Comyn castle at Inverlochy.

Some sources suggest the stone castles in Northern Ireland didn't arrive until later centuries so that, in the 13th and early 14th centuries, Dunseverick and Dunluce Castles would have been promontory forts or manors. The record is sufficiently unclear to me that I went with stone castles. I found the same thing when I did the research for *Summer Warrior* where timber castles may have preceded stone but they were still considered castles. (Dr. Kathleen MacPhee's book *Somerled, Hammer of the Norse,* is an excellent source for the list of castles that existed in Somerled's time.) It is also likely that Richard de Burgh's main castle was Carrickfergus on the east coast of Ulster but, as Dunluce was one of his holdings and close to Dunseverick, I have used it for this story. Irish kings held territories both inside and outside the administrative boundaries of the Norman Earldom of Ulster.

Finally, I should probably add a note about the form of names and address. "Macdonald" (one word, no capital "d") represented the lordship patriarchal title, as in "The Macdonald". While most other clans used a capital letter for what followed "mac" (meaning "son of"), the Macleans, Macleods, Macduffies and Clanranald were exceptions. I have my friend Ian Macdonnell to thank for that bit of information. As for Robert Bruce, the family name is spelled in different sources as le Bruce, de Bruce, Brus, Bruis, Brix, Brusse and even Broase. The Norman style would have been Robert de Brus but I have chosen the simpler path for the sake of my readers and used Robert Bruce. The address "Your Majesty" wasn't used until the 15th century, so at the time Robert I was crowned, he would have been addressed as "Your Grace", "My lord", "Sire" or "My lord king".

The next book in The Clan Donald Saga will be the story of Angus Og's grandson, Donald Macdonald of Islay, Lord of the Isles, the Hero of Harlaw. My working title is *The Strongest Heart*. For notices of future releases, follow me on Amazon.
amazon.com/Regan-Walker/e/B008OUWC5Y

You can also sign up for my infrequent newsletters on my website. I give away a free book each quarter to one of my new subscribers.
www.reganwalkerauthor.com

And, should you be on Facebook, do join the Regan Walker's Readers group.
facebook.com/groups/ReganWalkersReaders

For pictures of Tirowen and Tirconnell in Ulster or the castles of Ardtornish, Dunyvaig, Dunaverty, Dunseverick and Dunluce, among others, and the books I consulted, see the Pinterest storyboard for The Clan Donald Saga. It's some of my research in pictures.
pinterest.com/reganwalker123/the-clan-donald-saga-by-regan-walker

In October 2021, I spent three weeks in the Isles doing research for this series. I have a special Pinterest board for the pictures I took on that trip.
pinterest.com/reganwalker123/regans-trip-to-scotlands-isles-october-2021

AUTHOR'S BIO

Regan Walker is an award-winning author of Regency, Georgian and Medieval novels. She has six times been nominated for the Reward of Novel Excellence (RONE) award. Her novels *The Red Wolf's Prize* and *King's Knight* won Best Historical Novel in the medieval category. *The Refuge: An Inspirational Novel of Scotland* won the Gold Medal in the Illumination Awards. *To Tame the Wind* won the International Book Award for Romance Fiction and Best Historical Romance in the San Diego Book Awards. *A Fierce Wind* won a medal in the President's Book Awards of The Florida Authors & Publishers Association. *Rogue's Holiday* won the Kindle Book Award. *Summer Warrior* won first prize in the Chaucer Award for Pre-1750s Historical Fiction and 2nd place in the Incipere Awards.

A lawyer turned writer, Regan's years of serving clients in private practice and several stints in high levels of government have given her a feel for the demands of the "Crown". Hence her novels often feature a demanding sovereign who taps his subjects for special assignments. The Clan Donald Saga, her newest venture into historical fiction, is close to her heart as it tells the stories of the chieftains of her own clan. She has made several trips to Scotland as a part of her research.

Regan lives in San Diego with her dog "Cody", a Wirehaired Pointing Griffon.

BOOKS BY REGAN WALKER

The Agents of the Crown series (Regency):

Racing with the Wind
Against the Wind
Wind Raven
A Secret Scottish Christmas
Rogue's Holiday

The Donet Trilogy (Georgian):

To Tame the Wind
Echo in the Wind
A Fierce Wind

Holiday Novellas (related to The Agents of the Crown):

The Shamrock & The Rose
The Holly & The Thistle
The Twelfth Night Wager

Medieval Warriors (England and Scotland 11th century):

The Red Wolf's Prize
Rogue Knight
Rebel Warrior
King's Knight

The Clan Donald Saga:

Summer Warrior
Bound by Honor

Inspirational

The Refuge: An Inspirational Novel of Scotland

www.ReganWalkerAuthor.com

Made in the USA
Columbia, SC
23 October 2023